STAR DRAGON OMNIBUS

BLAZE WARD

KNOTTED ROAD PRESS

Star Dragon Omnibus
Blaze Ward
Copyright © 2019 Blaze Ward
All rights reserved
Published by Knotted Road Press
www.KnottedRoadPress.com

ISBN: 978-1-64470-116-4

Cover art:

ID 11056051 © diversepixel | DepositPhoto.com

Cover and interior design copyright © 2019 Knotted Road Press

Never miss a release!
If you'd like to be notified of new releases, sign up for my newsletter.

I will never spam you or use your email for nefarious purposes. You can also unsubscribe at any time.

http://www.blazeward.com/newsletter/

ALSO BY BLAZE WARD

The Jessica Keller Chronicles

Auberon

Queen of the Pirates

Last of the Immortals

Goddess of War

Flight of the Blackbird

The Red Admiral

St. Legier

Winterhome

Petron

CS-405

Queen Anne's Revenge

Packmule

Persephone

Additional Alexandria Station Stories

Siren

Two Bottles of Wine with a War God

The Story Road

The Science Officer Series

The Science Officer

The Mind Field

The Gilded Cage

The Pleasure Dome

The Doomsday Vault

The Last Flagship

The Hammerfield Gambit
The Hammerfield Payoff

Shadow of the Dominion
Longshot Hypothesis
Hard Bargain
Outermost
Dominion-427
Phoenix
Princess Rualoh

Earth Force Sky Patrol
Birth of the Star Dragon
Flight of the Star Dragon
Call of the Star Dragon
Shadow of the Star Dragon
Trial of the Star Dragon

BIRTH OF THE STAR DRAGON

PART ONE
CRIMINALS

DESPERATION

"YOU DO REALIZE that this is the stupidly, most completely-insane thing you've ever suggested, right?" his partner asked pedantically.

"So far," Morty corrected sternly, focused on the long control console in front of him. "Only so far, Xiomber. I'm sure it's going to get much worse before we're done."

"You truly believe that a *human* is the only being that can save galactic civilization from utter ruin?" Xiomber rattled on, leaning against the side of the control board but carefully not touching anything.

"Hey, a human's going to destroy everything if nobody stops him," Morty snapped. "And they even have a phrase for this, those folks: fighting fire with fire."

"Aren't two fires going to burn the house down twice as fast?" Xiomber sneered.

"We've got to find the right human," Morty replied. "The one Sarzynski is always going on about. Would you talk that way about anybody if they weren't your worst nemesis?"

"I talk about you that way all the time," Xiomber reminded him.

Morty didn't have a good response for that one. But he and Xiomber were egg-brothers, partners in science as well as in crime. And a lizard needed a friend watching his back. The galaxy was a big and dangerous place.

It had just grown bigger and more dangerous since the boss, the old boss, had decided that what he really needed was a human assassin as part of his team.

What other species could do violence without the slightest drop of empathy in them, after all? Humans weren't part of the *Accord of Souls*. Hadn't been *Uplifted* by the Elders, the grand and now long-vanished Chaa, and bound into a single, psionic whole as a way to bring peace between diverse solar tribes.

Hell, when the Chaa left, humans were still banging the rocks together, hoping someone was listening.

Who knew that they would suddenly evolve into an intelligent species and discover technology? It was all the *Accord of Souls* could do to keep humans isolated in their own home system and ignorant of everyone else. Safer that way, by far.

"You going to help or not?" Morty finally asked, looking up from the panel of knobs and gauges in front. "'Cause if not, then you need to go into the other room and not call the cops until I'm gone. That, or shoot me now, before I go and commit the worst crime imaginable on the books. Again."

He looked over at Xiomber, waiting for the damned lizard to make up his mind. Most species had a hard time reading emotions in the Yuudixtl. The Warreth probably came closest, since they had feathers that could semaphore to communicate, so they had half a clue.

Yuudixtl just had scales. Stripes and blobs and patterns that didn't really mean anything, since the Chaa had fixed their genetics when they uplifted the intelligent lizards to be one of the galactic custodians.

Xiomber was keeping his scales flat and starkly uncommunicative.

Like Morty, Xiomber was mostly kinda a gray-green somewhere a little darker than sage, but not down in that totally sexy range of a Terran crocodile. It was a shame that Yuudixtl couldn't be upgraded any further. Crocodile would be freaking awesome.

And probably useful right now, since a renegade human assassin had already killed the boss and pretty much taken over the whole organization, murdering anybody who tried to stop him or even looked at him funny.

The Yuudixtl were the smallest intelligent species in space. And maybe the smartest. They followed the basic uplift design the Chaa had selected: symmetric biped with sense organs on the head and opposable thumbs. If they were only half the height of the Vanir, and a third their mass, they made up for it in smarts.

Or had, right up until he and Xiomber had listened to Cinnra, the old Boss, and built him an illegal wormhole generator to capture a human killer, one step ahead of the human cops catching the guy, back in the Earth system.

Probably the dumbest thing they'd done, but only so far.

Morty looked forward to topping it in about five minutes.

Xiomber's dark green eyes slitted down hard and his scowl intensified.

"You're nuts," his partner repeated. "But what's the worst they could do? Throw us both in prison for two lifetimes instead of one? Scoot over."

"Me?" Marty razzed. "Why do I have to move?"

"Because you'll probably screw it up and pull the wrong guy through again."

"That was one time, and it was a chicken," Morty defended himself. "And you're the one who swore the machine was calibrated correctly."

Still, he leaned back and let Xiomber kinda hip check him out of the way. Quickly, four green hands flashed over the long rows of dials, tweaking things down and refining the target zone. They would probably only get one shot at this, because the power surge when they tripped all the generators would get someone's attention.

Maximus Sarzynski, wanna-be ultimate crime lord, would not take it well, him and his egg-brother digging up the guy's worst enemy and pulling him halfway across the galaxy as an insurance policy.

And unlike the Uplifted Species in the *Accord of Souls*, *Maximus* could kill them without the slightest hesitation or provocation. Just what old Cinnra had wanted in an hired gun.

He had only really screwed up when he thought that he could control a *human* afterwards.

"You figured out how we escape?" Xiomber asked out of the side of his mouth. "Those damned birds will roll over as soon as the new Boss yells *boo*. Then they're coming after us. And we sure as hell can't go to the cops with something like this."

"Kinda planning on cheating," Morty replied. "That's why I wanted you in the other room if you weren't going to help."

"Oh, *fardel*," Xiomber snapped. "Now what?"

"After we grab the human, I was going to redirect him right through another wormhole, and jump in after him," Morty said carefully. "This controller is kinda programmed to overload and eat itself, so nobody can chase us, or figure out where we went."

"Are you sure we came from the same egg batch?" Xiomber growled.

"'Cause I don't remember any of my siblings being that dumb. Where do you think they'll look?"

"I'm not sending him to *Yuudixtl*," Morty replied. "Like you figured, first place Maximus will look."

"Where then, Morty?" his partner got serious. Way serious. Like maybe *thinking-about-overcoming-the-empath-bond-so-he-could-kill* him serious. "Where you are dumping us out?"

"*Orgoth Vortai*," Morty said in a quiet, careful voice, expecting to get punched in the snout.

Instead, Xiomber turned and stared at him for several seconds, jaw agape. And then he started laughing.

Morty relaxed and zeroed down the last few gauges. The range was stupid long for a shot like this, doubly so on a bounce-tube, but they also had an exact match of the psionic coordinates that had located Maximus the killer in the first place. All Morty had needed to do was flip them end for end and find the man who was Sarzynski's psionic opposite.

A good guy.

"You ready to do this?" Morty asked as Xiomber settled down.

"Why the hell not?" Xiomber said. "I always wanted to visit the world of the tentacle-heads. With any luck, they'll look at the whole, damned thing as a monstrous art installation. Maybe a performance piece for the ages."

"That was actually part of my original logic," Morty admitted. "They already do crazy shit. What's one thing more?"

He reached out and grabbed the second-to-last slider, ramming it to the top of the scale with a hard click. Several floors below, a dozen generators began to hum. In moments, they were singing. Shortly, the metal would begin to scream.

Around them, overhead lights flickered and then a few exploded, throwing rooster tails of sparks and smoke in all directions as Morty's device started pumping too much power through the entire building. At least nobody would be using this tube generator station again.

But boy, was Maximus going to be pissed.

"Ready?" Morty yelled.

"Do it," Xiomber shouted over the rising din. "We're not going to hold this much longer."

Morty grabbed the last slider and pushed it slowly forward.

"Energizing," he hollered back.

In the area beyond the control console, a golden nimbus of energy formed, and quickly resolved itself into a pair of tube openings, like a hose that had been sliced neatly in half.

Morty stared hard at the zone controls, watching the screen's targeting array home in on the target he had selected.

"Almost got it," he yelled, starting to smell smoke rising.

The console was probably close to catching fire, with the energy they were processing through it.

"Now, Morty," Xiomber screamed. "It's not going to stay intact much longer."

Morty slammed a fist down on the big, purple button and listened to the generators reach for that last two percent.

Definitely getting bright in here. Maybe a little warm.

"Let's go," he scrambled around the console and began to run towards the nexus of the bounce-tube.

"What if you missed?" Xiomber was a step behind him.

"Then our goose is right cooked when Maximus finds out, and we've got nobody to hide behind," Morty replied.

Something was coming through the first tunnel. Morty could see the left-hand tube pulsate, like a snake swallowing a rat. Hope to the Gods this worked, because he also saw a door open at the far end of the lab.

"What's going on in here?"

FIELD AGENT

GARETH ST. JOHN DANKWORTH. Field Agent of the Earth Force Sky Patrol.

Gods, that sounded awesome. And looked even better. He had finally made it. He was a Field Agent now. Lawman extraordinaire. Respected across the entire Solar System.

Gareth stared again at his reflection in the wall mirror of his quarters. He was at **The Arsenal**, Sky Patrol's base in the Earth/Moon L2 point, over beyond the dark side of the moon. Affectionately called ***Shadow Base One***.

His new uniform was amazing. Still the black riding boots and white hotpants of a Sky Patrol Agent, but now his maroon tunic finally said *Field Agent*. Three white rings around the big, stylized SP in the center of his chest, offset by gold buttons up both sides of the bib and the gold wing-protectors on his shoulders like short fins.

He tugged the tunic down a little, settling it a little tighter beneath the black, Sam Brown belt. He ran a hand back through his curly, blond hair, just getting long enough to blow in the wind, so it was probably time to get it shorn again, as it had reached the maximum length that the regulations allowed.

Field Agent.

Damn, he looked good.

Best of all, he could finally propose to Philippa, after they had both waited for so long, both of them staying chaste and pure, until he could make it all the way to Field Agent and they could be married. Gareth reached a hand down into his pocket and pulled out the tiny, leather pouch he kept with him at all times.

From inside, he extracted the gold ring with the single, white diamond in the middle, surrounded by ruby and gold stones representing Sky Patrol. Tonight was the night. He'd catch a shuttle over to the Earth/Moon L1 point in an hour. She was working as a research assistant for her father these days, at Earth Force Headquarters, so it would be easy enough to take her aside after dinner, during a walk along the Promenade overlooking the Moon's bright side, and propose to her properly.

He was a Field Agent now. All that waiting would be over, and they could finally become man and wife.

He smiled at the ring, tucking it back into the pouch and stashing it in his pocket.

Not long now.

A sound brought his head up.

It was a strange humming sound, almost imperceptible, hovering right at the point of audibility. Almost as if a fly was trying to sneak around the room behind him, but wasn't succeeding.

Gareth looked all directions with a concerned scowl on his face. He was in his personal quarters at The Arsenal. Nobody ever came in except the cleaning crew, so the room was as pristine as his bunk had always been in school, bed made so taut that a shilling coin could bounce a foot high.

Except that the room had taken on a golden hue. Odd.

There was nothing wrong with the lights. They still put out the perfect, crisp white of the fifth generation organic diodes, but the air itself was turning golden.

Bizarre.

And now something faded into existence across the room, like a film of fog melting, only run in reverse. This mirage appeared to be the source of the gold, and it was growing, both in size and intensity.

Panic woke up at the back of Gareth's brain. He had always been noted for his bravery and leadership, but today, those parts of his mind seemed to be having second thoughts. There was no science he could think of that explained a portable whirlpool suddenly appearing in the air in the middle of his cabin.

Maybe it was time to do something.

A wind came up suddenly, inside his cabin at the center of a space station, ruffling his hair as greedy fingers began to pluck at his soul.

His soul?

Very much not good.

Gareth sprang into action, like the hero he had always been. He raced to the door, keying the internal telephone system and picking up the headset.

"Base Operator," a woman's bored voice answered.

"This is Field Agent Dankworth," he said, voice struggling to remain calm. "Cabin 24-575. Something's happening in my room. Something bad."

"Could you be clearer, Field Agent?" the laconic operator replied. It sounded like maybe she had one hand up, inspecting her nails as she spoke.

"I've got an emergency here, miss," he yelled, feeling those golden fingers begin to caress his back.

The wind was stronger now, tugging insistently closer to the hole in the universe that was growing over in the corner.

Hole in the universe?

"Please state the nature of your emergency," she replied, maybe reading from a script now.

Gareth tried to think of the right words, but the pull of the tempest was too great now. Fight it as he tried, the force literally dragged him across the cabin, stretching the cord of the handset until it was pulled right out of his hands, falling to the wall with a thunk as Gareth's legs went numb.

Looking down, his lower half appeared to be fading out of existence, right at the event horizon of that golden light. The golden fingers crept up his nerves, pulling him under with grim determination.

Oh, shit.

WORMHOLE

IT WAS like going down a waterslide as a kid, vacationing with his parents at a theme park dedicated to the South Seas, back home in Indiana. Gareth couldn't see anything except the sides of a golden tube of light, but when he put his hand out to touch, they pulled back.

He couldn't fall any slower, or faster, regardless of what he did. And it felt like he was simultaneously the size of a mouse and of a whale.

Screaming like a little girl didn't seem to help, either. Or rather, nobody was listening, which was probably good. Gareth wondered if he was going to keep on falling forever.

There, in the distance between his toes, Gareth saw something. Darkness, perhaps. A gap. Maybe the end of the tunnel, thank God.

He seemed to be slowing down. Or something.

Yes. The tunnel ended there. He could sense a room just beyond it.

Gareth felt his brain and his soul drop back into phase with the rest of the universe. What the name of Heaven was that?

He found himself standing in a clearing. Surrounded by trees out of the worst nightmares the ancient artist Dali had ever dreamt up: bark the wrong color, trunks somehow the wrong shape, and with leaves that looked like nothing so much as feathers.

The space here was that same golden hue of his cabin, and the tunnel.

Standing in front of him were a pair of three-foot-tall lizards, dressed in pants and t-shirts, standing upright and eyeing him like dinner. Gareth would have given a month's salary to be holding his Sonic Stunner right now, but it was safely locked up, back at The Arsenal.

Wait, lizards?

The room howled as well. Gareth considered joining it, but one of the lizard-men hopped into the air and tossed something into his mouth, rather like a jelly bean.

Jelly bean? What the hell is wrong with you people?

Gareth went to spit it out, but the bean had already dissolved and melted itself to his tongue, like the best peanut butter on a PBJ sandwich.

Gareth chewed frantically, trying to escape its clutches.

"That work?" the closer lizard-man asked.

Gareth turned, utterly shocked that these things spoke English. Had somebody slipped a Mickey Finn into his drink at dinner? Was this all some sort of hallucination as part of a failed seduction attempt? Who would he wake up next to in the morning?

He chewed, unable to speak. The one who had spoken wore a logo on his shirt, but it honestly looked like an old, ratty concert T-shirt, rather than the more stylized *Sky Patrol* **SP** on Gareth's chest.

"You can understand me?" the lizard asked. "Just nod."

Gareth complied, nightmares of Alice and toadstools haunting him. He scanned the feathered trees nearby for Cheshire Cats.

"We need to get gone," the other lizard-man told the first. "Somebody's going to remember us."

"Okay," the first said, staring hard at Gareth like he was a badly-trained puppy. "You need to come with us, so we can get someplace private and I can explain everything. This is not a dream, but it could become a nightmare, without too much effort. Are you safe to touch?"

"What?" Gareth managed around the peanut butter. "What's the meaning of this?"

The lizard-man sighed and his shoulders slumped. A twinkle came into his eyes after a second and he smiled.

"Humans are the most dangerous, lethal species in the galaxy, okay?" he said. "You've been kept confined in your solar system until you matured enough to not be a threat to everyone else, which is not today. Except one of your kind got loose, and it threatening to destroy all galactic civilization. Nobody can stop this killer, so we took a gamble and kidnapped you. You might be the only person who can save us."

Gareth felt a surge of pride rush through him. Earth Force Sky Patrol. The Good Guys.

Field Agent Gareth St. John Dankworth, ready to serve.

He stood taller, shoulders back and head up. Which kind of ruined the scene, since these two might have been three and a half feet tall.

"Who is my foe?" Gareth announced boldly. "What do I need to do?"

The two lizard-men shared a glance, and a smile, it seemed.

"Marc Sarzynski," the first one said. "Called *Maximus*."

"That bastard's here?" Gareth growled in shock. "No wonder he escaped me. Where are we?"

"The planet is named *Orgoth Vortai*," the second one said. "Home of a species known as The Grace."

"Species?" Gareth wasn't sure he heard the word right.

"You got it, pal," the first said. "There are over a dozen sentient, technological species in the *Accord of Souls*. The Grace are not quite the weirdest, but they're close. And when one wants to talk to you, and they will, be prepared to be touched. Now, can we go get some tea and hide out?"

"Maximus is here?" Gareth reiterated.

"Not on this planet, but we know where he is, once you're ready," the tiny lizardman said.

"And I'm not stoned out of my mind on Bennies and Smack?" he continued.

"On what?" the second one asked.

"Mind-altering, hallucinogenic narcotics," Gareth explained. "Humans take them as an escape from everyday life."

"Nope, we need you sober, pal," the first lizard-man said. "It's already going to be weird enough as is."

"What was that thing you put in my mouth?" Gareth asked, finally having swallowed the last bits. Or maybe they had dissolved completely.

"A transform virus programmed for humans," the little man said. "It inoculated you against most diseases, as well as programmed your brain to be able to speak our language. You don't think the rest of us spoke English, do you?"

"Oh," Gareth said. "Maybe I do need a drink."

"Tea first," the lizard-man said. "I'm sure we'll need something stronger later. Ready to join us?"

"Yeah, I think so," Gareth said, pretty unsure of all of this, but willing to stay put. Maybe.

"Good," the first said. "Now, we're going to exit this park, cross a couple of blocks, and hit a tea shop nearby. If anyone asks, you're just a runt Vanir, okay? Humans are the absolute embodiment of evil, as far as anyone knows, but nobody really knows what a human looks like, and you're close enough to pass for a Vanir for now. We good?"

"What are your names?" Gareth asked. "I am Field Agent Gareth St. John Dankworth, of the Earth Force Sky Patrol, Missile Division, 6th Cavalry Troop."

"Yeah, and if you ever mention that again, your ass will be in a jail cell so fast your head will spin, pal," the one said. "Ours right beside you. We'll never see the light of day again, and Maximus will end up Emperor of the Universe. So keep it quiet. We'll just call you Gareth, for now. I'm Morty, and this is my egg-brother, Xiomber. Let's go."

Gareth found himself following the first little lizardman. He had been so focused earlier he hadn't even really processed the fact that he was standing in a small clearing of an arboreal forest of some sort, next to a thing that looked remarkably like a bizarre garden maze, except the walls were only four feet tall and made of a weird mix of metal, wood, and flowering plants, with lots of open spaces allowing sunlight and breezes through.

He glanced up, trying to measure the time, and stopped so fast that Xiomber ran into him from behind.

"Hey, friend," Xiomber barked. "Little warning next time?"

"The sky…" Gareth's words tapered off.

It was close enough to noon, with the sun more or less overhead. But the sky was pink-orange, somewhere between cotton candy and first-run salmon from back home.

THERE WAS NO BLUE, ANYWHERE IN THE SKY!

"Quieter, please, Gareth," Morty smacked him on the thigh, breaking the hypnotic spell that had fallen over him. "You're not on Earth anymore, m'kay? This is *Orgoth Vortai*. C'mon."

Right.

Gareth fell in behind Morty again, walking in a calm daze. Alien planet named *Orgoth Vortai*. Sure. Surrounded by talking lizardmen. Why the hell not?

The trees ended suddenly and Gareth was on a sidewalk. Maybe. Whatever the local, planetary equivalent was.

And it was moving. Both of them. Wow. There was a path moving to the right, with a second one, closer to the street, moving to the left.

And people.

People? Sure, why not? I'm completely stoned now. Whatever they gave me has gone all the way in and now I'm riding the lysergic acid all the way to the end of the rainbow, where I'll find the leprechaun level monster, waiting for me to fight him to the death for his pot of gold.

Gareth must have stopped walking again. Xiomber just stepped up and took his hand, like a child leading a parent around a theme park.

They got on the moving sidewalk, and Gareth smiled politely at the woman in front of him as she turned and studied him.

Except it wasn't a woman. Or, maybe it was. She had curves. A fantastic bottom, narrow waist, ripe bosom contained in some sort of silky wrap that looked like a fairies' cocoon.

But her skin was green. And her eyes had slits, kinda like Morty and Xiomber, rather than irises. Like a snake, or a cat. Except she looked like a snake, with long, green-black hair. Except that wasn't hair. Those were snakes.

She was a medusa.

Gareth nearly screamed again, but Xiomber jerked his hand hard enough to nearly make him fall over. He rounded angrily on the little man.

"You're staring," Xiomber growled quietly up at him. "It's impolite. And she might take it as invitation to talk. Those tentacles on her head? You know, where you have hair and I have a bone crest? Those are sensors pods that combine touch, taste, and smell. The Grace are a very tactile species. Let's not today, okay?"

Tactile. Right. All those snake-hair-thingees slithering over his skin?

If he ignored the tentacles, she was an amazingly beautiful woman.

Medusa.

Something.

Maybe she'd turn him to stone, if he wasn't careful.

Or if he was lucky.

Gareth smiled weakly at her and turned his attention to the rest of the city.

Oh My God!

Earth had nothing like this. It was like a fairy tale, with impossibly tall buildings of all shapes and colors. Some were stone. Others were glass. A few appeared to be forests that had been transformed, like a giant's banzai tree experiment, plopped down in the middle of a city.

The woman behind them on the sidewalk smiled as he accidentally made eye contact.

Gareth managed not to scream. And pulled his mouth shut and held it there by grinding his teeth. She was a cat. No, a lynx, covered over with cream and gray fur, standing more than five and a half feet tall, wearing harem pants and loose top in matching baby blue silk. The face was close enough to human that it might be a mask, once he got past the magnificent, muttonchop sideburns and the ears on top, except that her ears moved, one rotating towards him like a radar dish as he watched in awe.

"Morty, we need to debark," Xiomber said loud enough that the other turned. "Now."

Xiomber tugged his hand and Gareth stumbled briefly as they landed on the sidewalk.

The lady-lynx kept riding by, but handed him a business card written in vermillion ink as she passed him with a hopeful smile. The smell on the card was almost enough to make Gareth chase after her.

"What are you?" Xiomber groused in awe. "Bottled animal magnetism? Morty, we gotta get this one undercover quick, before we've got a mob of horny women after us. That's two already."

There was a break in the traffic going the other way. The one called Morty bolted through it. Xiomber followed, dragging Gareth along numbly.

He was still holding the card, sniffing her scent. She made him feel all tingly inside, and kinda goofy. But it also let Xiomber pull him easier.

Traffic magically seemed to part around them, and Morty ducked into a shop, the other two in quick pursuit.

Now he'd gone blind.

Except, not blind. Sun blind. There. Man, it was dark in here. Okay, table. Bench. Sit. Good. Sniff card. Wow.

"Put that away," Morty snapped. "I need you coherent. Not dunk on the scent of a Nari in season."

"A what?" Gareth asked weakly.

"That woman on the slidewalk," Morty pointed back over his shoulder. "She's a Nari. She gave you a scent marker. Didn't think Nari did that, outside of their own kind. It's frightening, the power you have over women, pal. In other circumstances, we'd put that to use, but right now we need to hide."

Reluctantly, Gareth pulled out his wallet and slipped her card in with the others he had accumulated from scientists and politicians he had met. It was sized close enough to fit.

The two lizardmen were eyeing him when he looked up.

"What?" he asked, nervous.

"Nothing," Morty said.

Gareth watched him signal to a waitress. She was another of The Grace, although not as voluptuous as the first. If she were human, Gareth would have guessed her to be a teenage girl, perhaps. Petite and thin.

This one smiled, too, but Morty growled for her to get the tea if she wanted a tip, so she just winked at Gareth and sashayed away. She also had a mesmerizing bottom.

"Hey, pal," Xiomber cracked wise. "Eyes over here, please."

"Right," Gareth reluctantly turned to the others, trying to figure out why he was here. Wherever here was. "So the two of you are criminals, engaged in a major felonious enterprise, and somehow I'm both the crime and the prize?"

"A little louder next time, maybe?" Morty snapped. "I don't think the cook heard you in back. You wanna be in jail?"

"Sorry," Gareth dropped to a murmur. "A little excited here. I've never been on an alien planet before. What's next?"

"Now, we hide you from Maximus until we can get you to a lab and make some improvements to you," Morty said. "Maximus has been doing the same to himself, but I don't think he dreams big enough. At least not yet."

"Maximus," Gareth growled, remembering he was a cop. "What's he doing now? And how do we stop him?"

Gareth watched the two share a guilty glance silently for a moment. Morty shrugged.

"So until about ten minutes ago, we were members of a criminal gang," Morty began in a voice so quiet Gareth had to lean all the way down close to hear. "Our old boss, Cinnra, was a Warreth scientist, with aspirations of taking over the whole criminal underworld, across the entire *Accord of Souls*."

"What's a Warreth?" Gareth asked carefully, trying not to talk so loud that he got arrested just when the little man got to the good parts.

Xiomber leaned in and cut his brother off.

"Think birdman, Gareth," he said simply. "Earth has lots of bird species, so imagine a humanoid a little shorter than you, about half your mass, covered with feathers."

"Birdman," Gareth acknowledged. "Got it."

Sure. Why the hell not?

"So Cinnra had us build a very illegal, psionic wormhole generator, and locate him a human assassin," Morty continued. "This would have been about, uhm…"

He paused, apparently doing some math in his head, eyes fixed on some strange spot on the ceiling.

"Maybe five Earth months ago?" Morty asked. "I think."

"That was when Sarzynski escaped me," Gareth snarled quietly. "We had him holed up with his gang. He escaped, and they all swore it was some weird gold light that did it. Oh, shit. Gold light. You guys."

"Yup," Xiomber noted with pride. "Boss nailed down the shape of the psionic signature he wanted in a human, and had us program it into the scanner. Bada-bing, bada-boom, and Bob's your uncle."

"Uhm, what?"

"He said we located our target and extracted him, one step ahead of the arm of law enforcement," Morty explained. "You, given all the bitching Maximus has done about you since then."

"Oh," Gareth said with his own surge of pride. "So you recruited an assassin?"

"Yeah, but Cinnra thought he could control the human," Morty said. "Found that out the hard way when Maximus turned on him."

"What did the rest of the gang do?" Gareth asked.

"Went along with it," Morty said. "The human's a freaking killer. Our choices were pretty stark here. Your kind are not known for being the forgiving types, you know?"

"We're not all like that," Gareth replied.

He wanted to say more, but the young girl with the tentacles returned with a cast iron tea pot and three mugs. She set the pot down in the center of the table by leaning past Gareth.

He flinched and nearly screamed when several of her tentacles caressed his hair and neck.

"Hey," Morty snapped. "You want me to get the manager out here?"

"Sorry," she purred, withdrawing dreamily.

Gareth watched her face turn nearly umber with blush as she stepped back.

His subconscious couldn't decide if the feeling had been feathers caressing him, or teeth looking for a place to bite. Or both.

Xiomber poured a mug and handed it to him, before serving them. Gareth sipped carefully, but the taste was yummy.

"So that thing you put in my mouth," he asked after a moment.

"How'd you know that would work? You said Maximus and I were the only humans here."

"We reprogrammed him the same way," Xiomber explained. "We can do that with humans, because they aren't part of the *Accord of Souls.*"

"What do you mean: *reprogram?*" Gareth felt an uneasy tide nibble at his toes.

"The Chaa uplifted all the species to sentience a long time ago," Morty said. "Before they left, as a matter of fact, and turned most of their own kind into the Vanir. *Those Left Behind.* But they also fixed everyone's genetics pretty hard. We can eliminate disease and all that, but nobody can be improved past where the Masters left us all."

"Except humans?" Gareth guessed. "And Maximus is upgrading himself? Like bad?"

"He's improved his brain, so he's way smarter than he used to be," Xiomber explained.

"That's bad," Gareth replied. "Marc Sarzynski was a renegade from the Sky Patrol. Part of my class of Agents, before he went bad. Turned criminal. But he was already at the top of the pack, then. If he's smarter now, you're in trouble. We're in trouble."

MAXIMUS

"YOU'RE sure what it was that you observed?" Marc Sarzynski asked again, scowling heavily at the men of his gang, arrayed below him in the space that he thought of as his throne room.

It had been Cinnra's personal aerie, once upon a time. Marc liked the vaulted ceilings above him, as well as the stone slabs stepping down from where he had put his throne. Each was about ten yards across by twenty wide, and the whole room was a series of steps. The only change he had made was to have a couple of Yuudixtl add stair steps everywhere, so all the non-gliders could get around here easily, and not just the Warreth.

He was recruiting more, these days, and going outside the insular Warreth clans that had been the basis of Cinnra's power. The gang would need to feel more comfortable in here.

Marc scanned the mob of aliens a level below him, nearly a hundred faces from strange nightmares staring back. Five months ago, he had never even imagined that aliens existed. And now he had at least twelve species actively serving him.

The Warreth male at the center flattened his headcrest some as he spoke, an unconscious reflex that Marc had finally learned was the equivalent of a dog tucking his tail under. Body language of submission. It was good, being in charge. Things would get done around here, finally.

"The generators had all started running at once, so I went into the lab to see what was going on," Deoar said, somehow pitching his voice loud while not sounding threatening.

The survivors of the takeover had all learned that lesson.

"When I got there, Xiomber and Morty had powered up the wormhole generator and were pulling someone through," the birdman continued.

The creature reminded Marc of a Stellar Jay, with blue and black feathers, even though his beak was nowhere near as long as it would have been. Deoar's was shorter, almost petite. Just enough to crack walnuts, rather than dipping into flowers.

"So somebody came through the first tube," Deoar said. "Just as I entered the room. Then they bounced him out using a second tube and jumped in right after him. About that moment, the console overloaded and I had to concentrate on putting out the fires, but I know what I saw."

"Describe it again," Marc said in a voice that couldn't help but be threatening. His nerves were shot this morning. It was not possible, what Deoar had described.

"Before I met you, boss, I would have said a short Vanir," the birdman continued. "But I'm pretty sure it was a human. Same build, but not as tall. About what you used to be, a little taller than me. Golden hair."

"Yes, yes," Marc said. "The clothing. What was he wearing."

"Garnet jacket with gold letters on a black logo and gold shoulder pieces," Deoar replied. "Three white rings around the logo on the chest. White pants. Black boots."

"And golden hair?" Marc confirmed.

"You got it, boss."

Marc slammed one first down onto the armrest of the new throne but otherwise contained his emotions. Fear was a useful thing, in small doses. It would not do to completely frighten his people out of their wits.

"Ladies and gentleman, I should be possessed of an anger for the very gods, right now," he pronounced, watching the five score aliens below him recoil half a step at the thought, anyway. Yes, fear of god was a thing they understood. "And I will exercise that rage on those two little traitors when we find them. Xiomber and Morty are to be killed, without mercy. But today is also our lucky day. They've managed to locate my worst enemy and actually bring to me, here in the *Accord of Souls*. The human Deoar has described is a Field Agent of the Earth Force Sky Patrol. For humans, the equivalent of the Vanir Constabulary, with just about as much sense of humor. That human is most likely Gareth St. John Dankworth."

Marc rose from his throne and began to pace. He had the entire top platform to himself. Skylights overhead cast him in alternate spotlights and shadows as he moved.

"They will probably not have taken him to Yuudixtl, but alert our agents there anyway," Marc commanded. "Instead, we need to be on the lookout for another human loose in *Accord* space. Perhaps we should alert the authorities, as well."

Marc picked out a Nari male off to one side. Unlike most of the gang, Zorge was older, well into Nari middle-age, with white fur coming in along the edges of the orange and gray stripes. And he had actively chosen a life of crime, rather than being forced into it by circumstances.

If the cat-man had possessed any greater ambitions in life, Marc probably would have had to kill him when he first took over, but Zorge was content working as a spy, maneuvering in the shadows. All he wanted to do was run his own little network of informants. It was good.

"Pass an anonymous tip to the Vanir," Marc ordered the old cat. "Let them know that there is a *human* loose in Accord space. Emphasize the golden hair, though."

That got a laugh as Marc ran a hand back through his own pitch-black curls. In that, he looked much more like a typical Vanir, darker of skin and hair than Dankworth. And a foot taller, these days. If the so-called, self-appointed, Custodians of Order weren't so damned tall, a human like Gareth could have easily passed himself off as one, but the women alone were six and a half feet tall, and the men usually seven. Freaking giants.

Like Maximus was now.

Morty and Xiomber had been in the process of researching how to rebuild him again, even better than the Vanir he appeared to be. He already had the perfect disguise, so perhaps their betrayal now was in his best interests. Internally, Marc shuddered at the thought of what those two damnable, lizard scientists might have done to him, had he put himself under their care for greater transformation when they were intent on duplicity.

The room had fallen silent at his introspective pacing. They knew better than to interrupt, but no new genius insight bubbled up right now. He was still getting used to having an IQ of two hundred by human standards.

"Find him," Marc growled to his mob. "Bring him to me."

TEA ROOM

GARETH HAD SETTLED DOWN SOME. The tea was amazingly good in this place, a gentle blend of vanilla, caramel, oolong, and some sort of berry that just seemed to fill in all the happy spaces in his soul.

Briefly, he wondered if the twins had added something to the jelly bean they had fed him, to make him calmer than he should have been. Probably not the worst idea, given their opinion of humans.

Morty was off, making a phone call to someone. And possibly having a smoke, if Gareth understood the vernacular correctly. He would need to have a chat with the Yuudixtl scientist later on the evils of tobacco, or whatever it was.

Xiomber had run to the men's room, leaving Gareth alone for the briefest moment.

Keelee had just delivered a second pot of tea, leaning so close that she briefly seemed to press one breast against his shoulder in ways that made Gareth extremely self-conscious. Worse, at least half a dozen tentacles had taken their time tasting him.

Or whatever The Grace called it. It was positively pornographic, the way her tentacles caressed his skin, ran through his hair, idled at the edge of his collar. She seemed to hum, or perhaps purr, as she did so.

Gareth realized he was never, ever going to ogle a waitress in a public house again. Or perhaps any woman. His own behavior had never been all that bad, but suddenly he was on the receiving end of what his men had frequently done to those poor women they had encountered at landfalls, trapped by the need to remain quiet in a bar, rather than staging a loud, emotional scene in public that would get them fired. If Gareth reacted loudly, called attention to the treatment he was receiving, he'd be arrested.

By the Gods, he would be much more of stickler for the rules, if he ever got home. This sort of thing was just embarrassingly rude.

As was the way he seemed to be enjoying the feel of Keelee's tentacles exploring his skin.

Thoughts of Philippa suddenly flashed to mind and he sat bolt upright.

"Keelee, you need to stop now," he demanded weakly. "Xiomber will be back soon, and I don't want you to get fired."

She laughed, throatily, but withdrew, the most polite sandpaper to ever set his nerves afire. Gareth breathed heavily and concentrated on pouring himself more tea.

Burning his throat seemed like a good idea right now, but he blew on the mug anyway.

Morty and Xiomber returned at the same moment from different directions.

"*Fardel*," Morty swore quietly. "You left him alone?"

"I wasn't sure if you were coming back, Morty," Xiomber snapped. "And I really had to pee. Besides, it's not like he was going anywhere."

"You okay, kid?" Morty asked Gareth. "You look a little flustered."

"Huh?" Gareth looked over at the tiny man. "What?"

"I know a guy," Morty said. "Had to skip my usual contact here, because she's a she and I don't need that level of complication right now. Let's go. We need to get you changed into something a lot less obvious, and then off this planet before any of the old gang tracks us down."

"You find us a lab?" Xiomber asked.

Gareth watched the other twin pull something from his back pocket and hold it up. It was almost a floppy wallet, but it was as big as his palm and barely half an inch thick. Looked like leather, though.

"Remember, I got everything here we need, but we still need to baseline the monkey-boy before we get crazy," Xiomber continued.

"That's next," Morty said, digging into a pocket and pulling out several coins that he dropped on the table.

"Did you leave a tip for Keelee?" Gareth asked.

"Who?"

"Our waitress," Gareth replied.

"How did you know…crap, she tasted you, didn't she?" Morty snarled.

"It wasn't that bad," Gareth protested defensively.

"Except now she can describe you to the cops," Morty hissed angrily. "We gotta get gone, right now."

Gareth followed them out into the street. Morty pulled out a pocketcomm similar to the one Gareth would have had with him, except it was sitting on his dresser, back at The Arsenal, along with his money, his ID, and his Sonic Stunner travel vault.

Morty pressed a button and looked up. Within moments, a flying car dropped out of the sky like a gray hawk, landed right in front of them, and a side door full-winged open.

"Get in," Morty commanded.

Gareth more or less fell into the vehicle, finding the back of the sky chariot a comfortable cocoon of crushed blue velvet. He sat on the bench facing forward, with Xiomber next to him and Morty across the way. The seat belts were more or less intuitive, but the two Yuudixtl didn't move to put theirs on.

"Seatbelts?" Gareth prompted.

"Seriously?" Xiomber glanced up, but he huffed and pulled the straps on. A moment later, Morty did the same. "Morty, we gotta talk about this guy."

"Dead or Jail, Xiomber," Morty reminded his brother. "Those are your other choices."

Gareth discovered that a Yuudixtl could roll his eyes, just like a human. With the same level of apparent teen angst and *ennui*.

Some things were apparently universal.

The car leapt into the air, driving Gareth back into the seat and reminding him why the seatbelts were such a good idea. A moment later, the car banked hard and shot off horizontally. Gareth probably would have ended up on top of Xiomber if he hadn't been already strapped down.

Xiomber looked up and came to the same conclusion. The grumbling under his breath ceased.

Outside, an exotic wonderland of a magical city swept by. Towers and sky bridges and flying cars.

And an angel.

Gareth found himself with his nose pressed against the glass of the window and his hands up, like a six-year-old on a long drive.

Maybe an angel. Human-looking, with wings that looked twenty feet wide as it flapped, holding a pocketcomm in his hands and watching something.

"Wazzat?" he almost drooled on the glass.

Morty leaned over and peeked.

"Elohynn," he said. "One of the *Accord* Species. Empaths. Damned good counselors. Right bastards as bankers, though.

"How many species are there?" Gareth asked, watching the man fade into the distance as the taxi sped away and then slipped around a corner.

"Seventeen," Xiomber asked. "Three others are candidates, in another few thousand years. Humans are not, however. Too freaking dangerous."

"You keep saying that," Gareth turned to the scientist. "Why?"

"The *Accord of Souls* didn't have a word for murder, Gareth," he replied flatly. "We had to use yours. Same goes for all the different levels of killing you crazy barbarians to do each other. Some people might pass out, just hearing the word *xenocide*. If the Chaa were still around, they might have either fixed you, like they did the other uplifted species, or just wiped you out. The betting's about even right now, but it's going to tilt pretty heavy if the galaxy ever finds out about Maximus and his gang."

"Why wouldn't they?" Gareth asked. "Don't human's stand out?"

"We were successful in turning him into a Vanir," Morty said. "*Those Left Behind* are what's left of the Chaa. When they evolved beyond material forms, only a few really wanted to go, so they took it upon themselves to become gods. Transformed the rest of their kin into the current form. But to keep them from getting lonely, so the story goes, they uplifted all the other species at the same time."

"And inhibited them from violence?" Gareth asked, making sure he had understood all the previous explanations.

"For the most part," Xiomber chimed in. "We're all bound up into a single, psionic entity. That's what the *Accord of Souls* is all about. Empathy. But some folks feel it more and some less. Those individuals who are at the low end tend to become criminals, like us."

"And we're completely outside of your empathy, so Cinnra wanted a human as an assassin," Gareth completed the thought. "Except I'm a police officer. A Field Agent with Earth Force Sky Patrol. The good guys. Shouldn't we be contacting a Vanir Constable to help them?"

"Pal, if they could stop Maximus Sarzynski, we already would have turned ourselves in and turned state's evidence. They got no chance in hell of stopping that guy. That's why we needed you."

"So now I'm a hunted criminal," Gareth observed. "And I'm supposed to help two other wanted criminals stop an entire gang of wanted criminals from taking over the galaxy?"

"You got it, pal," Xiomber cracked wise, leaning back into his seat.

"Who the hell do you think I am?" Gareth rasped.

"A hero," Morty replied in deadly seriousness.

Gareth slammed his mouth shut when it fell open. Scowled hard, but the Yuudixtl scientist was immune to his look.

And the little lizardman was right. That was all he had ever wanted to be.

A hero.

THE ARSENAL

PROFESSOR LOUGHTY MADE sure everyone else stayed at the door, including his daughter Philippa. Given his druthers, she wouldn't even be here, but his headstrong, only, daughter was not one to be easily thwarted. Especially not when her beau was the one that had disappeared.

Royston Loughty, *PhD*, *FRS*, *CBE*, *CStJ*, already thought of Gareth as his son-in-law. The young man had pressed his case early on, and then spent several years reminding Royston and Philippa of his love. But nobody and nothing could crack that man's hard head that he had to be promoted to the rank of Field Agent before he would formally propose. And Royston had tried every trick he could think of over the years.

Worse, he had known that Gareth was all prepared to finally propose, but Royston couldn't tell Pip that. She was already on the verge of tears, standing in the doorway with a fist to her mouth, the short, red shirt and tunic of a Sky Patrol Auxiliary reminding everyone how tough she was.

Royston smiled at his daughter as his portable scanner went to work. She had her mother's red hair and green eyes, rather than his own darker complexion, but Pippa had gotten her height from him, as well as his bones, in comparison to his dear-departed Elizabeth.

However, Pip had had gotten Elizabeth's strength, and her force of will, which served the young woman well, both in dealing with Gareth and her father, and also with society in general. The world frowned on a woman of science, such as Pip had become. She had earned her university degree, but no college would admit her to higher studies, so he had brought her with him to Earth Force's Headquarters in orbit where she had met and fallen madly in love with a rising agent.

Who had just vanished.

Royston would have considered the entire thing to be an elaborate practical joke, even after listening to the audio tapes of Gareth's last call, except that the portable scanner kept returning bizarre radiation signatures, no matter how he tuned it. Nothing dangerous or he would have never allowed his only daughter in here regardless of her impending engagement to the man in question.

No, just *strange*. Nothing he could explain, and he was Earth Force's preeminent expert on stellar radiation.

Something must have shown on his face.

"What is it, Father?" Pippa asked in a serious voice that still could have filled opera halls with its musicality, had she been of the mind.

"Sir?" Sector Marshal Alvin Siddall asked from over Pippa's shoulder from the hallway.

Royston found it amusing that the commander of The Arsenal itself was so deferential, but the situation was well outside anything Earth Force had ever encountered. That was why he had called in Royston. Plus, it had been Gareth. Everyone knew about that connection.

"There is something here," Royston admitted. "I cannot explain it. However, I can see it, and thus, it must exist and be explainable. Seal the room off for now. I will need to return with better equipment."

"Where is he?" Siddall asked. "Where could Gareth go?"

Royston drew himself up fully. Like the Sector Marshal, he was over six feet tall. Unlike the other man, Royston was only a little pudgy around middle and not turning fat like the man who spent too much time behind a desk.

"I don't know, Marshal Siddell, Pippa," he acknowledged them both, especially the depths of fear in Philippa's eyes. "Nothing I know can explain a man just vanishing like that. But I will find out."

DISGUISED

GARETH LOOKED around the strange office where the flying taxi had deposited them. The room was large and airy, but mostly empty, except for a few racks of clothes near one gray wall and a couple of triple mirrors standing in the back corner on his right, plus a pair of blue couches in the middle.

Still, Morty seemed at home, and Xiomber as well. Both took seats on the one couch and gestured Gareth to the other.

Outside, the taxi dove out of sight and the balcony door closed, sealing them off from the cotton-candy skies of *Orgoth Vortai*.

"Welcome," a disembodied, male voice filled the oversized room. "What'll it be, Morty, Xiomber? You two finally ready to dress better?"

Gareth had to agree with the voice. Both lizardmen were wearing something rough equivalent to common dungarees in blue, with pull-over T-shirts, Xiomber's in black and Morty's red with the strange design on the front. Gareth felt desperately overdressed in his Field Agent uniform. The two lizardmen dressed like a couple of machinists out for a beer after work.

"Nothing so grand, Jorghen," Morty called back. "And I sure as hell wouldn't have you do my wardrobe. Need to make the Vanir here look less memorable. His name's Gareth."

Vanir? Oh, right. Not human. Short Vanir. That's the cover story. I can do that.

"Gareth?" the man asked. "Stand up and walk to the mirrors on your right."

Gareth did, nervous, but not too much. Socially awkward, maybe.

His image came back in triplicate from the nine-foot-tall mirrors. A light flashed in his eyes, and the image in the reflection was suddenly wearing black pants, baggy enough that they covered his boots instead of tucking in. The Sky Patrol tunic was gone, as well. In its place, a plain, white t-shirt, underneath a button-down, button-up shirt in Sky Patrol plaid colors. A jacket appeared over top of that after a moment, blue denim like the Yuudixtl pair's pants, with bronzed buttons and a small SP button stuck through the flap of the left breast pocket.

Hey, that wasn't bad looking.

"Why not just take him to a department store?" Jorghen's disembodied voice came from all around a moment later.

"He gets self-conscious, shopping in the kids section, Jorghen," Morty fired back. "You, of all people, should appreciate that."

Jorghen had a crude laugh. Ugly. The bully at school picking on the other kids, at least until Gareth put a stop to it. But discretion was still called for here.

"You like that, Gareth?" Jorghen asked. "The fashion's a little offbeat, but that's what your subconscious wanted."

Gareth turned a nervous eye to the two Yuudixtl scientists. Morty nodded. So did Xiomber.

"Yeah," Gareth admitted.

He couldn't remember the last time he had dressed as a civilian. It had to be before he went off to school, ten years ago. The guy in the mirror looked like a cowboy, in the good ways. Like maybe if he added a hat, he could star in Westerns. Add a seven point star and he could be the town marshal.

"Okay," Jorghen said. "Take me about thirty minutes to kick it out. You leaving the other outfit here?"

Gareth panicked. Give up my Field Agent uniform? Never.

"Uhm, no," he settled for, rather than unleashing a blistering stream of the sorts of profanities he had first learned from the enlisted Chief on his first command.

"Put it on my account, Jorghen," Morty said. "And spin him up a set of formal robes, as well. Something High Street, but without all the flash of an investment banker. Low profile, as it were. We need to be able to eat at a fancy restaurant with a dress code."

"Add about ten minutes then," the man said. "Coming right up. Have some tea while you wait."

Gareth thought about it, but he really needed to pee. More tea would make it worse.

Instead, he leaned close the two criminals.

"Uhm, I need to use the facilities," he whispered.

"Through there," Xiomber pointed.

"But…"

"Erect bipeds, Gareth," Morty said. "Same design. Find the target at your height. Simple as that."

Gareth blushed and nodded.

When he got up this morning, peeing in an alien toilet was not anywhere on his list of things to consider. Still, he was Sky Patrol. He could do this.

The door opened easy enough. A counter with a mirror and a sink on the left. Stalls and urinals on the right. A red light came on as he stepped close to one.

Motion sensor.

Still, he managed, even with all the extra publicity. It flushed itself as he backed up and looked around.

There were no handles on the faucet.

None.

He got lucky and it went off when he passed a hand underneath.

Huh.

That was smart.

Out in the main room, the boys were sipping more tea. Gareth passed, for now. There was enough caffeine in his system for one day. And it was close to midnight, back on Earth. He would need to sleep soon.

In fact, the couch looked comfortable. He sat down, leaned back, and closed his eyes.

"WAKE UP, SLEEPY HEAD," a merry voice intruded. "You need to change and put your stuff in the bag."

Gareth climbed out of his bizarre dreams, into his bizarre reality. Hopefully this one was better.

He really didn't want to see a tentacled cow again. Like, ever.

The outfit from the mirror was hanging on hooks next to the mirror itself. Quickly, Gareth transformed himself into an Undercover Agent working a deep mission. A cowboy, even. The boots were wrong, but hopefully none of the locals would notice.

The Field Agent uniform got folded up exactly to regulation and put away, atop a piece of fabric that appeared to be a thick, soft black silk, shot through with red and cream glitter. It was the most beautiful piece of fabric he had ever seen.

"Thank you, sir," Secret Agent Gareth said to the room as he picked up and bag and slung the strap over his shoulder.

"Any time, Gareth," Jorghen said. "It's interesting, watching the machines locate the clothes you want to wear, as opposed to what society would inflict on a short Vanir."

"Let's go," Morty groused. "Time's wasting."

Out the door and onto the balcony. Another taxi settled in and opened for them. Gareth followed the little men into the cabin and leaned back, seatbelts in place.

"Now what?" he asked sleepily.

"Now we've got a little bit of a jaunt," Morty said. "Why don't you sleep for now, and we'll wake you up when we get there."

"I could never..." Gareth began to say as the day caught up with him and darkness descended.

CONSTABLE BAKER

"YOU HAVE GOT TO BE KIDDING," Constable Eveth Baker rasped into the telephonetics handset as she furiously wrote notes into an old-fashioned, leather-bound notebook with an even older-fashioned pencil.

The written word calmed her. Words on a page, rather than a screen, somehow rearranged themselves in her imagination to create new links between clues that she didn't think about consciously.

"Fine," she continued. "But you better be right, or the weekly stipend we pay you for these sorts of leads just might dry up."

Eveth slammed the handset down angrily and looked around the police bullpen where she was working. The space always felt dingy in her memory, when she wasn't here, but the room itself was clean and spacious. Well designed for calming psychology. It was just her that wanted it to reflect some of the squalor of the job.

Across the shared desk, her partner looked up from his reading with studied casualness. Senior Constable Jackeith Grodray was a by-the-book cop. The old man of the precinct they had paired her with in an effort to tone down some of the crazier things Eveth knew she did when pursuing the criminal element.

He was tall for a Vanir male, more than seven foot, two inches in stocking feet, but skinny. The man weighed barely three hundred pounds. Grodray was an intellectual cop. Divorced with two kids in school. Forty One Standard Cycles old, the light brown hair on his temples was turning gray now, and while he might have lost a step in a footrace, the Senior Constable had gotten that much better at outsmarting the bad guys so he never had to chase them down.

And he had Eveth, if it came to that. She liked pursuing criminals who thought they could get away.

Even his uniform tunic somehow conveyed the image of a staid academic, well-tailored to his overall shape with the bright, cerulean-blue ring of the *Accord of Souls* over his heart. Hers were always wrinkly and dusty, but that was the time she spent crawling under desks and into dark corners looking for clues.

"Something interesting?" her partner asked in a quiet, droll voice.

The room was mostly empty this afternoon. Quiet, save for a drunk snoring loudly in a cage in one corner of the office. Everyone else was out doing things, so they had almost the entire floor almost to themselves right now.

"One of my secret informers," Eveth shrugged and took a calming breath. Getting emotional with Grodray never did any good. The man was deduction, boiled down and decanted into a glass bottle. Emotions just washed off his narrow, sturdy chest like rain. "Usually, the man's reliable. This time, he claims that they heard rumors of a human, of all things, running loose on *Orgoth Vortai*, right here in Punarvasu."

"Again?" Grodray asked. "Haven't we had enough of these wild goose chases?"

"Get this," Eveth said. "Completely different description, this time. A pretty detailed one, at that."

She relayed everything off of her notepad slowly, letting her partner digest the words. He was all about processing things like a prospector seeking gold flakes. Swirl the water slowly, let it settle, add some more water, swirl some more. Eventually, the good stuff would settle to the bottom of the pan, once all the dross was removed.

Something caught her eye as she repeated it. Intuition snuck in and bit her on the ear, like it did.

"What?" Grodray asked as he realized she had stopped talking in the middle of a sentence.

Eveth turned her attention to the keyboard on the desk before her and typed furiously.

Suddenly, the screen flashed bright red and a beep chimed angrily at her.

WARNING. Information classified. Enter Level-7 security authorization to proceed.

"*Fardel*," she grumbled angrily under her breath.

A Constable like her was only Level-3.

"What are you trying to do, Baker?" he asked warily, standing and walking around towards her side of the desk.

She showed him the description of the clothing the human was supposedly wearing, written hurriedly as the informer had spoken.

"See?" she asked. "Red jacket. Black and gold design on the chest. I was trying to look something up about the humans that I thought I remembered, but the system wants a Level-7 clearance. Not worth trying to ask a Senior Inspector. They'll just tell me I'm imagining things."

"What are you imagining, Eveth?" Jackeith questioned quietly.

"A uniform," she said, flipping back through her notebook unsuccessfully. "Or something. It was part of a throwaway line that one Inspector made, back when they briefed us about humans during the first scare, last winter. Damn it, this notebook is too new. I'll have to look it up when I get home tonight."

"Here," Grodray said, leaning over her shoulder and typing something into the keyboard.

The screen flashed a welcome and brought up an image of a Vanir male. Except it wasn't. This was a human.

And Jackeith Grodray had typed his password into…

"How in the nine hells did you do that?" she stared up at him in surprise. "That was a Level-7 authorization."

"Uh huh," he smiled back serenely. Like always.

"But you're only a Senior Constable," she continued, confused and maybe a little frustrated. "That should only grant you Level-4, maybe Level-5 at best."

"I only ever wanted to be a Senior Constable, Eveth," he answered calmly. "Plus, I had to do some things several years ago. This was back before we were partners. They had to read me in on some very dangerous secrets."

Eveth flushed with a moment of pure avarice at the thought of the crimes you could solve with that level of clearance.

"So what have we got?" Grodray continued, still serene, damn it.

Eveth pointed at the screen, going back and forth between her notes and the image.

"White pants," she observed. "Check. Dark red tunic with weird gold things on the shoulders. Check. Black background a foot wide, center of chest, with some weird logo in gold in the middle. Check. The description also included three white rings around the black, separated by red lines."

"Three, you said?" he asked in a voice suddenly gone cold and stern.

She looked up again, feeling her face harden. It matched Jackeith's in that.

"Yes, three," she replied. "What's going on, Grodray?"

She watched him call up a menu item quickly and toggle something. The image changed, and now the chest had three rings around the black.

"The thing in the middle are two letters, Baker," he said carefully, glancing up to make sure they were still alone in the room. "From the principle language on Earth. *SP*. Stands for Sky Patrol. Part of the Earth Force that humans have over their single solar system."

"A military?" she asked, suddenly scrambling to her feet. She needed to be out on the streets, if there really was a human, a warrior, loose in this city.

"No," Grodray placated her with one hand and a calm voice. "That's the uniform of an Earth Force Sky Patrol Field Agent, Baker."

"Meaning?" she asked.

"He's a cop, like us."

UNDERWORLD

"WHAT DO WE KNOW?" Marc asked harshly as the two Warreth females entered his personal chambers.

He generally didn't like dragging everyone into the throne room, except for special occasions. That kept the mystique going. This was business.

"Got a lead, but we've got a problem, Maximus," Maiair replied.

They were sisters, Maiair and Yooyar. Primarily crimson in their feathers, with black and white highlights. Maiair was taller, but only slightly, and a year older.

Yooyar was probably the more dangerous of the two, however, the older sister was the cannier opponent.

"What happened?" Marc asked, moving across the outer chamber to grab a bottle of wine.

It wasn't worth making a scene with these two. They were loyal, and could be lethal if he needed to point them at someone needing to be disciplined. He grabbed a glass and poured some wine into it while he listened.

"Morty and Xiomber indeed found themselves a human," Maiair said. "The description fits."

"Where?" Marc looked up as the glass was full. He didn't bother offering any to the sisters. They wouldn't be here long enough to drink any, and this wasn't a social call.

"*Orgoth Vortai*," the older sister replied. "Witness puts them in Punarvasu a couple of days ago, but they've gone dark."

"They're on the run," Marc said. "They can't get far."

"Somebody made the human," Yooyar interjected. "The Constabulary got a tip. We've spotted a pair of cops in the place where Morty and Xiomber were confirmed."

Marc swirled the glass and sniffed the bouquet as he thought. Suddenly becoming a genius was incredibly useful if he needed to solve a math or physics problem, but not in the messy, complicated tides that represented the street. Still, he could use this to his advantage.

"Follow the cops," he decided. "Keep an eye out for the two traitors and the human, but let the cops do the leg work. If we get lucky, they'll flush the trio for us and we can swoop in. If not, they'll all end up in a cell somewhere and we can take care of them."

"Second problem, boss," Maiair said. "We've been down in the lab. Morty cooked everything good. Sabotaged the controllers to fry all the panels when they completed the jump. Plus, about half the generators overloaded and functionally melted."

"How bad is it?" he asked.

"Fixable," she replied. "But it will take time to build a whole new, completely-illegal, wormhole generator. Plus, if the authorities are jumpy about humans being around, someone is going to be looking at all the parts vendors, wondering who brought him here. If we suddenly buy a lot of gear, it's likely to show up on someone's radar."

"Understood," he said. "If the cops do catch them, one of those two shits are likely to offer us up as a way to either cut their sentence, or make sure that we end up in the same cell with them."

"So what do we do?" Maiair asked.

"Let's get ahead of the curve," he replied, taking a drink as he cycled down all the branches of the new decision tree faster than anyone he had ever met could match. "Keep together the hard core of the organization. Just the twenty or so we'll need for action. Have everyone else go to ground as fast as you can shut this facility down. Assume a police raid in five minutes and wipe everything. Put the A-team on the transport and get us jumped over to *Orgoth Vortai* as a tour group."

"Why there?" Yooyar asked.

Warreth didn't have a mouth that could be used to communicate emotions, like humans did. They used the feathered headcrest instead. The younger sister was confused, but that was inexperience. She had only joined the organization barely long enough ago to meet Cinnra, before Marc supplanted the old boss. She and her sister had understood which way the winds were blowing.

She was trying to figure out which way he was moving, so she didn't put a foot wrong, rather than challenging his authority. Learning, which was good. There were still a few of Cinnra's people he would need to ease out.

Or arrange lethal accidents for.

"There is no place better than anyplace else," he explained. "But they're likely to run, so we need to be in a position to give chase. Either them or the cops. This is about being close enough to force their decision curve the way we want it."

"Oh," she said, nodding firmly.

She didn't understand, but Marc expected her sister to fill in the details once they left.

He nodded them out and drank more wine.

Having Sky Patrol here changed things. The cops just might listen, if they knew what Dankworth really represented, and Sky Patrol wouldn't give up on their prey.

He should know. Packed carefully away, he still had his old uniform.

WITNESS FOR THE PROSECUTION

"YOU'RE SURE?" Eveth asked the Borren publican of the tea house, pointing at the picture in Grodray's hands.

She and Grodray had ended up back in the office with the tea house keeper. It was a tiny space with high ceilings and little art on the walls. The door was open, but that just let them see back into the kitchen, rather than the public space.

They had printed the image of a Sky Patrol Field Agent, minus all the explanations of what the thing actually was, but even then, it was never allowed out of Grodray's immediate control.

"Indeed, officer," the man said, tapping the chest. "The design was quiet interesting. I have considered doing it as a piece of art. Could I get a copy of that?"

"No," Grodray said with quiet emphasis. "In fact, if you were to put it up, *Accord* Security might take exception. I'd rather your shop not be shut down for potentially-criminal behavior. What say you?"

"Oh," the man said.

Eveth watched the manager blush, which was always interesting on one of the Borren. They were the standard biped design, but exceptionally tall, often nearing eight feet in the male, and over seven for a female. But they were also stick-thin. At a full six-foot-seven, Eveth probably outweighed the man, despite only coming up to his shoulder.

The eyes were large, compared to most species, with a long, flat, narrow nose, and a tiny mouth, but it allowed them to see in far lower light than most species.

And they were pacifists, as a rule. Great shopkeepers, though.

He leaned back as politely as he could, putting emotional space between himself in comfortable robes, and Eveth and her partner.

"And they left after an hour?" Eveth pressed, raising her voice just enough to keep the shopkeeper's attention.

"Indeed," he agreed. "Keelee served them, and they left a good tip."

Eveth turned to look back to the kitchen.

"Keelee," she said in a loud voice at the few employees lingering and probably listening.

One of them looked up in shock, while the others edged away. She was a young Grace. Her tentacles still weren't to their full growth yet, so not that long out of school. She turned utterly umber under the force of Eveth's gaze.

"Join us?" Eveth ordered in a polite fiction that only sounded like a question.

She had left her jacket in the car today, so her armored bodysuit with the badge over her heart was obvious. Normally, a nice tunic covered it with softer lines, but today, the harshness of the blue-gray scales stood out. As did the knee-high armored boots, the holster on her hip, and the utility belt normally hidden under the tunic. Eveth had tied back her hair, but the bangs needed to be cut. She blew one up to clear her eyes.

Next to her, Grodray still had his jacket on. It made him look diplomatic.

Eveth was here to play bad cop.

Keelee shuffled over, head hanging and tentacles nearly motionless with embarrassment. The rest of the employees made themselves scarce.

Eveth caught the girl under the chin with her right hand, lifted the face up to look at her. A few tentacles carefully explored Eveth's suit, but none made it as far as her hand.

"Two Yuudixtl, and a small Vanir?" Eveth pressed, pointing at the picture. "The Vanir dressed like this?"

"Yes, sir," Keelee answered quietly.

If anything, the young woman's blush got worse. She nearly turned brown and her pupils dilated.

Eveth played a hunch.

"Did you taste the Vanir, Keelee?" she asked quietly.

That was frequently a major *faux pas* with strangers. But if he was what Grodray thought, then the stranger might not know any better.

"Girl?" the manager bellowed.

Eveth silenced the man with a hard glance. After a moment, she stepped out of the doorway to the manager's office and pulled it shut it behind her. The Senior Constable could keep him in line.

And Grodray was a guy. He might not understand.

"You can tell me, Keelee," Eveth said carefully. "They're fugitives from justice, but you had no way of knowing that."

"I did, sir," the young woman said.

Her head would have fallen, but for Eveth holding it up. Having more than a foot of height, and the muscles to match, helped.

"What did he taste like?" Eveth asked, disguising her tone as well as she could.

Keelee didn't need to hear Eveth's disgust.

Some species knew no bounds, but Eveth had never considered anyone that wasn't a Vanir. And precious few of them.

Most men were either too timid around her, or too competitive.

But Keelee had stopped breathing.

Eveth nodded.

"He wasn't a Vanir, was he?" she asked.

"No, sir," the girl said. "I've never tasted anyone like him. So warm. So purple. So dreamy."

Shit, they really did have a human on the run in the *Accord of Souls*. And a witness.

"You can never tell anyone about him, Keelee," Eveth said. "Except me or the Senior Constable in the office. Not your family. Not your coworkers. Not your boss. If you did, and I found out, someone would have to arrest you and probably put you in jail for decades."

It was a serious threat. Eveth Baker was a serious cop making it. And a decade sounded like forever when you were twenty.

"Do you understand me, Keelee?" Eveth asked, trying to be reasonable while firm.

"Yes, sir," Keelee said. "I just couldn't help myself. I had to find a way to taste him."

Huh.

"Have you ever been that way before?" Eveth asked.

"No, sir," Keelee wailed quietly. "I've always been a good girl. I'm still a virgin."

"Well stay away from that creature and you'll be safe, Keelee," Eveth instructed. "Find yourself a good boy or girl of the Grace and make art instead."

"Yes, sir," she said. "I'm sorry."

"No, you've done well, Keelee," Eveth reassured her. "Now we know where to start, so we can find them. But you need to keep our secret. Can I trust you?"

"Oh, yes, sir," Keelee brightened.

Eveth sent her on her way and knocked on the closed door.

The Grace were all about art. Being able to see, touch, taste, and smell with those tentacles meant they lived in the richest sensory world possible.

Eveth figured she'd go nuts in a hurry, surrounded by that level of sensory bombardment, all day every day, but she wasn't an artist. Nothing like the Grace.

No, that wasn't true. She did have an art. A passion.

Hunting down criminals and bringing them to justice.

The Senior Constable emerged a moment later, shooting the manager a significant look that probably mirrored what was on Eveth's face. Perhaps a touch more refined and polite, but no less adamantine.

She nodded and headed for the front of the shop.

Out on the sidewalk, the sun was pleasantly warm, but not enough so that Jackeith would remove his jacket.

"What did the girl tell you?" he asked as they got some privacy.

The uniforms ensured that. The Constabulary were the *Accord's* police. There were other, more dangerous agencies, hidden deeper in the shadows cast by the cops, but most people still gave them a wide berth. Eveth assumed everyone was guilty of something, however small, and could use that as leverage. She was rarely wrong.

"She confirms we have a human on our hands," Eveth said. "Alien of a type she had never tasted, anyway. I didn't tell her what he was. The manager confirmed the uniform, so we know what we're dealing with. Where do we go from here?"

"Cinnra's organization were the ones behind the last human scare," Grodray mused. "But he's no longer in the picture, according to some sources. One theory was that he did manage to recruit a human."

"So did some other underworld organization decide to engage in an arms race?" Eveth asked. "Get their own human? But could they get a worse target than a human cop, Jackeith?"

"Maybe it wasn't random luck on their part?" he contemplated. "Maybe it was intentional?"

"Are you nuts, Grodray?"

"Let's employ deduction," he began.

Eveth knew to shut up at those words. Anything she said trying to derail her partner now would just extend the conversation that much longer. He would not be budged. Not when he got like this.

She nodded, trying not to hustle him or roll her eyes.

"Suppose Cinnra got himself a human, an assassin," Grodray pondered. "And lost control of the creature, since a human killer wouldn't necessarily only kill the people Cinnra wanted."

"Speculation, but sure," Eveth injected into the spot she was supposed to say something.

"And the human killed Cinnra," Jackeith continued. "That explains some of the upheavals and shenanigans we've had to deal with on various worlds. Turf war and maybe a new boss shaking things up."

"With you so far."

Without a single eyeroll, even.

"Who would want a human cop?" Grodray posed the million-credit question.

"Someone in Cinnra's band of criminals who wants to cover his ass?" Eveth guessed. "They would be the only sort of people who would know how to get a human, outside of some very shadowy agencies that would have never let one run around unchaperoned. And they might want someone who wanted to take the first human down, and had the human violence to do it."

"Holds water, Eveth," he said.

"*Fardel*," she replied. "That means we've got a potential race war on our hands. Two uncontrolled killers, gunning for each other, with a whole *Accord* worth of innocents potentially in the way."

"Worse," her partner noted. "I'm not sure we can tell anyone, with as flimsy as our evidence is. And if we do, they'll take it away from us in a heartbeat."

"You want to take Cinnra's gang down as hard as I do?" Eveth pressed.

"Probably more, Baker," he replied. "I know things about those bastards than you do not."

Eveth wanted to ask. So desperately wanted to know the truth. It probably included an explanation of how her partner, a lowly Senior

Constable, managed a security clearance at least as high as a Senior Inspector.

But she didn't dare ask. If they trusted him that much, he had no choice but to keep quiet.

Eveth wanted that level of trust placed in her by those same people, one of these days.

First, she had to take down at least one human genocide machine.

Maybe two.

TRAVELERS

"WHERE ARE WE?" Gareth asked, still a little fuzzy from his nap. They had apparently let him sleep a while. The sun was down.

"In orbit, aboard a ferry," Xiomber replied.

"Oh," Gareth said.

And then his brain woke up with a strangled cry.

In orbit? But there were no rockets firing to wake the dead. No high-thrust run at five G's to clear the atmosphere, on the way to an orbital rendezvous with Sky Patrol Headquarters or The Arsenal.

He leaned as far forward as his seatbelt would allow and stared out the window.

Sure enough, deep space stared back.

"How?" he turned to Morty, eyes as big as grapefruits.

"The taxi took us to the ferry terminal," the Yuudixtl scientist explained. "From there, a commercial wormhole bounce to orbit. In a few minutes, we'll debark at the terminal and walk aboard a tube ferry and hop over to *Hurquar*."

"That's a planet?"

"That's a planet, Gareth," Morty reassured him. "Primarily Yuudixtl, with a bunch of Vanir and Elohynn, so we'll just kind of vanish into the crowd."

"Then what?"

"Then we talk about upgrading you to take on Maximus and save the galaxy," Xiomber said firmly.

Gareth turned to look at the other brother. He wasn't sure what *upgrade* entailed, but if that was the only way to stop Marc Sarzynski, then so be it.

Some sacrifices were always worth making.

The taxi rotated and Gareth found himself staring at the side of a gorgeous space station. It was a long torus design, a tall donut with a hole in the middle, slowly rotating as he watched.

Gareth finally realized he was in zero-g, floating but for the seatbelt holding him in place. The taxi puffed suddenly and began to ease into line with hundreds of other, similar vehicles, headed into a port in the side of the station.

Inside, the taxi reversed course suddenly and flew along the mildly-inclined deck until it found a little dock and slipped in, like an egg in a carton. Heavy, metal hands grasped the sides and a small airlock door extended.

The hatch gull-winged up and Gareth followed the two brothers into a hallway long enough that he could see the curve of the station at the upward horizon, feeling like no cowboy he had ever seen.

But he looked good.

Women's heads turned as he walked through the thin crowds, all headed towards a stairwell.

Gareth heard Xiomber whisper to Morty as they walked.

"When this is done, I got a couple of long cons we need to run, using our boy here," the lizard chuckled.

Morty joined in with him. Gareth blushed. He would be in their debt, if they helped him bring Maximus to justice.

And they had talked about doing a little swindle, so that he could help pay them back for giving up everything. That wouldn't be such a bad thing, would it?

Assuming they all managed to not be in jail when it was done.

Up a deck, Morty led them to a private booth, well off in a corner.

"Get in, sit down, shut up," Morty ordered. "I'm going to go get us some food."

"Everything good?" Xiomber asked.

"I thought getting him new clothes would make the guy less memorable," Morty shot back. "Shows what I know about women."

"I know how little you know about dames, buddy," Xiomber cracked.

"Grab us some dim sum. I'll keep Gareth safe from bands of horny chicks."

Morty sighed and closed the door.

"Now what?" Gareth asked again.

He had a feeling he would be saying that a lot.

"In about thirty or forty-five minutes, the ferry will drop into a wormhole and we'll emerge on *Hurquar*," Xiomber said. "Not sure who he talked to or where we're going, but Morty's got connections everywhere."

"Why not take a personal wormhole?" Gareth asked. "Like you did me?"

"Because those are extremely illegal, highly dangerous, and incredibly expensive to operate," Xiomber replied. "If you managed to accidentally cross-connect two of them, you might vaporize half a hemisphere. Cinnra was desperate enough to build one in order to get Maximus. Morty and I were desperate enough to get you. Plus, we blew that one up when we left. And everyone travels commercial. Established corridors and times. Safe and comfortable. Was your first trip comfortable?"

Gareth shut his mouth. Xiomber didn't need to know about him screaming like a little girl lost in the forest.

"No," Gareth admitted. "Not really."

"Yeah, and multiply that by hundreds of inhabited worlds," Xiomber replied. "So everyone's inside a big, safe ferry with no outside windows unless they want to go to the observation deck."

"Huh," Gareth said. "But we're still going to stop Maximus?"

"Pal, we're going to try."

HURQUAR

IT HAD BEEN a different taxi that took them to the surface of the new planet. Gareth had been awake this time, to follow the reverse process. Undock from the little egg carton, join the stream of vehicles splitting into five different groups, apparently to transfer to five cities down on the surface.

Morty had opaqued most of the the windows, but left one for Gareth to watch.

He felt like a golden retriever allowed in the car on a winter day, nose against the glass and tail wagging.

Into a cubical zone marked by eight satellites the size of small space stations. Park briefly. Flash of gold as they rode into a hole in space.

The tube was a short ride, compared to coming here from Earth, but that made sense. How many light centuries, compared to fractions of a light second?

The sky over Olehmmishqu was closer to the blue Gareth expected. Still a little too green, and there were two small moons visible on the horizon when he looked.

The ground looked like a city.

Well, no.

On earth, the cities were either really old and organic in shape, or more modern and square as a rule.

Olehmmishqu was built on a series of interconnected hexagons.

Xiomber had produced a pocketcomm and let Gareth spend most of the trip reading about the Moisa. All he could think of to compare them to was a giant praying mantis, with four arms (two primary, two delicate), and six legs coming off of a very short abdomen, like a weird centaur or something.

They built hexagonally, in memory of the great nests they had established before being uplifted.

Gareth had a hard time imagining a flightless bumblebee, but that was sort of the niche they had filled on *Ticcia* and brought with them into the galaxy, like at *Hurquar*.

They apparently made fantastic architects. Gareth could see that, looking down at the various buildings, laid out like a map from above. The towers and such were every shape under the rainbow, and every color he'd ever considered. Or something like that.

This was all still a little weird, even for a Field Agent of the Sky Patrol.

But eventually, the taxi brought them to the roof of a mid-sized building, kinda sorta near the south(?) edge of town. It was cold up here. Gareth was glad he had the denim jacket, although he would need something heavier if they got into winter on some planet.

And a raincoat.

This was an advanced, galactic civilization. Couldn't they do something about weather control?

The elevator wasn't a box. It was a hollow tube. Morty stepped into air like a coyote accidentally running off a cliff chasing a road runner.

"Level forty-seven," he said and then vanished.

"You next," Xiomber prompted.

Gareth peeked over the edge of the hole to see a rapidly-receding Yuudixtl scientist.

Sure. Free-fall and trust the building to catch you. What happens if the power goes out?

Gareth gulped. He had an audience, and this was no time to ask for a stairwell. He gritted his teeth and stepped forward.

Something held his foot, but he didn't dare look down to see what.

Just pretend you know what you're doing.

"Level forty-seven," he said, maybe a little louder than necessary.

He plummeted, but there was no feeling of wind. It was like he was in his own, little cocoon. Thirty-three stories raced by faster than he could count, and then he was magically standing on the deck, next to Morty.

The little lizard's knowing grin broke the ice around Gareth's soul.

"Fun?" Morty asked.

"Efficient," Gareth countered, thinking back to the times he had to take a lot of stairs because there were too many people trying to use too few elevators.

When he got home, he was going to have to find a way to invent these elevators. Or hire a Moisa architect to rebuild The Arsenal.

Xiomber was there a moment later, grinning as well.

Huh. Yuudixtl didn't really have lips like humans did. The grin was there in the eyes and the way the skin around them pulled tight and folded in. And the jaw dropped open just a shade.

Maybe he had spent enough time around the brothers to understand the non-verbal communication better. It had been two and a half days now.

Or maybe the magic PBJ sandwich was still modifying his brain. There was always that.

Morty suddenly walked forward, drawing the other two into his wake.

Gareth squinted at the writing on the door where they stopped, and suddenly the letters transformed into something he could read.

Biomimetics Heavy Southern Industries LLKR didn't make any sense, though. Maybe a cultural thing?

Morty went in, so Gareth followed, through a boring reception area into a bigger space.

Now this was a mad scientist lab. Beakers, burners, racks of tubes arranged on black, heavy workbenches. It even smelled mad, with that cloying hint of ammonia he always associated with danger in a laboratory.

There was a Nari standing across one of the black-topped desks, writing on a white board with some sort of electronic pen. She was making adjustments to an animated image as he watched.

She turned, and locked eyes with Gareth. And smiled.

Gareth felt uncomfortable, like he was back at the teashop, but this one might not settle for just sniffing him.

"Heya, Talyarkinash," Morty said, circling the tall desk.

The beautiful woman finally broke the stare and Gareth remembered to breathe. And start walking again.

Xiomber rolled his eyes when Gareth glanced down, but the little scientist kept quiet.

Hey, it wasn't his fault.

"So what have you brought me this time, Morty?" Talyarkinash seemed to purr, glancing back in Gareth's direction.

He stayed on this side of the big workbench, just in case.

She was just gorgeous, even if she was a bipedal lynx with upright ears and whiskers. Bright cobalt eyes complemented a resplendent pelt in what Gareth thought of as Imperial Blue. He had had a cat that silver-blue shade when he was young. He found himself clenching at the thought of this one also climbing into his lap and kneading.

She had that look in her eyes.

Yup, staying over here.

"Talyarkinash, this is Gareth Dankworth," Morty introduced them, shaking her hand and then pointing.

Xiomber also got a polite shake.

Then she turned and stepped close enough to the workbench to hold out her hand.

Gareth took it gingerly, watching her nostrils flare and her eyes slit, just the tiniest amount.

"Already got a Nari girlfriend?" she asked.

Purred, maybe?

"Huh?" Gareth managed, losing himself in those deep eyes.

"Knock it off, Talyarkinash," Morty chided her. "Random dame on the slidewalk literally handed him a scent card out of the blue yesterday. You still got it with you kid?"

"Huh?" Gareth managed to repeat. "Oh. Yeah."

He pulled out his wallet and extracted the card, holding it up, but not out. It was his card and he was keeping it.

But he could smell the other woman's perfume on it. Or her musk.

Uncomfortable here.

"So she doesn't have a claim?" the cat woman asked silkily.

Claim?

"Uhm, not really?" Gareth supposed.

"Good," Talyarkinash said. "So what can I do for you? Or to you?"

Gareth carefully stuck the card back in his wallet as an excuse to look down. He was sure his face had turned the color of his hidden uniform right now.

"So, you remember that project we hired you for, about five months ago?" Morty asked delicately.

"Sure," the woman said. "You needed me to modify an alien. Brought me another one?"

Gareth did NOT like that gleam in her eyes when he looked up again. He held his breath and considered if he should just find a cop and try to explain everything, in spite of what the brothers had warned him would happen at that point.

He was not supposed to be a criminal. It went against everything Earth Force Sky Patrol stood for.

But he wasn't a Field Agent here. No, this was time to be a *Secret Agent*.

Gareth held his calm. He hoped. The way her nostrils kept working suggested that she was studying him far closer than a casual acquaintance in a lab.

"Gareth is a human," Xiomber said baldly.

That helped.

Talyarkinash stepped a whole pace back from her edge of the desk, and her ears rotated in different directions: one still pointed at Gareth, and the other now locking in on Morty.

Gareth felt better. Maybe she wasn't about to make unusually-personal suggestions now.

"You brought one of *them?*" she snarled. "Here?"

"Another one," Morty snapped back at the woman, reminding her.

She was twice Morty's size, and really angry right now, but the two brothers almost looked like they were challenging her to say or do something stupid.

Who knew what a pair of Yuudixtl scientists could do against a Nari?

The woman retreated another step but otherwise held her ground. And her peace.

"Maximus is a human," Morty continued. "Or was before you. I'm not sure quite what he is these days. You upgraded the physical to a Vanir. And Xiomber and I did the mental afterwards."

"Bastards," she hissed. "You brought a human into my lab? Do you want to get me shut down?"

"No," Morty said. "I want your freaking help making Gareth here at least a match for Maximus, before that bastard takes over the whole criminal underworld, and then follows that up by taking over the entire *Accord of Souls*. You think that sort of thing's going to help business?"

"You think a race war is going to help?" she snapped angrily. "Two them hunting each other through the planets? I might be shady, but I'm not going to be party to mass casualties of innocents, Morty. You can take your business elsewhere right now."

"He's a cop, Talyarkinash," Xiomber added.

"And you brought a cop into my lab?" she growled. "What in the nine hells is wrong with you people?"

"It's the only way to stop Maximus," Morty said simply. "Nobody but a human has the necessary violent tendencies *and* lacks the psionic resonance of the *Accord*."

"You're a cop?" she sneered at him.

Gareth felt like she was sizing him up for a physical assault now, rather than an emotional one. But that was the sort of thing he could deal with.

Even if he had to let a woman hit him first. Hopefully, she wasn't that strong.

It would probably still hurt.

"My name is Gareth St. John Dankworth," he explained slowly, enunciating each syllable. "I am a Field Agent of the Earth Force Sky Patrol. Like Morty said, an officer of the law. Marc Sarzynski, the man you know as Maximus, is a renegade agent with a bounty on his head, back on Earth. And I will see him returned to Earth and brought to justice."

"Back on Earth?" she scoffed, before turning to the two lizardmen. "You haven't told him, have you?"

"Told me what?" Gareth felt his stomach go cold.

"No," Morty said acidly. "We hadn't. Not yet. That was supposed to come later, but I guess we'll have to cover it now. Thank you, by the way."

"I did owe you one, for bringing a cop in here."

"Told me what?" Gareth focused on Morty and Xiomber now.

"No Earthman knows about the *Accord of Souls*, Gareth," Morty explained. "Such knowledge is forbidden, because humans are the single most dangerous species known. But you're here now, and you already know too much."

"Meaning?"

"Meaning you can never return to Earth," Xiomber said, possibly with a wistful trace.

Gareth felt his vision go gray. Something was wrong with his balance and both hands slammed heavily onto the top of workbench, catching his weight.

Never go home?

Never see his friends and crew again?

Never hold Philippa in his arms again? Unable to propose to her? Marry her? Start a happy life as man and woman?

For the briefest moment, rage threatened to overcome him. To make these two, these three, pay for what they had taken away from him forever.

Gareth sucked a breath deep into his soul and focused on the far wall.

The Nari woman had backed up another step, ears back and eyes showing white around the edges.

Gareth suspected he looked like all their worst nightmares brought to flesh before them. He certainly felt like it.

But Marc Sarzynski was here. Running loose in the wider galaxy. Who knew what terrible grief the universe would come to if that man wasn't stopped.

And they had upgraded him, whatever that meant. These three people, he suspected, held all the guilt at such work.

What was it Xiomber had said? Only humans could be genetically engineered to go beyond the limits placed on everyone else by the Chaa?

Marc had always been a fantastic athlete back at Earth Forces Institute. He and Gareth frequently alternated first and second with everyone else vying for a distant third.

Academics had been the same way, with only three thousandths of a point finally separating them on graduation. It was one of the few times Gareth had actually been better, however thin that razor.

And then Deputy Agents with the Sky Patrol.

And Philippa.

She had chosen Gareth, and something had died in Marc Sarzynski. Turned him to darkness. Got him cast out of the Sky Patrol one short step ahead of his arrest.

And then he disappeared, until Gareth came that close to catching him in the process of breaking up a band of smugglers and slavers operating out of the UnderHives of Mars.

To apparently come here, to the *Accord of Souls*.

Gareth hoped it wasn't all a fever dream leading his subconscious over the rainbow.

Another breath.

Gareth forced his fists to unclench, noting how nervous the two Yuudixtl were in addition to the Nari woman.

Yes, he was capable of devastating violence. They all were. It was part of what made humans what they were.

And why Earth Force needed the Sky Patrol.

"He's here, and he must be stopped," Gareth finally said heavily, eyeing each of them individually. "Whatever the cost."

"Are you sure?" Xiomber asked. "We might could somehow try and erase a chunk of your memory instead, if we got lucky."

"Whatever the cost," Gareth repeated.

PART TWO
HUNTERS

EXAMINATION

GARETH STUDIED the secret lab Talyarkinash had taken him to. They had passed through a door hidden by a swinging bookcase, gone down a level, and entered into a smaller space that reminded him more of a dentist's office than anything else.

The scents in here were almost nothing, layered over with floral hints and something subtle his brain kept wanting to interpret as Talyarkinash herself. Recessed lights filled the room with bright white illumination.

One wall was a glass window that felt heavy enough to stop bullets when Gareth had tapped it.

She and the two lizardmen had gone through another door and sealed it up tight behind them. They were on the other side of that glass now, watching him intently.

"First, I'll need to scan you, Gareth," the Nari woman said over a speaker. "Please make yourself comfortable in the chair and let it adjust itself to your body."

Dentist chair. Mad Scientist Dentist's chair.

Xiomber had said that a male Vanir could be over seven feet tall, with the females close behind. This chair would fit them.

For once, he actually felt rather like a juvenile Vanir, by comparison.

But he climbed in. Let the cold leather warm slowly against his back, with his jacket and flannel shirt hanging on a hook by the door. He had only the tight, white, t-shirt against the chill, but that cold was in his soul.

The air in the room was a pleasant seventy degrees.

Slowly, the chair moved. Gareth would have jumped up, but she had warned him.

It seemed to shrink under him, adjusting and accommodating until it fit like a hammock.

After a moment, it tilted itself back, giving Gareth a view of a device hanging from the ceiling that was in no way something so simple as the X-ray machine to take pictures of his teeth.

"Ready?" the woman asked nervously.

She sounded more emotional than he felt right this moment, but Gareth supposed she was expecting a Viking Berserker to break loose in her lab. He just needed to get this over with so he could go out and hunt down the man who had once been his fiercest rival.

And his best friend.

"Ready," Gareth said.

"I'll need to hold you in place while I scan you, Gareth," she reminded him for the fourth time. "Tell me when you are comfortable."

"Go ahead," he called, holding all his emotions tight inside.

They were long since past the time to panic. Or to stop.

Gareth locked all his muscles as the dentist's chair seemed to unfold itself a second time. Metal bars slid over his wrists and shins, binding them tight against the chair. Another strap crossed his chest, and a helmet lowered itself to cover most of his head, leaving only his mouth and part of his nose uncovered.

He wasn't claustrophobic, but the feelings weren't that far away right now.

"This is only supposed to tickle, Gareth," she said over the intercom. "Please let me know if you start experiencing pain."

"Will do," he said.

Ants. Walking across his skin but not biting. The leaves of a weeping willow as he walked through them. The cool chill of a morning fog as he jogged around the track, back at the Institute, watching the sun come up higher on every lap.

A bright light passed through his eyelids and bored a tunnel into his mind like a three-quarter inch bit being driven by a three-quarter-horse-power motor.

Gareth ground his teeth together and refused to make a sound.

"Everything okay?" Xiomber asked. "Vital signs just jumped."

"Sharp, but controllable," Gareth called back, willing everything to stillness again. "Keep going."

Hunt the man down. Bring him to justice, whatever that looked like here.

Whatever the cost.

The ants were biting now. Nasty, Texas fire ants pouring acid into his veins. The willow was a rose bush, slashing him with thorns. The fog was an icy pond he had just fallen into, through the ice.

Whatever the cost.

Something changed in his brain. The pain was there, but pushed to one side. He could think through it, or at least around it. Gareth focused his will, pushed, and the pulsing turned outward, as though he was somehow driving the drill bit backwards and closing the hole up, faster than the machine could tunnel.

Everything let go so suddenly Gareth thought he would pass out.

The pain was gone. The fire. The cold. Everything.

The chair let go and moved him more or less upright.

Gareth swung his feet over and stood up, only wobbling slightly.

"How are you doing in there?" Morty asked carefully.

"Headache," he replied. "But it's going away now.

"You had pain?" the woman asked. "It's not supposed to do that."

"I overcame it," Gareth growled. "What's next?"

"Come in here and we'll watch the readouts," she said. "It will only take a few minutes to process everything."

The door unlocked noisily and swung open on silent hinges. Gareth stepped through into a sound studio.

One long console sat under the window, filled with hundreds of gauges, knobs, and sliders. Gareth had no idea what it all did, but he recognized the human outline on a large monitor beside the window.

The writing on the screen was mostly words he could make out, but Gareth was completely lost as to what they said.

He took a chair in a far corner and concentrated on breathing and reducing his heart rate.

It felt like he had just run from Marathon to Athens in a single instant.

A machine spit out a long strip of paper, clucking to itself like a hen.

Talyarkinash was studying the readout, holding it low enough for Morty and Xiomber to read it as well.

Someone whistled, low and startled.

Gareth looked up and studied the three scientists.

"Gareth," she said carefully. "Where would you say you rank, in terms of expressed, human potential?"

It took him three tries to process her words into something that made sense.

"Probably near the top, in terms of mental, physical, and emotional," he replied through his exhaustion. "Sky Patrol Institute is a grueling test that lasts four years. I graduated at the top of my class. Marc Sarzynski was a very close second."

"You went to school together?" She was aghast.

"I told you that."

"I thought that meant you knew of him," she countered. "How close were you?"

"He would have been my best man at my wedding, one of these days," Gareth said firmly. "Now I'll see him buried under the jail, if it's the last thing I do. Why?"

"So we scanned him then, but not to the level we just did with you," Morty explained as the Nari woman fell mute. "Plus, I know roughly where we put him, so I was looking for what we could do to improve you. We'll probably only get one shot to do it, and I want to get all we can. You'll be facing both Maximus and the Constabulary at the same time. Neither will play nice."

"So what did you learn?" Gareth felt some level of anxiety creep into his voice.

"It's just that…" Morty's voice tailed off.

Xiomber stepped up and gave Gareth a level gaze.

"What he's trying to say, I presume diplomatically, is that you appear to be using fourteen percent of your expressed, genetic potential, Gareth," Xiomber said. "For comparison sake, members of the *Accord* are generally fixed at right around ninety-eight percent. We can tinker with ourselves, but nothing significant."

"Meaning?" Gareth asked. He was tired, sore, and his head hurt.

"Meaning we were able to turn Sarzynski into a genius-level Vanir, Gareth," Talyarkinash explained. "But we stopped there because we apparently didn't dream any bigger."

Genius-level Vanir.

Seven feet tall. Three hundred, twenty-five pounds of hard muscle, trained to be as dangerous as an Agent of the Sky Patrol could be. With an IQ of two hundred.

And that was dreaming too small?

"How big should we dream?" Gareth finally asked.

THE ARSENAL

ROYSTON PULLED the ticker-tape readout from the side of his radiation scanner, made a note, and scrolled backwards on the tape nearly three feet to another set of results. Briefly he wondered if the radiation machine was broken.

Or if he had tuned it too sensitive and it was reacting to just the movement of the air at this point.

Except, Gareth's room was the only place where the readings changed. Royston looked around, but nothing was out of the ordinary. The place was as standard and regulation as they came, which was to be expected of Gareth. His pocketcomm was still sitting on the desk, next to a book the young man had apparently been reading when the emergency happened. The bed tucked tight, except where he had pulled the covers slightly while sitting on them.

Uniforms all arranged in the drawers and closet exactly according to specification.

Royston had even scanned both chester and closet, on the possible chance that Gareth had brought something home with him from a recent mission, but nothing reacted.

No, the only time the machine pinged at all was when he pointed the detector at the telephone's handset, or at a spot in the middle of the floor, almost in the center of the triangle between bed, dresser, and closet. And in both of those, the radiation reading went off the charts. It made no sense at all.

Royston turned the machine off and moved to the door. He opened it and looked out at his daughter, patiently waiting on a chair just outside.

"Any news?" she asked as she looked up.

"No," he replied. "Come inside, please, Pippa. I want to review what I've learned."

She rose with all the grace of her mother and flowed past him, holding a book of Tacitus written in Latin that she had been reading while she waited.

Closing the door, he found her seated on the one chair.

"I don't know how to tell you this, Pippa," he began.

"I'm made of far sterner stuff than you think, Father," she replied with a primness she inherited from dear Elizabeth.

"If I believed in angels and devils, I would have to only presume that one such opened the fabric of space/time itself and grabbed him," Royston said. "But since we know that to be impossible, I'm at a loss."

"Why do you presume the impossibility of such a thing, Father," she asked, eyes glaring. "In science, you have always taught me that we use deduction to eliminate the obvious, and thus, what remains, no matter how far-fetched, must be the explanation."

"Gareth Dankworth disappeared from this room in a way I cannot explain. And did so without opening any doors ," Royston said. "The air vents are too small to admit anything larger than a mouse. But he is absolutely gone."

"Then your understanding of physics are insufficient," Pippa stated flatly.

"What?"

"As you said, science cannot explain it, and yet it happened," she retorted. "Ergo, our knowledge of science is too rudimentary to explain that angel or devil and how they were able to open a portal through space and time to kidnap Gareth. Prior to Newton, we were still bound by the laws of gravity, even though we could not explain them. Gareth was here, and then he was not. The door did not open and there is no other method of egress. Therefore, something opened a different type of portal, one we do not understand. What did your radiation detector find?"

"Something my simple understanding of physics cannot explain," Royston said, granting her the warmest smile the chills in his heart would allow.

Indeed, sterner stuff than he gave her credit. Stronger than many of the men he knew.

She was like Elizabeth in that. He missed his wife less, knowing how well their daughter had turned out.

"Tell me," Pippa commanded, Queen of England facing down the Armada.

"There is a signal when I scan the handset," Royston said, moving to the middle of the room. "The only other place I find it is here. I have scanned countless other places and rooms, and only here do I find that signature."

"What does that tell us, Father?" Pippa continued. "It tells me that Gareth was talking on the telephone when this indescribable portal opened, right where you are standing. It pulled him through before he could resist, then the handset fell. The radiation only touched those two places, as you said."

"But how did someone open a rift in space and time itself, in order to kidnap the man?" Royston asked.

"No," Pippa stated flatly. "There is a more important question we should be asking. Namely, why did they want Gareth?"

BR'ER RABBIT

"IT HELPS that the perp is so damnably memorable," Eveth said, turning away from the foot traffic on the street to study the scowl on Grodray's face.

"I agree," her partner conceded. "But now things will get interesting."

Jackeith began to walk, so Eveth fell into stride beside him.

They were at the star ferry office downtown. Had just left, headed back to their own precinct building. The sun was clouded over, giving the day a soft and uncertain taste.

"How so?" Eveth asked. "We know they made it off-planet using the ferry."

"We suspect," Grodray corrected her. "We've got a witness putting them in an auto-car in the right time window. Records show that car deposited them at a haberdashery nearby. You haven't called the operator of the shop, because we don't want to tip our hand, and to get a warrant would require that we tell someone important what we think is going on, but more of your witnesses confirm the car's arrival."

"I've got a gut feeling on this one, Grodray," Eveth said.

"And I have learned to trust your intuition, Eve," he replied. "But all a raid gets us at this point is confirmation of who was there, and maybe an actual picture of the...*perp*."

They were on a public street. Not even her by-the-books partner would use the word *human* here, for fear of starting a riot.

"What's next?" she asked, knowing his penchant for deduction.

"So the next step was tracking auto-cars from the haberdasher," he said. "Once you had the building identified, I went off and tracked outbound cars, assuming that they think they are safe. Pretty sure I found a target. Certainly, the credit account they are using belongs to a Warreth insurance salesman living on the southern coast. He'll be in for a surprise when he gets his monthly bill, unless we warn him ahead of time. That also gives too much away."

"It does," Eveth said. "I don't want to share this one bit more than I have to. Any judge we tell is going to call a Senior Inspector in."

"They will, at the very least. That's wherein the problem lies," Grodray said. "Based on what we've run down today, all the other cars that left that address over the next two hours are accounted for, except for three that went to the orbital boost for the ferry, first stop: *Hurquar*. We have to presume they caught a ride up to space, and then left the system."

"And walked right out of our jurisdiction," Eveth grumbled.

"Perhaps," Grodray countered. "Is it worth raising a fuss now?"

"Have you got the jets to lift this one, Grodray?" Eveth asked suddenly. "You've got a Level-7 Security Authorization."

"And I am very careful about how I use it, Baker," he replied. "I can go to a judge and fill out a probable cause request. That gets us a warrant to access the haberdasher's records, but any judge we ask is likely to put in a call to a Senior Inspector, possibly the Command Inspector herself, and ask for clarification. That starts an avalanche of questions."

"In for a penny, in for a pound," she stated her position. "I want what you have. I want to be on the inside of some of those investigations you obviously can't talk about around me because I'm only Level-3. And if we've got a human loose, maybe *another* human loose, then I absolutely want to be in on that takedown."

"Even if it means being stuck running to get coffee for a Senior Inspector?" he asked. "Just being on the back of the stage while the big shots get all the credit for the work you did? The sweat you gave? The blood you shed?"

Something in his eyes told Eveth that Jackeith Grodray had been there. Had done exactly that. And let the politicians have all the credit.

But it also made him very quietly a Level-7. Almost the top of the ladder. Hunting renegade humans would be at that level.

"We are the law, Grodray," she growled. "I would rather see justice done than worry about getting my face in the newspaper."

"In that case, we need to split up," he said in all seriousness. "I'll go make a few personal calls and get things rolling. You go home and pack some clothes for a sudden, extended vacation."

She stopped cold and grabbed his arm to halt him. One hand indicated her uniform, even minus the outer tunic he was wearing.

"This uniform, this badge, is all I need, Grodray," she said.

"No, Eve," he replied. "Where we might be going, that sort of thing will get you killed."

Eveth studied the calm certainty in his eyes and let go of his arm. There was only one place that her uniform would be a hindrance. A liability.

If they were going undercover, into the very shadows where folks like Cinnra hid.

DREAMS

IT WAS something like Chinese take-out, on an alien world that had never heard of China, or dim sum. Still, it fit the bill, more or less. White, cardboard-like boxes, filled with a variety of things that had the textures of meat, or vegetables, or fish. Half a dozen bowls of sauce, arranged on the workbench on front of Gareth from sweet to hot, according to his palate. The Nari woman preferred things less salty, and the two Yuudixtl were looking for better *umami*. Whatever that was.

Gareth had a low-sided bowl in front of him, and had learned to snag a quick sample and eat it before pouring more out. So far, he was batting better than average for taste, as long as he didn't ask what anything was.

He was quite confident he didn't want to know.

The smells, however, kept him eating.

Talyarkinash sat directly across from him as she ate, watching him like a hawk. He couldn't tell if she was still interested in him or fearful. Probably both, if her ears moved the same way a Terran cat's did.

Morty was next to her. Xiomber was on this side. Both were face-down, shoveling in food as fast as they could chew. Gareth was actually tasting his food.

"What are the established capabilities of genetic engineering in the *Accord of Souls*?" Gareth finally asked the table, unsure who would answer.

All three took turns staring at each other, hoping someone else would go first. They had been that way all afternoon.

Gareth had decided it was finally time to wrestle with the eight-hundred-pound gorilla.

"What answers are you looking for, Gareth?" Talyarkinash finally asked,

"I realize the first question I want to ask is too open-ended," he replied. "As you said earlier, the limits might be in our imagination and not in your science. Could you undo it later?"

"Undo it?" Morty asked. "Kid, we're grappling with the need to maybe make you over into a god, for lack of a better term. The most powerful being since the Chaa left. You want to give that up?"

"Morty, you're talking about making me something God never intended me to be," Gareth said. "I get that. But if you can make me into a Vanir, could you reset me to a human later? Could you possibly undo what you did to Marc?"

"Crap, Gareth," Xiomber joined in. "Nobody's ever wanted to downgrade. This has always been about trying to work our way around the Chaa's limits and not die in the process."

"I'm not a god, Morty, Xiomber," Gareth said. "I went to Sunday School when I was a kid, and there's only one God."

"First off, up until very recently, humans had lots of gods, kid," Xiomber said with authority. "Some of your cultures still do, from what research I did when we went looking for Maximus. So maybe you need a better pantheon."

"I need to know that we can undo it," Gareth was firm. "I can settle for being a hero out here. That's all I ever wanted to be. But making myself over into a monster just to fight Marc, makes me just as bad as him."

"There are no humans in the *Accord*, Gareth," the Lynx woman pointed out. "Maximus is a Vanir now, by both scope and genetics. He could breed true with a Vanir woman."

"And if you also make me one, like you plan, you've forever taken away from me the only woman I've ever loved," Gareth replied, trying to hold the heat and anger in, at least as much as possible.

"Who is she?" Talyarkinash asked carefully.

Gareth stewed for a moment and then reached for his wallet. The scent card was still there. But so was a picture he pulled out and handed to the woman criminal scientist.

"Philippa Adeline Loughty," he said. "Pippa. A human woman I've been in love with for many years. I was just about to go see her and finally propose when someone opened an illegal, cataclysmically-dangerous, private wormhole and upended my entire life. If I'm a Vanir, we can never have kids. Never raise a family. Nothing. That's what you'll have taken away from me."

"Gareth, you can never go back to Earth," Morty said. "You know that."

"You don't know that, Morty," Gareth anguished. "Like Xiomber said, maybe you'll be able to completely wipe my memory, one of these days and just deposit me back at the Arsenal like nothing happened, except for a hole in my memory."

"Would she wait for you? Talyarkinash asked.

"Yes," Gareth stated categorically, thumping the tabletop with a finger. "She already has, because I wanted to wait all these long years until I made it to Field Agent. If she disappeared, I'd wait for her."

"Wow," the woman murmured.

The others fell silent. Gareth listened to his heart pound, sure they could hear it as well.

Gareth poured a cluster of purple things that looked like barbeque pork slices onto his plate and added a dollop of the yellow sauce from the middle. It wasn't mustard, but that wasn't pork, either.

He was eating ashes, either way.

"I have an idea," the Nari said quietly. "I don't know if it would work, but it might be worth a try. Gareth, what do you know about biomimetics?"

"I'm not even sure how to spell it, Talyarkinash."

"It's a study of natural creatures and how evolution has produced various biological solutions to mechanical needs that we can mimic, shaving off development time in prototyping and adapting things," she tried to explain.

Gareth listened, but the words went over his head.

"Modifying spiders to make their webbing super strong so we can use it as thread. Or inserting useful vitamins directly into milk in the cow. That's our cover here. The lab upstairs does a little work, but mostly it's a front for money laundering and giving people new lives by modifying their face and genes to hide from cops."

"Okay?" Gareth asked.

"I'm frightened with the raw potential that humans have for manipulation," she said. "But also a little excited. We absolutely need to make you over into a Vanir just so you can hide in plain sight afterwards, but maybe we can limit the major modifications by using biomimetics as a basis."

"Did any of that make any sense to you?" Gareth asked the two Yuudixtls.

"She's talking about building you toys, Gareth," Xiomber finally said. "Baking all the powerful enhancements into biologically-powered genetic systems that you could maybe undo later. Or at least turn off."

"That true?" he turned back to the woman.

Excitement brought out the beauty in those tanzanite eyes. Brought it back, and pressed the underlying fear of a berserker loose in her lab to the back. Mostly.

Probably about as good as it was getting for now.

"More or less," she said. "The possibilities are absolutely a blank page. I'm not even sure where I want to start. But I can turn you into a pseudo-god, with a little effort."

"Dream bigger," Gareth said.

Morty and Xiomber turned to him, jaws agape. Hers fell open a moment later.

Gareth just fixed them with a hard gaze.

"Whatever it is, you're already thinking too small," Gareth said.

He drew his inspiration from the two scientists across from him. Two criminals that were responsible for him being here, but were also going to give him the chance to stop Maximus and make it all right.

Two hard-headed Yuudixtl that reminded him of dreams from when he was a kid.

If he could not go home, he could still become a hero. He would just never allow them to make him a God. Mom and Dad wouldn't stand for that level of arrogance from their oldest child. Pastor Jacob would cast him from the kirk. And rightly so.

"I've met Nari and Grace," Gareth said. "Seen Vanir and Elohynn, Borren and Moisa, at least at a distance. Yuudixtl, however, give me an idea. I could look it up, but I'm pretty sure the Chaa didn't do it, or the Yuudixtl would have turned out differently."

"What are you babbling about, Gareth?" Morty sputtered.

"You're going to make me over into a Vanir," Gareth conceded. "I get that, since the only other choice I could see easily made would be an Elohynn, but I don't want to have to deal with wings all the time, as cool as that might be, and every kid's fantasy when they're eight."

Talyarkinash started to say something, but Gareth cut her off, even as rude as it was when a woman was talking.

"You're building me tools?" he asked her, eyes boring in. "Weapons that I'll need to fight Maximus and his gang? Going to make me a god, according to the old stories?"

She nodded, apparently breathless with anticipation.

Gareth shook his head firmly. Locked eyes with Xiomber first, and then Morty before returning to her.

"No," he told her firmly. "I want you to make me a dragon."

THE HUNTER

MARC REALIZED he had finally been in the *Accord of Souls* long enough to learn the patterns of a multi-species population, but cities as *things* never really changed. Olehmmishqu, on *Hurquar*, was really no different than New Metropolis, or reborn Shangdu, north of the ancient capitals of Nanking and Peking.

People were people, regardless of shape, color, or religious affiliation.

He was surrounded now by an entire restaurant full of them, unknowingly sharing their air with the single most wanted person in the *Accord*, at least until more people heard about Gareth Dankworth. After all, Marc was a cipher, a Vanir with a shady past working in the shadows of crime. Dankworth was still the thing parents warned their children against, human.

The man couldn't hide for long.

Marc sipped a glass of wine and studied his three dinner companions. The two Warreth sisters, the crimson raptors Maiair and Yooyar, were part of his inner circle for this mission. Zorge, the Nari scientist/spy, took the other spot. Marc might have brought others, but these three were fitting well into his needs, and some of the others might be a little too well known to openly dine at a fancy joint like this.

And Marc really had a hankering for a good ribeye steak, something close enough to a baked potato, and a slice of pie afterwards. Gareth was out there, but he could wait. Marc knew how this city flowed.

Money went to the nice places. Here, that meant down on the river that ran slowly along a park-like Promenade. At least for the younger set. If your wealth was established and generational, you had a place up on the hills to the west.

Both were places he didn't really want to see. The two traitors wouldn't have ended up there, even trying to hide from him.

No, he needed to look in the rougher places. The warehouse district, out at the edge of town, where miles of identical blocks held tomorrow's stock in trade. Or the meat-packing district, where refrigerated transports from various farming counties and planets coalesced with their exotic products, feeding their stock to the middlemen that served the boring, banal, cultural backbone of the *Accord*: the middle classes with their presumptions and small-minded ways.

Marc needed to be down with the bohemians, the artists, and the hustlers if he wanted to find a man trying to hide. The places where crime could be contained, and concealed, but still readily ignored for a good enough bribe to the right people.

Not the Constabulary. Those people had no sense of commerce. But they also weren't that thick on the ground. No, Marc preferred the local beat cops. The men and women who knew their neighborhoods and would overlook the petty crimes for a little money on the side, as long as you kept a lid on your activities and the only victims were outsiders.

Always protect the neighborhood. Being in Olehmmishqu was really just like being home in Little Krakow, back in New Metropolis.

"What have we learned?" Marc turned his attention to Zorge, seated directly across and just finishing his salad with a crunch.

The older scientist also had the best manners of anyone Marc had kept when he thinned out some of the less-loyal elements. Zorge paused, set his fork down, dabbed at his mouth with a napkin, and sipped a bit of water.

Most of Marc's crew probably didn't know which of the forks on the table did what. At least the sisters had learned quickly when Marc told them what they needed to do to get ahead.

"I'm working on one fundamental assumption that you should pause and reconsider," Zorge said, at once vague and specific. "You are now seven foot two. Dankworth is only six foot one, from what you've said, and thus will stand out as a very short Vanir, anywhere he goes. My presumption is that Morty and Xiomber, being geneticists, will want to do the same thing to him as they did to you, possibly with a five percent increase in his physical capabilities, if that's possible."

"That was my thought, as well," Marc agreed. "I don't see him becoming an Elohynn, as interesting as the symbolism of that would be."

"Sir?" Maiair asked, obviously a little lost at the turn of phrase.

"Back home, one could make the case for me as the *Fallen One* of one of our primary religions," Marc said. "An angel who was cast out of heaven. A man who would rather rule in hell than serve in heaven. Giving Gareth Dankworth wings would make him over into Michael, the warrior archangel. Rather fitting, all things considered, but not worth discussing at this time."

"Right," Zorge said. "But that brings me to a possible logical fallacy. Would he try to outthink us by turning himself into a Nari, or a Grace? He could walk right up to this table, disguised, and none of us would be the wiser."

"I don't think so," Marc said, racing the newly-enlarged confines of his mind back over the years he had spent next to the man who had once been his best friend and greatest rival. "His ego would never let go of being human, so he'll want to stay as close as possible to that baseline. Vanir are the best place to look."

"Good," Zorge looked relieved. "I have my teams out pounding the pavement, looking for shadow-shops that specialize in that level of genetic modification. There aren't many, and we have to approach them quietly enough, politely enough, so that we don't burn bridges later with any of them that aren't hiding our prey. Second question. Do we think they went to ground on *Hurquar*?"

"It is an interesting parlor game," Marc replied. "They didn't want to bring him to *Zathus*, because that was our base and I have fingers everyplace they might have wanted to hide. They didn't stay long on *Orgoth Vortai*. Really just enough time to distract us and vanish. My guess is that their ultimate goal was *Hurquar* and no farther, at least until we find them, or the cops do. They'll need time to do whatever they have planned, so they needed to get ahead of us, but they have to stop running at some point so as to complete the work. After that, they can hide better. Yuudixtl and Vanir are two of the most common, least-insular species in the *Accord*. What do the authorities know?"

That last in a quieter voice as their waiter swooped by to refill water, replace bread, and pour more wine. This place really was top notch. Marc couldn't remember the last time he had eaten bread that good.

Possibly Gareth's mother's bread, at a winter break celebration, but that would have been nearly eight years ago. He would have to come back to this town more.

"They got really quiet, there at the last on *Orgoth Vortai*," Maiair took up the thread. "We're facing Senior Constable Jackeith Grodray, one of Cinnra's worst enemies, and his new partner, Eveth Baker, another Vanir like Grodray."

"How good is Grodray?" Marc asked. "I've read Cinnra's notes, but he left out too much and self-aggrandized with the rest."

"He's good," Maiair replied. "Came close to unraveling us on a couple of occasions, back in the old days, when Cinnra first deposed Jeffrak and hadn't gotten rid of all the trouble-makers with axes to grind. Forced us to go much deeper underground than we ever had been before."

"Grodray's not the problem," Yooyar injected. "Baker is."

"How so?" Marc turned his attention to the youngest member of the gang, both in age and seniority. But the latter was just a matter of time, as he stared to recruit again. Then, she would suddenly be in the middle and need some responsibilities, to see if her natural talents could be honed down and polished into something like her sister.

"Grodray is methodical," Yooyar said. "Slow, careful, numbers-oriented. According to some of the old timers, he actually tracked us down with bank statements, wading through all the different transactions as we laundered things, spending a year just reading printouts. That's well and good. We learned to hide better. Baker is all action. She'll be the one that kicks in the door and stuns everyone in the room just so nobody gets away while she sorts out villains from innocent bystanders."

"Interesting," Marc observed. He turned to Zorge with a thin, cold smile. "When you nail down a probable target chop shop, let's feed the constables an anonymous tip. I want to see these two in action so I know what to prepare for. We know they're here. But they've gone to plainclothes work, so tracking them is harder. Let's flush everyone out at once."

"Understood," Zorge said.

Further conversation ceased as the food arrived. Marc considered the two pounds of rare steak in front of him, with all the fixings. He had rarely eaten this well back on Earth. At least not since he got drummed out of the Sky Patrol.

Maybe he needed to bring in a few more folks from the old

neighborhood, once he was well and firmly in control around here. The *Accord of Souls* was an old lady walking home in a poorly-lit alley, just waiting to be mugged.

Maybe Marc needed to make himself king.

PLAINCLOTHES

IT FELT WRONG. Just wrong.

Eveth wasn't naked in public, but she sure felt that way, wearing civilian clothing as they chased down leads. Back home, she would still be in her bodysuit with the scale armor and the ring badge over her heart.

That intimidated people, however unconsciously. Vanir weren't the tallest species in the *Accord of Souls*, but they were the biggest, in terms of size and bulk. Eveth liked to use that to her advantage.

Here, she felt like an insurance salesman, cold-calling for new clients. Most of the people they had interviewed so far today had initially reacted that way when she and Grodray walked through the front door.

People got a lot less antagonistic when she dropped her wallet on the desk and flipped it open to reveal the badge inside, however

Still, they were making maddeningly-slow progress.

Slacks and a blazer did nothing to improve her humor.

Eveth checked the next address. Biomimetics Heavy Southern Industries LLKR.

The local Constabulary office had suggested that the place might be a cover for criminal activities. At no point, however had anybody ever been able to find anything even good enough to get a warrant that they could use as a wedge in the door, turn the place upside down with a fishing expedition.

She wondered if that just meant that the owners knew which local cops and politicians to bribe, to make sure that the authorities never knocked on their door.

She smiled to Grodray, checked the stun pistol tucked inside her jacket next to her insulating undershirt armor, and turned to her partner.

"Ready?"

"Let's go," he smiled sternly back.

Eveth stepped into the lift tube.

"Level Forty-seven," she said aloud.

What will those folks upstairs do when the Constables just show up out of the blue?

There couldn't be that many places left on *Hurquar* to hide. Three or four more stops, max, and they would have to rethink their approach. Maybe the human wasn't going to go out in public, and someone just had him on ice for now, until his violence could be unleashed.

In a way, that made her more comfortable. The thought of a human scaled up to Vanir-size was truly frightening. Most of the Accord were more of a size with humans, as she understood the file Jackeith had showed her. She could take a human in physical combat, unless he had been trained to mastery in one of the amazingly-common hand-to-hand fighting arts that all human cultures seemed to invent.

Did everyone on that planet study violence from the day they could walk?

The lift deposited her on the right floor without providing any answers or solace. Grodray was there a moment later.

"Good cop?" she asked him as she strode down the unremarkable hallway towards a nice, wooden door at the end.

"Bad cop, Eve," he replied, telling her to take the lead. "The humans call it turning on the light in the middle of the night, to see what scurries for cover."

She nodded. Like her, he was getting tired of knocking on doors to bland faces and innocent shrugs. She could see that in his eyes. At least three of the places they had hit so far in the last two days had something about them that suggested to Eveth that a future police raid might be entertaining, but this case was too important to randomly kick over ant hills.

They needed to find a human on the loose, and do it without anybody who didn't already know finding out.

The office door was locked, so Eveth pressed the comm panel to the right side.

"Who is it?" a woman's voice answered a few moments later. A little light came on next to the speaker, indicating that the camera was working.

Eveth held up her badge, close enough to almost obscure any view of the hallway, and then lowered it so they could see how cross she had gotten today.

"Constabulary," she said simply. "We'd like to ask the principal researcher a few questions."

There. Nothing more. You don't need to know, if you're innocent. I don't need to spell it out, if you're guilty.

A fine game to play. A thin line to walk.

Long pause on the other end. Perhaps vermin scurrying? There was a team back at the precinct, watching for all auto-traffic in and out of this building right now. Anybody running would have the vehicle's controls remotely overridden and get them deposited nicely in a police parking lot for questioning.

And Eveth could run down anybody on foot.

That left only Elohynn, but there weren't that many in this city, and there were enough cameras available. They didn't prevent crime, because it was impossible to watch all the screens at once. Instead, they solved crime by letting investigators go back and track your every step afterwards.

The lock buzzed suddenly.

Eveth gave Grodray a shrug and opened the door. Inside was a corporate reception area so standard they might have all come out of the same decorating catalog. Desk where a receptionist would sit, currently empty. Polished wood walls with art. Two chairs and a sofa for people waiting for meetings.

This place varied from the basic design by including a *Brag Wall*. Eveth quickly scanned the images of a Nari woman: shaking hands with local politicians and others, accepting awards at various dinner ceremonies, and a couple of scholarly journal covers indicating a woman named Talyarkinash Liamssen published something really big inside.

Blue eyes. Fur just lighter than stone blue, with faint grayer stripes and black highlights. Eveth guessed her to be perhaps in her early thirties. Probably one of those brilliant researchers that finished all their degree work and realized that they would make more money opening a clinic catering to people trying to recapture lost youth, than trying to find gaps in the programs left by the Chaa or curing disease.

But there were always going to be people looking for immortality, however they could arrange it. Most of those folks would get scammed out of their money, but that wasn't Eveth's problem. It was the ones who might succeed that she had to handle.

Or folks willing to transform a human to hide him from the authorities.

Doctor Liamssen emerged from an inside door a moment later. The photos really didn't do the woman justice, or perhaps she had used her art on herself. Eveth would have said this woman was barely out of school rather than old enough to have established a corporation like this.

Eveth made a note to look her up later. Something just didn't smell right, already, and woman hadn't even spoken.

"Good afternoon," the Nari woman said carefully, pulling the door closed behind her so that three of them were alone in the front room. "I'm Doctor Liamssen. How may I help you, officers?"

"Constable Eveth Baker," she flashed the badge again, watching the woman's eyes for a reaction. "This is my partner, Senior Constable Grodray. We're investigating a smuggling case, and your organization came up in an offhand way. Normally, nothing, but the sensitivity of this case requires us to check off on every box individually, so we need to ask you some questions. Is there a conference room where we could talk?"

"I was actually in the middle of something…" the woman began.

"And we won't keep you very long, Dr. Liamssen," Eveth overrode her. "But we don't really have any flexibility here, and we'd like to get back to our case before the good leads grow cold."

Sharp blue eyes. Intelligent. Calculating the odds right now.

Everyone has something they want to hide. How hard did the good doctor want to push back on a pair of unknown Constables that just popped in for a bit of tea?

Eveth smiled. Dr. Liamssen smiled back, but it was plastic and brittle.

"Yes, I suppose," the doctor said. "If this won't take long."

"Just a few minutes, Dr. Liamssen," Grodray suddenly spoke up, his baritone voice drawing the woman's eyes and face back sharply.

The doctor was perhaps five foot eight, not counting her ears. A little taller than normal for a Nari female. Eveth was six foot seven, and out-weighed the woman by probably eighty pounds, all of it bone and muscle.

But Jackeith, the quiet one behind her, was seven foot one and three hundred pounds. Even as a skinny guy, the Nari would probably feel like a child next to a serious adult.

The look in the woman's eyes gave that much away.

She quickly led them back through the door into a large, spacious work area, with several black-topped workbenches that had seen hard use. Lighting overhead was bright and sharp, rather than friendly. Every blemish in anything would be shown.

Good thing to know about the occupant.

Eveth scanned the various things on workbenches, but couldn't even begin to describe them, let along classify things. Biomimetics, she seemed to remember, was about studying natural systems to replicate them in scaled-up formats, but how you did that wasn't something Eveth had ever bothered with.

At least this place wasn't breeding better food animals so she didn't have a wall of scared rabbits staring out at her, and all the fear/shit smell that went with it like that one time.

This place was almost a showroom, by comparison. Utterly clean ad lacking any personality.

The doctor led them to a small conference room off to one side, with a picture window looking back over the main room.

Eveth sat and pulled out her notebook to record a few thoughts.

"So what can I do for you, officers?" Liamssen said in a voice that was too forced to be calm and innocent.

But nobody was innocent.

"Smuggling," Eveth challenged the woman. "What do you know?"

It was a throwaway question. The sort of thing they taught you in police school to knock a subject off kilter. You didn't care what words came out of the suspect's mouth. Instead, you were watching how her mannerisms change when she's surprised.

When she forgets what lies she has prepared for them.

"Huh?" Liamssen replied, utter confusion resculpting her face, ears headed different directions, whiskers twitching a-harmonically.

"Sorry," Eveth wasn't, but it sounded good. "An organization that has dealt with you in the past has been accused of smuggling controlled chemicals without clearances or tax stamps. We need to eliminate you as fast as we can as a suspect. However, this is a very confidential case, so we can't tell you who they are. I was hoping we could take a quick scan of the premises and get a copy of your last ninety days' worth of inventory, just so we can mark you off the list and move on to the next place."

The eyes gave her away. She was good, but the nostrils flared a little too much, as if trying to smell the lies Eveth was peddling. The pupils expanded.

Eveth would have been willing to guess that the fur on the back of the Nari's scruff was standing up right now, hard as the woman was trying to hide it.

"I don't believe we keep those sorts of records on site," the doctor deflected well. "This is the lab, and most of the paperwork is in the main office. Is there something you can tell me? Perhaps I might be able to show you the right things?"

Eveth glanced significantly over a Grodray, as if asking permission. She was making it up as she went, and he knew that, but cops were never required to tell suspects the truth, except on the witness stand.

"Unlicensed genetic engineering," Eveth said in a conspiratorial tone, dropping her voice a little and adding a quaver of emotion.

She did it quite well today. Must be on.

"Oh?" the doctor countered, still off-balance.

"Someone is conducting experiments that go well beyond younger skin and different eyes, Doctor Liamssen," Eveth admitted on an awkward voice, watching the scientist's reaction. "Those require specialist chemicals that most labs have no need to maintain, so we just need to check your hazardous materials placards and refrigerator, and then we'll be on our way."

"Oh," the Nari brightened suddenly, like Eveth had just taken a weight off the woman's shoulders. She stood like an excited schoolgirl. "That we can do. Right this way."

Eveth smiled and rose, innocent as the dawn, and fell into the woman's wake. Out into the main room, so clean and well organized. Right to a four-ring binder thick with laminated cards and stamped with dates.

Eveth made it look like she was carefully checking things, flipping through them one at a time and making interested noises, plus occasional chuckles and harrumphs.

She had no idea what ninety percent of them even were, let alone what a geneticist might do with them. Didn't matter. She wasn't watching the notebook.

"The refrigerator?" Eveth asked after she had finished the notebook.

"There are two," the Nari doctor pointed across the room. "Or rather, the large one is at thirty-five degrees, and the small one is at fifteen below zero, depending on the materials we're working with in our experiments."

Eveth took the big one first. Inside, lots of vials and bottles for a pulse injector, plus a few larger bottles, none of which she could identify. Still, she pulled out her pocketcomm and dutifully took a couple of pictures so she had labels to inspect. The freezer differed only in that the bottles were usually metal, with screw-on lids and ice rimed on the outside. More pictures. More evidence, as it were.

"I think we've got everything we need, Doctor Liamssen," Eveth said brightly. She turned to her partner. "On to the next one?"

"Very good," he said. Grodray even bowed to the Nari woman. "Doctor Liamssen, thank you for your help."

"My pleasure," the woman said. "Will there be anything else?"

"No," Eveth said. "I've seen everything I need to. And we can show ourselves out. Thank you."

Grodray led. Eveth followed, twitchy because she didn't have her usual armor on, if a shot was going to strike her in the back she had turned.

But they made it to the door, unlocked it, and exited.

Jackeith didn't even look back, but walked right to the drop-tube.

"Ground floor," he said, vanishing.

Eveth was a step behind him, and a beat back at the first floor.

He stepped to a quiet corner and looked significantly.

"How soon can you get a warrant for that place?" she asked. "That woman's hiding something so big I thought her heart would explode."

"Agreed," he said. "I'll need twenty minutes or so to pass a message to the right people. They'll need another twenty to get us the paperwork we need. Think they'll wait that long up there?"

"Don't know," Eveth said. "I tried to play it casual, but she might have made us. You noticed how excited she was to show off the main room?"

"I did."

"I've never been in a working lab that clean," Eveth said. "Day one, something gets spilled, or set on fire, or broken. The only way that place is that clean…"

"Is if it has never been used, and what we saw was a stage for folks like us, if we broke in," he completed the thought. "We might have found our target. We've certainly found somebody. You wait here. I'll call this in and have all auto-traffic to the building locked down until we can land a Heavy Response Tactical Group on the roof."

Eveth moved to the front atrium of the building. A hex like this was impossible for one person to cover, but she found a tea shop table with a great view of the big, open space and settled herself in. Anyone emerging from the drop tube would be visible to her before they could slink out a side entrance.

And she could run down any human.

MADE

GARETH LOOKED up as Talyarkinash came down the secret stairs three at a time. He hadn't noticed before, because he was always studying her face for clues, but she was wearing shoes with no heel and barely any cushion, instead of the two to four inch heels most women, most *human* women, wore in public as a matter of course. And baggy, maroon pants that gathered at the ankle, vaguely like harem pants, plus a long, green tunic.

But the shoes were what threw him off. She wasn't human, so applying human fashion standards to the woman felt wrong. Off.

And human women wore skirts, not slacks. Right?

"We're made," she called out as she came into sight.

Gareth had found another room beyond the dentist chair and the music studio. There was a whole suite of rooms through there, as a matter of fact, but he was in a common room right now, seated on one end of a couch reading about the history of the *Accord of Souls* on a space tablet Talyarkinash had gotten for him.

Morty was on a barstool that telescoped down for a Yuudixtl and up to a Nari-height bar. Xiomber was at a low table, eating a sandwich he had made from ingredients in a refrigerator in the kitchen, down the north hall.

Gareth had slept in a room down the south hall. At first, he had been concerned that the woman might try to slip into his room, in spite of his

92

commitment to Pippa. He had locked the door just in case. But after that first afternoon, if she was going to do that, Gareth was pretty sure she'd be bringing a gun.

"What do you mean, made?" Morty asked. "We watched you on the screen. You did great."

"I don't know how, but that cop saw through everything," Talyarkinash said. "There should have been far more questions. Intrusions. Inspections. Annoyances. The last time the city wanted to check something, I had people in here for three days."

"She gave up too easily," Gareth observed, calmly powering off the magical book and placing it on the end table. Something had not felt right, but he hadn't been able to put a finger on it until Talyarkinash said something.

"Yes," the woman said. "I don't know why."

"She already knows you're guilty," Gareth said. "She left so that she could call for reinforcements to seal off the building without you being aware that the trap was closing."

"How would you know that?" Xiomber asked and then stuffed the last two bites into his mouth at once.

"That is how I would do it," Gareth said. "And I'm a cop. We need to run. Right now. If we're overreacting, we can come back tomorrow, but I doubt the building will still be an option in an hour. I've done this too many times to folks like you. I know what it feels like."

He rose and stretched. Action made him hungry, but there wasn't time to make a sandwich, and instinct told him their freedom might be measured in minutes.

"*Fardel*," Morty suddenly yelled, punching his pocketcomm. "We're screwed."

"What just happened? " Xiomber mumbled around his chewing.

"Two things," Morty snarled, lowering his chair and leaving the pocketcomm behind on the bar. "One, I tried to call a taxi, and the map somehow shows no available vehicles anywhere, in the middle of the afternoon. Two, the credit account I had been charging everything to suddenly locked up and shut itself down."

"Oh, crap," Xiomber rose.

"Yup," Morty agreed. "Normally, losing a credit account is nothing. We go through them all the time. Timing is exceptionally bad right now. Rather suspicious."

Gareth turned to see Talyarkinash pulling a duffel bag from a previously-closed cabinet.

Good idea. Gareth raced to his bedroom and grabbed his own bag. Everything had been cleaned and folded, ready to go.

Or run, as the case apparently was.

Amazingly, both of the brothers had also already grabbed bags, a soft sided satchel case for Morty, and backpack for Xiomber.

"What's the plan?" he asked.

Three days with these folks, and he had not really spent a lot of time on possible escape routes.

At first, sitting in that damned dentist's chair three more times and getting his brain psionically drilled had left him fuzzy for hours afterwards. Then watching as Talyarkinash and the brothers sketched out designs for a suit he could wear. Except it wasn't a suit, exactly.

Gareth hadn't really come to terms with what they had come up with.

But they had started designing something.

And now the clock was about to expire.

Its midnight, Cinderella.

"Yuudixtl are pretty common on this planet," Morty said. "If we split into two teams, Xiomber and I should be able to blend into a crowd well enough. Vanir and Nari tend to congress, so you two won't raise that big of an issue together. Talyarkinash, I'm sorry that we blew your cover with this. Do you have a bolt hole we can make?"

Gareth watched the woman pass through the stages of death in a few, quick seconds, lingering on anger for perhaps a touch too long, before she reached acceptance. She gave the brothers an address and fixed Gareth with a hard scowl.

"You better be worth it," she said.

"If I don't stop Maximus, I'm not sure anybody else can," he replied calmly. "The only price you're risking is jail."

That got through the woman's hard façade. The ears flickered forward and her whiskers even relaxed.

"We should go first," Gareth continued, turning to Morty and Xiomber. "If the Constables don't know you two, they'll key on me and you might be able to escape in the confusion."

"Where are we without you, Gareth?" Xiomber asked.

"Go back and build a new machine, Xiomber," he replied calmly. "Any Field Agent of the Sky Patrol you kidnap will be on your side as soon as you explain the situation to them. Invoke my name when you do."

"You're nuts, kid," Morty said.

"I'm Earth Force Sky Patrol, Morty," Gareth said. "That means something."

"Let's go," Talyarkinash snapped peevishly, pulling open yet another hidden door and stepping into the hallway only a few steps from the drop-tube.

"Second floor," she called, rather than first, and dropped from sight.

Gareth was right behind her.

The second floor of the building was a mezzanine that ran all the way around the outside of the building like a balcony. It was apparently made of glass, or aluminum that was functionally transparent, because for a moment Gareth thought he was floating in the air.

Talyarkinash had slung her bag's strap over a shoulder and added a jacket in the same rich maroon as her pants. Gareth was wearing what he thought of as his cowboy outfit: black pants, plaid shirt, blue denim jacket, no hat. The bag holding his clothes was more of a soft suitcase, so he had it by the handle, an oversized, pine-green briefcase as he walked.

The beautiful scientist had paused long enough for Gareth to come up on her left. She held out a hand and grabbed his. Bright blue eyes with a hint of fear in them looked up at him.

"Pretend we're on a trip together," she said calmly as she started to walk. "Maybe a honeymoon on a new planet. Walk like I'm your girlfriend."

He stared to say something, but swallowed it when he saw the abject terror in her eyes.

Being arrested and thrown in jail forever still didn't frighten her anywhere near as much as being this close to a human.

What in the nine hells did people in the *Accord* learn about humanity? Sure, we could be a rough folk. And probably too violent, especially since all species in the *Accord* had an empathic bond to them, but we aren't that bad.

Are we?

But he was Earth Force Sky Patrol. If nothing else, he had a duty to uphold the highest standards of conduct.

Gareth smiled at her and set off at a normal pace. Her ear tips were about as tall as he was, and their legs were roughly the same length. Her hand was clammy in his, and he didn't hold too tight.

Two young lovers, just landed and walking to a hotel. He could do this. And not even blush all that hard, because his heart was still true to Pippa, no matter how beautiful or forward some of the women of this new galaxy were.

Like he would have expected at home, there was an escalator to the ground floor. Six of them, in fact, one at each corner of the building. She led him to the one farthest from the front of the tower.

The atrium wasn't completely empty. It was mid-afternoon, and there were people coming and going. Tourists standing around. Messengers delivering packages.

Cover.

They rode the escalator down in the immediate wake of a Warreth mother and three chicks just about of an age to start school, back on Earth. They were full of questions about everything and kept their mother distracted.

Rather than stare, Gareth leaned against the side of the escalator and looked around the interior of the building. The architecture was unlike anything back home, with soaring, curved ribs like a giant whale holding the building up, instead of the normal squat pillars a human designer would have used. Curved panes of glass all around the outside made the inside feel like an aquarium, with him a prized fish on display.

Or a piranha.

Something drew his eye to the northeast corner of the ground floor. A tea shop was doing a brisk business this afternoon, catching people at that point in the day when they needed a jolt to make it through the rest of the work and then get home safe.

Someone was seated at the closest table to the center, sipping tea and amiably watching the crowds ebb and flow around her.

He had never seen her in person, only through a remote camera hidden up in Talyarkinash's lab, but he had no doubt that the figure was Constable Eveth Baker.

Even across more than one hundred yards of space, Gareth felt her eyes lock on to him.

Gareth turned to Talyarkinash and nodded back to indicate the Constable. His eyes turned deadly serious.

"Run."

GAZELLES

EVETH WAS WATCHING THE DROP-TUBE, but like a good cop, she made sure to track the rest of the space. Jackeith would be back with reinforcements in under an hour. All she had to do was bottle them up, nice and cozy on the forty-seventh floor in their cute, fake, lab.

Until she had that Nari liar handcuffed in an interrogation room, sweating, while a heavy-armed strike team cleared the space with live weapons.

Eveth was looking forward to that part. This had been a hard week.

She saw the Warreth and chicks descend from the mezzanine. Probably taking pictures of the river before heading home for dinner. Two other tourists followed, quietly enjoying their trip.

Something about the male caught her eye. Vanir male. Nari female. The light was bad at this distance, odd afternoon shadows distorting things, but something wasn't right. Something about the image of the male.

He wasn't anything special from this distance. Casually dressed in a style she didn't recognize. Blond hair. Broad shoulders. A little short.

Short.

Nari females tended to run about five and a half feet tall. The Warreth woman in front of them looked about the same, so the man was a little over six feet tall. Short for a Vanir.

Tall for a human.

The man turned and made eye contact with her like he was seated across the table, rather than nearly one hundred twenty yards away.

Recognition, like an electric shock running through both of them, apparently.

He turned to say something to his companion, nudging her forward as the Warreth mother gathered up her brood and started across the tile plaza.

Eveth was already out of her chair and moving.

The human had the woman by the hand and was tugging her along now. She resisted at first, until she saw Eveth moving, and then those long, Nari legs started to churn.

Eveth didn't bother to yell. The distance was too great, and those two weren't about to listen to her.

And the last thing Eveth needed to do today was to start a panic about a human loose in Olehmmishqu.

Civilian clothes drove her almost to distraction as she picked up speed. In her bodysuit, there was a pouch on her right thigh, opposite her holster, for a pocketcomm. In mufti, she had been forced to stuff in into an interior breast pocket of the blazer.

The two fugitives had made it to the exterior door now. Hopefully, they would try to call for an auto-taxi, gambling that the vehicle would arrive before she did, except that Grodray's contacts had already set up a hard lock on all calls, two blocks in every direction.

She pushed harder, closing the space to the door as they turned right and began to move.

All the two fugitives would get was an angry cop closing as fast as her Vanir legs could carry her.

She was at the door, jammed it open with her immense mass moving at high speed, and took off after them.

Eveth was confident she could run down any human.

Still, she needed backup. And help cornering them.

She pulled out the pocketcomm and triggered a call to her partner.

It rang twice before he picked it up.

"Talk to me, Eve," he said urgently.

"I've got two runners, Grodray," she said.

Any other words were lost as she plowed squarely into a pedestrian coming around a corner from the alley, one of the Tree People, built about as sturdy as an oak.

All the breath whooshed out of her and Eveth felt her skull crack hard on the man's trunk. Fortunately, she had a really hard head.

But her pocketcomm slid away, still moving when she stopped.

The Tree Person looked down at her in surprise and offered a hand up, along with an apology.

Eveth took it, but couldn't see her pocketcomm through the wobbly stars dancing circles around her head. Down at the far end of the block, the human and his accomplice had already crossed a street and were threatening to melt into the afternoon rush hour mobs that were just starting to emerge from buildings.

She had a choice, but it was never really in doubt.

Eveth could always track down her pocketcomm later. It would lock up in ten seconds, and Grodray could send a pulse to make it scream fit to wake the dead, once he realized she had lost it.

But in the meantime, the human would vanish into the underworld, and Eveth was pretty sure they would never get another chance like this to capture him. He had a top geneticist helping him to escape. In three days, he might look like anything at all.

Eveth growled out her rage and began to run. Since she couldn't call for backup, she would just have to do this on her own.

She reached inside the jacket and pulled out her stun pistol. The range was too great now, but that was just a matter of anger and patience.

Right up her alley.

HUNTED

GARETH COULD HAVE EASILY outrun Constable Baker on a track. One of the horror elements of the species descriptions in the book he had been reading spelled out the immense endurance and stamina of humans compared to every other species in known space, including the presumably-horrifying little fact that some human societies had been known to chase their pray to death, jogging lightly along for hours until the creature simply collapsed of exhaustion and died.

Only Terran dogs, Humanity's secret weapon, could match humans for endurance.

He would have liked to tell the writers of such lurid squamph that the average human worked in a factory or at a desk, and was about as dangerous as the average citizen here, but they wouldn't listen. He was a human, after all.

And it wasn't Gareth against a single Constable. He had Talyarkinash to protect, and a strange and wondrous city into which he could easily become so disoriented that he became an easy target for some innocent beat cop.

Gareth would not kill an authorized law enforcement agent doing their job. He wouldn't even hurt one any more than necessary to escape.

He had to represent all humans to the *Accord of Souls*. On his life would be their eventual welcome into broader galactic society.

Fortunately, rush hour was apparently the same, the galaxy over.

Happy hour had dawned and people were starting to sneak out of offices a little early to get a head start on family life, or extra time down at the corner bar.

Just in the few seconds since they had emerged from the building and gone a block, the number of people on the sidewalk had practically doubled. Gareth was hard pressed not to run into people hard enough to knock them down, especially while also not losing Talyarkinash's hand.

She was his lifeline right now, and he needed her like a lifesuit in a hull breach. Fortunately, she needed him just as much. Without Gareth and the brothers, she would have nowhere to go when the police did come back and started going through her files.

He tried not to shout out his internal joy that another criminal ring would be broken, because that meant he was about to go down with them. A cop like Eveth Baker would shoot first and he would wake up behind bars for the rest of his life, while they tried to figure out a way to completely wipe his memory without taking the rest of his mind with it.

That woman had the look about her.

And she was chasing them, gun in hand and down by her side like a well-trained operative. Gareth understood instinctively how dangerous she would be.

At the corner, the light held them for a second. Gareth glanced back and picked her up through the mass of bodies as she came after them. He watched Baker run into a walking tree (*A **WALKING TREE?***) and lose her communications device, the handheld sliding under a car parked at the curb.

It gave him an idea as the light turned to walk.

"Talyarkinash, I need you to trust me," he said as they pressed their way forward through the growing mob of strangely-smelling folks.

He felt her dig her heels in hard, because she stopped moving and he nearly pulled her over accidentally.

"Trust you?" she snarled quietly. "You?"

"I think I can get us away from her, but I need your help," Gareth said. "Your trust. I swear that I will do everything I can to protect you, on my honor as a Field Agent of the Earth Force Sky Patrol."

"Are you insane, Gareth?" she hissed.

Gareth decided that they were losing ground to Constable Baker while arguing. He pulled the Nari scientist along by sheer strength.

"Maybe," he admitted as she allowed herself to fall into stride again.

It was like pushing against ocean waves to get to the calmer, open water, getting through the press of bodies.

There. An alley way between two buildings, possibly allowing industrial vehicles access to interior loading bays. The asphalt was worn and dirty, and no plants lined the walls.

He looked back and Baker had chosen pursuit over assistance. She was holding her gun and had foregone her radio for backup.

Gareth pulled Talyarkinash into the alleyway, like two young lovers sneaking off for a quick smooch out of the flow of traffic. Nothing could be further from his mind, but anything to confuse people worked in his favor.

Like New Metropolis back home, the streets were movie set facades, pretty on the street, but unwashed, ugly, and industrial in the alleys. Gareth counted dumpsters, trashcans, a parked delivery truck, and several overhead balconies, possibly good, old-fashioned fire steel escapes. None of the latter provided him the cover he needed, but the rest of the space would do.

Gareth measured off the strides he needed, pulling Talyarkinash along with him.

"She'll be here in seconds," he said urgently. "I need you stretched out on the asphalt here, like you've tripped and twisted your ankle, and I didn't stop. She'll see you, and come to arrest you. I'm hiding close by. I will jump her when she gets here. Can you do that?"

"The alternative is jail?" Talyarkinash asked.

"The alternative is Maximus finds out you've been helping me and the brothers, and kills you," Gareth said simply. "I'm trying to prevent that right now. Later, I need your help to save the galaxy."

The terror was still there in those ocean-deep eyes, like icebergs floating on a storm-tossed, angry sea. But something else appeared.

He might have been bold enough to call it hope, if he wanted to push his luck.

"You'll protect me?" she asked quietly.

"I promise," Gareth stated.

Before he could react, she lunged forward and kissed him, one arm around his neck and whiskers tickling his face. She felt ice-cold initially, but warmed in the second he held her.

"Go," she ordered, tossing her bag further down the alley and stretching herself out, just as he had explained it.

Gareth loped over to one of the dumpsters and crawled into a shadow cast by the delivery truck, face all a-blush. Now all he had to do was hope that the driver was too busy having a smoke to come out in the next thirty seconds.

"Come back here, you bastard," Talyarkinash suddenly yelled at the top of her lungs. "You can't leave me."

Gareth nearly surged out of his hiding place, then stopped himself. He peeked anyway.

Talyarkinash honestly looked like she was watching him run away from where she had fallen, as a cowardly Gareth had panicked and fled.

Like he had done the absolutely unthinkable and left one of his own behind.

But humans had no reputation for honor here, either.

"Gareth," Talyarkinash yelled. "Come back."

"Freeze," an angry woman called.

Gareth recognized the voice from the building.

Constable Baker, right on time. Hopefully alone.

Talyarkinash stopped yelling. Glanced back and moaned wretchedly.

"Oh, you bastards," she cried. "All of you."

"Where is he?" Baker yelled.

From the volume, she had entered the mouth of the alley. Probably in a two-handed stance, one hand cupped under the other to steady her pistol, since she didn't have the walkie-talkie with her. Most likely turned thinways to her target to reduce her silhouette.

Gareth held his breath.

"Where is he?" Baker repeated.

"Bastard abandoned me," Talyarkinash replied angrily. "I fell down and couldn't get up, so he just ran."

"Show me your hands," Baker ordered.

Gareth couldn't see the Constable when he slid an eye even with the edge of the dumpster, but Talyarkinash was in clear sight, ignoring him as she faked a bum leg and held her hands up.

"Roll over on your stomach, hands behind your back," Baker called.

She had to be walking slowly closer, as the echoes softened. Gareth might have done the same thing, approaching carefully and by the book.

Knowing who he was dealing with, Gareth might also have just shot the criminal on the ground with the stunner, to be sure. Talyarkinash had a dangerous edge underneath that scholarly brain.

But the Nari woman complied. Laid out flat with her hands behind her.

Trusting Gareth to save her life.

The surge of pride made him feel ten feet tall.

Shadows on the pavement as Baker got close. Gareth could track her now, with enough sun behind her.

He would be reaching for handcuffs about now. Moving towards his weak hand side so he could hold the pistol while snapping a cuff over a wrist.

Baker was left-handed, she would be shifting towards him, and turning her back on his hiding place.

He hoped.

There.

Now or never.

Gareth rose on silent feet and exploded out of his hiding place.

He had to pretend Baker wasn't a girl as he was about to tackle her. All of his soul cried out in shame at hitting a woman, and doing it from behind as well.

Her being half a head taller, and almost as broad in the shoulders helped. He was back on the muddy turf, bringing down a burly tight-end short of the goal line to save the play, the game, and the season.

Slamming into her felt like that tackle had been. Damn, she must outweigh him, too.

The woman must have had a sixth sense. Something warned her and she glanced back at the last instant, tangled up with gun, cuffs, prisoner, and rampaging human.

They ended up in a jumble of bodies, but Gareth used all his training to force his way on top. She was muscled like a tight-end as well, so he didn't have time to wrestle with her. Not if he wanted to survive.

God only knows what kinds of martial arts *Accord* cops were taught.

Instead, he broke every rule his mother had hammered into him as a child. He had hit a girl. Knocked her down and pinned her to ground.

Gareth punched her in the middle of the forehead, as hard as he could. It was like trying to open a coconut with a fist.

But it worked. Her head bounced off the hard pavement almost as hard as it had his fist and her eyes lost focus.

He punched her a second time, wailing inside at the thought of his father finding out when he came home. Another bounce.

This time she stayed down.

He checked her eyes. They were half rolled back, unfocused, but symmetric, so he had just knocked her out cold and into a mild concussion.

Still, he climbed up and rolled her onto her side so she wouldn't somehow choke. The handcuffs had fallen just about with them, which was fortuitous.

Gareth grabbed Agent Baker and lifted her enough to shift her over to the dumpster he had used as cover. A quick snap and the handcuffs latched her to a ton of steel. He had no idea what a key might look like, but hopefully this would be enough of a peace offering.

He was a human. He was supposed to be a mindless, killing machine threatening all civilization with bloodshed.

Maybe, just maybe he could communicate with them by *not* using violence.

"Not bad, buddy," another voice said. High tenor, nasty tones.

Gareth looked up at a Warreth male, standing in the mouth of the alley, holding a gun on him.

This one didn't look like a cop. Too slovenly, compared to Agent Baker and her partner.

Gareth was willing to gamble that he had just found one of Sarzynski's men.

"Stand up slowly, human," the birdman said, confirming the first estimation.

Only one of Maximus's men would know him by species on sight.

Gareth complied, hands out but not overhead. His mind was racing with options, but the birdman was far enough away that he could probably shoot Gareth without a problem.

He needed to get out of this alley, and quickly.

And he really needed to be away from all of this before somebody's backup arrived.

"You work for Maximus?" Gareth asked carefully.

"That's right," the Warreth gunman said with a sneer. "Told us to watch the cops. Follow them around, in case they led us to you. And lookie what we have here."

"I'd rather not," Talyarkinash said.

She shot the man with Baker's gun, both of them forgotten in all this excitement.

Gareth realized just how lucky he could be.

"Thank you," Gareth told her as she emerged from behind the delivery truck, pistol in hand pointed at the thug.

"I did owe you one," she smiled up at him. "What do we do with them?"

"Is that a stunner?" he asked.

"Yes," she said. "Hers."

"Can you adjust the stun?"

"Sure."

"Put it on the highest setting and shoot him again," Gareth said. "How long will he be out?"

"Probably hours," she replied, adjusting something with her other hand and then shooting the birdman again. "Now what?"

"Now I would like you to put the gun back in Agent Baker's holster," Gareth said. "And then we're going to run like hell."

"You just knocked her out," Talyarkinash said. "She'll be awake long before he is."

"And she'll have her handcuffs, badge, and gun," Gareth agreed. "I'm trying to send them a message."

"What message?"

"That we're on the same side," Gareth said.

RESCUED

"I DON'T CARE," Eveth growled, holding an icepack to her face and forehead. "He's mocking us."

"And he could have killed you, Baker," Grodray replied mildly.

It didn't help that her partner was probably right. She had come to, handcuffed to the dumpster with her own manacles. Badge and gun were tucked into their spots. Unconscious thug with a rap sheet a mile long stunned and laid out at her feet.

She had just managed to free herself when Grodray arrived with half a dozen uniforms holding weapons out.

Now, they were all back up on the forty-seventh floor, taking Talyarkinash Liamssen's life apart. No reason to waste a perfectly good warrant. And she had found an icepack in a personal refrigerator, down a set of steps concealed by a bookcase and hiding a medium-sized apartment.

Grodray had taken charge of things at that point, setting her down in that sterile conference room upstairs with instructions not to move while forensics teams went to work.

"What do we know?" Eveth asked, raging inside but controlling it.

She couldn't believe she had fallen for something so obvious. The human was dangerous, that much she knew. Half a foot shorter, but roughly the same mass, and extremely strong. And he had a punch like a wallop. Her head was still ringing.

"The two Yuudixtl were probably here with them," Grodray said, reading off his notes. "We've found indications four people were staying downstairs, and at least one was the right size. They had been here three days, from the trash in the can and the food missing."

"Missing?" Eveth asked, still a little fuzzy.

"Count slices of bread missing from a loaf, divide by two, and you have meals served," Grodray smiled. "Things like that. Crude but effective."

"Right."

"The Yuudixtl obviously disappeared when you went after the others, and we have no witnesses," Grodray continued. "Cameras probably caught something, but it will take time to track that down. I'm sure they made it outside the lock-down zone and called a cab with a new credit account they had stolen."

"Sirs, you might want to see this," one of the cops, a young Grace officer with good instincts, had appeared in the door and motioned them to join in.

"What have you got?" Grodray was first, only because Eveth had to stand up, wobble the tiniest amount, and then follow.

"Not sure," the male cop said. "We think she was in a hurry to destroy things, but missed this."

They followed him out into the main room, down the stairs, and into a small work area off the main control room with the worthless music studio deck. Liamssen had done something to the computer controlling it all, and none of the knobs or sliders did anything now, as far as anybody could tell.

Another officer was standing there, holding a piece of paper that had been crumpled up at some point, now flattened out on the desktop.

Eveth leaned over the Grace cop's shoulder to look. The tentacles were almost painful on her head and neck, but she could deal with that. Except that everywhere those tentacles touched, the pain receded.

She glanced down at the officer in surprise. He smiled sheepishly and blushed.

"Thought it might help," he offered.

"It does," Eveth replied. "Thank you."

He leaned closer. She leaned closer. It was almost like they were kissing, except both were faced to the side. It was still a bizarre experience, one that should have been erotic, under almost any other circumstances.

The paper was a sketch, drawn freehand but by an extremely skilled hand. It showed a wing, such as an Elohynn might have, coming out from the back and down to a central elbow joint, before running up to a rough point overhead.

But the scale was all wrong, if the lengths on the side were any indication.

An Elohynn male, roughly six feet tall on average, had wings that were roughly nine feet long, with a twenty-foot wingspan on a mature adult.

This wing would be almost three times that.

"Any ideas?" Grodray asked.

Eveth pulled clear of the forest of helpful kelp and stood fully upright with a nod of thanks to the cop.

Grodray was deduction writ large. Eveth had always suspected the reason she was paired with him, once the bosses realized that they wouldn't hate each other, was that she brought induction to the equation.

Leaps of intuition that the evidence just wouldn't cover.

"Ornithopter?" she tossed out.

It was utterly inefficient, since something like an auto-car rode powered lifters and could also maneuver in low planetary orbit once a transport tube had lifted you. But the Elohynn preferred personal flying to anything else, including walking.

But why would a human want to build an Ornithopter?

She shrugged after a moment.

"Where did you find this?" Grodray pointed at the page.

"Crumpled up and behind the waste drop, sir," the Grace cop said. "Looks like someone didn't like the design, but missed the incinerator bucket, and were either too lazy to get up, or didn't see it fall long."

"Tag it and scan it into the files," Grodray instructed the man.

Eveth followed her partner into the main common room where obviously the criminals had been waiting. There were remains of a sandwich on a low table, a pocketcomm that one of the Yuudixtl had been using to access a stole credit account on the bar, and a reading tablet on the end table next to the sofa.

"Three of them in here, watching us upstairs?" Eveth asked, taking it all in at a glance.

"That's my theory, Eve," Grodray said. "Given the timelines, Liamssen came down stairs as soon as we left, everyone panics. They run, taking the time to grab go-bags from that cabinet over there, and to tell the computers to kill themselves."

"So we've found them, and lost them," Eveth said. "Now what?"

"Now we turn up the heat," Grodray smiled with a cruel mouth and lips pressed thin. "Assault on a Constable. Flight From Justice. And we have Dr. Liamssen's full bio signature, plus a good description of the other three."

"Do we lock the city down?" Eveth asked.

"Had you been hurt, or killed, I would have gotten nasty, Eve," Grodray said in a voice that managed to make even a hardened cop like Eveth shiver. "The perp did the absolute minimum necessary to escape you, plus he left us a prize, like a cat bringing home a mouse. I want to sweat that Warreth hard and open up a second avenue of the investigation, but we're going to hand the punk off to another team so we can focus on the perp."

"Can you do that?" she asked, suddenly breathless with anticipation. This was up there with Level-7 Security.

"I talked to the Planetary Inspector while the medics were checking you out," Grodray stated. "She's cleared us to act like free agents here."

Free agents. Just a tiny step short of Prime Inspector, the dream of every cop, to be able to pursue any crime they thought warranted their attention, on any planet of the *Accord of Souls*, and demand the full cooperation of the local authorities.

Not request. Demand.

Jackeith Grodray had said he never wanted to get to that level. Hell, he had never gone farther than Senior Constable, but that was a personal choice that Eveth would never settle for.

But Grodray had a Level-7 Security Authorization. Had they offered him Prime Inspector at some point and he refused?

Eveth made a note to learn as much as she possibly could from the man while they were partnered. Jackeith Grodray had always been exceptional, spoken of in the department in reverential tones. Was he even better than that?

"Step one?" Eveth asked after she got her thoughts under control.

"Dinner," Grodray said. "I know a good take-out joint not far from here, so we can move quickly if we get a hit on an All-Points Bulletin in the next hour. Then I'm going to turn up the heat and see what boils."

Again, Eveth felt a shiver at the tone. She wasn't sure she had ever seen Grodray lose his temper, but that was what this felt like.

Which was good, because she was well past that point with the damnable human running loose in her city.

ESCAPED

MORTY BREATHED a sigh of relief as the *maître d'* settled them in a semi-private room just outside the kitchen and left menus.

"Shouldn't we be making our way to Talyarkinash's backup place?" Xiomber asked soberly before taking a long drink of water.

"Yes and no," Morty replied, studying his brother for signs of wear or fear. "The lab's been burned now. And we know the other two got away, or the cops would have made a much bigger stink about catching a human. Somebody would have leaked that to a news crew, regardless of the situation."

"Okay, so we all got away," Xiomber agreed. "And?"

"So now we have a secondary duty to look after ourselves, egg-brother," Morty said. "Like Gareth said, if he gets taken, it will be up to us to build a new generator array and kidnap another cop from Earth, if we want to stop Maximus. We can't do that from inside a jail cell."

"You think Talyarkinash's other place will get raided?" Xiomber asked.

"I don't know," Morty admitted. "But we're hiding from the cops, the Constables, and Maximus now. That doesn't leave us a lot of places to go, because Talyarkinash would have needed underworld help to set up her bolthole in the first place. Somebody knows. The question is how quickly they'll talk, and that hinges on either fear of Maximus or a good enough reward from the cops."

Xiomber followed Morty's logic as he emptied his water glass. It had been a nerve-wracking couple of hours. He was a scientist, not a bank robber. A good salad and a pasta right now would help calm him, because they needed to find a way to set up their own bolthole on this planet. One where they could hide from agents of Maximus and the law at the same time.

"How long can we run?" Xiomber asked, calming enough to go through the implications.

"We spent a month setting this gig up," Morty reminded the man. "Once we realized that Maximus wasn't going to just settle for being the kingpin of the criminal underground but wanted to rule everything. It was only a matter of time before he brought in more humans to help. I've got eight more credit accounts we can access right now, and connections to a couple of brokers for more, so we're good for money. I know a few places we might could hide, but it depends on the Constabulary now. I'm expecting random, armed raids on a number of them tonight, expressly looking for any of four known fugitives. We cleaned up Talyarkinash's lab well enough, but we were in a hurry and the cops will find enough."

"So hiding in plain sight at a restaurant is a good idea?" Xiomber rolled his eyes.

"Cops aren't going to roust this place," Morty replied. "And there are probably thirty other Yuudixtl in here right now, so we don't stand out. This buys us another couple of hours, then I know an all-night tea house in a nice part of town, over by the university. We can hang out there, as long as you don't mind open mic poetry night."

Xiomber rolled his eyes again, but Morty expected that. His egg-brother was not a bohemian by any stretch of the word. But cops would never look in a tea house filled with weird kids playing guitars and chanting bizarre performance art to total strangers.

In the morning, if they were still able and the idea still sounded good, they could make their careful way to where Talyarkinash was hopefully hiding with Gareth, and move on to the next step. Or just run and find themselves another place to hide while they worked on a different plan to save the universe.

Damn the Constables for being good enough, smart enough, or maybe lucky enough to have broken things so wide open, so early. Morty had been counting on having at least a another week, and then it would have been someone from the old gang sniffing around.

Talyarkinash could have deflected them long enough, and then Morty and his brother could have unleashed an avenging angel on people who seemed to want to take the whole damned *Accord of Souls* down.

Didn't those fools understand that you had to have a working society first?

Morty could see a dark future where Maximus got himself made over into an emperor. He would have to institute a reign of brutality to keep power, which would mean more humans, until all of the old species of the *Accord*, bound by their psionic empathy, became a permanent slave class to a caste of humans and other murderous criminals.

If Morty had realized all this a year ago, when Cinnra decided he needed a personal killer to keep power, Morty might have quit and turned state's evidence then. Better jail than the sort of dystopian future Morty might have personally helped give birth to.

He could only hope that it truly was possible to fight fire with fire.

At least he and his egg-brother had managed to destroy the wormhole station back on *Zathus*. Maximus wouldn't be able to bring in more humans until he built a new one, and that would take time, especially if the cops were watching, and the overlord had lost his two best physicists to crises of conscience.

The waiter came and took their orders. Morty had wanted some wine, just to help with his nerves, but Xiomber overrode him. And he would let his brother do that. It was only fair, if he was going to drag Xiomber to a poetry slam later.

"I hate you, by the way," Xiomber mentioned as the waiter left.

"What did I do this time?" Morty asked.

"You're going to turn me into one of the good guys, you bastard," his brother snapped. "All our lives we've wanted to be criminals, you know. Could have gotten legitimate jobs, but that was too staid. And now I'm running for my life from every goomba and cop in this town."

"Sorry," Morty offered.

"Is it ever going to get better, you suppose?" Xiomber asked.

Morty shrugged.

"We have to save galactic civilization from a madman first," Morty replied. "And then deal with a human cop that we've turned into a god, and a criminal underworld that won't forgive us, either way. I'm happy enough to be in the frying pan right now, because the alternative is the fire itself."

"Do we turn ourselves in?" Xiomber asked. "Tell the cops everything, including what we plan for Gareth, and see if they can stop Maximus?"

"They won't believe us," Morty said. "We've already shredded the law books at this point. *Fardel* only knows how many centuries we'd be sentenced too, even with time off for good behavior. Gareth would be in the cell with us, or a zoo, which is the same thing. Maximus would dance right around any traps they thought they could set to catch him, and then end up grand poohbah of everything."

"No," Xiomber countered. "I mean *everything* we know. The crooked cops. The suborned prosecutors. The Constables Maximus secretly recruited. Everything."

"We wouldn't live to see the inside of a jail cell, brother," Morty replied mournfully.

"It might be worth trying," Xiomber said.

"We'll give Gareth a shot first," Morty said. "I think he has what it takes to do this."

"And if he succeeds, brother?" Xiomber snapped. "We're still guilty of breaking just about every law on the books. You think they'll just kiss us on the snout and send us on our way?"

"I think that I would enjoy spending the rest of my life in the next cell over from Maximus," Morty retorted. "At least the rest of the *Accord of Souls* would have survived, at that point. That's way better than some of the options I can see right now."

Xiomber wanted to say something sarcastic and biting to that. Morty could see it in his eyes, almost taste it in the scent his egg-brother gave off. But Xiomber held his silence.

Morty knew why.

He was right.

In the end, if the *Accord* didn't survive, being outside the jail wouldn't mean much of anything.

Because Morty had been the one who had done the most to tear it down.

SAFE

GARETH OPENED THE DOOR FIRST, Talyarkinash standing off to one side in case somebody was waiting inside and opened fire. Not that there was much of anything he could do if the game was indeed up, but it made him feel better.

In addition to a couple of bags of takeout food they had grabbed a few blocks over, she still had the pistol she had taken off the thug, to replace Constable Baker's sidearm. That punk wouldn't be needing it again. It was in her hand now, only shaking a little bit as the toils of the day took their toll on the Nari woman.

Talyarkinash wasn't nearly as fragile as the human women he had known. Most of them, anyway. Pippa might have had a heart of gold, but there was still a spine of titanium. She and Talyarkinash might have seen eye to eye on many things, although they would never meet.

Thinking about his beloved helped him frame the Lynxwoman scientist better. Women in the *Accord* weren't soft creatures that needed to be protected at all costs. That cop had almost been tough enough to take him singlehandedly, after all.

And Talyarkinash hadn't shrunk from shooting the Warreth in the alley to save his life.

Gareth took a deep, confused breath, and pushed the door open. It was made of some light but extremely durable plastic and swung inward on silent hinges.

Inside, he found a traditional flat, with a compact kitchen and dining area on his right, and a long, skinny salon on the left. The furniture in here was odd, but Gareth put that down to Talyarkinash's personal tastes.

The couch was an open, wooden frame with a single pad that folded in the middle, rather than the sort of thing he had known growing up, overstuffed and upholstered, with lace doilies on the back.

A chair in the front corner appeared to be a square, metal-tube frame with a kickstand back. A single piece of black canvas had been sewn around the frame in such a way as to form a person-sized hammock, for lack of a better way to describe it.

Instead of a big wooden armoire to hold the entertainment system, there was a single flat panel thinner than his thumb, maybe a yard across, hung from the wall across from the couch-thing, with odd-looking shelves below it. Each shelf appeared to be a wooden box about eighteen inches deep and eighteen or thirty-six inches wide. They were stacked up and leaned against the wall, providing a variety of flat spaces to put books and other knick-knacks.

Down the left side of the center wall, Gareth could see a door he presumed was a restroom, and another to her bedroom.

Nobody was visible when Gareth entered the room. He quickly confirmed the other two spaces were what he thought, and empty, returning to find Talyarkinash standing in the salon, arms wrapped around herself and shivering.

Gareth wanted to walk up and wrap his own arms around the woman to help comfort her, but that didn't sound like a good idea. It might remind her she was supposed to be afraid of him.

Instead, he moved to the counter where she had set the food and began unpacking things onto the table. Protein and calories would be a good idea right now, as he had missed dinner while they slunk through back alleys and quiet streets, making sure they didn't have a tail of any kind.

"Food?" he asked, trying to break through the wall of frost that had seemed to settle itself around the scientist.

She visibly shuddered once, drawing a deep breath, but she joined him, pulling two bowls from a cabinet and filling glasses with water.

They sat at a low table that reminded Gareth of ancient Japan. Pillows on the floor in various colors instead of chairs, so he kicked off his shoes and knelt. The table itself appeared to be a two foot by four foot sheet of three-quarter inch plywood, painted black and enameled over. Looking underneath, it was held up by an overturned, red milk carton.

Weird.

Gareth presumed it was an artistic statement of interior decorating, rather than poverty. Maybe a cover as a poor student, since this was where she went to hide, expecting the police to be waiting at her regular apartment.

She joined him, digging into the food with chopsticks. He had never learned the trick to eating with two sticks, so Gareth had to settle for an odd, plastic device that combined a spoon with short tines from a fork.

"Do we know when Morty and Xiomber will arrive?" he asked after selecting a random mix of colors and shapes into his bowl.

She shrugged and chewed. After a moment, she took a drink and fixed him with a focused gaze.

This was when a medusa would turn him to stone. Fortunately, his associate tonight was a Nari, and not a Grace.

Gareth surprised himself by not freaking completely out to be surrounded by aliens of all shapes, sizes, and colors. Pastor Jacob would probably expect that they were all going to hell, but they really were good people, the ones he had met so far.

"We can't even be sure *that* they will join us," she said in a cold, hard voice. "If we get caught, you told them they had to build a new machine and get another human agent to help. They might have gone off to do that as an insurance policy."

"Oh," Gareth commented neutrally. "I had not considered that."

"And I think we should move quickly ourselves, regardless of when we see them," Talyarkinash continued. "I have all my notes, even if I had to destroy everything at the lab. And it will be extremely experimental, beyond anything I've ever tried before, and dangerous, but I'm not sure what I can do to mitigate that, so we don't gain much time by waiting."

"You were ready when the Constables showed up?" Gareth asked. Nobody had told him that.

"Close enough," she admitted. "The next step was to mix reagents and test them against human DNA, and I can do that first thing tomorrow."

"You have a lab here?"

He was shocked. Just in case, Gareth had examined every room, but detected no sign.

"The back of the linen closet has a hidden door," she said. "I own the next flat over on this floor and I converted it into a small lab, just for this exact circumstance, the need to do something when I couldn't work downtown."

"Wow," Gareth managed.

For a Field Agent of Earth Force Sky Patrol, he was certainly getting a first-class education in the criminal mind this week. The bad guys back home were never going to escape him. If he ever found a way to return.

Dinner went quickly. Gareth watched her put a few containers in the refrigerator and the rest into an incinerator slot on the wall. He moved to the weird-looking sofa and decided it was wide enough. He grabbed a blanket from the linen closet in the bathroom while she watched and took off his boots.

"What are you doing?" she asked.

"Going to sleep," Gareth replied. "I'm tired and tomorrow already feels like a busy day."

"But on the couch?" Talyarkinash pressed.

Gareth fixed her with his own, serious gaze.

"Yes," he said firmly.

As a contest of wills, it was over quickly.

Gareth thought he detected a sag in her otherwise-rigid spine, and then she walked past him.

"Okay," she said mildly. "Good night."

"Good night," he replied, stretching himself out as much as he could.

When his weight shifted, Gareth discovered that the back and bottom moved on sliders built into the sides. He got up, tugged experimentally on the bottom, and was rewarded when the entire thing slid out and flat, providing him a bunk wider than he had back at the Arsenal, and long enough, if he slept diagonally, to stretch out.

Lovely invention.

He got horizontal and started to relax.

Up the hallway, the light under Talyarkinash's door went out after a few minutes and the apartment fell into silent darkness.

Gareth knew he should be sleeping. However, the day had been too much for him to unwind quickly, so he listened to the building creak. The walls themselves were thick enough to obscure the sounds of neighbors, but fans blew warm air about, and the refrigerator hummed to itself occasionally, keeping his mind too alert.

After fifteen minutes or so, Gareth heard the bedroom door open, and bare feet pad quietly across the carpet. His eyes had adjusted to the dimness, so he could see Talyarkinash, dressed in a pair of long, silken pajamas, walk into the center of the room.

Rather than speak, Gareth waited, unsure what was going through the beautiful alien's mind. At least she wasn't holding a gun.

She knew he was awake. Her eyes were better than his in this light, and his were open, watching her.

He would be true to Pippa. Period.

Nothing could change that rock-solid conviction.

"I'm cold," she said in a soft voice just above a whisper.

Cold? Then add another blanket, or turn the heat up.

But he didn't say that.

Because it wasn't a physical chill that had gripped her.

No, this one was spiritual. The sort of things he had been grappling with for four days, lost on an alien adventure in a land he had never dreamt of.

Gareth was fully dressed, except for his boots by the couch and his denim jacket hanging on a hook by the front door. Talyarkinash was wearing silk pajamas with a floral print on them. In the darkness, he would have guessed the fabric to be salmon, with crimson designs.

It might cover the body, but it left almost nothing about her shape to the imagination.

Still, they were both fully dressed. And it said a lot that she might trust him that much.

Gareth pulled the blanket back as an invitation for her to climb in with him.

She did, pulling the blanket around her and sliding backward into him. Gareth rolled onto his side, one arm under her head and the other wrapped around her arms to give her heat, even though he could feel the woman's warmth through the layers of clothing separating them.

After a few minutes, she fell asleep, astounding Gareth.

After another few minutes, he joined her.

PART THREE
HEROES

MORNING

GARETH AWOKE to light leaking past the curtains in the front of the flat. He was alone on the sofa, which helped. He had no idea how he would have dealt with the beautiful Nari woman waking up in his arms.

But she had wakened first and managed to slip out with rousing him. He heard her now, making tea in the kitchen, on the other side of the central wall, metal spoon clinking on a porcelain mug.

Gareth threw back the blanket and stood, taking the time to fold the thing back into a sofa and fold the blanket up.

"Gareth?" she called quietly.

"Yes, ma'am," he said.

"I'm sorry," she said. "I didn't meant to wake you."

"You didn't, I don't think," Gareth recalled. "This is my normal time to wake up."

"Tea's almost done," she appeared around the edge of the wall. "Or you can take a quick shower in the sonic fresher first."

Gareth nodded and headed to the bathroom.

That had been the single coolest thing he had found about the *Accord of Souls*. Instead of walking naked into hot water, he could step into a small booth without taking off his clothes, just stand there for sixty seconds while the device bombarded him with some sort of sonics and radiation, then stay there while another machine vacuumed him in a way that left both him and his clothes completely clean. He hadn't even had to do laundry once since he got here.

Taking that technology home to Earth might put a lot of people out of work, but it would save so much time that everyone should come out way ahead.

The only thing that had been a problem was that he didn't have a razor. Morty had brought one before, made for a Vanir male, but they'd forgotten to stop at an all-night grocery where they could get a new one. Fortunately, his stubble was blond, so it wouldn't show up for a few days. He felt bad being out of uniform.

Except he was already out of uniform. It had been packed early, and hidden. He was undercover. Should he grow a beard?

He'd never gone more than three days without shaving, since he started.

What kind of Undercover Agent could he be, with hair already a week past the point he should have gone to the barber, and a beard?

Gareth hadn't come to any conclusion by the time he rejoined the woman scientist, but his brain was percolating like a proper coffee pot.

She must have been up for a while, because she had already gotten cleaned up and changed from her pajamas into an outfit similar to yesterdays: harem-like pants in baby blue with a lavender tunic over that, wrapped by a cute belt in black leather with all sorts of decorative, silver bangles.

She handed him a mug of steaming tea and smiled.

"How are you feeling this morning?" she asked.

"Refreshed," he discovered as he said the word.

Really spot-on. Like he had just slept twenty-four hours after eating the best ribeye possible.

"Good," she said. "Come with me."

He followed her into the bathroom. She pressed a hidden catch and the back of the linen closet opened into a hidden room beyond. They went through, and Gareth found himself back in the room with the dentist chair, but the walls were more of a brown color.

Beyond it, the same kind of control room as at her lab.

Back where her bedroom would have been, in the other apartment, a working space like what he was really expecting. Just a single workbench with the black top, scarred and stained and melted in a few places.

A computer on a desk in the corner.

Restaurant-sized refrigerators took up the whole back, three of them.

She moved around the workbench and gestured him to stand across from her.

"You here," she ordered mildly. "I need to take some blood, and then test how it will react. Take off your outer shirt, please."

She was more relaxed today. That much was obvious. Maybe it was escaping, and being saved, and escaping again. Plus a good night's sleep, even if she had to have a human to do it.

The plaid shirt in the colors of Sky Patrol came off, leaving him with only the tucked-in white t-shirt. Talyarkinash pulled some strange medical device out of a drawer and held it out. With her other hand, she grabbed his wrist and turned his arm over.

She touched the inside of his forearm briefly. It was more like a puppy's lick than anything, and then she pulled it back.

Gareth looked down and realized that it had left a tiny, red spot. Had she just drawn blood? That painlessly? That quickly?

There was another invention to take home, if he ever could.

The machine beeped after a few seconds. Talyarkinash hmmm-ed a bit and read some readout.

Rather than speak, she put it down on the counter and began to pull vials out of the farthest-right refrigerator. From underneath Talyarkinash pulled out a small crucible and a pair of eyedroppers.

It all looked incredibly sciency.

First, she poured some of a vial into the crucible. Then she added exactly three drops from the second bottle. The second eyedropper went into the side of the first device, and came out filled with a bright red fluid.

Blood? Wow.

"Ready?" she asked, looked up at him with an unexpected smile.

Gareth smiled back and nodded.

Talyarkinash dropped a single drop of Gareth's blood into the crucible, and stirred it with a glass rod that had appeared from somewhere when he wasn't looking.

At first, it started to steam a little.

And then a lot.

Before Gareth knew what was happening, the sides of the crucible cracked and the mixture inside poured out and started to melt the surface of the counter.

When Talyarkinash managed to splash it with some fresh water from the sink, it had eaten a disk about an eighth of an inch into the surface, which looked like a plastic of some sort.

"*Fardel*," she whispered under her breath.

Gareth felt like he should blush at this point, to listen to a lady curse in public.

"Everything okay?" he ventured, unsure of his footing.

She looked up and there was almost no color in her eyes, just slitted-open irises like it was all black to bottom of her soul.

She sucked a loud breath in and blew it out.

"Had that been my blood, Gareth, or Morty's, or anybody else's, there would have been the slightest puff of steam," she explained. "Just enough to see, but you might miss it if you blinked. Normally, the second experiment is to do the same thing in a genetic spectrometer to see where we might manage adjustments, if someone had any space left."

"Okay?"

"I didn't do this with Maximus," she continued. "We were just upgrading him slightly by causing him to resize into a Vanir, so it was a simple enough cut and slice job."

"Cut and slice?" Gareth felt his hair want to stand on end.

"I program a virus like a phage, Gareth," she looked up in deadly seriousness, even if the meaning of some of the words eluded him. "Once we inject it, it infects every one of your cells and reprograms them to make you someone else. In the case of Maximus, he went to sleep for a few hours, and then ate like a horse for a week as his body suddenly grew a foot and he put on almost a hundred pounds of mass. After that, I never saw him again, but Morty and Xiomber said they did something similar to raise his IQ to genius levels."

"But we aren't stopping there," Gareth observed.

"We're not," Talyarkinash agreed nervously. "Especially with all the changes I needed to program. This goes well beyond just making you Vanir-sized, since I need to program the changes with a morphic level clear out at the limits of anything anybody has ever done."

Gareth reached out and took her hand before she could pull it back.

"This is necessary," he said. "I understand that you might kill me accidentally in the process. It might be the single dumbest idea I have ever had, but it was the only context I could find for myself to encompass what I needed to stop Marc from taking over the entire galaxy."

"Are you absolutely sure you want to do this?" she asked in a quiet voice.

"No," he said. "I'm sure it is probably suicidal. But I don't know any other way to handle it. And the clock is running."

WARLORD

"THAT FOOL SHOULD CONSIDER himself lucky that he didn't get away from the police," Marc snarled as Maiair finished her report. "He had the human dead to rights, and let Dr. Liamssen shoot him? Let him rot in prison. Make sure nobody posts bail for that fool. If someone does, I want them both brought to me in chains."

"As you command," Maiair replied, turning to signal to her younger sister with the message to convey.

Once the younger woman was gone, Marc was alone with the older in his outer chamber. He moved to the table and took a seat, gesturing for her to do the same. Normally, he would enjoy a glass of wine right now, but he was too angry for that to settle him.

This was why he needed to go get some of his old gang, even if he had to break them out of prison. He knew of the perfect tool for a jailbreak. However, right now he was surrounded by fools that would rather talk than shoot. Cleveland Eddy and Two-gun Kowalski wouldn't have made that mistake.

"What do we know about Talyarkinash Liamssen?" he asked, rubbing his eyes in frustration.

"Best in the field," Maiair replied. "At least among those willing to work for us under the table. Probable a few better geneticists out there, but not that much better."

"Make your plans on the assumption that the man coming after us is my size and at least as smart as me," Marc warned her.

"As smart?" Maiair asked.

"She's the one who did my physical structure, Maiair," Marc said. "Morty and Xiomber did the programming that upgraded my mind. At a minimum, you're now facing me, but as a cop."

"Then we might have a problem, boss," she said carefully. "You've managed to whip the rest of the gang into shape, but in doing so, you've intimidated the hell out of them. Which was a good idea at the time. Will another human echo that and cause them to freeze up? We don't know what happened to Cheepsath. He might have frozen, thinking about facing a human."

Marc sighed.

"That's my one fear here," he said. "Having to rely on a gang I didn't build, to go up against the most competent, most capable enemy I've ever known. Once I get past you, your sister, and Zorge, I'm not sure how many more managers I've got, versus a lot of make-weight street criminals."

"Managers?" Maiair asked, at a loss.

"This organization is going to have to get much bigger, Maiair," Marc replied. "And soon. We'll have to come out of the shadows at some point."

"But we are the shadows, Marc," she said, headcrest bobbing in confusion. "Why would we come out?"

"Because I've got bigger plans than just ruling *Zathus*'s underground, Maiair," he explained. "At some point, we need to take over the whole godforsaken planet. We've already made a good start on that, with corrupt politicians we can bend."

"What's your ultimate goal, Maximus?" Maiair asked, headcrest now fully up and puffed sideways a little bit. Not challenging, but fierce.

"Taking over the entire *Accord of Souls*, Maiair," he said simply, saying it out loud for the first time.

"How in the nine hells do we do that?" she probed, headcrest puffing even more sideways with energy.

"I have a check list, actually," he said with a small laugh. "Fringe benefit of a bigger, faster brain. Who to turn. Who to kill. Things like that. At some point, I plan to import some of my old killers from Earth and their families, and start a new government."

"Would you make them Vanir, like you?" she asked carefully.

"No," Marc understood where her mind was going. "We'll leave them as humans. That way, the Vanir can still fight them on relatively even terms: Vanir might against human ruthlessness. The only real advantage the Vanir and other species will have over the next millennia will be numbers, because I won't bring that many humans over. Who knows where I'll be in a thousand years."

"Won't you be dead, Maximus?" she asked. Her headcrest had bobbed back down again. It was better than watching eyes and mouth on a human, to read their internal monolog.

"Not if all goes to plan," he explained. "The Chaa never programmed limits into humans. Why bother, since we were still stone-age cavemen, little better than animals, when they left. No, I will need a few geneticists to work on a project I have in my head, but I should be able to live forever."

"What about the rest of us?" Maiair asked.

The way she said it left a question in Marc's mind, but Maiair was a Warreth. Not the sort of creature he was interested in, except as a means to an ends.

Still, he fixed her with a stern gaze.

"You'll have as much responsibility as you can handle," he said. "For as long as you can handle it. That's decades, for your kind. I'm just sorry we can't do anything to extend that."

Her headcrest collapsed. Her head hung as well.

This creature couldn't have been hoping he would make her immortal, as well? Perhaps more? Did she think he needed a Warreth empress to rule with?

Marc's mind flitted back to the one woman who might have been a perfect queen, a decade ago. Before she made her choice. Maybe one of these days he might bring Philippa Loughty, the little maid of the lake, here, just so he could show her what a bad decision it had been, picking Gareth Dankworth over Marc Sarzynski.

If the machines were still available, he might have even chosen to bring her here now, just so she could be there when he finally caught up with the man and finished him off.

Perhaps another day.

But he would need to return home and scout for a future wife at some point. Someone he could turn into the physical form of a Vanir, while he made the changes she would need to breed up the generation of advanced humans he would need as a new nobility for the star empire he envisioned. Which he planned to rule forever.

But first, he needed the loyalty of his closest people.

"Maiair," he said softly, causing her head and headcrest to come up some. "I would grant you immortality, if I could. And we'll look into what gaps your genetic bonds have to improve you. I fear that the Warreth generally got the short end of that stick from the Chaa, along with the Tree People and the Borren. But who knows what we might be able to do with human science thrown in."

That brought some color back to her eyes. Some luster to her feathers. As much as he could do, for now.

It wouldn't do to alienate the very criminals he needed.

At least not until he didn't need them anymore.

Once he had enough humans to rule the rest, all bets were off.

SQUARE ONE

EVETH WAS BEGINNING to develop a deep and abiding antipathy towards Olehmmishqu. It was still a beautiful place, well ordered and filled with wonderfully-grand buildings and park. They were close to the river today, running down a tip that had turned out to be a miscommunication about a Moisa hairdresser. Or an old enemy with an axe to grind.

Because right now it was the people of this town that were driving her a little crazy.

Since the local police had put out a full description of the Nari scientist, Dr. Liamssen, she and Grodray had been overwhelmed with tips and leads, all of them leading to dead ends.

Grodray had made a few calls, and the Constabulary had dropped a number of officers into place around the fringes of the investigation as help, but kept things exceptionally quiet, otherwise. According to her partner, she was getting as much rope as she wanted to buy, until she decided to throw in the towel on this one.

The city was reasonably well locked down, but there were still over three million sentient creatures to watch coming and going. Any Nari, Vanir, or Yuudixtl in an auto-taxi or taking a ferry got a second look, to make sure it wasn't one of their four quarry making a run for it. All that had happened so far was that a number of innocent civilians were being inconvenienced for reasons nobody would explain.

Most of the officers involved couldn't anyway.

Worse, the words of that dumb punk kept coming back to haunt her.

A camera on the back of a smoke shop had caught enough audio to be cleaned up and useful. The man had known about the human. And worked for someone called Maximus, which was a new name circulating, one connected with some sort of crime ring thought to operating out of *Zathus*.

And the human had a name now. *Gareth*.

But she was under observation by those same criminals. Her, personally.

Someone on the inside was feeding the thugs her itinerary. Had been for several days. Possibly, any clues that might be good ones were being filtered out by corrupt members of the local police.

Who could she trust, besides Grodray?

This Gareth fellow had tried to suggest to the crooked doctor that they were on the same side.

A human? Please. Got a sued spaceship you want to sell me?

"Let's lunch," Eveth offered as they walked out of the latest office and back onto the main street.

The river itself was two blocks over, just past a long park fronted by a variety of interesting restaurants with sidewalk dining. But she wanted an inside table today.

Grodray raised an eyebrow, but nodded and gestured for her to lead.

She found a Borren-homeworld-style café, heavy on fish in cream sauces, that had the layout she wanted. Asked for and received a booth clear at the back, as far from the restrooms as possible. Got far enough away from anyone that nobody would ever have a need to get close enough to eavesdrop.

Had even flashed her badge quietly when asking to be seated away from everyone.

It was as much privacy as she could get on short notice.

"What's up, Baker?" her partner asked as they got their orders taken.

Food wouldn't be long, as they were on the early end of lunch and had the place almost completely to themselves.

"I'm not sure our communications or our investigation are secured," she said simply.

"The information we're getting makes no sense unless someone is filtering things before they get to me. Normally, we would have several decent leads, none of which was critical, but all pointing in the same rough direction. We've gotten nothing here."

"I agree," he nodded. "Asked a few friends to look into some things without sharing with the locals."

"You think the local Constabulary is bent?" she pursued.

"No," he replied. "The police probably are, given how much underworld activity we seem to keep finding. They should have kept the place cleaner if they were doing their jobs. My gut says that we have a couple of bad apples inside our organization."

"You never listen to your gut, Grodray," she snapped.

He actually smiled at that. A twinkle came into his eyes that she had rarely seen before.

"Let's hope they believe that as much as you do, Eve," he grinned. "A reputation is a powerful thing, especially if you can lead folks astray with it. So, what do we do to shake things up?"

"I want to rattle some cages," Eveth replied. "Liamssen disappeared, which suggests that she planned ahead, and had help. We need to find who might have helped her set up her escape plans. What have we got that we could offer a low-level punk to roll on someone?"

"If we could trust the prosecutors on this planet, I would say we could offer some punks sentencing bargains for information," he noted. "But I don't know which ones are the safe ones. I can promise you that a couple of forensic accountants will be making unannounced visits in the near future."

"What do they do?" Eveth asked, lost at the term. Forensics and Accounting seemed miles apart.

"They follow money around," Grodray smiled. "How it comes in, when it comes out, where it goes, how it comes back. Most criminals aren't smart enough to hide their tracks well enough from those sorts of Prime Investigators."

Prime Investigators. The true free agents. Had her partner called in some favors from old friends at that level? Was it that necessary? Were things that bad?

Eveth wondered if the *Accord of Souls* was closer to tottering than she had ever suspected. She had always thought that crime was just a little worse than it used to be. Maybe she needed to go back generations and compare? Was that something a Prime Investigator might do?

"Okay, so we can find corrupt politicians and the people holding their puppet strings," Eveth said. "But that's still going to take months. I have a feeling we have days at most. Liamssen is a geneticist. That suggests they plan to recast their human so he can hide. What do we know about human genetics?"

Or rather, what did you know that you haven't been able to tell me before, but which might be utterly critical right now, Jackeith?

She saw Grodray do a lot of processing quickly, from the way his eyes shifted back and forth on some invisible horizon.

Finally, those internal voices reached some consensus.

"This is Level-7 stuff, Eve," he began slowly. She nodded with the gravity of that pronouncement. "Humans are not part of the *Accord of Souls*. Were never modified by our ancestors, the Chaa. They look like smaller versions of the Vanir, *Those Left Behind*, but that's just convergent evolution, we think."

"Okay," she said, holding her breath.

"Most geneticists can work with basic things," he continued, pausing to glance over his shoulder to make sure they were along. "Fix problems at birth. Alter hair or skin or feather color. That sort of thing. Non-threatening to galactic order."

"What about the humans, Grodray?"

"There might not be *any* limitations on them, Eve," he said quietly. "They might be a blank slate onto which a geneticist with a lot of skill and no scruples might be able to paint."

"So those killers…"

"Might be turned into one of us easy enough," Grodray nodded. "Vanir are the closest match, if you want to hide. Plus you add size and mass to an already dangerous species. Look at what that human was able to do to you in his native form. Now make him my size with those muscles."

"Would she stop there?" Eveth asked.

"What do you mean?"

"Would a criminal geneticist just stop at making him Vanir, Grodray?" Eveth asked. "If there are no limits, would she go crazy? Most doctors have some level of god-complex, trying to either make the world a better place, or prove that they are smarter than everyone else. What might she do?"

Again he turned to look out of the booth. Nobody was anywhere close.

"Six months ago, we had suspicions that Cinnra, on *Zathus*, was trying to get himself a human killer," Grodray said. "Not long after that, about two months ago, Cinnra was dead and there was a new boss. One nobody had heard of before. A renegade Vanir, according the very little we've been able to piece together."

"A modified human?" she gasped.

Grodray shrugged meaningfully.

"And somebody in the gang went and got themselves a cop, to try and stop this Maximus?" Eveth leapt into the darkness. "But they'll need to upgrade him to a Vanir as well. Will they stop?"

"That's why we're functionally acting like Prime Investigators on this, Eve," her partner said, deadly serious. "Go wherever the crime takes us, without *being* Prime Investigators, because that might attract attention."

"Are you really just a Senior Constable, Jackeith Grodray?" she asked, making another intuitive leap.

Another grin. But not a no. Or a yes.

"Then we're back to the top," she said. "I don't think we have time to do anything but kick over an anthill and see what happens. If Maximus is really a disguised human, and Gareth is about to become a Vanir, we're potentially facing a war among literal gods, right here on our beat. You need to find me a door I can kick in."

His eyes got a faraway look to them, like he was checking files for the right address. Someone that wasn't normally worth rousting, or maybe a criminal he knew about, because those were easier to keep track of.

Instead of answering, he pulled out his pocketcomm and dialed.

"Yeah, me," he said to whoever answered.

Pause.

"I want a name," Grodray said. "Someone at mid-level that is wired in enough to give me the information I want when my crazy partner has him dangling out a window by one ankle."

Longer pause. Probably some hemming and hawing at the other end. Like maybe she already had that sort of reputation on *Orgoth Vortai* and someone might know that.

She had never actually let go. But it made a fantastic threat, when a woman who was bigger than you could hold you by one leg, upside down, over a thirty-foot-drop.

"And remember, you're the one signing this check," Grodray added his own threat when he got an answer.

If whoever it was wasn't on the level, Jackeith Grodray might be coming for them next. With an angry partner in tow.

Food arrived as he hung up, so he sat silently, but she could see that twinkle in his eyes again.

When they were alone, and he checked, the man smiled like a shark spying a wounded seal.

"I might have someone for you, Eve," he said.

Good.

She had to stop two gods from destroying the *Accord of Souls*. And she absolutely had to do it tonight.

AWAKENING

GARETH WAS BACK in the dentist chair. The walls were brown, so he knew he hadn't fallen into a nightmarish dream, reliving those few days in the other chair, being slowly eaten by the psionic drill.

Talyarkinash was in the other room, tuning things as well as she could.

She had gone as far as her extensive experience and creativity could take her, she had told him. And he believed her, having watched quietly all day as the woman alternatively calculated and cursed under her breath.

They both felt the pressure coming to a head. Angry people out there were looking for their scalps, and he had only one option to protect this woman who had come to trust a human.

"Gareth, are you ready?" she said over the intercom.

"I am," he said, taking a deep breath.

"Stand by."

The chair grabbed him in iron bands. Wrists, shins, chest, head. He was back in that technological iron maiden, waiting for the mad scientist to press the door shut on him.

"I wish I could say otherwise, but this is going to hurt," she offered an early apology. "Normally, we would space the six injections out over as many days, with stops to monitor your medical condition and feed you a proper, balanced diet. But as you know, they could kick in the door at any moment."

Lunch had been everything left over from dinner, plus a can of pasta and some canned fruit, until he felt like he would explode if he took another bite.

"I understand, Talyarkinash," he replied. "Thank you for doing this my way. I can handle pain. I am Earth Force Sky Patrol. There is no other choice. And if it fails, keep notes so you can fix it for the next agent you recruit, because we both know nobody in the *Accord* can stop him."

"I will, Gareth," she said quietly. "And thank you for last night. I really needed a friend."

Gareth started to say something. Started to blush. But she must have hit the button as she spoke, because something tapped him on the left shoulder, the one closer to the heart, and suddenly his entire body was on fire.

He might have screamed. Wanted to. Told his lungs and throat to carry through, but his body was no longer his to command.

Instead, Gareth was composed of a roaring fire that someone else was trying to extinguish with acid. Every nerve. Every muscle. Every neuron.

Gareth could never remember experiencing a tenth, even a hundredth as much pain. Diving across death pressure without a helmet, in order to save the ship from detonation, hadn't hurt as much.

His eyes were on fire now, or perhaps his optic nerves were slowly being eaten by miniature piranha, one angry bite at a time.

After an eternity measured in the lifetime of stars, the pain seemed to ebb.

Gareth found he could think again. His throat was raw, but that might have been the screaming he was hoping he was able to do. His arms and legs felt like wet spaghetti sliding off a plate.

"Gareth?" the Angel of Death called his name. "Can you hear me?"

No, not the Angel of Death. Retribution, perhaps.

That would make her *Nemesis*, the bringer of retribution. Except that was his job.

The helmet retracted and Gareth found that he could see again.

He looked up and saw Talyarkinash's azure eyes staring down at him with concern.

Yes, he had become Nemesis. That would in turn make her the goddess of night, Nyx.

He rather enjoyed that thought.

"Are you okay?" she seemed to be asking.

Gareth nodded and grunted, not quite willing to trust his tongue right now.

"Good," she continued. "Because somebody just kicked in the door to my apartment, across the hallway. We've run out of time."

CLOSING THE TRAP

"WE'VE GOT THEM," she said as Marc let Maiair into the other chamber.

Yooyar was with her, and both had their headcrests at full display. Marc was pretty sure what that signified among the Warreth, but now was really not the time.

"Where?" he asked. "And are you sure?"

There had been a couple of false alarms so far today. Those two Constables were getting progressively less communicative with the local cops, which suggested that they had finally figured out what was wrong. Probably, they were on the verge of cleaning up the local police and Constabulary, which would seriously dent his operations on this planet, but that was a problem for tomorrow.

Today, he needed to kill Gareth Dankworth. After that, he had time to put longer-term plans into action.

"We leaned extra heavy on someone who should have told us sooner," Yooyar said with the sort of grim tone that suggested she just might be capable of killing in cold blood, which made her a rarity in the *Accord of Souls*. If she could do that, he would have as much work for the young Warreth as she wanted to undertake. "When we threatened to hand him over to the cops, he gave us an address. Supposedly, around two years ago Liamssen hired him to build her a secret lab not far from the university campus."

"Good," Marc exclaimed. "If it really is the place, then we'll turn him over to the Constables later for holding out on us now. If not, I want you to kill him. I'm done playing around and the stakes are too high right now."

"Who do we take with us?" Maiair asked the million-credit-question.

Who did he trust, when he was about to take on a human? Maiair had been right. Most of the team he brought to *Hurquar* were only really dangerous to their own kind, those inside the *Accord of Souls*.

What he really needed were killers. Men he had used back on Earth.

This group would have to do.

"Get me a driver who knows his stuff," Marc commanded. "You two, plus Zorge. Bring stunners only, as I may need to torture information out of the four of them later, and I want them all alive for now."

Yooyar nodded and departed. Maiair waited an extra second, as if about to say something, before she nodded and departed as well.

The way the women had reacted to the word *torture* just exacerbated the difference between the human, ruling caste he would need to build later, and the pitiful pacifists that had inherited the galaxy from those people who really should have done something about humans fifty thousand years ago.

That, or they needed to come back now and set it to right.

The failure of the Chaa to stop him was evidence enough to Marc that he was indeed destined to live forever and rule the galaxy as a newly-born god.

ANT HILLS

EVETH HAD TAKEN the time to change before they set out. She was back in the blue-gray bodysuit, covered over with armored scales and sporting a holster for her pistol on her left thigh. The blue ring over her heart seemed to be filling her with white-hot plasma from the surface of a star. Grodray had changed too, but he had gone the full route, including the white, dress beret and tunic over the top of his armor, so that made him look like the good cop.

That was okay. Eveth was angry enough already. And Grodray had said they were acting as Prime Inspectors on this case. That meant she had a great deal more leeway on rules and regulations than a mere Constable.

Time to put that to the test.

The auto-taxi had dropped them on a side street not far from the main tourist area, down by the river. They had eaten lunch not a mile from here, but by night it was an entirely different world.

Neon signs competed for attention Music pulsed a low, rumbling bass she could feel in her sternum, even from here. There was a line of people at the door, waiting for one of the bouncers protecting the joint to let them in, assuming they passed the requisite coolness test inherent in clubs like this.

"That's it?" she asked, nodding the direction of the target as they came around the corner. The music hit her like a wet towel.

Grodray just nodded.

"What exactly are you planning to do, Eve?" he asked in a simple voice, falling into stride with her as she moved.

"Kick over an anthill, Jack," she smiled back, almost biting her lip with anticipation.

No more deduction. No more intuitive leaps into the darkness. Just heads that needed cracking together.

She approached the line and went around the rope holding the unwelcome at bay.

Two of the bouncers in black shirts at the front door were Nari. Big specimens of determination that probably intimidated the hell out of tourists and artists. The one in the middle was a Vanir. He was maybe Grodray's height, and had lots of mass, but much of it was turning into a pot belly around the middle.

Eveth flashed her badge as she got close and slipped it into her thigh holder so it was out of the way and her hands were clear.

"You can't go in there," the fat guy said. "It's a private party."

"Stop me then," Eveth said.

Apparently, they bred them dumb on *Hurquar*, or wherever this guy was from. He actually reached out and tried to grab Eveth's shoulder as she walked by him.

It had been a day. A whole week of days like this.

Eveth grabbed the hand on her right shoulder with her own right hand. She twisted it forward hard as she kept walking, forcing him sideways and down if he didn't want his arm broken.

One of the two Nari looked like he might want to cause trouble, until a stun pistol appeared in his face, at the other end of a long, Vanir arm belonging to her angry partner.

"Official business," he said, invoking the kinds of dread-bringing words that would get the other two thrown in jail for weeks until Grodray or Eveth decided they had suffered enough embarrassment.

Interfering with a Constabulary investigation was a felony everywhere, just for situations like this.

Both Nari turned white around the eyes. Ears went flat against skulls and the two men backed away.

Eveth would have expected to see tails tucked under, if they weren't wearing baggy pants.

She turned her attention to the big guy, still trying not to have a broken arm. He had a look about him of a bully boy. Just the kind of guy you wanted at the front door of a club like this. She twisted a little more, and he was on his knees.

Eveth pulled her spare handcuffs from a belt pouch and hooked this bastard to the door handle. The only way he was going anywhere without her now involved a cutting laser, patience, and a high pain threshold.

Grodray nodded his approval.

Inside, the wall of sound was almost a painful experience. Eveth wondered what subsonics might be bathing the crowd in emotional manipulation, but it wasn't her problem.

She looked to the right, and saw a crowd pressed up against a long bar like a rising tide. On the left, tables filled with sweaty patrons. In the middle, a dance floor and a light show so bright it might constitute an optical assault.

The door she wanted was on the far side, back on the left, near where risers went up to tables in the back with a good view.

Two more goons protected it as she wended her way through the mob, not exactly elbowing folks out of her way, but taking full advantage of the smaller species around her, who couldn't resist her angry mass.

Another Nari guarded this door, with a Grace on the other side. Both wore the same black shirt of security employees, and had noted her approach with concern bordering on hostility.

Eveth smiled as she got close enough for the men to move to block the door. With one hand, she flipped open the wallet with the badge. With the other, she drew her pistol and pointed it at the one on the left. Grodray's pistol was there a split-second later, like he had known how this was going down.

Maybe he secretly was a Prime Investigator, hiding out with the little people?

"Your choice," Eveth yelled over the music.

The Grace nodded and backed down first, sliding across from the doorway and more or less pushing the Nari against the wall and whispering something in his ear as he did.

Like what a really bad idea it might be to resist the angry, giant woman with a badge and a gun.

Through the door the sound fell to a dull echo in the middle distance. The walls were rough wood covered over with old concert playbills, and the floor badly scuffed tile. Eveth passed a kitchen that extended behind the wall on the bar side, and then a blank space that was probably the back of the restrooms.

The hallway ended in a wooden door, older than the hills, and with a name on it in gold letters. The name Grodray had gotten for her earlier.

She had always wanted to do this, but it had never been an option, even in this line of work.

Without breaking stride, she stepped up and kicked the handle with all the anger she had accumulated since she came to this planet, shattering the strike panel out of the frame and a good chunk of wood from the door.

Inside, a fat Grace was talking on the telephone and looked up with a surprise that turned his tentacles nearly white.

"I'll call you back," he said. "Something just came up."

The rest of the office was empty. Just the short, fat man behind a battered desk, two chairs, and wall-to-wall pictures of famous people who had been here or played the club at some point in their careers.

Eveth still had the gun in her hand, so she sat in the nearer chair and smiled at him.

"I want information," she said primly. "You have three options. One: you can just tell me what I need. Two: you end up spending the rest of the night and maybe a week or two in jail while badly-misfiled paperwork gets untangled."

Pause.

"What's option number three," he asked, falling for it like any good straight man.

"You have to stop at the hospital first," she smiled.

CONFRONTATION

GARETH WAS in no shape to fight, but he had no choice. He stumbled upright as Talyarkinash put his arm around her neck and wobbled with him towards the door.

A crash nearby signaled the secret door being broken open, and suddenly there were people pointing guns at him.

Gareth tried to manage his drunkenness, but his body was only vaguely under his control at this point. He recognized two Warreth females, both holding what looked like stun pistols pointed at he and Talyarkinash. Both women were cherry-red, with the taller one having black and white highlights and the shorter one having mostly yellow underplummage.

A Vanir male entered a second later. He was magnificent. At least seven-foot-four and built like a linebacker. Handsome face with dark, curly hair covering the man's head. He seemed to be familiar.

"It looks like we're too late to stop *her* from upgrading you," the man said in a cruel voice. "But that just means that I'm not too late to stop *you*."

He smiled down at Gareth, but it was more of a sneer.

After a moment, Gareth finally recognized the man. The scale had thrown him off.

Intellectually, he had known it was a fact, but coming face to face with it was something entirely else.

"Hello, Marc," Gareth said slowly, trying to sound more coherent than he was. "Or should I call you Maximus now?"

"Either will work, old friend," Gareth's worst nightmare smiled. "Welcome to the *Accord of Souls*."

And then the bastard shot him.

OVERLORD

MARC SMILED as the bolt took Dankworth square in the chest. For good measure, he shot the woman as well. Stunners were a cheap way to handle prisoners.

"Find the other two," he ordered brusquely.

It became clear within moments that Morty and Xiomber weren't anywhere in the suite of rooms, and there were no more hidden doors to blow open. Nothing but this operating theater, a control room, and a small lab, and no indication a pair of Yuudixtl had ever been in here.

In a way, that made it worse, because it suggested that those two knew he was going to catch up with Liamssen and Dankworth, and had already moved on, probably hoping to find another Field Agent from Earth Force Sky Patrol, or maybe even a Special Agent.

He couldn't put any of his other plans into action until he had cauterized this wound. And now he might have to start over.

How long had those two been planning to betray him?

"The place is empty, Maximus," Maiair confirmed. "What's next?"

"You two grab her," he said, pointing at the doctor on the floor of the operating theater. "Bring her along to the truck. I only gave them a medium stun, but they won't be conscious for at least thirty or forty minutes. Then I need to know where the other two are."

"What about the human?" Yooyar asked.

"I'll bring him myself," Marc said.

It was almost like picking up a ten-year-old child, using his enhanced muscles to lift up the man who had once been his best friend and toss Dankworth over a shoulder in a fireman's carry.

"What about the rest?" Maiair pressed.

Marc looked around at the space. There was no way to hide the kicked in front door of the other suite, nor the destroyed hidden door between the two flats. It would only be a matter of time until someone called the police, and the place would be crawling with badges.

Still, he had the doctor. He could get what he wanted out of her before he killed her. And still had enough connections to the authorities to get copies of her files once the police impounded them. He was pretty sure all of the corrupt locals he owned would be in jail fast enough as a result of this fiasco, but not before he could get that much out of them.

"Leave it," he decided. "I've got what I really need."

The girls were gone first, lugging the Nari traitor between them. Zorge was covering the front door when Marc emerged from the bathroom with his own burden.

"So that's him?" Zorge tsked. "Doesn't look like much."

"Neither would you, stunned," Marc snapped. "This man, this human, is orders of magnitude more dangerous than you ever dreamed of being, Zorge. He might be the only person in the universe that could stop me."

"Why haven't you killed him, then?" the spymaster asked abruptly.

"I need to know what he knows first," Marc promised. "After that, it's a whole different ballgame."

GETAWAY

MARC'S TRUCK was right where he had left it, double-parked in a loading zone at the bottom of the short tower. The *Accord* wasn't big on personally-owned vehicles, but there were always a few, so most buildings dedicated a couple of floors of the big towers to landing bays.

He had brought a simple panel truck tonight, painted on the outside with the name and phone number of a local plumbing service as a way to vanish into the scenery. Let the fools drive around in big, black limousines that screamed *"I'm important. Somebody arrest me!"*

He would settle for a quiet time in the shadows, building his power up until he could simply explode out and take what he wanted. Liamssen's notes on what she had done to Dankworth would be invaluable for that.

What little extra did they think would give that man the edge he needed to take on Maximus?

The girls were carrying the rogue geneticist towards the back of the truck as he approached. Zorge had gone ahead and was sitting up front with the driver for the word to move.

Lights suddenly appeared at the near edge of the garage as an auto-taxi landed and deposited two figures on the balcony apron outside. Something about them just had Marc's hackles up, so he crouched down, carefully setting Dankworth's body behind a window-washing repulsor craft.

The two were Vanir, and the way the female walked just screamed *cop* as Marc watched. When she passed into the internal light from the darkness outside, Marc also saw the badge on her chest.

For a moment, his rage burned crimson at the thought he had been betrayed by someone in his organization, but he stopped himself cold. Cops looking for him would have surrounded the building with heavy teams and be storming the place right now, so maybe they had just gotten lucky tip and arrived too late to keep him from his prize?

"You there," the woman cop yelled as she saw Maiair and Yooyar, carrying a body between them in unfortunate circumstances. "Stop and hands in the air. Police!"

One of the reasons Marc had chosen a Vanir as his final form, in addition to the amazing physical size, were the reflexes.

Warreth were gliders, with human-like upper arms that had been extended and flattened into wings that ran along past their hands. They were more like bats that way, and couldn't truly fly, not like the Elohynn. But that latter race was a true hexapod, a body that could usually pass for human in dim light, plus wings like an angel, except they hinged down instead of up.

The two Vanir cops had guns out and pointed before either sister could even consider dropping their package. Zorge was up front, probably with the door closed. He would suddenly find a stunner in his ear, if he wasn't paying attention.

And the cops were coming up at a bad angle for anyone in the cab to see them before it was too late.

Good thing Marc was sneakier than everyone else.

He pulled out his pistol and adjusted it to the highest settings. The beam attenuated with distance, and this would be a pretty long shot for a hand-held stunner. But he only needed to soften them up enough that they couldn't evade follow-up shots.

"What's going on here?" the woman cop yelled in an angry voice as she closed.

Her partner was a few steps back and to one side, concentrating on the rest of the garage and possible ambushes. Like Marc.

He decided to take the male first, trusting that he had enough cover to protect himself from the female cop. Yooyar would also be able to get involved if the cop stopped covering her.

Marc stayed perfectly still, aware that Vanir, like humans, had eyesight keyed to motion and color. He measured the shot in his head and watched the two cops come to rest, too far away for the sisters to attack them, but close enough to track everything happening with the truck.

The male risked a glance the other direction.

Marc exploded into motion, raising his pistol into view and triggering the shot almost before he had the barrel down, trusting that the gun itself needed a fraction of a second from the trigger pull to the primary coil energizing. About the same amount of time it took a bullet to exit a barrel under the high pressure of burning cordite.

The shot was a little high, but still tagged the male cop in the shoulder. Hopefully, it would be enough, because Marc was already tracking on the woman.

She was spinning in his direction, targeting on sound as her eyes searched for him.

Time slowed to molasses on a Nova Jersey winter day.

Marc fired.

She fired.

Marc felt the brush of her stunner, like the kiss of a tree branch whipping by, but most of it went into the vehicle in front of him. Still, his eyesight grayed out for a moment.

He fired a second shot blind. Memory said he had gotten her harder than she had gotten him, with that first shot, but he had never seen anyone with reflexes as good as his.

He needed an Empress like her, one of these days, but a modified human. Still, he had a pattern upon which to base that future wife, if he got out of this situation alive.

A third shot rang out as Marc's vision cleared.

A fourth.

Silence.

Marc managed to make out the scene.

The cop was unconscious. Both cops.

Maiair had gotten her pistol out and taken both cops down by herself, once he had distracted them.

Marc made a note to pay better attention to the older Warreth sister. She was making herself look better and better as a potential second-in-command for the organization, just as her younger sister was turning into a dangerous gunsel.

Maybe he really did need a harem after all, as a way to bind them more fully to the throne he intended to create.

"Good job," Marc said as he holstered his pistol and gathered up Dankworth's body.

"What do we do with them?" Maiair asked, covering them with her pistol anyway.

"Bring them along," Marc decided. "If they're here, there's a leak in the organization, and we need to plug it. I'll find out what they know before we work on the other two."

Marc deposited the Field Agent into the back of the van as Zorge emerged, eyes wide with surprise.

"What happened?" he asked.

"You missed all the fun, old man," Yooyar's sarcastic tones could have been used to paint a building.

"Constables?" Zorge inspected them as he helped Maiair lift the female. "How'd they find us?"

"That's your job, Zorge," Marc said coldly. "Find out who talked and have them brought to me for punishment."

"Yes, sir," the Nari spymaster nodded.

Marc pulled the unconscious male to the van and then lifted him inside, noting that the man was skinny, but still a solid block of mass. Older cop, wearing the insignia of a Senior Constable, what Marc would have called Detective Sergeant back home,

Nothing else was moving in the garage.

Before they lifted off, Marc pulled the pocketcomms from both cops and tossed them under a nearby car, aware of how easily they could be tracked, if someone was suspicious. The rest of their belongings went into a sack someone had grabbed: guns, badges, wallets, handcuffs.

Accord cops used cuffs that keyed on bio-signature, rather than the old-fashioned iron key. Marc assumed that a competent cop would put herself and her partner into the tiny, electronic brain, so using their own cuffs on them was a mere annoyance, rather than a useful tool.

Still, they would be out for a while. Long enough to get back to the warehouse he had been using as a base.

After that, he would have all the time in the world, and all sorts of interesting tools, to torture these four for all the information they had, like squeezing a sponge completely dry, before he discarded them onto the ashheap of history.

PRISONER

GARETH WOKE TO PAIN. Millions of microscopic ants marching through his veins, biting him with every stride. Hot coals scorching his flesh on a slow smoker.

A groan escaped his lips.

"Ah, you are awake, my old friend," Marc Sarzynski's voice intruded on Gareth's nightmare.

He tried to open his eyes, but the light in here stabbed his brain with icepicks.

Gareth squinted to the merest slits and tried to focus on something beyond the torture in his soul.

"Too bright?" Marc asked.

Gareth groaned again and nodded. Tried to. He wasn't sure how much of what was happening in his mind made it to the nerves and muscles of his body.

Sudden darkness reached out and embraced him in coolness.

"Better?" Marc asked. "I remember when I first awakened, as the growth began to hit. Everything hurt and I was nearly blind."

"Thank you," Gareth managed to slur out.

"Anything for my oldest, dearest friend," Sarzynski sneered. "We want you comfortable for what comes next."

Gareth heard the emphasis on that last word and knew what Maximus had planned.

He had failed. They had been too late to get everything done and escape.

Or rather, Talyarkinash had done everything she could, but Gareth had needed more time for it to happen.

Time he had run out of.

Gareth managed to open his eyes enough to see, this time. Through the fire in his body, he understood that he was hanging from a pair of manacles holding his arms up, those in turn attached to an I-beam running horizontally on some sort of frame. Another pair gripped his ankles.

The space smelled like a shipping warehouse, all dusty and oils and dry. The ceiling was far overhead, with a crane on rails up there for lifting things out of railroad cars, just like home.

Gareth was on his knees, so he fought with his body to stand. It was like lifting the old Empire State Building, but he managed, hanging forward on the chains to find his balance and drive upwards.

He couldn't stand right now. Not really.

But he wasn't about to be on his knees for Marc Sarzynski.

A breath pulled down into the base of his stomach seemed to quell some of the fires coursing through his blood. His mind might have even cleared a little.

Gareth focused on breathing and learning to think again. This was worse than the hardest concussion he had ever sustained, and his head was ringing like a church bell in synch with his heart.

"My," Sarzynski exclaimed. "You do look better already."

Gareth managed to turn his head far enough to find Maximus, seated on a chair on a small platform, like a king on his throne. The rest of the royal suite stood around him, arrayed in layers of power and access, from the dumbest rookies at the edge of the crowd to the two Warreth women standing closest to Marc, the taller one whispering in his ear.

Gareth looked down and realized his favorite cowboy outfit was gone. Hopefully not destroyed, since he wasn't sure who that tailor had been and wanted to go back soon for more wardrobe.

In its place, Gareth was wearing a long robe of a heavy, white linen. It hung long on his feet and wrists, as if it were for a Vanir, rather than a human. The white suggested something angelic, which was probably appropriate, given the roles he and Marc had chosen to play.

But the oversized nature also sent an important message. Sarzynski understood. Knew that Gareth would be growing as the various viruses worked their way through his body, reprogramming things and triggering all manner of changes. Hopefully, he would miss the important changes when focusing on the obvious.

"Are you ready to talk yet?" Marc asked a polite, even pleasant voice. "The others haven't woken up yet, so I can't put them to the question and find out what they know."

"Why, Marc?" Gareth asked simply, as he managed to gain control of his mouth.

"Power, Gareth," the man replied. "You had always managed to thwart me, back home, mister White Knight on a Charging Steed. Here, we are a whole new thing, and the *Accord of Souls* lacks the fundamental tools to prevent me from taking over."

"Emperor Marc the First?" Gareth asked sarcastically.

"Indeed, old friend," the criminal overlord smiled grandly. "I had even considered who I might need for an Empress…"

The way he left the phrase dangling left no doubt in Gareth's mind as to whom Marc was referring.

"If you hurt her…"

"Relax, Dankworth," Marc said. "She made her choice, and I honor that. She'll make a lovely little housewife for you. Or would have. I will need a woman with grander dreams to create a new species of rulers here."

Gareth had a better view of the crowd than Marc did. He watched the implications of those words ripple out, a pebble dropped into a still pond. Useful information, long term, but Gareth didn't know how long he had. That Sarzynski hadn't killed him already meant that there was something the man needed to know, and needed Gareth to supply it.

Knowing Maximus, the man would resort to torture at some point. Gareth steeled his soul to resist as long as he could.

Another deep breath and the fires seemed to bank, turning down to a small hearth of coals, just keeping him warm on a chill night rather than threatening him with a foretaste of hell.

"So what do you want, Marc?" Gareth even managed to sound calm, he thought.

"I want to watch you change, Gareth," the man replied with a smile. "See what *she* did to you, so I can figure out what I might want to add to the current repertoire."

Gareth followed Marc's eyes and saw Talyarkinash strapped down to a chair off to one side, head lolling as she was still out cold. Beyond her, a pair of Vanir in steel-blue uniforms. Gareth looked close and recognized Constable Baker and her partner, also captured.

Only the brothers seemed to have escaped. Hopefully, they had enough money and connections to remain at large while they assembled another wormhole generator and sought more help. Nobody else in the *Accord of Souls* was left who could stop this madman.

"She made me a match for you, Marc," Gareth said gruffly, turning his eyes back to his foe. "That's what the *Accord of Souls* needed, after all. Someone who could stand in your path and say *No*."

"Well, then you both failed," Marc said. "Not even the strength of Samson will save you now. I will cut your hair and blind you, so you can listen to the others spill their secrets first, and then their blood."

"Marc, you can just walk away, you know," Gareth retorted quietly. "Take your little mob of pitiful losers and vanish back into the shadows. I'll even give you a head start."

"You think I should fear you, little human?" Marc voice suddenly turned to rage.

"Because if you hurt her, or the Constables, I promise that there will be no place in the galaxy or in hell that will save you from my wrath."

"You don't seem to understand, Dankworth," Marc's anger towered as high as the great ceiling overhead. "I've been waiting for this moment for years. I was always second best when you were around. Anything I did was almost, but not quite as good, as the great Gareth St. John Dankworth of the Earth Force Sky Patrol. Have you any idea what that's like?"

"I wasn't competing with you, Marc," Gareth said simply. "I was simply trying to do the best I could. Trying to make the Solar System a better place. I will do the same with the *Accord of Souls*, since I can never go home now."

"Fool," Sarzynski thundered. "You'll be dead."

Gareth watched him rise from the cheap, imported throne, just an over-sized metal chair, and stomp down to ground level. The criminal gang around him had already fallen silent. Now they parted like the waters at his approach.

Maximus came close, but not close enough for Gareth to grab him. Still, Gareth got his first major shock. Marc Sarzynski was only half a head taller now, so Gareth had reached something like six-foot-nine as his body expanded under the force of all the chemicals and transformational virii.

A hunger took root at the bottom of Gareth's soul, but it wasn't just for nourishment.

This one was for justice.

"Now, you will watch what your foolhardy gambles have brought," Marc snarled.

It felt like they were the only two people in the entire vast auditorium of the warehouse, the rest of the people hanging silent on pins and needles.

Gareth watched his foe stomp over to where Talyarkinash was strapped to the chair. A nearby table had been covered with a cloth, one that Marc pulled back now and cast from him.

Underneath, what looked to Gareth like the contents of surgical theater had been laid out in careful order. Gareth felt his stomach clench.

"Do I have your attention, Dankworth?" Sarzynski yelled angrily.

Without pausing for a response, Marc reached down and picked something up. Gareth struggled against the chains binding him as Marc stepped around behind the Nari woman, but the criminal did not touch her.

Instead, he snapped something and held it under her nose. Even from here, Gareth picked up the rank assault of the smelling salts.

Talyarkinash moaned and stirred, struggling weakly and vainly against the ties binding her to the chair.

"Good," Marc said in a cruel voice. "You're awake, Dr. Liamssen."

It dawned on Gareth that he had never heard the woman's last name, having been apparently on a first-name basis with her from the first moment. He would apologize to her later for his social failures.

"Whaa…" Talyarkinash fumbled to find a context.

"Welcome to *my* lab, traitor," Marc continued. "I'm going to ask you questions, and you are going to answer them. If you don't, I am going to use pain as a tool and an art form to slowly rip away your sanity, until I get what I want. If you please me, I might kill you quickly."

"MAXIMUS!" Gareth roared across the space. "This is your last warning."

"YOU DO NOT GIVE ME ORDERS, HUMAN!" Marc screamed back in a voice of cruelty that transcended human or Vanir.

Gareth watched the man pick up something from the table and step around behind the woman again, so Gareth that had an unobstructed view.

"My friend needs to understand his situation, doctor," Marc hissed.

"And I need you to understand that your only choice now is how much pain you will suffer before you tell me what I want to know."

Gareth growled, low in his chest, as Marc held out the thing to Talyarkinash's left arm. It was a fine-pointed, surgical knife, but Gareth wasn't sure how he knew that from this far away. It should have appeared as a steel pencil, considering the distance.

"We begin," Marc said in a voice dripping with venom.

He took the knife and turned it sideways.

Talyarkinash struggled, but she was bound too effectively to move anything but her ears.

Slowly, Marc ran it down the outside of her arm in a move that made no sense, until Gareth saw her fur fall away in a strip an inch wide and several inches long.

He and Marc locked eyes across the space for a moment, rage swirling back and forth like a storm's tide. Lightning bolts of fury seemed to pass between them, at least in Gareth's imagination

Marc turned the blade again and plunged it directly into Talyarkinash's arm, right in the center of the bald spot, dragging it far enough to make a deep cut. Bright red blood welled up and began to drip.

Talyarkinash whimpered in pain.

Gareth saw more red, but this time it was in his soul. Anger, previously banked, waited no more. Those coals, calm and waiting at the center of his being, they were no longer quiet. Hot wind blasted them and they exploded into the sort of white heat necessary to forge steel.

The pain Gareth felt was worse than anything he had previously endured, but this was driven by wrath, not confusion.

Gareth squinted his eyes and howled. Felt the sound echo off the far walls of the warehouse as Marc smiled at him, pulling the blade free and wiping it clean on Talyarkinash's tunic.

Gareth looked at his left hand now, the manacled arm closer to the heart, where six injections had forever altered his life.

Nothing would alter his soul, but the flesh of his hand seemed to melt under his gaze, showing the faintest tint of bronze as his fingers extended a little in the fury of a molten forge.

He looked back up at Marc and smiled.

Something had changed in the man's face. Fear, perhaps, had taken root and begun to spread its tendrils.

"What are you doing?" Marc called in a voice twinged now with doubt, supplanting the towering anger that had been there a moment ago.

"Being born," Gareth said simply.

He closed his eyes and reached down into the depths of his soul, plunging both hands into that pile of white-hot coals, seeking something. What he wasn't sure.

Perhaps Excalibur.

Gareth had been raised on all the great martial tales of history: Arthur who was known as Pendragon. Saint George of Lydda, reputed to have slain a dragon, and Theodore of Amasea, another warrior for his faith. But others as well, including Bilbo who fought a dragon in his own way and lived to tell the tale.

All throughout the Western Literary canon were sprinkled great beasts who tormented men. Creatures known as dragons that had become receptacles of dreams of flight and fancy, powerful immortals who challenged men spiritually as often as they did martially. Symbols as well as monsters.

Gareth had no desire to face Samson's fate, even as he considered the manacles binding his arms and legs to an iron frame. Nor would he accept the imagery of another man so bound, with the Spear of Longinus plunged into his side.

There was only one God, according to Pastor Jacob, and Gareth lacked the arrogance to challenge that notion, even as the desperate, criminal scientists of the *Accord of Souls* sought to make him over into one.

But he would accept a dragon as a powerful totem.

Gareth howled again as the fire crept out of his soul and immolated his physical form, Talyarkinash's greatest success coming to flesh and fruition around him.

Dragonsong.

But this roar was not pain.

No, this was retribution.

Gareth turned his face on the rest of Marc's gang and snarled his rage at them, watching them shrink beneath him as he did.

Except that they were staying the same size.

Gareth was growing. Elongating.

Transforming.

The four manacles shattered as he flexed mighty limbs, covered over now with bronze scales inspired by two scared Yuudixtl scientists, willing to risk everything to undo the evil they had unleashed on the galaxy.

Reptilian Pandoras trying to find Hope at the last.

Marc Sarzynski stood frozen in shock as he watched.

Gareth leapt into the air, trusting the instincts Talyarkinash had programmed as mighty wings unfolded from his back and began to beat. A tail swished behind him like a great rudder as he was suddenly airborne, racing towards the suddenly low-hanging ceiling overhead.

A sound below drew his attention. A stunner pistol firing. At him.

The range was too great for such a small weapon to be effective, but both of the Warreth women would not let that dissuade them. They continued to fire. A gray-furred Nari male joined in after a second.

Gareth had no interest in finding out if the weapons would stun his new form, but he also didn't want to simply annihilate them all, as much as the beast in his breast called for it.

He banked at the far end of the warehouse and set his eyes on the array of species representing Sarzynski's gang. Wings beat a tattoo on the sky and he dove, weaving back and forth to avoid the fire.

He would not kill them unnecessarily. Fear of dragons was a thing all humans seemed to be born with. Gareth hoped that these other species, who had already learned to fear a human, might acquire an even greater fear of a dragon.

He took a breath and opened his mouth, screaming pure fury at them like a physical assault.

Dragonfear.

They broke, scattering in mindless panic as they tried to find a door out of the building.

Anything to escape their worst nightmare made flesh before their very eyes.

"GARETH!" Marc screamed as Gareth pivoted on a wing and began a second pass.

Gareth found the man. He had not moved at all, except to grab Talyarkinash by the fur on the back of her head and pull it back to expose her throat.

"I'll kill her," he warned, almost touching her with the tip of that scalpel.

Gareth swung around in a tight arc, watching the rest of the gang flee, including the three with enough anger to shoot before. Just to make a point, he picked out a spot, high on a nearby wall, and trusted Talyarkinash again.

Fire erupted from his open snout, a great gout of flames that licked the wall and scorched it down to the metal in an instant, raising the temperature in the room several degrees as metal oxidized under that assault.

The rabbits ran even harder.

Gareth turned his attention back to Marc, holding a hostage he would kill, even knowing that Gareth could immolate him a moment later.

It was time to talk, finally.

Gareth circled one last time and swooped in to land, nowhere close to the one known as Maximus and his hostage, but instead crushing Marc's throne under the immense weight of a twenty-meter-long dragon. One of mankind's greatest terrors, soon to be something the criminals of the *Accord of Souls* learned to fear as well.

He felt his tail flicker angrily behind him, knocking things over with a variety of sounds. Rear paws had grown talons, which he dug into the wood of the small stage, splintering it loudly. Front paws came down and flexed as well. His wings folded to half-mast, not retracted, but not spread to full extension.

"What have you done?" Marc screamed, almost mindlessly.

"She made me into something that could stop you, Marc," Gareth said in a voice that sounded like his own, down an entire octave of resonance and anger.

"You're no longer human," the man raged, amazed.

"Nor are you, Maximus," Gareth replied coldly. "Remember that. You have chosen to become a Vanir, among your other enhancements. You are no longer human either."

Gareth let his weight settle forward, like a cat resting, except he kept all four paws out for quick movement. His eyes had enough peripheral vision to see nearly the entire space of the warehouse behind him. He watched the last three, the dangerous criminals: the two Warreth and Nari, get to an outside door and flee into the night without once looking back.

Let them go. They had the fear of a dragon carved into their souls now. As he had intended from the start. They would take that with them and infect the entire underground with it, fighting half of his future battles for him.

"Stay back," Marc threatened, jerking Talyarkinash's head hard enough to elicit another yelp of pain from her. "I'm warning you."

"I will make you a deal, Marc," Gareth rumbled. "Put the knife down without hurting her and walk away. If you do not, you will never make it out of this building alive. But I will let you go, right now."

"Let me go?" Marc's mind seemed to have snapped. "What kind of a deal is that?"

"I will make you that promise on my honor, Marc Sarzynski," Gareth said. "For old times' sake. We were both members of the Earth Force Sky Patrol, once upon a time. You know what my word is worth."

"Just walk away?" Marc asked, sanity creeping slowly back into his voice. "Just like that?"

"Just like that, Marc," Gareth promised. "Tomorrow, I will begin to hunt you again, in earnest, but today you and your kind are free to go. The price is the lives of Talyarkinash Liamssen and the two Constables."

"Your word?"

"Yes, Marc," Gareth acknowledged.

Talyarkinash hissed in surprise when Marc Sarzynski suddenly let go of her hair. Gareth watched him step to the table and replace the knife he had picked up earlier, grabbing a bandage and strapping it around the oozing wound in the woman's left arm.

Marc reached down and undid one of the straps holding her in place, freeing her right arm. He placed her hand over the bandage, so she could hold it in place.

Gareth held his breath as Marc Sarzynski, the criminal mastermind known as Maximus, turned to face him one last time.

"Until tomorrow, Gareth," he nodded.

"Until tomorrow, Marc," Gareth replied.

The Vanir warrior, who had once been his best friend, when they were both humans, turned and began to walk away.

"That's it?" a new voice raged into the empty silence.

Gareth and Marc both turned to Constable Baker, apparently awake now. She must have been silently biding her time, but Gareth could understand.

"That's it, Eveth Baker," Marc said.

He turned and quickly made his way to an exit.

"You're letting him go?" she turned and directed her bile up at Gareth.

"For now," Gareth reassured her as the door slammed shut on Marx Sarzynski.

Carefully, he made his way down from the platform, kicking the uncomfortable, crushed remains of Sarzynski's throne to one side as he did.

Gingerly, he reached out a giant paw and tugged as the bindings holding Talyarkinash to the chair, snapping them with the razor edge of his talon.

"It worked," she said with an awe-tinged voice. "Thank you for saving my life."

"No, Talyarkinash Liamssen," Gareth replied. "Thank you for saving mine."

"Release me," Eveth Baker demanded as Talyarkinash rose and hugged Gareth's serpentine neck with her good arm. "That bastard's getting away."

Gareth turned to the female officer, noting with interest that both of them were awake, and that the dangerous-looking man was watching with steely eyes even more interested than hers.

"Tell me, Constable Baker," Gareth asked. "What is your word of honor worth?"

CONSTABLE

GARETH THE VANIR looked up as the door to the hospital room opened, admitting Eveth Baker and Jackeith Grodray. He saw another pair of armed Constables guarding the room from the outside before the door closed again firmly.

Talyarkinash had been seated next to Gareth's hospital bed, where she had been eagerly consuming some medical article on her pocketcomm. She put it down now and looked up expectantly.

Gareth considered the several empty dishes on the tray stretched across the bed. He hadn't felt the need to be in a private clinic, but had been unable to convince anyone else that he felt fine.

At least they had been feeding him better food than he remembered from his previous hospital stay, and enough for three people. And he had been able to transform himself back into a human, well, a Vanir, although that had left him so exhausted that he had been at the mercy of the two cops. But they had only brought him here.

On each trip to the tiny restroom in the last three days, Gareth had measured his new, Vanir body against the door frame, until he had finally stopped growing.

Seven feet, four inches. Three hundred and forty pounds, but he would need to get back to the gym and PT soon. It had been almost two weeks since his last morning run around the gym level, back at The

Arsenal. He hadn't shaved in a week, and his hair was far too long for Sky Patrol regulations.

Eveth Baker was closer, with Grodray standing off to one side and a full stride behind her. Something about the man left Gareth concerned. The eyes were too bright, too knowing for a simple police detective.

"Some of them got away," Baker began without preamble. "Maximus, Maiair, Yooyar, and Zorge being the most important to elude capture. We've caught many others. Your two helpers, Morty and Xiomber, have also vanished. For now."

"For now," Gareth agreed. "I only promised Maximus a one day head start, so he's already gotten more than I bargained for."

"You think you'll be chasing after him, Dankworth?" she challenged.

"I am a Field Agent of the Earth Force Sky Patrol, Constable Baker," he responded solemnly. "A cop, among other things. So yes, I'll be going after him as soon as you let me out of this hospital bed."

"How?" she asked.

"I can't go back to Earth. Ever. That much is certain," Gareth said. "I had to sacrifice everything, with Talyarkinash's help, to do something crazy enough to defeat that man, however temporarily he escaped me afterwards. He becomes my next mission."

"You're not a cop here, Dankworth," she noted angrily. "You are an illegally-enhanced, alien creature whose very existence is a crime."

"Yes," he agreed. "That still doesn't change my task."

"And if we won't allow it?"

"You let me know when you have someone who can stop Marc Sarzynski, Constable," Gareth retorted. "Because nothing I've seen, read, or heard in the *Accord of Souls* suggests the sort of ruthlessness to fight that man nose to nose."

"I could," she suggested.

Gareth studied the woman for a second. Six foot seven. Built like an East German Olympic swimmer, with a long, feminine frame covered over with muscles.

And a brain like a computer.

"You might," Gareth made a peace offering. "But I know how that man thinks. He was my best friend for many years before he turned to evil and lost himself. And you are at the top of what a geneticist like Talyarkinash here could do to improve you. Marc's not. Especially now that he knows what lengths I was willing to go to in order to stop him."

"You're it, then?" Eveth sneered.

Gareth shrugged, and addressed his next words as much to the Nari scientist next to his bed, who had become his friend, as the cop looming over him now.

"If I could deliver you his head on a platter today, I would happily walk into a cell for the rest of my life tomorrow," Gareth said. "Or ask you how to erase enough knowledge from my brain that you could shrink me back down and send me home. Until then, I might be the only thing standing between you and the darkness."

He expected Baker to say something more, but her partner placed a silent hand on her shoulder.

Baker nodded and stepped to one side silently.

The Vanir man, Senior Constable Jackeith Grodray stepped up now, into her place.

"You don't know our ways, Gareth," he explained in a calm, deep voice.

Gareth shrugged again, rather than answer. That much was a given. He had been here for all of a week.

"Back home, you were a Field Agent of Sky Patrol, correct?" he asked.

"Correct," Gareth nodded. "Only about a month ago, I got my third ring, and was all set to propose to the woman I loved, the night this all happened."

Grodray nodded in turn, his face turning pensive and serious. He turned to the fourth person in the room.

"Dr. Liamssen," Grodray began in a heavy voice. "You belong in the cell next to Gareth, and normally I would be happy to put you there."

Talyarkinash surprised both of them by standing slowly. She couldn't look the giant man in the eyes, but that was a physical thing, not a measure of her stature. Gareth felt a surge of pride in the woman.

"And?" she asked in a hard, unforgiving voice.

From the look on Grodray's face, she might have gotten the same response, the same look on his face, had she just slapped him. Baker shared Gareth's grin from behind the scene.

"Under the auspices of the Official Secrets Act, I can deputize you into a posse for purposes of supporting efforts of the Constabulary to fight crime, in extreme circumstances."

Gareth had spent enough time around the Nari woman to measure her own shock at those words, ears flat backwards, pupils slitted all the way open, jaw hanging, fur on her neck and arms standing up.

Something niggled at the back of Gareth's mind. He had spent the last three days eating, sleeping, and reading.

"I'm sorry," he said in a concerned voice. "But I don't believe that a Senior Constable has that authority. I don't have the book in front of me to quote the statute, but I have been studying your manual."

Grodray's eyes got big. So did Baker's.

After a moment, the man nodded once and reached into his back pocket. He pulled out his wallet. The badge inside was the standard blue ring of The Constabulary, but then the man opened what looked like a secret compartment to reveal a second badge, smaller and made of platinum.

Eveth Baker gasped.

"You would be correct, Gareth," Grodray conceded carefully. "However, Senior Constable is a cover. I am actually a Prime Investigator with the Constabulary, something roughly equivalent to a Senior Special Agent with Sky Patrol. And that kind of person does have the necessary authority."

Gareth nodded, his own jaw almost on the floor next to Eveth Baker's.

"And under the Official Secrets Act, any disclosure of that information will result in a jail sentence of not less than ten years, so you have been warned."

"How can I help?" Gareth asked. Then he turned to Talyarkinash to include her in the conversation. "How can *we* help?"

"My superiors have come to the same conclusions you have, Field Agent Dankworth," Prime Investigator Grodray intoned seriously. "Your help will be necessary to stop Maximus and his gang, and to return some level of honest government to the systems of the *Accord of Souls*, where too many of them have become infected with corruption. We're not sure how we'll use you, yet, but you represent an entirely new option in our fight against crime."

Gareth nodded.

The underworld had an overlord who had once been one of the most dangerous criminals in the Solar System in Marc Sarzynski.

The Constabulary would need a Star Dragon.

FLIGHT OF THE STAR DRAGON

VANIR

IT HAD BEEN a month since Gareth's transformation. A month of looking at a new face in the mirror in the morning.

Talyarkinash had printed a picture for him, a photo taken back when he was still human. He had grown into his Vanir face, but it was still damnably odd, comparing the man he had become with the man he had been as recently as six weeks ago.

The ears were probably the hardest part to adjust to. On a human, they were rounder, both on the top and the bottom. His new Vanir ears were almost pointed at the top, like cartoon depictions of elves. Sleeker. Taller too, by maybe a whole inch.

Gareth couldn't tell if it was new ears that had made his hearing any sharper, or all the other modifications that had come with what Talyarkinash had done to him, with the help of the two Yuudixtl scientists: Morty and Xiomber.

Similarly, his eyes were ever-so-much bigger as a fraction of his face. And wider, coming out to sharper corners that almost made him feel half-Japanese, if there was such a thing. Cheekbones had grown more angular, sharper planes than his more-rounded face and head had been.

At least the soft, blond beard covered part of his face, and blurred some of the changes. It had finally grown in enough that it stopped itching, but it still threw him off when he saw that person in the mirror.

It was Gareth St. John Dankworth. Field Agent of Earth Force Sky Patrol, Missile Division, 6th Cavalry Troop. Except it wasn't, anymore.

Probably never would be again, unless something magical happened.

More magical.

More bizarre than all the things that he had seen since Morty and Xiomber pulled him through an illegal wormhole from Earth Force's base in the Earth/Moon L2, *The Arsenal.* Dragged him into the wider galaxy. To the *Accord of Souls,* which humans could also never become members of.

But he was still a cop. A protector of the innocent. He would do that here, as long and as well as they allowed him.

Gareth wiped both hands down his face, watching the stranger in the mirror do the same. He ran his hands back though blond hair that should have been cut six weeks ago. At this point, he was likely to turn into a bohemian, a surfer pretty soon, with long, curly locks already touching his collar and perhaps down to his shoulder blades in another year.

A Field Agent would never be that far outside of regulations, unless he was a Secret Agent operating under cover. But Gareth wasn't a Field Agent these days. Might never be again.

Would most likely never see Earth again. Or his friends. His family.

Or Pippa.

Gareth reached into a pocket of his pants and pulled out the tiny, leather pouch his still kept with him at all times. From inside, he pulled out the gold ring with the single, white diamond in the middle, surrounded by ruby and gold stones representing Sky Patrol.

Today, they represented *Loss.* The life he could never go back to. The sacrifices he had been called upon to make, in the name of duty.

He had considered asking Talyarkinash to find a way to clone his body and turn it back into the human he had been, so that they could return it to Earth and he could be declared formally dead. Pippa might wait the rest of her life for a man who could never return. And even if he did, she was still human, so they could never have children. Never be a family.

He tucked the ring and the pouch back into his pocket and sighed heavily.

Never *be.*

Gareth emerged from the small bathroom into his suite. It was as identical to his cabin, back at the Arsenal, as he had been able to make it, both in layout and content. A single bed, or whatever the equivalent was when he was seven-feet-four-inches tall and had a seventy-inch chest. The chester had been scaled up as well, but still had four drawers, white paint, and a flat top. A reading chair by the bathroom, warm and comfortable. A table and two chairs by the door.

Home. Or a reasonable imitation thereof.

He grabbed his tunic from where he had dropped it on the bed and pulled it on. Constabulary Blue, like his pants. Almost the color of his blue-gray eyes. So tight as to be a second skin, but somehow woven with a layer of triangular scales covering much of the exterior and providing protection against blunt and edged weapons.

The uniform of a Constable. Or whatever Gareth was. He hadn't been to their police school, but had come back to his cabin after dinner every night and studied and read everything he was allowed access to. Back home, he had been a Field Agent of Sky Patrol, so he knew how to be a cop.

Here, he was introduced to anyone who visited this facility as an Explorer, roughly equivalent to a Patrolman, or a Deputy Agent back home. It was a good enough cover story. The fewer people that knew the truth, the safer everyone would be.

He had no idea what the actual truth was either.

Gareth turned and found the digital clock sitting on the chester, counting slowly. Getting used to a twenty-eight-hour day had been possibly the smallest thing, as well as the weirdest, in a month of complete nonsense.

Fourteen meant local zenith. Back home, time for lunch. Here, breakfast was at six, lunch was at eleven, dinner was at sixteen, and supper was at twenty-one. Four meals, instead of the three he grew up with, but Gareth just pretended that third meal was the equivalent of English High Tea and that all sort of made it all work in his head.

Dr. Royston Loughty, PhD, FRS, CBE, CStJ, and Pippa's father, would have called it a serious case of culture shock, and he would have been correct. But there wasn't anything Gareth could do but roll forward and figure it all out as he went.

That was all any of them could do, but their lives hadn't been nearly as upended as his.

Gareth held his elbows out and flexed, making sure his tunic stretched right. According to Talyarkinash, it would move with him when he changed forms, becoming somehow absorbed into his flesh when he did, and adding an extra layer of dermal armor when…

How did you explain it to a complete stranger that had never seen it happen? That Gareth St. John Dankworth, as a human, did not have any of the limitations to his genetics that the Chaa, the **Elders** who had uplifted all of the species of the *Accord of Souls* and then bound them into a psionic unity, had put on all the others.

What vocabulary did you use to explain that you could turn into a thing he called a Star Dragon?

Gareth shrugged and headed towards the door of his cabin. He didn't want to be late to his meeting. Constable Baker and Senior Constable Grodray would be there.

Gareth hoped that meant that there would be action soon.

CONSTABLE

EVETH BAKER CONSIDERED the view as the vehicle cruised through the late-morning sky of *Irron*. It wasn't an auto-taxi, but a similar vehicle, privately owned by the Constabulary to transport officers around. The craft was low and sleek, done in the Constabulary's traditional steel blue inside and out, with a comfortable cabin that would seat eight Vanir or a dozen Grace on the two benches running parallel to the sides. She and Grodray had the plush, warm seats to themselves.

According to her partner, Jackeith Grodray, the blue overhead was among the closest to the planet *Earth* where Dankworth had been born and lived his whole life. Hopefully, that had helped with his acclimation.

She didn't like it, any of it, but they were going to need his help.

The sky was clear and a blue that just seemed artificial to her eyes, but she was used to more urban places like *Orgoth Vortai* or *Hurquar*. *Irron* was almost a nature preserve, by comparison, with few cities of any note and vast wilderness areas covering much of the planet still.

The Constabulary maintained one of their largest training facilities out here, away from civilian eyes that might not react well to loud noises and activities of the men and women training to protect the many worlds of the *Accord of Souls*.

Below, a plateau stretched out, overlooking a gorge that seemed bottomless in the fog and spray of a tremendous river waterfalling over one thousand meters into a lake so blue it might have been tanzanite.

"Kopek for your thoughts, Eve?" her partner asked, looking up from his digital book as the cruiser banked and started its descent to the base revealed below them in the trees.

"You'd get overcharged, Jack," she said. "Still not sure what we're doing here. What I'm doing here. What the hell happens next. You know?"

"You're here because you impressed the hell out of my bosses and helped break open a major smuggling and genetics operation, Baker," the man turned serious. "Lot of sunlight suddenly shining in on places where it never should have left. We'll be years cleaning up all the corruption revealed. This might be one of the biggest cases in our lifetimes."

Eveth shrugged. She was a cop. That was why she had joined in the first place. Stopping bad guys.

"And Dankworth?" she turned to face him. The ground was rushing up to meet them, but she had been here before, and this runway wasn't all the impressive, once you had already flown next to the waterfall overlooking a kilometer drop.

"He's here because he has nowhere else to go," Grodray nodded once. Sharp. Fierce. Decisive. "He's a cop, like us, trying to save the galaxy. And everybody is still trying to identify a way we can stop Maximus without him, but nobody's come up with anything better."

"He's a monster, Grodray," she snapped.

"We're all monsters, Baker," he replied in that cold, flat voice he got when he was past teasing. "Sane people do not take up arms and put on a badge. They become musicians. Or shopkeepers. Something predictable. That's why Kathra divorced me and remarried. Too many nights alone when the kids were young. It's why she found a second husband who's a sales manager. Safe. Quiet. Comfortable. But someone has to do this job. Someone has to hold the line against all the people trying to cheat the system and make an unfair profit. Without the *Accord*, you have chaos."

"Or Maximus," she mused, mostly to herself, but apparently loud enough for him to hear.

"Or something worse, yes," Grodray acknowledged. "I remember Maximus telling Gareth about his plan to become Emperor Marc the First, an immortal human who was planning to take over the entire *Accord* with the help of more humans, and rule forever."

"So we have to trust another human to save us?" she sneered. It wasn't meant to come out that bitter, but even she heard the tones in her voice.

So did Grodray. His eyes got hard.

"That man has sacrificed everything, Eve," Jackeith's voice dropped to a murmur. "Everything. And I've not heard any reports of him complaining about it afterwards. He's lost his past, his present, and his future. All his friends and family. The woman he loved. And he would do it again tomorrow, if we asked. Keep that in mind."

"I know, Grodray," her own voice dropped as the cruiser landed lightly. "Will it be enough?"

"I don't know, Eve," he said. "But we've got to try."

CRIME BOSS

IT HAD BEEN a month from hell. Marc had no other way to quantify it. Six weeks ago, he had been the functional ruler of the entire world of *Zathus*, living in the shadows yes, but with his tentacles into almost every aspect of that world's economy and polity.

Granted, he had inherited most of that power from that idiot Warreth, the birdman Cinnra, but the gang Marc had taken control of, the small army of corrupt officials and merchants, did his bidding. Nobody did anything major without a nod or a word.

And then those two lizardmen had turned on him and ruined everything.

Even Marc had been shocked at how tenuous his organization had turned out to be, so maybe it had been for the best that it had all gone down the way it had. He had shut down the main facility on *Zathus* and sent everyone into hiding before going to *Hurquar*, bringing on twenty-five people with him.

Of those, ten had made it out of the trap that he had managed to spring on himself.

Even Marc wasn't so arrogant as to suggest it was anybody's fault but his own. He could have killed Gareth instead of taking him prisoner. But he had wanted information that the Nari woman had. And the two Yuudixtl. They had been the ones that had upgraded Marc in the first place, taking a lowly human and turning him into something even more dangerous.

Seven-foot-four. Three hundred and forty pounds of muscle. Genius-level intellect to go with it.

And he was still human, underneath. At least in all the ways that mattered. Everyone else belonged to the *Accord of Souls*. Psionically linked to one another in such a way that intramural violence was almost impossible.

Almost.

There were a few. There were always a few who slid into the cracks. Criminals born wrong, to hear the locals talk. As if that was a mental-health issue that could be fixed with a little genetic surgery. Just undo those miswired neurons and you'd be right as rain.

And boringly obedient.

Humans didn't have those limits. Marc Sarzynski wore the physical form of a Vanir, but his soul was still human. Some of his old gang have lived in fear of that. Many of them had turned on him.

Like this stupid bastard.

Marc looked down on the Elohynn tied to the chair with cruelly-tight leather straps. They were in a warehouse, another in an immeasurable string of them, where Marc and his closest associates had hidden like rats when the Constabulary had suddenly known too much about too many things.

Like perhaps someone had started feeding them tidbits, not realizing that he was the only person who knew some of them, so things could be traced back to him.

The room was cold, but Marc was sweating with effort. He had stripped down to dungarees and a T-shirt with some band he had never heard of on the front.

The Elohynn was sweating, too.

They were alone in this office. Several of Marc's people were outside, where they could watch though the big picture window if they wanted, but he doubted most of them had the stomach for it. Maiair and Yooyar probably, the Warreth sisters who were fast becoming his indispensable right and left hands. Zorge, the Nari physicist-turned-spymaster. They had been there when Gareth Dankworth had unleashed his ultimate abomination on the galaxy.

When he had transformed into a dragon.

Damabiath the Elohynn had obviously thought that he could get away with it. Too many raids had gotten too close. Maybe the Elohynn planned to make a little profit feeding the cops tips about Marc's whereabouts for the reward money. Something. It had worked.

Right up until he forgot that he was dealing with a Vanir that had a 200 IQ and absolutely no qualms about doing violence to one of his fellow sentient creatures.

Marc missed his medical theater equipment. It had been perfect for slowly torturing his enemies into revealing the little tidbits that he had needed to take control of the gang, and the underworld, and eventually the cops and prosecutors on *Zathus*.

But he didn't want anything from Damabiath.

Well, technically that wasn't true. There was just nothing that the Elohynn could tell Marc that he didn't already know. Or wanted to know.

No, they had a much more personal conclusion, and it was at hand.

The Elohynn was naked. Marc understood the importance of removing the clothes from a victim. The psychological effects of being completely unmasked.

This particular species tended to run taller than humans, perhaps six and a quarter to six and a half feet for the men. The slightest bit smaller for the women. Plus those gorgeous wings.

Mark Sarzynski was a head taller now.

The angelic criminal was seated, which just emphasized the size difference. The straps holding his arms and legs to the chair were too tight, cutting off circulation in ways that would start to be troublesome in another hour or so.

If it mattered.

His wings were stretched out as far as they would go sideways, and then held in place by spikes Marc had personally punched into the tips and attached to chains in the walls, far enough back that Damabiath couldn't pull them loose by tearing skin. Not without breaking bones first.

The man's mouth was gagged with a piece of leather that showed intense bite marks, but had resisted all attempts for the Elohynn to get through it. Maybe if he had a few more hours he could have managed.

Marc reached down and picked up a pair of pliers. They were already covered with blood and down at this point, so he wiped them slowly on a messy towel that had been clean a hour ago.

Marc examined his victim closer. All the feathers had been individually plucked from the left wing. From his studies, that was the single most debilitating fear any Elohynn could face. Many chose self-termination, rather than lose the ability to fly and be relegated to the "two-dimensional crowd," as they tended to view the rest of the *Accord*.

Marc watched the eyes follow the pliers, rather than the wielder. There didn't appear to be any mind left inside there at this point. Marc hadn't asked a single question once he got the man trussed up like a turkey for the plucking.

Just pain. Artfully applied, as if a psychotic Grace had needed to create a new sculpture installation.

Idly, Marc wondered if he might locate a Grace who viewed such torture as art. With their sensory tentacles, they might be perfect for this sort of thing if he could break their operant conditioning hard enough. Elohynn, conversely, were among the most empathic species in the *Accord*, so they could never really abide with pain, unless they were so crazy as to be dangerous. It made them good counsellors, and reasonable bankers, but lousy criminals.

Slowly, Marc replaced the pliers on the bench and picked up a knife. Damabiath had betrayed him. Sold him to the Constabulary for thirty pieces of silver and the hopes for a pardon. Expected that he would never be identified. Wouldn't have, but for an inside leak, a data clerk with a gambling problem, trying to reduce her debt with information for Maximus.

"And now, we have reached the final stage of our conversation," Marc said in a low tone.

Damabiath tried to say something through the gag. Tried to scream, perhaps, with what little was left of his mind and his soul.

"You, of all people, should have known how I deal with traitors, Damabiath," Marc scolded the man. "You were there. You watched the punishment. Helped even, by providing me the proof I needed to unearth one of the conspiracies against me. My, how the mighty have fallen."

Marc considered the being. His eyes were all whites at this point, painting a masterpiece in red blood and sweating skin.

"I do not feel good about this," Marc admitted quietly. "Any of it. But you people have forgotten that I'm not one of you. Am not bound by your ridiculous morality. And even then, I probably wouldn't have been reduced to something so petty as this, but someone had to become an example. The children of the night need to fear me more than they do the Constabulary. In that, your life will provide one, last, valuable lesson."

Marc stepped forward and slammed the blade into the Elohynn's chest with all his augmented might, driving it straight through the fragile keel bone and cutting his heart in two. There was precious little blood, and the light went out of the man's eyes quickly.

Marc pulled the knife from the cooling corpse, cleaned it, and set it with the other tools, taking the time to methodically pack things away. Hopefully, this would send the correct message and he would never have to do this again.

How in the nine hells had Marc Sarzynski, Deputy Agent of Earth Force Sky Patrol, fallen so far? He considered all the tiny steps that brought him thus. None of them included a concrete commitment to evil.

And yet, here he was.

This road wasn't even paved with good intentions. No. Easy clips. Corners cut. Mistakes when he tried to finally come out ahead of Gareth St. John Dankworth once and for all, only to fall ever so short, time and again.

And worse, he knew in his soul Dankworth hadn't been competing. Or rather, not with Marc. Gareth had been competing with himself to become the best agent he could imagine.

Marc's jealousy at second place was just a terrible taskmaster.

The door opened and closed, noisily enough as to be obvious. Marc glanced up. Maiair, her red crest at half-mast. Powerful, but not threatening. Supportive.

He would make her a queen, once he had regained his power. Not an Empress, but close. He would need her and her sister, and there was no better way to bind them to his throne.

"The body?" she asked simply, standing more or less at attention, but turned in such a way that she didn't have to see or acknowledge the mess. Yooyar and Zorge waited outside the office, still visible through glass, but separated by the closed door.

Middle managers, as it were.

Marc considered his options. Terror was an effective tool, but it must be used like the edge of a razor, slicing a little at a time and withdrawing. Overuse would render it comically less effective. People could become inured to such atrocities if they became commonplace.

Once should hold everyone in fear for a year or more.

"Leave him," Marc said in a heavy voice.

It was acceptable for Maiair to know that he took no pleasure in this task. No pride in a well-tortured opponent. That he still had his humanity, underneath it all.

"After we have made it to safety, contact a journalist," he decided. "Give them the address and leave the door unlocked. Damabiath on the evening news will send the message to anyone wavering at this point."

"Won't the Constables know it was us?" she pressed.

"They already know we're on this planet," Marc said. "I need the local underworld to hide me. They must fear me more than they do that damnable dragon."

"Understood," she said as she turned. She hesitated.

"What?" Marc snapped, as he faced her.

"Are you all right?" she asked in a quiet voice. Nervous about overstepping an undrawn boundary.

"If I never have to do that again, it will still be too soon," he replied. "But this has become a war. And bad things are likely to happen."

SCIENTIST

"ARE you sure this is the sort of place you wish to go, father?" Pippa asked Royston as they approached the front door of the concert hall, surrounded by youngsters, teenagers frequently flirting with hooliganism but still safely on this side of the line.

Royston nodded, watching the scene with his pursed lips set in a firm, disapproving line.

There was no choice. Science had demanded that he try alternate methods to find the answer to the puzzle he sought. They were in a neighborhood he wouldn't have come on his own, down by the wharves of East London, but all his logical deduction had led him to this conclusion.

"Two, please," Pippa said to young woman inside the little kiosk at the front of the theater, sliding several shilling coins across the counter.

The young woman pushed a button and several strips of rigid, white paper emerged from the machine underneath with a mechanical clunk. The woman pulled them clear and handed them to Pippa, leaning forward just a little so she could observe Royston, standing next to his daughter.

"Rock on, grandpa!" she called with a smile that did nothing to assuage the doubts plaguing Royston as to the rightness of this task.

Still, everything else had failed.

Royston Loughty, PhD, FRS, CBE, CStJ, had discovered enough new aspects of mathematics and physics in the last month to probably be considered for a Nobel Prize one of these days, and possibly the Fields Medal, but he had still failed in his intended task.

Gareth St. John Dankworth had disappeared from his cabin aboard *Shadow Base One*, the Arsenal, and nobody could explain how. Royston had even considered it to be perhaps a practical joke, but there was something there when he looked. Radiation signatures he could not explain with any science, in places that lent credence to the story and defied him in all other things.

Pippa, dearest only-daughter who reminded him too much of departed Elizabeth, had suggested baldly that obviously his understanding of physic was simply insufficient. Royston Loughty, possibly the greatest expert on Stellar Radiation in the entire Solar System, was out of his depth.

He had laughed then.

And yet.

Nights spent with a pad of paper, his favorite pipe, and a forgotten martini had gotten him nowhere. His favorite syncopated jazz music, from the bizarrely-experimental down to the coolest hep-cats, had left him cold. Rachmaninoff and Chopin, Tchaikovsky and Beethoven, even Gilbert and Sullivan. Nothing had provided him the inspiration he needed.

Royston escorted Pippa into the noisy auditorium on his left arm, as was proper. He felt desperately out of place here, wearing his traditional tweeds and a broad, silk tie that had been a gift from Pippa for some father's day long forgotten. Even his porkpie hat made him stand out in a room full of youngsters that probably considered Pippa an old maid at twenty-seven, with their slicked-back hair greased into pompadours made to look like little duck tails.

The mass of humanity around him probably had a median age of twenty, and he suspected an analysis of the mean would be even lower if he wishes to apply scientific procedures.

He did not.

Pippa was a bright spot of color, in her uniform as a Women's Auxiliary of Earth Force Sky Patrol. Crimson skirt just past her knees. Matching tunic as long as a blazer, double-breasted over the left with gold buttons and gold embroidery lacing. A yellow stripe edged the tunic and the collar, making her look like a professional woman, emphasizing the red hair and bright green eyes of her Scots heritage.

The children around them on all sides seemed to be in their own uniform. For the boys, blue dungarees, rolled up twice at the ankle. White T-shirts tucked in, frequently with a pack of cigarettes in the sleeve. Often a black jacket, sometimes leather and sometimes cotton denim.

The girls were identifiable by socio-economic class as Royston watched. Long poodle skirts gave way to simple skirts of a cut similar to Pippa's, growing progressively shorter until they barely covered more than a beach costume, as one tended down the scale of their father's income and profession. Finally, at what he considered the bottom, some daring souls were so androgynous as to ape the clothing of their male peers, even going so far as wearing pants in public.

Thankfully, Pippa's rebellious stage had never progressed farther than experiments in hair colors. Even his reputation might not have protected her, to be seen in dungarees, somewhere other than a farm.

They made their way to wooden, fold-down seats closer to the rear than the front of the auditorium. Three teenage-looking girls in too much makeup politely slid sideways a seat to make space for he and Pippa to sit together.

The youngster Royston found on his left looked up at him and then touched him silently on the arm with a smile, her palm placed flat in a welcoming gesture that left him perhaps both more and less terrified at the same time. Pippa's grin when he looked at her did nothing to assuage his embarrassment.

After a few moments, the lights came down and the restive crowd began to settle. Red velvet curtains across the stage withdrew slowly to the sides, revealing a band already in place, dressed in matching, slender black suits, with narrow ties and slicked back hair like so many of the men down front.

At the front, a young woman stood alone at a mic stand, eyeing the crowd like a predator stalking the high grass. She wore a turquoise, skin-tight dress, cut high on the sides to reveal too much thigh, like a nightclub's torch singer. Her long, brunette hair was wild and loose, billowing lightly in the breeze of a fan down front and centered up on her.

Black opera gloves covered her to elbows, and the dress itself was only to mid-thigh. At least she had sensible pumps on her feet, rather than the black, lace-up boots that she seemed to project with this image.

Royston tore his eyes aware from the mesmerizing female as the drummer began, a hard backbeat so at odds with the light brush of good jazz.

It was primal. Powerful. Unyielding.

After sixteen full measures, the crowd had fallen to utter silence, perhaps snakes charmed by the man with the pungi as they emerged from the darkness of the basket into the sun of this woman's music.

The bass player joined now, a harmonic beat walking back and forth on chords. His instrument was played upright in the classical style, but is was barely wider than the fretboard, with a plug emerging from the bottom to connect to the immense, black speaker stacks Royston saw threatening the crowd from both sides of the stage.

Two electric guitarists framed the woman, once closer to the front and one a step back, nearer in depth to the bass player. If he understood the mechanics and politics of the modern music, they represented a lead and rhythm guitar to offset the rhythm section of drums and bass. He did not see any horn players, so this would not be jazz as Royston understood the concept, but rock and roll.

He would survive the experience, come hell or high water.

A spotlight suddenly illuminated an upright piano off to one side, it's battered, wooden shell perhaps older than the young man playing it, as he slid a hand down from the top of the scale to draw all mesmerized eyes to the keys.

He began to play. No, that did not do the act justice.

The young man attacked the keyboard as though mortal combat had begun.

Hard, rhythmic, almost *bombastic*, if one could use that term to describe someone with the apparent technical chops to challenge Rachmaninoff instead throwing himself into rock and roll. Royston found his foot tapping with that back beat, head bobbing ever-so-slightly to the immense, lyrical complexities of the pianist.

One guitarist joined him. A full measure later, the other man gave meaning to the term *Lead Guitar* with a power and emotion that Royston had only known the best violinists and saxophonists to achieve. It was like a squall line had emerged from the stage and washed over the entire audience, a tide pushing them a little closer to shore, before the rip currents began to suck them out to sea.

And then the woman opened her mouth and sang.

Jazz was not generally known for its singers. The art form was in the instruments and the technical sophistication of the players. The few good scat singers had to work more to keep a hard beat with the musicians behind them, but rarely dominated, instead providing another piece of the rhythm section. Torch singers, on the other hand, were slow and emotionally-laden, immersing the hearer in sadness and longing.

This woman was power. Raw and unrestrained. Anger and love, sophistication and destruction.

It was like the ancient Hindu goddess Kali-ma stood before him on the stage, proclaiming the end of the world.

Somewhere in the middle of the performance, Royston noted that the singer had an easy working range of three octaves, and had touched four across the breadth of her songs.

At no point had a Master of Ceremonies emerged to work the crowd, and the woman never spoke. One song ended, everyone stopped to take a quick breath, drink some water while the crowd roared and clapped, and tune instruments.

And then the next song began, without even an explanation from the girl. Just the next notes in her ritual magic.

Royston felt one upbeat song end and the enchantress on stage transitioned into a love song that would have made the most embittered torch singer weep. He was suddenly nineteen again and meeting Elizabeth at that dance. In the middle of the first chorus, he realized that he had a young woman on each side leaning against him and weeping. Pippa and the unknown teenager had both unknowingly mirrored themselves, hooking an arm around his and pressing their heads against his shoulder while they listened.

As a sociological experiment, it was astonishing, but Royston did not move. Could not move. Both young women apparently needed something like this, and his mind was still too focused on the music, the syncopation, the skills on display. The raw emotions that the woman could invoke.

At the end of the song, Royston looked down at the young stranger on his left. She gazed up at him, blinked, and blushed so hard he thought she might pass out. He grinned a secret grin to her as she untangled herself and leaned away, lips pressed together to keep from speaking.

Pippa just grinned at his discomfort.

The woman on stage stood still in the quiet, and looked out over the audience. Her eyes seemed to find Royston in the stygian depths of the auditorium, boring into his soul with her medusa's gaze. Royston fell into darkness with the rest of the auditorium as the stage went dark, but for a single spotlight on the girl.

"One more," she intoned in a throating alto. "Best for last."

And it was. The previous hour had been a tour-de-force of emotional manipulation unlike anything Royston had ever witnessed, in any jazz bar or orchestra. The last song was Joshua at Jericho, bringing the very walls down with his music and the power of his faith.

Silence fell as the piano finally walked the last bits of tune away into the darkness. The spotlight went out and there was only darkness. Only emptiness.

Royston felt beads of sweat wick into his undershirt as his emotions tried to return to anything approximating normal. It would be hours before something so mundane was possible.

The lights came up suddenly and revealed the red, velvet curtains closed, sealing off the sorceress from her worshippers. The crowd of teenagers came alive and quickly made their way out of the auditorium, voices only slowly rising back to normal.

His was not the only soul in shock.

Even the teenager girl on his left stopped and gave him a chaste kiss on the cheek before turning and fleeing silently with her cohorts.

Within minutes, Royston found himself alone in the space, with only Pippa as company. She was withdrawn and quiet, but that was an understanding on her part that his brain was seeking some higher answers.

Finally, he rose, handing her to her feet.

Royston Loughty, PhD, FRS, CBE, CStJ, felt thirty, perhaps forty years younger. Energized in ways he could not remember.

He smiled at Philippa as he made his way to aisle.

Syncopated Jazz was a controlled thing. Technically sophisticated but somewhat emotionless. Symphonic music had more of the emotion, but it was filtered through a hundred musicians before it reached the audience.

This had been powerful. Primal. All the amazing skill of the best jazz musicians, but raw and uninhibited.

He nodded at Pippa and took her arm, emerging into the warm night at the tail end of the crowd.

"Did you find it?" she asked hesitantly. "Whatever it was that drew you here?"

"Perhaps," he replied quietly, drawing a breath of the magic deep into his lungs to take home with him to orbit.

Mathematics and physics were like jazz. Sophisticated and technical, without the powerful emotions that rock and roll brought to the table. They had not led him astray so much as merely fallen short of that place where his mind, his soul, needed to go.

He had needed rock and roll to show him the path.

Yes, perhaps he indeed had found the way.

HUNTERS

"HE DID WHAT?" Omerlon demanded angrily.

Rage drove the Elohynn to his feet, which was an impressive task, considering how far overweight Omerlon had grown, over the years. On bad days, his wings could barely lift him into the sky, and he didn't have the endurance to fly for long.

But no Elohynn ever walked.

That was why he had dedicated vehicles, customized to carry him around. That, and it was far easier to hide inside a closed vehicle than be out in the open where any goomba thug might take a shot at him. Or narc him to the cops.

This vehicle had been converted from a panel van, giving him three meter ceilings and a thick, brown shag rug. He used it to pace right now. They still had time before arrival at the next destination.

The Warreth stayed seated across the way cringed, but didn't clam up.

"Reporters got a tip, boss," Danzeekar replied. "Damabiath had been tied to a chair and his left wing had been stripped to the flesh. Not a single feather left. And he was dead."

Omerlon hissed in rage. There was no greater insult anyone could give to an Elohynn. None. Anywhere. Bodies would pile up at the morgue over something like this. His Warreth captain agreed, from the set of his headcrest and the way his feathers all puffed out a little.

"And Maximus did it?" Omerlon snarled. "We have confirmation?"

"I got someone close to his inner circle, feeding us tidbits now and again," Danzeekar replied. "Never much, but never wrong in the past. They know which way the wind is blowing, but can't get out right now. Maximus is a wild card and nobody's sure what he'll do next."

"If he wants a war, I'll give him one," Omerlon growled.

All his life, he had been an outsider kid. Too heavy compared to those sleek bastards at the aerie who made fun of him. Too short. Too ugly.

Always too something.

He didn't know if he had been born broken and didn't find out until later, or if the anger had just built up over enough years and twisted something inside him. Most people couldn't kill someone without a lot of anguish up front, as well as afterwards.

Omerlon had gotten over that crap pretty quick. It had gotten him in with a series of ever-more-dangerous criminal gangs, until he ended up in charge of the biggest on *Orgoth Vortai*. An Elohynn ruling an underworld largely composed of Grace, but still the dregs of any society.

Omerlon stopped pacing and turned to face Danzeekar. They would be close to their destination and landing soon. He needed time to get himself together and look the part of the lord of the underworld, especially if he had to go to war with Maximus.

"Do we know where the bastard's hiding?" Omerlon asked quietly, his voice honed down to a razor's rusty edge.

"Negative on that, boss," Danzeekar said. "I get my notes third-hand through delivery boys right now. Hasn't been worth trying to push back up the chain yet, because we're likely to blow our mole and it hasn't been that important yet."

"And it still isn't," Omerlon decided.

He flexed his head back and snapped a shudder through his wings to loosen them up. Had there been space in here, he would have run them out to points. He would probably need that level of intimidation shortly, especially with some of the people around here having second thoughts.

"Find me those two physicists that disappeared," Omerlon ordered. "We'll use them as bait to bring Maximus to us, and then crush that weasel."

"You got it, boss," Danzeekar nodded.

Outside, Omerlon felt the truck shift as it started its descent. The Mayor of Londra, the biggest city, needed to be reminded how little wiggle room he had if he wanted to stay out of jail, and keep his entire, corrupt family free with him.

Omerlon looked forward to venting some of his spleen on the bastard. Maximus wasn't going to get away with killing his people.

FUGITIVE

"HEARD ANY NEWS?" Morty asked as he emerged from his bedroom.

Xiomber looked up from his morning paper, tea mug in one hand and a sour scowl on his face as he sat in the dining space and enjoyed his quiet.

"News news, or real stuff?" Xiomber asked.

Morty walked over to join his egg-brother at the table. The place was cheap, but their needs weren't all that great right now. And a month on the run had given Morty a far-greater appreciation of the simple things in life, like hot food that didn't come out of a convenience store refrigerator. And a roof over his head when it was raining.

The table even a had a pretty good view of the city from about seventy stories up. *Churquark* was the name of both the city and the planet. It was mainly a Grace world, so there was art everywhere, but the window next to the kitchen table looked out over a two hundred meter tall bronze statue of a Chaa, one of the Elders, poised apparently at that moment of awakening that had transformed them from amazingly-advanced scientists into gods.

And that wasn't even the weirdest thing Morty could see from here, as he pulled up a seat and poured himself some tea.

"Whatever news you got, Xiomber," Morty replied to his partner. "You always wake up at dawn and scour the boards and papers for things. I need my beauty sleep."

"Ain't that the truth?" Xiomber nodded.

Morty just grinned and let his egg-brother's sarcasm roll off his scales. He was feeling especially feisty this morning.

"So talk to me," Morty prompted.

"We been here three days, Morty," Xiomber sighed.

"And we've been on the run for five weeks," Morty countered. "Maximus ain't taken over the galaxy in that time, and nobody's heard anything about Gareth or Talyarkinash, so either they got away, or the Constables really did catch them and have been hiding them someplace."

"We better hope that the Constables didn't catch them then," Xiomber paused and sipped his tea noisily, like an alligator running low in the water, eyes and snout above the steam. "Prices for gear had gone through the roof on the black market."

"Everything?" Morty felt a metaphorical scorpion perch on his shoulder and eye the side of his head hungrily. Never a good way to wake up.

"Everything we would need to build a new lab," Xiomber explained. "Generators, control surfaces, secondary coils, even the sensors like we used to locate Sarzynski and Dankworth in the first place."

"They know the truth, then," Morty was sure.

"That's my guess, too," his partner nodded. "Somebody rolled, or maybe they finally raided the palace back on *Zathus*. Rumor on the street was that Maximus shut the place down when you and I bailed, and nobody cleaned it up afterwards. Wouldn't take much to put two and two together, ya know?"

"No way to build a new lab?" Morty asked, just in case.

"Not an underground one," Xiomber said. "And I'm guessing all the legitimate physicists in the family are probably cursing our names right now for the amount of paperwork they suddenly have to go through to replace or upgrade anything."

Morty shrugged. Small price to pay, if they wanted to ensure that the *Accord of Souls* was still here in a year.

Ya burn the house down, you don't get to complain about sleeping in the backyard when it rains. Summoning a human like Maximus had to be the dumbest idea he'd ever let himself be talked into. Summoning Gareth to stop him had perhaps balanced the scales a little. Hopefully enough.

If the Chaa really were gods, he was going to have to do a lot of hand-waving, when he got to his final reward. Angry deities weren't going to be happy at what he had done to the galactic commons they had carefully built and arranged before leaving. And they sure weren't going to like humans running around outside their house.

"Any good news from all that?" Morty continued after a moment of thought.

"We're connected into the underground here," Xiomber said in a careful voice.

"But?"

"But both the Constables and Maximus are hunting our asses, Morty," his egg-brother said. "And offering threats and rewards that are going to get somebody to roll on us, eventually."

"You're the street etiquette expert," Morty replied. "Is there anybody who could protect us? I'm willing to work for my keep, as long as they don't go down Cinnra's path and decide they need more humans. Even cops. At some point, someone will talk."

"Or a human will walk into a teashop and get tasted by a Grace?" Xiomber sneered.

"Hey, you left him alone, too," Morty said. "If she knows what he tastes like, my greatest hope is that the cops scared the wits out of the girl. You saw what that Vanir chick was like when she took off after Gareth."

"Yeah," Xiomber shuddered, eyes flickering with memory. "Ain't going there again."

"So find us someplace to set up shop," Morty said. "Even half-legit works for me. I haven't completely forgotten how to write code for responsible companies. I really don't want to have to go back to *Yuudix* and hide among a billion grains of sand. Don't think that would stop the Constabulary."

Xiomber nodded in agreement. He started to say something when his pocketcomm beeped.

The two Yuudixtl looked at each other for a moment, and then Xiomber shrugged and answered it.

"They're your kopeks," he said into the phone and then listened.

"Yeah?" Xiomber said a moment later. "Okay. Thanks. I owe you one for that. Later."

He hung up and stared at Morty

"We got a problem."

OFFICER OF THE COURT

GARETH WALKED into the briefing room expecting to find a mob waiting. Instead, he found an empty conference room with Talyarkinash Liamssen quietly waiting, sipping from what smelled like a glass of juice from here. Gareth blushed slightly as he realized that no human, nor Vanir, should be able to smell that well. Even a Nari like her might be hard pressed to match it.

And yet.

She rose as he entered and stepped away from the big, rectangular table to hug him. Nothing more, just physical contact that she seemed to find reassuring. If Gareth had given up everything in order to stop Maximus, Talyarkinash had come close in terms of cost.

She had lost her entire existence, being arrested at the same time Gareth was and quickly disappeared into police custody. However, she had been a willing witness once everything was explained to her, turning over names and addresses to the two Constables. It was the least she could do to help undo all the evil she had done, unwittingly or not.

She had burned all bridges, but still had a future in front of her. She was still Nari. Still five-foot-eight, approaching six feet at the tips of her ears. Her Imperial Blue fur was still sleek and shiny with gorgeous stripes, complimenting her eyes. Gareth had even gotten used to a woman with bigger and more luxurious muttonchop sideburns than any man he had ever known could grow.

He would have guessed that the Chaa, the Elder race responsible for the *Accord of Souls*, had taken a Canadian Lynx and transformed it into a woman-like creature. The eyes slitted vertically. The snout was ever-so-slightly prominent. She smiled with teeth that had more points than his did when she smiled at him.

But she had become a friend. And he, hers. She would have gone to prison forever, according to the Constables, but for her willingness to work with them to understand everything she had done to Gareth. And what some greater fool might do, next time.

Someone like Marc Sarzynski.

Gareth took his seat and considered coffee. Or whatever the thing in the silver urn on the side table should actually be called. It was close enough for his taste buds, raised on the instant stuff kept in a big can in the freezer, rather than freshly-roasted beans ground on demand.

Sounded like too much work. Like shaving had turned into as his beard came in. Or getting his hair cut.

Gareth wondered if he was going through teenage rebellion, or a very early mid-life crisis. Being turned into a giant alien creature would probably have that effect on a guy.

The side door opened before Gareth could decide. Eveth Baker and Jackeith Grodray entered, and nobody else. Just the four of them in the room.

He looked around the room at the other three people with an inside giggle. He and the two Constables were all wearing the exact same uniform, the steel blue bodysuit with triangular scales. Grodray had added the outer tunic that made him look more formal, while he and Baker had not.

Talyarkinash was wearing purple. Skin-tight, cheongsam top without any sleeves. Baggy, Samurai pants in a broad straight-leg cut, with a high waist that flared out at the top, almost like a pirate girdle. Everything she wore was embroidered with silver, in some arcane design that almost looked like something he had seen once in a Shia Mosque in Samarkand.

"What's so funny?" Baker asked as she took the seat directly across from Gareth.

She wasn't angry. Or it wasn't at him, anyway. At last not that he could tell.

Grodray had ended up across from the Nari woman, but his face was more closed.

"Wondering if there was any symbolism in fashion," Gareth replied.

It didn't make any sense, but she had asked.

Baker looked like she wanted to say something, then looked like she was trying not to roll her eyes at him. Finally, she huffed once and settled.

"Will it be just us today?" Talyarkinash asked in a serious voice, dividing her attention between the two.

Eveth Baker was probably the more dangerous, from a purely physical standpoint, although Gareth had been her match back when he's still been human. Grodray was still a more interesting foe from a strategic standpoint. He only looked like a Senior Constable, a role he played to mislead watchers. The man was really a Prime Investigator, a free agent allowed by his superiors to go wherever the crime might lead him.

As far as Gareth knew, Baker wasn't one. Not yet, but she had something like a candidate status, so she probably would be in another year or so, if all went well.

Gareth really didn't know where he fit into the whole mess. Talyarkinash was at least a scientist, and had been working closely with some of the staff here, but only a few people and most of them were not *read fully into* the project that was Gareth St. John Dankworth, renegade human, genetically-engineered monster.

Baker paused and looked deliberately at Grodray.

The older man suddenly looked angry enough to chew nails, where he had just been serious before.

"The fewer people that are aware of this operation, the better," Grodray said ominously.

Gareth heard the echoes of vast, bureaucratic arguments in the background of those words. Complaints taken all the way to the highest authority, rather than being worked out down in the trenches.

When you have a human on the loose, things could get ugly. Two of them doubled the problems.

"How can we help?" Gareth asked the man simply.

That was why they were here. Nothing else would require the two of them to physically travel this far, when they could send a message or a courier.

"I understand from Dr. Liamssen that you have gained better control of your…powers," Grodray began.

Gareth nodded silently.

"I need to see you in action, Gareth," the Senior Constable said. "That will tell me what I need to know about how to use you, going forward."

"Here?" he asked.

"No," Grodray said. "Too many witnesses. We need to go up-country to the gunnery range. I've had it locked down for the next two days, so there will be nobody but us."

Gareth whistled unconsciously at the astounding display of authority in those words. He caught the slightest flinch in Baker as well. Talyarkinash had never been in part of a major bureaucracy, so didn't understand that it was almost never possible to simply snap your fingers and just have something *happen*.

"I can go whenever," he said, turning to the Nari woman next to him. "Talyarkinash?"

"I suspected that was why you were here," she allowed. "I have some equipment in my lab that we will need, specially prepared for Gareth when he's in the field."

"What kind of equipment?" Baker spoke up now.

"When he transforms, his clothing and anything he is carrying somehow become absorbed into the new form, and then returned to normal later," Talyarkinash replied. "After a month, I still don't understand it, but humans have vast, latent psionic powers that might eventually put them on a par with the Chaa."

"And?" Baker almost growled.

"So the first round of bio-sensors I put on him went perfectly blank for the entire time he was transformed. Constable Baker," the Nari woman returned the challenge. "I have a new design that I want to try. Hopefully it will work. Science is about attempting and failing until you succeed. I do not know if I am there, yet, but I am getting closer."

"Oh." Baker backed off, which Gareth found rather interesting.

She was a big woman. Slender and athletic, but muscular and a whole head taller than the scientist. However, she was apparently willing to learn, and maybe even admit when she was wrong, or maybe pushing a little too hard.

"Gareth?" Baker asked.

Which was kind of astounding, but he hoped he hid it well. Usually, she only called him Dankworth to his face.

"Whatever you need, Constable," Gareth replied evenly. "Maximus is still out there."

SCIENTIST

IF THE GODS would have allowed it, Talyarkinash would have rebuilt herself to be seven feet tall, just so she could lurk above Eveth Baker for once, to give the woman a dose of her own medicine. Among her own kind, Talyarkinash was usually an inch taller than any Nari woman she met.

Being around Vanir all the time was wearing on the soul.

She kept her grumbles to herself though, as she climbed into the Constabulary Transport and buckled herself in, followed by the three giants from some fairy tale. Her small equipment bag, almost a purse, went between her feet.

Gareth was the most perfect gentleman. Had been from the first moment they had met. Had remained so even after she had discovered he was human. He gave lie to all those horrible threats and fairy tales her mother had told her as a kitten, even going so far as to confirm her seatbelt was done before attaching his own harness when he got in just now.

Baker, on the other hand, had been a major burr in her tailfur from the beginning.

Talyarkinash was willing to allow that she had been with the bad guys at the time. And guilty of some of the worst crimes on the books. Technically. Conspiracy and Being an Accessory to Treason were not particularly good things to list on her C.V., so she was planning on leaving those off, if she ever managed to make to a class reunion.

At least one outside prison. She had a pretty good idea how many of her old associates would probably be able to make one of those in another few years.

Eveth Baker was a bully. Emotionally. Psychologically. Even physically. It made her a good cop, Talyarkinash supposed. It also made her a pain in the ass, most of the time.

At least Baker appeared to be completely immune to the charms of one Gareth St. John Dankworth. That helped.

Gareth still had the card from some other Nari woman in his wallet. Seriously, the woman had given a complete stranger from another species a scent card.

What the hell?

Not that Talyarkinash hadn't considered doing the same, from time to time. Being human, Gareth had just possessed a magnetism that would have made her rich, had she been able to identify it, bottle it, and market it. After becoming Vanir, it was all she could do some days to not run her fingertips through his mane.

The craft lifting off concealed the way her fingers curled in her lap.

Post-zenith sun in a clear sky out the windows. Cool up here from the elevation, but she could have found a place out of the breeze, if she wanted to just bask on a warm rock. Instead, she had added a jacket that hung to her knees and a wool-lined cap with the perfect ear holes, for when they got even further up the enormous valley and the temperatures began to nip, even in direct sunlight.

This much wilderness was unnatural to a city kitten like her, but it was the hand she had been dealt. Rumors had been circulating that Maximus was currently in a war with his own people, deep in the underworld, to retain control. Or regain it. She was much safer with Baker and Grodray protecting her.

And Gareth.

If she was in the city, any city, someone would have found her, eventually. Maximus had done some amazingly savage things, even for a human, according to Gareth. She would have been on Sarzynski's list. Especially from where the two of them had started, her and Maximus.

Much better here.

The flight took all of about fifteen long, silent minutes. Gareth was lost in his sightseeing. Baker was scowling at something, but she always did. Grodray had grown introspective.

Gareth had explained to her the armies of earlier centuries on Earth. The tremendous wars fought over things she still couldn't quite parse. But more importantly, the science of destruction that his species had worshipped for so many millennia and the amazing advances they had driven in human culture, over just a few millennia.

Bronze Age to Space in three thousand years? Without outside intervention? Amazing.

And frightening. Where would they be in another thousand years?

The Gunnery Range they were about to take over was designed to give Heavy Rescue teams from the Constabulary a place to practice, working with weapons that could kill, rather than just stun, when you needed to blow things up, or destroy vehicles.

When you were reduced to the sorts of savagery that humans apparently just took for granted.

Talyarkinash shuddered, in spite of herself as they landed.

She had been here twice before, working with Gareth as he flew and practiced things like the breath weapon he had insisted almost all human cultures expected that dragons were born with.

Was there a more violent species, anywhere in the galaxy?

Today, the place was abandoned. Completely empty.

Even the vehicle bringing them had been auto-piloted, so the four of them might be the only people within twenty kilometers in any direction.

The old Talyarkinash would have had serious qualms about that sort of situation. Too easy to be brought up here and vanish without any trace that a crime had been committed. But Baker and Grodray weren't that sort of cops. And there was Gareth.

This might be one of the few situations in her life that Talyarkinash was confident she could take at face value.

She turned in place to view the magnificent arena formed by a bowl of mountains all the way around her as she emerged. The tarmac where they had parked was probably over one thousand hectares by itself, with a line of six enormous hangars on the right and a set of office buildings and warehouses on the left. Space for five, or maybe eight thousand people in a pinch, although last time she had been here, the population had been barely two dozen, sworn to secrecy but still gawking in the afternoon sun at a bronze dragon flying overhead. At least they had all had an occasional friendly smile for her.

The air was crisp, but not enough to penetrate her coat. If a breeze picked up, the hat would go on, but she was fine for now. It even smelled faintly of pine sap, a sticky, green pungency at the lower end of her range. Gareth almost certainly could detect it, but she doubted the cops would be able to.

That brought the faintest smile to her face as she fell in behind Grodray, with the other two behind her.

He led the column to a tower, a five story square cylinder where flight control would be able to see aircraft coming and going, and keep them organized in the sort of emergency where auto-pilots might not be smart enough to all maneuver in synch.

The stairs warmed her, as did being inside, to the point she pulled her coat open and considered taking it off.

Talyarkinash found the echoes in the stairwell amusing. Grodray walked with a lighter step than most Vanir, while Baker seemed to be trying to punish each tread as she stepped on it. Gareth made almost no sound, just a whisper more than she did.

The step into the brightness of the top chamber, after the dimness of the stairwell, caused her eyes to slam nearly shut for a moment, before they flickered sideways again.

Empty.

Four sides where up to eight controllers could work, although one was normal. She followed Grodray to the side where they had the best view of the long runway. He turned and gave them his best grouchy stare.

"Wanted to confirm we were completely alone," he said simply. "Dr. Liamssen, you said you had mechanisms that would not necessarily be part of Gareth's translation?"

"I do," she said, reaching into the bag she had brought with her and pulling out a small, clamshelled container that she handed to Gareth. "Attach this to your ear like an earring, and flip the tip into your ear canal."

He took it and opened the box warily. Simple enough, for now. A clip for the cartilage, hinged. He pulled it out and put it on. She saw a little red light appear.

Talyarkinash pulled out the communicator and pressed the button that would send a beep. He nodded in response, so she handed it to Grodray.

"Gareth's side is voice activated," she said. "Press the button on the side when you want to talk."

"Gareth, I've seen the videos of you in action," Grodray said. "I've read Dr. Liamssen's reports, plus a few others from around you. Those were relaxed, controlled circumstances. I want to see you in something like combat circumstances. Questions?"

"Anything in particular?" Gareth asked, himself falling into the seriousness of the other cops.

"Speed, maneuverability, fire," Grodray said. "We're reaching a point where talk now is about putting you in the field to hunt Sarzynski."

"Stalking horse?" Gareth asked.

"Do you know a better way to hunt lions?"

Talyarkinash shuddered. Maximus was at least that dangerous. Hopefully Gareth was as well.

DRACO-FORM

GARETH EMERGED from the bottom of the tower and sniffed the air around him. Nobody. It was odd, being able to smell like a hunting dog when he concentrated.

The base had been occupied until recently, but everyone had left at least a day ago. All this, just for him.

"Checking in," he said, assuming that the earpiece would pick it up.

"Go ahead, Gareth," Grodray said.

Deep breath. Reach down and grasp hold of the power that Talyarkinash had placed inside his soul when she given him the ability to transform. It no longer hurt as much to turn. Instead, it was a friendly heat that wrapped around him like hands, rather than scorching them. Even the pain of transformation was manageable.

Gareth paused, and took a second breath. The fire seemed to engulf him physically, although he had seen videos where he transformed, and everything was internal.

Just his imagination that he was burning.

And his perception changed as well. Eyes moved outward as his skull reshaped, granting him peripheral vision almost good enough to see all directions at once. Chitin formed from his blood and bone created a ridge of dragon plates that ran back his skull and all the way down to the new tail that was extending outward.

Fortunately, the uniform really did subsume itself into his flesh. The first attempt Talyarkinash had given him had shredded under the stress, coming apart and leaving him naked when he shifted back.

Dragons could blush, but right now nobody could see it under the bronze scales covering his face. He smiled, as much as he could with the new form of his jaw, too much like the Yuudixtl who had been his inspiration.

Crocodile smile.

"Can you still read me, Constable Grodray?" Gareth asked, his voice rumbling a rich bass in his own ears.

"Affirmative, Dankworth," the man replied. "Go ahead."

Gareth took several running steps and threw himself at the sky. He could fly from a standstill, pumping heavily to gain altitude, but this was much more efficient, using the tiny amount of breeze to gain a little lift.

Quickly, he was twenty meters in the air, racing along at sixty kilometers per hour as he rose higher. Grodray had given him no directions, other than to show off, so Gareth decided to stretch his abilities today.

Up and up, slowly orbiting the tower as a central beacon for his column, until he was nearly a thousand meters in the air. He rolled over and aimed himself to glide a little, back along the runway back to where their transport was parked.

There were a few birds up this high, but most had fled at the sight of the monstrous, strange beast breaking up the afternoon sky. A few predators continued to circle at what they thought might be a safe distance, but even they kept their orbits far wider than his, reacting like scalded cats when he turned one way or the other.

Finally, he turned, finding the line of the runway and pulling his wings in until just the tips stuck out, like tiny ailerons providing him control as he nosed over into freefall. Below, the equivalents of eagles and hawks scattered to the four winds with surprised cries.

Gareth rumbled a laugh, forgetting for a moment that the microphone was live.

"Everything okay?" Grodray asked, but it sounded more like a formality than anything.

"Speed drop," Gareth replied. "Locals are a little nervous."

"Roger that."

His draco-form was streamlined. The final size he had reached when he had stopped growing as a Vanir was twenty-seven meters from sleek snout to spiky tail. Pulled in tight, he quickly reached a terminal velocity far greater than a human skydiver ever could.

And he had learned early on how much torque his wings could take before they buckled under the stress, so he slowly stretched his wings out, forcing his flight flatter and flatter as he went, transforming into the horizontal from the vertical that he had started.

He didn't have an airspeed indicator gauge to track his speed, but his inner eyelid had dropped down, making everything just the slightest bit fuzzy while still letting him track large targets. Still, Talyarkinash had built him a communicator.

What else might it do?

"Can you track my airspeed?" Gareth asked as he flattened out and pumped his wings to keep him level and running, about twenty meters above the concrete apron below.

He would pass below his audience, if he was careful.

"Two hundred and eighty kph, Gareth," Talyarkinash replied after a few seconds. "Peak during your dive was three hundred and fifteen."

Wow. Faster than anything on the ground, and fast enough to catch most flying vehicles under computer control.

For fun, Gareth pulled back a little and shifted into an Immelmann maneuver, holding his wings still as he went straight up and stalled. An aircraft losing forward momentum like this would have to flip over and undo a stall, falling initially onto its tail.

Here, Gareth started his stall like normal, and then folded himself in two, pulling his wings in, reversing course like a diver coming off the high board. After a moment, he extended his wings again and flapping hard enough to hover in place fifty meters in the air.

For fun, he slowly pivoted on his tail at the same time, until he was facing the threesome in the tower from around seventy-five meters away, like the galaxy's biggest hummingbird.

Not the meanest. Hummingbirds back home had attitudes like tiny T-Rexes, all bluster and fury, while still small enough to fit in your hand. He could gulp one down in a single bite if they decided to get feisty with him today.

Let's see, speed, maneuverability, and hover displayed.

Gareth winged over and landed, more or less below the control tower window. Glancing up, he could see three faces leaned out and looking down, so he reared back and triggered the two glands in his upper chest, pressing out paired streams of liquid that ran up into his mouth.

One turned into a spray, and then the second mixed with it and ignited, reacting to the oxygen in the air and the misty spray to turn into a column of fire nearly thirty meters long for a second. There was nothing to burn, but he knew he would leave a scorch mark on the concrete that newcomers couldn't explain.

Folks who had been there to watch him before would know. He was sure rumors were already floating about the *Accord of Souls*.

Fire-breathing-dragon. Gareth was pretty sure that both Grace and Nari would react with the same awe and trepidation as humans did.

"Did you need a strength demonstration?" Gareth rumbled. "I could lift one end of the transport, but I don't think I could get the whole thing off of the ground."

"That's okay, Gareth," Grodray was back on line. "Go ahead and return to normal for now. I want to talk about next steps."

Gareth had landed on all fours for stability. He reared up now and let go of the terrible fire in his soul, feeling the energy collapse back down inside somewhere.

Talyarkinash had said that the ability was psionic, whatever that meant. Except that he didn't have any biology or physics that could explain what he did. Neither did she.

Magic was as good a description an anything, he supposed. He wondered if Dr. Loughty would be able to do any better, but he doubted it, as far beyond Terran culture and technology as he found himself these days.

Still, he was happy when he looked down and his skin was covered in a blue scaled jumpsuit. He had believed the Nari scientist and her equipment, but there was always that least bit of doubt in the back of his mind.

Grodray emerged first, with Baker close on his heels. Talyarkinash was several seconds behind, but she probably went down every step, when the taller twosome didn't have to. Not necessarily fair, but not a lot he could do about it.

"I had to see it with my own eyes," Grodray said by way of apology. He held out a hand for Gareth to shake.

"Understood, sir," Gareth replied. "I still don't always believe it myself. What's next?"

Something in the man's face was off, the way Grodray's eyes found Talyarkinash and he lost all emotion.

"Field work," he said.

Gareth was confused. Doubly so when Talyarkinash smiled.

PRIME INVESTIGATORS

EVETH WAITED until they had returned Dankworth and Liamssen to
the base, and then cleared that on their way back to town.

"Out with it," Grodray said from the bench across from her. "You've
been stewing for an hour, and too polite to say anything in front of those
two. What's eating you?"

"Is he ready?" she asked simply, compacting any number of arguments
into those few words. Grodray was her boss, and a Prime Investigator,
however secret that designation was. He made his own job, as he saw fit.

And the highest echelons of the *Accord of Souls* would back him. She
could have opinions, but she was only a candidate to become a Prime
Investigator herself, so she needed to be a team player right now, working
within Grodray's framework.

Grodray surprised her by smiling.

"Not really sure it matters, Eve," he said. "I'm up to no good here."

"How so?" she asked, a little lost.

Normally, Jackeith Grodray was deduction itself. Cold, calculating,
logical. That was one of the reasons she had been given about why she'd
initially been paired with the man, as her own approach was much more
inductive. She could make fantastic, intuitive leaps, so he balanced her, so
the story went.

Since the mask had come off, revealing that a well-respected Senior

Constable, a simple Level Four, who was actually a Level Seven, she had seen a side of the man she had never really imagined.

"Playing a couple of hunches," Grodray said.

"You?"

He laughed and leaned back into the chair with a twinkle in his eyes.

"One, Maximus has a deep and abiding hatred of Gareth," Grodray said. "You've read the debriefing reports and the bio that Gareth helped assemble on the man."

"Stalking horse," Eveth replied, nodding with understanding. "Put him out in the open and see if you can draw Sarzynski out of the shadows to take a shot at him."

"Correct," Jackeith nodded. "But there's a second element at play, and I want to see how that works."

"What's that?" Eveth pressed. What else could there be?

"I've watched a number of female officers and researchers around Gareth," Grodray said. "Plus the original reports, and that young woman in the tea shop when he was first pulled through to *Orgoth Vortai*."

"What about him?" she asked bluntly.

"And that's the best part," Grodray said with a dry chuckle. "You appear to be immune, but every other female Gareth Dankworth comes into contact with has a serious, visceral reaction to the man. And they did even when he was human, but becoming Vanir hasn't changed it."

"The fact that every woman wants to jump his bones?" Eveth asked.

"Except you," her partner grinned.

"He's human, Jack," she snapped, finding a seam of coal underneath her words to ignite. "That's disgusting."

"They don't know that," he countered. "And if it works, I want to turn him loose in a few places, to see if that charm and magnetism can get us into a few areas where pure police work has failed."

"And if it does?" she sneered.

"Then he breaks our case even further open, Eve," the man turned serious. "I'll get all the glory on this one, but you're doing the hard work, and you'll get credit in the right places."

She liked that thought. On the one hand, that would be her ticket into the big leagues.

And maybe, if she was lucky, the two humans would manage to wipe each other out and save everyone else a lot of trouble.

OMELETS

IT WAS GETTING OLD.

Morty knew they were in the top ten most wanted people in the entire *Accord of Souls*, but it would be nice to be able to stay in the same apartment for more than a week before somebody tipped either the cops or his old friends from *Zathus*, as to where he and Xiomber were staying.

Today, supposedly, it had been the bad guys who got the call.

Fortunately, Xiomber had friends. Or was owed enough favors. Or maybe owed enough other people that they wanted to be able to collect on those debts in the future and couldn't if he was dead.

Whatever. The phone had rung. A message had been conveyed. And they ran like hell for the door.

Somewhere, there was still a pot of tea cooling on a kitchen table with a fantastic view of that giant bronze statue: *"Walking into Discovery."* It was a stupid name for a piece of art, but the Grace were weirdoes to begin with, so he wasn't going to argue.

And Xiomber had found them a nice dive on the edge of downtown to get breakfast. Not too close to the old place, where someone might see them accidentally, but only three stops away on the first bus that had driven by.

Fortunately, after a month on the run, Morty's entire life pretty much fit into a single bag. He had a few bolt holes scattered around the *Accord*, and he and Xiomber had set up a few joint efforts beyond that, but these days it really was possible to grab his comm off the counter, and his bag by the door, and walk out of an apartment forever.

"So who called?" Morty asked as the waiter delivered menus and a fresh pot of tea.

They were seated clear down at the back of the narrow joint, tucked into a tiny table that was invisible from the front door and most of the windows, back around where the counter wrapped and led to the restrooms. The joint had been decorated in white: walls, counter, floor, aprons; but it still had a dinginess that no amount of soap would ever get out. Too many cigarettes and plates of greasy bacon and eggs had passed through here over the years.

And the crowd was just starting to wind themselves up, but Morty could see three tables left for whoever managed to get here next. After that, he was pretty sure the line would be out the door, just from the smells coming from the kitchen.

Seriously, there were what looked like a couple of farmers at the counter, enjoying a break between milking cows and whatever else folks like that did in the morning. Except they had to have come all the way into town to eat here, because the nearest farms were like thirty kilometers away. Above them, a television was showing two pretty talking heads doing morning news and fluff, but the sound was off.

Morty studied the menu while Xiomber ruminated on the question he had posed.

"Nobody you know," Xiomber finally said. "Old girlfriend I did striped scales for, back when she got married."

"Ah, her," Morty said. "She must still like you?"

"Enough," Xiomber allowed with a vague shrug. "She got a whisper and put two and two together."

"Do we need to get off this rock?" Morty asked, pouring some tea and letting it warm his mug.

"I don't think we're totally screwed yet," his egg-brother nodded, pouring his own tea. "The old gang didn't have many fingers here, so finding us requires that they use the locals. People will talk."

"Yeah, but how soon until you run out of friends, or they get lucky?" Morty asked.

Xiomber shrugged.

"I had hoped that we could drop down the rabbit hole here, Morty," he said. "Find someone to take us on faith and let us work for them for a while, at least until the heat died down, ya know?"

"The old man's getting more desperate, not less," Morty noted. "You saw what he did to Damabiath. I don't want to know what a scaleless Yuudixtl looks like, m'kay?"

A sudden sound caught them both short, a low moan of surprise and shock rippling through the crowd. Morty and Xiomber both turned, but Morty had to half-stand out of his seat to see over the counter and know what was going on.

All heads had turned to the television screen over the counter, by the front door.

"Turn up the sound," somebody yelled.

A Warreth waitress fumbled with a remote control for a few seconds before she found the right buttons.

"…repeating our top story, an explosion occurred just a few minutes ago in a downtown apartment tower, blowing out windows across the street, but apparently confined to just one apartment. Fire and police are responding, and we've got the first images from our **Morning Three** *Eye In The Sky* drone," the female, a Grace, was saying.

The image was zoomed in on a blackened window, smoke oozing out, before the camera pulled back to show the rest of the tower and part of the street. The operator slowly rotated the hovering camera in place to show windows shattered, but it looked like a pretty clean explosion.

It helped that tower blocks like this were generally self-contained reinforced-concrete shells. All the boom would tend to go outward, and usually a fire would be contained to just one flat. Defensive architecture was a hallmark of the *Accord*. Keep everybody safe.

Morty blew the air out of his lungs and sat down hard, muttering profanities under his breath.

"Yeah," Xiomber said. "I saw the same thing. Now I'm really glad we left when we did."

Morty wasn't sure exactly how somebody had killed their apartment. Explosive shaped charge on the front door? Missile in through the kitchen window?

Maybe they had kicked in the door, found that Morty and his egg-brother gone, then lost their temper? Morty would have been tempted to stake the place out, on the off-chance that the two fugitives would return, but apparently Maximus and his people already knew they had flown the coop.

That looked like a message. And an unpleasant one.

Morty sighed and picked up the menu.

"We owe your old girlfriend big time," he muttered.

"That's exactly what she said," Xiomber smiled back grimly. "She said it would probably make the morning news, whatever it was, and we should walk out immediately. Thoughts?"

"Omelet with everything," Morty replied absently. "Gimme lots of carbs and protein this morning because I got a feeling it's only going to get worse from here."

"I meant about us," Xiomber groused.

"That's what I'm talking about," Morty snapped. "I'm beginning to wonder if we're out of rope, Xiomber. Like we have to finally do something amazingly stupid if we want to survive all this. Lots of broken eggs in our future."

Xiomber's eyes slitted down tight, and his lids dropped halfway.

"How stupid?" he asked.

The waiter interrupted at that moment. Morty went all in, obviously afraid that this might be his last nice meal for a while, and he could always stuff the other half into a to-go box and carry it with him for lunch.

Xiomber started easy, but saw something in Morty's eyes that appeared to unsettle him. He ordered the ribeye with eggs and hash, instead of a fruit and greens salad. The waiter smiled and departed.

"How stupid?" Xiomber repeated, but his heart wasn't filled with anger. Morty could see that.

"Let's find Gareth," he said quietly.

"You know who has him," Xiomber snapped, keeping his own voice as low as possible.

"Yeah," Morty acknowledged. "But I'd rather spend the next forty years complaining that I've read the entire prison library than be dead by lunchtime, okay? We can always get ourselves rehabilitated later."

"You think they'll let us out of prison in this lifetime, egg-brother?" Xiomber sneered.

"The crazy lizard who started all this has had a significant change of heart, brother," Morty said. "I screwed up, big time, and nearly brought the entire *Accord of Souls* down. I own that, yes, but I've spent the last two months trying to save civilization from all those crazy bastards. Do you want an immortal super-human ruling the *Accord* for the rest of time? No. Hell, I'd be happy if anyone ever figured out how to summon back the Chaa and let them fix everything."

"You'd be in hell, Morty," his brother said. "And I'd be with you."

"And the galaxy would survive, Xiomber," he snapped. "Maximus would be dealt with. Gareth's people would either be stuffed back into their hole or modified enough to be added to the *Accord*. People like you and I could go back to whatever petty crime and juvenile shenanigans the Elders left us as crumbs if they didn't just wipe us from existence. But the galaxy would be *safe*."

"Gareth?" Xiomber asked morosely after a moment. "You realize all the cops on this planet are pretty bent, right?"

"Yeah," Morty said. "I figure either *Hurquar* or *Orgoth Vortai* should be our next step. Those two Constables were from *Hurquar*, but I don't know if they went back."

"No, I like *Orgoth Vortai*," Xiomber said. "Let's take it back to where it began. Is *Orgoth Vortai* going to be safe? That's the next question."

Morty nodded.

"No place is safe," Morty said. "But Omerlon's got no reason to like Maximus. Less if that's who did Damabiath."

But Morty liked the thought of *Orgoth Vortai* as well.

Knowing the Grace, they would see the whole thing as a giant piece of insane performance art.

But for the bombs going off, Morty would, too.

TIP

A KNOCK at the door brought Gareth's head up. He had been quietly reading criminal statutes, and making notes on a pad of paper as a cross-referenced index, comparing the *Accord of Souls* legal system to Earth Force. The table was covered with piles of paper and note cards, but he was almost done. After this, time to begin memorizing some of the more interesting details of the seventeen species that made up the *Accord*.

"Come in," he yelled.

The door was never locked. He had no reason to lock it as most of the people at this facility generally stayed well away from him anyway.

Oh, they were friendly enough, but all of them belonged to species that were within two or three percent of the absolute limits of genetic engineering and there was always some element of jealousy as to what he could do.

And nobody else could turn into a dragon, so he had to be an alien of some sort, masquerading as a Vanir. Eventually, someone would probably figure it out. All hell would probably break loose when they did.

The door opened slowly. Talyarkinash poked her head in and looked around before opening it the rest of the way and stepping in.

"I forget that you need so little sleep as well," she began, a smile that went all the way to her ear tips lighting up her face. "I was afraid I would be waking you up."

Gareth rose and smiled back.

"Homework," he gestured to the stacks of paper on the table between them.

A thought struck him as he looked down.

"Did you modify my brain?" he asked suddenly. "This didn't used to be this easy."

People with fur on their face could hide a blush. But he had spent enough time around the Nari woman to see the subtle signs. The way her whiskers twitched back. Her ears turned a quarter rear as well. The pupils opened wider than necessary for the light in here.

"Maybe a little," she said in an off-hand way as she entered. "Maximus was already a genius, so I thought you could always use a bump."

"How much?" he pressed, sitting back down as clues and hints began to coalesce.

"There is a line, according to what Sarzynski told Morty and Xiomber," she offered, stepping fully into the room and closing the door behind her. "On the other side of that line, you get genius, but frequently human artists are also insane, according to his understanding of human history. To us, that is a relative concept, since all humans are completely deranged to begin with."

She said the last with a grin that brought a smile to Gareth's face as well. Nobody had worked as closely with any human as she had with him over the last six weeks. She was now the *Accord's* certifiable expert.

"You said on the other side of that line," Gareth prodded her.

"Correct," she agreed. "You were already well above average for humans, by your standards, but there was still space to bump you up further, so I did. Right now, you straddle that line, but that just means your memory is sharper and your reactions have improved some. Oh, and all your senses are sharper than before, but not so bad as to overwhelm you, but you already knew that."

"Thank you," he said. "I was beginning to wonder how I could memorize so much material, so quickly, but there was just too much I needed to know, so I come back here after dinner and read and take notes until after zero."

"I'm glad it has worked out," Talyarkinash admitted. "So much of what I was doing was guesswork, taking you and extrapolating along predicted lines to what I hoped were logical conclusions. And turning you into a dragon."

He grinned from ear to ear.

"Every kid wants to be a dragon, when they're about seven," he said. "Right after the dinosaur phase and before astronaut. It's a human thing."

"I see," she nodded and shrugged.

Being the best expert on humans they had didn't make her an expert on the species. Gareth was better for that, but nobody could bring themselves to fully trust him. He knew that.

Maybe Talyarkinash, but that was about it.

"You have news?" he asked, prompting her back from where he had derailed her.

Talyarkinash moved to the table and pulled the other chair. It was Nari-sized, so she could join him for tea or to chat.

"We've received orders to pack our personal gear," she said nervously. "Senior Constable Grodray is relocating us to *Orgoth Vortai*."

"Why there?" Gareth asked.

She shrugged meaningfully.

"Perhaps they have a tip?" she offered. "Maybe they just want someplace relatively used to strange things. You can't get much weirder than the homeworld of the Grace."

Gareth shrugged in turn.

"How soon until we leave?" he looked at his piles and began sorting them into things to keep and things to recycle.

"There will be a shuttle for us mid-day tomorrow," Talyarkinash said. "Around fifteen hours."

Gareth turned and looked at the closet door. It was closed, but he could have picked out every outfit in there blindfolded.

There wasn't much to begin with. Beyond two Constabulary uniforms, there was his Secret Agent/cowboy outfit that he had been wearing when Marc captured him. A set of lovely robes that Morty had bought, but he had never worn. And his Sky Patrol uniform.

None of them fit him, being sized for the human he had been, once upon a time, but he wasn't about to lose them. Any of them.

At least in the future, laundry was a much easier task. Walk into the booth fully clothed and let all the various beams and radiations clean you and your clothes at the same time. Gareth had two more of Talyarkinash's special uniforms, designed to morph with him. One tunic was for normal duty, while the other was a touch fancier and would be for those weird, formal occasions where he was expected to be in dress uniform.

He hadn't been to anything like that yet, but supposed that he might have just graduated and be ready to become a Deputy Agent again.

Starting at the bottom was okay. He was a cop and there was work to be done.

"Thinking about your past?" Talyarkinash asked when he turned back to face her.

"My future, actually," he said. "The past is lost. I haven't made peace with that yet, but I'm working on it."

"You miss her?" she said. It was more of a statement, but it sounded enough like a question.

"Every day," Gareth sighed. "If it wasn't such an amazingly bad idea, I'd sneak back to Earth and bring her here with me. Have you turn her into a Vanir so we could live happily ever after. The Constabulary would never accept it, though. There are already too many humans here."

She wanted to say something. He could see it in her eyes, but she refrained. There wasn't much to say at that point. He could never go home, and he would probably end up in a cell, once he captured or killed Marc.

It would be apocalyptic, their final battle. Gareth had no doubts about that. Hopefully, he would prevail, and could bring peace to the *Accord of Souls*. Whether Marc would allow himself to be taken alive was another question.

Either way, the end of Marc Sarzynski's reign of terror would also be the end of Gareth's freedom. He wasn't sure how he felt about that, but duty was duty. Stop Marc first. Then deal with spending the rest of his days in prison as an illegal alien who was too dangerous to allow to roam free.

Rather than speak, Talyarkinash held out a hand. Gareth took it and held on.

It was nice to have friends, because they both knew whatever was coming was likely to get ugly, before it might ever get better.

INTO THE SHADOWS

"WE KNEW THEY WEREN'T THERE," Marc heard Zorge explain. "But, following orders, we planted a small bomb anyway and annihilated the place with fire."

Zorge paused at that point. When Marc turned to stare at him, the Nari spymaster was looking for the right words. Something that would get to the heart of the matter, without offending the crazy human boss who had cut such a bloody swathe across the *Accord*.

The group had taken over a small resort on the outskirts of the city of Uwethis, on *Kani*. It was about as far from the civilized core of the *Accord* as one could get and still have indoor plumbing, as the joke went. Planetary population still under a half billion souls, but a good mix of species in the city. And one of the lowest rates of cops to citizens in known space. A safe enough place to hide while he rebuilt the organization.

Marc relaxed on an overstuffed chair done in green, while the Nari was on an equally-over-stuffed couch in gray and yellow squares. Hideous, but he wasn't an interior decorator.

"*Why?* you were wanting to ask?" Marc smiled as the pause stretched.

"Something like that, yes," Zorge replied defensively.

"They weren't there, but had been," Marc explained. "The criminal underground on *Churquark* isn't as well organized as *Zathus* had been. Not as powerful either, relying too much on corrupt politicians and mid-level folks to get by. They might have considered letting things slide."

"So bombing the place sends a message?" Zorge asked. "To whom?"

"Everyone," Marc actually felt a smile on his face. Those were rare, these days. "It tells those two that I can find them, and that I won't accept their apologies. It reminds the local underworld that anyone wanting to shelter the two lizardmen will be dealing with me, personally. It tells the Constabulary that things are more rotten than they think, so they'll concentrate more effort on *Churquark* than they had been."

"Net result, drive Morty and Xiomber off planet, right about the time the cops drop a ton of bricks on the place," Zorge concluded. "They escape the dragnet, and nobody else?"

"Exactly," Marc said. "Think of it as a shell game. Everyone will be looking on *Churquark*, where the marble is not hiding. I don't know where they'll go, but we've made the rest of the people around them unwelcoming, so they'll have no choice but to run. Eventually, we'll find them. Or the cops will."

"Won't they talk?" Zorge asked. "Tell the cops everything they know, trying to buy a reduced sentence?"

"Everything they know doesn't include what I'm up to now," Marc smiled. "You're still thinking defensively."

"And we're rebuilding, while bringing down all the other gangs," Zorge breathed. "But won't that make it harder for us, if they start bringing in honest politicians? Or clean up the local police departments?"

"For a while," Marc said. "I've been studying the *Accord's* history, and one thing is clear. The structure they built was never going to last forever. Too fragile. The Vanir might be all law-and-order as a rule, but their place at the top of the hierarchy of things tends to rub a lot of the other species the wrong way. And so you get an underclass that don't see how they can get ahead when the Vanir are so dominant."

"Which breeds resentment, and creates the conditions for the underworld to thrive," Zorge agreed.

"And I don't see that pattern changing," Marc said. "At least not for several more centuries. At some point, the Chaa might just have to come back and fix things if they want to go back to the old days, but I'm here now, and nobody's done anything about it, so either they don't see me as a threat, or, more likely, they don't care."

"And you plan to be around for that long still?"

"Correct," Marc said.

He studied the Nari closely, but the man didn't have any obvious qualms. Of course, without Maximus protecting him, the man would be a cell quickly enough. They were all in the chute now, and they knew it.

Victory or death.

Zorge shrugged.

"So I have my teams watching for all the key players," Zorge continued. "Grodray and Baker disappeared for three days last week, but they're back on *Hurquar* now, working to unravel everything there."

Marc nodded.

"My theory is that they went to visit Gareth Dankworth, wherever he had been hidden," Marc replied. "Now they're getting desperate enough to use him."

"Should we target him for anything?"

"No," Marc said firmly. "Just watch him for now. Perhaps he'll lead us to Morty and Xiomber. If he does, we'll sweep them all up, but I need better weapons, if I'm going to take on a star dragon."

"That's Maiair's department," Zorge said.

"Indeed," Marc agreed. "Anything else? Then send her in next."

"Yes, sir."

And the Nari spymaster was gone.

Marc looked around the room. Not bad, as resorts in the middle of nowhere went. Wood paneling on the walls made them feel small and intimate. Strange knick-knacks seemed to cover every free space on the abundant bookshelves, although he had no interest in ever reading the vast array of cozy mysteries and romances that the *Accord* writers seemed to generate on an annual basis.

He had a small front room with the couch, the overstuffed chair, and a writing hutch that could fold down. Down a short passageway was a tiny bathroom on the left, a kitchenette at the end, and a sleeping room barely big enough for the bed on the right. But this wasn't a place tourists stayed all day.

They were close to a variety of what Marc would have called nature preserves back on Earth. Places to hike and camp, all a short ride away. The resort had a kitchen and a small bar up in the main building, but Marc had arranged to rent the entire facility for a month. It was the off-season on *Kani*, not far past the middle of winter at this latitude, so the owner had made them a great deal, especially when Marc didn't need staff on hand for cooking and such.

He could have the place to himself for a while, cheap, and let his people work. Singles and doubles coming and going wouldn't excite any gossip with the locals. They had been given a cover story of a small religious group on a retreat, so they could be self-contained.

Let the storm blow over the *Accord* right now, while he was sheltered. The fundamental mechanics had not changed, so all Gareth and the Constables could do would be to imprison the current batch of criminals, until Marc could bend the new batch to his will.

It might take a decade, but Vanir were long-lived folk to begin with, and he had plans for upgrading this body.

Emperor Marc. Not even Marc the First, as he planned to live as close to forever as medicine and genetics would allow, so he would give up the throne when it was taken from him in death, or when one of his sons finally impressed him enough to take over.

God/Emperor. Yes, that sounded more accurate.

A knock at the door, and then Maiair entered a moment later. Her crimson headcrest was carefully at half-mast. Unsure but firm and proud. Not challenging his authority, but not backing off of her own.

Good.

He had been afraid that the stress of the last month might have ground the Warreth woman down. Used her up. Broken her.

He could see he had been wrong.

"You wanted to see me?" she asked in a voice that found that perfect spot between subservient and sarcastic.

"Yes," he smiled at her, gesturing to the sofa for her to sit. Hopefully, she would be at ease.

Like Zorge, she was poised at the edge of the seat rather than putting her weight back.

"Things are beginning to move," Marc began. "Shortly, all of the enemy pieces will be on the table again, and we can begin our more complex gambits."

"What do I need to concentrate on?" she asked, her headcrest perking up some, fluffing a little as she grew more confident in the direction of the meeting.

"Gareth St. John Dankworth is a wild card, Maiair," Marc said quietly. "Zorge has his people trying to get me information from the Constables, as to what his capabilities truly are, but without Liamssen's notes, we're only guessing. I need you to find me a competent geneticist that we own, or can turn."

"Kidnap?" she hazarded.

"No," Marc replied flatly. "I'll be putting my life in his hands, so I want one with a god complex and so much intellectual arrogance that he sees me as a challenge for his brilliance, rather than as an opportunity to destroy me in one shot."

"They come in flavors," she observed. "What kinds of upgrades were you needing for yourself? Liamssen was among the best as a generalist, and the rest are being prodded enough by the Constables enough to be looking over their shoulders constantly."

"I am bigger and stronger than most Vanir," Marc noted. "Smarter than just about all of them, as well. But Dankworth and the others didn't stop there. He can turn into a flipping dragon, for God's sake. I need something to counter that, but I'm not sure what, yet."

"Draco-form?" she asked carefully.

"This is a genetic change, Maiair," he replied. "If Dankworth ever had children with a Vanir woman, it would probably be a trait that was passed down. If the *Accord* isn't ready for humans, they really won't be able to deal with lycanthropic dragons. No, I'm looking to found a dynasty, so I need to get as close to immortality as we can get, which won't be that hard, but I want to be able to do something nobody else in the *Accord* can do."

"Which is?" she hesitated, sensing something that left her nervous.

More nervous than she already was.

"Breed with other species," Marc replied carefully, almost tenderly. "There's no reason all my children should be Vanir, Maiair."

She sucked a nearly-silent gasp and froze perfectly still, like a rabbit in the grass hearing an owl's cry.

Marc left the silence hanging. She had hinted at such things earlier, but she probably never realized that Marc Sarzynski was capable of going there intellectually. The various species of the *Accord of Souls* had been fixed in place by the Chaa when most of them were *Uplifted*, and the Vanir became *Those Left Behind*. They could marry and live happy lives, but never cross-breed.

Hell, most of them had different chromosome counts, so fertility was truly impossible.

But if he told a conference of geneticists that something was simply impossible, a few would stand up and challenge him. Those were the ones he wanted. Immortality wasn't a red flag they could look at on a readout. It had to be inferred from a host of indicators all being too healthy at the same time.

Perhaps one who would make him immortal, and a second who could help Marc create a whole series of ruling castes over the current species. He had been serious about bringing in a few humans and adding them in as dons and capos. And his own children would probably require fifty years before they were stable enough as a royal family.

But Marc was measuring time in millennia.

"You're sure?" she finally spoke.

Her headcrest had nearly collapsed, but now it had risen again. Puffed out feathers around her head had relaxed as the moment of shock passed.

"We have the opportunity to reshape the *Accord of Souls*, Maiair," Marc almost whispered. "I see no reason to limit things to the Vanir. The Warreth should have a chance to shine, as should the Nari and even the Grace. I'm less confident in some of the other species, but we can look. Can you find me the right doctor?"

He paused again. This was where things got tricky.

On the one hand, she knew he was going to create a ruling caste of humans, led by a royal family of heavily modified Vanir. On the other, he had just offered her the chance to place her own offspring into that level of power as well.

Permanently.

And the best part? All of his children would not be bound by the *Accord of Souls*, so he would have a permanent underclass of peons that were generally incapable of doing the kinds of violence necessary to stop him.

He would only have to worry about the humans he brought over, and his own children.

And Gareth St. John Dankworth.

COTTON CANDY SKIES

GARETH JUST COULDN'T WRAP his head around the color of the daytime sky overhead. Not quite as pink as cotton candy, but not so far down into orange as to be salmon-colored. It haunted him, but that had been the moment when he truly understood that he stood under alien skies. Looking up and not seeing blue.

Xiomber had explained it to him eventually. The weird bacteria and things that floated in the sky, plus a soft, constant haze of dust from the deserts on the continent of Mishalque. *Orgoth Vortai* had more land than *Earth*, only some forty percent being oceans, rather than the seventy-five percent back home. Heat made that desert largely uninhabitable, except by researchers who burrowed down into the rocks by day for coolness.

But he was back in *Londra* now. Gareth hadn't even known the name of the city as he was passing through it. One minute he had been at The Arsenal. The next, he was in a park on the other side of town, headed to a tea shop…

"You have a very far-away look on your face, Dankworth," Eveth Baker said in a voice strong enough to jar him out of daydreams.

"Last time I was here, six weeks ago, I was on planet for all of about six hours," he replied. "Still completely trapped in culture shock and trying to figure out what the hell was going on."

"And it made that big of impression on you?" she asked. Her voice had lost some of the ragged anger that had been with her all day.

She started to walk, so Gareth fell into stride with her. It was weird, working with a female partner. Back home, the few Women's Auxiliaries of Earth Force were more secretaries and such, rather than agents. Although, come to think about it, Gareth could think of a few women he had known who could have done this job at least as well as him. Maybe better.

Here, he was the junior agent, but Baker was treating him like a peer, rather than a semi-feral animal she needed to keep on a tight leash.

Pippa, for example, could have done this. She had graduated third in her entire class from college, but couldn't go on to get an advanced degree because no reputable program would enroll her, so she was doing something like *Reading The Law* to do advanced stellar physics with her father. She could have certainly handled this.

He had been raised that way, but Gareth wasn't sure now why women were thought to be such frail, fragile creatures, to be protected at all costs. Eveth Baker was one of the toughest people he had ever met.

"Dankworth?" Baker prodded.

He had fallen silent in thought.

"The city? Yes," he said, finding his way back to conversation. "Still culture shocking over all the things females do here as a matter of course, where back home they can't."

"That sounds stupid," Constable Baker decided.

Gareth shrugged. He really couldn't argue, having just spent the last six weeks surrounded by competent, capable females doing things that he had always thought of as a man's job.

"What's the next stop?" he asked instead.

They were dressed like cops today. Both in the steel-blue bodysuits with the bright blue ring over their hearts as a badge. Like always, she wasn't wearing the extra tunic over the top, but Gareth was trying to be the spit-and-polish rookie cop here, so he had everything exactly to regulation, including the white beret.

That also included a stun pistol like hers. Plus strict instructions from Eveth Baker never to draw it. He would probably do so automatically, if danger appeared, but he would argue with her over it afterwards.

She really meant in most situations, and he found that acceptable. They weren't going to find Marc Sarzynski while randomly checking bars and dives.

No, he was out here beating the bushes in order to drive the game towards Senior Constable Grodray. There would be no glory for Gareth

Dankworth, but that was acceptable as well. The fewer people that knew he existed in the *Accord of Souls*, the better everything was likely to be.

"Here," Baker pointed to a building that had remained behind when the neighborhood was gentrified and redone at some point in the recent past.

The apartment towers behind him had a recent feel to them, like a row of houses had been leveled and a massive stack of flats with a giant picture of a rooster on the side put in instead, with two stories of retail and office space at the bottom.

This was a solitary building in front of them. One story tall. Sitting on a corner facing the main street they were on as well as the side. The outside walls were wood, with neon signs for things Gareth presumed were local beers. It had that kind of feel to it.

Weirdly, the front door was Dutch. The top half was open, and the whole sat recessed at a forty-five degree angle, facing the center of the intersection rather than either street. Baker unlatched the bottom half and pushed it in.

Gareth followed her into a space that managed to carefully surf that line between upscale restaurant and neighborhood dive bar. Four booths ran down the right hand wall, with a hallway indicating restrooms beyond.

On the left, high and low tables filled the bulk of the space. Maybe forty of them, all told, with a waist-high, wrought-iron fence separating the space from a bar that ran halfway across the back wall. A window and a door beside the bar showed a kitchen, but Gareth could already tell that from the smells. Outside had been nice, a smell like a Sunday afternoon grilling.

Inside, the smells trebled. Gareth's stomach rumbled in anticipation of the meat and yummies to be had here.

Three people sat at the bar, their backs to he and Baker as they came in. A Grace bartender watched them from under hooded eyes and restive coils, but gestured to the room.

"Anywhere you like," he called in a voice that was just about as friendly as he was required to be to cops walking in in the middle of the afternoon.

Baker led him to one of the booths and slid in, tapping the other side to indicate where he should go. He ended up with his back to the front door, the bar on his left, and the hallway in front of him, over her shoulder.

The menus were meat. It came grilled, fried, barbequed, sous vide, and probably tartar. Gareth could recognize about half of the animals that were the source by now. Vegetables came grilled as a side, or possibly in a salad for someone that had been dragged along kicking and screaming by hungry carnivores.

Baker studied the menu, while Gareth looked over at the inhabitants.

The Grace woman on the closest end of the bar looked over as they sat, blanched, and quickly paid her bill and vanished. A Borren drunk at the other end leaned back enough to look over and then went back to his beer. Or whatever it was in his glass.

The man in the middle was a species Gareth had never met before, though he had studied them. Th'Tarni.

They reminded Gareth of wood elves, as portrayed in stories. A little over five feet tall, with a dusky skin that wasn't gray and wasn't brown and wasn't smoke, but somewhere in the middle of all three. Back home, he might have belonged to the negro subgroup, based on the color of his skin and his flat nose. They weren't that common in Earth Force Sky Patrol, so Gareth had never really interacted with them.

This man's eyes were the most fascinating. They didn't have an iris and pupil, like most species, but simply a transparent orb for an eyeball, lit from within with a shy, baby-blue light that stood out against the gray-brown skin. Similar dots of color on his skin were freckles, or the roots of his hair. That same hair faded to gray and then black quickly, but always had some of the cerulean along all edges, like it was part of a neon sign.

The ears were pointed, like Gareth's were now, but instead of going straight up, this man's flowed backwards and then rose to points nearly even with the back of his skull. They also glowed with the same internal light.

It was like the man was made of light and given a shell. Or maybe he was a gigantic lightning bug given human form by the Chaa.

The man turned as he watched and glared at Gareth, almost challenging. Gareth realized he was staring and quickly turned his head down to study the menu again, blushing furiously.

He thought he heard a snicker come from Baker, but couldn't be sure and wasn't going to ask.

Suddenly, music engulfed the room. Gareth glanced over and the bartender was responsible. Probably to keep conversations more private. Maybe it was just late enough in the day that this was when he normally turned the jukebox on.

And pigs might fly.

The bartender meandered over, making it clear from his stance that he was serving them because they had walked in and had badges, and not because he liked their kind in his joint.

"What'll it be?" he called over the music in a rasp that bordered on rude.

Gareth checked the small section at the bottom of the drinks menu. Seventy-three kinds of beer and hard cider. Eight things without. Half of those were mixers in hard drinks.

"Cola," he said simply.

"Anything in it?" the man almost sneered.

Gareth fixed him with a hard stare.

"Ice," he said in a growling tone.

The Grace blinked and recoiled, ever so slightly.

Two can play at that game, buddy.

"Coffee," Baker added. "Hot and black. Preferable strong enough to stand a knife up in it."

"See what I can do," the Grace man moved away quickly.

Like they were toxic to his physical being, not just his state of mind.

"We eating?" Gareth asked quietly, letting the music cover his tones. "And is it safe to eat here?"

Baker actually let go of her hard-ass persona long enough to give him a genuine smile.

"Very safe," she said in a similar, quiet voice. "Best bacon on the planet, as far as I'm concerned. And don't let Ray's demeanor fool you. He's been a source for me for years. This is all just an act, so feel free to bad cop him as much as you think he deserves."

"Roger that," Gareth acknowledged.

The bartender, Ray apparently, returned a few minutes later with a brown-black glass for Gareth, *with ice*, and a mug of coffee and additives for Baker. She ordered a pulled pork sandwich and a plate-of-bacon sampler. Gareth got a mac and cheese with all the bacon added it.

Seriously, they had bacon made from three different kinds of animals. None of them were pigs. How weird was that?

About the time that more customers started to wander in, the Th'Tarni man paid his bill. He fixed Gareth with a long, appraising stare, and then sauntered out of the room like the King of Brooklyn, robes swishing to show off elaborate embroideries over the front and sleeves.

Gareth decided the man needed a small hat, maybe a kufi or a chador, to make the outfit perfect, but maybe the colorful hair didn't like a lid.

It must be happy hour, Gareth decided. By the time food was delivered, nearly a quarter of the tables in here suddenly had custom, and a Vanir waitress had come on duty.

She wasn't as tough-looking as Baker, nor all that attractive as a woman. Tall and kind dumpy, with too many tattoos visible and a paunch around the middle. She did had a smile for him, every time she caught him looking over, though.

The food was absolutely fantastic. Nothing like what his Mom would have cooked, but his mother wasn't that good of a cook, preferring to pull something out of the freezer and either toss it into the stove or the microwave-emitter. Or better, when Gareth had finally gotten old enough, to have him do it himself.

He looked down and considered licking the bowl clean but his tongue wasn't long enough. If he had gotten any bread, this would have been the time to smear it and pick up any cheese sauce left.

Baker was watching him with mirthful eyes when he looked up, rather at odds with how she had been for the last three days. Gareth studied her carefully, like she was about to ask him a final exam question that counted for twenty-five percent of his grade.

"You're very quiet for a rookie," she observed.

"I'm only a rookie in your department, Baker," he said sincerely. "I've been doing this for almost eight years in mine. Plus, I don't want to screw up your investigation, so I'm trying to listen and learn."

She nodded slowly. The grin hadn't left her eyes, even as the rest of her face fell into seriousness.

The bartender, Ray, approached in his casual, unruffled-by-cops saunter, and placed a small, black binder on the table with a "Whenever you're ready," before he fled back to the bar.

Baker pulled out her wallet from a thigh pouch, extracting a credit card plus something else. Gareth thought he saw her palm a piece of paper and stick it into the binder with her card, closing it and laying it flat on the edge of the table.

Gareth concentrated on what was left of his cola, the music, and the crowd. He could tell the place had gentrified and done so fairly recently. A young Nari woman walked in and one point and asked about a job, but Ray explained that everybody loved this place so much that nobody ever quit. She left, but Gareth could tell she was from the old neighborhood, not the place that it was turning into.

Others at various tables had the feel of businessmen out for a late meeting happy hour beer, or an early dinner before heading out for a night on the town.

Ray came back and retrieved the binder. Gareth thought he detected a ghost of a nod between Ray and Baker, but it might have been his imagination.

Baker didn't say anything, just kept watching over his shoulder.

A few minutes later, Ray emerged from the back and slid the binder in front of Baker, again retreating, almost disdainfully, rather than make small talk.

Baker opened it, fiddled around with the papers inside, and then signed one. Again, Gareth thought he saw her palm a folded piece of paper, but she slid out of the booth quickly and stood before he could ask her about it.

Gareth joined her. In addition to being a cop in this joint, he and Baker were the only two Vanir, other than the waitress. Gareth almost felt like he was walking in a middle school lunch hall, being a head or two taller than almost everyone else.

It might have been his imagination, but there seemed to be a small bubble of silence that rippled along with them as they exited. Each table they had passed had seemed to quiet down for a beat, perhaps as the occupants looked over, before it picked up again.

Back out on the street, Baker retraced her steps with a jaunty stride. Gareth had to stretch his legs just to keep up with her, which was another strange feeling.

"You done good in there, Dankworth," she said after they had gotten two blocks away. "Professional without looking like a rookie. Not letting anything throw you off. Nicely done."

"Why was *Tornado* so important?" he asked, referring to the restaurant behind them.

"Ray, the bartender?" she said. "He owns it, and has for a long time, but it has always been something of an underworld hangout. Neutral ground. Everyone minds their manners in there, and nobody says anything. Probably a quarter of the people in there with us had criminal records, possibly active warrants."

"And you let a place like that exist?" Gareth was aghast.

"Better the devil you know," she replied carefully. "Plus, Ray provides a forum where enemies can meet and work things out. Better than bloodshed. Even cops can have conversations with criminals in there, as long as nobody raids the place."

"What would happen if they got raided?" Gareth asked.

This was so far outside his normal expectations of law enforcement that he couldn't wrap his head around it.

"Everybody would make common cause on the person responsible," she said in a serious voice. "That includes the Constabulary helping the local dons take someone down. It's not the best arrangement, but it keeps a lid on things, at least until we can do more to get rid of the rotten elements in society. That's where you come in."

"Me?" he asked, almost faltering in his stride.

"You," she agreed. "When those two Yuudixtl brought you here, they started a chain of events. Sarzynski overplayed his hand and we nearly broke his organization. Right now, he's spending more time fighting with the underworld than with us. More thugs have been arrested in the last month than the previous year. Crooked prosecutors are suddenly having to go to court because of the increased visibility, and bad guys are going to jail rather than getting off on technicalities and witnesses refusing to cooperate."

"Huh," Gareth replied. "I've been off training and studying, so I didn't see any of this."

"Yes," she said. "We've intentionally kept you in the dark up until now. But Grodray wants you visible now. Being seen with me. Word will get around."

"Who are we looking for?" Gareth said.

Baker stopped walking now and pulled out her comm. She called an auto-taxi and turned to him.

"Anybody that panics when they see you," she said with a predatory smile. "You don't exist, so you're just another Vanir cop. But if they know anything different, I want to put them in a small room and sweat them."

"Okay," Gareth said as the car landed and the door opened.

He followed her inside and buckled his belt.

"And that note you passed Ray?" he continued.

That got him another smile. Gareth wasn't sure he was a ready for an Eveth Baker who smiled a lot.

"I told him I wanted a name," she said, pulling the paper out.

She unfolded it and read it quickly, nodding to herself.

"Now the fun begins," she smiled at him.

Gareth wondered if a shark smiled like that, right before he took a bite out of your leg.

"What's next?" he asked.

"Now we put your superpower to work," she replied.

Gareth really didn't like the sound of that.

POSSIBILITIES

SHE FOUND the closed door intimidating, but Talyarkinash didn't let that stop her. It was unlocked she found, so she pushed it in and entered the room.

From the outside, this was just another tower in Londra, the art capital of *Orgoth Vortai.* And that was all the Grace really cared about. Art.

The actual capital city, where politics got done, was Burich, but that was a sleepy, college town two hundred kilometers up the Temin River. All the action was in Londra, or possibly down in Xarxe, the port city down on the delta where so many musicians had gathered together.

Talyarkinash preferred Londra. Living in a tower with a mix of flats and offices, depending on the floor and the lift tube you used. There was supposedly an indoor arcade filled with shops and restaurants, taking up the first two floors above ground and three below, but she had never seen it.

She was still in police custody, even if everyone was too polite to call her a prisoner to her face. She did not leave this floor without an armed escort, so she could call it what it was.

The room she entered was bland and meaningless. That took significant work on the homeworld of the Grace, since they saw any blank wall as an invitation and excuse to commit art. Someone had consciously undone this room. White walls greeted her, with pedestrian watercolor pictures on two walls, plus a large picture window looking out over the rest of the city. Brown carpets as bland as the walls under her feet.

Senior Constable Jackeith Grodray was already seated across from her, with a stack of folders off to one side. The small room was dominated by a cherry-oak table, Vanir-sized, that worked as either a desk or a conference table for a small group. Another Vanir, this one a woman, was seated on Grodray's right.

Like him, she wore the generic uniform of the Constabulary. They didn't wear names or ranks indicators of any kind, unlike most of the police departments she had ever known, so Talyarkinash had no way of identifying the woman's place in things, except by age.

She had been skinnier when she was younger, that much was obvious, but the Vanir woman was much older now. Not plump, but not the lean huntress the younger version had obviously been. More senior. Possibly into her eighth or tenth decade. Dark hair was now streaked with silver and white. The flesh of her neck was slack, and her eyes and forehead were a maze of wrinkles that Talyarkinash suspected led one to the minotaur, rather than the treasure.

Grodray rose as Talyarkinash closed the door carefully.

"Dr. Talyarkinash Liamssen, this is Dr. Dalton Fitzroy," Grodray introduced the woman. "Prime Investigator with an emphasis on biology and genetics."

Indeed? Talyarkinash had never heard of a Constable with advanced degrees in those sorts of things, but considering the uses to which they were generally put, the woman most likely would have been undercover. Or recruited as a cop later. Or the Constabulary had a secret university where only cops were trained. She made a note to inquire at some point.

Talyarkinash had spent the last decade in her lab ignoring the outside world, getting filthy, stinking rich. Some of it was still hidden away, in places that might not have been discovered yet. Cops like Grodray had already taken the rest of her life apart and confiscated most of her ill-gotten gains.

Fitzroy rose and held out a hand.

"Dr. Liamssen," she said in a pleasant, alto voice.

"Dr. Fitzroy," Talyarkinash replied, shaking the hand.

The woman was almost as tall as Grodray, standing. Talyarkinash willed herself to stillness, expecting the woman to show off her strength by squeezing, but she didn't.

"Please, be seated," Grodray said, putting deed to word.

Talyarkinash found that they had given her a seat that could telescope up enough to make the Vanir-height table comfortable, as long as she didn't mind her feet swinging in the air.

Fitzroy's eyes bored into her as Talyarkinash watched.

"I have studied your work extensively, Dr. Liamssen," the woman cop began suddenly. "It is a pleasure to finally meet you in the flesh."

The tone was nice enough, but Talyarkinash had a feeling that there were layers of cop ugliness concealed underneath. How long had they been trying to pin something on her and failing? How many of her former patients had they found? Or only suspected?

So many of her files had been carefully hidden away and encrypted, but that was before she became a ward of the state and turned them and the decryption key over to Grodray.

Which only made it funnier, since the crime that finally got her taken down might be the most honest thing she had ever done.

"You have me at a disadvantage, then," Talyarkinash replied. "How may I be of service?"

"I would like to talk about Gareth Dankworth," the older cop began. "And then the one known these days as Maximus."

Talyarkinash nodded. As she suspected when she opened the door. She was the expert right now, but the *Accord of Souls*, and very specifically the Constabulary, needed more experts on humans.

It was entirely possible that they would never cram that djinn back into the bottle, three wishes or not.

"You've reviewed my report on Gareth?" she asked carefully. "Both the baseline values and the upgrades?"

"I have," Fitzroy replied. "But those were written for the lay officer. The men and women who do not have a deep understanding of species genetics. Jackeith Grodray, for example."

Talyarkinash nodded again. Entirely accurate, as that was exactly what he had asked her to produce.

"You wish to understand the implications of the baseline?" Talyarkinash hazarded a guess.

"I do," the woman said. "Unlike most of the Constabulary, I have studied humans in great detail, something that brought me out of retirement six months ago when it was feared that a human had escaped into the *Accord of Souls*. Before anyone knew the truth."

"That one Marc Sarzynski, AKA *Maximus*, was born a human on Earth, and illegally transported to *Zathus*," Talyarkinash acknowledged.

"Before being illegally upgraded by myself and the two Yuudixtl scientists known as Morty and Xiomber, no known last names. How well do you understand humans?"

"At one point, research was done to determine if the *Accord of Souls* should send an agent to Earth to introduce a virus that would completely eliminate the species while not destroying other life forms," Fitzroy answered in a calm, bland voice.

Talyarkinash gasped and felt her blood drain to her stomach. Wipe out humans? Just like that?

But it also made a cruel sense. They were not part of the *Accord of Souls*. They were not part of the psionic collective, not bound by non-violence. Such a thing was monstrous, but at the same time logical. And practical, if humans were that dangerous a species.

"And you did the research?" Talyarkinash guessed.

"I did," Fitzroy smiled grimly.

Talyarkinash turned to Grodray with an angry face.

"I am never going to see the light of day again, am I?" she hissed. "I know too much to even see the inside of a prison cell, if you decided you no longer needed me?"

"On the contrary, Talyarkinash Liamssen," Grodray smiled back grimly, still nodding in acknowledgement. "While that was exactly the case five weeks ago, I have had agents paying close attention to your every word and action since then. You are never without some level of surveillance. And you never will be. Make no mistake there. Yes, you know too much. But you have also thrown yourself whole-heartedly into trying to undo the mistakes you had made. Into making Gareth into the monster he became, because you and the other two believed that it might be the only way to save the *Accord* from utter destruction. You have provided the records we needed to arrest more than fifty prominent criminals that you had previously modified to let them escape justice. Those factors also weigh in your favor."

Huh.

"Knowledge is dangerous, Dr. Liamssen," Fitzroy spoke up. "But heart and soul matter. Gareth Dankworth has proven himself to be even more willing than you to face whatever consequences arise, whatever sacrifices he must make. That has impressed even the most surly agents, such as myself."

Talyarkinash kept her eyes on Grodray, aiming her sensitive nose at the messages he was giving off, even unconsciously.

"So I'm not to be just drained like a lemon and tossed onto the ash heap of history?" Talyarkinash snarked.

"According to my cohort," Grodray gestured to Fitzroy, "you might be the single most capable geneticist in the *Accord of Souls* right now. It would be the utter heights of folly not to take advantage of those skills. We have Gareth on our side. They have a rogue in Marc Sarzynski. Dalton Fitzroy is here because we may need more."

"More?"

"How much more capability could we engineer into Gareth?" Fitzroy asked in a serious, scholarly voice. "Should we consider recruiting a second Sky Force officer?"

Talyarkinash laughed before she could smother it or cover her mouth.

"If you have studied baseline humans, how would you rank Gareth Dankworth on their scale?" Talyarkinash asked the older woman.

"In the top one percent physically." Fitzroy replied. "In the top four percent mentally. I've actually been able to study his records from Earth Force, to compare them to his current form."

"How?" Talyarkinash gasped. "No. Don't tell me. It's obvious you must have spies and systems in place, if you need to keep this close of a track on them. Gareth was using fourteen percent of his genetic capabilities as a human, the moment before I hit him with the six transformation virus injections. Marc Sarzynski, according to Gareth, was so close to him in all ways as to be identical, save for hair color and ethical standards."

"Fourteen?" It was Grodray's turn to gasp. "Where did you take him to?"

"Roughly thirty-one percent," Talyarkinash replied. "I haven't been given access to the quality of lab I had at home, or my full notes, to nail it down closer than that. Gareth is now the strongest, fastest, and toughest Vanir you will probably ever meet, excepting only Sarzynski. Both are in the top one hundred for intelligence, but Maximus has an edge there because I purposefully kept Gareth on this side of a line that frequently risks significant mental instability in humans."

"What about the dragon?" Fitzroy asked, leaning forward and staring intently.

"Gareth's idea," she admitted. "He wanted something that apparently instills fear in humans, and would probably do the same in the *Accord of Souls*. He wanted a symbol. So the transformation makes him hexapodal and grants him scales as a layer of dermal armor. The costume I built for him uses his own DNA as a signature, so that it will become part of the transformation and undo later."

"He can fly and breath fire," Fitzroy noted. "What are the limitations there?"

"I don't know," Talyarkinash admitted with an honest shrug.

"Why not?" Grodray leaned into the conversation. "How is that possible?"

"Gareth's abilities tap into a vast, unconscious pool of human psionic energy," Talyarkinash said. "I gave him the power to reshape himself as he needed, but I can no more explain how it works than you could describe blue to a man born blind, Constable. She might be a better expert there."

"Fitzroy?"

It was Talyarkinash's turn to sit back and watch. And it was fascinating, watching the woman pick and choose her words carefully.

"I suspect Liamssen speaks the bald truth, Jack," she said.

Talyarkinash had never heard the man called by the diminutive of his first name, which told her how close these two must have worked in the past. Teacher and pupil?

"Gareth once told me his limitations might be his imagination," Talyarkinash offered. It was like tossing gasoline onto a fire, to watch the two of them flinch.

"And Maximus?" Grodray asked.

"The same," she concluded. "Except that all I did was modify him into a top of the line Vanir physically. Morty and Xiomber did the mental work, so you'll have to ask, if you can locate them. I went well beyond the basics with Gareth. There's no reason another geneticist worth her egg couldn't do the same."

Grodray reached out a hand and opened the forgotten files, flipping through it until he found the page he wanted.

"Both you and Gareth have referred to the form as a Star Dragon," Grodray asked carefully. "What does that mean?"

"I used his terminology, Grodray," Talyarkinash replied. "But the basic form of the dragon could survive in space, at least as long as he could hold his breath, which we have not tested extensively. And fly there, if I understand things correctly. We haven't yet tested that either."

"Fly? In space?" Fitzroy asked. "How?"

"Again, the power is psionic, and not physical," Talyarkinash said. "Those wings could not lift his mass, nor carry it to those speeds, using simply physics. He does it, himself."

"And we have not tested it?" Grodray probed.

"We have not," she smiled. "He and I have been in custody since the moment his powers manifested."

"Huh," was all the man said.

Abruptly, he folded up his notes, gathered the folders in his hand, and stood.

"I will leave you two to talk, then," he said. "You'll both nerd out so quickly that I would become lost, but I look forward to talking to both of you tomorrow and learning your conclusions."

He left with a nod and Talyarkinash found herself alone with the older cop. This woman was still at least as dangerous right now as Eveth Baker had ever been on her best day, even as old as she was.

But Talyarkinash was here to save the galaxy, as weird as that would have seemed to her six months ago.

"What would you like to know?" she asked the woman.

HABERDASHER

GARETH RECOGNIZED the type of room, but this wasn't the same one he had visited with Morty and Xiomber. That had been a tower on the other side of town, if he remembered the layout of the streets correctly. It had all been culture shock at the time, and then meeting Keelee and getting tasted by a Grace for the first time.

He still shivered at that memory. Grace were weird, with tentacles instead of hair and vertically-slitted eyes, like a Nari, but otherwise could pass as a human, if they wore a hood.

But those tentacles…

What must it be like to be able to smell, taste, and touch with dozens of acutely-sensitive fingers at the same time? No wonder they all seemed to grow up to be artists, to live in a world that rich with sensory input.

Gareth had followed Baker into the room. It was big. Twenty meters on a side, with five meter ceilings, which was rare, even for Vanir offices. Two sofas on one side. A triple-mirror on the other.

This only differed from Jorghen's shop in that there was an desk with a computer console making the third point of a triangle. And a young Grace officer operating it. He looked up with a smile as they entered.

"Constable Baker," he nodded. "What can I do for you today?"

"Explorer Dankworth needs to go undercover, here in Londra," she said, gesturing for Gareth to walk closer to the man. "I need him to look like a mid-range punk, capable of fitting in with a party crowd while still looking like a tough guy. He'll be armed, so put an ankle holster into the mix."

"Fop or grinder?" the man asked, losing Gareth in the process. "Londra's nightlife is running down those two paths, this year. By next year, historical reenactments will be the rage, according to the fashion designers I'm in touch with."

Baker surprised Gareth by turning to study him, green eyes squinted in appraisal.

"Let's go grinder, right now," she replied. "But keep his measurements in the system in case we need to kick him out a second outfit on the fly."

"Will do," the Grace officer said. "Explorer, if you could move to the scanners?"

Gareth complied. Unlike Joghen's system, this one didn't have the light at the top that apparently looked inside his brain.

Gareth stopped and turned to the officer.

"Last time, there was a light," he said, rapping on the top of the center mirror. "Right here."

"You've done this before?" Baker was suddenly standing right there. "Been hard scanned for a new outfit? Where?"

"Here in Londra," Gareth said. "When we passed through *Orgoth Vortai* on the way to *Hurquar*. I thought I included that in my report?"

"You did," she nodded. "But I didn't realize that it had brain-scanned you fully."

"Is that a problem?" Gareth asked. "He pulled the outfit I wanted out of my subconscious."

"Do you remember the name of the place?" she pressed. "The name of the tailor?"

"Jorghen," Gareth said. "Last name unknown. Never saw him, as his console was in a different room and we talked over the house comm. Tower somewhere on the south side of town."

"Interesting," she said, reaching for her comm. "You get done and I'll talk to Grodray. Somebody might need to have a chat with this tailor."

Gareth nodded, a little lost, and turned back to the mirrors. He stood perfectly still as the other agent worked his controls, until there was an image of Gareth in all three screens. Instead of steel-blue, he was wearing mostly black, highlighted with emerald green.

Black, shiny, leather boots came up almost to his knees, done with green laces. Knickerbocker shorts met them in the middle over black socks, the pants baggy but not jodhpurs in cut. These used a black and green tartan pattern with a little gold thrown in. Looking close, the fabric appeared to be a really nice wool, like a Scottish Laird might have worn.

The jacket was a blazer, sort of, except it had poofy patch pockets attached to the front instead of them being inside slits. Three buttons covered the front with a narrow lapel, but only the middle button was hooked. Instead of a dress shirt with a tie, he was wearing a black, knit pullover that tucked into the pants behind a brown, leather belt.

"Where's the holster go?" Baker asked abruptly, bringing Gareth back to the job at hand.

"Tucked into the bottom of the shorts," the Grace replied. "Accessible via the clasp that hold the knee hitch closed and generally concealed by the pleat and gather on the thighs. Are you right handed or left, Dankworth?"

"Right," he said, watching the Grace type something into the keyboard.

Gareth stopped himself from speaking. If this was a grinder, what must a fop look like? He had been expecting leather with chrome spikes, or something equally outrageous. This was almost something he could take golfing, if he could get the man to add threads for spikes to the bottom of the boots.

And he looked good.

But the best part was the new beret. It was huge, almost a tam-o-shanter in size, done in a coarse, black wool, with a gold medallion on the left side and a pair of feathers poking up that looked like they came from Stellar's Jays, bright, fierce blue.

"You like?" Baker asked, suddenly standing right next to him.

"I do," Gareth replied honestly. "Rugged but distinguished. I could wear that outfit many places without being self-conscious."

"Good," she smiled wickedly. "Because you're going to be bait."

Gareth suppressed a shudder at the way her voice sounded.

But who ever asked the worm how he felt?

ON THE RUN

"THOUGHTS?" Morty asked as the auto-taxi deposited them on the sidewalk and bounced back into the sky.

"We stay away from any spot where we took Gareth," Xiomber said. "Past that, we need a roof and I've got the munchies."

Morty nodded. Jorghen hadn't been his favorite tailor in Londra, but he had needed to keep Gareth's scent away from the woman who normally dressed him and his brother. He could imagine what it would have been like introducing her to Gareth.

And he would miss his favorite tea house, but the poor girl who had waited on them had probably been utterly traumatized by the time the cops got done with her. Seeing them again would likely bring it all back in a screaming flash that would end up with he and his egg-brother under arrest.

"Right," Morty said, turning right and heading east down the street. Downtown Londra was commercial, but there were all sorts of places on the east end that got deep into the Bohemian side of things. Just the place for a couple of renegade physicists to hide.

A bus dropped them at the edge of a park. The weather was passable nice today. Just warm enough that people were outside, but not warm enough to encourage the kinds of nude debauchery Morty had seen around here in the middle of summer.

Still, his favorite hot dog stand was doing a brisk business. He got five, figuring Xiomber would stop at two, like he normally did, and they'd have to hit the pastry shop on the far side of the park afterwards, as always. The coffee was bitter dark, but Stanz didn't like tea and Morty didn't want to stand in line for any of the other shops or stands.

They ended up not far from the water fountain, leaned back against a couple of rocks in a bushy area with a good view of the ball fields and generally out of sight. The fountain was off and the fields were abandoned right now, but both would change within a week or three.

They ate in silence, watching the few students studying and a couple of young mothers with strollers, but the park was amazingly empty. Just the way Morty liked it. So much harder for someone to sneak up on them.

Morty checked his watch as a private sedan landed clear across the way. Omerlon's people might be cut-rate punks, but they did understand punctuality. Three people piled out, two Grace and a Warreth, and started across the field, leaving the vehicle and the driver over in the parking lot.

From their seats, it would be almost impossible for the guys coming to spot them, which was how Morty preferred it. Smuggling themselves across the galaxy was enough of a pain in the tail. Trying to get guns from a reputable fence at the same time was too much.

Plus, Omerlon didn't have any reason to hate them, as far as Morty knew. Nobody outside Sarzynski's gang even knew the new boss had been human once, not counting the cops, let alone knew that he and his egg-brother had been responsible for it. Better for everyone to keep it that way.

Nope, hopefully this was just a job interview, and they could settle in and do nice, simple, criminal things for the folks around here for a while, at least until he or Xiomber figured out a way to turn themselves into the Constables, or somebody actually managed to take Maximus down and they might be safe.

That happened, and Morty could see retiring to a nice desert somewhere, living off the ill-gotten gains of a disreputable life of crime without having to look over his shoulder constantly for assassins.

The two Grace thugs pulled up short and took up a spot off to one side. Visible, but not close enough to listen. The Warreth moved to the edge of the fountain and sat.

Morty turned to Xiomber.

"Last chance to change your mind," he said.

"Oh, hell no it isn't," Xiomber chirped. "I got lots of chances to sell your stupid ass down the line and set myself up as a king."

Morty smiled.

"You aren't rich enough to buy the right babes, Xiomber," he sneered merrily. "Best you could do it rent them by the hour."

"And they'll still charge me half what they would you," Xiomber countered. "Let's do this. The dogs were good, but I want a turnover now."

Morty shrugged and rose. He emerged from the bushes first, with Xiomber close behind. Like the Warreth, they were wearing light jackets and heavy dungarees today, but everyone kept hands in the open, like polite thugs meeting in public.

"You Xiomber?" the Warreth asked as they got to speaking distance.

"Nope. Morty," he said, pointing over his shoulder. "That's Xiomber. You Danzeekar?"

"Correct," the Warreth replied.

The two Grace appeared to relax a little, turning each a little sideways to make sure nobody else suddenly decided to join this shindig, like, say, cops. Or assassins.

Morty had no doubts that all three were armed, but that was just part of the game these days.

He walked close enough to talk, but didn't feel like climbing up on the bench.

"So we're out of work and looking," Morty said.

"That's the message I got," Danzeekar replied. "Why is that?"

"Because Maximus is nuts and getting worse," Morty snapped. "Turning into a killer. Smart money's getting out now, while all the parts are still attached."

"So, free agents?" the Warreth asked haughtily.

"It's you or the cops, pretty boy," Morty sneered. "Nobody else has enough moxie to keep us safe from assassins. You need a couple of high-end physicists in the organization?"

"Rumors say that you two also do genetic work," the birdman observed in a neutral voice. "That true?"

"Yup," Morty smiled. "We did some of the upgrades on Maximus, along with Talyarkinash Liamssen."

"What kinds of upgrades?"

The beak was pointed this way now. Morty smiled as the headcrest popped up to full extension. He had the guy's attention and interest, finally. Dumb-ass punk.

"That's above your pay grade, pal," Morty said. "And sure as hell not something to talk about in the middle of a park in the middle of the day, *capiche?*"

"So you want to come in from the cold?" Danzeekar said. "Just like that?"

"We got information your boss will find interesting," Morty said. "Plus our skills and experience. You make us a good offer on salary and benefits, and we can do a deal. You empowered to negotiate at that level, or should we talk to the big guy?"

Morty held his breath while the Warreth considered. They really didn't have a lot of leverage, but Omerlon's folks wouldn't know how hard he was bluffing.

Hopefully.

And wouldn't call his bluff, either, because most of this was bluff.

"You got bonafides?" the man asked.

Bingo.

Morty nearly laughed out loud. Pretty boy was just a messenger, sure, but high enough ranking to dicker. Bonafides were secrets presented in good faith. That first taste of the cake before you bought the rest.

"Yeah," Morty said as he stuffed his hands into his front pockets. "We upgraded Maximus to a full genius intelligence level as part of the other things we did to him. Liamssen wasn't involved in that part."

"How the hell did you do that?" Danzeekar was shocked. "He's Vanir. They're already about as fixed as you can get."

Morty just smiled. Kinda rocked back and forth with his hands in his front pockets. Not *quite* mocking the guy.

"Oh, and the only other person who knows any of what we did?" he continued. "Talyarkinash Liamssen? She's in Constabulary custody, and has been for several weeks. I imagine, from my own sources, that she's spilled everything she knows. You saw how fast *Hurquar* has been dismantled in the last month, right? Wanna talk yet?"

"Yeah," the Warreth's headcrest bobbed three times. "You got a number we can reach you? Boss will want a sit-down after I talk to him."

"Nope," Morty said. "You leave a message with Stanz, the hot dog vendor. He's an old comrade of ours. I'll check in with him later and see where you'd like to meet. Dinner at an expensive joint, reasonably public, would do nicely."

Morty turned and walked back into the bushes. Xiomber was kinda crab-walking, to keep an eye on the Grace, but they made it to cover.

There was a little creek tucked in down there. Morty led his partner to it and skittered along the shore as fast as his stubby legs would allow.

When they emerged from the park ten minutes later, that sedan was gone, so Morty picked a side street with some traffic and headed north, Xiomber walking about forty meters behind so they didn't appear to be together, to a watcher looking for a pair of Yuudixtl males.

They settled into the pastry shop for turnovers and more coffee. Better, but still not tea.

"Think they'll go for it?" Xiomber asked around a mouthful of blueberry jam threatening to run down his front.

"Hope so," Morty replied. "They really are our last chance. After that, we either have to go straight, or go to the cops."

LIFEBLOOD OF THE GRACE

GARETH CLOSED the book and placed it atop a pile of three others on the sidetable next to his comfy reading chair. Two days and four books on the topic wasn't going to make him an expert on art, but he could at least have a reasonable conversation at the event without looking like a complete fool.

Plus Grodray had brought in an older man, a Grace of some note as an art historian, to prep him for tonight. Apparently, the older a Grace got, the longer their tentacles grew, so he must have been ancient, since some of his had come down to nearly his waist when they hung still.

And he knew everyone that was going to be at the show. This was *Orgoth Vortai*, so that would be critical. Gareth wasn't native to the planet, but even he had been impressed. The *Accord Ball* was the social event of the season, and everyone who was anyone on the planet had been trying to get tickets to attend.

It was a fundraiser, so the major players either bought seats, or an entire table, for astronomical sums that supported the *Accord* Hall of Arts, the gravitational center of Grace culture. Lesser players were admitted as far as the front hall, where everyone could watch the beautiful people arrive, and then they were allowed into the hall itself after dinner, where they could mingle.

Rumor had it that the deals done every year at this event represented a serious percentage of the planetary output. At least in total cash.

How the Constabulary had gotten three tickets, Gareth didn't know, but obviously, strings had been pulled. Or they had the cash for something like this in their operating budget.

Or they just sent a few officers undercover every year on general principle.

He checked the time on his nightstand and decided he was close enough to ready. A quick look in the mirror hung on the wall to confirm everything, and he stuffed his new pocketcomm into the breast pocket of his blazer. The palm-sized stun pistol was on his thigh, hidden away inside the pant leg. He picked his beret up off the nightstand and went to the door.

He was supposed to wear the beret inside, but that just didn't fit with how he was raised, so it could wait until he was in the auto-car.

Grodray and Baker were down in the Operations Center when he arrived, chatting with Talyarkinash. Interestingly, while he was in the so-called grinder outfit, undercover, both of them where in their uniforms. Baker had even gone so far as to wear her outer tunic, like she was taking this sort of thing quite seriously.

Both women turned to him when he entered and gave him a critical once-over. Actually, all seven women in sight did the same, but Gareth tried to ignore that fact. And the intense interest and smiles on those faces.

"Beret?" Talyarkinash asked, so Gareth put it on, draping it just right.

"Yes," she said a moment later. "You'll do. Quite nicely."

Gareth blushed at her tone. It was not entirely friendly. Or it was, but not just that. No, he was the center of a lot of attentions, right now, like a beautiful woman who had walked into a room full of sailors who had been to space for too long.

Uncomfortable. Unpleasant turnabout. He would have made a note to say something about that sort of behavior when he got home, but he quashed that thought before it ever took shape.

There was no home. Not anymore. There was the *Accord of Souls*. And whatever he did to fit in here. For the rest of his life.

Gareth found himself standing at attention, like this was an inspection, so he forced himself to relax. It was an inspection, and he had apparently passed, from the looks, but he wasn't being graded.

Much.

"We'll depart first," Grodray announced simply, coming over to stand close.

He was a tall man, but skinny. Standing next to Gareth just emphasized his own, massive bulk.

Gareth nodded.

"You just smile and make small talk, Gareth," he said with a friendly grin. "Nobody knows you here except us, so it makes a good way to quietly introduce you to *Accord* society in a way that doesn't require a lot of legend-building on your part. You be aloof and mysterious. Talk art as if you'll be writing all this up for some magazine under a pseudonym later, and everyone will be polite."

"Then what?" he asked, still a little fuzzy on the overall picture.

"Then we'll see who nibbles at the bait," Baker said. "Nobody knows who you are, so you can make a whole range of new connections that can turn into contacts later."

"Okay," Gareth agreed. "I get that, but why don't I have business cards to hand out when they ask? I'm really just supposed to give them my first name and a comm box?"

"It forces them to perk up," Grodray said. "Makes you a galactic man of mystery, especially as an unknown who could afford a seat at this table, and had the connections to get in. Everyone will want to know who you are. Make them work at it."

"Okay," he shrugged. "Never really done undercover work, but I can at least talk art."

"And on *Orgoth Vortai*, that is all that matters, Gareth," Talyarkinash smiled up at him, reaching out a hand to flatten his lapel a little and run her hand down the wool of his blazer. Maybe a little too long. "I can't wait for you to tell me all the details later."

"And that's our cue," Grodray said. "Your vehicle will arrive in ten minutes, so you should arrive just as the red carpet starts to get interesting. Remember, aloof and mysterious."

Gareth nodded and watched them head to the door. He had his pocketcomm, his wallet, and his stunner. If he was lucky, he wouldn't embarrass himself, or the nice man who had walked him so carefully through so much art history.

All he had now was that and those four books of modern art history and biography he had largely memorized.

Hopefully, it would be enough.

THE RED CARPET

IN ONE OF the books the older gentleman had suggested Gareth read, walking the red carpet was occasionally referred to as "The Pole Dance," which conjured up images of a scantily-clad woman doing all manner of athletic maneuvers on and with a floor-to-ceiling brass pole on a stage. Similar to burlesque, but far more physical in nature and requiring a great deal more effort to make look effortless.

And a little seedy, when you got right down to it. Tonight's arrival, too.

The auto-taxi deposited him at the curb behind a massive, hopefully-only-gold-*plated* limousine that delivered a well-dressed Grace and his barely-covered companion. They walked up the red carpet and were politely accosted at each of several reporter station, with cameras rolling. Famous people. Gareth hadn't seen either face to be sure, but he had narrowed the options down to about four, all of them important.

He himself emerged to a flash of lights and whistles, but the man holding the vehicle's door made it clear that he was to simply amble inside, in full view of everyone, but not stop and chat with any of the reporters, unless specifically accosted.

Aloof and mysterious.

And really, freaking self-conscious, but he mustered himself under the gravity of the scene and strode forward in a relaxed manner. He could ignore the various whistles and cat-calls emerging from the dimly-lit crowd behind the barriers and holding up cameras.

Right?

Five reporters, each interviewing someone. Gareth breezed by them at a slow cadence, glancing right and left, but not seeing anything outside his imagination.

Four identical Nari men, dressed almost as silly as the Pope's Swiss Guard, defended the main hall from the riff-raff. The looks of appraisal sent his way were more along the lines of checking out the guy that had just walked into the wrong bar, to see if anybody really felt like doing anything about it. He had a head and at least one hundred pounds on the any of them, so they smiled.

"Ticket, please?" the closest one asked as Gareth approached.

He pulled the ornate card from an inner pocket and handed it over.

"Gareth?" the man asked in obvious confusion. "No last name?"

"That's right," he smiled ambiguously.

Let people fill in their own stories, Baker and Grodray and others had told him, time and again. That was the key to undercover work. Keep it all vague and you don't have to track your lies later.

"Very good, sir," the Nari handed the card back and stepped to one side.

And with that, Gareth was in the Great Hall itself.

Because of the Chaa, and their lasting impact on the culture, everything was huge. The building was an eclectic mix of Ionic and Gothic that shouldn't have worked, but did. White marble flecked and striped with precious metals held up the roof and covered the floor.

The ceiling in here was forty meters at the peak of the low-pitched roof, with colorful banners hanging from everywhere and idly drifting in the breezes generated by open doors and the air conditioning system. The red carpet continued a four-meter-wide path up a flight of twenty, deep stairs. A Vanir could walk them individually, but anyone shorter would take two steps on each.

At the top of the stairs was an impressive bronze bust, fifteen feet tall, of a cyclopean Grace, tentacles in wild disarray and one, angry eyeball scowling out of the middle of his forehead.

Gareth checked the small placard at the bottom as he approached. He had seen pictures of the enormous head, but had never realized how big "*The Art Critic*" was in real life. Or what a lovely play on words it was, subtly tweaking all the artists in here and their fiercest enemies.

It put a smile on his face as he entered the atrium of the space at the top of the stairs, trying not to ogle the people around him. There were seventeen species represented in the *Accord of Souls*, and all of them appeared to be present tonight, in an array of outfits that left him too stunned to even comprehend, let alone describe.

Except there was a lot of skin visible, on both male and female, as well as fur, scales, and bark, depending on the direction he turned. Gareth concentrated on keeping his mouth from falling open, and headed in the direction of the open bar on the side wall.

He wasn't there to be noticed, unlike many of the people around him. If pressed, he could only name on sight perhaps two dozen, at best, of the three hundred or so that would be joining him for dinner. Many would be offended at his ignorance, however unintentional, so he would keep to himself.

The bartender was a tall, skinny, Grace woman. Lanky and over six feet tall, she was probably used to looking down on her patrons. The expression on her face as she turned to her right to serve him was sour.

She stared at the center of his chest for a moment, and then leaned back to see him smiling above her. Her own smile seemed to emerge from behind the dour shell.

"Sir?" she asked, voice turning hopeful, after the gruffness she had sent after the previous victim.

"Red wine," Gareth said simply. "The house blend is good enough for now."

Gareth had no way of guessing which of the dozen bottles in front of him he might like, and wasn't going to more than sip this glass anyway.

She overpoured him anyway and handed the glass up. Gareth took it with a nod.

"Thank you, ma'am," he said, turning away before she pursued any conversation.

He did not understand the effect he had on women, but there was no denying it. Gareth knew he was considered attractive, but had never seemed all that impressive, back home.

Or maybe he just never paid any attention? There was only one woman for him, even if he might never see her again.

Gareth took a sip and meandered into the slowly-thickening crowd.

———

"NO, IT'S JUST HIDEOUS," Gareth overheard two Grace, and older man and slightly-younger woman, well-dressed if conservative, discussing a painting that was hanging on a pillar.

Back home, art was something you observed from a safe distance, frequently behind a velvet rope, with the picture itself perhaps protected by a sealed, transparent container against aging.

But this was *Orgoth Vortai*, and these were the Grace. That was far too pedestrian.

One approached the painting and leaned close enough that a dozen or more head tentacles could touch the picture, absorbing a full-sensory experience of smell, taste, and texture to go along with the light. Many other installations in here included a musical element as well, so all senses would be engaged.

To allow the pitifully-under-sensed (the Grace's occasional term for the rest of the *Accord*), there was a small table to one side, near the picture. Sets-of-three shot glasses held a red, an umber, and a green liquid: just a taste of each, with a number indicating the order to consume them.

Gareth stepped to one side of the two Grace, still arguing, and studied the painting itself. The oil appeared to be a land- and sky-scape at sunset, perhaps. Fierce crimsons bled up into salmony-orange and down into violets, but the over-all image was scarlet in nature.

Gareth nodded to himself and emptied a red glass into his mouth first. It held barely enough to give him a taste, but that was the point. Umber followed quickly, and then green.

One held the three in one's mouth for a moment, swishing them around like a *sommelier* at a good wine, before swallowing. It was a complicated taste, almost sour at the outset fading down to an earthy sweetness after a few seconds.

"Mm-hmm," Gareth hummed to himself.

The nearer Grace turned to him.

"Utterly atrocious, am I correct?" he almost demanded.

Gareth checked the image of the artist herself by leaning well forward, just to make sure, before he leaned back and turned to the two critics. They didn't appear to be man and wife, although they might be of a similar age.

And he had absolutely no idea if the picture was any good. Or bad. Or how a Grace might experience it differently from a Vanir, or an Elohynn, like the one he saw over there.

But it didn't matter, as the old master had explained to him this morning. Art was art.

Gareth fell back on the best line the man had taught him, for exactly situations like this.

"I like the way she exhausts her reds," he opined breezily. "Refreshing."

Both gawked, and then leaned close to taste it again, afraid they had missed something terribly important that a Vanir, no less, had caught.

Gareth giggled privately to himself and departed before he was called on to explain the random remark. As if he could.

Art was art.

He made his way to the next installation, wondering what any of it meant.

SHOWTIME

"SERIOUSLY?" Morty demanded. "The *Accord Ball?* That bastard wants us to hang around outside like paparazzi for him, and he'll mingle with us after dinner? Screw that shit."

Xiomber shrugged. He handed the letter over to Morty and took a step back. Likely moving out of range before he got an angry fist to the snout.

Morty controlled his temper and read the note. Yes, that was exactly what it said. He and his egg-brother had tickets to the after party, while Omerlon would be at the banquet itself, being seen and famous.

"Hey," Xiomber said to get his attention. "There's another card in here. It's for a tailor who owes the man a favor. We're supposed to call him and get fitted for something nice, on Omerlon's dime."

Morty found that at least mollifying. Power, showing itself off. Omerlon was one of the power players on this planet. He was making that point, aggravating as it was.

But if he was willing to throw in a new suit as an enticement, Morty was willing to be enticed. He had worn nothing but grungy jeans and T-shirts for so long he might not even own anything nice enough for a public event like this. So even if they didn't end up getting a job offer they liked, they'd come out ahead.

Not that he'd be able to wear it in prison, but at that point, maybe something else would come up.

"Fine," Morty groused. "Anybody we know?"

"Nope," Xiomber said helpfully. "Want me to look him up?"

"Yes, please," he said. "Don't want to end up looking like a clown here."

"More like a clown?" Xiomber asked serenely.

Morty growled at the Yuudixtl. Xiomber laughed and pulled out a pad, typing furiously with one hand.

"Let's see," Xiomber said after a few moments. "Shit's gone really weird, this season, with an emphasis on flesh and glitter, if I read the guy's brochure correctly."

"We're scientists," Morty reminded his egg-brother. "We're supposed to look like nerds. Dark and severe would be my preference."

"Yeah, you ain't got the gams to pull off an outfit like this," Xiomber turned the screen to show him something a self-respecting Nari woman might hesitate to wear to the beach, let alone a ball. "We doing this?"

"Make the call and set us up an appointment," Morty groused some more. "I'll find us a place close for dinner reservations. Might as well try and make this stupid charade work."

Seriously? They wanted a quiet, sit-down kind of meeting to talk turkey with Omerlon, and the man wanted a spectacle.

Were all the criminals these days turning into congenital idiots?

DINNER

"GARETH?" the Borren woman seated on his left asked as she turned away from a conversation on her other side. "That's it? No last name."

"More mysterious that way," he offered, turning away from the overweight, middle-aged Vanir guy on his right that had wanted to talk about investing in art futures.

Whatever that was.

"I see," the woman leaned a little closer.

Borren were even taller than Vanir, so it made sense that they would be seated at the same table, itself a foot taller than normal. And Gareth had only seen a few of her type, and only at a distance, and not actually talked to one, so he couldn't tell her age at a glance.

She wore a headpiece in turquoise that sat on her bald skull like an ancient Chinese temple, as much as he could find words to compare it, looking at her. The species was apparently hairless, with spots bigger than freckles on their pate, as well as interesting color patterns like a giraffe trailing down all the parts of her shoulders, chest, and stomach that were naked flesh.

Which was most of them.

Twin ridges of bone emerged from the sides of the large, flat nose and flared away over the eyes, providing shadows that looked rather like eyebrows. Her eyes were simply huge, at least twice the size of Gareth's, with the points at the inner bottom and outer top corners of an invisible square.

She wore a dress that seemed to cover her back and encase the long, giraffe-like neck, covering only the tops of her shoulders and her arms down to the wrists. White, flexible, plastic sheets had been wrapped around her thorax like an open-fronted corset, resting on her hip bones and coming up to more or less cover her breasts from the sides.

More or less.

The fleshy top of her belly button was pierced, with a ruby pendant dangling in the hole. And if he was understanding the physics involved, he had to guess that her nipples were pierced as well, connected by a silver or platinum chain, hidden by the open-front corset device, connecting them. Not a question that he sought to answer, thank you kindly.

Gareth cleared his throat, sipped his wine, and concentrated on her face. It was weird, but looking up kept him from looking down. The way she leaned towards him and seemed to flex her long torso didn't help his state of mind.

"And what do you do, Gareth-with-no-name?" she purred warmly.

Gareth fell back as hard as he could on the training and books. Those had been for this question, but the role-play he had done to get ready had been with fully-clothed agents, many of them men.

This was…

"I'm a writer," he offered, as blandly as he could. "Mostly magazine work."

"Anything I'd know?" her gravity seemed to be off, or her balance. She kept easing closer, like a tide coming in.

"All written under a pen name," he tried to relax. "Fewer enemies that way."

"You must have friends, to get this invitation," she smiled easily with soft, blue lips.

"Favors for important people," Gareth suggested. "And I'll write this all up tomorrow."

"And when will it be in print?" she was almost breathing on him now. It was like dating that volleyball player in junior high school, when she had been almost a head taller than him, too.

"Who's to say," Gareth shrugged, using that as an opportunity to eke out a little more distance.

If he wasn't careful, she'd be in his lap very shortly.

Not what Constable Baker had planned for him tonight.

Hopefully.

The steward rescued him, delivering a mixed salad and refreshing the bread bowl. Another one filled water and took drink orders.

Gareth had no idea what the salad was. And didn't really care. The colors were probably fake anyway, or they grew pink carrots here. Didn't matter. He used the fork in one hand and a hunk of bread in the other to defend his turf like the Russians at Moscow facing the invaders. Any of them.

The woman seemed more bemused than insulted. The man on Gareth's other side was still bending the ear of the man on his far side about investment opportunities and tax breaks.

All conversation seemed, of universal volition, to subside for an hour, replaced by the tinkling of knives and folks on plates and glasses being set down loud enough to clunk. Salad was followed by a cold soup that would have been proudly served by any Ukrainian café in the solar system.

Gareth hadn't ordered the main course. Apparently, that had been handled by whoever got him the invitation. They had selected the beef. He hoped it was beef. Now was not the time to ask. Nor was this the place. The sauce was lavender. And rather sweet/sour in the way of certain Chinese dishes he had encountered in his travels.

Gareth pretended he had a boneless ribeye in a redwine reduction, and attacked it with gusto. And it was close enough, with the occasional sip of red wine and some buttered bread in between bites.

When the stewards removed his plate and filled his coffee cup, Gareth found the woman on his left suddenly much closer than he remembered her chair being before.

"Diệu Ahn," she introduced herself. "Since we don't have last names tonight."

Gareth shivered, but only inside, he hoped. That sounded like too much of an invitation on her part. Letting her hair down, although she didn't have any, just exquisite, tiny ears and that huge headpiece.

Gareth lifted the coffee cup like it was a shield, holding his left elbow out in such a way as to hopefully keep her at arm's length. But then the other patrons began to rise and make their way towards the front of the building, from the auditorium at the back where dinner had been served.

Before he was fully standing, Diệu Ahn had her arm wrapped around his.

"I think you're one of those fashion writers that always goes by a secret identity at these sorts of things," she murmured down to him. "That or a secret agent. What do you think, Gareth?"

"Something like that," he replied evenly. It was even true, more or less.

Just not the parts she was expecting.

"Have you seen the entire hall?" she continued, leading him towards a grand flight of stairs he had ignored earlier, when he had been scouting the people more than the terrain.

These steps were more polished white marble, overlaid with a burgundy carpet that bullnosed at each step.

"I have not," he replied.

Gareth felt like a dog on a leash, or one with his head out the window, as she politely led him up the stairs. That she was at least seven inches taller or more, depending on the heels below that dress, didn't help. Everything about her was turquoise and white tonight, except her skin, which was too pink to be alabaster, and those freckles, which might cover her entire body in geometric shapes.

Gareth really, REALLY didn't want to do any math tonight.

The mezzanine was lovely. Gareth regretted not coming up here earlier. The view was perfect to observe all the beautiful people below, while keeping them at a polite and impersonal distance. He and Diệu Ahn shared the balcony with a number of other folks, some he recognized from dinner, and a large number of photographers making their living. Steward with trays came by, and she snagged them both glasses of what Gareth guessed were champagne, from the color and bubbles.

She giggled as they tickled her nose. It was a pretty, girlish, distracting sound that kept Gareth's attention wandering to places it had no business going.

Pippa. Only Pippa.

At the far end of the hall, the flood gates had apparently been breached. A wave of species poured into the grand hall from the front, those people with second-class tickets to the after-party.

Dinner had been showy and self-congratulatory, as various awards had been given out while everyone chowed down. Now came the grand event. Everyone coming in with the tides had a camera in one hand. Drones were forbidden indoors tonight, and nobody wanted to miss anything.

Diệu Ahn still had her free hand around his elbow. Gareth watched her set her glass down on the wide, marble balustrade and reach inside her corset, thankfully below her breast instead of across it. She did something and withdrew her hand, reaching towards him.

Gareth nearly flinched. He wasn't sure what to expect, but his mind kept seeing a giant spider in her hand. His nerves were apparently shot.

Instead, she had pulled a business card from in pocket inside the corset-thingee. Rather like his blazer had pockets inside, but his were empty.

She leaned in close and languidly slid her hand inside his blazer, searching for his pocket for several seconds in the wrong places with a smile and a quiet, coquettish giggle. Finally, she dropped the card and withdrew her hand. Gareth's breath was short.

"Got something for me?" she purred, twisting her torso around a little to make it obvious where he might put such a thing.

Inwardly, he said a small prayer of thanks to Constable Baker. Even accidentally.

"My, uh, boss actually forbid me from carrying any tonight," Gareth replied dejectedly, at least he hoped it sounded that way. "Under threat of extreme sanction. And she was serious."

"She?" Diệu Ahn looked interested in a potential rival to battle.

"Complete and total hardass editor," Gareth freelanced the relationship. It sounded close enough, from what he had seen of newspapers on the video tube. "If I wasn't bound under a tight contract, I'd shop my services elsewhere."

Wrong thing to say. Her eyes perked right up.

"Oh," Diệu Ahn smiled. "Need a good lawyer to help you break a contract? I have several on staff."

Gareth blinked and remembered his manners.

"It dawns on me that we've only talked about my life tonight," he tried to deflect the statuesque woman. "What do you do, Diệu Ahn?"

She grabbed her glass and sipped, telegraphing a shrug with her entire body in such a way that Gareth kept losing focus on her eyes.

"I'm an art patron," she said modestly. "I buy, I sell. I collect things that catch my eye."

That last in a purr that felt like a bear-trap closing.

"I'll have to remember to call you next week for an interview," Gareth suggested.

"Call?" Diệu Ahn smiled. "That, too. Nudge, perhaps?"

Gareth smiled and sipped his wine, hoping that he wasn't beet red right now.

Pippa.

She seemed to sense some of his discomfort and withdrew her fangs, just a little. She tugged at his arm, turning him to the right, where he could see a new gallery through a narrow archway.

"We should enjoy the art," Diệu Ahn announced in a quiet, authoritative voice. "Broaden our horizons."

Gareth nodded and read the name of the space over the door. His heart really wanted to stop beating right now. Just keel over and die, but it refused.

Inter-Species Erotica it read in a lovely, Helvetica font. Small enough to be discrete.

In a Grace museum. The sort of place where art exhibits were expected to be *interactive.*

Gareth's eyes refused to dwell on it. He was undercover, making contacts which he hoped would lead him to useful places in the underworld. Baker and Grodray had them. His job was start building his own network.

However unsavory that task might turn out to be.

Instead, his focus drifted back to the crowd below. The mad rush was over and people were settling into clusters and currents.

Gareth stopped dead, dragging Diệu Ahn to a halt as well.

"Hey," he muttered absently.

"What is it, Gareth?" she asked, leaning close and rubbing herself against his side.

"I know those guys," he said aloud.

Down in the main hall. Morty looked up and locked eyes with him. The Yuudixtl said something that was covered by the noise in the auditorium, but that was okay. Gareth was pretty sure it would have gotten the lizardman's mouth washed out with soap, were either of their mothers here right now.

Morty turned and nudged Xiomber, the two them talking to a fat Elohynn with a couple of obvious bodyguards.

The frozen tableau held for a moment, and then the two Yuudixtl bolted.

THE CHASE

"HEY, YOU TWO," Gareth yelled, but Morty and Xiomber weren't having any of it.

He was still tangled up with Diệu Ahn, so he took the moment to set the wine glass down and smile up at her.

"Fashion writer with a secretive past?" he said quickly. "Also secret agent. Those two are bad guys. My most profuse apologies, but I must give chase now,"

She leaned in and quickly kissed him on the lips before he could react.

"Call me," she said, stepping back and letting go of his arm.

Gareth threw caution to the wind and grabbed her to return the quick kiss, only the third woman he had ever done that to, and the second one taller than him.

He turned and spotted the two runners. They were making their way to the front door, with the fat Elohynn lumbering along in their wake. Given the nature of things, Gareth assumed another bad guy with a guilty conscience.

Considering what Morty and Xiomber did, he wondered if the man was another crime boss, like Marc. One way to find out.

The stairs were too flat and wide to take them more than two at a time, and there were people on them that were too fragile for him to brush against. Especially with a forty foot drop off the side.

He ran anyway, weaving like a wingback that had made it through the defensive line and was facing open field and a goal line. He had always been athletic and a jock. As a Vanir, he was even better than he had been then, moving like a ballerina.

At the bottom of the stairs, two of the fat person's bodyguards had decided to fight a rear-guard action of some sort. One was a Vanir like him. The other a burly Grace. Gareth smiled.

The *Accord of Souls* was a peaceful place, by design. Team sports were all about skill and athleticism, but they had nothing like rugby or American football.

Too violent.

Too bad.

Neither of the goons had a weapon in hand, so Gareth didn't bother trying to pull his stunner from his knee. Instead, he transformed on the fly into a halfback, punching a hole in the defensive line for his tailback to streak to glory. He lowered a shoulder and pulled in his right arm close to his body, just like the old days.

The Vanir facing him was awkwardly balanced and had obviously never faced a blocker coming through the line. You had to get under the runner in order to stop him. Gareth had been a defensive end in school, faster and smaller than the monsters in the interior, and taller than the linebackers.

Now he was bigger and faster than any player he had ever faced. And running full tilt. He smashed into the Vanir and bounced the poor man onto his ass while stiff-arming the Grace to the face in a way that would have been good for a fifteen-yard penalty and a stern talking-to from Coach, if the man were around to witness it.

Needs must.

Both villains were down and Gareth was in the backfield, with the safeties still trailing their receivers and their backs to the play. He put on a burst of speed towards the front door and the goal line.

Out of the corner of his eye, he spied Baker and Grodray suddenly wake up to the situation, but he was moving as fast as his upgraded legs could carry him, and not even Eveth Baker could run him down now, as much as she might want to dispute that in other circumstances.

From the top of the entry stairwell, he saw the trio exit through the front door, the glass thrust open hard enough to ring when the metal frame slammed against another door. Neither broke, but that just meant they were reinforced.

And the Elohynn was in the lead now, with the two lizardmen trailing him as fast as those stubby legs could churn.

These steps were so wide that Gareth had to take them individually so he didn't trip and face-plant going down. It slowed him some, but not enough. He could see a plain van land outside and the trio enter through the back. It wasn't an auto-car, so there was probably no way that the Constables behind him could override the controls. At best, they would have to call for backup pursuit, which may and may not arrive fast enough to corner them.

Gareth hit the closing door hard enough that it did shatter this time. Or at least spiderweb into a million pieces held in place by a film of clear plastic. The panel van was just taking off and he had only a split second to make a decision.

He jumped onto side of the vehicle by the driver's door as it leapt into the air, the ground falling away quickly behind him.

Now was when it would probably get ugly.

PAPARAZZI

MORTY HAD TO ADMIT IT. He looked good tonight. Purple tights tucked into low, pull-on boots in a black suede. Lavender tunic almost to his knees, with a white belt and lots of showy pockets embroidered in white.

Even if the night was a bust, he could get into the nicest restaurants and parties in this rig. That dude must have really owed Omerlon a big favor. Even Xiomber was presentable, though he looked more like a banker, or a mortician, in severe black pants and blazer over a black shirt and black tie. Seriously, that lizard was a hole in the night, standing next to a supernova of awesome.

It wasn't Omerlon's champagne, but the house stuff was still damned good, as the three of them chatted about nothing and sipped. Omerlon was wearing a white toga tonight that made him look like how the Chaa were always portrayed on television. Even down to the purple stripe around the edge.

"Enjoying yourselves, gentlemen?" Omerlon asked, looking like a cat with the best cream in town.

"Indeed," Xiomber replied with a nod. "Ravishing."

Morty expected his egg-brother to click his heels together or something. What had come over the boy?

"This is a mark of my control of *Orgoth Vortai*," Omerlon swept a hand out and nearly whacked a goon in the face.

Both bodyguards took a step back in unison, so Morty presumed that the man gestured a lot when he spoke. Useful to know.

"We're convinced," Xiomber said. "Right now, we're down to brass tacks. Retirement plans and profit sharing."

"Is that how Maximus did it?" Omerlon half-sneered and looked half-interested in the information.

"Among other things," Morty heard Xiomber reply.

Morty's attention was suddenly riveted onto a figure up on the balcony. Huge, even for a Vanir, if the Borren next to him was a good measure of size. The blond hair was long enough that it would get shaggy soon, and the beard was a pretty good disguise, but Morty had helped Talyarkinash with the basic upgrade designs.

That was Gareth. As a Vanir. Here. At this party.

Looking this way.

Their eyes met. Locked.

"*Fardel*," Morty ejaculated before he could contain it.

"What?" Xiomber turned towards him, but Morty nudged him and gestured to the balcony with his chin.

Even Omerlon grew interested enough to glance over his shoulder.

"Oh, shit," Xiomber muttered under his breath before raising his voice just enough for Omerlon to hear. "We're blown."

Morty was gone as soon as Xiomber said the word. If Gareth was here, there would be others.

There. The crazy Vanir cop chick from *Hurquar*. The other guy was probably her partner, the two them in dress uniforms tonight while Gareth had been in mufti.

Definitely time to skedaddle.

He could hear Xiomber right behind him, those mortician shoes slapping angrily at the marble with every step, while Morty's boots squeaked.

A heavier tread close behind was Omerlon, trusting their instincts and joining them in flight.

Across the hall and past the giant head of the crazy Grace. Morty cursed whatever damned Grace architect had decided that stairs should slow you down to enjoy the art. Gareth was running after them with Vanir legs, and Morty couldn't just throw himself forward if he wanted to make it to the bottom without any broken limbs.

And that fat bastard Omerlon cheated. Hit the top of the steps and stuck his wings out sideways to glide to the ground floor while Morty and his egg-brother were only halfway down.

At least he opened the door for them, hard enough that the catch hadn't swung it back in their faces by the time they got there.

Morty heard the crime boss calling for his car on a comm, so maybe they had a chance to get out of this, if they stayed close to the guy. He had been planning to hit the door and bolt sideways, making the cops pick who to chase down in the darkness, but a personal vehicle just might get away.

The truck landed. It looked like something a plumber might own, minus only the name and comm number on the side, but the back sprang open and the fat angel waddled up the steps inside.

Morty was right on his ass when he cleared the doorway, and Xiomber slammed it shut with all his might as he got in.

"Go." Morty yelled at the driver, a head visible through a window to the cab.

Omerlon had landed himself in a throne, gasping for air like a grounded whale shark. Morty grabbed Xiomber and pushed him into a pair of seats at the front, backs to the driver and facing the fat man as the engines surged with power.

He took the moment to hook his seatbelt, laughing to himself while Xiomber did the same. They had both picked that up from Gareth, the very man chasing them.

The driver had slammed the throttle to the stops. The whole vehicle seemed to squat for a moment on its haunches, before it leapt into the night sky like a jaguar pouncing on a bird in a tree.

Morty and Xiomber shared a secret grin as Omerlon was nearly dumped on his ass before he managed to grab onto the arms of his seat. The truck was pulling something like two G's, more or less straight up. Hopefully enough to get some distance before a local cop car could start after them.

After that, it was a matter of getting underground and hiding before the Constables brought in everybody in town down here to chase them.

A thump on the outside hull beside Morty sounded an awful lot like a big Vanir landing on the running boards next to the driver. A moment later, a thump that sounded like a fist hitting the window.

Knowing Omerlon, they were bullet-proof, but the crime boss had only been expecting a normal cop. That sort of thing might not stop Gareth, if Talyarkinash had actually pulled it off.

This was about to get ugly.

"Boss, we got a passenger on the outside," the driver yelled as the vehicle kept surging upwards into the night sky.

"Dump him off," Omerlon called back.

"Hang on," the driver replied.

Morty and Xiomber were already buckled in. Omerlon managed to do the same just in time as the vehicle turned almost fifty degrees to the left.

It was like being on a ride at a carnival.

Another thump on the side of the panel truck. Louder.

Angrier, if Morty had to put a better adjective to it.

Yeah, that sounded like a modified human losing his temper out there.

"Who is this guy?" Omerlon fixed them with a hard stare.

"Constable," Xiomber offered. "We've run into him a few times. Mean SOB. Even worse than Grodray and Baker."

"And he just happened to recognize you at the Ball?" Omerlon sneered.

Morty just shrugged. No way to explain that without getting himself killed.

Outside the vehicle pitched again. The thumps on the driver's window got louder.

Suddenly, the glass shattered, letting a ripping wind into the interior of the van.

The vehicle leveled off some, as the driver was suddenly too busy wresting with Gareth to try to shake him loose.

Omerlon reached inside his toga as the noise grew worse. He came out with a pistol and Morty felt all the blood pool in his stomach.

"Since you know the guy, I'll let you die with him," Omerlon snarled.

Before Morty could react, Omerlon shot the flight console twice. In a flash, the fat man moved to the rear door, pushed it open and stepped out into the night.

"See you in hell," trailed back into the cabin with the wind.

The words were quiet, but Morty could still hear them clearly. All the engines had gone silent as the craft slowed to a halt, paused, and began to free-fall.

RELENTLESS

GARETH FELT his upgraded muscles strain to hold onto the side of the truck as it pitched over until his back was parallel with the ground. He had a boarding rail in one hand, where the driver could reach up when climbing in, and a running board under his feet.

And about three thousand feet of warm night sky below him.

He managed to swing his right foot loose and get it under the running board, using that and the rail as a pair of anchor points to hold himself up.

Gareth punched the driver's window with an angry fist, but it bounced off. Safety glass, he presumed.

The truck righted itself for a moment, and then rolled again hard, like an angry gator with fresh prey.

Now he was losing his temper. They could manage to dump him, but Gareth wouldn't be killed, unlike any other officer in the service. That still made this attempted murder.

He snarled.

One thing Gareth had learned about his new form was the ability to trigger it in pieces, for lack of a better term. He didn't have to fully transform his body, but could instead just dramatically escalate his strength beyond anything an unmodified Vanir could do. It helped that rage just fueled him right now.

He leaned into a minor transformation, even as the vehicle righted itself a second time. Instead of just punching the glass, the Star Dragon put all his might into annihilating it.

Nothing was capable of resisting that might. And it did not.

Even the most bullet-proof glass wasn't dragon-proof,

Gareth reached in with a hand that had started to turn scaly and green. The driver grappled with him, trying to do something. Knock him loose, perhaps? Force his hands away from the controls?

Gareth would never know. A raygun suddenly blasted the entire console in front of the driver and the truck's engines died.

"See you in hell," a sour voice rang clear in the sudden silence, and then the vehicle's upward trajectory abruptly slowed as it discovered gravity.

Gareth snarled.

Now, attempted murder of a Constable had moved up to mass murder. At least four people, including himself, Morty, Xiomber, and the driver, plus whoever else might be in back, plus anyone who would be killed when an out-of-control panel van slammed into the ground at terminal velocity.

And there was nothing he could do about it.

Or was there?

Gareth was supposed to keep his powers secret. A surprise weapon to spring on the bad buys at the best time. At least, those that hadn't already been there, or heard the stories.

But if he did that, innocent people would die tonight. Even criminals who didn't deserve this end.

Gareth let go of everything but his left hand on the boarding rail and let the rest of the transformation take hold.

Even a Star Dragon couldn't lift a heavy vehicle like this, but he had to try.

"Mayday," the dragon's immensely deep voice called out, hoping that someone was monitoring the channel.

Someone who could help.

"Gareth, this is Baker," her voice came back instantly. "What's your situation?"

Gareth felt the truck reach the top of the parabola and pause for a second at its highest point. He shifted around so that he could grab the two front windows with his front paws and hammered his claws into the armored sides of the back. His wings caught the night air and bit as the immense dead weight pulled him towards the planet below.

"Total vehicle failure," Gareth said precisely. "One Elohynn criminal in flight. At least three others trapped in the vehicle. Can anyone help?"

The strain on his shoulders felt like they would tear loose at any moment. He flapped, but barely made any headway, until he had a thought.

Gareth pushed his entire body backwards, letting the weight of the vehicle shift itself forward. The nose of the truck went down, and Gareth could see better where he was going.

He didn't have to slam into the ground when it got here, but the others didn't have that option, and the ground would be here faster than anybody could arrive that might be able to prevent the giant anvil in his grip from smashing itself to pieces on the ground, plus any towers or restaurants that managed to be in the way of falling death.

"Can you make the river?" Baker asked calmly. "Ditch there where we might be able to rescue survivors?"

Might.

It was night, and that water would be dark and cold. The men inside would have seconds to escape, assuming the van survived impacting the water, before they were pulled to the dark, murky bottom.

And from this height, hitting water was going to be like hitting concrete, because there was no way he was going to flatten them out enough to matter in the next thirty seconds.

"Negative," he said.

Gareth looked other directions. The river was just too far away, and the towers beside it too tall. He'd probably end up slamming into one as he went by, trying to avoid killing people.

He was back to Ethics 101 at school. Do you choose to send the runaway vehicle crashing into a tree to save pedestrians, thereby killing the driver, or do nothing and let the vehicle kill the pedestrians instead?

How do you decide who has to die today?

In some ways, that wasn't even a thing to discuss. The three inside might have to die, but Gareth would not put anybody else at risk to die, possibly with them, rather than instead.

Blinking lights on the ground caught his eye. The tube station was close. But the entire facility was dark right now. Gareth had learned enough to know that meant there were no ferries currently in orbit overhead.

"Can you contact the station?" Gareth strained to make the words intelligible as he pushed everything he had into his shoulders, trying to turn the massive dead weight to starboard. At the very least, there were open fields in that direction, so he would only kill the two men who had brought him here, and the driver.

Hopefully.

"What station?" Baker asked.

"The tube station," Gareth roared. "Have them turn on the generators and open me a tube into space. Do it now."

He took a breath and leaned over to the left.

"Morty, can you hear me?" he called.

"Is that you, kid?" the Yuudixtl physicist called back in a hopeful voice.

"It is," Gareth replied. "Can you find the emergency oxygen masks?"

Every flying vehicle had to have them, by law, on the presumption that they might go through a wormhole at some point, and all of those were in space. Because the law said emergencies and mistakes happen, you had to be able to survive suddenly losing a vehicle seal and facing vacuum.

This vehicle was turning. Falling in a different direction, perhaps. Not into the heart of the art district, nor the Hall of Arts.

If he could only make it that far before his friends had to die.

"Got 'em, Gareth," Xiomber's voice came back. "What are you doing?"

"Put them on now," Gareth roared in a voice that much of the city below might have heard.

Baker had gone silent on him. Hopefully that meant that she was calling someone over at the tube station, waking them up. Doing something that would prevent a lot of unnecessary deaths tonight.

Gareth strained through the pain. It felt like his wings were being pulled out of their sockets to the point that he might not be able to escape when this thing hit the ground. He would just have to deal with that.

Or watch his friends die. He could always just let go right now and survive with nothing more than bruises and pulled muscles. Three presumed criminals would suffer the ultimate sanction, and they would never again be a threat to the *Accord of Souls*.

That wasn't why he had joined Earth Force. Wasn't what made him an agent of Sky Patrol.

Gareth St. John Dankworth was not a man who surrendered.

He pulled harder. Growled. Metal actually began to deform under his grip as his claws ripped into the steel of the truck's carcass.

Ten seconds to impact.

Gareth howled in pain and frustration. They hadn't dreamed big enough, back when they created a Star Dragon. He should have gone for something big enough to lift a tank or a star shuttle off the ground.

Then Morty and Xiomber and the poor driver wouldn't be about to die from his failures.

Five seconds.

Light.

NIGHTFALL

THERE IS no air in space, Gareth thought to himself as the flash of light ended, replaced by an endless darkness broken by a billion points of light. He was suddenly in freefall and vacuum.

Beneath him, the air in the panel van exploded outwards through the shattered window and the opened back door, a snow storm that ended as abruptly as it had begun.

A pinging began in his right ear in spite of the soundlessness of space. It matched a flashing red light that suddenly reflected off his hide and tail.

Emergency beacon on the truck. Automatic. The vehicle has suffered a failure in space and the onboard systems had triggered their own mayday. His earpiece was picking up the distress beacon, and it was tucked in deep enough that he could feel it click in his bones.

Gareth's inner eyelids clicked shut and held in moisture, as did his nostrils. He kept his mouth shut and let his own unconscious systems come into play. Talyarkinash had designed the Star Dragon to survive in deep space. He was airtight and insulated against cold, air loss, and radiation for several hours, if his held breath lasted that long.

The men inside the van didn't have that option. If they were wearing their air masks, they could at least breathe, but vacuum damage and cold would do them in quickly. He needed to do something.

He hadn't come this far just to lose them now.

Without gravity's greedy clutches, he could move the panel truck more easily. It was a giant medicine ball in his hands now, rather than a Sisyphean impossibility. He flapped his wings and imagined bringing the vehicle to a stop, since he had nothing in the vicinity against which to measure his speed.

Still, it seemed to work. He let go with rear claws and right hand, and flowed himself around to the open front window. The one he had shattered earlier.

The driver was gone.

For a moment, Gareth panicked, looking every direction in case the man had been blasted into deep space by the sudden decompression, but he was alone in the darkness and silence.

Nothing.

He stuck his head into the window and looked at the rear. Morty and Xiomber, at least, had been back there, and hadn't gone out the back door either.

Then he saw why.

Inside the rear cabin was a giant bubble. One Grace and two Yuudixtl sat inside, pale white and darkest green, respectively.

Morty waved cheerfully. The driver flinched.

Huh. Emergency lifeboat system. He hadn't thought about that. Trigger it to inflate and then seal it up around you. Probably up to an hour of air, depending on how many people it had to contain.

"Gareth, this is Baker, can you hear me?" a tinny voice came in his ear.

"I can," he said.

It was weird, talking without moving his jaw. The bones in his head would carry the sound via induction to the microphone in his ear, with some distortion. No complicated speeches, but basic communication would work.

"Thank you," he continued. "It worked."

"What is your status?" she asked, obviously relieved.

"Vehicle dead in high orbit," Gareth murmured. "Three people in a survival bubble."

"Okay, stand by," she said. "We're trying to find a truck big enough to rescue you at the same time we do your prisoners. Nothing like that here."

Gareth considered his options. He actually couldn't remember seeing anything but a transport shuttle capable of holding his twenty-seven-meter-long dragon form, and he couldn't shift back to his base form without a space suit. Up here, there would be no time to get into one.

He'd be facing the same freezing death he had feared these three men had gotten into.

Then a thought struck him.

"Do you have an auto-car that had can open to space?" he asked.

There was a long pause before her voice returned.

"We do, but what about you?" she asked.

"Rescue them first," he said. "I have an idea for me."

"Okay," Baker said. "Stand by."

Gareth pulled his head back out the window and stuck a paw in instead, giving them a thumbs-up signal he hoped was universal. His current face wasn't capable of smiling like a Vanir or a Grace could, and he didn't have time to teach them.

Instead, he moved around the truck, finding the spots where his rear claws had actually managed to punch holes in the sides in spite of the armor.

Of course, in the *Accord of Souls*, everything was a beam weapon of some sort, rather than a high-velocity shell, so you needed insulation and thermal barriers, rather than inches of hardened steel plate and ceramics to protect you.

The men inside were trapped by the narrowness of the door. Gareth had no idea how much squeezing and reshaping the bubble could take, trying to pry it out of the back of the vehicle, and it would only take one mistake to kill the three men inside it.

He braced his feet into those holes again, but facing rearwards this time. In space, there is no gravity to hold you down. And no friction to stop you from moving, You are actually in constant freefall, but moving sideways such that it looks like you can never hit ground.

Everything becomes leverage.

Fortunately, Agents of Earth Force Sky Patrol had to be experts in extra-vehicular activities in order to earn their badge. Gareth had lost track of all the times he had needed to move outside a vehicle in deep space, from rescuing a lost puppy to stopping a runaway ship from destroying Shadow Base One, back in the Earth–Moon L2 LaGrange Point.

His dragon form was long enough to clamp onto the top of the truck and hold himself firmly, while also stretching his front to the aft of the craft. The door opened out and was just getting in the way, so that needed to go first.

Or did it?

He relaxed his chest and inspected the metal of the craft more closely. In this form, he could have licked it and gotten almost as good an understanding as a mass spectrometer, but that would waste precious air. Plus he might end up sticking his tongue to a frozen sign post.

He twisted around until he was looking in the rear. Morty and the others had turned to face him from much closer. Apparently, one of them had said something to the driver, because the Grace seemed a little more relaxed than before.

Like maybe he wasn't expecting a Star Dragon to have him for lunch.

Heh.

Gareth held up a single finger, again hoping it was a universal signal, and pushed the door closed until he felt it latch through his claws.

In space, nobody can hear you laugh. That was good, because this was the single silliest thing he had done since he came to the *Accord of Souls* seven weeks ago.

He let go.

It stayed where it was.

He flapped lazily until he was lined up with the passenger bottom corner of the truck.

There is no air in space, but he didn't actually use mechanical lift to do this, according to Talyarkinash Liamssen. It was all in his mind, somehow, a leftover from somewhere, or perhaps a trace of the very godhead that the Chaa had tapped when they moved past physical forms.

Was that why they had uplifted all the other species in the galaxy and left humans alone? Did we have the potential to someday join them on their exotic quest to find God and sit at his feet?

Gareth had always been punctual about Sunday school as a child. And visited Pastor Jacob whenever he had home leave, plus whichever priest was assigned to the base he was at. The religions really didn't matter that much to Gareth, as long as they *believed*. As ship's commander, he had even had to act as priest for his own crews, making special readings every seventh day to help bind them into a greater whole that was Earth Force Sky Patrol.

Gareth blinked in shock. He wondered if this radical idea was something he could ever share with anyone. The *Accord of Souls* was comprised of species that had been Uplifted by the Chaa and then set into their current form.

Did that mean that nobody but a human had that potential? Did it mean Marc Sarzynski really could achieve godhead if he worked at it hard enough? That Gareth could himself?

Whoa.

Still, not a problem for today. Right now, he needed to save these three men from certain death, and that meant that he needed to get them out of the vehicle safely.

The hatch was closed and latched. He hadn't seen it move. Everything *should* be safe enough.

Just to be sure, he started low and away, like a good curveball coming in over the plate.

The Star Dragon had a binary chemical weapon. It didn't need oxygen, as one of the two chemicals in the mix contained enough. More would help, but he needed controlled destruction today, and not psychological terror.

Gareth opened his mouth just a little. It was almost like that disgusting habit of chewing tobacco and spitting the juice into a cup. He had set down strict rules on any crew he commanded that something like that was not allowed aboard ship, because it could be so messy.

Squeezed his chest slowly and carefully. Aimed his snout and focused the sudden blast of superheated fluid.

And discovered that Newton was right, when he was suddenly tumbling backwards ass over teakettle.

He hadn't been pushing forward, and had done the equivalent of lighting a rocket engine in his mouth. Hopefully, nobody had a camera pointed this direction.

He flapped a few times and stopped his tumble, just the slightest bit queasy.

Getting closer, the tail of the truck was certainly scorched, but not in a single spot, as he had planned. It looked more like a badly done crème Brule.

Okay, focus on incoming pressure and hold yourself stable this time, dummy.

He moved again to the right spot and focused his will. Another jet of flames.

This time, he flapped his wings, leaning into the heavy wind that was his own personal rocket engine in deep space. He'd need to remember this trick, sometime.

The blowtorch hit the corner of the truck and started it tumbling as well. Slower, but noticeable.

Crap.

Gareth quickly pounced on the vehicle and pulled that damned medicine ball until it felt like it was sitting in space again. The riders probably wouldn't notice a moderate spin, but he didn't need them puking on the inside of that emergency bubble and then having to sit in it for an hour or more.

Okay, fine.

Gareth stuck his toes back into the holes he had gouged earlier. Newton was right, and physics were physics. He would just have to do this upside down.

Third try.

He had a better idea of how to flame in space by now. And could bring it down to a fine, cutting blade of plasma. He was pretty sure the door was insulated, and probably a good chunk of the rear and sides, but the welds where the vehicle had been assembled would still be vulnerable.

It was just going to take patience.

Fine.

Up the sides, and he could see the welds weaken. He didn't want to actually penetrate the interior, because his breath weapon was too dangerous to the soft tissue of the emergency bubble.

No, this was just to soften them up a little.

"What are you doing?" Baker's voice came across the radio.

It sounded like she was watching him.

Gareth stopped flaming and looked up. Sure enough, an auto-car hung in space about thirty meters away. Almost close enough that he could touch both at the same time if he stretched, but far enough distant to stay out of his way.

The aft airlock hatch was open and she was standing in it, wearing a light EVA suit and clamped to the interior with a secondary line. Good professionalism on her part.

He wondered who was driving, if anyone, and what they though to see a dragon in space.

"Watch," Gareth smiled.

He returned to his work. Across the top. Down the driver's side. Back across the bottom.

"Could you move up and to my starboard?" Gareth asked.

"Stand by," she said.

Silence, so she was probably on a different channel, talking to the car or the driver.

Gareth puffed a few places that looked a little stronger than the rest, and then delicately opened the door. He leaned his head in and scanned as much as he could with his peripheral vision.

So far, so good. Probably would have set things on fire if they were down on the surface, but there was no air to burn up here.

Morty and Xiomber looked quite thrilled at the spectacle. The Grace had turned almost green by now. Probably not the day he envisioned when he got out of bed.

Baker's car had moved off and out of the way. Physics was physics, and this was probably going to be impressive as hell when she replayed the video later for Grodray and whoever else was cleared for this level of secrecy.

Okay, now to get crazy.

Strength, like flight, was a matter of mind. Or mind over matter. Or something. He hadn't been strong enough to lift this truck when it was falling, but maybe Talyarkinash could upgrade him again later. Maybe a Greater Star Dragon form to improve upon the first?

But he didn't need to carry the damnable thing, just damage it.

Eight, razor-sharp, front claws found the weakened seams where the pieces had been welded together, once upon a time. But heat/cool cycles unquenched metal, had it ever been done right, and made things brittle.

And Gareth was still a little angry at having failed earlier. He sank the tips through the welds like butter and pulled.

In space, everything is relative leverage.

And dragonrage.

He heaved.

A seam parted. Not much, but a crack suddenly ran nearly a meter. Good enough. He shifted his grip to the other side of the stern and did the same thing. This was easier. He had a feel for where it was going to tear.

The sides were going to be harder, except that he could just shift himself around the truck ninety degrees.

Oh, yeah.

He slithered to his right and found a new spot to dig in his toes. Couple of good, solid kicks and he was firmly anchored to the carcass.

This might even work.

Reach around the aft end and grab the side. This weld felt softer than the others. He wondered if the verticals hadn't been anchored as heavily as the horizontals. That would certainly make this easier.

Torque, and he could see a gap run the entire side of the vehicle.

Gareth had planned to hit the top next, but a lazy welding crew might make this far easier than he had planned. He shifted one hundred and eighty degrees this time, so he could get a grip on the passenger side and attack across.

Sure enough, this set of welds had been seals, rather than structural, like the top and bottom. Possibly to make it easier to get at lights and wires later, but he gave it a good tug and the side came across from the quarter panel.

Okay, now the fun part.

Gareth returned to his original overhead spot, rather than climbing underneath, like he had planned originally. Quick double-check, but Baker was back and staying out of his way, about fifty meters off to his right.

He took a deep breath. Or whatever a Star Dragon did in deep space where there wasn't any air.

Settled his toes into their holes and grabbed on, foot-fists holding him tightly in place.

Stretch out and over the back of the truck. Grab hold of that panel, right below the door, where the seam had failed earlier.

Pull.

Nothing.

No, unacceptable.

PULL.

Movement. Not much, but proof of concept.

Gareth focused his entire being on that top weld and flexed all the way to the tip of his tail.

It started slowly, failing by millimeters and fighting him for every bit, but it moved. After about three centimeters, something snapped somewhere inside, and the metal began to deform. He pulled more, but the door was warping now as much as it folded. Still, good enough for his purposes.

He let go and flowed around into the opening he had ripped. The back plate gap was about a meter wide, which was enough to get his head, arms, and shoulders inside.

His snout was actually touching the emergency bubble now, and Morty, being Morty, just had to boop him on the snoot with a finger and a laugh that the membrane transmitted.

Gareth rumbled with a laugh, and then set his arms on the floor, using the Elohynn's throne-like chair as an anchor point. He flexed his shoulder and back up and out, growling with the intensity. The metal moved more, failing under the torque Gareth was forcing into it.

It failed with a snap, breaking loose.

Gareth had hold of the chair, so he didn't embarrass himself again, with witnesses this time. Instead, he glanced back and caught the back plate with his left foot, holding it in place, more or less. The throne was in the way, so he found the pins holding it to the deck and snapped them off. He slid it around to the side and stuffed it into the front seat, out of his way and the bubble.

He let go and backed out of the cabin, flowing up and over to the driver's door. His arms weren't long enough in this form, so he pulled open the door and stuck his head in.

Just because Morty had started it, Gareth head-butted the emergency cocoon once, his own boop that picked it up and shoved it softly out into space, now that the entire rear of the vehicle was wide enough for it to get out without catching on anything.

"Baker," Gareth rumbled over the radio. "All yours."

He moved to the top of the truck and snagged the floating panel. After a moment of thought, he stuffed it inside and wedged it well enough to hold. At some point, a tow ship would have to grab the truck and move it to an impound yard. Otherwise, it might fall to earth and maybe have enough metal to survive reentry.

Not good.

Baker was EVA now. Her suit had little jets on the backpack that she used to capture the cocoon, like a sheep dog, and herd them into the open rear door of the truck. The door closed and the three were safe.

Under arrest for a variety of crimes and in really deep doo-doo, but safe from death today, and that was all that mattered right now.

"What about you?" Baker asked, turning her jets to face him as she waited outside the airlock for it to cycle.

"When you get back, open a tube and I'll fly through it," Gareth replied.

She was silent for a moment, deep in thought or maybe talking to Grodray on another channel.

"Sun's coming up over Londra," she observed. "You'll be visible."

"You would never be able to keep something like this secret now anyway," Gareth retorted. "Might as well make a splash."

More silence.

"You sure about this, Gareth?"

He heard Grodray's voice on the line this time. Senior Constable Jackeith Grodray who was secretly a Prime Investigator. A Level-7 instead of a Level-4. The man in charge, but still keeping a very low profile. And he could hide even better in the shadow of a Star Dragon.

"I am," Gareth rumbled back.

"Very good," Grodray said. "Stand by."

A golden portal opened in front of the rescue truck, and the vehicle moved carefully into it, disappearing like a soap bubble on a sunny day.

Gareth waited.

"Okay, Gareth," Baker said. "We're clear of the landing point and moving away. You have a clear flight path."

"Thank you," he said.

The golden tube in front of him represented all the weirdness that had upended his life over the last two months. Perhaps it was appropriate that it would open the next phase in his cursed, or perhaps charmed existence.

The underworld had been rife with unbelievable tales of a giant, flying lizard hunting bad guys. Nobody would doubt them after this.

And he was also a good guy, rescuing people from certain death.

That legend would take shape as well.

For the briefest, scariest moment, Gareth wondered if his appearance might trigger some bizarre new religion. None of the known species could become a dragon, and nobody would know the truth except a very few on both sides of the law.

Would people think he was one of the Chaa, returned to the *Accord of Souls* to help fight evil? Would they worship him?

He was sad that Pastor Jacob wasn't here to advise him, but the man had helped shape him along the way. Gareth would do what was right.

Whatever the cost.

He turned to the golden portal and began to flap, building up speed.

There was a flash of light, over almost before it began, and he was suddenly at gravity's mercy again.

Down became down, and the morning air had turned so cool that his breath steamed when he let go and drew a new breath into his lungs.

The sun was just above the horizon over Londra, painting the cotton-candy sky almost the same reds as that painting he had experienced last night. She hadn't been painting the sunset, that Grace woman.

She had been facing the dawn. The new beginning.

Hope.

Gareth let loose a cry of pure joy as he banked over and began to slowly orbit the Hall of Art.

His story was finally beginning.

YET HIGHER MATHEMATICS

"I'M concerned about his paper, Loughty," the man said.

Royston held his tongue. The cluttered oak desk between them, stacked with papers and old tomes, might as well have been a battlefield drawn up between two armies. He had expected what was coming, and wasn't about to back down one scintilla on this.

Not even to this man could make him: Dr. Sir Westfield van Duren-Abbott, PhD, FRS, GMU, KCB, GBE.

Fellow of the Royal Society. Past Guardian of the Mathematical Union. Knight Grand Cross, Order of the British Empire. Knight Commander, Order of the Bath. Even the best-selling author of a popular book on the shape of the universe and humanity's place in it.

Sir West was probably the only mathematician alive that the man on the street might recognize by name. Professor Emeritus, King's College, and all that.

Royston smiled grimly at his old mentor and set his teeth to prevent the growl from escaping his mouth. Now was not the time. Even with Sir West's office door closed, this was not the place.

Royston leaned himself into the wingback chair and forced his muscles to relax. The walls on three sides of the oversized office were covered with bookshelves, and at least four of his books were in here somewhere, along with all twenty-three of Sir West's.

When the man realized that Royston wasn't going to rise to the bait, Sir West sighed.

The man looked every one of his eighty-three years, with a wild fringe of white hair surrounding a sea of liver spots on the bald top. Even his tweeds might be older than Royston. The eyes were hazel most of the time, and gave utter lie to the rest of the man's unkempt appearance as a fussy old duffer headed down to the pub for a pint.

Sir West had lost barely any of the genius that put him at the top of the field sixty years ago and kept him there.

"Yes, concerned that you've gone about this all wrong, Loughty," the man repeated himself.

"Why is that, Sir West?" Royston finally asked.

If they were going to have to play this game, he was going to make the old man work for it. Simple as that.

"Your co-author, Roy," Sir West intoned in a severe, almost condescending voice.

"Oh?" Royston fired back innocently.

As if he hadn't woken up this morning and spent his breakfast and the flight down here to England preparing for this battle.

"I appreciate that she is your daughter," Sir West equivocated. "And a very sharp girl, but this paper has the potential to utterly destroy your reputation, Loughty. I wouldn't want hers to suffer any collateral damage."

"What's wrong with the contents of the paper, Sir West?" Royston challenged, letting just the thinnest edge of his pique show through.

The man had been his mentor for nearly three decades now. Challenging his genius was like arguing with God himself about things.

"You claim to have invented an entirely new mathematics, Loughty," the older man was exasperated. "As if your place in history is to rival Newton and Leibniz. Higher dimensions of space? Wormholes? Ye gads, man, that's the fanciful conjecture of the worst speculative fiction writers. Newton was surpassed by Einstein, but nobody in the last five hundred years has been able to prove the German wrong. And everyone has tried."

"I'm aware of that, Sir West," Royston replied with a sniff.

"This paper will get you laughed out of the Royal Society, Loughty," Sir West pleaded. "Burn it, before anybody else finds out, and I swear I will never mention it again."

"I've already begun designing the first generator, Sir West," Royston replied.

"You've what?"

"The theory supports a certain type of radiation, previously unknown anywhere in any proposed model of physics, being a residue from such a device as an electromagnetic signature," Royston said.

"So?" the man shifted uncomfortably in his chair.

"I've seen that radiation," Royston replied, eyes squinting with fury. "Detected it under circumstances that were utterly impossible to explain. If the security clearance around the incident wasn't so high, I could tell you about it. Instead I might suggest you ask the Queen when you next have lunch with her. Perhaps a tour of The Arsenal and a look at the bleeding edge of research might be in order, sometime soon."

He left it at that. That was exactly as much hint as he could offer without getting himself in trouble, but Sir Westfield van Duren-Abbott was a bright enough fellow to understand the clues and follow the breadcrumbs to enlightenment.

If he really wanted to know the truth.

"And this?" he gestured at the folder between them on the desk.

The paper was amazingly thin, as those things went. More than half of it was an Appendix filled with the new vocabulary of terms and symbols Royston had been forced to invent, to try to explore the ideas that took shape under the influence of that young lady's rock and roll.

The paper itself was an exploration of several higher orders of dimensionality, arranged like layers in a puff pastry and separated by walls of radiation that might be some bizarre, previously-unsuspected residue of the Big Bang itself.

That awaited a future paper to explore. And possibly entire generations of science fiction writers to prove right. He looked forward to dropping a small and rather polite bomb on the Royal Society sometime soon. Possibly by opening a wormhole across the length of a desk and rolling a marble through it. That demonstration might require an entire atomic pile to power it, but the expressions of shock on those old fart's faces would be worth every pfennig.

"How would you classify this?" the older scientist pressed.

"A roadmap to the future, old man," Royston snapped. "I don't know what's out there, or who, but I have strong suggestions that we'll find someone when we get there. The rest is just the work of some extremely competent and creative mechanical engineers. I have a number of those on call, up in orbit."

"So you're going to go through with it?" Sir West demanded abrasively.

"Indeed," Royston smiled. He leaned back again, when he realized he had leaned forward far enough to put his hands on the desk again.

"And you will share credit with a woman?" Sir West's voice got ugly.

"Did you know that King's College used to admit women into their doctoral programs, Sir West?" Royston purred icily. "That many schools did, back in the old days before Earth Force? Back at the dawn of the Space Age?"

"And next I suppose you'll tell me that the Etruscans were a co-equal society. And the Vikings and so many others. Ancient history, and she has nothing more than a basic degree."

"Truth," Royston acknowledged. "And since no admissions council would grant her leave to attend, she has instead been my principal assistant for several years, when she might have been successfully pursuing such advanced degrees. After me, she's the only other expert on the topic. If people intend to be snotty enough to me on the matter, I might send her to make all my presentations and remain in my lab in orbit."

That got the man's attention. Royston could see Sir West envisioning a woman standing before the Royal Society, dressed in that red skirt and tunic, representing Sky Patrol. They had admitted women once, as well. In the so-called Dark Ages of Technology.

Royston smiled at the possibility of her on the talk shows, describing the work as an equal partner, and not just the daughter of the inventor.

Sir West leaned back in turn, cooling his ardor by force of will. He could see the precipice that Royston had walked him to, like a bear trap hidden in the low grass.

"Let me make a few inquiries," he half-promised, suddenly understanding the lever Royston held.

Archimedes had warned these bastards, but not enough of them had listened.

"How soon until you build a device?" Sir West asked carefully.

"This one will exceed my current budget," Royston replied. "I'll be sending this paper up the chain at Sky Patrol, requesting additional funds and assistance. They have a powerful, vested interest in the topic that I am not at liberty to discuss, currently."

"Would you consider building it at King's College?" Sir West asked, dancing expertly around the topic.

"When the Sky Marshal asks me to present my theories to the Secretary, it might be helpful if Her Majesty was willing to chat with the Chancellor on the topic," Royston allowed.

The Americans would also be quite interested, and willing to throw money at him. And they dominated both Earth Force in general and Sky Force in particular.

Very interested.

Because someone had kidnapped Gareth St. John Dankworth.

The Americans would want to have a friendly chat with those folks.

At least it would start friendly. Americans were like that.

"I shall make some inquiries, Loughty," Sir West finally temporized. "Will this really potentially give us the galaxy?"

"That is my hope, Sir West," Royston replied. "That is my goal."

WITNESS

CONSTABLE BAKER SMILED as the six people were marched onto the low stage and lined up under extremely bright lights. She was on the other side of a thick window, sitting in darkness with a pair of Yuudixtl men who were practically vibrating with excitement, in spite of the handcuffs around their wrists.

This was all just a formality anyway. Six Elohynn were lined up. Two of them slouched in the uniform of the Constabulary. One of those and another were female. Another was a well-known, local sports reporter with a sense of humor. One was a random stranger off the street, willing to take an hour off and get lunch in the deal.

And one fat, old man Elohynn that had been utterly bullet-proof until yesterday.

She smiled some more, letting it spread so far across her face that she was afraid she might start to glow.

"Number four," the neared Yuudixtl crowed.

She had only met Morty in the flesh a few hours ago, but she had been reading reports and hearing stories from both Dankworth and Liamssen about the lizardman for nearly two months now. He was just as silly, as sarcastic, and as sharp as they had warned her.

Eveth picked up a microphone and spoke into it.

"Number four, step forward," she commanded.

It helped that he was the only one wearing cuffs in there, but this was just a formality.

Omerlon took an angry step forward. He looked like he wanted to punch the glass, had his hands been in front. Perhaps he might head-butt it yet.

"That's him," the other one said.

Xiomber. Supposedly egg-brother to Morty. Partners in crime and mischief. And willing to spend the last three hours, on tape, detailing every crime they could remember, with names, dates, places, and amounts. And not just Sarzynski's gang, as these two had spent twenty years being bad guys for a number of outfits.

It would take her weeks, and maybe months to suck these two dry. And they seemed even more excited at the prospect than she did.

Bizarre.

"Morty?" she asked.

"Correct," Morty said. "Number four."

"The rest of you may go," she said into the mic. "Thank you for your service."

"You bastards got nothing on me," Omerlon snarled.

"On the contrary, Omerlon," Baker said with an infectious smile that the other two seemed to have picked up. "I have you on four counts of attempted murder, including attempted murder of a Constabulary Officer."

Three of the folks in the line-up had departed. The two Elohynn officers were pushing Omerlon the other direction, towards the holding cells.

"May I?" Morty hopped off his stool and approached with a hand out.

Baker shrugged and handed him the microphone.

"Hey, Omerlon," Morty cat-called the Elohynn crime boss. "You were right. See you in hell."

He handed her back the mic and moved towards the two officers at the back of the room, almost skipping with glee.

She had no idea what was going on, but this was going to be fun.

Because Omerlon? Yeah, he was about to enter hell.

HOME

GARETH ENTERED the research lab as quietly as he could. Talyarkinash was working on a screen with her profile towards him, tracing something on the screen with a nail painted green today. It looked like his silhouette on the screen, so she was probably calculating new options.

He cleared his throat as he got closer.

Talyarkinash turned and blinked in surprise. She took three steps across the lab and engulfed him in a hug, as short as she was.

"You did it," she said. "I saw you on the morning news. It was glorious. You were glorious."

Gareth untangled himself a little and leaned back enough to smile at her.

"You did it," he said. "I was able to rescue Morty and Xiomber in that truck, along with another man, by having Baker bounce me to orbit. I could have never done anything like that without your help."

"Morty? Xiomber" she cried with joy. "You found them?"

"And arrested them," Gareth said. "They're in custody downstairs while Baker and Grodray work out what to do with them."

"What will happen?" she asked, leaning back herself until they only touched where hands contacted ribs.

"There is a precedence," he grinned slyly. "Ex-criminals willing to turn state's evidence and work with the Constabulary."

"Like you?" she teased.

Gareth's grin turned into a smile. Technically, he was an illegal alien, illegally upgraded. And trying to do good.

"I might know others," he teased back. "Have you had breakfast? I've been using the Star Dragon form for hours and I'm famished. Plus, I want to talk to you about some things. I had a lot of time up in space alone, since the others were trapped in an emergency cocoon. They could wave, but I had nobody to talk to except Baker and Grodray."

She stepped back and turned to her workstation, hitting a button to save everything and power it down for now.

"I would love to join you for breakfast, Gareth," she said. "What did you need?"

"On the one hand, I have a few questions about maybe upgrading the Star Dragon," he replied. "Or maybe creating a second, larger form I could shift into when I needed to go beyond the normal for size and strength."

"Okay," she said, moving towards the door and opening it. "That's actually along the lines of what I have been working on up until now. What was the second part?"

"How will the average person react to seeing me as a dragon?" Gareth asked. "I will become a symbol of fear to the criminals, which was what I intended, but will the rest of the *Accord of Souls* see me as one of the Chaa returned? Will they think I'm a god?"

"Oh, Gareth," she leaned close and placed a palm on the chest of his grinder wool blazer. "That's not something I can help you with. You'll need a priest, or maybe a philosopher."

"No," Gareth corrected her. "What I need is a friend."

CALL OF THE STAR DRAGON

GUILTY

GARETH SUPPRESSED a heavy sigh when the Bailiff paused, turned the page he was reading, and looked up at the judge, defendants, and court room.

"Last page," the man promised wearily. He stopped and took a long drink of water from a glass sitting on the counter in front of him.

The rest of the room seemed to relax as well. It had been nearly three hours, just reading all the charges publicly for the first time. As public as this room was, anyways.

"And finally, the defendants are accused of four counts of High Treason," the bailiff continued. "And one count of Attempting to Overthrow the *Accord of Souls* By Illegal Force."

Gareth grinned as the man picked up the enormous stack of papers, tapped them into a clean pile, and walked across the court room to rest them on the bench in front of the presiding judge.

That worthy rested a weary hand on the pile, nearly an inch think, and scowled at the defendants seated in front of him at a low table, the Yuudixtl scientist criminals: Morty and Xiomber.

The judge was an older woman, Gareth would have guessed. Perhaps his Mom's age, with all the wear and lines of a hard, disciplined life.

Not a woman to trifle with, even today. Again, like Mom.

He wondered how well she could bake an apple pie.

"How do the defendants plead?" she asked it a fatigued voice.

They had been at it all morning, and it was almost lunch time.

Morty turned to the attorney representing them with a confused look. That man was rather exhausted as well, but holding up well.

"That's only six hundred and twenty-seven charges," Morty said quietly.

The room was still so silent that the words carried.

"The State skipped all the jaywalking, speeding tickets, overdue books, and parking violations you two listed," he muttered back.

"Oh," Morty chirped. "Gotcha."

Gareth watched Morty, dressed in an orange prison jumpsuit, push his chair back, stand with great ceremony and solemnity, in spite of being hand-cuffed, and grin at the judge. Next to him, Xiomber did the same, perhaps a little slower. Maybe he had been napping.

Gareth would have liked to see the smiles on the two Yuudixtls faces, but he was back in the galley, several rows behind the two scientists, so he had to settle for listening to their voices instead. He could imagine it, though, just from the gleeful tones.

"Guilty, Your Honor," Morty called cheerfully.

"Also guilty, Your Honor," Xiomber joined his egg-brother a moment later.

The Judge, for all her seriousness, seemed non-plussed.

"You understand, gentlemen, that you intend to plead guilty to the only two crimes in my statute book that carry the possibility of capital punishment?" she asked slowly, waiting patiently for the two goofballs to suddenly realize what they had said.

"I do, Your Honor," Xiomber said, maybe morosely. Maybe it was just tiredness.

Gareth felt the need for coffee, and he'd been able to slightly doze over the last few hours. Talyarkinash, sitting beside him, had nudged him in the ribs a few times when he had started snoring.

"You betcha, Lady," Morty said.

For the briefest moment, Gareth wondered if the woman judge was going to lean forward and fling her gavel across the court room like a throwing knife, to bash Morty square in the forehead like a bolt from Zeus.

She looked capable of it.

But after a moment, she reconsidered.

"In light of other circumstance, and requests from the Prosecution, the defendants are hereby found Guilty of all charges and remanded to State Custody, pending a sentencing hearing currently unscheduled," she said evenly, bashing that gavel onto her desk top instead. "This Court is dismissed."

The entire room rose as one. Talyarkinash was obviously expecting it as much as Gareth, so she didn't miss a beat.

After all, she was the only other person in here besides Morty and Xiomber who weren't wearing the uniform of the Constabulary. Blue-gray bodysuits and tunics, for the most part, although a few of the more senior officers and officials present were in really fancy attire. Even the judge under her black robes.

Two Constabulary Explorers, the equivalent of Deputy Agents that Gareth would have seen were he back home in an Earth Force Sky Patrol courtroom, led the two convicted criminals off to wherever they were going to be fed lunch.

Gareth watched Senior Constable Jackeith Grodray and Constable Eveth Baker turn and approach from the front row, surrounded by other men and women departing. Several paused long enough to offer congratulations and such to the two officers, which they took good-naturedly.

Grodray was a serious cop. Intellectual and stern, but affable for the most part. As a Vanir, the man was seven foot three, but rather lanky and skinny, coming in at barely three hundred pounds.

Since he had been transformed from human to Vanir, Gareth now had an inch of height on the other man, but at least forty pounds of bulk, mostly muscle.

But Grodray was also a cypher. He appeared as a Senior Constable in public, a Level-4. A simple detective, back home. But in reality he was a Prime Inspector, a Level-7. A free agent with authority to pursue any crime, anywhere, and expect the willing assistance of every cop and civilian he encountered along the way.

Eveth Baker was smaller than Grodray, but still big for a Vanir woman. Six foot seven and two hundred and forty pounds of grit, muscle, and tough rolled up in an athletic brunette body. Not that Gareth would ever consider her more than a cop.

He had Pippa to think about. Back home, waiting for him. Pippa unknowing that he was even alive, and that he could never return to Earth. Even if he somehow did manage it, he would be a monster.

That he wasn't even human anymore.

He had been modified. Talyarkinash, Morty, and Xiomber, the only three civilians present in the courtroom today, had reprogrammed his DNA to make him a Vanir. Bigger, stronger, faster, and smarter than ninety-nine percent of even that impressive species.

And then they had gone beyond that, even if it had been at his insistence. They had tapped into something Talyarkinash called his *latent psionic potential* to let the former human Gareth trigger a transformation into a twenty-seven-meters-long flying lizard form that could breathe fire.

A Star Dragon.

It had been the only thing Gareth could think of at the time to make him dangerous enough to take on Marc Sarzynski. *Maximus.* Another human, the only other human in the *Accord of Souls*, Gareth hoped. The man vying to become the overlord of the underworld. The Master of Crime.

And a man who, at one time would have been Gareth's Best Man, on the day he finally wed Pippa. Maybe it was just as well that such a day was never coming now.

Grodray came to a halt before Gareth, looking slightly up at him with a stern glare.

"That's done," he announced so quietly that perhaps only the two of them and the two females close by heard. "Now the next part. Come with me."

Gareth waited for Grodray and Baker to pass, and then nodded Talyarkinash to precede him. They were the last four out of the court room, a sanctuary of law in the midst of a semi-secret, Constabulary research facility on *Irron*.

Gareth had been brought here so the Constables could study the genetic engineering Talyarkinash had programmed into him.

Every other one of the seventeen species in the *Accord of Souls* had been fixed by the Chaa, the Elders, fifty thousand years ago. Sixteen of the those species had been uplifted into their current forms at the time, and most of the Vanir had been reduced to a rough equivalence. The few remaining Chaa had then transformed themselves into gods of some sort and gone looking for the One True God who had created everything.

Nobody had expected humans to suddenly become a technological species in that time, so the Chaa had left them alone.

Which was a dreadful mistake on their part. The rest of the *Accord* was stuck in their forms and could not be modified in any significant way, beyond fixing flaws and changing hair and skin color.

Nobody but Gareth could become a Star Dragon.
Except, perhaps, another human.

ALTERNATIVES

MARC SMILED as he considered the machine in front of him. It was off right now, but that was purely a safety measure.

On, it could be lethal.

Standing next to him in the small lab workshop was Zorge, an older Nari scientist turned spymaster who was still with Marc after so many of the others had fled or been captured.

"What am I looking at?" the Nari asked as Marc touched at the machine.

It was manlike in silhouette. Around six feet tall. Bipedal. Two arms ending in human-like hands with opposable thumbs.

"My kind called this an android," Marc purred.

Zorge only slightly flinched at the implications.

Humans were considered so dangerous that all knowledge of the *Accord of Souls* was blocked. There was a whole astronomy division dedicated to making sure that no signals from any *Accord* planet ever made it to Earth to be picked up and possibly give those xenocidal maniacs any clue that they weren't alone in the universe.

Marc had been human, once. Had been kidnapped via wormhole and brought here by a crime lord who wanted his own personal killer. Before that man realized he couldn't control such a beast.

So Marc took over. But Zorge stayed.

"Android," the Nari man mused, his ears flickering back and forth in a rhythm with his whiskers. "What do you do with it?"

"At one time, it was considered a labor-saving device," Marc replied. "You could program it to do things instead of humans having to. All the boring and mundane, or the very dangerous. Androids fell out of fashion a long time ago and never got used in any numbers."

"Why not?" Zorge asked. "Sounds like a useful thing, to be able to just tell a machine to clean the floors, or rush into a burning building to rescue people."

"Oh, humans still have *robots*," Marc stressed the difference. "But those are automated systems that are engineered and optimized for to do one thing only. Like a small disk about a foot across and six inches tall that has a brush and a vacuum built in, to automatically sweep the rugs on a daily schedule. Or mighty factory robots that pick up three pieces of a vehicle, drop them into perfect alignment, and weld them exactly true every time. Androids are generalists."

"Okay," Zorge reached up with one paw and scratched at his muttonchop sideburns absently. "So why are we needing one?"

"Androids can be programmed to do a few, repetitive tasks that lets them replace human workers. Or Nari, or Grace. Whoever," Marc smiled. "And they will be obedient to me, because they have been programmed that way."

Marc saw the lightbulb come on in Zorge's eyes. The old Nari liked to pretend to be a simple scientist who dabbled as a spymaster from time to time, but Marc knew the truth. Knew how many citizens of the *Accord* had met an untimely end at the hands of the Nari man.

Even Maiair and Yooyar, his Warreth cohorts that, with Zorge, formed his inner council, had only killed half as many people as the Nari had in his rise within the crime organization.

"They won't rat you out to the Constables," Zorge breathed heavily. "And they'll carry guns, but they aren't bound by the *Accord*, unless you program them thus."

"Exactly," Marc's grin turned feral.

"So what about the rest of us?" Zorge asked carefully.

Marc turned more fully to watch the scientist. It was important that his inner circle stay loyal. They were the basis of building his new empire.

"These do one thing," Marc explained carefully. "They will kill things. That's all. They don't talk to people. Don't build. Don't do anything else except protect me, us, from Constables and other criminals."

"Do they have to kill?" Zorge asked, obviously uncomfortable, in spite of his own background.

Very few members of the *Accord* were born broken enough that killing didn't do something bad and strange in their heads. People like Zorge had managed to overcome it, usually in rage or fear. Flight or fight syndrome.

"It has a hand," Marc said. "What you put in that hand is your choice. These things are tools, just like hammers or guns. We will retain control. But I am never going to put my safety in the hands of someone I don't trust again. That comes down to you and the girls. Nobody else. When we rebuild the organization, maybe there will be others."

"Understood, boss," Zorge nodded. And then he paused for a moment.

Marc watched the furry scientist walk slowly around the machine again, studying it from all angles before he stopped and looked at Marc.

""Does it have to be this size?" Zorge asked, his whole face screwed a little sideways in concentration. It was almost of a height with the Nari.

"As opposed to?" Marc asked, intrigued.

He had expected a major argument with the man. After all, killer robots on the loose was almost as bad a threat as humans. Like he had been.

But something about the machine had piqued the scientist in the Nari, obviously.

"Two thoughts," Zorge answered distantly. "One, why not make one nine or ten feet tall, to scare the hell out of even the Vanir? Or maybe fifteen feet tall? Something huge."

Marc paused and considered. He had been thinking in human terms again. Six feet tall, as a labor-saving robot soldier who wouldn't discretely call the cops and narc on him when he slept.

But Vanir males were often over seven feet tall. He himself was seven foot four, these days, as was Gareth. Maybe he did need something that could overawe even *Those Left Behind*, the Vanir who liked to think of themselves as the direct descendants of the Chaa, in a galaxy where everyone else had been uplifted?

"I'll consider it," Marc said, listening to both the angel on his left shoulder as well as the devil on the right. "Two?"

"Two," Zorge replied grimly. "Do we need one big enough to wrestle with a Star Dragon?"

SEEKER

ROYSTON LOUGHTY, PhD, WMU, FRS, CBE, CStJ, considered the massive, complicated device resting on his lab bench like a beached whale. He was the man affectionately known on this station as "The Big Brain" but even he was half-certain that much of what was resting in front of him could be just as adequately explained as magic as it could physics.

But he was a scientist. Doctor of Physics. Warden of the Mathematical Union. Fellow of the Royal Society. Commander, British Empire. Commander, Order of St. John. One of the preeminent physicists in the solar system, and certainly the top expert on the types of solar radiation that Earth Force employed.

Only a handful of men, and one woman, could even follow the details of the paper he had written. Dr. Sir Westfield van Duren-Abbott PhD, FRS, GMU, KCB, GBE was one of them. The Grand Old Man of science himself.

Royston expected that one of the two of them would eventually have to write a second paper, just to boil it all down into terms that the average genius mathematician or physicist could follow, to say nothing of the man on the street.

Magic, indeed.

The door to his vast lab opened as he pulled a pipe from the pocket of his tweed jacket and considered stuffing it into his mouth. Something to chew on, to keep him from grinding his teeth in frustration.

"So it must be going well," Philippa Loughty, his only daughter, smiled and laughed as he walked in and spied him. "You only smoke that damnable pipe when you think you've hit a dead end and haven't yet convinced yourself you've solved whatever problem confronted you."

"Eh?" he looked up, surprised and perhaps abashed.

She might be right. Pippa usually was. That was why he had taken her on as his assistant, when all the major universities refused to admit a woman into their PhD programs in higher math or astrophysics. Nobody else was willing to admit that a woman might be the intellectual equal of a man.

Fools.

Pippa walked close and kissed him on the cheek. She was a bright spot of color in her uniform as an Women's Auxiliary of Earth Force Sky Patrol. Crimson skirt just past her knees. Matching tunic as long as a blazer, double-breasted over the left with gold buttons and gold embroidery lacing. A yellow stripe edged the tunic and the collar, making her look like a true professional woman, emphasizing the red hair and bright green eyes of her Scots heritage.

"Is it done?" she asked, spreading a hand to indicate the machine on the desk.

Royston put the pipe back in his pocket, aware that he just might bite through the stem in frustration.

"Theoretically," he announced in an irritated growl. "The gentlemen who built it to my specifications and designs had to do some fancy work inside in places, and could not actually test it."

"Why not, Father?" Pippa's beautiful face scrunched up in confusion.

"Well, for one, the power requirements would require at least eighteen percent of the full output of this station's power plant, dear," Royston replied. "I have not yet gotten approval to set up such an experiment, even to try to configure the machine. Plus there is the safety aspect."

"Safety?" she asked. "How dangerous could it be?"

"We'll be opening a wormhole in physical space, Pippa," Royston scowled at her. "It might suddenly turn into a black hole and destroy this entire station. If we were on the ground, it might destroy the Earth."

She grinned and kissed him on the cheek again, lacing her arm through his elbow.

"And Oppenheimer had the exact same concerns at Alamogordo, Father," she reminded him. "At a standard deviation in the same rough neighborhood as a cash register spontaneously turning into an ice cream machine. Certainly, if it requires that much power to simply open, it won't have enough to trigger any sort of feedback loop faster than you could cut the feeds, could it?"

She reached out a hand and tapped the one device he had insisted be external to everything else. A guillotine large enough to kill a rabbit perhaps, poised on powerful springs to sever the immense power cables that would feed the ravenous beast when he activated it.

Without enough power, the theory said that the wormholes would collapse back into Einstinian physics immediately, leaving only a trace of radiation. That trace that had first set him on this mad quest six months ago.

Even in his own mind, it sounded like the worst mixture of a lurid spy thriller combined with the silliest, most over-the-top scientifictional tale.

Open a wormhole in space. Reach through and kidnap a man from his own cabin, never to be seen again.

To what end?

And yet, six months ago, Gareth St. John Dankworth, Field Agent of Earth Forces Sky Patrol, had vanished. Gone. Leaving no trace at all, except a detectable type of radiation that had no place in the current Extended Model of Physics. The understanding of the universe accepted by everyone else.

In pursuing that, Pippa had accused him of having an incomplete understanding of physics and the universe. Which had galled him all the more, when he realized that she had been right. So he invented more physics, more mathematics.

And built himself a machine. One that frightened him as much as he thrilled at the possibilities. Could they really travel through wormholes to other worlds? Explore the universe?

What would they find out there?

But, more importantly, *who* would they find?

It had not been a natural occurrence, when Gareth vanished. Someone had opened that tube, Royston was sure.

Why? And why Gareth?

"Father?" Pippa broke into his train of thought.

"Hmm?"

"Is this device safe enough to test?" she asked, voice suddenly a bit more abashed.

"Indeed, Pippa," Royston tried to assuage her. "The cut-out will function perfectly, severing the line with non-conductive blades that are irresistible. I have considered a dead-man switch as well, so that if something were to happen and I lost control, loosening my grip would trigger the blades as well."

"So why then are you so frustrated?" Pippa stayed close, leaned against him.

With her mother gone, it was just the two of them. Had been for nearly two decades. And she was as brilliant, and as stubborn as her mother had been.

"I think it will work," Royston mumbled nervously.

"And?"

"What if we are not alone in the universe, dear child?" Royston asked.

TROUBLE

GARETH FOLLOWED the other three into a small conference room that had been set up for lunch, glasses and linens already laid out. Stewards were just placing plates of hot food and filling glasses, and they quickly departed.

Must have been following the trial and just waiting for everyone to get out.

Quickly, they sat, three Vanir at a table full-sized for them and a Nari whose chair and foot rest had been elevated until she was comfortable enough to eat with the others.

Lunch wasn't cow, but the meat was close enough. And the vegetable wasn't a potato. Wasn't even remotely related to a potato, but it served a close enough purpose to hold butter, sour cream, and bacon. Or the gustatory equivalents thereof.

Food went quickly and they settled for coffee. Gareth was glad that none of the others smoked tobacco. That smell would just undercut a fine meal.

Grodray fixed him with a professorial eye.

"It has been five months," Grodray said in a characteristically terse tone. "People who saw you flying above *Orgoth Vortai* have largely written the entire thing off as some sort of crazy, massive public relations stunt organized as part of the *Accord* Ball. We have not worked to dissuade them of that notion."

Gareth nodded. He had done his duty that night, saving Morty and Xiomber and the driver of the van from dying when the crime boss Omerlon shot out the controls of the flying machine. That had gotten the man convicted of attempted murder of a Constabulary officer, so he was going to rot in prison forever.

But they had also laid low in the time since.

Partly, that was Grodray and Baker suddenly breaking open one of the biggest corruption scandals in the history of the *Accord of Souls*. They had been too busy chasing and catching all the cockroaches revealed when someone turned the kitchen light on.

Gareth had returned to *Irron* with Talyarkinash to train and study his abilities more, and eventually Morty and Xiomber joined them, to try to understand what a Star Dragon was, and what it could and couldn't do. The boys were now permanent convicts, but that really didn't mean anything, as far as Gareth could tell.

"Now that things have calmed down, the decision has been made to put you back out in the field," Grodray continued. "Maximus has vanished completely this time, and nobody is even talking about the man. We can't tell if that's good news or bad, but all leads have dried up in the time we spent dismantling Omerlon's organization. And dealing with a number of bent or criminal officers of the courts that needed to be removed as well. Baker?"

Every eye turned to Grodray's partner now. Eveth Baker would be a Prime Investigator soon. Of that Gareth had no doubts. She was young, barely four years older than Gareth, but she was being groomed for big things.

Like running Gareth in the field. Possibly being the senior officer to him, if Gareth was made a full-fledged officer in the future, rather than just…whatever he was now. Trying to do the right thing as best he knew how.

She took a deep breath and seemed to transform herself away from the ball of angry energy she usually presented, to something calm and almost scholarly.

"Gareth, I went back and read your report about the *Accord* Ball," Baker said simply, eyes locking with him across the table. "Before you spotted Morty and Xiomber, you were in the process of establishing a very useful contact with Diệu Ahn Jamart, an extremely wealthy art collector."

Gareth blushed as he thought back to the night. Her outfit that night had barely covered her enough for polite company, even in that crowd, showing off an extraordinary amount of pinkish, tanned skin marked all over with large freckle patterns, from the bits he had been able to see. And imagine. It had been like standing next to a bipedal giraffe.

"That's right," Gareth said. "I have not contacted her as yet, pending orders. I am not sure I would be able to."

"The number she gave you was her personal comm," Baker said with a smug smile. "We've confirmed with the right people that it still works."

Gareth felt all the blood drain out of his entire body, rushing instead into his face. That night, he had been moments from being pulled by the incredibly tall Borren woman into an interspecies erotica exhibit at the *Accord* Hall of Arts.

An interactive exhibit.

It was a Grace museum. A people who were human-sized bipeds that could pass for human at a distance. Until you got close enough to realize that instead of hair they had a mass of writing tentacles equipped with extensive sensory capabilities. And that they liked to touch.

Finding those two criminal scientists at the last moment had been the greatest breakthrough in his life, as far as he was concerned.

Gareth gulped again. Baker seemed to be enjoying his discomfort as she watched silently.

Talyarkinash wasn't any better at hiding her grin.

"Enough," Grodray growled. Dad cracking the whip.

Baker sobered immediately.

"You will contact her," Baker said. "You will continue to use the cover of a traveling art critic and reporter with no last name. One who writes under a penname. It is our hope that she will provide you access to elements of society that the Constabulary is excluded from."

The dissipated wealthy, Gareth supposed. Those people with so much money that they couldn't spend it all if they tried. The kind who collected esoteric art. The really weird stuff.

"Am I real?" Gareth scowled at Baker

"Real?" she replied, utterly confused.

"Is there actually a bi-line somewhere?" Gareth said. "Some authentic art critic and fashion reporter from the Constabulary who does write this sort of thing, when you need to send someone under cover?"

Baker paused and looked sideways at Grodray.

The older man smiled like he had just won a bet.

"Indeed there is, Gareth," Grodray said. "You'll travel to meet him shortly, and we will supply you with a collection of things you supposedly have written over the last few years, so that you can be prepared, in case someone tries to trip you up later."

"How many of me are there?" Gareth said. "No, don't answer that. Above my pay grade and I don't really want to know."

Grodray just smiled.

"At present, we do not have any leads," Baker continued. "Nor do we necessarily expect anything out of such contacts, but you are to keep your eyes open. If something comes up, your job is to call me or Grodray and let us handle it. You will not get yourself into trouble, nor will you display your capabilities. Am I clear?"

"Yes, ma'am," Gareth nodded sharply. "Deep cover."

"Deep enough," Grodray spoke up now. "As your cover is a reporter, you can remain in regular contact with your editor. Baker will run you just like an editor would. You will write up reports as if they were going to be edited and reviewed before publication in some magazine, so keep your language clear, and don't be afraid to include whatever background materials you feel appropriate."

"What do we actually know about Diệu Ahn?" Gareth asked. "I read a brief bio five months ago, but nothing since."

"She divorced one enormously wealthy husband, and outlived a second one," Baker said grimly. "Somewhere in the top five hundred richest people in the *Accord*. Collects things that catch her eye. She will attempt to seduce you."

"She can try," Gareth growled under his breath.

"Understood," Baker acknowledged. "This is more a warning than an expectation of success."

Baker turned the firehose of her attention to Talyarkinash now.

"Doctor Liamssen, now that the two Yuudixtl have been officially remanded into custody, you will be transferred with them to work directly with Dr. Fitzroy, with whom you have previously consulted. Until we can capture or eliminate Marc Sarzynski, there is a significant risk that he will try to bring in more humans, as well as potentially performing experiments on himself to match Gareth."

"Okay," Talyarkinash replied evenly. "What part will I play?"

"We need the three of you to build me a human detector," Baker smiled savagely. "Gareth is supposedly Vanir now, as is Sarzynski, but the transformation does not appear to have made either of them part of the *Accord*, at least that psionic link we all share to one degree or another."

"I see," the Nari geneticist said. "And we need to find out how to identify a transformed human?"

"The four of you, with Dalton, are the principal experts on humans I have available, Doctor," Baker replied simply. "We cannot protect the *Accord* unless we can identify infiltrators. How they are dealt with is another department, and one I'm not interested in. We're the hunters."

"Will we remain on *Irron*?" Talyarkinash asked.

"You will for now," Grodray spoke up. "Eve and I will trail Gareth at a safe enough distance, working mainly from a private office on *Orgoth Vortai*. Dalton Fitzroy is a Prime Investigator, like myself, so she will be able to punch through any bureaucratic issues that come up. Questions?"

Gareth and Talyarkinash both shook their heads. It was too early to know anything, but they had been planning for this. Now it was time to put everything into action.

Gareth just wished he had Pippa here to talk to. Diệu Ahn as likely to make unacceptable demands on him, and he would have to find a way to navigate the Scylla and Charybdis of the case.

It would not be fun.

PRISONER 1000786128

MORTY PUT the book down as the lock to his cell rattled loudly.

It was a compact space, if a bit roomy for a Yuudixtl, being Vanir-scaled. Bed permanently attached to the wall as a shelf. Sink and toilet in a corner. Small bookshelves hanging from another corner. Light switch by door that only worked to lower things to dimness, not darkness.

Learning to sleep with the lights on had been the hardest part of prison. Even the food wasn't all that bad. Of course, until today, the cops had wanted to keep him and his egg-brother cooperative.

This morning, he had sealed his fate.

Now, he got to find out what that would be.

The big cop entered as the door opened. Grodray. The terror of the underworld, according to everything Morty had known about the man, back when he was still a full-time criminal scientist.

Grodray brought a wooden chair into the room and sat on it as Morty put his book off to one side and concentrated on the man.

The door closed loudly and the locks shot home with a thump.

Silence fell.

Vanir were huge. Seven feet tall. Twice Morty's size. Nearly three times his weight. Skin without scales, but with fur in strange places. Grodray might actually look pretty good, if he grew a beard. It had made a helluva change in Gareth.

Course, might also come in completely gray now, too. There was that. Yuudixtl just got yellower in the scales as they aged.

Expressive and communicative face, at least compared to the hard ridges and bone of a Yuudixtl. Pointy ears that looked like they should move, catlike, like Talyarkinash Liamssen's did, but didn't.

Oh well.

Not a lot of communication going on with that face right now. Maximus had been like that. Hard, cold stare designed to unnerve people. Usually worked.

Morty wasn't that impressed. He cocked his head to one side and just sort of grinned at the guy.

What more can you do to me besides sentence me to death, officer?

Silence.

"Why?" Grodray announced suddenly.

Morty cocked his head the other way.

"Could you narrow that down, Grodray?" Morty asked. "I've done some amazingly stupid shit over the years, so I'm not sure which bad decision you want to talk about today."

Pause. Hard-ass cop stare.

"So let's start with Gareth," Grodray said. "I've read all your statements and reports, Morty, so don't give me that line of crap. Tell me the truth about the man."

Morty took a deep breath. Only Xiomber knew that story, as far as those sorts of things went.

Not that he expected a cop like Grodray to get it. But what the hell? They would be recording whatever he said for posterity anyway, after he was dead.

"Because I thought I was God, the first time," Morty finally replied.

"God?" Grodray's grunt was not all that amused.

"Cinnra wanted himself a human," Morty said. "A killer. So I got him one. Well, me and Xiomber did. He's the smart one. I'm the sneaky one. Went and located the baddest, most dangerous human criminal I could find. Turned out he was a renegade cop. He came, he saw, he conquered. Cinnra's dead and Marc Sarzynski takes the name Maximus. And now we're going places."

"Such as?" Grodray asked.

"If we'd done nothing to stop him, Maximus would have taken over the entire underworld on *Zathus* once and for all by now," Morty said.

"Then the government itself. Because nothing could have stopped him. Nothing at all, okay?"

"Okay," Grodray allowed.

I mean, if we're going to be honest here, cop, let's talk turkey.

"But then I woke up one morning and my house was on fire," Morty continued. "Just a small one, but what do you do when the stove is suddenly on fire and it's too big for you to put out alone?"

"Call for help," Grodray nodded.

"Yeah, but what kind of help?" Morty felt his face and voice get all growly now. "And it is my fault that Maximus is likely to take over the whole shooting match. If I hadn't thought I was a God, I wouldn't have built the machine to grab the guy, one step ahead of his own cops arresting him, back home. Turns out later that Gareth, of all people, had Sarzynski's gang cornered, and had caught most of them. But they missed out on the big guy."

"But—" Grodray started to say, but Morty cut him off.

"So if I burn the whole damned house down, I don't really get to complain about sleeping in the backyard when it rains, do I?" Morty snapped. "Once I woke up to that, the rest was easy. Set the psionic parameters almost exactly the opposite of what they had been before, look for a signal that matches, and realize the guy's a cop. A human cop, of all things. But he's the best fit I can find if I want to stop Maximus from taking over the whole damned galaxy. Kidnapping Gareth and bringing him to the *Accord* might be the biggest crime I've committed in a lifetime of debauchery, but let me tell you this. It was also the smartest thing I've ever done. And I'd do it again, if I had to. When we got separated from Gareth that first time, on *Hurquar*, he told us to find another Earth Force Sky Patrol Agent if we had to, and explain it all to them, using his name."

"Treason and Attempting to Overthrow the *Accord*," Grodray quoted at him, but Morty wasn't having any of it.

"That was Maximus," the Yuudixtl said angrily. "Gareth was to stop Sarzynski and save the damned *Accord*."

"And the Star Dragon?" Grodray asked.

"Kid's crazy as a junebug, Grodray," Morty replied. "We were just gonna turn him into another Vanir, so he had an even chance to hide and stop the crooks. He wanted something big and splashy. Something that would strike utter terror into the hearts and minds of criminals everywhere. If I thought I could have wings and breathe fire like that, I would have stayed in legitimate business, buddy."

"Okay," Grodray nodded. "So what do I do with you and your egg-brother?"

"I told Xiomber that I'd rather spend forty years complaining that I had read the entire prison library twice, than be dead," Morty said. "I can't imagine you trust me, whatever I do or say, so what can I do?"

"You willing to work?" Grodray asked in a hard voice. "You and your brother? To spend the rest of your lives trying to save galactic civilization?"

"Yeah," Morty said simply. "Can't talk for him, but you and Gareth are the only things protecting us from Maximus."

"I've got the entire Constabulary, Morty," Grodray growled back.

"And it won't be enough, cop," Morty snapped. "Unless you know something I don't."

"We'll see."

Grodray rose suddenly. Lifted the immense chair easily and carried it to the door. One mighty fist banged three times on the metal door and it opened.

Morty found himself alone in his cell again as the door slammed and locked, wound all the way up to the point he hopped off the bed and began to pace.

How the hell would *he* stop Maximus, it was up to him?

REPORTER

THE HOTEL LOBBY was vast enough to have its own telephone zone, as Gareth walked in from the busy street.

Cream and tan marble on the floor, supporting white, stone columns that dominated a three-story vaulted space with two mezzanines wrapped around the edge, with glass fronts of their own so people could see everything. There were people here, but most of them looked like they were trying to be seen, rather than actually waiting for anyone.

This hotel had that kind of reputation. Famous people passed through, staying and making their reputation as much as the hotel's. Perhaps they were here to be interviewed on their next project. It was a good place for an undercover fashion and art reporter to use as his base, while he penetrated the world of elite luxury.

Gareth had studied all the things he had supposedly written over the last few years under a pseudonymous penname. Fashion and art, for the most part, with the occasional foray into writing puff pieces on fabulous vacation spots for the extremely wealthy.

The kinds of places where your name was on a secret list, or you weren't even allowed to know it existed.

Being undercover and not being required to be dressed as a dandy, he had fallen back on a replica of the outfit he first got when he came to the *Accord of Souls*. Baker had approved the replacement for the identical outfit Gareth still kept in his closet. The one that was still only human sized. Gareth had considered adding a cowboy-style hat, but decided that would be too much, most of the time.

So comfortable cowboy boots with a heel high enough for roping, but low enough to walk considerable distances, and not too sharp a toe. Black dungaree pants, baggy enough that they covered his boots instead of tucking into them. He still missed his Sky Patrol tunic, but in its place he had a plain, white T-shirt, underneath a button-down, button-up shirt in Sky Patrol plaid colors. So he was almost home. A blue denim jacket with bronzed buttons on the breast pockets and a small SP button stuck through the flap of the left breast pocket completed the look.

The only addition of note had been a plain, gold ring on his left hand. He could lie and pretend to be engaged, and use that as an excuse to turn down invitations gracefully. Explaining the truth to someone was impossible, anyway.

So here he was. Dressed up and ready to go.

As it was, he already felt like if he added a pair of toy, nickel capguns in twin holsters, he'd be seven years old again and all set to play Cowboys and Indians.

But this outfit worked. All he had to do was wear it into Talyarkinash's lab and watch her eyes light up. Or walk up to the lunchroom and sit where the female members of the Constabulary could watch him.

He had no idea how or why, but it was apparently *a good thing*, to hear Baker and Grodray talk. And it helped keep him out of a jail cell, where he really, honestly deserved to be, all things considered.

Or a freak show.

Gareth didn't let himself go down that path.

A self-important Grace in a fancy suit accosted him as he crossed the floor, looking around. The tentacles for hair just added an edge of weird to Gareth's day.

"May I help you, sir?" he asked in a voice filled with serene, superior doubt on the topic.

Obviously, one of *those* people who had wandered into the wrong building by accident. Or not known to use the delivery entrance around back.

Something about the man's silent sneer just rubbed Gareth entirely the wrong way.

Rather than answer, Gareth drew himself up to his full height, glaring down at the man from a head and a half higher. He reached inside the comfortable jacket and pulled out an oversized card.

"Is my room ready?" Gareth snapped at the Grace in a peremptory voice.

Mother would have taken a wooden spoon to his bottom for such a tone, but she wasn't here, and the role called for it, apparently.

The difference in the Grace was night and day.

Suddenly, Gareth wasn't an imposter, but *Important People* who must be fawned over, and how could the Grace man have possibly make such a terrible mistake?

"I'm sure it is," the Grace said, carefully taking the card from his hand to inspect it before swiftly leading Gareth to the discrete desk off to one side.

A cute Nari girl, barely out of her teens but composed and professional, stood behind the counter and took the card from the man.

"Mary will take excellent care of you, sir," the concierge promised in an utterly obsequious tone. "Did you have luggage?"

"It will be delivered this afternoon," Gareth noted absently, drolly. Playing a role he barely believed himself.

Seriously, were people normally like this?

"Very good, sir," and the Grace was gone.

"Just Gareth?" Mary asked carefully. "No last name?"

"That's right," he said, playing the role Baker and Grodray had assigned him. Mysterious and aloof.

"Everything is already taken care of, then, sir," Mary said, looking down at a screen on her side of the desk.

She paused for a moment, sniffing him. He had enough experience with Talyarkinash doing the same thing to note the way the nostrils worked. And the whiskers and ears twitching out of tune with each other.

"May I escort you to your room, Gareth?" Mary asked brightly.

Gareth swallowed the snarl that wanted to blister the girl. He would just have to get used to a world where females could be just as forward as males, bizarre as it was. Where he would be absently propositioned for meaningless sexual encounters by strangers in hotel lobbies, if he wasn't careful.

Worse, once he dove into this world, they would frequently be people with money, who were unused to being rebuffed.

Tough, buddy.

"Absolutely," Gareth allowed, rocking his weight back onto his heels.

She came around the counter with a plastic keycard in one hand and a small envelope that she handed him, passing too close for politeness. Just barely brushing herself against his side.

The elevator ride was pleasant, as long as he focused on the lights and not the young girl focused on him.

The room was larger inside than Patrol Cutter *Bellerophon*, his first independent command, had been. Huge. Suite didn't do it justice, as it had a full kitchen and dining room, three subsidiary bedroom suites, and a salon large enough for his junior high chess club to hold tournaments in, plus a balcony that was four meters deep and ran the entire width of the suite, which was a significant radius of the hotel itself.

Mary had to show him everything. He smiled and thought happy thoughts until he managed to get her out the door and drop the deadbolt into place. He considered sliding a heavy chair into the way as well, but stopped himself and moved out to the balcony to relax and enjoy the view.

They were on *Morthri*, the original homeworld of the Nari. The skies weren't the blue of *Earth* that he kept expecting when he looked up. Nor the greener skies of *Irron* where he had come from most recently. But at the same time, the reddish hue overhead wasn't the cotton candy of *Orgoth Vortai*.

The Underhives of Mars were probably the closest comparison he could make, in those rare times when you got out onto the surface to walk around, rather than staying safely below ground.

Watching the sun slowly set as he stood on his balcony, he could see the inland sea in the near distance, and a swimming pool so close below that a cliff diver could have made a living.

"Well, hello," a voice came from his right. Female. Cheery. Welcoming. "It is so good to see you again."

Gareth turned at the voice and located the speaker. He watched Diệu Ahn lift her head up to smile at him, from where she had been lying face down on a lounge chair sunbathing. Hopefully, she had a towel below her, because as near as Gareth could tell, she was completely nude otherwise.

DESTROYER OF WORLDS

ROYSTON SURVEYED the walls of the massive bunker where his experimental equipment had been installed. The Sector Marshal had tried to insist that someone else be here conducting it, but Royston had put his foot down rather angrily at that suggestion.

The man had only subsided when Royston pointed out that the only other person qualified to handle the machinery was his daughter. It was a low, cruel blow, forcing the man to confront his own cultural chauvinism, but it was still God's honest truth. And Royston didn't always play nice.

As a consolation, they had lengthened many of the cables. It put Royston two meters away from the machinery, instead of lurking over it, but he couldn't see what difference it might make. The radiation involved was not working on anything like an inverse square model here. He would be just as exposed. Just as at risk.

But anything to assuage the Sector Marshal. Alvin obviously feared that losing Royston to an accident would be a blot on his career that nothing would ever remove.

And while he might be right, the Sector Marshal had nothing he could actually do here except sign off on the final approvals that made it all happen and let him build this little fortress.

So Royston was standing in a secured, insulated bunker located in the middle of the Arizona desert. Inside walls nearly a meter thick and reinforced with armor cladding over that. Air conditioning kept the space cool and moist, as though he was still at a LaGrange Point station in space.

The machinery on the wooden bench had seen better days. Scars from energy, chemistry, and brute force had left their marks on the glossy, black surface. Two power cables thicker than his arm passed through holes in the wall on his right and went off to the massive generators that had been installed nearby outside.

There were no other humans within fifteen miles at this point, so if he did manage to blow himself up, hopefully nobody else would be hurt in the process.

Oppenheimer had grown apocalyptic in his old age, convinced that he had personally opened the way for the destruction of the world and death of all humanity. Royston had his doubts about this particular theory, and the tools to exploit it, but at the same time, there was that element of risk in the back of his mind.

Certainly, this was possibly the greatest step forward for humanity in centuries. Since Einstein, perhaps.

But Royston was here because someone else had shown him it was possible. Had opened the door in his mind, just as they had opened the portal into Gareth's cabin.

They wished to remain anonymous. Whoever they were. And Royston was likely to wander up to their front door and knock at some point soon.

Hopefully, they would be charitable hosts, along the old Nordic model, and not cannibals.

No time like the present.

Royston walked once around the apparatus to confirm everything in his mind.

"Activating power," he said aloud, knowing his words were being communicated to the Sector Marshal via several radio microphones. Possibly a few others. Sir West had suggested that Her Majesty might be listening in surreptitiously, as might an American President and a few others.

This was bigger than one country. Bigger than the Sky Patrol. Possibly bigger than all of Earth Force.

A small rocker switch had been installed on the right. He flipped it now, and listened to the machine slowly hum to itself.

"We read power on, Doctor Loughty," a man's voice replied quickly. "Edging towards the high end, but still within the band you set previously."

Royston grinned silently. Those bands had been picked arbitrarily. To use the vulgar vernacular, a SWAG. *Scientific Wild-Ass Guess.*

Half of his theory would need to be revised and refined after this, in light of experimental observations. By him if he survived. By Pippa otherwise. But which half was the question to explore.

Royston moved to study the two big gauges set in the face of the machine. Both read zero right now.

He stepped close and turned a dial slowly, watching the needles begin to move, ever so slightly. Again, *SWAG.* Not that he could ever tell anyone that. Except perhaps Sir West. That man understood the nature of pushing the edges of an envelope.

The air took on a golden hue around him as the machine's quiet hum built up to a low C on a concert grand piano.

"Radiation readings at one point eight, Dr. Loughty," the man said aloud. "Stable. Nothing dangerous detected on other bands."

No, there wouldn't be. Either it would work perfectly, or it would fail. Or he would somehow open a portal large enough to annihilate the Earth, and do it so quickly that nobody was likely to notice.

There was that.

He adjusted the knob one last time, getting right to two point zero and letting it hum to itself for several seconds before it decided it was happy.

So far, so good.

Royston moved around to the long end of the bench and studied the Rube Goldberg contraption that his young engineers had made for him. A simple, elevated track starting at shoulder height and running straight and true for about four feet, to a spot eleven inches above the table top itself, where a final curve would bounce the marble coming off the tracks onto the work top.

That much was Newtonian. Almost Gallilean. Simple and safe.

At the far end of the bench, a bowl had been placed. White porcelain with a blue flower pattern around the rim. Six inches deep and a twelve across. Someone's wife or mother might miss it, come fall when it was time to make casseroles again.

Royston addressed himself to the set of switches installed here. These were larger. They reminded him of mad science in ancient horror movies from the early cinema era. The kind you grabbed with your whole hand and slammed shut like a gunshot.

Hopefully, they had just run out of rocker switches in the

construction, and it wasn't the case that someone was making a socio-political statement on Royston's work.

Not that he would blame them, for this truly was mad science.

And yet…

With his left hand, Royston reached into the pocket of his tweed jacket and pulled out a simple marble. A catseye he had owned for fifty-some years. Just the right thing for this.

It grounded him.

"Activating primary power," he said to history.

With his right, Royston took hold of the first switch's handle and closed it.

Somewhere nearby, the generators would come to a higher level of activity, preparing to feed their enormous river of power into the ravenous beast before him.

The lights flickered ominously, but Royston was prepared for that. At least in his mind. If he lost all lights, he had a pocket flash he could pull out. And the doors were locked from the inside with simple mechanical devices, rather than electronics.

The golden hue in the air was brighter now. The air had a smell of ozone and something else he couldn't place. Almost sweet, but that made no sense at all, except as a detail to be noted for later.

"Initiating portals," Royston announced grimly.

It was hard keeping a note of triumphalism out of his voice. Especially since Sir West was standing in the other bunker with Pippa and the Sector Marshal. Doubting, as the man would.

Still, this would be like being whacked upside the head with a four-days-rotting sand shark, if it worked. Even Sir West would be forced to come around.

Royston closed the second big switch and quickly moved to the last one. The guillotine. He was poised to kill the machine at the instant there was a problem. Probably a flaw in his math in that case, as the mechanical construction had been relatively straight forward and the men he hired to perform it worked frequently in movies, constructing amazingly detailed models and mockups as sets. Their skill and professionalism was not to be doubted.

A glowing, golden dinner plate opened beneath the ramp in front of him. Four inches above the surface of the workbench. Possibly eight inches across, and barely one deep, except that Royston suspected he would see infinity if he looked down. Like lining two mirrors up and watching reflections of reflections.

If he dared.

Across the way, a matching golden glow as a reciprocal plate opened.

He hoped.

"Releasing the payload," Royston said as he placed his catseye on the track and let go.

It rolled happily down the middle of the metal tubes, slowly accelerating, until it hit the curve and plummeted six inches into eternity.

A heartbeat passed. Rapid, yes, but measurable, still.

A tinkling thump as a catseye marble emerged at the far end of the workbench and bounced once, before rattling loosely around the bottom to bleed off inertia.

Royston had been holding his breath. He released it now and watched the future explode out of his mind to reshape humanity.

It was a heady load, but he had done it. This was not the conquest of the entire galaxy, but he could see it from here.

Like Jim Ryan breaking the four minute mile centuries ago, this was as much a psychological hurdle as a scientific one. Others would suddenly have their blinders removed and would no doubt expand and improve on his theory.

But he had just teleported a marble across the length of a workbench, without it seeming to cross the space in between. Technically, he had connected the two points via a fifth-dimensional structure that acted like the inside of a half-torus, in layman's terms. Dig a tunnel underground from A to B and emerge over there.

"Dr. Loughty, is everything all right?" the technician at the other end grew concerned. "Respond, please."

"I'm here," he finally managed to say. "The experiment was a success."

He cut the power feeds and powered the device back down without lobotomizing it in the process, and the walked over to retrieve that marble.

It was a lucky one. That was why he had traded two silverfish and a bloodstone to Tommy Wilson for it, when they were both six and those sorts of things were important.

He would need that luck.

In the back of his mind, Royston expected that he had just grasped the lamp and had summoned forth a djinn.

IMPOSTER

TO BE SAFEST, at least in his mind, Gareth had insisted on a semi-public dinner, rather than having Diệu Ahn get room service delivered to one of their suites. Where she could have him privately.

She had indeed been sunbathing nude, but had transformed herself into an ingénue when she saw the effect her nudity had on Gareth. Which had somehow made it worse, as she pulled a beach towel into place, mostly, when standing.

Gareth had found himself staring rudely, hoping to catch glimpses of the things he had forbidden himself, like a teenage boy again.

It hadn't helped that she was Borren. Eight feet tall to his seven. Skinny, like a praying mantis. Perhaps a giraffe was more appropriate, when he considered the elaborate pattern of freckles that covered her *entire* body, most of which he had now seen.

She had a tiny jaw and a beautiful smile. Small nostrils emerged at the bottom of a flat, plate nose that extended up to smoothly integrate with her forehead. Hers irises were a green/gray color he found fascinating, especially with black eyeballs. And her eyes were set at angles, low at the inner bottom of an invisible box, and high at the outer corner. Twin ridges of bone and skin served the save purpose as eyebrows, he presumed.

Diệu Ahn, like all Borren, had fine hairs on her skin, like a human woman, but no other hair on her body. Just the various freckles like a giraffe's camouflage.

And a pretty smile.

She wore red tonight. A long tunic dress, almost a sundress, except it was too tight and she wore nothing under it, as far as he could tell. And as Borren were mammalian, at least her small breasts weren't outlined against the thin fabric of the dress.

For a headpiece, she had gone simple, with a structure that rested on her ears and skull and presented almost as a pillbox hat, done in red and black, with a small fascinator attached that reminded Gareth of an Aztec temple.

Gareth had stayed in his almost-cowboy outfit. He also had a black tie tuxedo and could go white-tie if the situation demanded it, but this one didn't. Or he could find several layers of formality in between with a few hours and the right haberdashery computer system.

The maître-d had seated them on a small, circular platform in the middle of the vast dining room. Where it felt like they were on display. Zoo animals, if you wanted to be rude.

Diệu Ahn ate it up like candy, while Gareth tried to maintain his equilibrium. There was undercover, and there was making such a splashy entrance that everyone might forget why you were here, except to be seen.

And here he was.

"So tell me about her," Diệu Ahn began, as they got seated and the first glass of wine served.

The only glass of wine, as far as Gareth was concerned. He could handle his alcohol, but didn't want to make a mess of himself if he had too much.

"Her?" Gareth answered blankly.

"You're wearing a ring, Gareth," Diệu Ahn smiled warmly at him and pointed with a long finger. "Hopefully that means you've found the woman for you, and it isn't just a cheap trick to keep me from sneaking into your bedroom at night and cuddling up against your back."

Gareth blushed. He didn't think she was joking. And wasn't wanting to find out, either way.

"Philippa Loughty," Gareth said. "Pippa."

"Is she the one?" Diệu Ahn's voice got serious.

"I hope so," Gareth replied. "My job takes me away for very long stretches of time, so I don't get to see her. At times, I hope she'll wait for me. But there are other times I wonder if she'd be better off finding someone else and settling down without me."

"Settle down, perhaps," Diệu Ahn said knowingly. "She wouldn't be better off."

More blush as the implications of her words struck home.

"So what brings you to *Morthri*?" Diệu Ahn picked up the conversation rather than letting them dwell in bad places.

Gareth brightened up immediately.

"Partly, my boss sent me on something of a vacation," he said. It was even more or less true. "Partly, she was intrigued that I might be able to contact you and finagle my way into your world for a time, where I could then be able to write some interesting pieces about the lives of the decadently wealthy. Her readers like that element of living vicariously."

"I see," Diệu Ahn pouted slightly. "So you didn't just come to see me?"

"Not just," Gareth let his tone grow soft. "You are still only the third woman I've ever kissed."

"Really?" that brought her back out of her shell quickly. "Such a disgrace. A handsome Vanir like you should have had his pick of the litter. All the litters."

Gareth shrugged. Part of his cover was to leave out pieces of his own backstory, but let the rest stand on its own. That way, you didn't have to keep track of the lies you had told later.

"When I was younger, I wanted to be a cop," Gareth said. "Worked my ass off for it. Even succeeded for a time, but then everything went wrong. Now, I'm just trying to get my life back on track, and find a way to make a difference in other ways."

"Unknown writer and occasional secret agent?" she asked, taking him back to his excuse for abandoning her on *Orgoth Vortai*.

"Something like that," he acknowledge glumly. That part wasn't even forced.

"Pity you wouldn't be happy as a kept man, Gareth," Diệu Ahn smiled at him, licking her lips carefully. "And hopefully, Pippa will wait. But in the meantime, I think we can have some fun. When was the last time you had a true vacation from work?"

Gareth picked up his wine glass and took a sip as he did math in his head.

"Eleven years," he answered honestly. "Just before I went off to school, I had an entire summer to myself."

"And what did you do?" she was intrigued.

"Built a cabin in the woods, on some land my family owns," he replied, letting his mind drift back. "Split the logs and fit them into the frame. Roofed it and then finished the interior from the shell inwards. Planted a garden for my mother. Swam in the lake when the day got too hot. Hiked when I didn't want to work."

"And that's your idea of a vacation, Gareth?" she was somewhere between amused and appalled, depending on how close the actual work part got to her.

"No, that's what I do when left to my own devices," he corrected her with a grin. "I have no idea how to actually vacation."

"Well, then," she raised her own glass in a toast that Gareth matched. "We'll just have to see what we can do to broaden your horizons."

They drank and smiled at each other as the waitress approached.

It would get him connected to a whole new stratum and element of society. The richest ones.

Grodray had insisted that most were good little *Accord* citizens, and that many of the so-called crimes he might encounter around them were barely worth noting in passing. But at the same time, the money to fund the criminal underworld in the galaxy had to come from somewhere.

Gareth was a bloodhound now, seeking a scent.

GENERAL

MARC and his inner crew had returned to the planet *Kani*. It made a helpful place to hide. Like when he was here six months ago, they had managed to rent an entire vacation resort area as a place to rest and work. That one had been in the midst of a major forested area.

Now, they were in their own desert, it felt like. In the cool and rainy season, this place was wall-to-wall with tourists and campers hiking hither and yon. But this was the high summer on *Kani* at this latitude, and it didn't get below thirty degrees Celsius at night, running up above forty routinely during the day.

That was okay. His Vanir body could tolerate that level of heat far better than his human one had. And the Warreth as a rule didn't start to lose mental efficiency until things got above forty-five degrees.

Only the Nari really complained. Well, the younger ones. Zorge commented that he was always cold as an old man, so the extra heat made him comfortable. The kids needed toughening, anyway.

So Marc had brought everyone to a resort for a month. Toughen them up, like Zorge said, by making them hike and exercise in heat. Put them through something like he had done in basic training, when he joined Sky Patrol. Make soldiers out of them, instead of just hired thugs. Washing out here meant demotion, since Marc was going to form his elite out of the survivors.

That meant everyone worked that much harder.

Today, Marc was on a mesa with Zorge, Maiair, and Yooyar, plus a few of the more science-minded of his crew: a couple of Nari and three Warreth troopers.

Mishalska, one of the Nari, had gone so far in this heat as to clip most of his tan fur extremely short, and then buzz strange patterns into the remainder, like tribal markings. The young man was standing close by, acting as a bodyguard today with a beam rifle held point down and eyes constantly in motion.

In the distance, a flying truck was approaching, beginning to circle prior to touching down.

"Is it safe?" Maiair asked quietly from close by.

"There are risks," Marc answered. "But we need to take them at this point."

She withdrew a few steps and drew her own pistol from the holster on her thigh, looking now like a copy of her younger sister, with both of them armed and alert. Both wore heavy cotton pants in taupe, with black hiking boots, and bikini tops in red that matched their feathers.

The Warreth had originally been uplifted by the Chaa from a creature similar to an emu, back on *Earth*. The Gods had transformed them into bipedal mammals that gave birth to live young, rather than egg-layers, when they patterned them similar to the Vanir, but they still had feathers covering their skin and providing communicative head feathers and short beaks instead of lips.

And they were both killers. That was all Marc really cared about.

The truck dropped down finally and landed with a small whirlwind of dust kicked up as it settled.

A man stepped out of the passenger side with a smile.

"Maximus, it is good to see you," he said.

Gonquah was Th'Tarni. On most worlds where they lived, the species formed something of a culturally- and socially-oppressed minority. Marc could understand why.

The man was short. Just over five feet tall, so short even for them. He had dark skin that was rough, almost like tree bark, and covered on his neck and the sides of his face with freckles that glowed with their own internal light, as did the eyes that had no iris or pupil, just a baby blue ball of fire staring out. His hair, like others, was black, pulled back and kept long, coming down to tips that looked more like leaves than anything, flat like blades with internal structures. And glowing with the same blue at the tips, edges, and roots.

Gonquah's kind were unsettling to look at, but Marc had seen worse in his time.

He stepped up to Gonquah and shook the tiny man's hand carefully.

"Do you have a prize for me, Gonquah?" Marc asked.

"Indeed, Maximus," he beamed. "Come and see."

The man led Marc and many of the others around to the back of the truck, a tarp-covered flatbed filled with several boxes the size and shape of coffins. Two more Th'Tarni waited back here, dressed in what looked like paramilitary uniforms to Marc's experienced eye.

"Open one up," Gonquah commanded.

One of the troopers unlatched a lid and flipped it open, reaching in and doing something.

The being inside sat up. Machine.

It was Marc's android, as he had designed it, except the face was alien. Two eyes, wideset to give it hunter's vision. A mouth from which words could emerge. Ears on both sides human enough. A steel helmet of a skull perhaps, on a steel skeleton designed to elicit panic among humans with superstitions. And most of the rest of the *Accord*, from what Marc had studied.

"Arise," Gonquah ordered the machine.

The android stood and stepped out of the box on careful feet.

"Come," the Th'Tarni continued.

The machine man leapt gracefully to the ground, but still made a racket when he landed. All steel and power systems.

Gonquah pointed at Marc with one hand.

"Maximus is your owner," Gonquah said. "Acknowledge."

The machine turned to Marc and studied him briefly.

"Maximus," it said in a dry, metallic voice and a quick bow of the head. "Acknowledged."

"What is your task, creature?" Marc asked loud enough that everyone could hear.

"To guard you, master," the robot said. "To follow your orders."

Marc reached down to the holster on his thigh and drew the beam pistol. It was just a stun model, but could have easily been something lethal. He handed it to the robot, watched the machine man take it in one hand comfortably, turning the weapon sideways briefly to check the safety and power level.

"Shoot those three," Maximum commanded, pointing at two Warreth males and a Nari.

The machine immediately snapped off three shot as fast as the pistol would cycle.

Amazingly, Mishalska managed to dodge to his right, nearly getting his rifle up to shoot back before the machine caught him with a fourth bolt that dropped him.

"Any others, master?" the android asked politely.

"No." Marc laughed, watching the utter shock play out on the other faces around him.

Most of the other faces. Zorge had only been a little surprised. Maiair and Yooyar were grinning. Gonquah's smile could have lit up the night.

"I take it this meets with your approval, Maximus?" the arms merchant asked with a feral smile. "I'm rather looking forward to making more for you. Perhaps a small army, once you have a chance to test these four out and refine anything that needs adjusting."

"And why is that. Gonquah?" Marc asked.

He knew the truth. Had done extensive research on the topic and the man before selecting the young industrialist personally for the manufacturing task.

Gonquah was a dedicated revolutionary. An angry young man willing to use the wealth he had inherited to build an arms manufacturing capability disguised as a white good factory. Killer robots instead of refrigerators, as it were.

"Because the Vanir have ruled us long enough, Maximus," the little man said. "Barring yourself, they need to be cast down from their privileged heights to live as my kind have been forced to for fifty thousand years."

Yes. Angry. A welcome fellow-traveler. A man who would help him break the Constabulary and the *Accord* itself.

Too bad he wouldn't live to enjoy the fruits of his labor, but Marc was thinking in centuries now.

"So, my friend," Marc said. "I will need a month or three to put these machines through their paces. And then we will have a nice, private dinner somewhere and discus the future."

"Indeed, my troublesome ally," Gonquah clapped him on the arm and returned to the truck. "I look forward to it."

The men unloaded the other three coffins and four robots took up their places in a line.

Marc had left his stunner on the lowest setting, so the three targets of his demonstration were stirring as the truck flew away.

Marc walked over to Mishalska and helped the man to his feet with a big paw.

"Impressive, Mishalska," Marc said with a friendly smile. "You shouldn't have been able to even react, let alone move. What other things can you do to astound me?"

"Just you wait, sir," the young man said, a little groggily.

Marc nodded. A month of hard training would make these men and women almost as dangerous as his killer robots.

And then, my friends, let us see how the *Accord* survives.

FIRST INSPECTOR

"YOU'RE SURE?" the Vanir woman asked, turning to look at the little communications handset on her desk. "We have independent confirmation on this?"

"We do," a male voice came over the intercom line. "They were broadcasting a radio communications signal at the same time, so we were able to synchronize with our scanners picking up the signal."

"And nothing at all was done at the time?" she confirmed, brushing a stray black hair out of her eyes as she concentrated.

"That's correct, First Inspector," the man replied. "Per your orders."

"Very well."

She cut the line and leaned back in her chair to think. Her office suddenly felt claustrophobic, in spite of being large enough to hold fifteen friendly Vanir for a meeting. Or thirty Grace.

Anen Wardson rose from behind her desk and began to pace, glancing occasionally at the early evening sky displayed out the window. From here, the horizon of *Almar* looked almost endless, as fit a world frequently referred to as the Axle of Time.

The capital of the *Accord of Souls*. The platform from which the Chaa themselves had leapt outward, leaving the Vanir behind to try to hold this new galactic civilization together.

Anen was First Inspector. The Commander in Chief of the

Constabulary. Not all of them had been Vanir, like her, but many had. The species held a special love for the *Accord*.

A place now threatened by the worst possible thing she could imagine.

On a warm, blue planet, clear out to the edge of the galaxy, a species that hadn't even been above the Stone Age when the Chaa left, had just opened their first wormhole. And done it more than a thousand years before the most ambitiously-paranoid speculation had suggested it was even possible.

It was a threat to the entire galaxy. Xenocidal maniacs let loose from their galactic prison to run roughshod over a place where violence was barely allowed, and war completely unknown.

Xenocide. To wipe out an entire species. Nearly impossible with star-faring technology, but that wouldn't prevent the humans from trying. They took any excuse to kill one another, frequently using skin tone as a distinction.

What would they do when they encountered the Grace? Or the Nari? Or the Borren? To say nothing of the more exotic species that probably factored into Human nightmares such as the Ramasayia or the Arawath.

Still, it was her job to know these things, as well as to deal with them. First Inspector was the principal law-enforcement agent in a galaxy that hadn't had words for war, until the humans had become a potential threat.

Anen returned to her desk and placed a call.

"Commissioner Diazal's office," a bright, cheerful voice came on immediately. "How may I assist you, First Inspector?"

"I would like you to find me a half hour in the Commissioner's schedule, as soon as possible," Anen replied politely, letting the content of her words convey the immediacy that she dared not spell out, even on an internal line, within the *Accord's* Hall of Government. "Preferably today."

There was a pause she put down to someone clicking hold. It stretched. Probably bouncing this up to the Commissioner's Chief of Staff, if that woman was still in the office.

It was late in the day. Possibly, most of the Commissioner's staff had gone home.

Anen was seventy-one. Her grandchildren would be starting families soon enough, and her current wife, Elloayn, understood the needs of the service, having retired herself five years ago.

A new voice came on the line.

"Hello, Anen," Commissioner Diazal replied in a warm, easy tone.

The Commissioner was known as much for his intellect as his

charisma. She needed the former right now. Obviously, he had done the math in his head, when the Prime Investigator of the Constabulary called and requested a meeting.

"Hello, Petim," she replied. "When can we have a chat?"

There. Leave it at that.

Pause. Weighing the things she would not say.

"I was about to head out for some dinner," he offered carefully. "Would you care to join me?"

"Would it be possible to get something delivered, instead?" Anen countered.

She heard the faint catch in the Commissioner's breath.

"Certainly," he decided after a moment. "You order something and get enough for two. Or order me some fish, if you would?"

"That will be lovely, Petim," Anen decided. "I'll be up in a few minutes."

"Yes," his voice fell just a trace. "I was afraid you would say that."

Fortunately, she worked late frequently. There were several places that she could call on, already cleared to deliver food to his floor. A quick message home to Elloayn that she would be much later than expected tonight, and Anen Wardson headed to the lift tube.

The Commissioner's office, when she got up there, was largely dark. One young Borren woman in front, more or less guarding the door. She gestured Anen right through to the back.

Petim's office was lit. It was large enough for meetings, although not as big as hers.

Anen entered with a smile and closed to door.

"That bad?" he asked, rising from behind his desk to greet her.

Petim Diazal was one of the Arawath. Many people had remarked over the centuries that they seemed to be smaller cousins of the Vanir. Tall, slender bipeds with hair on their heads and skin elsewhere. Slightly smaller than Grace overall, or even humans, if you wanted to make that comparison.

Blue skin marked the significant difference, as they were a fully aquatic species that could walk on dry land, as long as they were able to immerse themselves frequently and let clean water run over the gills on either side of the necks.

Today, he wore a muted, russet suit in a herringbone pattern. Expensive and well cut to make him even more impressive.

Petim was short and slender, even for his species. But he had worked hard on his physical presence, and in turn had been elected to the *Accord* Commission at a very young age. A well-deserved accolade, though.

He was not the Proctor of the Commission, but many expected that to happen when the current worthy retired in another few years.

"Sit, please," he said, directing her to a sofa and two chair off to one side.

She chose the closer chair and watched Petim recline on the couch.

"How bad?" he asked after a moment. "What do I need to plan for?"

"Possibly a worst-case scenario, Commissioner," she replied, letting him know that it wasn't just a personal thing, but a business issue.

She watched the man steel himself and swallow once.

"Tell me," he directed her.

"Within the last few days, we have detected, observed, and confirmed the human scientist, Royston Loughty, successfully demonstrating a very primitive, short-range wormhole generator," Anen said. "The humans are possibly within a few generations of breaking out of their home system and threatening the *Accord*."

Even a man with blue skin can pale appreciably, if all the blood drains out of his face. And his diving membranes flickered down over his black eyes once in shock before they withdrew.

"Who knows?" he asked, assuming the report and moving on to the implications.

"Nobody outside of my organization, as yet," Anen replied. "I got off the phone and called you immediately. This will need to be handled with the utmost care and diligence, but at the same time, speed is off the essence."

"Why is that?" Petim asked, suddenly leaning forward and dropping his hands onto his knees.

"Loughty is an unknown quantity," Anen said. "Our wildest fears would be that it would take them only another thousand years to reach a technological sophistication sufficient to even understand wormhole physics," Anen also leaned forward, placing them close enough to almost whisper now. "We're not sure how to stop him, short of considering the ultimate sanction."

Petim recoiled. Assassination was always possible. At one point, the Commission had even explored the necessity of eliminating the humans entirely, using biological warfare to destroy the species while not wiping out all the other life forms.

"Genius?" Petim asked. "Loughty?"

"At least," she said. "And I fear we are partly responsible for the entire thing. I am, personally."

"How?"

"Gareth Dankworth," she reminded him. "His kidnapping by the criminal Maximus seems to have set in motion the chain of events that drove Loughty to consider the higher physics. And then to successfully unravel them well enough to become a threat. I made the decision not to have Gareth transformed back into a human, killed, and returned to Earth, which might have deflected Loughty from this path. In light of events, that might have been a mistake."

Petim blinked again. The Commission generally had clean hands, but only because many decisions had to be made at much lower levels. He was seeing the sausage-making now, probably in ways that had not been quite so clear before.

"Do we destroy the humans?" he asked. Again, the leap of logic, without having to slowly work his way through all the possible dead ends. His snap caused her to flinch. "Just like that? Or somehow stop Loughty?"

"I do not think we can stop Loughty at this point," she replied. "And the technology has been proven successful, so it will metastasize over time. The humans are like that. But this is not my decision to make."

"Indeed, First Inspector," Petim nodded. "Something like this must come from the very top. You will provide the Commission your report how soon?"

"Tomorrow," she said. "If you believe they will be ready to calmly and rationally consider it. Xenocide is a powerful action that cannot be undone later. Nor can assassination."

"No, it cannot, Anen," Petim agreed. "But I have a much greater fear to address."

"What's that?" she asked, wondering what could possibly top something so drastic.

"What happens if the Chaa take exception to the situation and decide to do something about it?"

VACATION

PERHAPS THERE WAS something to this concept of relaxation.

Gareth stood on the top-most deck, slightly sheltered from the wind as the yacht cut a white swath through the outer harbor. Below, there were at least five different species lounging somewhere on the rear deck in the late morning sun. Male and female. Diệu Ahn was among them, in a red string bikini he wasn't sure had enough material to make him a handkerchief.

The others wore less. Sometimes nothing, in the case of one Nari woman with fur just on the verge of faded mustard. Gareth tried not to stare, but the xenobiologist in him was fascinated by the wide range of humanity below him. And the likenesses.

Except he shouldn't call it humanity. None of them were humans, not even him. Vanir, Borren, Nari, Grace, Ramasaya, even a Moisa which reminded him of an uplifted praying mantis that had four arms hanging from her torso and six legs off of a small abdomen. Like a compact centaur, maybe.

Possibly the weirdest species, to hear the others talk, the Moisa had huge, compound eyes on either sides of her skull, nostril slits inside that, and a tiny mouth. The species were generally herbivores that went heavy on pollen and plant life.

They were the builders. The architects who designed the fantastic hexagonal buildings so common throughout the *Accord*. Gareth had grown up with square buildings and the occasional round tower, but the hexagon was so much prettier, especially when the Moisa went to such effort to make them blend in, like a forest of giant trees masquerading as a city.

As Gareth listened to the quiet churn of the big twin propellers driving the massive yacht forward, he wondered about the Chaa. They had uplifted sixteen other species at the same time they downgraded the Vanir, setting everyone on a rough parity that had lasted for at least fifty thousand years before he and Maximus came along.

No war. Very little disease. No hunger.

Poverty, if it existed, was contained as well.

He had seen representations of the Elders. Usually Grace interpretations, so done with some level of artistic license or bombast.

Erect biped with bilateral symmetry, assuming the Vanir had looked the most like them before. Human-like, to most degrees of classification, with only the pointed ears and greater scale truly marking the species different, at least externally.

If one thing stood out, it was that the Vanir were always so much bigger than everyone else. Borren might be taller, but they were spindly enough that he was always afraid he would hurt Diệu Ahn while dancing. The other species were all done to human scale, more or less. A few were half that size.

If a Grace covered their hair, he was pretty sure one could walk the streets of New Metropolis, or maybe Shangdu and nobody would notice.

He wondered if one ever had.

"Enjoying the day?" a voice intruded on Gareth as he day-dreamed.

Gareth turned to see a much smaller man standing next to him. Gonquah was Th'Tarni, a species he couldn't help but think of as wood elves. The dangerous pixies of European legend, living in the forest and playing tricks on humans. Five and half feet tall with black hair that had glowing blue at the ends and roots, and matching eyes and freckles.

"Absolutely," Gareth smiled and shook the proffered hand. "I can't remember the last time I was actually on vacation. Normally, I'm on assignment here or there, and too busy paying attention to my surroundings to actually enjoy them."

"I understand," the man laughed and turned to watch the bevy of beauties on his boat's fantail. "Diệu Ahn tells me you are a reporter?"

The voice sounded just a little off. Like maybe he thought Gareth was a muckraker gone undercover to expose crime and corruption to sell papers? Which was kinda the truth, at the end of the day. Maybe.

"Fashion and art," Gareth stuck with his cover story. "High end magazines with limited subscription bases, rather than the red tops. The glossies that let wealthy people show off and make other wealthy people jealous. Or let the average Jane dream about marrying a prince."

"Oh," he suddenly turned much brighter and chuckled. "Then remind me to take you on a full tour of my little boat, so you can make all the others unhappy. Got dinner plans later when we get back to dock?"

Gareth shrugged.

"I'm here as Diệu Ahn's Plus One," he nodded. "At some point next week, my editor expects me to check in, but I don't have to be on my next mission for at least another week after that."

"Good, Gareth," Gonquah decided, snapping his fingers. "You two will dine with me tonight and we can talk politics."

"Oh, I never talk politics," Gareth warned.

"All art is politics," Gonquah grinned up at him.

"And those conversations are even worse," Gareth allowed a small chuckle. "The statue at the top of the *Accord* Hall of Arts entryway sums it up greater than anything else I've ever seen."

"*The Art Critic*, yes," Gonquah agreed. "But I'm sure you have a much different outlook on those sorts of things than most of the people I encounter regularly. Either they are businesspeople whose only art is the hustle, or people like Diệu Ahn, who never bother with the business end and just let their portfolio managers handle everything. I would be interested in an outsider's take."

"I can try," Gareth offered. "So what do you do for money, Gonquah? You seem to fall somewhere in between those two groups."

"My father was much older than normal when I was born," the man's glowing blue eyes shifted to focus on the blue horizon. "I inherited his vast business empire just out of school, and have spent the last decade adjusting its focus. He was content to just serve the frivolous desires of the common people."

"And you?" Gareth asked.

"I want to change the *Accord*, Gareth," the Th'Tarni man turned a serious face back this direction. "It has grown stale and predictable. All the old lines have calcified. It's time to shake things up."

Gareth grunted and nodded, but remained silent. After a moment,

Gonquah smiled and headed forward again, down the steps to the main cabin and bidding him adieu until later.

Something about his tones had Gareth's back up. This didn't sound like a simple suggestion of a new fashion trend. No, it had felt like a call to arms. He made a note to ask Diệu Ahn a few misleading questions to see if she had any background on the man. Most of the people he had met in the last few days were like Gonquah had said. Either hustlers chasing after business or *bon vivants* with so much money that eventually it turned into oxygen, something you only noticed by its absence.

Gonquah might be something else.

SUNSET FOUND them atop the tallest tower in Narvanie, the capital city of the world. Gonquah's penthouse spanned an entire city block, because the Moisa who had designed this building had narrowed it at the waist, like a tree, before swelling it back out at the canopy.

Gareth had been able to look straight down from slanted windows at the world below, so far away that even the auto-taxis looked like ants.

It was not an impromptu dinner party, as several other couples had joined, some from the boat and some just meandering in. If pressed, Gareth would have called it an open, rolling party, running all day, and centered on Gonquah's presence. The man felt like that. The situation felt like that.

The mob were all scattered around the suite now, having consumed a wide buffet meal, rather than sitting in formal elegance with salad forks. But Gareth and Diệu Ahn had ended up in a smaller, homier salon with the tannish Nari woman from the boat and a Ramasayia male whose name Gareth had missed, then been too embarrassed to ask later.

The Ramasayia reminded him of nothing so much as an Australian wombat, with a fine gray-brown fur covering their body and expressive eyes, plus a nose that never seemed to stop twitching, as if it was tasting the room more than watching it. And he had a pouch, where Gareth watched him pull out a pocket comm, type something, and then stuff it back in. In spite of the pockets on his loose pants and vest.

Gareth thought jealously about all the times he could have used a stomach pouch.

"So Gareth," Gonquah's voice pulled him back to the present. "Where is art going to be in say, five years' time?"

The man's eyes had an odd gleam to them as Gareth swished the glass of something he had been nursing for the last hour. He looked at the far wall and let his eyes wander, taking in the expensive silk paintings, the rich ornamentation on flat surfaces, and the books all leather-bound on a case nearby.

This wasn't just a general question. No, it was a test. A chance to out him as a fraud, perhaps, when what it might really do it suggest he was a cop, if he answered it wrong. That was the tone of voice Gareth had picked up. And Diệu Ahn, as well, as she leaned close and put her weight on his arm, seeming to distract him as he looked up and smiled at her.

"I'll go out on a limb and suggest that the Alternative Realism School work will begin to be considered too pedestrian in another year," Gareth said, zeroing in the on the man. "Everyone will have a collection of some flavor, and it will lose that element of exclusivity and cache that it has now. You'll see cheap knockoffs starting to show up in middle class catalogs by then."

"And what replaces it?" the Th'Tarni pressed. "What can I buy now that sets a trend everyone else will have to pay extra to emulate when they arrive too late?"

Gareth smiled. There was always that. The man wanted to show everyone else up by beating them to the punch. But why ask a stranger? Unless you suspected him of being deeper than just an interested observer.

Sure. Let's play.

"I know an artist working on *Yuudix*," Gareth said evenly, somehow sensing everyone as they leaned forward to catch his words, afraid that they might miss out. "A Moisa woman whose name eludes me now but I could look her up in my contacts list later. She's doing ultra-miniature cities, one building at a time, each custom designed for an overall aesthetic to fit the space into which it will be viewed."

"How miniature?" Gonquah asked, dollar signs suddenly appearing, however metaphorically in his eyes.

Gareth held up his right hand and measured four centimeters between his thumb and forefinger.

"This tower," Gareth said, "Maybe a little bigger. I only got to hear about her from someone else, and see some two-D pictures and one blurry hologram she had produced as a simple advertisement. She forbids most photography, but these had been captured in the background while snapping stills of her in her studio. They were blown up and indistinct, but took my breath away, even then."

Gareth felt a spike of conscience run through him like a frozen knife. But her work had been amazing, and she was working on the very fringes of art on *Yuudix*, a world more focused on science than the pleasurable pursuits. It had been a background interview someone in the Constabulary had done, and she had mentioned scraping by on a regular basis, subsisting on the Universal Basic Income and living cheap, so as to have time for her dreams.

From the hungry look in Gonquah's eyes, she would be getting a call soon, and probably an offer no sane artist would turn down. Hopefully, success wouldn't completely ruin her life. But at least she would have that choice. And a lot of people attached to this party, or even in this room, making inquiries about prior pieces and available prices.

Art made no sense, except that it made the artist happy to create, and the buyer happy to own. And Gareth was tired of bombastic bronzes of super-life-sized godlings.

It reminded him of the stranger he saw in the mirror in the morning.

"Is it truly that impressive?" Gonquah breathed in apparently disbelief. "Her cityscapes?"

Gareth shrugged eloquently. She had been ignored by the major schools of art as being too far out there, but there was so much money sloshing around, just in this room, that she could live comfortably on a few commissions and survive when the wheels of interest turned to something even more bizarre, five years after that.

He hoped she would eventually forgive him. The people around him looked like they wanted to bolt the room so they could make private inquiries one step ahead of everyone else.

He suspected the party would end up moving to *Yuudix* tomorrow somehow. Possibly the day after. He wondered if Diệu Ahn would accompany it, trying to slice off a piece for herself a rock-bottom prices today.

Gonquah pulled a device from the inside pocket of his dinner jacket and pressed a button.

"This calls for a toast," he said into the thing, apparently. "Five glasses of champagne delivered."

"Arriving shortly," a female voice replied. Except it sounded mechanical rather than organic.

Gonquah slid the device back into his pocket and smiled at everyone.

"I have a surprise for everyone tonight," he announced in a broad, conspiratorial voice. "Something completely new that I'll be offering shortly from one of my factories."

Everyone waited on pins and needles.

A mechanical man entered the room, carrying five flutes on a tray. The people around Gareth all cooed and squawked with surprise.

It was about six feet tall. Looked like a robot from a bad scifi vid to Gareth, with thin arms and legs, and big joints. The surface reminded him of nickel steel with a satin finish. The face was human-enough, as well, with eyes, nose, and mouth, plus ears, but they looked like something you drew with simple geometric shapes rather than having a Grace or Moisa artist do the work.

It paused in front of Gonquah and bowed, lowering the tray until everyone took a glass.

"What in the name of Zaffan is that?" Diệu Ahn asked. "Some kind of mechanical being?"

"I was commissioned to begin production of them by a Vanir designer," Gonquah said. "It is indeed a mechanical servant. He called it an *Android*."

Gareth hoped he kept his flinch deep inside, where nobody else would detect it. Even Diệu Ahn seemed focused on the new arrival, so he prayed she was too distracted.

Android was a human word. And Gareth could only think of one Vanir that would use it.

It frightened him to consider what an android might do here, where they could be programmed to do anything the owner desired. Anything. Just like back home.

That included turning into an army of killer robots.

Because Marc Sarzynski was the only other person Gareth could think of who would know that word. And he was a Vanir.

How much worse would that man be next time?

VINDICATED

ROYSTON HAD NEVER BEEN INVITED to the palace as an individual. He had certainly attended significant events here, but only as part of a larger group.

Not one where he was the guest of honor. Worse, he was being escorted today by an extremely mature, fourteen-year-old Crown Prince Henry, as they traversed these ancient hallways, teeming with history and culture dating back more than a millennia in many places.

Henry was a ninety-percent-sized copy of his father, the Prince Consort, and would probably grow into his full height in another year. Right now Royston had an inch on the young prince, but that would change. His father was nearly six foot three.

They were both dressed professionally today. This was not a major, public ceremony, to be witnessed by friends and cameras. Instead, a polite Tea was happening. As Henry opened a door and ushered Royston through with a hand.

Inside, Prince Daniel, the Royal Consort, tall and fit. A man who still played polo regularly in season, and showed his service in the Household Guards in his erect carriage. Indeed, young Henry would follow in his footsteps in another few years, unless he chose to do his service in Earth Force Sky Patrol instead, which would be a welcome first for this ancient family.

The other two children, Sarah and Emily, were too young to attend today, Royston presumed, being eleven and nine, but would no doubt grow up just as involved as their older brother.

Sir West was here already, seated to one side in a suit that showed all the hallmarks of having been freshly pressed. Possibly the suit he wore solely to the palace, and no other time, so that it didn't smell of tobacco or have stains from whatever Sir West had eaten most recently.

Her Majesty rose to shake Royston's hand as he was presented. Elizabeth III, Queen of England. She was a tall, willowy blond approaching forty. A long face with a prominent nose could have rendered her homely, but the high cheekbones offset that in such a way to convey a raptor's face instead. Especially when those blue eyes focused on you.

Like now.

The Prince Consort served tea steeped to the perfect thickness, into exquisite porcelain cups. The Queen first. The Crown Prince. Sir West. And then Royston himself. Just a mathematician and physicist, as it were.

At least today.

This meeting might change all that.

The small talk had eventually evaporated, like the little sandwiches and the first mugs of tea. Now they were into the second round. Where things would get interesting.

Her Majesty had a cold, intellectual gleam in her eyes as she blew on her second cup of tea and studied Royston. He felt like a dormouse awaiting the chef's pleasure. The door to the chamber was closed, and locked.

"Prince Henry has recently begun to study advanced sciences, Mister Loughty," she began in an offhand way, gesturing to the youngest member of the group.

The young man blushed awkwardly, but that was probably the fact that such studies would not doubt include reading one of his books and three to five of Sir West's, depending on the field studied. And the young man was having tea with them today by way of introduction.

Royston nodded politely to both of them. She hadn't asked a question, nor invited a comment.

"He has also recently begun to be more active in the affairs of the Household, so that he can represent Us in public in the future," she continued. "So I thought it appropriate that he join us to discuss your most recent activities."

"Just so, Your Majesty," Royston replied carefully.

She probably knew more about his experiments than even Sir West did, because the security classification around it would be that high. But as supreme executive of one of the founding members of Earth Force, she could pull rank, if someone like Royston had suggested to Sir West that she do just such a thing, as he had. The PM was the only other person who could do that, and that worthy was really a shopkeeper from Scunthorpe at the end of the day. Not a physicist. Nor a Queen.

"I understand you were successful, Mr. Loughty," she dangled the bait in front of him expertly.

"We were, madam," he replied, carefully taking note of his language that it never grew too personal. Sir West could possibly call the woman by her Christian name in private, but he had known her since she was Emily's age, at least. "The theory bears out soundly, but now I must go back and revise the paper, in light of experimental evidence. Some of my assumptions were simply wrong. Others were too cautious. But we can press forward in careful steps."

"How soon do you envision building a larger device, Mr. Loughty?" she asked, eyes boring in on him.

Royston leaned back carefully, paying extra attention to his body language as he did. This was where things would get interesting.

Whoever hosted the first large transporter machine would have a significant political and economic edge over the rest of the planet. And the solar system as well, if goods and personnel could instantly move from London to the Neptunian mining colonies without requiring transit time and delta-v burn calculations. It would open up the entire solar system in ways that not even the jet airliner had done to the surface of the globe, centuries ago.

"That is contingent on two things," Royston replied judiciously. "One, the entire apparatus will need to be dismantled and examined by specialists to make sure there are no issues inside that will cause us problems when we scale things up. And two, budgetary constraints. This task is currently being handled as part of Earth Force Sky Patrol, related to certain internal investigations they are pursuing."

"Yes, the disappearance of Field Agent Gareth St. John Dankworth from his cabin aboard the Arsenal," she acknowledged smartly. "I understand that the Americans are deeply interested in that aspect of your research. And contemplating that he may have been kidnapped by forces currently unknown on *Earth*."

Royston couldn't help but glance at the other three men in the room, counting the young Crown Prince as grown up enough to be involved, if his mother shared that opinion.

Her words suggested that she had followed his original train of thought. That a previously-unknown alien species had kidnapped the man. But why Gareth? And why do it in such a public place? There were many others that could have been taken instead, and done in such a way that perhaps nobody would even have noticed.

"And I have cleared everyone in this room to discuss any sensitive materials related to Dankworth, Mr. Loughty," she continued in a voice forged of steel.

She could do that. As Head of State, it was within her ancient prerogatives to appoint her own advisors, which had long included Sir West on the scientific side. And presumably the Prince Consort so that she had someone outside of the formal government at close call.

"I have a theory, Your Majesty," Royston offered diffidently after a moment to gather this errant thoughts together and lick his lips. "I cannot lend any scientific credence to the claim, but at the same time I also cannot refute any portion of it, using the old standards of Doyle and Holmes."

"Go on," she said in a breathless tongue.

"Gareth was kidnapped by removing him through such a wormhole as I have now proven can be constructed and used," Royston turned deadly serious. "No one else in this solar system was, at the time, capable of replicating the feat, as far as I, and by extension Earth Force, have been able to tell."

"In this solar system?" Prince Consort Daniel spoke up now for the first time, the military officer in him coming to the fore. "Did I understand you correctly?"

"You do, sir," Royston nodded to him. "My pet theory is that he was taken by an unknown alien species from outside our sphere."

"But why?" young Prince Henry spoke up. "Why him? Why then? Why there?"

"It is the *when* that drives my theory, young sir," Royston said. "Sir West and I have spoken in loose terms about it before now, only because he is not a member of any Earth Force Directorate at present, so I could not share certain classified details with him before this moment. But Gareth is, was, one of the top agents in Sky Patrol. A hero, if you will. I have an irrational theory that whoever it was had identified him as the person they needed, perhaps for some heroic task elsewhere. Had you known the man, you would understand. But they needed him at a specific moment in time. That he was alone in his cabin was just luck on their part, as they might have just as easily taken him while he was at dinner, and the event witnessed by dozens, or potentially hundreds of people."

"So you ascribe benevolence to them?" Her Majesty's tone was tart.

"I do not necessary ascribe malice, Your Majesty, which is not the same thing," Royston carefully corrected her assumption. "It all comes down to *why Gareth* and *why then*. Whoever it was could have just as easily taken other men whose disappearance would raise no fuss."

"Have they taken others?" Prince Henry asked suddenly. "Do we have other men missing who might fit the characteristics, the circumstances you have identified? Whom we have not previously associated with the disappearance of this agent?"

Royston remembered to close his mouth before any flies took up residence. The two proud parents beamed. Even Sir West grinned at his shock, having previously remained a touch aloof from the whole event that was Royston's presentation to the Crown.

"It strikes me that if they have the confidence to capture this one man, it might not be their first attempt," the young prince continued carefully. "Who else have they taken?"

"I do not know the answer to that, sir," Royston admitted, shocked almost out of his wits by the penetrating question. "But I intend to task certain people with looking into that exact question when I return to the Arsenal. I may have missed the forest for the trees. Thank you."

He nodded gratefully to the boy, the young man, who was blushing furiously now.

"Well done, Henry," his mother rescued him. "Now, Mr. Loughty, let us return to the other topic. The question of budget, as to where the first large-scale demonstration project of your engine might be constructed."

"Indeed, Your Majesty," he replied,

They began to discuss locations and costs, but Royston's mind kept circling back to that one question that might answer why Gareth had been taken at the time he was.

Who else had gone before?

SECRET AGENT MAN

THEY HAD RETURNED to the hotel late in the evening. Or early in the morning, depending on how you wanted to look at it.

Gareth figured the sun would rise in about two hours, given the lightening sky in the east, so he should have gone to bed a long time ago. These people liked to follow the darkness, rather than the day.

Diệu Ahn had invited him up to her suite for a nightcap, but it was clear she wasn't using that as a thin veil for a proposed romp. She had gotten a little withdrawn and pensive over the last few hours as he had watched the Borren woman.

They sat on her balcony now and watched the night sky now, across a low table from each other in comfie canvas sling-chairs and covered with light blankets against the chill. Gareth had made himself a simple hot chocolate. Diệu Ahn had originally planned on something stronger, but the smell turned her head, and she had done the same, with a small shot of something like apple schnapps in hers.

He would already sleep well, just from the exhaustion of a twenty-seven hour day. And he was safe here, as he could simply climb over the low rail separating the balconies and get into his suite if he didn't feel like the long stroll inland and back to go something like fifteen feet.

"Is everything okay?" he finally broached the topic as they settled in the dimness and cool breeze off the water.

Nothing more. Leave it at that. He had never learned how human women thought, and Diệu Ahn was both alien and from a radically different socio-economic background from him. They might be talking foreign languages, depending. Plus, he didn't want to pry.

"Is she real?" Diệu Ahn asked.

"Is who real?" Gareth sipped his mug and tried to figure out which conversation they were having. Never an easy chore with some women.

"That artist you mentioned tonight," she said, still pensive. "The one who makes miniature cityscapes."

"Oh, her," Gareth nodded, glad that the woman didn't want to talk about Pippa right now. "Yes, she's real. And hopefully, if she ever finds out about me, and tonight, she'll forgive me for sending people with a lot of money after her."

"Why is that, Gareth?" she probed.

"The woman is an artist," he said. "I read a thing on her and it included her desire for more support, but she was really only looking for a few people willing to buy her work and tell their friends. I've possibly put her on magazine covers as the *Next Big Thing*. It might ruin her life."

"We call that failing upward," she smiled in the shadows, teeth suddenly flashing and disappearing from otherwise darker skin. "I had wondered because…"

She stopped there. Just hung the phrase like she had run out of words in the middle of the sentence. Gareth let it dangle until she found what she sought.

"Something you said, back on *Orgoth Vortai*," she continued, pausing again.

He continued with silence. He could remember every single one of those conversations, but had no idea what bit she might have latched onto.

"When you suddenly disappeared from the party," Diệu Ahn breathed slowly. "We had joked that you were a fashion writer with a secret identity, so you could get in places. Or a secret agent."

He let himself grow perfectly still.

That was exactly what they had talked about.

"When you left, you said *also* a secret agent, Gareth," her voice had fallen to a whisper. "Was that true?"

He took a deep breath. She would have found out eventually, if he wanted to cultivate her as a source. It was just his luck that she was also that smart, but he hadn't doubted that, having read more on the woman's background.

"It is," he said, just as quietly.

She paused.

He wondered if she was going to erupt in anger and throw him out. Or out him to the people he was trying to investigate.

"For who?" she finally asked quietly.

Gareth was still poised to throw himself to the side in case her hot chocolate was flying at his face, but she deserved an honest answer. At least as much of one as he could give.

"The Constabulary," he offered.

"Are you after me?" she asked in a small, frightened voice.

"Oh no, Diệu Ahn," he warmed, smiling at her in the low light. "My bosses consider you a good bet. Safe. They were hoping that you could innocently get us into some of the parties where the bad guys were."

"Like Gonquah?" she asked, her voice growing firmer, if not louder. "He's always been a bit of a scoundrel."

"Actually, this really was supposed to be a vacation for me," Gareth said. "Get to know you and meet some of your friends. Maybe spend some time being seen, so that later on, when I needed to be on a mission, I would be a face someone recognized, if we needed to do something, rather than a stranger off the street to be viewed suspiciously. Planting seeds now for fall harvesting."

"Something happened at the party last night," her voice turned in a new direction. "You reacted to the mechanical man in a strange way. Different from everyone else. Why was that?"

How much to tell her? Obviously, not much, or she would become terrified, and possibly turn on him anyway. But she would detect any falsehoods. He had so very little experience with lying, and women seemed to have a sixth sense for that sort of thing anyway.

"There are limits to what I can tell you," he decided to go with some of the truth, and ruthlessly cut away the dangerous bits. "It wasn't the mechanical man, per se. It was the term that Gonquah used to describe it."

"*Android*, he called it," she repeated the term. "So fanciful. What does it mean?"

"Roughly, *in the shape of a man*, in an archaic, lost language nobody speaks anymore," Gareth shaded his truth carefully. "A female version would be a gynoid."

"What languages are forgotten, Gareth?" she was surprised. "This is the *Accord*. There is only the one language, that of the Chaa, plus some older dialects that are species-specific, and usually cultural terms, slang, to any one planet. Where does *android* come from?"

"I can't tell you, Diệu Ahn," Gareth replied. "And you are better off not knowing. But there is only one other person I am aware of in the entire *Accord* that would use that term, and he used it correctly to describe the mechanical man when talking to Gonquah. That machine is what I might also call an *Ellis Device*, after the first futurist that conceived of them in the modern context."

"He's your enemy, isn't he?" she asked, stepping past her confusion to lock onto his tones, perhaps, the anger that never left Gareth at what Marc had turned into. "That other."

Jealousy was a cruel taskmaster and a fickle mistress.

"That's right," Gareth nodded, even though it was almost too dark for him to see. "He is the man I have dedicated my life to stopping, primarily because he represents a threat to the entire *Accord of Souls*, if we fail."

"Do you need to leave again?" she asked, perhaps a little hurt. "To chase after him?"

"Actually, if I could, I would ask your help to get closer to Gonquah, so that we can find out more," Gareth replied. "To find that man, and stop Gonquah from helping him."

"Why is an android so dangerous, Gareth?" she leaned forward, voice sharp and insistent now. "Why is it a threat to the very *Accord*?"

"It is a tool, a device that can be programmed, Diệu Ahn," he said. "The men and women of the *Accord of Souls* are bound into a single psionic resonance that prevents violence and had held the peace between species for fifty thousand years."

"And?"

"This man can program those robots to kill without any pity or remorse," Gareth said. "He can conquer the *Accord* because he will be able to murder anyone who might try to stop him."

Her tiny gasp spoke volumes. But he had also read up on her life closer than perhaps anybody but her physician or her solicitor, so he knew where he might find safe ground with this woman.

"And you think you can stop him?" she finally asked, voice again tiny and frightened.

"I've got to try," Gareth whispered.

SEEKER

ANEN STUDIED the young woman seated across the desk from her for cues, but she had never met a human, so she had no easy way to identify if it would work.

The youngster did make her feel old, but Fatima Darzi was already a veteran officer, a Senior Constable whose acting skills had made her invaluable as a deep cover agent in several previous investigations. She could literally become someone else, almost before your eyes.

But these were humans. And she dared not consult her resident experts on that dangerous species, lest she tip her hand to what might have to come next.

Fatima was a Grace. That was the only species that could come even remotely close enough to the human bioform to try to pass as one without extensive and possibly irreversible surgery that would take far longer than the available time.

Vanir were more structurally similar, but even a short Vanir would be so much taller than a human as to stand out. Nari were the right height and build, but you would never get past all the fur, and without it, they would look even more strange.

So a Grace was going to have to walk into the lion's den alone.

At least there was a human culture the young woman could call upon in this instance to aid her disguise. Fatima wore a crimson outfit apparently tailored exactly like a Women's Auxiliary of Earth Force's Sky Patrol. Knee length flowing skirt, with a long tunic-style jacket over that and a gold edge on both. The top was double-breasted down the left side with a series of gold buttons and embroidering in a complicated diamond pattern connecting the buttons on both sides. It had a tall, folding collar, edged in gold like the rest of the tunic, with more embroidery on the cuffs. A black belt around her waist could hold a holster, according to the pictures Anen had seen, but Fatima would not need one.

Or rather, if she did, she would already be running for her life and need more help than a mere firearm would give her.

Fatima would pretend to be Persian, according to the notes. Anen had studied just enough of the background to understand the religious garb the young woman wore on her head today, a thing called a hijab. It was a long piece of cloth, almost a wide scarf, worn centered on the forehead and wrapped around and tucked in such that only the face was visible. And none of the woman's sensory tentacles.

Without them, Fatima did look human. It was rather eerie, staring at her, but the young agent just sat patiently and smiled back demurely.

"Tell me about the origins of the costume," Anen said suddenly, watching the woman for things that might give away her alien nature.

"Persia is an ancient land on Earth," Fatima said easily, adding an interesting accent to her tones, as though one who had learned another language growing up and transitioned later. "It has been a center for intellectual activity and scholarship going back to the late Bronze Age, for humans, but in modern times has remained something of a cultural backwater, far removed from the major centers of power in Earth Force."

"And the wrap on your head?" Anen asked.

"The religion of that region of Earth is called *Islam*," Fatima answered easily. "A follower is known as a Muslim, one who has submitted to their one God: Allah. A Muslim woman is supposed to dress conservatively, covering herself with modesty. Depending on the sub-culture, that might be as little as a hair scarf such as you might wear, or as much as something called a burqa, which completely engulfs the woman, except for her eyes. In some sects, even the eyes are then covered over with a mesh. All one might see are the hands. However, Persia sees itself as more open to educated and liberated women, within limits, so the hijab is generally sufficient. Among the English or the Americans of Sky Patrol, they will most likely not even know the term, but will immediately understand me as a foreigner, and a non-threatening one, so that will hopefully give me some level of flexibility to make cultural mistakes, being an obvious outsider. It will be a dangerous game we play with them, already."

"And your sensory tentacles?" Anen pressed.

"I have been working hard to keep them still," Fatima nodded. "Additionally, I will take certain drugs that will minimize movement, at a small cost to myself in terms of sensory input. As our Grace joke goes, I will become one of you instead."

They shared a smile. The Grace lived in such a rich sensory environment at all times that it was a wonder they only became artists, and not complete madmen.

"And you are prepared to escape?" Anen turned serious now.

"I have my transmitter, which will remain with me at all times," Fatima nodded, sobering. "It also has a dead-man capacity on my heartbeat, as well as triggering an alarm if I am separated from it by more than thirty meters. My backup team here has instructions to pull me out if that happens, on the theory that anything the humans see can be later discounted, if there is no body or evidence that an alien walked among them."

"You said body," Anen noted.

"These are humans, First Inspector," Fatima's voice was serious now as Anen listened to the underlying tones. The unsaid. "Not counting Dankworth, they are known to be dangerous and prone to unprovoked violence, even to their own kind. A true alien risks immediate death at their hands. In addition, we must penetrate to the heart of one of their most secure military facilities and discover what one of the most intelligent humans known has discovered."

"I do not like the idea of sending anyone on a suicide mission, Fatima," Anen said. "In this case, it is my hope that we can somehow find a lesser solution to the human problem. Even now, the High Commission is quietly discussing whether or not to simply wipe out the species, possibly with a biological weapon of some sort. Your mission is to give me other options. As humans are not part of our psionic pattern, it may be enough to kill this scientist, this Royston Loughty, and anyone else who could replicate his work."

"I understand, First Inspector," Fatima said.

"Find me a way to save as many people as you can," Anen ordered her.

"I will do what I can."

Anen hoped it would be sufficient. She had become a cop to protect and serve. But that wasn't supposed to be limited to only the *Accord*. What kind of officer was she if she couldn't protect those ignorant savages as well?

ANOTHER MAN TAKEN

ROYSTON PROBABLY SHOULD HAVE WASHED his own mouth out with soap, due to the vile profanity that escaped when he first opened the report that had been compiled by the Women's Auxiliary Service. It didn't help that Pippa was seated close by in his office, reading Plutarch in the original Latin as a way to relax.

She merely looked up with one tart eyebrow raised at him, which caused Royston to blush all the more furiously.

No parent likes being caught being naughty by their own children, however grown and mature the latter.

She powered her reader down and set it primly on the edge of his desk with an expectant eye, the very image of innocence while still radiating a type of intellectual curiosity in his direction.

Without ever mentioning the profanity he had used.

Which made it worse. He had heard her use the same word previously.

"I had described the entire experiment in as particular detail as I was able," Royston explained to her. "And then trusted that most magical of quantities to pursue it."

"Oh?" she tilted her head just enough that he nearly laughed out loud. As if she could fool him.

"Woman's intuition," Royston supplied. "I told them what happened and asked if anyone else had ever disappeared thus. They went back and

367

culled through the records, eliminating all the obvious false leads put out by people suffering some established levels of delusion or *Munchhausen By Proxy*. What was left was then rated in order of reliability, which was, in most cases, akin to asking how many angels could dance on the head of a pin."

"And what did those vile witches in the Records Department find for you, Father?" she batted her eyelashes at him, which did make him chuckle.

Until he glanced down at the folder in front of him.

"One incident, a little more than a year ago," he sobered instantly. She did the same, watching his face change. "The golden glow and unexplained disappearance were what whichever woman who did this keyed in on. And she found this one in the official records."

"Who?" Pippa asked, color draining out of her face.

"Marc Sarzynski," he supplied.

Rather than curse as he had, Pippa gasped, and her hands flew to her mouth. Not that she didn't know those words as well, but she was less likely to use them than he was, even in the privacy of his office.

After a moment, she calmed, resting her hands in her lap again.

"That would explain why Gareth then, Father," she offered. "As well as possibly the timing, if they needed him to go be a hero, as you suggested to the Queen."

"Yes, indeed," Royston nodded. "The man had disappeared entirely, right at the moment when Gareth had cornered his gang and was able to arrest the rest of them. I remember now, him mentioning their stories about a bizarre golden light, which at the time suggested that Marc had somehow used some unknown device to hypnotize those hard men into believing he had vanished, so they couldn't turn on him when he got away from them."

"But suppose he really did vanish?" Pippa asked. "What would that mean?"

"Perhaps, like Gareth, someone decided they needed a man like Marc," Royston suggested. "That might, in turn suggest why someone else would have chosen Gareth, in order to thwart him."

"So now we're reduced to suggesting the hosts of heaven and hell are girding themselves for some final battle?"

Her tone only mildly suggested the heavy weight of sarcasm behind it, but Royston had to shrug.

"Information insufficient, Daughter," he said. "I do not know how long the radiation residue might last that would at least confirm a level of similarity."

"No," she said peremptorily. "But you have built a detector for it."

"I have," Royston agreed.

"Perhaps we need to build warning devices," she said. "Like vacuum detectors, but warning about someone opening a wormhole such as you did. As the ancients like to say: *Once is chance. Twice coincidence. But three times is enemy action.* Are we perhaps suborned with enemy agents? Aliens able to hide in plain sight because we've never even considered their existence?"

"Or are we overreacting?" he countered. "Seeing patterns where none actually exist because we so desperately want to see it? Worse, will I become a laughingstock for suggesting it?"

"Don't tell them why," his daughter turned sharp. "Just build the thing, and leave a few around with instructions to contact you immediately if it goes off. Let them draw their own conclusions, as most people only understand that you have detected a new kind of radiation. Only the ones in the know will appreciate that it might be a portal warning."

"Yes, I believe that would be the most prudent course of action, Pippa," Royston agreed. "What would I do without you?"

"Get yourself into even worse situations than the ones you do now?" she smiled tartly and winked at him.

Royston smiled back, but underneath he felt the chill of death when he looked down at that report again while she went back to reading. There hadn't been a more dangerous criminal alive than Marc, once that man turned to evil and threw away his entire past. And did it because the young woman across from him had chosen Gareth instead.

If those two men were matching wits now in some broader, alien galaxy, might it not risk being considered *Götterdämmerung?*

INSIDE JOB

GARETH WAS EYE CANDY TODAY, and he knew it. Diệu Ahn had contacted Gonquah, or perhaps just knew the itinerary of the ongoing party around the man, so they had ended up at another event where Gonquah was. It wasn't one of that man's parties, like the one on his yacht, but had started off at a musical performance of a small mixed chorus before eventually ending up in the private wing of a casino.

Gareth had never seen many of the games being played, nor the card decks, so he was fascinated. Unlike the rectangular Hoyles of home, these were triangles as big as his palm, with about an inch cut off of the points to make them strange hexagons.

Gareth leaned nearby against one end of a bar, well away from the players at the big table centering the medium-sized room, as Diệu Ahn, Gonquah, and several other high rollers played for pots roughly equal to the annual salary of a shipping clerk in a major *Accord* corporation. He had a glass of something fruity and only mildly alcoholic to sip at, as well as a hexagonal plate with a variety of exotic dim sum piled up.

And several young women smiling at him from around the room, but he just smiled back and patiently ignored all of their attempts to flirt. Like a boy-toy that was attached to Diệu Ahn and unwilling to risk his meal ticket.

It was a weird place to live.

But it was obvious that this wasn't the first time the facility had hosted this sort of thing, and perhaps not even this group. There were bars on three walls, doing a brisk business in wines, spirits, and teas respectively. A kitchen was through a door on the fourth wall, with a staff back there apparently dedicated to this room alone, because no order took very long to be delivered.

Gareth enjoyed himself as he munched. People-watching had always been one of his hobbies, trying, as a cop did, to suss out everything he could about a random stranger just from the way they walked or dressed.

Most of the people in this room fell into one of three major categories, excluding the employees in black shirt, black pants, black aprons, and various species, or the managers in nice suits with white shirts and ties.

The fabulously rich were playing at the table. A dozen of them, roughly, with piles of chips in front of them done in that same cut-triangle hexagon as the cards, made in copper, silver, and gold colors. Some of those piles matched the annual revenue of medium-sized companies, relatively.

The next tier down were mostly people not quite as fabulously wealthy, or perhaps not as addicted to the games of skill and personality that poker represented. If less wealthy, they dreamed of becoming big enough to get invited to play at this table. Others apparently had the wealth, but not the interest, so instead were people-watching like Gareth was.

The final tier were attached to one of the other groups. Gareth wasn't so prudish as to be offended that many of the men and women in here had Plus Ones that weren't their legal spouses. After all, that was the role he himself was playing, and at least a quarter of the big shots in here were female. Frequently the powerful men and women in here had what the vice teams back home had once taught Gareth to call boy-toys or rent-boys, depending on the gender combinations involved.

It was generally illegal on Earth, but many of the off-world colonies took a more libertine approach to those sorts of things. And Earth Force Sky Patrol didn't pass judgement, it just enforced the laws as they were in the jurisdiction asking for help. Crimes involved someone getting hurt physically or financially, not socially.

And he had a role to play, so he watched people watch people. It kept his mind and skills sharp.

A man approached Gareth as the game built to one of those massive pots where the egos of three people got personally involved. Diệu Ahn had presumably-wisely folded early, as she watched the men: a Nari, a Vanir, and Gonquah himself, began betting utterly ridiculous amounts of chips.

"Garrette?" the man asked as he sidle his massive bulk up and leaned against the bar, watching the spectacle innocently if you were far enough away to not hear anything.

"Gareth," he corrected the man, never looking over, even though he had never been this close to a Vratha before.

They reminded him of the massive pachyderms of earth, especially the semi-prehensile trunk that emerged from the center of the face and was nearly as long as a businessman's tie. The skin was heavy as well, rough and with that same sort of grayish tinge. Big ears on the sides weren't quite as semaphoric as a Nari's, but came close. The only big difference between a Vratha and a bipedal elephant was the crest of hair on the head and running most of the way down the back, rather like a horse. Other than that, the species had fine hair like a human covering most of their body.

"Ah," the man said. "I stand corrected. I understand you are a friend of Diệu Ahn's and she said you're a reporter?"

"I dabble," Gareth's tone suggested that anything like formal work was a stretch, and that perhaps he was more of a trust-fund child, as so many of the second tier in this room were.

You had to own something that generated an amazing cash flow to have enough wealth to play with the big kids.

"Oh?" the Vratha replied innocently. "My name is Aning Nocia."

Gareth smiled, but only on the inside, as the man's first name was pronounced exactly like awning and now Gareth would forever associate the man with umbrellas.

Nocia was perhaps six and a half feet tall, but probably weighed as much as Gareth did, built more like a mobile tree trunk than anything else. Vratha women occasionally had some suggestion of hips and bust, but also tended to be mistaken for Ionic columns in nature.

"Gareth," he replied. "How can I be of assistance, Mr. Nocia?"

Keep it polite and simple. Gareth didn't have to impersonate the type of airhead that many of the men in here went for.

Diệu Ahn had played him off to strangers as an intellectual type, reminding folks around here that he was probably a secret agent art critic, a tale that people from that other party, like Gonquah, would no doubt be spreading as they started to outbid each other for miniature copies of Londra or other places from a woman who worked by hand over months.

"I'm something of an art collector, Gareth," the Vratha said in a low, friendly tone, speaking out of the side of his mouth like two strangers watching the horses and just happening to be leaned at the bar. "But I have a bit of a problem on my hands and wondered if I might bribe your expertise?"

Gareth was intrigued now, but kept things inside. Strangers, randomly met.

He was really watching Gonquah play a hand of poker for astronomical sums against two other men he assumed saw themselves as experts and mistook the Th'Tarni as a mark.

Gareth could have corrected their foolish assumptions, had they asked. He had watched Gonquah selling them rope earlier in the evening, but the tiny man was now in the process of setting the hook and reeling it in with just enough slack to draw them, rather than fighting.

You had to tire a swordfish out, not drag it kicking and screaming aboard the boat.

So Gareth glanced over at the Vratha man, rather than speak. It was a kind of side eye that suggested Gareth was listening, but not committing to anything.

"I have acquired a few paintings in my time," the man murmured, pausing to grab and take a gulp from a glass as a steward brought a tray around. "I've trusted my hunter in the past, but I'm beginning to wonder if he's in on a scam of some sort, passing off fake masters into private collections."

"I see," Gareth suggested a greater depth of knowledge on the field with his tone than he actually had, but he knew criminality probably better than most of the people in the room.

Probably not all of them, but he wasn't sure which few warranted greater vigilance.

Not yet, anyway.

"And you haven't asked a professional expert because...?" his words dangled. Setting that hook in the swordfish's mouth, as it were.

"Well," the man hemmed a bit. "Some of these pieces supposedly still hang in other collections. But I wonder if perhaps there weren't multiple copies made, and the original left alone."

"And how might I help, Mr. Nocia?" Gareth glanced over now, making eye contact to express some level of interest.

He found it terribly amusing that he might suddenly stumble into art fraud as a second Constabulary career, if he managed to stay out of prison once Marc Sarzynski was stopped. Still, crime was crime. Stopping small time lawbreakers prevented them from growing up into major menaces at a later date.

And Diệu Ahn would probably giggle at the thought. As near as Prime Investigators on Almar had been able to determine, looking very closely, the woman didn't even have a parking ticket to her name. But she had inherited more money than even she knew what to do with, and employed experts to watch the experts watching her money. It helped that she knew accounting and signed her own checks for any amount larger than dinner.

And was smart enough to bail out of hands like this one playing out in front of everyone. It might be the end of the evening, as Gonquah had both men matching outrageous bets and running low on table stakes as the last hand of cards was dealt face down.

Nocia cleared his throat with a sound like a subway passing underneath the streets of New Metropolis. Low and subsonic, deep in your bones.

"Might I host you two at my palace sometime soon?" he asked diffidently. "Perhaps show you a few things in a more private setting and get your opinions?"

Gareth let a smile form briefly before returning to the neutral look as the tension built over there. The rest of the room was so riveted on the card play that he might have been able to rob one of the bartenders and get into a shootout with another one and not have anybody notice.

"I understand that my dance card might be booked up for a bit," Gareth murmured back to the man. "But you can ask her and I won't object."

"Thank you," the man Gareth thought of as an umbrella nodded and made his way quickly off as Gonquah turned over his last card to cheers as well as cries of anguish and disgust.

That was not a man you should ever bet against. Unless you knew what cards he was holding.

INTRUDER

THE NIGHT WAS dark and calm. Perfect hunting weather for something like this.

Marc's team was in an alleyway near the delivery gate of a small, urban estate.

Watching.

For Marc, the best part of all the training this last summer had been watching his people move to a level of professionalism almost on a par with the sorts of gangsters he had been able to take for granted back home. Lots of *Accord* citizens were broken to one degree or another, he had found, but few had the capability to do intentional violence to one another.

Finding such people had been like sifting hay for needles. Or diamonds in a coal mine. But he had succeeded. In addition to the original trio he had kept, Mishalska's anger at being bested by the android had broken something in the youngster.

It gave him an odd symmetry on the team, as Marc watched them prepare. Two Warreth females, barely out of their teenage years, and two Nari men, one older and scientific and the other a young Turk who had taken Marc's advice and let his fur grow back out to a single length.

Never leave the cops a visual identifier when they go back and review the tapes of an event.

Not that there would be much the tapes would be able to show that didn't just confirm everything the cops already suspected, but they should be in the habit of not making it easy. Everyone was dressed in baggy black clothes that would hide identities, if not races.

After all, a Vanir male, two Warreth females, and several Nari males committing crime was going to identify him to Gareth and those other two Constables without any doubt. Assuming that they could do anything about it. It didn't matter what they thought of the sixth figure, dressed for now like another Nari.

Marc had spotted the standard cameras in the obvious places. Effective enough to deter amateur criminals, but this particular model didn't even come equipped with microphones to record ambient sound. There were probably a few other units he had missed, but these people simply had no understanding of violence as a tool, or crime as something to be solved later by experts with as much information as possible.

Amateurs.

"Android," he quietly addressed the machine dressed as a person. "Are you ready?"

"This unit is prepared," the machine answered back, drawing two pistols from shoulder holsters and holding them out for inspection. "The disintegrator and the stunner are fully charged and have been tuned to acceptable levels of accuracy."

"Very good," Marc said. "Stand by for action."

"Standing by," it said.

Marc turned to the others. Maiair and Yooyar held disintegrators, while the Nari had stunners. Like the machine, Marc had one of each in thigh holsters, where he could get at them quickly, but for now would rely on size, speed, and wits.

"Zorge, Mishalska, shoot anything that moves inside. Am I clear?" he asked them, towering like a redwood above the shorter men.

Both nodded. Mishalska might have gulped, but this would be his baptism by fire. The others had been there with him before at least once.

Marc turned to the women.

"The boys are out front," Marc reminded them. "You are responsible for doors and things that a stunner will not affect."

Maiair nodded. Yooyar grinned with her head crest and eyes.

Marc moved out of the deeper darkness to the gate and tested the handle with a gloved hand. Locked, but he knew that. Getting it unlocked would either require someone inside hitting a button, or someone outside spending a lot of time fiddling with electronics.

Marc preferred a more direct approach.

"Android, destroy the lock and open the gate," he ordered quietly, stepping to one side to watch.

The Ellis Device raised its left hand and fired. There was a small popping noise as metal sublimed under an intense explosion of sudden heat. The machine stepped forward and hipchecked the gate out of the way, scanning the interior courtyard with careful eyes. He shot two other cameras a quickly as he could process their locations and cycle the weapon.

One of the reasons Marc had been willing to try this place was the lack of outside guard dogs. Not that he had anything about shooting dogs, but they would make a lot of noise and might wake neighbors at the wrong moment.

The backyard was empty. A nice patio for hosting small parties. A pool and hot tub for summer fun. Old trees and a small garden for kitchen herbs. It had a very homey feel.

Marc wondered if the current owners would eventually sell the place rather than live with the memories of what had happened tonight.

Marc led his ragged convoy of killers across the piazza quickly and approached a rear door to the garage. The android reached out and shot something even as Marc spotted the small camera above the door.

There was a small hole there now. About big enough for a chipmunk to take up residence later, if this planet had an equivalent creature like that.

The second shot went into the door, annihilating a portion of the sill and the strike plate in a quick flash of light. Just like he had laid it out for the machine earlier.

Inside, the garage had just enough night lights on to see the door to the house. This one was heavier, fireproofed against events in the garage.

"Hinges," Marc ordered quietly.

The machine shot the right hand frame in three places, bursting quick holes in the pseudo-wood and revealing the destroyed hinges holding it upright.

"Remove the door quietly and set it to one side," Marc ordered.

He would have done it, but even with gloves on the immense heat would scorch his hands.

The android holstered both pistols and grabbed handle and middle gap. It pushed forward and Marc was sure he heard metal tearing inside the door itself. He drew his own stun pistol now and watched the widening gap as the android stepped into the kitchen and pivoted to lean the door against a wall.

There were no dogs present. Or, they weren't fed and watered in the kitchen, which was what he would have expected. Thus far good.

The android drew his sixguns again and took the lead. The kitchen and dining room were empty. The salon and entryway as well.

Nobody in the library or the downstairs bathrooms.

The last little hallway led to the laundry room, and the first risk on this venture. They moved like ghosts, another benefit of six months training in the desert. There. A door tucked in behind the pantry.

"Destroy the lock and stun the inhabitant," Marc whispered.

He presumed the *au pair* would have a locking door, just in case the father got drunk and decided to make a pass at a teenage girl. He had heard rumors about the gentleman. It was one of the reasons this house had been chosen, rather than one of the others. People who were already crooked were easier to bend.

The android studied the situation for a moment, and then moved so quickly that it was probably a blur to everyone else. But they weren't used to high-speed mayhem. The lock shattered with a hard kick, the door swung open but the android caught it with the barrel of the disintegrator before it could slam into the wall.

On the bed, a young Grace girl slept. Marc guessed she was barely eighteen, only because that was the legal minimum age for a job like this.

Eyes opened, but the android shot her before she managed to come fully awake. Hopefully, this would be nothing but a bad dream she would forget on waking. There was nothing a teenage Grace girl could have done to stop him tonight.

Best she not be hurt trying.

Marc moved to the bottom of the stairs and scanned the balcony above. This space showed fantastic wealth. Old money that had been collecting items for a long time and putting them to best show.

He turned to Maiair and Zorge.

"You two watch front and rear from downstairs," he ordered quietly. "We'll clear the upstairs."

Both nodded silently and moved: Zorge to the kitchen to cover their retreat, Maiair to the front door, in case someone had called the cops and a badge might come knocking, even at this time of night.

Up the stairs, noting that they were almost too small for Vanir, but that made sense. The owners were Traakna, and their shorter legs wouldn't appreciate a house that would make Marc comfortable.

The killer robot led, with Marc in its shadow. At the top, Marc pointed to Yooyar and indicated she should watch their rear, the far end of the hallway that faced a closed double-door right now.

First door revealed a bathroom, empty though showing indications of a youngster living here, with various bath toys piled haphazardly in a blue, plastic laundry basket. Cute, mermaid nightlight over the sink.

Back out into the hallway. Door open halfway into a room with lots of nightlights.

The android peeked in and rotated its head like an owl to look back at Marc.

"Female juvenile Traakna, master," it said in a quiet, mechanical voice.

Marc nodded and stepped around the machine man.

The Traakna girl, little Ariela, indeed slept, sprawled on a double bed in the middle of the room, surrounded by toys and decorations that made the place look like a fairy tale castle owned by unicorns. Her antennae twitched to some inner rhythm as she dreamed.

Marc studied the room quickly, identifying several targets before he aimed his own stun pistol and shot the child while she slept. He had specifically tuned his weapon down to for the task. Had the android done it, the weapon might have risked permanently damaging the child. An adult would be out cold for mere minutes if Marc shot them with his. That would still be enough for this group.

Marc knew himself to be a cold, evil man, but making war on innocent children was absolutely a bridge too far, even for him. She would sleep peacefully, and awaken in a new place with strangers, so Marc needed to identify the toys to bring along with them to keep her mollified for the few days or week he would need to keep her.

He turned to Mishalska and the robot. The Nari was showing a little too much white around his eyes, but Marc wasn't about to tease the man. Anybody who would hurt children for no reason had no place in his gang.

It was good.

They checked the library. A full office showed all manner of locked file cabinets Marc might have found interesting, but he simply didn't have the time. Another bathroom, this one decorated for company. An upstairs reading room that reminded Marc of the private chapels some old castles had maintained, but with only one bookcase, overflowing, and two plush chairs that looked like they were for midgets. Or Traakna.

The double-door at the end of the hall had remained closed when they joined Yooyar again. Marc gestured the others to move a little closer and tested the handle.

Unlocked.

He drew his pistol again and turned to the robot.

"Take the male and render him unconscious," Marc ordered. "I will stun the female."

"Acknowledged, master," the machine said.

Marc turned the knob and pushed quietly unsure what he would encounter.

The four of them spilled into a sitting room, large and comfortable and opening onto a balcony through closed, glass doors that admitted just enough moonlight to make the place cozy. An open door showed the sleeping quarters beyond, so Marc led them quickly to that door and peeked in.

There.

Elgannohn Shevskara and his wife, comfortably asleep.

Traakna reminded Marc of Yuudixtl, to some degree. At least in the sense that both had evolved from marine lizards, much like humans and Vanir had both started their evolutionary conquest as arboreal tree shrews.

Traakna had the bright green scales of a gecko, with a reverse-hinged legs like a dog or chicken and a long, almost prehensile tail. Two sensory antennae grew backwards out of the sides of their foreheads like gazelle horns. Big, expressive eyes were wider set than on most *Accord* species, giving them a tremendous peripheral vision. Nostrils and ears were just slits, and the mouth had almost no lips. Just a long, shockingly-pink tongue almost as prehensile as the tail.

The wife stirred in her dream, but Marc was shooting her anyway. The machine shot the husband almost as quickly.

"Check the room," Marc said unnecessarily.

Yooyar and Mishalska were already investigating the massive bathroom and his and hers walk-in closets.

"Clear," Yooyar announced a few moments later.

Marc nodded. He hadn't expected any troubles so far. Shevskara was a businessman, not troublemaker. And he would be even less so with a hostage involved.

"Android, carry the male," Marc ordered. "Mishalska, grab him some clothes to wear. Yooyar, with me."

Marc strode quickly back down the hall with the lethal Warreth woman in his wake.

He paused at the doorway to Ariela's bedroom, but she was out cold still. Good.

Marc moved quickly to grab a bag and stuff clothes and toys into it. A plush doll from the bed that reminded Marc of a sasquatch went into the bag, as well as a collection of unicorns and a few other things.

Yooyar watched from the door.

"Books," she said aloud.

Marc cast an interested eye in her direction. She was among the least-maternal females he had ever known, but she was still a woman. He grabbed several books off a nearby shelf and stuffed them into the bag, along with a twirly skirt hanging over a chair.

The bag went to Yooyar to carry.

Carefully, he picked up Ariela and wrapped her in a blanket. She was so small, relative to his new, massive size, that it was almost like holding an infant, even if the girl was the developmental equivalent of a six-year-old human.

He returned to the master bedroom and surveyed it, pulling an envelope from an inside pocket and resting it on the bed where Elgannohn had been sleeping and turned to leave.

"Just like that?" Yooyar asked. "It's really that simple?"

Marc smiled at her like a crocodile.

"Yes," he replied simply. "Kidnapping for profit is a time-honored way to make money, if you get a reputation for both ruthlessness and respectability in the process. And we will. I just need to train you how to handle it. And who to hunt."

"And Shevskara?" Yooyar asked as she followed him out the door and down the grand staircase.

"Something like this doesn't work nearly as well on an honest man, Yooyar," Marc said over his shoulder, tenderly watching that his bundle was safe. "But Shevskara can't even spell truthful."

Out the back, across the yard, and into the alley. Mishalska and the android had already tied the Traakna into a seat in the back of a passenger van, with Zorge in the driver's seat just waiting.

Ariela went into a child seat and got buckled fussily in. She would be returned to her mother in just a matter of days, regardless. Her purpose now was to get her father's undivided attention while Marc held the man captive. After that, knowing Shevskara, the man would be happy to buy his freedom as well.

"What was in the letter?" Yooyar asked as they pulled away.

"I have your daughter and your husband," Marc quoted it from memory. "You will follow my instructions to the letter. If you do not call the authorities, you will get Ariela back in a few days, after which we will discuss the ransom for your husband. We will be in touch."

"And humans do this thing for sport?" her face was scrunched up.

"Our reputation for ferocity with your kind is well deserved, Yooyar," he turned and smiled at her. "Here, it lets me do things that your kind can't even fathom, for the most part."

"And we're returning the child without getting anything for it?" Yooyar followed up. It was obvious she was learning, not questioning.

"We're buying silence and collaboration," Marc said. "The wife will remain quiet. Elgannohn will be much less likely to be obstinate when I show the man that I have his only child in my possession. And then he will convince his wife to give us a significant amount of money, which will help fund the organization for a long while. If all goes according to plan, we will return him unharmed in a couple of weeks."

"And if they refuse?" Maiair asked from the front seat.

"They she gets her husband back in pieces."

LIONS

FATIMA FELT ALMOST BLIND, walking out of the Arizona sun and into the transportation center in her disguise, dressed as a Woman's Auxiliary and carrying a bag with spare uniforms and such.

At least she could barely smell the bizarre human scents wafting about her as she got inside and away from the dry desert heat, but at the same time, she had to rely on her eyes for nearly everything.

No wonder the rest of the *Accord*, and perhaps the rest of the galaxy was so mundane. Everything with them was limited to a two-dimensional perception field that left out so many things.

But she was as prepared as she could be in the time given to assimilate. She had pills she could take that would help her process and absorb nutrients and vitamins from human food, and keep much of it from poisoning her in the process.

It helped that Earth Force Sky Patrol cuisine tended to be extremely bland, based largely on American or English cooking, which gravitated towards well-cooked meat, possibly in a mild sauce, with grilled or boiled vegetables on the side. This would be so much more of a dangerous adventure, if the standard was Javanese, or Pekinese, or perhaps Ecuadorian.

Stew she could handle.

And the clothing was outrageous, but again, she understood the bizarre cultural underpinnings that drove it. Males had returned to a peak of utter cultural dominance over the last few centuries, after reaching near parity at a previous juncture. Females of most cultures were relegated to a socially-subjugated state, expected to serve a man, defer to him, even cook for him upon marriage.

Just one more reason why this species was unfit for galactic civilization.

But she wasn't here to be a fashion critic. And the skirt she was forced to wear in public wasn't all that bad, as it had been specifically cut to give her a little more freedom to move than it should, and to moderate her temperature, depending on the situation and location. Even her brassieres had labels suggesting it came from a human factory, but someone had taken the time to fit them to her so that she would be comfortable in them, when the placement of her breasts was apparently closer together on her chest than most human females.

She had several identical uniforms, in gradually heavier weights of fabric, from the lightest silk for equatorial heat to a heavy wool gathered from a true Merino sheep on this very planet. In the field, she would be expected to add a prim, scarlet kepi matching the rest of her clothes, with a gold band, but that was inappropriate on a station or ship, as she would be boarding shortly.

Each uniform had been vacuum-sealed according to the Earth Force Sky Patrol regulations she had studied, to be as flat as possible and then packed into a carryall, along with personal items and an electronic reader with a variety of human-entertainment options and books programmed into it, in case she wanted to learn more about some of the more interesting bits of the amazing number of cultures on this single planet. And boredom was likely to be her biggest risk, if everything else went well.

English words on a monitor as she entered the hallway directed her to a smaller corridor on her left, away from the larger mass of humans in the process of moving to her right into the larger facility. Down a short hallway tiled in white or black rectangles and through a door, Fatima found herself in what she guessed was a small waiting room, with a woman seated behind a counter, wearing the identical uniform to hers.

"May I help you?" the person asked brightly. Guard, security, or official wasn't readily obvious from the arrangement of things, but Fatima suspected that to be an intentional thing.

She took a quiet breath and approached the counter, reaching inside her tunic to withdraw a set of papers that she placed on the counter.

"I have orders to report here for transport," Fatima said simply. Perhaps adding a level of confusion to her voice as misdirection.

Certainly, she wasn't entirely sure of this process. She would be writing up most of the infiltration manual for future female agents, if she was successful.

And if humans were still an ongoing concern in another year.

The official pulled the stack of papers apart and sorted them. Passport. Sky Patrol Identity Card. Orders To Report.

Fatima rocked back into her heels and crossed her hands behind her, a close enough approximation of the at-ease posture she had never learned in Earth Force Basic Training.

"Fatima Darzi?" the woman asked. "Persian physicist on detached duty?"

"That's right," Fatima nodded.

Leave it at that. I am on a secret mission for Sky Patrol and you do not have the security clearance to even know who I am, let alone why I am here.

The woman nodded in turn and began typing into a computer hidden on the other side of the tall desk.

Fatima measured the steps to the door, if she should have to run. And if the door wasn't locked by the time she reached it.

Humans relied extensively on computer networks for information, which was bad, but they also didn't trust them, so the systems were not highly automated, nor efficient, settling on massive redundancy instead. And they were greatly fragmented, with no organization trusting any other to host critical data or information.

As a result, it made their information security a nightmare to penetrate, but only because you had to do the same job twelve times, rather than just changing one setting and letting it ripple out through the rest of the electronic forest.

And it took time. But it also took time to look something up, and to cross-reference it, if necessary. And something missing from another system might merely mean that you didn't have the clearance to see it there, or maybe it hadn't been typed in already.

Primitives who have only just barely begun to look on information as a tool, rather than a weapon.

Fatima managed not to goggle in surprise when the woman opened her passport and stamped it with a mechanical device made from chrome. One that left ink on the page.

How utterly antiquated. And easy to fake later.

"Here you are," the woman said with a smile. "I've checked you in for the flight already and assigned you a window seat. The kitchen is prepared for a halal meal. Right through there."

She handed everything back and Fatima stuffed it back into the inner pocket of her tunic, on her hip under the flap, rather than higher, across her breasts.

Fatima wondered if having the pocket higher up on her chest where it would be more comfortable was forbidden. Where perhaps something in the pocket might alter the shape of the breast so much, or cover it, that male commanders had vetoed it at some previous juncture. Sexism run out of control. Men had such a pocket and didn't give it a second thought.

Still, she kept her opinion to herself as she circled the counter and approached a door. It buzzed loudly at a signal from behind the desk and she pulled it open, emerging into a much nicer lounge.

Red carpeting with a thick shag. Soft blue walls. Floor to vaulted ceiling windows looked out over one of North America's southern skyports. Comfortable chairs. Even a refrigerator with a transparent front and filled with bottles of various kinds.

She retrieved a glass bottle of orange juice and grabbed a bag of salted nuts from a nearby bowl before retreating to one of the seats and relaxing. Even the smells were better in here. Less industrial cleaner and perhaps more floral orange and rose. It at least smelled natural, in her greatly-reduced olfactory state. Her tentacles probably could have measured the exact chemical signature to a degree that she could either identify the source chemicals, or tell when the flowers had been cut and then infused into an alcohol base for dispersion.

It was still so much better to not have to deal with the smells of the humans in here.

None were close to her, but she was being covertly watched by several. Two Anglo men in Earth Force uniforms looked like middle-aged managers returning from a business conference. A pair of East Asian women in Women's Auxiliary uniforms similar to hers. An African-looking male in a Sky Patrol Field Agent uniform confused her for a second, because she hadn't emotionally prepared herself for the fact that humans occasionally got large enough that they might pass for Vanir with a little work.

She kept thinking of them as being at her scale, and yet just the human diversity in this lounge put paid to that. Interesting. It had been an academic exercise before, as white Anglos were so dominant in Sky Patrol, and shared responsibilities with the teeming masses of East Asia and South Asia inside Earth Force itself.

Fortunately, her hijab served the secondary purpose of marking her out as a stranger. Persia was a member of Earth Force, but rarely contributed forces to Sky Patrol, as they had almost no off-world colonists. Further west from Fatima's supposed homeland, the folks of the Levant had perhaps taken up that slack, being over-represented both in Sky Patrol and among the merchants and traders of deep space.

So the various people in the lounge left her alone, except for a brief, commiserative smile from the African male she suspected was meant to convey a comradeship over being outsiders here. She lacked the genetic background to automatically make sense of human mannerisms that apparently transcended culture.

By the time the juice and nuts were gone and being slowly processed in her system for useful nutrients, another woman had joined them from the hallway behind her, and several men from a different doorway. They were all Earth Force, but not Sky Patrol, so apparently the flight today was a mostly-civilian sort of thing, and not a military transport.

A woman appeared from a third door at one side and spoke into a microphone that projected her words cleanly across the giant lounge.

"Good afternoon, ladies and gentlemen," she said professionally. "Flight *Arizona-Seven* to Earth Force Headquarters at the L1 LaGrange point, with subsequent service to The Arsenal at L2 is now ready to load. Please have your ID and orders ready and we will board the bus to take us across the field."

Fatima joined the group lining up, and found herself behind the East Asian women and just in front of the African man. She could feel almost at home, if she pretended they were Nari and he was Vanir.

The bus was a large box with comfortable seats, riding on vulcanized rubber tires and powered by batteries. She had a fantastic view as they crossed the landing field, watching sub-orbitals, ballistics, and simple airliners moving about in a complicated dance.

Again, so strange, when she was used to flying auto-taxis that would take you to a tube station, from which you would simply transit a wormhole to a second location, or jump up to orbit and board a liner making a set run of stops, like an enormous space freighter.

Arizona-Seven was a small, winged aircraft, located at the farthest end of the field. A white tube lying flat, with portholes to see out of, and a tall fin like a predatory fish at the rear. Four large engines made up the stern of the craft, currently being fueled by a pair of tanker trucks.

Fatima was indeed in a window seat. The flight was small enough that she had nobody in the aisle seat next to her, but she couldn't be sure if that was luck, or if the agent at the desk had decided to isolate her from the others, lest her strange, Persian ancestry infect them.

Little did they know.

She grinned to herself and set to connecting all the appropriate straps and buckles.

The seat was deep and comfortable. The safety briefing far more complex and detailed than any back home, but her culture also had been flying in space since before this species discovered metals. Fatima worked to calm herself that the speech was to cover multiple eventualities, rather than representing probabilities.

Was it really likely that they would face a water landing? Possibly, given that the planet itself had just a large water surface ratio, and so much land was farther away from their equatorial flight path.

It was mind-numbingly loud when the engines ignited. She was so happy to be nearly deaf already, without her tentacles. She could only imagine the migraine that so much noise might trigger.

The Arizona desert was flat and brown as the craft lifted off and began to climb to a much higher elevation. Eventually, the air would thin and the wings would retract to just stubs as they relied more and more on the roaring thrust behind her.

It took hours just to reach orbit, and the better part of a day to reach the gravitationally-stable high ground over the planet/moon system. She slept through some of it, relaxing in the absence of gravity. Two meals were eaten that were neither here nor there, and she spent the rest of her time reading current news from various sources on the planet below, and the stations ahead. Humans being humans, which was to say dangerous monsters, but they did appear to be trying to better themselves, once they managed to not hate each other over differences in color, shape, size, or religion. At least according to some of the news she read.

Fatima didn't have a lot of hope for most of them, but the First Inspector had sent her here to try to find a way to save the species, in spite of themselves. She could do that. Earth Force and Sky Patrol did represent an attempt to unify the humans into a better whole, however pale a shadow of the *Accord* it was at present.

Perhaps someday the Chaa would find a way to integrate these people as well.

The business managers and most of the females debarked when the vessel docked at Sky Patrol Headquarters, with a number of Sky Patrol officers and staff boarding in their place. This next flight was more crowded, but she was still did not have anyone in the seat next to her to bother her during her meals and sleep patterns, so she presumed a level of discrimination by that first woman, as other females on the two flights had been seated with males. Only the Muslim was kept isolated.

Good to know, and useful to her disguise.

Arizona-Seven was close to her destination before she finally caught a glimpse out her porthole, of the place called alternatively *The Arsenal* and *Shadow Base One*, for its location at the L2 LaGrange point, the so-called *Far Side of the Moon* from the system's sun, having run a slingshot from the inner point to the outer.

The base itself was a huge, spinning cylinder seen edge on, like a hollow tube just about than four kilometers across with massive spokes running from the central axis column out to the living quarters around the inner edge. She was looking forward to being back in pseudo-gravity again, after several days in free-fall. Again, primitives that had only just managed to make it into space on the backs of basic physics, and nothing more advanced.

And hopefully she could help to keep it that way.

Arizona-Seven docked to one end of the hub and she debarked with the others, floating out to the edges of a small chamber under the watchful eyes of several, male, Sky Patrol officers who reminded her of nothing so much as mother ducks with happy ducklings intent on meandering about.

Into a small elevator, where each of them was seated into a quick harness and inspected, before this platform was sent on its ways, with gravity going from a suggestion to a force as they descended outward to the edges of the station.

Inside, one more quick check of her paperwork and orders, and she was assigned to an unwed females barracks, with her own private room and shower attached to a communal eating and study facility. She unpacked her various uniforms and stowed them into a closet, set out her items supposedly issued by a quartermaster back in Tehran, and then settled herself on the bed to meditate.

She had entered the lion's den. Shortly, she would have to meet the lion himself.

UNDERCOVER

HIS INSTRUCTIONS HAD BEEN SUCCINCT, detailed, and a little strange, but Gareth had assumed they were the product of years or perhaps decades of deep-cover experience that he didn't have. Heck, until this, he had never had any interest in even becoming an undercover agent. Of course, if his secret got out to the general public, that would no longer be an option.

Unless Talyarkinash could somehow transform him again and not kill him in the process.

It was weird being the only person around who could dream of becoming someone else. Well, not counting Marc, and Gareth wasn't. After so many years as that man's friend, he couldn't see Marc radically changing his appearance. Even the new ears and the altered shape of his skull to make him Vanir was probably as jarring in his mirror as it was Gareth's. Marc wouldn't go any further visibly. Probably just stronger and faster if he could.

The joint Gareth had entered was what he would have called a truck stop, back home. Located out on the edge of town, he had taken an auto-taxi, jumped clear over to *Datha*, which was one of the newer worlds in the *Accord*, then followed the directions.

This place was nobody's homeworld, so it was an interesting mix of Yuudixtl, Vanir, and Nari, already three of the most common species in the *Accord*, along with Enjev, Moisa, and a fairly significant group of Tree People.

Gareth grinned to himself as he walked in, contemplating that a tribe of Tree People, or Quarrie as they were more properly known, really was called a Forest. There weren't any in here, but a group was standing in a nearby clearing, probably absorbing sunlight and dew for breakfast.

The restaurant itself was about as divie as he could have imagined. Booths down both sides with tables in the open middle. The dominant table coloration was a polished cherry oak, with black leather, so it was rather darker than most of the ones he had known as a kid or young agent, where white was the main color. A counter stuck out into the middle like a horseshoe, and a window behind it showed the kitchen.

Gareth was dressed down today. Back from his nicer duds to dungarees and his denim jacket. It fit in well with the midafternoon crowd as he looked around.

Baker was in the last booth on the right, opposite the bathrooms located on the left side of the counter. Gareth walked over and sat with his back to the room, but he wasn't too concerned about someone sneaking up on her.

"I got your message," she said, sipping some coffee from an ugly, green mug. "What needed to be discussed in person?"

"I have a lead on Maximus," Gareth said quietly. "Or rather, someone that Maximus has possibly hired to make him weapons. Rather than just arrest our target in a big, public event that warns Maximus, I would like to break into the man's facility and gather up more evidence first."

"Why?" her eyes bored in on his like a laser cannon.

"Because what I have won't stand up in front of a grand jury, Baker," Gareth grimaced.

He explained the series of parties to her as they ordered and ate, including the reference to the Ellis Device that Gonquah had called by the English name: *Android*. The implications didn't register with her any more than they had with Diệu Ahn, but they were all *Bound*.

Only he could envision an army of killer robots turned loose on the general populace of the *Accord*, which was exactly what he feared might happen if they waited too long.

"Killer robots?" she still sounded dismissive.

"Think of them as guns with legs, then, Baker," Gareth snapped, still trying to keep his voice down as the waiter approached to clear plates and refill coffee. "They are about as controlled, considering the circumstances."

"This might be enough," she suggested after the they were alone again. "We could take it up the chain of command and get an opinion."

"You do that," Gareth said. "Or better yet, have Grodray. But in the meantime, I don't think any laws have actually been broken, other than providing goods and services to a known criminal, and I'm sure there are enough layers of obfuscation involved that he's safe there as well if his lawyers are any good."

"Gonquah has been on our list for a while, Gareth," she admitted finally. "As you surmised, nothing could be made to stick, but that's not the same as we haven't been trying. How would you build a killer robot?"

"The word he used was *android*," Gareth replied, his voice staying low and quiet as the restaurant's clientele came and went. "That suggests a bipedal silhouette, like a human or a Vanir, but I would make it roughly Nari sized to blend in better with the general public. All the usual sensors on the head, like a uhm…like one of me. Hands as well, with opposable thumbs, following the standard model. The only point at which you start breaking laws then becomes the moment you hand the thing a pistol and tell it to kill people."

"And they would not be programmed against such an occurrence?" she asked.

"You already have automation and robots in your factories, Baker," he said. "Immobile and massive and stupid. That's one of the reasons we invented the term android. To distinguish a special kind of machine. And Sarzynski isn't about to have them custom built for him with the standards Laws of Robotics baked in."

"Laws of Robotics?" Baker's face scrunched in confusion.

"A set of programming imperatives," Gareth said. "No robot can harm a human. Robots must follow all orders given them by humans, except when it would hurt a humans. Etc. They can get quite detailed, according to the Ethical Technologists who taught me at school. Those won't exist here."

"Okay," she finally nodded. "I'm convinced. You have really good instincts at this sort of thing. What do you propose?"

Gareth blushed at the compliment. This wasn't the hardass Constable he had known for so long. Perhaps having her prize in sight had made her a little less antagonistic all the time?

Or maybe people were finally valuing her like they should. Eveth

Baker was one of the best cops Gareth had ever met. She deserved to be a peer of Grodray and the other Prime Investigators.

"I want to break in during the middle of the night," Gareth said. "Gonquah mentioned which factory had made the one in his suite, that first night when he told someone that they weren't ready for everyone to order yet, as they worked out the final specs and tested some in the field."

"Was he telling the truth?" Baker leaned forward abruptly. "Not ready yet?"

"Maybe," Gareth suggested. "It might also be that he didn't want others to have a chance to figure out what they were capable of. And if it were up to me, thinking like Maximus, I'd order a few and then find someplace very remote and quiet to push them as hard as I could to find their exact limits in the process of breaking them. Then come back and order a second batch with improvements and refinements."

"Does Earth have such armies?" Baker's eyes were showing white now.

"No," Gareth tried to satisfy her. "There was a stretch a few centuries ago where they did, and the violence and warfare got so far out of hand that a global government had to be formed to stop it and then prevent future wars. That's Earth Force. Sky Patrol are the cops that deal with criminals who want to break loose and return to those terrible days. But there are also groups that will come in and crush anyone trying to start a rebellion against the peace."

"So you think you'll just waltz in there by yourself and find what you need?" Baker's voice had a sharper note now.

Gareth nodded, unwilling to give her more details, as he would be most likely faking it every step of the way.

"No," Baker decided.

"No?" Gareth was shocked.

"No," she repeated. "You're not going in there by yourself and risk it."

"Why not?" Gareth asked.

Her sudden smile was almost more frightening than Eveth Baker angry.

"I'm coming with you."

DEFENSIVE MEASURES

ROYSTON WAS confident enough in the design of the machine that he didn't need to go back through the entire, convoluted process of opening a new wormhole, down in Arizona, just to confirm that this detection device worked. His older machines had registered the sudden appearance of this new type of radiation in a concentrated form, and his original sensor worked well enough, when he went into Gareth's abandoned and sealed off cabin to test it.

The radiation itself was fading at a slow but measurable rate. Royston estimated it had a half-life of roughly eighty-three days, so he knew it would be too faint to detect in another year, swallowed back up into the cosmic background radiation it seemed to have been derived from in the first place.

Royston's lab was, as always, the dark mirror reflection of his office. Perfectly clean, as though a movie set put into storage, with every tool put away into a labeled slot in a drawer, clean and polished. Nothing at all on the countertops themselves that wasn't there all the time. As opposed to his office, where books, papers, and old coffee mugs frequently competed with one another for space.

The two newest detectors waited patiently on a work counter, quiescent and poised, but Royston hadn't opened any portals in here. Nor, as far as he could tell, had anyone else. One device was small, a pocket-sized case no larger than necessary for holding cigarettes had an effective detection range of only a few meters, while the larger one was more the size of a desk phone, or perhaps a cigar box, and would both detect and then triangulate to a range of sixty or eight meters, depending on the materials blocking the signal. Neither had found anything new.

Hopefully, that situation would remain thus. He had woken from more than one nightmare fearing that his hypothetical aliens had learned of his new discoveries and were in the process of returning, in order to do something about it.

Something ugly.

He had no way to preventing a portal from being opened, if they wanted to just chuck a bomb through and destroy The Arsenal. That was one of the reasons that information about the generator he had built, including the fact that it had even worked, was so tightly controlled.

Someone else could teleport a bomb anywhere they wanted, if they took a fancy to the notion. And then the wars would return.

Royston made a mental note to take a week off, preferably with Pippa, and see if they could locate that one singer and her rock band. He hoped it would give him another chance at the sort of inspiration that had led him to this new mathematics in the first place. He could not imagine that the physics of the universe were not so well balanced that it was impossible to build a device to disrupt such a wormhole from forming.

He just needed to find them.

The outer door opened and Sector Marshal Siddall stepped through. The last few months had aged him badly. Royston had known Alvin for more than twenty years, and in that time, the now-Head of The Arsenal had always been a tall, heavy-set man. Over the last few years, Alvin had spent too much time behind a desk, growing progressively rounder and less like the agents he led. Or he himself had been.

But now, the stress was showing. The man's hair was thinning appreciably and coming in all white. He had dropped weight, but that was due to not eating, rather than exercising more, so he moved stiffly, rather than the long, determined strides Royston had in his memory.

"Good morning, Sector Marshal," Royston smiled and tried to put a brave face on things. He was happy Pippa wasn't here to see how gray the man had turned in the last little bit.

"Hello, Royston," the man replied with a bit of a rasp to his voice as he walked over and shook hands. "I understand you have a new gadget for me, but that I needed to come down here to see it in private?"

"Indeed, old friend," Royston said. "This must remain at the highest security level for the time being."

Royston picked up the smaller device and handed it to the Sector Marshal.

"This is for you, to carry with you at all times," Royston's voice turned serious. "It will detect a new portal opening and sound an noise similar in volume to a breech alarm, which should awaken you and anyone close by that they are in danger."

"Thank you," Alvin took it and slid the device into his pants pocket. "And the other?"

"The other is a more powerful version, with a greater detection range," Royston said. "It will also project a small hologram showing you a vector to a portal it detects, with a reasonable range, but it not enough to cover the entire base."

"Should we build more?" Siddall asked. "Cover both this base and Headquarters with them? Perhaps the Hall of Governments down in Zurich, as well?"

"Perhaps, my friend," Royston said. "But if you do, it must be done quietly. Most people are not aware of the ability to open portals, and if such knowledge gets out, we will have other problems."

"Crime, yes," Alvin said. "It is driving me crazy, trying to find a way to prevent some Lawless Joe from just stepping into a bank vault and making off with all the gold. Or worse, pushing a bomb through and committing acts of terrorism."

"Just so," Royston said. "I can't prevent them. Not today. But I can know now that something happened, if it becomes necessary to solve a crime. So we must not let the lesser angels know of the solar system know of such a machine."

"What about the aliens?" Alvin's voice fell to a hoarse whisper. "Can we stop them?"

"We cannot." Royston was apologetic. "And I have no way of reaching out to them to even find out if they are helping us or setting us up for some grand invasion later."

"Welcome to my nightmares, Royston, old chap," Alvin said.

"I have a few ideas, Alvin," Royston said. "I plan on taking a week or three off shortly so that I can pursue them in a non-academic setting."

"What does that even mean?" the Sector Marshal's brow furrowed.

"Rock and roll, of all things, provided me the inspiration last time, Siddall," Royston grinned. "Teenage rebellion. I'm hoping something like it can show me the way to deflect portals, or prevent them entirely over a volume."

"I might sleep again, if you did," the big man grinned back. "Consider your vacation request approved in advance. And anything else you might need along the way."

"Thank you," Royston said, picking up the second machine and handing it to the Sector Marshal. "Put this in the station's Command Chamber and instruct them to contact you or I, or even Pippa, if it goes off, and then wait for orders."

"Your daughter?" Alvin scowled, mildly offended by his tones.

"My intellectual partner, Alvin," Royston fired back. "She is more knowledgeable about all of this than anyone else, including Sir West. And she had a good head on her shoulders in an emergency. I truly wish Earth Force would get over their male supremacy tendencies and realize that they are leaving out half the population as useful, contributing scientists."

"That is out of my hands, Royston," he said. "But I will set this up and leave those orders. And perhaps that will help others see past the Women's Auxiliary Uniform to the mind and heart underneath."

He nodded and turned the go, pausing suddenly and pivoting back.

"Oh, dear," The Sector Marshal said. "I had forgotten. You have a visitor that that arrived on station late yesterday. We've been clearing her paperwork and following up. She's Persian, so we don't have a lot of background or context, but she's apparently a niece of your old nemesis, Firuz Alinejad."

They both smiled at the reference.

"Firuz was hardly a nemesis, Alvin," Royston laughed. "Except perhaps during the World Cup. The world lost a great mind when he died in that accident."

"Just so," Alvin nodded. "But his niece apparently inherited his brains and is a member of the Women's Auxiliary, in the same sort of situation as Pippa. Basic degree and nowhere to study the advanced stuff to challenge what the files say is a first-rate mind. Someone in our Persian office approved her to come here, with an eye to studying."

"Why is she here?" Royston asked.

"You apparently have a soft spot for letting women learn, Royston," Alvin laughed and headed for the door. "She checks out, but I wanted to prep you, rather than just letting her walk in an introduce herself to you."

"Thank you, old friend," Royston said as the door opened and the Sector Marshal departed.

Firuz Alinejad's niece? All well and good.

Except that he remembered getting half-drunk with the man as they watched a World Cup final more than a decade ago, listening to him kvetch that nobody in his family had the brains Allah gave a goose.

So who was this woman?

NIGHTFALL

NORMALLY, Gareth knew, it would have required a bit of work to track down all references to all the Gonquahs in the system. Especially as Gonquah belonged to a culture that didn't do last names, but just usually combined two or three syllables as a first name and called good. Or rather, all of the Th'Tarni used the exact same last name, which was the same thing, so *Accord* systems didn't even bother with them.

At the same time, the Constabulary had been gunning for the Th'Tarni merchant for years, however secretly and unsuccessfully, so getting Gareth everything known about the man and his business had only taken them a few days. That included the rough layouts of the factory Gareth wanted to break into, as they had to be kept up to date with the local fire suppression forces.

So he knew where he was going, and what he would see when he got there. He hoped.

The night was dark and warm. A little overcast, as if perhaps it might make up its mind to throw howling thunderstorms later, but it was still just pregnant with heat and potential at this point.

That worked to their benefit. Gareth and Constable Baker were a few kilometers away, and more than a kilometer in the air, watching.

Gareth had never flown a lifterpack before, but it made perfect sense, once the mechanic had explained it to him and fitted him for the device. Small anti-gravity lifters neutralized your weight until you were effectively buoyant. Internal induction fans with vectored thrust nozzles could move you around like a hummingbird, or let you chase down a hawk if you needed to.

Baker was watching through a set of helmet optics that included magnification and light amplification. They were talking on a low-powered radio so they could be extremely quiet, even if they stumbled into the guards walking the facility.

"You ready?" she asked, flipping the scanner faceplate up into her helmet so he could see her eyes.

"Yes, ma'am," Gareth replied, pitching himself forward and pushing the button to accelerate his fans. This was almost as much fun as free-swimming in an orbital facility, a skill all Sky Patrol agents had to master.

She was a beat behind him, but slid onto his flank like a wingman flying a patrol in a fighter jet. Below them, the city stretched out, quiet like it was already anticipating trouble later.

Gareth told himself he was just being paranoid, but at the same time, Gonquah was also someone who dealt with Marc Sarzynski, so he wasn't sure it was possible to be too paranoid. Just in case, he had a stun pistol on his right thigh and a heavy disintegrator on his left.

The latter was a weapon capable of destroying an auto-taxi, but Gareth had no idea what the capabilities of a killer robot might be. He also figured that he wouldn't be liable for damages if the man was selling them to Maximus.

And Gareth still had the slightest juvenile delinquency streak, if he was being honest with himself. A standard disintegrator might do the trick, but the heavy version would be so much more entertaining if push came to shove.

They approached the building slowly. It was several stories high, but most of that was just vaulted space with catwalks connecting various manufacturing lines and machine systems. The roof itself was only slightly pitched from a central keel, and made of metal, so Gareth presumed landing on it would still make a noise like a drum.

With that in mind, the plan was for them to land in a quiet corner and force open a door, hopefully by picking the lock, but he could still annihilate it if he had to. They had the warrants duly signed and executed, so it wasn't criminal destruction. He just wanted to sneak up on that bastard if he could.

The outside was mostly dark on this side of the building. A loading dock was mildly busy on the other side, filling and emptying trucks at night, when most of the employees would be off, so they wouldn't be in the way.

Gareth and Baker just had to stay away from the few people moving around. Unless he wanted to arrest everyone and unscramble it all later. There was always that.

He suspected Baker was actually looking forward to that sort of thing. She could be like that.

They landed in a back yard with grass and tables. The map had it marked as a break area for employees, but the folks on the docks had their own, several hundred meters away around a corner, so hopefully they didn't need to walk clear over there for peace and quiet.

It was dark enough here.

"Should we leave the lifters?" he asked.

That had been the original plan, but she was in charge.

"Yes," Baker decided. "They are too obvious if someone sees us, while from a distance we might just be two employees walking along."

Gareth stripped quickly out of the oversized backpack, leaving only a set of black clothes built by Talyarkinash for covert missions. Baker did the same, drawing a set of compact tools from a pocket as they approached the door. Gareth drew the stunner for now and shifted to one side to keep watch behind them.

He had never picked a mechanical lock before. The theory itself was relatively simple, but it took a lot of practice to do it without breaking the lock or leaving a trace that you had passed through.

In his time, Gareth had always knocked politely. Or kicked the door in with beams blazing. But he could learn.

Eveth had it open almost as fast as Gareth suspected he might be able to get it with the key in one hand, but he didn't ask how. She was a cop. And a damned good one.

She passed through first, with him a step behind. Inside, they were in a space that reminded him of an enlisted man's wardroom, with a number of tables where people could eat their lunch without having to leave the building. From which they could then step outside and have some sun. Or a smoke. Or something.

They crossed the space quickly and emerged into what Gareth thought of as storage. That spot where you put things you didn't need immediately on hand, out of the way of the folks on the floor, and not taking up precious loading dock space.

It made a useful spot to sort of hide in while they studied the interior.

Gareth was reminded of a factory for making automobiles, with large overhead cranes that would carry a big piece along as teams did things to it, before you attached the wheels at the end and it could roll on its own.

He followed Baker from there to a stairway that got them up onto one of the catwalks. They were more exposed up here, but had a much better view in all directions. The lights were turned way down over most of the facility, so they should be okay as long as they moved slowly and stuck to shadows.

Carefully, they crept forward, staying out of sight as much as possible.

"And I'm telling you that somebody in your department signed for it two days ago," an angry voice suddenly echoed up from right beneath them.

Gareth froze, his stunner pointed down as two men walked exactly beneath he and Baker. She had drawn her own pistol and remained utterly still watching.

"And I wasn't here two days ago, so I got no clue what the hell you're talking about pal," the other man answered angrily. "Ask him where he put it."

"He's not here, so I gotta ask you," the first man yelled. "Maybe if your people weren't all fuckups we wouldn't have this problem. You ever imagine that?"

The angry noises faded as the two men turned a corner, but Gareth suspected that they would be going at it for a while. Or things would get out of hand and somebody would throw a punch.

That would actually work in his favor, as a fight back over there would draw more people from the inside of the factory and give he and Baker space to work.

As long as nobody walked out that rear door and saw a pair of lifterpacks stashed against the side of the building. Then the gig would be up.

They moved again quickly, just in case the men came back. To the end of the current run and sideways, it got them over a massive machine that Gareth thought might be a welding robot. It really didn't matter, as long as it got them out of sight.

Baker stopped so suddenly that Gareth nearly walked into her back.

"I had my doubts," she said as she quickly knelt down, using a handy I-beam pillar as cover.

Gareth studied her eyes and turned to see what had gotten her attention.

Robots. Two of them. Just exactly the sort of things he would have built, had he been commissioned to build *Androids*.

They stood watch on either side of a closed door to a section of the factory sealed off from the rest.

Each of them carried a disintegrator pistol in its right hand. Gareth would have expected Gonquah to arm them with stunners, but you apparently had to cross some level of security to get as far as that door, so anybody reaching those robots knew what they would find.

Or were up to no good and needed to be stopped.

Gareth had found what he had suspected from Gonquah's stories.

Now, he had to find the rest of the story.

ANDROID

SHE HAD HAD HER DOUBTS. However, even Eveth Baker was willing to admit she had been wrong. She kept thinking of humans in terms of Gareth Dankworth, but that man was a born cop who lived and breathed doing the right thing. While his suggestions weren't always the legal thing, he was possessed of an innate ethical standard that had challenged even her from time to time.

Marc Sarzynski, on the other hand, was the death of all civilization boiled down and decanted into the form of a Vanir devil. A killer with absolutely no remorse, willing to say or do literally anything that would bring him closer to ultimate power.

Now, was one of those times when she wondered how bad things would have already gotten if those two idiot Yuudixtl hadn't had a change of heart and tried to stop the human on their own. Not that she would have believed them, if they had just walked into a Constabulary Station and turned themselves in. And that assumed that they had found honest cops.

Eveth was simultaneously appalled and outraged at how many bent cops had been discovered over the last few months as her and Grodray's investigations caused organizations to unravel and paperwork listing crimes and bribes to be revealed.

But this, this was something entirely else. There was no word for it in the *Accord*, so they had been forced to adopt a human word, like so many other situations.

Warfare. The systematic, industrialized killing of organic creatures, most of whom would be innocents caught in the middle. For that, Eveth could see the ultimate sanction being applied. She would make that case with Grodray and whoever else might listen, all the way up to the First Inspector, if necessary.

Two of Gareth's *androids* guarded a door. She and Gareth were wearing their Constabulary bodysuits, with black, civilian jackets thrown over that to make them look less like cops at a distance.

If someone got that close, it would already be time to either start shooting or call in Grodray with the Heavy Rescue Team he had on tap a few kilometers away. Gareth didn't know, because…

She wasn't sure why Grodray hadn't decided to tell Gareth. Maybe to inspire the man to be even more self-sufficient? Gareth was willing to go in alone already, so her quietly bringing up some heavy artillery wouldn't have changed anything.

And Gareth could be trusted. Nothing the man had ever done suggested otherwise. She made a mental note to ask Jack later. It hadn't seemed important then, but neither of them expected this, either.

The whole universe had just changed, if people like Gonquah were willing to supply people like Maximus with killer robots.

She measured the distance to the machines, but her disintegrator might not do the trick from here. Gareth's would, but they would still have a major distance to cover, even if he managed to destroy both machines.

"Back up," she ordered. "We'll circle around."

The big Vanir nodded and moved like a jungle cat, so utterly silent and fluid that Eveth felt a twinge of jealousy. And she was among the best.

But she knew what Dr. Liamssen had done to the human. Frighteningly, she also knew how much more capacity the form had, if they chose to go further at a later date.

Would the Chaa be offended if a new god was born in their ancient home? Eveth had never been a religious type. She knew the old stories handed down, and didn't doubt them, given all the other species that made up the *Accord*, but were people like Liamssen playing with fire now?

How far would be too far?

They moved. Back up the catwalk and to a space dark enough she felt comfortable descending to the factory floor. It was cooler down there, cold concrete underfoot acting as a heat sink and all the warm air rising up to the catwalk.

She kept two walls of equipment she couldn't identify between her and the machines on her right, and the loading dock on her left, tracking both locations on a detailed mental map as she moved. Gareth remained three steps behind her and to the right, but she still had to glance back occasionally to make sure he hadn't vanished.

Utter silence, from one of the biggest Vanir she had ever known.

There was no way to know how good the sensors on the machines were, short of opening one up in a shop or locating the design specs that had been supplied, so Eveth had to guess when she would be close enough to hurt those machines, but not so close that she triggered a response from them first.

Fortunately, she was an even better shot than Gareth was.

This was probably close enough. At least she hoped.

"Just around this corner, at an angle of approximately forty degrees," she whispered up to Gareth. "I will shoot the one on the left. You shoot the one on the right. Then we'll get through that door and see what's inside. Questions?"

"Negative, sir," Gareth said.

It sounded automatic, rather than insulting. Gareth returning to an younger version of himself, fresh out of whatever the Earth Force Sky Patrol equivalent of Constabulary School was. Snapping to.

Eveth checked her pistol one more time. Charged. Safeties both off. Beam setting standard, rather than the short-range focus you might use to open an armored door or a safe. She noted Gareth doing the same and felt a surge of power go through her.

She had never tried to storm a building with Grodray, but she suspected that the man was hiding extreme competence in that field as well under that phlegmatic exterior. Gareth Dankworth was a Vanir of action, who had done this sort of thing before numerous times. She wouldn't have to worry about him freezing up.

Eveth took a breath and shifted just a little to her left. Not enough to be seen, but it gave Gareth a touch of space, since he would be a step behind her.

"Go," she said quietly.

Eveth stepped around the corner at a normal pace, but immediately knew she had misjudged the machines. Or their orders.

A pair of disintegrator pistols started to rise, so she snapped off a shot at her target. It was hurried and a little low, but good enough, even at thirty meters. She caught the machine in the right leg. Its knee exploded in a flash of sparks and superheated metal, knocking its torso forward and off-line.

That was good, because a wooden crate not far in front of Eveth exploded when the robot's own pistol fired.

She snapped off a second shot as fast as the weapon would cycle, aware that the android was doing the same thing. This one went center mass, but the machine was on its face on the concrete floor, so the head exploded, scalloping a divot out of the chest that shot sparks for several seconds.

Beside her, Gareth's heavier beam had struck his target center and a little high, ripping the top half of the torso away from the bottom and scattering metal parts everywhere.

It hadn't sounded all that much like thunder and lightning, but she hoped that whoever might have heard it in the building had presumed that the storm outside was either moving closer or had finally broken.

As she moved forward at a hard jog, it dawned on Eveth that Gareth was so much faster than she was that he had taken an extra step forward and still gotten a kill shot on his first try. She suspected that anyone other than her might be subject to an inferiority complex, knowing what Gareth could do, but Eveth also knew that she was still close to the top one hundred of her kind, across however many millions of Vanir there might be in the galaxy.

She could live in a world where Gareth was in the top three, as long as she could remove Maximus from the running. Preferably personally, given the opportunity.

Gareth arrived first, pulling the disintegrator pistol from the dead robot before removing the power pack and stuffing it into a pocket. She did the same as Gareth lifted the first machine and slid it behind some nearby crates, where it was more or less out of sight for now.

Eveth drew her stun pistol in her off hand and kept watch while he moved the second robot. She was ambidextrous with pistols, but having a stunner in her off hand meant that she had options.

If she wanted.

"Do we kick the door in, or pick the lock?" Gareth asked quietly as he stepped close.

"Is it locked?" she asked, watching his face fall and turn red in embarrassment.

He was a good cop, but still a little too linear.

Instead of answering, he grabbed the handle in his left hand, the one without the heavy disintegrator that had done such a good job on the first machine, and turned the knob.

"Me first," Eveth said, stepping forward.

Gareth pressed the door in just enough to clear the jamb, and then stepped back.

Eveth put her shoulder into the reinforced metal and pushed slowly.

Now, they would see what the hell Gonquah was really up to.

PENETRATION AGENT

THE ELEVATOR RIDE WAS QUICK, and then there would be a good deal of walking and riding on a sliding sidewalk to get there. Fatima took the time to be something of a tourist, understanding that no one from the *Accord* had ever actually been aboard this facility before. Just visiting Earth itself had been enough of a risk for the few anthropologists who had done it over the last few centuries. Now they were reaching that perilous stage where anything might be possible. Or necessary.

Including xenocide.

Fatima hoped that it was a good sign that the Sector Marshal himself, a human named Alvin Siddall, had come to escort her to the laboratory of her target, Dr. Royston Loughty, PhD, WMU, FRS, CBE, CStJ. Doctor of Physics as a Stellar Radiation expert. Warden of the Mathematical Union, apparently representing advanced, human scholars of mathematics. Fellow of the Royal Society, an insular, British organization of scientists dating back to the pre-Industrial Age. Commander, British Empire, and Commander, Order of St. John, representing prestigious awards for service to the British Throne, itself on a small island located off the northwest coast of the tiny peninsula called Europe, from which so much recent human history, for both good and ill, had originated.

Loughty was going to be a formidable opponent, of that she had no doubts. On the simple basis of the two Yuudixtl criminals kidnapping the Star Dragon, Gareth Dankworth, Loughty had come to envision and then articulate a higher level of physics than his culture should have been able to even imagine existed.

Worse, he had successfully translated that understanding into the very first wormhole generator in human history, a machine that would eventually allow them to access the entire galaxy, including invading the *Accord of Souls*, once they found out that they were truly not alone among the stars.

Fermi had been right to question things, according to her recent studies of human science. And she could fill in a very good set of approximations for Drake, if the folks around here wanted to run the numbers on his formula and extrapolate out to the rest of this massive galaxy. And all the other ones in the neighborhood.

Thankfully, there weren't many advanced civilizations out there. Some had already come and gone over the last billion years, either *Ascending* to a higher form of existence like the Chaa, or managing to wipe themselves out entirely by luck, anger, or technology run amok. Most of the rest were simple and primitive, as humans had been fifty thousand years ago when the Chaa uplifted the *Accord*, by means of taking semi-intelligent animals that represented the peak of mental development on *Orgoth Vortai*, and turning them into the *Children of the Accord*.

And the Chaa had specifically excluded humans, but even then the species was intelligent and tool-using. Philosophers had argued for millennia as to the *why* of that decision, with no better understanding now than they had had then. Hopefully, she would never find out why it had occurred, because there was only one way to get the truth, and that would be from the very beings that had made that decision, fifty thousand years ago.

So she followed the Sector Marshal. He was an older human, as she understood the physical signs of aging from her crash course on them. He did not appear to be all that healthy, if she was interpreting things correctly, but had apparently known Dr. Loughty for decades, as well as having known the man whose niece she was impersonating, the real Fatima Darzi, a rotund housewife who had served in the Women's Auxiliary for several years before meeting a salesman and marrying him. They were happily living on a farm several hours north of Tehran, far from most modern civilization.

Fatima had never met the real woman, but studied her, and more importantly, their uncle, Firuz, enough to talk with the Sector Marshal. It helped that Uncle Firuz had been killed in a tragic automobile accident while still rather young. That gave her an opening that she could exploit, once the right computer records had been doctored to show an entirely different career path for one Fatima Darzi than had been the actuality. Being Persian, there were few people around who might be able to gainsay those records in person.

"So not really much of a football fan?" the Sector Marshal asked, apparently trying to make pleasant conversation as they rode.

"Afraid not, sir," she replied. "I was always too busy studying, frequently in secret while my football-starved family was concentrating on the day's match."

It even sounded reasonable.

Fatima had never watched the so-called World Cup, but did understand the sport humans called *football*. The *Accord* had a similar sport, usually separated down species lines at the professional level, as the Vanir had such a tremendous physical advantage over their neighbors.

"Shame," the human said. "We used to have tremendously fun parties watching the tournament. Your uncle and Royston would make outrageous bets on matches that were more practical jokes on one another than anything."

"So I've heard," Fatima offered as a deflection.

She could smile at the human and let him ramble. Apparently a match eleven years ago had been one of the highest scoring finales in Cup history, and everyone still talked about it like it happened yesterday. Fatima could enjoy the conversation. Football was a team sport, rather than an individual thing. And it did serve to rally large groups of humans into something less violent than war, even if those sorts of things were frequently seen as a substitute.

Anything that made humanity less violent, as they developed, should be supported, however outrageous it might be. She had even wondered if geneticists back home could come up with some chemical or organism they could introduce into Earth's various biospheres, that might render humans less violent and dangerous.

Knowing their luck, it would end up killing most of the population instead and turn the rest into cannibals, another human term with absolutely no equivalent in the *Accord*.

Maybe wiping them all out really would be the only option.

"Here we go," the human said as the slidewalk reached a break point.

Fatima watched carefully as the human disembarked, ready to catch the man if he stumbled, but he was apparently stable enough on his feet to make the transition. They moved to one side as others followed from behind them, and then went up a side corridor into a secured area.

Both of their badges worked to open a door into what smelled, even to Fatima's reduced senses, like a scientific facility. Exotic chemicals signals were strong enough she could pick them up with just her nose, rather than her tentacles, layered over with the kind of heavy ammonia smell she associated with destroying organic experiments that had gone awry.

Still the best way to clean a petri dish. Unless you wanted to expose it to deep space and then have to scrape the freeze-dried gunk off afterwards.

A second door opened to a third and then a fourth. Fatima found herself in a mechanical laboratory. The sort of place where a scientist could play with physical toys to extrapolate from mathematics and physics, as a way of perhaps building better gadgets.

Probably weapons, knowing humans, but sometimes a better dishwasher might come out of it as well.

The smells were greatly reduced here. The most prominent was a rich, sweet smell she could not identify for a second, before something in her brain registered tobacco smoke from her studies.

Dr. Loughty frequently carried a device called a pipe, wherein he burned the dried leaves of a particular type of plant that had been soaked in a variety of chemicals to give it a specific taste. Fatima didn't smoke, and didn't know anyone who did, but was aware that it happened.

"Where the Devil are you?" the Sector Marshal called out. "My secretary said you were around."

"In here, Alvin," a voice called back.

It was richer in tone than the Sector Marshal's. Deeper and more authoritative, but also friendlier. Presumably Dr. Royston Loughty.

Her target.

"This way, my dear," the man said, leading her around the big work bench and to another door that was open.

Inside, an older human male. Not quite as tall as the Sector Marshal, but in much better health, by comparison. Perhaps the same age, from the color of hair and lines on the face. Late-middle-age, she would have guessed, but this man was well-preserved, even as the Sector Marshal felt used up.

The human rose and smiled at her. He was dressed in English Tweeds, as she had expected from her studies, right down to the leather elbow patches on both arms. A clean, wooden desk separated them.

A second human rose as Fatima came into view. Female. Beautiful for any species. Much younger than the scientist, perhaps Fatima's apparent age, or just a few years older. She also wore the crimson and gold of the Women's Auxiliary, and was taller than Fatima.

She had very light skin, compared to the duskiness of Fatima's Grace heritage. Shoulder-length red hair and a freckles suggested a Scottish background, so this must be Philippa Adeline Loughty. *Pippa.* Daughter of Royston and Elizabeth. Intended fiancé of Gareth Dankworth, in other circumstances.

"Royston, it is my inestimable pleasure to introduce to you Ms. Fatima Darzi of the Women's Auxiliary," the Sector Marshal's voice took on new strength as he spoke. "Ms. Darzi, Dr. Royston Loughty and his daughter, Pippa."

Fatima shook hands with both in the human style, a thing apparently invented to show that you did not have a weapon in your hands as you approached a stranger.

"I will leave you in extremely good hands," the Sector Marshal said with a quick bow. "Hopefully, you will have a most pleasant stay with us and make great contributions to both Earth Force and Sky Patrol in your future."

He departed with a grin. Pippa closed the door and Fatima found herself finally alone, sitting politely with two of the most dangerous humans alive.

She took a deep breath and prepared for the conversation of her lifetime.

MONSTERS

IF HE HAD BEEN ALONE, Gareth would have raged fit for the gods themselves, but that wasn't an option here. Eveth Baker didn't need to see him angry enough to chew nails. To break things with his bare hands.

She needed to know he was capable of restraint in the face of this kind of adversity. That the Star Dragon was a tool he could call upon, rather than an example of the deep anger churning in his soul at what Marc was trying to do.

Even Earth had moved past the phase of using killer robots to solve their problems. The whole existence of Earth Force was dedicated to never letting things get that bad again. That Marc Sarzynski had gone there showed just how far he had fallen from the man Gareth had once been proud to call a friend.

It wasn't going to be enough to merely stop the criminal warlord Maximus. Dragging the carcass of the android off and hiding it brought home to Gareth that perhaps he really did need to destroy the man who had been his best friend. Bury him under the jail, as the old saying went, rather than ever letting him see the light of day again.

Gareth suppressed an angry sigh and made it a point not to grind his teeth. Eveth Baker needed him calm, rational, and effective.

Burning this entire facility to the ground and then salting the earth would have to wait for another day. And probably a calmer Constable. He could trust her and Grodray to see it done right tomorrow.

"Do we kick the door in, or pick the lock?" Gareth asked in a low, ambiguous tone, trying not to let his emotions color the situation. The heavy disintegrator would probably do an awesome job of demolition.

"Is it locked?" Baker replied with a quick glance up.

Damn, he hadn't even considered that option. How far off true was he, right now?

Gareth grabbed the handle in his left hand and turned just enough to confirm that Baker was right. Not even locked. Just guarded by killer robots.

"Me first," she said, stepping into him from the side before he could move.

She would have hipchecked him out of the way, too. Well, at least tried. He still outweighed her by eight stone, give or take, but he gave way anyway, pushing the door in just enough to clear the jamb, and slowly letting go of the handle.

He watched her ease into a dark space, then stepped after her.

Gareth found himself in a hallway with two doors on either side. They felt like offices.

Past that was a wide opening that felt more like a storage garage than a factory. Low ceilings and wide walls beyond created something like the hall where he had once gone to see a bunch of antique automobiles from the petroleum era and early electric period. The floor had a black and white parquet checkboard set into it, but most of the near space was clear.

Deeper back, the hall fell to darkness, but he could see light reflecting off metal back there. Hopefully nothing bad.

Baker led them to the first door on the right. It was an office space, generic and sterile. No pictures on the desk or backboard. Mass produced copies of water colors on two walls. Just a chair, a working surface, and a telephone, like a traveling manager would use this space when he was here, but would share it with a number of others.

She grunted, but made no other comment, so Gareth concentrated on calming thoughts, rather than setting fire to the desk and watching the flames lick walls hungrily. Now was most definitely not the time.

Across the hall, another office. This one looked lived in, with flowers and a picture of a Nari family: Mom, Dad, and two kits; on the backboard. The desk was locked, but Baker didn't try forcing any of the drawers.

Gareth figured that she could probably just rip the first drawer open, if she wanted to, then trip the switch to open the rest, but she could also get out her picks.

Maybe later, once they knew what was about.

The third door was another generic office. Unlived in and almost abandoned feeling.

The fourth space was the jackpot, as far as Gareth was concerned. A big table dominated the space, with several four-drawer file cabinets along the rear wall.

Someone had been working in here, and had not bothered to clean up when they left for the day. There was an android head resting on the table top like a victim of Dr. Guillotine's device. Around it, a number of blueprints, actually printed on off-white paper in blue ink, like back home, rather than just electronic files to be transmitted from machine to machine wirelessly.

Gareth studied the blueprint while Baker lifted the head and studied it. After a moment, his unconscious fascination with the document became clear. On the one hand, it did remind him of home, and did so in a good way, taking him back to the days of his first drafting class, when you had to start at the very beginning, with paper and pen, and only later learned how to use modeling software in your second semester.

On the other hand, it also looked familiar because he recognized the handwriting. How many years had they spent checking each other's homework to make sure they hadn't missed anything? He missed that guy, too, but they were long past those days, and would never get them back.

He was holding the proof in his hands, signed **MS** in the bottom right, just like the old days.

Marc Sarzynski, Destroyer of Worlds.

Gareth tore off the top page and folded it up enough to stuff into a pocket on his belt. If nothing else, that one piece of paper was all the evidence he needed to shut this place down and have Gonquah hauled away, even if killer robots with disintegrators guarding the front door somehow bizarrely failed to meet a standard necessary for a grand jury to indict.

Now, he had the connection he needed back to Maximus. He could burn this place down. Or rather, have it seized. Gareth let go of his anger long enough to consider all the men and women who would be out of work tomorrow if he destroyed this factory, much as he wanted to.

He let the heat simmer, since there was no way to turn it off.

"You okay?" Baker was suddenly standing next to him, concern etched on her face.

"Angry," he replied, figuring that honesty was the best choice here. "But we've got them both."

He pointed to the remaining stack of papers, tapping the MS signature on each one. And Gareth would be happy to testify as a handwriting expert personally familiar with Sarzynski's scrawl.

He doubted that he would ever be able to take the man alive, though. He would still try. That was who he was.

"MS," Baker said. "Marc Sarzynski?"

"That's his handwriting," Gareth murmured. "Know it as well as my own."

She tapped the page and studied it.

"Simple enough," she said, tracing lines and pistons. "Amazing that it could be so dangerous."

"The programming for safe robots back home is the product of thousands of man-months of work," Gareth noted. "Here, you just skip all that and aim the damned thing. Do we have enough to call in the Constabulary and turn this place over?"

"Let's see what's in the space beyond this," Baker said. "But yes, this will be enough to blow up in Gonquah's face and let us sweat him. Hopefully, he'd rather give up Sarzynski than take all the heat himself, but this will be more than he can wriggle out of, this time."

Gareth nodded and kept his opinions to himself. Death by fire breath was not the solution right now. He was a cop, not a rogue elephant.

By the book. By the law. By the standards of justice.

Not just revenge. Much as he was seeing red right now.

Tomorrow, hopefully, he could start hunting his old friend.

And kill the man.

Baker watched him like she could see the internal monologue. Maybe she could. Gareth wasn't trying to hide anything right now. Just control it and get the damned job done.

"Let's go," she finally said, when she had decided that he was under control.

He nodded and followed her back out into the hallway.

Right, and they entered that big arcade. It was dark in here, with just the standard emergency exit lights and a few others. Gareth was still absently holding the disintegrator in one hand, mostly as a security blanket rather than a threat, so he reached for a flashlight from his belt.

Baker turned and walked to the side of the doorway. She ran her hand up to flip several switches, and suddenly it was as bright as day in here.

Gareth apparently muttered the word out loud, instead of just inside his head. That, or Baker was thinking the same thoughts, because she said the profanity much louder as she turned back to the room.

It was a showroom, of sorts. Fifty meters wide and at least one hundred and twenty deep, it was, mercifully, mostly empty. That was good, because Gareth guessed there were perhaps as many as a hundred more of the androids at the far end, lined up perfectly still, like troops awaiting an inspection.

Gareth found the scene drawing him closer. Baker came along in his wake, but neither of them spoke.

He was just thankful that these machines were not armed, like the two they had destroyed out front. One hundred was an entire company, going back to the days of organized armies. God only knew what someone could do with that sort of force here in the *Accord*.

Up close, they were even more frightening. All-steel bodies with protective knobs around the joints. Human sized, so they felt to Gareth like twelve-year-olds, but he could see how intimidating a six foot tall robot would be to Nari or Grace, who tended to be a shade smaller. And if he was designing them, and he knew the man who had, they would be at least as strong as a Vanir. Probably more, since Marc knew what Gareth had turned into.

Metal heads like motorcycle helmets. Eyes and mouth, with just a suggestion of a nose and simple holes for ears. At least Marc hadn't added antennae or something, like a Traakna had, and this model just had hands.

Gareth could imagine a dedicated model with a heavy blaster of some kind permanently attached to the forearm, or perhaps replacing it altogether as a walking anti-tank gun.

This all needed to be destroyed before it got loose into the *Accord*. They might never recover.

"That's it," Baker announced in a voice that even came close to approximating the rage in Gareth's breast. "I'm calling this in."

He watched her pull a comm from her belt, but suddenly the android closest to her turned his head and stared right at Baker.

"Intruder alert," the android said in a crude, mechanical voice.

It started to step forward, arms coming up to apparently grab Baker, and Gareth did the only thing he could think of.

He punched it across the jaw. Which was a stupid thing to do, since it was metal, and he was holding a heavy disintegrator in his other fist, but something had snapped in him.

And while he knocked down the first android, all of the rest of them began to move.

END TIMES

EVETH HAD BEEN CONCERNED about how close to the edge Gareth seemed to be. Or rather, just how shallowly buried the man's intense anger was right now. But she was also impressed by the level of control he exhibited. That scored a lot of points in his favor, as far as she was concerned.

She would trust the man less if he was a true teenage Nature Scout, and not a grown adult with a full range of emotional potential. He was working to act like an adult, but she could almost smell the brimstone coming off of him, presumably at what Maximus had done, and might still do.

She could only imagine a hundred or more of these killer machines loose with beam weapons. Most cops only carried stunners because it was the easiest and safest way to stop a criminal from getting away, or if two people were fighting and wouldn't listen to commands.

That lit some of the same fire in her that apparently Gareth had been experiencing for the last few minutes, but he understood the implications in his soul, while she was only now truly wrapping her mind around the term "a threat to the entire *Accord of Souls*."

This wasn't academic. This was a conspiracy to overthrow everything and presumably institute a reign of terror as only humans could imagine and enforce.

"That's it," she said firmly, keeping her own emotions in check as Gareth had done. "I'm calling this in."

Eveth reached for her communicator as the android closest to her suddenly woke up and turned to look up at her.

"Intruder alert," the machine announced, reaching for her as she tried to back away.

Gareth surprised the hell out of her by punching the machine, and doing so hard enough to knock it over. But the others were moving. Waking up. Coming for her soul.

Eveth quick-drew her blaster and shot the closest one square in the chest before it even took its first step, but one hundred more were coming.

"Run," she ordered, turning and starting to move. Unless Sarzynski had programmed them to her sort of specs, she could make it to the door.

Behind her, two quick shots rang out, followed both times by the sort of sound you might get throwing a box of anvils down a staircase.

"Gareth," she yelled to get his attention. He seemed to be in a fog, backing away from the machine and shooting them, rather than fleeing. And she could see both wings starting to move forward and around the man. He would be encircled and possibly killed, depending on how these things reacted to intruders.

What would someone like Gonquah program into them, to keep his secrets safe?

Something about her voice broke through Gareth's attention.

"Baker," he yelled, acknowledging her and starting to come away from them. "Get help."

Yes, they were in trouble. The robots were moving faster now, as Gareth started to jog backwards. Like horsemen, they were about to flank him.

Eveth stopped and turned back.

"Mayday," she said into the comm. "Officers under fire. Require backup now."

Not entirely true, but that would get Jack and his team here the fastest. She fired a shot at the right side, winging a robot and knocking it down. A second shot grazed a closer one and hit one further away, damaging both but stopping neither.

Gareth was moving, but he had waited too long. That much was obvious. Hands began to clutch at him, even as he fired back over a shoulder and tried to run.

"Jack, this is Eve," she yelled into the comm. "Now, damn it."

More shots. Hers and Gareth's. It felt like trying to stop the tide from coming in with a shovel, but her partner was back there, and had been trying to protect her when they got in over their heads.

Gareth screamed in pain as one of the machines clipped his leg and he stumbled into another that grabbed on and held tight. Several more arrived and held.

She couldn't shoot into that melee without hurting Gareth, possibly killing him.

"Jack?" she yelled, suddenly afraid that they had gotten inside of a scrambler field as well, and nobody would ever come for her.

Eveth was about to abandon Gareth and run when her comm squelched.

"Inbound, Eve," Jack said in a hard, angry tone.

Gareth's anguished scream nearly stripped her soul raw, and then it changed, deepened. And it grew loud enough that anyone in the factory probably heard it. Or at least felt it in their own souls.

The Star Dragon. That was what the monster sounded like as it was reborn tonight.

Pure rage.

Eveth knelt and took a careful aim, blasting everything that moved close to Gareth. If she could get him free, maybe they had a chance.

The androids knocked Gareth down, and several more piled on top of him. For a moment, she wondered if they had been programmed to kill Gareth as their first priority, but a large group suddenly turned towards her and began to run. Faster than a Vanir could escape them.

Eveth gave up shooting and ran for her own life. Gareth had the Star Dragon. She only had whatever Jack could bring.

And however long it took that team to get here.

She reached the hallway, just as a flying android slammed face first into the wall beside her and went clear through into the office beyond.

She looked back, to see the Star Dragon in full form, rolling and swatting with arms, legs, and tail as he was beset by a plague of bipedal rats.

A gout of flames behind her suddenly lit the entire room brighter than noonday sun. "Gareth?" she yelled, slowing just a little.

"Run," he commanded. "He made them fireproof."

Or course, she thought. Wouldn't you, after seeing that thing being born?

She almost made it.

Got her hands onto that outside door when two of the robots grabbed her from behind.

Eveth managed to kill one of them, but the other got hold of her pistol and ripped it away from her hard enough that she might have broken bones in her hand.

Not that it would matter, if they were both about to die.

The Star Dragon screamed in a rage so loud, so primal that she nearly almost screamed back in reaction, the sound ripped from her very soul.

A scaled hand suddenly grabbed the machine holding her and squeezed.

Even over her pounding heart, Eveth could hear the sound of metal deforming under that assault. She could do the same to a soft drink can, and that's what it looked like.

"Go," the Wyrm ordered as he blocked others from getting into the hallway to come after her.

Simple math, she realized as she fled.

Without a gun, she couldn't do anything here to alter the outcome.

Except die. There was always that.

Gareth was going to sacrifice himself to keep her alive, dying in the process of destroying as many of these androids as he could.

Eveth suppressed the profanity and put her energy into her legs.

She kicked that outer door hard enough to bounce it off the far wall, barely slowing as she ran.

Outside, a mob of men was running towards her.

Eveth was just going to have to kill all of them before they could help the robots kill Gareth. Jack would be here soon enough to avenge them both.

"Get her to safety," the closest man yelled.

Eveth focused on the speaker, and realized that it was Grodray, wearing his own lifterpack, with a matched pair of heavy disintegrators in his hands.

One of the others caught her and shifted her out of the way of a dozen men and women with rifles and pistols as they charged back up the hallway.

"Are you hurt?" the medic asked.

That woman had her own heavy disintegrator in a cross-draw holster under her arm, but was doing medical things now.

"Broken hand," Eveth held it out. "The rest is bruising."

From behind her, screams of pain gave way to the thunderous roll of several weapons firing as fast as they could cycle. The medic pulled her to one side.

Eveth truly wondered if the fabled End Times was upon them, just from the sound, so loud that it was a physical thing.

It felt like eternity has passed, but silence suddenly broke out.

"Gareth?" Eveth said.

"You need to stay here, Constable," the medic said firmly, trying to see how badly she was hurt.

"That's my partner," Eveth growled. "Give me your pistol. I'm going in there."

The medic started to argue, subsided, and handed Eveth her pistol. She moved to follow Eveth in.

"Medic," Grodray yelled, so the woman started to run.

Eveth kept pace.

The inside of the space looked like how she always envisioned a true battle would, if the humans ever escaped into the *Accord*. There were pieces of broken android every direction she looked, including embedded in the roof. There was blood everywhere, as well. Lots of it.

Grodray was kneeling next to one of his troopers.

When Eveth got there, she realized it was Gareth.

He looked like hell, but he was still breathing. Both eyes were blackened. As was most of his face. Blood from a cut in his hair had covered much of his chest and was dripping onto the floor.

His hands looked like he had slammed them in door, and then used a hammer to finish the job, gnarled and bloodied.

"Lie still, damn it," Grodray yelled, trying to hold Gareth down. "We got them."

"Baker?" he cried so pitifully it nearly broke her heart.

"I'm here, Gareth," she yelled back, falling her knees across from Grodray.

That seemed to get through to him. His head turned towards her and the medic slid in and just hit him with a heavy-duty pain-killer. Gareth had to be blind from all the blood and swelling, but she saw him smile for just a moment, before he passed out.

"Eve?" Grodray stood and lifted her to her feet.

"We've got Gonquah, Jack," she said. "Evidence is in one of the offices back there. I want him nailed to a wall this time. I'd be dead right now, if it wasn't for Gareth. And he'd be dead without you."

"Understood, Eve," Grodray said. "I've already got another team kicking in the man's front door as soon as a message gets there.

"Good," she said. "He and Sarzynski have started a war with the entire Constabulary. I'm going to destroy that son of a bitch."

FRAUD

AS A MATTER OF COURSE, Royston would never have met with a young, single woman in the privacy of his office. They would have gone to one of the coffee shops on the station, or some other public place where nobody might be free to whisper things that would damage such a woman's reputation, even with a fussy old duffer such as himself.

He had his memories of Elizabeth, and a most wonderful daughter, so he did not foresee himself ever marrying again. Not that he would ever say never, but…

Today's meeting needed to be as private as it possibly could be. He needed an unimpeachable witness as well, one that would be believed, regardless of the story that she might tell later.

Pippa would make sure you were listening.

The three of them were alone. The door was closed. Presumably the Sector Marshal was returning to the Command Chamber, where he would count this as a successful meeting.

At least until Royston told him otherwise.

Royston smiled to put Ms. Darzi at ease. Pippa smiled as well. After a moment, the stranger relaxed, more or less.

"I remember Firuz Alinejad quite well," he announced, savoring some of those deep-into-the-night discussions and arguments over tea, as well as all the louder hijinks around the World Cup.

Truly, he missed his old friend.

"He was a good man," Darzi replied. "Warm and brilliant at the same time, when that so rarely happens."

"Indeed," Royston smiled at the young woman. "So how may I be of service, madam?"

"There are rumors that you are studying higher mathematics," this stranger, this *imposter* said carefully. She nodded politely to Pippa. "As with your daughter, I was unable to pursue my studies, as many people were offended that a woman might take such a slot at the university, when it should go to a man. If possible, I had hoped that I might be able to study under you."

Royston noted Pippa's look of mild surprise, but she had never really met Firuz, except when he and Elizabeth had hosted the man for an Eid dinner, or some other things where he might be one of the only Muslims around. And she had been only a teenager when the man died.

Pippa would only know about Fatima Darzi what the records showed, and not the sorts of things that might have never made it to a computerized record, where someone with intent and capability might tamper with it.

Royston let the moment drag, perhaps a little too long. Pippa turned to him, as if to silently reproach him for rudely not responding, even if to let her know he was thinking about the topic.

He was indeed thinking about it. Just not the way either of these two women probably expected.

At least whoever it was had respected him enough to not throw a floozy at him. He could deal with them playing to his vanity and intellect. It would be downright insulting to suggest that a honeypot might have worked.

He would thank them for that, perhaps, if he ever got the chance.

"Father?" Pippa finally asked, perhaps amazed at how rude he was being.

But then, he was being rude.

And it was about to get worse.

Royston smiled at Pippa. He smiled at Fatima Darzi, or whoever she really was.

Mildly, he pulled open the top drawer to his desk and pulled out the pistol he had put in there earlier, when Alvin had mentioned Firuz's niece.

He had met the young lady. Well, teenager then, twelve years ago when he and Firuz had secretly snuck down to Tehran to watch a football match at his sister's house: Yasmina Darzi, born Yasmina Alinejad. Fatima

Darzi had been an angry teenager in those days, plotting how to escape her family and run away from the city she saw as being so decadent as to threaten the very future of Persian society.

Too intellectual, when Allah offered all the answers a woman needed, none of which included western mathematics, even if the Persians had actually been the fathers of so much of the learning that Western Europe had later stolen and claimed for themselves.

He knew the woman had later served a quick tour of duty, just enough to appease her family, but he also knew she would never leave the surface of the Earth again voluntarily.

Royston centered the pistol on this imposter's chest and flipped the safety off rather noisily.

He had a smile, even as both women registered the immense shock of his appallingly bad manners. Pulling a blaster pistol in conversation could be like that.

"I think we can dispense with the silly notion that you are Fatima Darzi," Royston said with a steely tone. "Why don't you tell me who you really are, young lady."

"Father?" Pippa spoke, but didn't twitch.

That was good. Any motion at all right now and he would pull the trigger, assuming self-defense at this point as he annihilated the woman across from him and a reasonable chunk of the chair and wall behind her.

Darzi appeared to appreciate that. She kept her hands down on the arms of her chair and her body encased in ice.

The moment stretched.

"Or I could just shoot you and turn your body over to Alvin to investigate," Royston offered. "Your choice."

"That would be…unwise, Dr. Loughty," she said in a slow, deliberate voice.

It was a different tone. Calmer. More centered. Like another woman was inhabiting the flesh than the one who walked in here.

Staring at your death from violent beam weapons was almost as good as a hanging to center the mind.

"Would it now?" Royston found his voice getting light, like a cat patting at a mouse. "Why is that?"

"I am not what I seem," Darzi said.

"Oh you seem to me to be an imposter and a spy," Royston said politely. "Why shouldn't I shoot you?"

"I would like to show you the truth, Dr. Loughty," she said carefully.

"I had hoped that it wouldn't come to that, but you've obviously thought much deeper about the implications of things than my superiors considered. If you will allow me to remove my hijab, much will become clearer, but I need to extract a promise from you, from both of you, that you will keep my secret. I can negotiate in good faith, if you will as well."

Good faith? From a spy? It would have probably worked, but for things nobody but he and Fatima would know.

"And if not?" Royston pursued the thread.

"Part of my mission was scouting, Dr. Loughty," she said. "But the First Inspector tasked me with finding a way to prevent a greater catastrophe, if that was possible."

"And removing your hijab will uncover the truth?" Royston was doubtful, but she wasn't as panicked as an amateur would be.

"It will," Fatima replied.

Royston considered it, and shook his head.

"You will remain perfectly still," he ordered. "Pippa can remove the cloth. I would hate to find that you had secreted a weapon of some kind up there and were able to get to it."

"Agreed, Dr. Loughty," Fatima said, nodding with her eyes and nothing else. "Ms. Loughty, the hijab is tucked in under the right side and pinned behind my ear. More or less."

"Father?" Pippa asked carefully. She was out of her depth here, but Royston had been his own kind of agent, back in his youth. Even Elizabeth hadn't known the full truth about some of the things he had done at Gareth's age.

"Go ahead, Pippa," he directed her, lowering his point of aim a bit to catch the imposter in the belly rather than the heart.

Pippa rose and slid out of her chair, never getting between him and his target. She moved carefully and deliberately next to Fatima and reached out with just her left hand, probing.

"What?" Pippa flinched, nearly causing him to kill Fatima, but something in the imposter's eyes held the shot off.

"It's okay," Fatima said, sharply but calmly. "You will understand shortly."

Pippa reached again and found the pin. She extracted it and stuck it into her own blouse to keep it out of the way. Then she grabbed the hijab and pulled it up and away carefully and deliberately.

Royston had thought he had steeled his soul for anything, including a bomb hidden up there.

The truth was so much worse.

"What?" Pippa said before she caught herself.

Fatima's eyes never left Royston's.

"Those are sensory tentacles," she explained carefully. "I have taken drugs to keep them from moving, and in the process nearly blinded myself to all normal sensory input. I understand that to a human, I would look like the medusa of your Hellenic legend, but that is not the case. I have no teeth, merely more senses, currently mostly asleep."

"What are you?" Royston's voice had fallen to a hoarse whisper.

"I am a *Grace*, Dr. Loughty," Fatima said. "One of the member species of a galactic organization known as the *Accord of Souls*. I have been sent here to find out how much you know, and how close you are to becoming an existential threat to the *Accord*."

"Threat?" he asked, aghast at this turn of events.

"Humans are seen as the greatest menace in the galaxy, sirrah," she snapped tartly. "Some members of the *Accord* have voted to wipe the species out, but they were always previously overruled, on the simple basis that humanity was trapped in this solar system and thus could not reach us. That has now changed."

"Wipe us all out?" Pippa asked.

Fatima turned slowly to look up at her, no other bit of her moving, except for the sluggish, snake-like tentacles she had instead of *hair*.

"It could have been a bomb as easily as a spy, Ms. Loughty," Fatima said coldly. "Or a bioweapon. We are trying to prevent that, if possible."

"We?" Royston asked.

"The Constabulary, Dr. Loughty," she replied. "I'm given to understand that it serves much the same purpose in the *Accord of Souls* as Earth Force Sky Patrol does here."

"How would you know that?" he demanded sharply.

"Gareth Dankworth told us," she replied.

SHADOW OF THE STAR DRAGON

IMPOSTER

OF ALL THE things Royston Loughty had steeled himself to believe about the young woman seated across from him, wearing an Earth Force Sky Patrol Women's Auxiliary uniform no less, that she was an alien police officer, something akin to an Earth Force Sky Patrol agent, like disappeared Gareth, simply was so far down the list of possibilities that he would have discounted it utterly.

And yet.

She called herself Fatima Darzi, after the woman she was impersonating, the niece of his dear, old friend, the physicist Farouz Darzi, killed eleven years ago in a speeder accident. Outwardly, she even looked human enough. At least, until Pippa had removed the supposedly-Persian woman's hijab to reveal…

Tentacles.

As though Medusa herself were come down to turn him to stone. Perhaps that would have been the better outcome, if the rest of what she spoke was the truth. That there were aliens out there, living in mortal fear of humans gaining access to any kind of stardrive that would let them escape the sub-light travel limitations of Einsteinian physics.

That Royston Loughty, PhD, WMU, FRS, CBE, CStJ might have sealed someone's irrevocable doom. That his arrogance had pushed the galaxy to the edge of perhaps *xenocide*. He should have been smarter than that. He was, after all, a Doctor of Physics and the principle stellar radiation expert in the entire Solar System. Warden of the Mathematical Union. Fellow of the Royal Society. Commander, British Empire. Commander, Order of St John.

And fool. There was always that, if what Fatima said was true.

Royston lowered the pistol he had been holding on the stranger and clicked the safety on, quickly placing it back into the top drawer of his desk. He nodded to Pippa's arched eyebrow and she returned to the seat she had had taken earlier, pausing only to politely hand Ms. Darzi the cloth of her now-removed hijab, a lovely peach silk.

"So we are to believe her then, father?" Pippa asked. She paused and turned back to the stranger. "By what name should we address you?"

"It would be for the very best if you continued to refer to me as Fatima Darzi," the woman, this Grace woman said rather politely, in that soft burr of a Persian accent she affected. "If news gets out beyond this room, the First Inspector and the *Accord* Commission may feel that they have no choice but to move to extraordinary judgments."

Royston was fascinated by her sensory tentacles, even as her words struck him to the quick. They looked like nothing so much as short, dusky snakes extruded from her scalp, with a ring of lighter-colored spots near the ends, that somehow reminded him of eyes, just back from a larger such *eye* at the tip.

Alien. Here, in his office aboard Earth Force's L2 base, **The Arsenal**. As far as he knew the most secure facility in the Solar System.

"What happens if your superiors do panic?" Royston forced himself to speak past the sudden lump that had taken up residence in his throat.

"There was talk of a bio-weapon capable of inflicting xenocide, but hopefully just limiting it to humanity, if I understand the human term correctly," the Grace woman replied. "We had no such word in our language as *xenocide*, so we have had to borrow yours. As we have with many such barbaric, linguistic aberrations."

"Aberrations?" Pippa inquired, sounding like a scholar who read Tacitus in the original Latin.

"War is unknown in the *Accord of Souls*, Ms. Loughty," Darzi turned her head that way. The tentacles appeared to be sniffing the air like a cat seeking treats. "Violence exists nowhere on a scale that humans everyday seem to take for granted."

"What is the *Accord of Souls*?" Pippa pressed.

Royston sat back and listened, trying to pass a camel through the eye of a needle in his mind to find a way out of this impasse.

"The collective of species that the Chaa uplifted, fifty thousand of your years ago, before they left to seek the Creator," Darzi explained in words that left Pippa apparently as breathless as Royston. "Seventeen species, psionically bound together into a greater whole, conducting art, commerce, and joy."

"Why did these gods, the Chaa you called them, skip humanity?" Royston asked, intently.

Fifty millennia was a great span, but modern humans had already emerged as an intelligent, tool-using, language-using species by then. Even distant, galactic gods should have noticed.

"You have touched on one of the great philosophical and ethical conundrums of the current age, Dr. Loughty." Darzi actually smiled at him. Even her tentacles seemed to convey amusement. "We cannot know without asking them, but they fixed the other many species into their current forms and departed, apparently to seek the *Face of God.*"

Good. At least the aliens still had some solid religion to ground them. Royston had always feared that a true atheism, as had been attempted a few times in the early periods of the Industrial Age, would tear all societies apart eventually. If they had Gods, they still had the opportunity for wonder and doubt. As well as a dread of ultimate consequences behind their behavior.

"And the *Accord of Souls* fears humanity? Correct?" Royston pursued an earlier comment.

"Yours is considered the single most violent, most dangerous species in the galaxy, Dr. Loughty," her voice turned serious. "Escaping your home system puts every other species in the universe at risk."

He couldn't really argue with that logic. Even a casual study of human history would bear out what a barbaric species they really still were.

"And your mission was to penetrate Earth Force, and Sky Patrol, and do what, Ms. Darzi?" Royston brought things back to a head.

She was an admitted imposter. An infiltrator. He had only her word for anything, and her supposed knowledge of things from Gareth Dankworth, hopefully. If there was a better man in the Solar System, Royston Loughty had yet to meet him.

"I am a scout, Dr. Loughty," she shrugged in a most human manner. "I was to find out what you had accomplished, and how it might be derailed before it grew out of control."

There. Those were apparently the table stakes they would have to play, but Royston had somehow known that as soon as this woman removed her hijab and revealed the stark, mind-shattering truth.

"Then you have already failed, Ms. Darzi," Royston concluded dispassionately. "The knowledge exists within certain circles, and can thus never be contained again. Humans are like that. Having proven that it was possible, it is only a matter of time before the next scholar figures out how it was done, and improves upon my work. Even if I were to inject my own failures into future experiments, it would only delay the inevitable. How do we convince your superiors not to destroy humanity?"

"Why should we?" Darzi challenged him.

It was a telling, near-mortal blow.

"Because of Gareth," Pippa spoke up firmly. "Because you know him, or at least know of him, so you know what kind of man he is."

"Indeed, Ms. Loughty, but there is also Maximus," Darzi replied. "The criminal who was once Marc Sarzynski."

Pippa gasped and her hands flew to her mouth. Royston felt his heart begin to pound hard enough that it might rattle its way out of his chest. He paused for a moment to find the words.

"I had a theory that someone in the *Accord* had opened a wormhole in space for the purpose of kidnapping Gareth Dankworth, the same as they had previously done to Marc," Royston fought to keep his tone on this side of fear and anger. "Is that the truth?"

"It is, Dr. Loughty, but not in ways you could imagine," she said.

Quickly, the alien woman related the whole story, or at least the bits she had been cleared to know by her superiors. Sarzynski being captured by a crime boss looking for an assassin, failing to understand he could not subsequently control a man like that. Royston was especially thrilled with the bit about the two, tiny lizardmen, *Yuudixtl*, who took it upon themselves to find the *Accord of Souls* a guardian angel in the form of Gareth.

And then she came to the next part, even more unbelievable than the rest.

"Could you repeat that, Ms. Darzi," Royston said. "He was transformed into a what?"

"They call it a Star Dragon, Dr. Loughty," she shrugged. "I have never seen it, but I have heard rumors and stories, that he could transform from his new, Vanir form apparently into a giant, fire-breathing, flying lizard form."

Pippa had fallen utterly silent. Royston turned to her just to make sure his daughter was still breathing. Her eyes were pools of dread midnight. Perhaps this Grace woman was a medusa, and had transformed his daughter to alabaster.

"And a Vanir?" Royston asked.

"Seven foot some tall and three hundred plus pounds, by human reckoning," Darzi continued. "The face is more angular than humans, and the eyes larger. They have ears that come to pronounced points, perhaps twenty percent larger than yours. Sarzynski is functionally identical, from a physical standpoint, without the secondary transformation."

"He's no longer human?" Pippa managed to gasp in a whisper.

"He is not, Ms. Loughty," Darzi said. "I'm sorry. It is my understanding that he refers to you even now as his betrothed."

That brought a splash of color to his daughter's utterly pale cheeks. Only Royston knew that Gareth had been literally on his way to propose to Pippa on the night when he was taken by Morty and Xiomber, to use their names.

Could he call it their *Christian* names?

Apparently, even Yuudixtl career criminals could be rehabilitated.

That gave Royston a jolt so hard that both women turned to him with some alarm.

"Father?" Pippa asked weakly.

He smiled at her and then turned his terrible gaze on the imposter.

"We will use your cover story, Ms. Darzi," Royston announced forcefully. "At least as part of a larger cover-up that I will need to cause to come into being immediately."

"Dr. Loughty?" the imposter, the Grace woman, asked.

"I had been planning to take a short sabbatical, Ms. Darzi," Royston said. "To find a particular human group, musicians as you will, and see if they could help inspire me to even greater heights of scientific creativity than I had achieved thus far. Pippa would have accompanied me, so you will be able to as well, with no scandal attached to either of our reputations."

Both women blushed at the same time and same rate. Apparently, it transcended species, so it was probably a factor of intelligence rather than biology.

"We will depart The Arsenal and return to the surface of the Earth, as I had intended," Royston continued. "In the course of actions, I will just drop off the face of the Earth, to use the colloquialism, while sending the occasional postcard to Alvin, that he does not grow concerned at my disappearance."

"I do not understand," Fatima Darzi's doppelgänger said plaintively.

"You will contact your superiors and endeavor to convince them to bring Pippa and I to wherever we may talk to Gareth and whoever else needs to be involved," Royston said with a firm smile.

"Father, that's insane," Pippa exclaimed.

"It is, indeed, daughter," he replied. "But if I am to be seeking the *Life Bohemian* to explore some new facet of my discovery, no other research will move forward, especially if I tell Alvin and Sir Westfield I originally miscalculated the risks of accidentally destroying the Earth with the wormhole generator I have built. That will buy us at least six months without question."

"And then what?" Darzi asked, leaning forward and eyes growing large.

"Then I have to figure out how to keep your superiors from destroying humanity, my dear."

AN ILL-MANNERED PATIENT

GARETH SIMPLY COULD NOT HELP himself this morning. He knew Talyarkinash meant well, but having to be fed by someone else, as if he was a helpless infant, had left Gareth grumpier than a wet hen. He waved the spoon away almost angrily.

The Nari woman leaned back and put down the bowl and spoon of stew she had been feeding him. Her whiskers twitched forward in alarm, as did her ears.

Gareth rested both of his cast-encrusted hands on the dining room table with probably more of a thump that was necessary.

"I'm sorry," Gareth managed to make his voice polite. "It's just too much this morning."

"Should I program the kitchen machine to deliver a liquid breakfast substitute with a straw?" she asked.

It helped that her voice contained no mockery. Gareth hated being helpless, even if modern, *Accord* medicine meant that his hands would be fully healed in days, rather than months. Both eyes this morning in the mirror had held only the faintest trace of raccoon patches, from the terrible bruising and cuts the fight with the killer androids had inflicted.

But his hands had simply been smashed too badly for mere splints. As it was, Talyarkinash had explained the month or more of physical therapy that would be necessary for him to play piano or guitar again.

"No," Gareth breathed in defeat. "I know I'm a bad patient. Being helpless to even feed myself was just too much this morning. And I realize that I should have been in bed for a fortnight after what happened, rather than two days. It's just…"

"You want to be out there with Baker and Grodray, chasing your old friend," she replied in a quiet, helpful tone.

"Stopping him from destroying the galaxy," Gareth sort of corrected her.

"I understand," Talyarkinash smiled up at him.

She was truly his closest friend in the entire galaxy these days. Nothing more than a friend, although he suspected she might have different desires deep down. He still held out hope that they could somehow reverse the entire process and turn him back into a human, that he could be sent home.

Pippa would wait for him. He knew that. Just as he would have waited for her. It would just take time.

A hatch opened and two new bodies tromped into the semi-private dining space where he and the Nari doctor were seated.

"Hey, kid," Morty exclaimed, carrying a booster block over to the chair next to him and climbing up to sit at the table. With the extra height, he was nearly on a level with Talyarkinash. "Doc Fitzroy said you were down."

Xiomber ended up on the other side. Both of the tiny Yuudixtl were drinking coffee this morning, although Morty had somehow managed to add nearly a dram of brandy to his from the smell.

Of course, Gareth didn't suppose anyone but him might smell it. Talyarkinash, perhaps, if she got close enough.

Gareth held out both hands, like boxing gloves in the rigid casts.

"Overly grumpy, yes," Talyarkinash informed the table with a smile. "Forcible inactivity apparently is contrary to his very nature."

"Yeah, not surprising," Xiomber chirped. "Kinda why we picked him the first place."

"So I have a theory, Gareth," Morty grinned. "Goes back to the weird shit we had to do to reprogram you in the first place. Talyarkinash probably knows most of it, but maybe not the weird bits."

"Weird bits, you scaly reprobate?" the Nari woman turned her stern look and chuckles on the other two scientists. "What have you done now?"

"*Reformed* reprobates, I'll have you know, madam," Xiomber

interjected tartly. "We have been adjudicated guilty and are currently serving our debt to society, thank you very much."

"Yes," she retorted with a sarcastic grin. "You seem so humble and reformed."

"So I got to thinking last night, when Fitzroy told us how bad Gareth got hamburgered on his recent mission," Morty said. "Couple of days of healing would be a really good thing, just so the body got over the shock, but we might be able to radically reduce the rest of his down time."

"How?" Gareth's cry was almost savage. Both Yuudixtl leaned back a notch. "Sorry."

"So if you ate a whole bunch of protein this morning, we might be able to convince Fitzroy to remove the casts," Morty said. "Then you go into full Star Dragon mode. The transformation has reshaping built right into it, so it ought to fix your hands, for the most part. Again, there's gonna be a crapton of pain, like you broke them both again, and it won't fully heal them. Soft tissue will need another week to recover. You game?"

"What does Talyarkinash need to feed me?" Gareth asked so intently that the other three laughed. "I'll be the best little chick ever, waiting to be fed. Anything to get out of these casts."

"It'll hurt, Gareth," Xiomber reminded him. "Things out of alignment now get forced back into shape. That means tearing and breaking."

"And?" Gareth smiled brittlely at the man.

"Make sure they take him someplace up in the mountains," Morty suggested to Talyarkinash as she picked up the bowl and spoon again. "And stay away from avalanche zones."

Outside the base, most of this hemisphere of *Irron* was in the depths of winter. The mountains reminded Gareth of family vacations to Colorado when he was a kid, especially the snow.

But to have his own hands back???

"Sign me up," Gareth pronounced, letting the Nari woman stuff a spoonful of stew into his mouth happily.

"Gotcha, kid," Morty suddenly hopped back down onto the floor and grabbed his lift. "I'll tell Doc Fitzroy you're in."

Xiomber joined him and the two departed.

"Better?" Talyarkinash asked as she filled the spoon again.

"I make a lousy patient, Talyarkinash," Gareth said. "As you have seen. Every minute I'm here is another minute Sarzynski has to perfect whatever plans he has , whatever trouble is coming."

Nobody knew Marc Sarzynski better than Gareth. They had been best friends for almost a decade, going back to ground school together. Until Marc turned to darkness when Pippa chose Gareth instead.

Dr. Loughty had once predicted that worlds would fall in their ensuing feud. But even that worthy had no idea just how right he had been.

DESPERATE MEASURES

BECAUSE MARC SARZYNSKI worked hard at being ruthless, he had developed an instinct for when to cut and run. It had saved his ass more than once, when the Constables had gotten a solid-enough lead to come knocking. When a Heavy Team kicked in the door to Gonquah's estate, the Th'Tarni man had been arrested almost without incident, but Marc have moved his base of operations absolutely immediately.

Several people in his gang had expressed surprise, but Zorge had just nodded and gone along without question, packing what he could and burning the rest.

Two days later, another Heavy Team had shown up at the resort Marc had been renting in the off-season, but he was already gone by then, leaving only one supposedly-innocent watcher to identify everything. The rest of the gang had been extra quiet after that.

They didn't understand violence, but that was because they were of the *Accord of Souls*. Even most of his gang still had some level of empathy with their fellows, broken though it might be. Marc was human, in spite of his exterior shell as a Vanir. He could kill anybody and everybody that got in his way.

Marc finished reading the details from his watcher's report. Sloppy, on the part of the Constables, but they hadn't brought a Star Dragon with them. Gareth would have made different suggestions about the approach.

That man understood how to kick in a door shooting.

Maybe he had been as grievously injured as one of Marc's moles still hiding in the Constabulary had suggested, from medical reports the woman had seen.

A knock at the hatch brought Marc's eyes up.

"Enter," he called.

The team was currently *seeing the galaxy,* as the old saw went. They had rented a long-term transport pod in which to stay, as they rode in between worlds on a cargo vessel. Technically, Marc owned the entire vessel around them, through a series of corporate shells he had inherited when he took over the gang by killing Cinnra, back on *Zathus.*

For now, they could travel incognito, hidden among a thousand other such containers in the big ship's belly. It would also let them visit any planet along the itinerary, as long as they didn't stay more than a day or two during the loading and unloading process.

Zorge opened the hatch and stepped in, closing it behind him. There were ten people with them right now, so the pod could be a little crowded, but nobody was complaining. Jail cells would be even smaller spaces to be confined in.

"We'll be over *Zathus* after lunch," the Nari scientist said as he entered. "We still planning to head down to the surface?"

Marc gestured the man to take a seat. The office was small for a Vanir, almost cramped, since Cinnra had been almost two feet shorter, but it worked for both Warreth and Nari.

"No offense to you and the girls, Zorge," Marc began. "But with Gonquah taken down, I only have four androids now, and likely we'll never be able to get more, or even possibly fix these if something happens to them. It's time I brought in some serious firepower."

"We're really going to build a new wormhole station?" Zorge asked. "The prices for everything went through the roof after the Constables cracked down. Under the table, it's even worse."

"That's why we kidnapped Elgannohn Shevskara," Marc said. "And took his cute, little daughter, Arieala. I'm just glad the girl saw the whole thing as an adventure, although I would have never marked you as the paternal type."

"I have grandkits about that same age," the Nari scientist said. "Probably never see them again, but I do know how to have tea with youngsters and read them to bed. What would have happened had the wife called the cops?"

"She would have still gotten the girl back," Marc's face turned hard.

"Unharmed. Never doubt that. All the pain would have been the father's to bear. But I'm glad that she listened to reason. And it's not like any of that money actually belonged to Shevskara. He skimmed it off others."

"We're likely to burn through all of it, just buying the gear we need and paying bribes to keep it quiet," Zorge's muzzle ruffled sideways in thought. His whiskers were back, but his ears were merely sideways.

"I can always take more hostages," Marc smiled coldly. "That's almost a bottomless well, when dealing with the kind of element that worked as middlemen. Bent, but only guilty of civil infractions, at the end of the day. The kind of people who budget for bribes and fines as part of their regular business. Use all of the money we got from Shevskara. I can get you more."

"What about the Constabulary?" Zorge asked. "Grodray's team apparently went through the androids without any hesitation."

"They saw them as machines," Marc said. "I would have. Plus, none of the Ellis devices had a weapon of any kind except themselves except fists. I would have liked to have seen what a hundred of them could have done with disintegrators. But when I have humans on the battlefield, even the Vanir will hesitate."

"You're sure?" the Nari hesitated.

"Their worst nightmares made flesh, Zorge," Marc sneered. "Coming for them. Baker and Grodray might be tough enough to handle it, but your average officer will freeze up, at least long enough that a human who doesn't care will be able to shoot them."

"Then what?" Zorge asked.

"Then we shatter the Constabulary," Marc growled heavily. "Sticks and carrots, but I'm willing to unleash the most nightmarish scenarios the *Accord* could possibly imagine. Maybe even worse, since they dream too small to truly encompass what I could really do when I'm angry. We'll bring the Constabulary down. After that, there will always be politicians who would rather kiss the ring than die for their principles. We'll use those to control the rest. That and fear."

"And those of us who aren't human?" Zorge asked. "Where does that leave us?"

"You three, and a few others, are the only people I trust," Marc said. "The humans I'm bringing over are killers, just like me. And they'll turn on me in an instant if they thought they could take over. You along with Maiair and Yooyar, will be the key advisors running things. I know what would bind the girls to the throne. What does Zorge desire most?"

"Me?" the Nari asked.

"You," Marc said. "If you have a vested interest in the future, you'll support it. What is that thing that brings you permanently on board?"

Marc was impressed with the way the Nari sat, deep in thought for several minutes. As far as Marc knew, just being able to run his spy networks and tinker in his labs was usually enough for Zorge, but Marc planned to live forever, once they could figure out the genetic engineering necessary.

He would need this Nari scientist/spymaster for decades.

"I've never really thought down those lines before," Zorge finally admitted. "I'll have to get back to you. What do the girls want?"

"Their own form of immortality," Marc said. "I'll need you to find me some geneticists on a par with Morty and Xiomber. And maybe Liamssen, since all three are now working for the Constabulary and I wouldn't trust them, even if they got rescued."

"That will be a rather tricky ask, boss," Zorge said. "Those three were among the very best on the market."

"You've got years, not days," Marc assured him. "I will bind Maiair to my reign by finding a way to use my genes to give her a son. Our son, who would then be part of the new ruling class I will institute when I turn the *Accord of Souls* into a proper, galactic Empire."

"Good to see you aren't planning small," Zorge grinned at him.

"I will live as long as science can manage it, Zorge," Marc said. "Maybe forever. Humans will break the *Accord* for me, but only so far as I will have a permanent underclass of serfs, unable to rise up and stop me. Those same humans will not be given the sorts of advanced modifications capable of making them a threat to me, so they can compete with those rulers from *Accord* species who had been broken free of the Chaa's conditioning, which can be done. It was already cracking when Cinnra brought me over. I will finish the job."

"Okay," Zorge said simply. "I will put that in the back of my mind while I go about building a new wormhole station. As you said, we've got years. At least, assuming we can stay ahead of the Constables."

"There are only three of them I worry about, Zorge," Marc said. "Grodray and Baker will be easy enough to take down, when the time comes. Then we'll go after Dankworth. Not even a Star Dragon will stop me."

COP

SHE KNEW she should have been happy with the current situation. Thrilled beyond measure at what she had achieved, but Eveth Baker was never one to rest on her laurels. This glass was still half empty. She looked around her impersonal flat and considered the space beyond these tiny walls.

Marc Sarzynski, the criminal mastermind known as Maximus, was out there, somewhere, along with a small core of hard, dangerous killers. And possibly one or more of Gonquah's killer android devices. Chaa alone knew what kind of trouble he might cause with that before they caught him.

But she and the Constabulary had managed to break yet another criminal enterprise. Better, one with extensive notes on delivery addresses and bank accounts. She might yet live to see the *Accord* put back on stable ground, after she and Grodray had been shocked to discover how rotten the foundation really was.

But for Gareth, everything might have fallen by now.

She checked the clock on the mantle. Early in the morning still, but she had already been up for two hours, working out and then reading a stack of reports. It was hard letting go of some of these cases, but she knew that Grodray and his bosses had a different mission for her.

The flat's system chimed with an incoming call.

"Answer," Eveth called out, sitting still on the couch and just breathing. Good meditation to get her day started. Wondering who might be calling this early. "Hello?"

"Morning, Eve," Jackeith Grodray said. "Figured you'd be awake, but thought I'd call instead of knocking too early on the one morning you decided to sleep in."

"I'm up," she smiled.

Sleeping in was something a Constabulary counsellor had suggested she try at least once each week. She had managed it twice in the last three months, but that was probably still more than the previous ten years.

"You had breakfast yet?" Grodray continued.

"I have not," she thought out loud. "Worked out, then read. Been sitting here for the last ten minutes waiting for you to call. Or someone."

"Good," she could hear the smile in the tall man's voice. "I'll be over in a few minutes and we'll get some food. Busy day ahead."

"What's up?" she asked, intrigued by the almost-playful tone. This was a man who was forever serious.

"You'll see," he said cryptically, cutting the signal.

Eveth stood and checked her uniform. The same, blue bodysuit she always wore, with an equipment belt about her flared hips and a thigh holster that was supposed to be more or less covered by a jacket she rarely wore.

Because Grodray had sounded serious, she went back into the bedroom and retrieved her jacket, putting it on and securing the first two buttons at the bottom. Enough to look formal, but still let her move quickly.

Her brown hair was getting long enough that she would either have to get it cut soon, or let it grow long enough to pull back. She hadn't decided which, and had been so busy over the last few months that most personal things had fallen by the wayside. A quick blow upwards was still enough to get it out of her eyes for now.

Jack was up to something. You had to know the man to see the humorous layer underneath that serious exterior. So she waited in the salon until a knock at the door.

Eveth opened it and smiled at her partner. Former partner, maybe. It was hard to tell. They had been paired together by her bosses to give an upcoming, Level-3 Constable like her a Senior Constable to learn from. And have him rein her in some, if that was possible.

Except that Jackeith Grodray was really a Level-7. A Prime

Investigator in disguise, able to pursue any crime, anywhere. The free agents of the Constabulary. That thing that she wanted for herself.

Eveth kept telling herself that the bosses, all the way up to the First Inspector, must be impressed with the cases she had helped break open, working with Grodray and Gareth Dankworth, the Star Dragon. They hadn't returned her to regular duty on *Orgoth Vortai*.

She had never planned to save the *Accord of Souls*. She was just a cop, not a messiah. But then, she had never expected it to be so fragile.

"Good," Grodray said as he eyed her. "Was going to suggest you look a little more formal today, if you weren't."

"Oh?" she asked, but he just grinned and stepped back, gesturing her to come with him.

Downstairs, there was a Constabulary private car waiting, rather than an auto-taxi. Something was up, but the man was mum.

At least the first stop was her favorite restaurant for breakfast. It wasn't crowded yet, but *Orgoth Vortai*'s sun was only just coming up over Londra's horizon, so most people were only now stirring. Or settling, as the situation demanded.

"Order heavy," Grodray suggested as the waitress delivered coffee. He proceeded to do exactly that, so Eveth followed suit.

Sounded like one of those days where they'd be in one meeting after another, with no time to eat until after sunset.

"Anything you are willing to tell me?" she finally asked when they were alone.

"Things are about to get more serious, Baker," he smiled grimly, but still with a twinkle in his eyes. "Nothing you can't handle, but a lot of levers had to move first, to get us to today. Now we'll see motion, where everything had been in a holding pattern for the last month or so."

"What about Gareth?" she asked.

Technically, Grodray wasn't her partner anymore, as she was now in charge of bringing the former-human on board, but the man was laid up in the hospital for a bit yet, even with everything that medicine could do.

His injuries fighting the androids might have killed anyone else. Even the Star Dragon had come close to dying, protecting her.

"He'll have a place in what's coming," Grodray nodded. "But there are folks at the top who still distrust him, in spite of everything that man has done for us. You and I will be driving. And it starts today."

She couldn't get anything else out of the man except cryptic smiles as he ate more food in one sitting than she had ever seen. Eveth took that as a sign and did the same, until she was so full she felt bloated.

Outside, the same car dropped them at the local tube station, where they rode to orbit in a different private vehicle and docked on a Constabulary transport rather than a civilian one. As soon as they docked, the transport dropped through a tube, which suggested that the vehicle had been waiting specifically for them to arrive, rather than following any sort of a commercial schedule.

Eveth knew she was home as soon as she looked out the porthole on the far side of the tube. There was something about *Almar* that she could identify just from seeing its disk from orbit.

So, whatever was happening was going back to the beginning. On the world usually know as the *Axis of Time*. Home of the *Accord* government, but more importantly, the home of the Constabulary and the legendary home of the Vanir themselves, when they descended from the Chaa.

The next tube ride dropped them out over Prime itself, the capital city of the planet and the *Accord*. It wasn't as artistically decorated as *Orgoth Vortai*, but then the Vanir who made up most of the population didn't do representative art as compulsively as the Grace did. Plus, the Vanir were the only ones who had the *Chaa* inside them, as children of those very gods who had created everything before Ascending in turn.

But it felt good to come home. Like discarding an old robe to step into a new one, just the sun in the sky seemed to wash Eveth clean.

She kept her mouth shut, though. Baker knew she would never live it down with her mates if they thought she was somehow less that solid granite all the way through emotionally. None of them needed to know that she did hear music in her mind. Stopped to smell the roses occasionally.

Granted, far more today than even a year ago, but she could chalk that up to somehow growing up. Or at least growing into herself.

The vehicle deposited them atop the Axis building, built on the very ground where, according to the Founding Legends, the *Chaa* beings known as *The Communion* had last stood, the most powerful of the new gods, before departing forever in their quest.

Landing on the roof was as serious a signal to Eveth as anything she had ever seen. Everyone else was supposed to land in the vast parking lot and front lawn, before entering the building through the grand foyer that contained an ongoing history of the *Accord*.

It didn't yet have a Star Dragon etched into the walls, but it might, one of these days.

Eveth followed Jack to a drop tube and fell quickly into the depths of the building, holding her breath in more ways than one. Below, Grodray led her through a series of hallways and secured doors until they ended up in a small conference room, somewhere in the interior of the building without any windows.

"Now what?" Eveth asked as Grodray sat and she joined him.

"Now we wait," he said, looking as relaxed as she had ever remembered seeing him.

The wait wasn't long. A door opened and several people filed in, standing at one end of the room and smiling at her.

Eveth was mildly shocked at the company, though. Several Prime Inspectors she had met at one time or another, including Doctor Dalton Fitzroy. In addition, several Command Inspectors and even a few Planetary Inspectors, Level-8's and 9's.

Grodray stood, so Eveth did as well, only then seeing the First Inspector herself, Madam Anen Wardson, somewhat obscured by the others.

Eveth tried to remember to breathe. Especially as the First Inspector smiled and stepped close to greet her, her hands behind her back.

"Eveth Baker," the woman smiled. "It isn't often I get to do this anymore, but I pulled rank here, in spite of tradition."

"Ma'am?" Eveth managed, somewhat at a loss.

It didn't help that Grodray was suddenly grinning from ear to ear. As were the others.

"Traditionally, Jack Grodray would be the one to do this, Constable Baker," the First Inspector continued.

She pulled out a flat box, perhaps twenty centimeters tall and twelve wide, but only two thick. Flipping it open on a hinge at the top, there was a Constabulary badge resting on a gold, silk cloth. Except this one wasn't cerulean blue like the one over Eveth's heart.

Instead, it was a simple, brass one, a ring about seven centimeters across with the outer band being about half a centimeter wide. Seventeen stars had been etched into the metal, three crossing lines each other to form a six-pointed shape, filled in with something black.

Eveth's breath caught ragged.

"Constable Eveth Baker, it gives me great pleasure to raise you to the rank of Prime Investigator," Wardson pronounced in a warm voice. "Welcome to the College."

The College. The organization composed only of Prime Investigators. The single most elite club in the galaxy, as far as she knew, because you had to be accepted by a group of people who had already proven themselves to be the very best cops there were.

Anen Wardson surprised Eveth even more by kissing her on the cheek after handing her the new badge in its case. Others followed suit, including Grodray.

By the time she had recovered her wits, there was a cake in the middle of the table and glasses of wine or juice.

The big breakfast made sense now. There would be a party later, and she might not have a chance to eat anything nutritious for a while.

Grodray had a smile where butter wouldn't melt in his mouth.

"You're evil," she accused him.

"Guilty as charged," he grinned back. "But you earned this. And did it more than a year ahead of where the rest of them had expected, so I get to collect on a number of bets along the way."

Grodray had bet on her making it earlier than anyone else?

Huh.

"So now what?" she asked as someone handed her a glass of red wine.

"Today we celebrate," he smiled warmly. "Tomorrow, we're going hunting."

LAST TRAVELER

LAST TRAVELER and the rest of the *Ascended Chaa* referred to the Vanir as *Those Left Behind*. Once, they had all been one people, until *First Immortal* had found the way to *Ascend*. Many others had followed once the way was known.

The others, the vast bulk of their kind, had chosen a corporeal existence instead, one that would eventually result in physical death. The twelve greatest of the *Ascended Chaa* had transformed that remainder into the Vanir and uplifted the other species to keep them company.

The gods all had personal names, but none of them thought of themselves in those terms, it having been so long since they existed as embodied beings. The others frequently referred to him simply as *Last Traveler*, as he was the final one of the *Communion*, the pantheon the Vanir and others called the Great Gods, to cast loose the bonds of flesh.

Even him *was* something a misnomer, as the Chaa had, by the very end, been able to take on nearly any form as their need or fancy required. But he had been of the male gender at birth, some sixteen Chitra ago, one hundred and sixty thousand years as the *Accord* measured such things. and still used such a pronoun internally much of the time.

As the last, he had also had perhaps the greatest sentiment and affection for the others, and volunteered to stay behind for a time to watch over the *Accord of Souls* as it found its place. *First Immortal* had already departed in her haste, as had *Seeker for the Knee of God*.

Docent, also known as *Great Teacher*, and *Magistrate* had taken the new thing, the *Accord of Souls* created by *Uplifter*, and given it knowledge and laws. It had been a magnificent thing to behold, both the departure of his kin as well as the dawning dreams of *Those Left Behind*.

Glory in Sunrise had led the final group, standing on the powerful shoulders of the one known only as *Mountain*, as they cast themselves into the great depths to seek the signposts left by the Creator of the universe. *Last Traveler* had waited nearly a third of a Chitra, more than three thousand years, before he leapt outward to join the quest, always yet keeping a tender spot in his soul for *Those Left Behind*.

For more than four Chitra, forty-seven thousand years, give or take, he had wandered, speaking occasionally with others as he encountered them, updating *Narrator of History* with his tales and sights. Always seeking evidence of God's Great Plan.

Time had brought him back to the tiny island of life from whence the Chaa had once departed, one galaxy among innumerable others in just this phase of the multiverse. He paused to look in on his far-removed descendants. So much had changed, and so little.

The chain of lights still crossed the galaxy back and forth, leaving only that one, dark corner where *Merciless*, at the behest of the others, had wiped an entire section of the galaxy clean of alien life lest that other species expand their militancy beyond the small cluster of stars that they had conquered before encountering proto-gods.

Last Traveler had argued the case for the others to be somehow preserved, contained, but *The Communion* had decided. It had been so great a decision that in fact all of the *Ascended Chaa* had been consulted for the first time since *First Immortal* opened the way.

Last Traveler turned away from the darkened stars and smelled the life of the *Accord*. It brought him such pleasure. Some things had not changed in five Chitra, but that was by design. The Vanir and the others had been placed in a stasis from which they could live out long and prosperous lives, but they would never be allowed to *Ascend*. *The Communion* would be the last of their kind, because they had already destroyed one sentient race, and had no wish to fight a second war, this time with their own children.

But a new smell caught his mind as he hovered above the ancient home. An eighteenth species was present, when the Great Plan called for no such thing for perhaps another Chitra at the earliest.

Last Traveler strode close to examine this upstart being. There were two of them present, both wearing the outward form of the Vanir, perhaps as camouflage.

The species called itself human.

He leapt across space to the place where the human smell originated. One world, well out to the fringe of the galactic spiral, along one of the lesser spurs not even on an arm. Ten billion humans, currently contained within their single system, *Last Traveler* studied them closely, took in all of human history in a few moments.

The species had been advanced enough for consideration, seven Chitra ago when the *Accord of Souls* was proposed. The vote had been lopsided, but not absolute, as the species was yet too warlike, and would have not fit in with the proposed Vanir, without significant modification.

The last human Chitra, as he studied them, had been one of unrelenting war. Killing on scales that took *Last Traveler's* breath away. Xenophobic to a degree that staggered the psyche, even though they themselves recognized this and worked to contain the dangerous elements with an organization called *Earth Force*. But still they knew failure, and so *Sky Patrol*, approximating The Constabulary of the *Accord of Souls*.

Worse, *The Great Plan* expected that humans would not have achieved even a space-capable civilization for another Chitra, had they somehow survived the many chokepoints available during the Industrialization Phases.

Last Traveler noted one last thing that left even his heart cold and frozen.

The humans had discovered the very wormhole technology that the Chaa had first used to explore the galaxy in embodied forms in their early days, before later *Ascending* into godhead. The species could break out of their single system and perhaps master the very galaxy that the Chaa had worked so hard to create. And do so in a manner of centuries, if not a single lifetime, taking their frantic and breakneck pace of scientific exploration into account.

He would need to contact the others and perhaps gather them into a single place for the first time since the very beginning. As he leapt outward, *Last Traveler* wondered if the efforts of *Merciless* would be called upon again.

FIRE

IT BURNED WORSE than the first time he had tapped the form. Gareth tried to clench his teeth and keep his snout shut, but the pain was too great to hold back. His bellow echoed back seconds later from the surrounding mountains, but he was mindless with pain to hear it.

Every transformation hurt. It required reshaping his human body, his Vanir form, and forcing it to grow into a giant, winged lizard. The Star Dragon.

Thankfully, the giant landing field where he frequently trained was empty today. Only the usual team on the training base, faces he knew well enough, even as he had been purposefully kept at a distance from them by security needs.

The morning air was crisp enough that Talyarkinash's breath steamed as he had watched her, but no snow had yet fallen. Perhaps in a few days, if the forecast was correct. Gray skies hung low overhead with potential, but nothing as yet fell.

Gareth opened his dragon's eyes and gazed out at the field around him. The giant Quonset-like huts used as hangars. The tower from which a few live people supervised the systems that brought auto-taxis and such as needed.

It being too cold outside, Morty and Xiomber were up in the tower, wrapped in silly, striped scarves they had acquired somewhere and sipping hot chocolate. Only Talyarkinash was down here with him on the tarmac in a heavy coat.

He gazed down at her now, noting the remains of the casts that had been cut off both of his hands and forearms before he shifted.

"Are you all right?" she asked simply.

She was one of the best geneticists alive, but lately her job was as much psychologist and friend as medical professional.

The Star Dragon flexed his front paws, resting on his haunches with his wings flapping just enough to keep his length upright.

If you could somehow take the burning itch of a bad sunburn and apply it internally, it might feel like this. But that was still ten thousand times better than it had been yesterday.

"Yes, I think," his low voice rumbled back to her.

Gareth always felt like he had a foghorn for a voice in his draconic form. That low, mournful sound calling across the fog-shrouded waters of the Golden Gate at night.

He twisted, this way and that to make sure that there were no kinks or burns left. Those androids, the Ellis devices that Marc had designed, had nearly done him in. Had Senior Constable Grodray and his team been three minutes later, they would have ended up burying Gareth with military honors.

Or whatever it was that the Constabulary did when someone was killed in the line of duty.

Even if he was a renegade human impersonating a Vanir while trying to stop his former best friend from destroying the galaxy.

"Everything looks good from here," she said, stepping sideways for a better view.

"One quick flight, then?" he asked.

She was in charge of his recuperation. And he would listen to the woman.

"A short one, but don't perform any flying stunts today," she replied. "Just up, around a bit, and back."

Rather than reply, Gareth took a running leap and threw himself into the sky, letting his programmed instincts find the thermals to ride, even on a chilly morning like this. It took work to gain altitude, extra energy reserves that he burned prodigiously at a time when he had barely been eating enough to heal himself. Gareth smile to himself and understood why he shouldn't push things, as much as he wanted to.

Up in a spiraling column, until he was five hundred meters in the air and Talyarkinash was merely an ant in the great distance. He nosed over but kept things controlled, rather than the mad dive he liked to do. Here, he merely fell out of the sky like a feather, swooping by the Nari woman at a lazy hundred kilometers per hour, rather than his craziest top speeds.

Just because, he opened his mouth and scorched a section of the reinforced tarmac with a cone of fire, a burst of binary liquid that burst into a ravening belch hot enough to destroy things.

Except Sarzynski had planned for that. Had made the androids tough enough to resist dragonfire.

Gareth would have to go back to outthinking one of the smartest men he knew.

He banked up and over, reversing his line of flight quickly enough. Because he could, Gareth swooped close to Talyarkinash and thrust himself up in the air, stalling with a big backblast of wings over her head, until he could land almost as softly as a cat.

She had a frown on her face. He had been expecting a smile. It got pronounced when she pulled out her pocket scanner device and aimed it at him.

"Could you drop flat and stretch your tail as far as you can?" she said.

It sounded like a question, but Gareth knew better. He complied, happy that his keel scales would protect him from the cold asphalt for a while.

The Nari woman walked down his right side, aiming the scanner at him. She stood still for a moment and then turned and walked back to his snout.

"Interesting," she said absently.

"What?" he asked, maybe just a little nervous.

"According to this, you are close to twenty-eight meters long now, Gareth," she said. "When you had been merely twenty-seven before."

"I'm still growing?" He was a little shocked. "I thought that you and the boys had set that."

"We did," she was still staring at the scanner's readouts. "You seem to be doing this yourself."

"Me?"

"We'll need to run more tests," she decided. "Could you change back, please?"

Again, she aimed the device at him. This transformation wasn't nearly as painful, but shifting back to human, Vanir, form never was. And his hands hurt less. Barely at all, or perhaps about as bad as if a nun had smacked him on the wrist with a ruler.

At least the bodysuit she had built for him was warm enough in this form, as long as he got inside in a bit. Or put a jacket on.

Talyarkinash walked close. The scanner beeped and pinged merrily.

"Okay, good," she said, eyes intent on the device. "Your regular form is unchanged. I had feared that you might be turning into a giant of a Vanir as well, but the shift appears to be limited to the Star Dragon."

"What does it mean, though?" he asked.

"I have no idea, but I'll talk to Xiomber and Morty, and perhaps Dalton, and see what they think. For now, you can be cleared for duty."

That was the best news he'd had in almost a week, so Gareth didn't mind the rest. He could get back to stopping Marc.

And saving the galaxy.

THE DESERT

WHILE HE HAD JUST BEEN in Arizona recently enough, it had been years since Royston had gone out into the desert itself, just to explore. Not since…no, best not to even think about that time. Those security clearances would not even be reviewed until at least fifty years after the last of them were dead, just to protect the reputations of everyone involved.

Still, some days, Royston missed being a Field Agent in Earth Force Sky Patrol.

It was morning. The sun was just beginning to rise in a pool of molten, red fire to the east as Royston navigated the vehicle north and west into the high basin. The Nevada Territory had been an American State once, when enough rain fell here to support human life at places like The Meadows. For the last century, it had been a ghost town hundreds of miles across and haunted by the memories of past glory.

He had requisitioned a personnel truck from the motor pool with the orders Alvin had sent along. Comfortable enough for eight to travel, it allowed the three of them space to bring extra gear and still stretch out.

Behind him in the backseat, in front of the only known human wormhole device, the two women had settled in as though old friends. Everyone was still on their personal clocks from The Arsenal, set to London time, so they had not minded catching the restaurant as it wearily opened and then gorging on a heavy breakfast, before driving out into the wilds of the desert.

The vehicle had a solar-absorbing skin to power the batteries, plus a tiny thorium reactor, so they would risk only running out of water, but Royston still had all of his desert skills from the old days, if it came to that. And radios he could use to call for help to drop on them in minutes, were the situation to arise.

"Is there any place better or worse, Ms. Darzi?" Royston called as they made their way along the ancient asphalt hardtop.

"There is not, Dr. Loughty," the Grace woman replied from behind him.

"Please, call me Royston," he said. "My daughter uses Father most of the time, so Dr. Loughty makes me feel too formal, especially with what is hopefully to occur."

"Royston," she seemed to try the name on for size, pausing for a long moment. "In another world, I might have once been known as Ilak Vorta."

"I shall endeavor to remember that," he smiled at her in the rear view mirror. "Especially if we are successful."

"Speaking of success," Pippa spoke up. "Why did we need to bring the machine with us, Father?"

"Much of the internals have not been adequately dismantled and scanned yet, my dear," he smiled at his daughter as well. "The original plans exist, but my mechanical geniuses that built this contraption had to use as much art as engineering to get it to where I needed the machine. Were we gone, Alvin or someone would have inevitably taken it upon themselves to produce a full as-built blueprint, which is the last thing we want. Especially as we know it works. We are buying time."

"I see," Pippa concluded. "And we are not supposedly traveling to England at some point to locate that woman and her band?"

"In time," Royston mused. "I suspect that she will be necessary, somehow, for the next steps, but I could not explain why I feel that way."

"I am intrigued by this rock and roll phenomenon, Dr.—Royston," Darzi said. Or maybe Vorta, but he decided to think of her by her human guise, at least for now. Less chance of making a mistake later. "You found the secrets to the higher mathematics contained in music?"

"I realize how strange that sounds," Royston began, but she cut him off.

"Oh, no, that much is clear, Royston," she said. "The Grace live in a world of such rich sensory experience that we feel constant sympathy for the rest of the galaxy, to live in such a dull, dreary place. I have had to explore it myself recently, with my tentacles so greatly limited."

Royston looked up in the mirror. She had shed the hijab that hid her secret once they left the restaurant, and apparently not taken the drugs that kept her tentacles quiescent this morning. They roiled slowly like a snake ball, tasting and sensing the cool, Arizona air and the rising sun.

"Depending on how the rest of this goes, perhaps we will be able to track down that young woman and enjoy another performance," Royston offered.

"I would like that," the Grace woman replied, a distant, airy smile on her face as she got to fully immerse herself in the desert.

They rode for another hour or so, climbing up into the mountains, from which they would in turn descend into the basin below.

"I think this would be a good place," Royston announced.

Royston slowed as they reached the peak of the road, along a vast shelf looking down a thousand feet or more into the dry wadi below, where a tributary of the mighty Colorado River had once strode forth.

Before the dry times.

He pulled the vehicle to the side of the road and parked it in a place that might have once been a scenic overlook, exiting to enjoy the morning air before it grew unbearably warm. A quick-deploying pavilion would provide them protection from the sun while they waited, and Royston had packed sufficient water and food for a week, if necessary.

"Now what, Fatima?" he asked carefully as they stood together.

"Now I will convey your message to my superiors, Royston," she replied. "I can only estimate what their reply might be, but hopefully they will allow me to return, if only to deliver it myself."

He nodded as the imposter, the Grace woman stepped back. Royston felt Pippa take his arm and they watched the other being activate a device disguised as a simple wrist watch.

From his jacket pocket, Royston heard an insistent beeping.

He had forgotten he carried the little alarm with him, but it was apparently detecting the first traces of a new wormhole coming open, so his theory and construction had been on the beam.

Royston left it beeping. He was too fascinated watching the golden haze that suddenly seemed to appear around the Grace agent, Ilak Vorta, sometimes known by some as Fatima Darzi. She smiled once, and then disappeared, fading rather like morning dew subject to golden sunlight.

"Now what, Father?" Pippa asked, once they were alone again.

"Now we wait," Royston said. "And perhaps, dear daughter, we should pray."

SHOPPING

"HOW DID IT GO?" Marc asked as Zorge slipped into the penthouse suite's office, having made it past several people with guns arrayed in layers around him, from the ground floor entrance to the outer chamber of the suite itself, to the door with the first android guarding.

"Clock's ticking, but we've got time," the Nari spymaster replied, throwing himself wearily into a chair.

Marc paused what he was reading to study the man. The fur around the muttonchop whispers was coming in more gray now than it had even a few months ago, as with the longer locks on top. Marc forgot how old the man was, because he himself hadn't yet made it to thirty, but the big, cuddly killer kitty was over fifty by some amount. In the last third of his lifetime, at least. The notes on his age were just estimates, plus known dates of what the man had been involved in, in his youth.

"What did they say when you arrived?" Marc asked.

"And I quote: *Crap, you're not dead?* Unquote," Zorge laughed lightly. "Your reputation will carry them long enough to get the job done, but we'll need to take all our parts and run away with them afterwards, rather than trying to build a new facility here."

"They've lost their fear of me?" Marc scowled.

It had been barely a year since the Constables had broken Marc's hold on the underground of *Zathus*.

"Oh, that's graven into their souls at this point," Zorge replied.

"Damabiath's death guaranteed that. Someone will overcome their terror at some point and whisper to a cop, and there are very few bent ones left on this planet. They'll be afraid that they're going to be next."

"Understood," Marc said simply. "I miscalculated. On *Earth*, that would have been sufficient, but the equations are different here. Plus, we look like we're losing right now, and morale, as they ancient Marshal once said, is three to one to the material."

"Meaning?" Zorge's eyebrows came down in apparent confusion.

"Momentum favors the Constabulary over the recent few months," Marc said. "So people want to be on the winning side, rather than digging in for the long term. Once we start winning again, all those people will come out of the woodwork again to explain how they were always supporting you, but had to make it look good to the authorities."

"Gotcha," Zorge leaned back. "We have untraceable cash in hand, and fear, so they'll provide us everything. The first double-cross will probably come when they arrange delivery."

"Assuredly," Marc agreed. "Keep watch on the delivery systems as much as you can. I'd be fine with us hitting a postal truck in route with our equipment aboard. We can pay up later, plus they'll be able to collect the insurance."

"And that won't piss them off?" Zorge's confusion was back.

Truly, the *Accord* confused Marc at times. Even simple things like casual violence seemed to be alien to their nature. And Zorge was broken, compared to the rest of them.

"I don't care," Marc growled sharply. "Once we have everything built and working, nobody will dare speak a word askance. Do we have estimates on timelines?"

"Some of it was already in hand, but I didn't make delivery arrangements, because like I said, I think we need to load it on a truck and then fly the truck straight to orbit and disappear."

"I agree," Marc nodded. "When the transport comes around again, time everything that needs to be picked up so we can do just that. Especially if we can hijack the rest in transit."

Something on Zorge's face caught Marc's attention.

"Second thoughts?" Marc asked.

"Thinking about the future," Zorge admitted. "About that place where you've won and have taken over the *Accord* and turned it into…what's the human word again?"

"Empire," Marc filled in.

"Yes, Empire," Zorge agreed.

"And?"

"And I'm feeling old and worn out today," Zorge said. "Can't find that thing that would break me out of this rut and ground me hard in your Empire, even though I know it should be there."

"Did you want to simply retire at that point?" Marc asked. "Be set up with a lab to tinker and a budget to play? Go fishing? I need you. Your brilliance. Your conniving. Your connections. You are an integral part of this future."

"I understand," Zorge said. "I think I'm an introvert and need time away from people to recover, and we've been on the run for a year."

"Two more months, and you can have all the time you want, Zorge," Marc promised him. "Just give me two months to get us all there."

"That I can do," the Nari sighed, falling in on himself for a few seconds. "Anything else you needed for now?"

"No," Marc said. "We'll need to plan some raids to steal some things legitimately, but nothing that needs to happen today. Can you send Maiair in when you go out?"

"Will do," Zorge said as he withdrew.

Marc sat and contemplated things. He had seen older conmen go through that phase, when they thought they had seen it all and done it all, and just didn't have the fire in the belly anymore.

"You needed me?" Maiair asked as she stepped in.

Like her Warreth sister Yooyar, Maiair's feathers were primarily crimson, with black and white secondary feathers around the edges. Her headcrest was at half-mast today, which he had expected, and her short beak was partly open.

"Sit," he gestured to the chair Zorge had just vacated. "We need to talk about Zorge."

She bristled and Marc caught a motion to her pistol, but it was only a twinge.

"What's he done?" she demanded.

Maiair was his Chief of Staff. The smartest person in the gang after him. Her younger sister was the second deadliest, but Maiair was no slouch in that category.

"He's feeling depressed," Marc said simply. "So we need to find him a smart, cunning, abjectly-criminal, young Nari woman who will play to his ego and experience."

"A bimbo?" she asked, almost angrily.

"No more than you or your sister are," Marc snapped. "He's been an outlaw too long, and now that endgame is approaching, he's rethinking about all the choices that have alienated him from his family in pursuit of power. That much, I understand. I want him re-energized. If he considered crossing-species, I would ask one of you to find me a cousin with the same fire in the soul as you two have, but it will have to be Nari. Perhaps, Grace, if we could find a psychologist in our ranks who could help him over this hump while being beautiful."

"Oh," she seemed chagrined, but confined herself to that one syllable.

"And while I'm thinking about it, we'll need to consider my needs as well," Marc said carefully. Her headcrest semaphored up, just a little. Not much, but he was paying attention. "I will need to locate an appropriate Second Wife when we are finally able to return to Earth."

"Second wife?" she repeated, confused.

Marc smiled at her. It was time to go beyond the occasional moments of pleasure they had stolen in the past year.

"You are, and always will be my First Wife, Maiair," he said, as tenderly as he could. "The second wife will be for the good of the Empire we will forge. And future generations."

"Oh," she said quietly, her headcrest collapsing as the shock hit home.

Marc let her stew for a few moments.

"What will she be like?" Maiair asked in a tiny voice.

Marc leaned back and considered. At one point, Philippa Loughty had been his perfect choice. Beautiful, intelligent, lively. But she had chosen the heroic one, as he had somehow always known she would.

It didn't still hurt any less, six years later.

"Tall and athletic," Marc said carefully, envisioning her in his mind. "Beautiful and erudite. A first-rate, scientific mind, but one not constrained by the sorts of antique morality that would prevent her from participating in our mission."

"A human version of Talyarkinash Liamssen, then?" Maiair asked.

Marc was gobsmacked. Yes, exactly her.

He even knew a few such women, back home, against which he could compare, rather than using Loughty as a benchmark. They would probably still be stewing that they could not be allowed into the refined heights of the sciences.

"Yes," Marc agreed. "Although we may need to kidnap our target, since I can't just walk into her life as a Vanir and expect a rational response."

"I remember you as human, Maximus," Maiair said. "Vanir is just an improvement, but I see no reason that would stop any smart woman."

Marc fixed his future First Wife with a hard eye, but could detect no conniving in her. Perhaps she was sincere. Time would tell, especially when there was a second generation of the ruling caste, chafing at the bit for power, and thrust against one another.

He just needed to get them there.

A CLUE

AT LEAST NOTHING had changed about their outward relationship. Eveth was still a mere Constable, as far as most people were concerned. At least in public. Jackeith was a Senior Constable. The two of them were partners investigating crime.

It was only in her secret heart that they were now both Prime Investigators, Level-7's, and tasked by the First Inspector herself to see this thing through.

She looked around the back of the large vehicle, flying across the afternoon skies of *Irron* on the way to the tube station. Grodray was reading something on his tablet device. Gareth and Dr. Liamssen were whispering like siblings, facing her. Xiomber was asleep, snoring ever so quietly.

"So why *Zathus?*" Morty asked quietly, turning and looking up at her instead of staring out the window.

Eveth considered her possible answers. On the one hand, this man was a hardened criminal with decades of crimes to his name that he had admitted to in court, and was eventually going to be sentenced, once the full scale of problems came out.

On the other hand, he and Xiomber had happily turned state's evidence, putting their eidetic memories for details to paper, including dates, payments, and witnesses to various conversations.

The underworld on *Zathus* had been shattered as a result, like a bug hitting a windshield at high speed.

But his question made sense, as the Constabulary had made such deep and terminal inroads into the various criminal organizations that had grown up slowly, like pearls accreting materials over the many decades.

"Because we missed something," she finally admitted to the little, Yuudixtl scientist. "With what you and your brother provided, we should have been able to round up everything, but Maximus stays ahead of us at each step."

"That's because there are that many bent cops out there, Baker," Morty sneered at her. "Them I can't name, because I never dealt directly with most of them, but the organization had massive inroads everywhere. You cleaned your own house out yet?"

Eveth blushed, in spite of her anger and her effort to suppress it. Gareth and Liamssen had fallen silent, watching, as had Grodray. Xiomber still snored.

"Yeah, thought not," Morty said. "So what can we find on *Zathus* that you missed? Otherwise, you wouldn't need me and Xiomber tagging along."

"What's the next step that Maximus will take?" Eveth replied simply. "That's what nobody has been able to answer. We've been two steps behind him for a year, but no closer than that, or we would have caught him quickly after the birth of the Star Dragon. He has to be getting help we've missed, so I want to return to where it all started and look again."

She nodded to Gareth, acknowledging their old argument about him sparing Sarzynski's life in trade for hers, Grodray's, and Liamssen. At the time she had been angry, but Jack had gotten her over that, with the expectation everyone had that it was just a matter of time.

"Could he have gone someplace else for help?" Morty asked.

"We've looked everywhere," Eveth snapped at the tiny man.

"No, you haven't," he said grimly. "I know that for a fact."

"Because we haven't found him?" she almost sneered the words

"Because you haven't looked on Earth for one," Morty said, turning to Gareth. "Would he go there?"

"He'd be trapped," Gareth spoke up quickly.

"Not if he had enough equipment to make two stations," Morty said. "Build one and open a wormhole. Chuck everything and everyone through, and then sabotage the machine to eat itself when it's done. Go hide somewhere on Earth and build a new machine, while recruiting people there. The killer robots were a great idea, but you smashed that, so he's got to be getting desperate for help he can rely on. After all, me and Xiomber double-crossed him. What's to stop someone else?"

"Gareth?" Eveth turned to their human expert. "Would that work?"

She noted that even Xiomber was awake now, but the vehicle was utterly silent save for the drives pushing them through the air.

"If he had a generator powerful enough, or plans to build one?" Gareth replied. "Yes. And there are any number of places he could hide, even as a Vanir. Gold is still a medium of currency exchange, so getting enough to buy friends and supplies on Earth would be pitifully easy. And he probably still has friends he could contact."

Eveth turned to Grodray, on her opposite side from Morty, in more ways than one, and caught his silent nod. Yes, they might have to look on Earth as well. What would the First Inspector say?

FIRST INSPECTOR

FATIMA TRIED NOT to grind her teeth as she told the story again.

At least they had taken her seriously, as mad as her story had sounded, even coming out of her own mouth. But Fatima Darzi, the once and future Ilak Vorta, had been nothing if not compelling. And the First Inspector's staff had listened to her. Then escalated things very quickly to the boss herself.

Fatima was inside the woman's inner office within twenty minutes of stepping through that wormhole from Earth. Anen Wardson sat patiently on her couch, while Fatima sat in one of the two chairs.

"Just like that?" the First Inspector asked as Fatima finished her explanation.

"We made mistakes," Fatima said, gesturing to the building around them. "In background research, planning, and execution. Some of them were pure bad luck, but others were failures of context on our part. Those I can help remedy later with new training and documentation, but for now, we are facing perhaps the single most intelligent example of the species currently living. Our one mistake, in selecting Fatima Darzi as the point of access, functionally confirmed what had been mere speculation on his part prior to that. That potentially hostile aliens were behind the disappearances of Dankworth and Sarzynski. Worse, that infiltrators might be coming and they should be on their guard."

"But the knowledge is contained?" Wardson asked.

"Indeed, madam," Fatima replied. "More than contained. Loughty has specifically isolated himself, his daughter, and the one piece of equipment capable of generating the tube. They are far from anyone else in a desert setting, awaiting developments."

"He does know that we could just kill him, correct?" Wardson pursued.

"We did not discuss that scenario explicitly, but I am confident he is aware of it," Fatima said. "I would almost consider this to be an offer of sacrifice on his part. His life, and his daughter's, for the continued existence of humanity. However, he is absolutely convinced that someone would eventually be able to replicate his work, for merely having known that it was possible in the first place. What he is offering us now is time. Without his direct effort, he does not believe that anyone else will be able to replicate the mathematics that currently only existent in his head, for at least another century."

"So the humans cannot be contained," the First Inspector's voice turned harsher.

"Not for long," Fatima agreed. "Once they have the technology understood, it becomes a matter of scale and power for them to reach orbit quickly, and then to their various colonies. After that, they will turn outward and look for other worlds to colonize, unaware how many are so close enough to their needs as to require minimal bioforming. To say nothing of all the worlds of the *Accord* itself, where humans could live easily."

"What have you promised him?" Wardson asked.

"To relay the message to you," Fatima said. "That he did not kill me when he had the opportunity, did not unmask me to anyone else, isolated himself where he could be eliminated with minimal risk to us, all of this speaks towards a desire on his part for some peaceable solution, if one can be found."

"Can one?" Wardson asked. "Is there some outcome that would work?"

"Royston seems to think that Gareth Dankworth would be able to find something," Fatima said. "I have never met the man, nor spoken to any of his handlers, so I have only the perspective from the humans, but the man seemed to have no enemies at all, from what I was able to determine, during my time with the Earth Force people, as well as Sky Patrol. That, hopefully, speaks well of him."

"It does," Wardson agreed. "Especially in light of the methodology originally used by the Yuudixtl criminals to locate Dankworth in the first place."

"Are we at a greater risk if we bring them here, or send a representative there?" Fatima asked. "Working on the assumption that you desire the Loughties to continue alive?"

"They are isolated?" the First Inspector asked.

"Yes," Fatima acknowledged. "But Royston seemed of the opinion that help could be only a short time away, in an emergency, so I would presume that watchers overhead could react to an incident."

"I, as well," Wardson said. She paused for a moment to think. "I will need to take this to the Commission."

The First Inspector rose from the couch and picked up her handset on the desk, dialing and smiling at Fatima.

"Commissioner?" Anen Wardson asked after a moment. "I have a situation that requires your attention, as quickly as you can spare some time."

She paused, eyes distant.

"Now? Yes," she said. "In my office."

She hung up and returned to her spot on the couch, facing Fatima in one of the chairs. Her hands clenched and unclenched in a nervous movement.

Petim Diazal joined them in less than ten minutes. The Commissioner was an Arawath, one of the amphibious species of the *Accord*, looking like miniaturized, blue versions of Vanir. The man was about Fatima's height, slender and rather short even for that species. He dressed sedately, in a charcoal business suit neither too expensive nor too flashy.

But his eyes burned with a charisma and brilliance that made it obvious why he was at the top of the government.

Quickly, the First Inspector related some background, and then Fatima repeated her story for the man.

"It seems utter madness," he said as she finished. "A century to go from this to invading the *Accord*?"

"Human science, from what I have studied, appears to be frequently the result of a lone genius trying something, which can then not be disproven by others, until eventually it becomes canon," Fatima explained. "The genius is the unpredictable element in the whole equation, as stochastic analysis breaks down."

"I do not know how the Commission itself would react," he said to both of them. "At present, I suspect that the tendency would be to overreact. To simply wipe the humans from the face of history defensively."

Fatima cringed.

"And yes, I understand what a significant stain that would be on my soul when I go to meet the Creator," he continued. "Suggestions otherwise?"

"I would like to bring him and his daughter here," the First Inspector said. "We can contain him then. Exile him from the rest, if need be, without necessarily killing him."

"What of the musician?" the Commissioner turned his attention to Fatima. "I do not understand her role in this escapade."

"It is a human concept, Commissioner," Fatima tried to explain. "The genius has a muse, frequently female to his male historically, who inspires him to ever greater heights. It exists in many of their creative arts, and apparently mathematics was close enough for Royston Loughty."

"Then you must accompany Loughty to such a performance before we can remove him from Earth, Constable," he replied in a hard tone. "See what her power is, since we all begin to see that humans have only started to tap their own abilities. Gareth Dankworth is an example of their unknown capabilities, as much as Royston Loughty. If necessary, she may need to be kidnapped and exiled as well."

"Could we hobble the humans that way?" Wardson mused aloud. "Remove their most dangerous elements secretly, that the rest might pose less of a threat?"

"It would not work, First Inspector," Fatima said quietly. "There is an old Irish proverb that covers this among the humans. When asked how many generations it would take to replace them all, if something were to happen to every poet and musician in Ireland, the correct answer is *One*."

"One?" the other two gasped in harmony.

"One generation," Fatima said. "It is, as I understand it, a human thing. And nothing can stop it."

QUEST

THEY HAD CAMPED OVERNIGHT and prepared a pleasant breakfast at sunrise. Royston was enjoying a bowl of tobacco and the last of the pot of coffee, while Pippa sat across the small fire from him and worked her way steadily through Plutarch. Without looking, he guessed it to be around nine in the morning, as the heat was just starting to sand the fine edge of chill off the air.

His pocket began beeping madly, signaling that a portal was about to open. Was in the process of opening near them. Would be here momentarily.

Royston rose to face his fate. Pippa closed her book and did the same. This might be the end of the world, depending on what decision the aliens had made.

An assassin might appear before them. Or a bomb. He would expect the former to be more likely, as they would need to collect the two bodies and then make the vehicle disappear.

Royston would face it unarmed. The pistol was in the truck, locked safely away against need, none of which rose to this occasion. He clenched the pipe in his teeth and turned in the direction of a metaphorical pull.

Psychic, perhaps. Not something that impacted on the physical senses, but his mind could still place it. They would emerge: *there.*

The air took on that golden hue. A slight breeze seemed to emanate from it, which made sense. A smart alien would want positive pressure, to keep human germs and viruses from somehow leaping across the galaxy to possibly infect innocent and unprepared worlds.

A shape took form as he watched. Briefly, he regretted not having a high-speed scanner camera set up to trigger now, so that he could go back and analyze the event.

Fatima Darzi appeared before them. He could think of her on those terms, as she had replaced her hijab with great fastidiousness, atop the crimson uniform of the Women's Auxiliary. And she was unarmed, so perhaps he would live to see another day.

And perhaps the Lords of the *Accord of Souls* had some hope yet for humanity. Or had simply not gotten far enough along in their planning and execution to finish the species off yet today. Darzi could always be withdrawn at a moment's notice, especially if you had the ability to release bio-bombs all over the Solar System.

Royston held out a hand, which she took in both of hers.

"Good news, perhaps," she offered with a thin smile.

She surprised him by turning and hugging Pippa, who had initiated out of habit.

Royston grabbed a spare chair from where it had been folded up against the side of the vehicle. He gestured them all to sit.

"Tell me," he commanded lightly.

"No decision had been made," she replied. "However, they would like me to visit this musician and evaluate her impact on all of this."

"Her impact?" Pippa asked.

"The First Inspector read me in one some details that I would need, in order to proceed," Fatima said. "Things I had not needed to know prior. Humans, at least as expressed by Gareth Dankworth and Marc Sarzynski, are possessed of a psionic potential that is only rarely tapped, and far in advance of any of our species. In Gareth's case, if provides him the ability to transform into a dragon. My superiors would like to explore the theory that it was only via the combination of Royston's mind and this woman's music that anything could create the psionic gestalt needed to achieve what you have done to date."

"How does that help our cause?" Pippa pressed, concerned.

"If it is such a thing, daughter," Royston interrupted, "then for another to replicate what I have done is a task of such long odds that they may rest easier. It maybe yet be out of humanity's reach to build a large enough device to threaten our neighbors anytime soon. Am I right?"

"You are," Fatima said. "The machine, as you have noted, requires an extraordinary amount of power to do something so simple as move a small glass sphere a matter of meters. Without significant technological breakthroughs, being able to move a man to The Arsenal from the ground here will hopefully be progress measured in centuries, rather than months. Given humanity's evolution over the last thousand years, there is hope that they may yet achieve true civilization in that time."

"Most war and crime is a result of want," Pippa said, bringing her lessons in the social sciences to bear. "Of poverty, both physical and emotional. As Roosevelt once said, freedom from want will lead us to freedom from fear. If we could move past poverty at a global and systemic scale, humans can be fantastically warm and giving people."

"So my superiors hope, Pippa," Fatima replied. "Based on your history, there are bright lights in the darkness that we can pursue."

"I am not the only possible genius that could do the work," Royston said. "The last thousand years of human history have been an astounding collection of small inventions that opened the doors to previously unimaginable things, just because of human propensity to ask *What if?*"

"Exactly, but if you are not a threat to break out of your home system in the next decade, the Commission does not need to panic and overreact in consequence today," Fatima said. "We can try to find another way."

"There are many who might welcome the *Accord of Souls* meddling in human culture," Pippa noted. "Moreso than you have. Perhaps more publicly, if you will."

"Yes, indeed, daughter," Royston nodded. "But there are others who would object strenuously. Demagogues forever threaten, and it would not take much to rouse a mob at the possibility that intelligent aliens are out there. Then you have the very war we are trying to prevent. Thus the tightrope we must walk."

"Could Earth Force be strengthened?" Pippa asked, more rhetorically than with any seriousness. "Would that help or hinder our cause?"

Royston noted that Fatima sat silently, observing and probably preparing a report based on this conversation. As she should.

"It probably harms us, at least in the short term," Royston mused, letting his mind wander over the things Earth Force was created to prevent, such as wars, and how Sky Force might be twisted by a charismatic, amoral charlatan. "What was fascism, the worst of the Twentieth Century ideologies, but the pursuit of power for the sake of power itself, rather than the betterment of humanity? Better that we shatter the edifice and allow a war that grinds us back down to the iron age, than we turn outwards and conquer a defenseless galaxy."

Pippa shuddered, but made no argument. Pain for a few billion humans, stacked against the deaths of how many trillions of intelligent beings? Royston had no expectations that the better angels of humanity would prevail, at least at first. And how the *Accord's* psionic harmony might react to a human invasion was something he could happily go to his grave without knowing.

The air seemed to have recovered that chill it had as the sun first rose, but there was nothing to do about it, except soldier on.

"I think it would serve us best if our trip across the badlands of the Nevada Territory was now cut somewhat short," Royston decided aloud. "England would, I believe, be a better choice at present, as long as we are careful."

"What would be the problem with home, father?" Pippa asked.

"I fear what devilment Sir Westfield might get up to, were he to discover we were close," Royston stated. "Unless you think a visit to Buckingham might aid our quest."

He rather liked the way Pippa's face turned to alabaster. Fatima's brows knit together in concern.

"Buckingham Palace," Royston smiled at the other woman. "The home of the Queen of England and her family. Sir Westfield, who was one of my mentors, remains one of her favorites, and the Queen has taken a keen interest in my recent studies. If our presence became known, we may not be able to escape a meeting, yourself most likely included. Given the sensitivities of the subject, I would rather forebear, at least this once."

He rose and began packing things up as the women processed the future. The fire was easy enough to smother with dirt. The pavilion undid itself with a simple button, converting down to a portable unit not much larger than a lunch box. The women quickly joined him in organizing things into the rear of the truck, as he and Pippa had put everything away after sleeping inside last night.

"Now would be a nice time to be able to just step onto a disk and emerge in London," Royston laughed as the truck slowly began to descend the mountains, turned around and headed toward the Gulf Coast again, eventually. "But those are the sorts of labor-saving inventions that might make things worse, so I will simply endeavor to drive us to a spot where the auto-controller unit might take over. Or not. Suffice it to say, we can be in London in a week, if we were to drive to someplace like Boston at a leisurely pace and then catch a flight."

"Perhaps we should not necessarily stop and smell the roses this time, Father?" Pippa noted from the rear.

"Yes, indeed," Royston sighed. "Our destiny awaits us in Merry Old England, I fear. Avoiding it will save us nothing."

Eat, drink, and be merry, indeed, as the ancient saying went. Tomorrow we may all indeed die.

ZATHUS

TECHNICALLY, Gareth had been on *Zathus*, according to Xiomber, but had only passed through the system for the briefest of instants, before being further shunted off into a second tube, to land on *Orgoth Vortai*, where the adventure truly began.

The sky overhead was a little too purple for Gareth as they emerged from the transport. The truck had dropped them at a new Constabulary facility, a small training base just outside the city limits of Seani that reminded Gareth of the ancient National Guard Armories that many states back home still maintained, mostly as vehicle depots for emergencies.

Tall, cyclone fence around the grounds. Red brick buildings two and three stories tall. A garage off to one side that was nothing but closed bay doors right now, with a gravel quad in front and grass over to one side.

Constabulary officers were coming and going as the group organized themselves in front of one of the smaller buildings, but nobody paid much attention, even when only three of the six wore uniforms. Morty and Xiomber had successfully pled their cases to be allowed out in their comfortable, blue dungarees and black t-shirts, although Morty's had a phrase across the front that was right on the borderline of rude and profane, even if it was apparently the name of a musical band.

Talyarkinash wore dark gray: pants, chemise, tunic, and light jacket in various shades and fabrics that flowed together well.

Grodray led them into the building at a pace that left the shorter half of the party almost jogging to keep up, but he wasn't doing it out of spite. Grodray was just like that when he got focused. Inside, the building was apparently unused, at least for now. Gareth was at once reminded of an armory barracks, empty most of the time, with things in storage except for the regular musters once a month and the big training formation annually.

The inside was a big, open bullpen filled with desks, rather like a Constabulary office where Constables and other detectives would work. Forty people could be active in here at any given time, without being too crowded, assuming that one of the other buildings had a canteen running, or you had access to a vehicle to take you to a nearby donut shop.

They were utterly alone in here.

"I have made arrangements for us to bunk upstairs," Grodray announced to the group. "We'll mess with the training cadres over in the main building, which include civilians, so not being in uniform should not present any difficulties. If you feel the need for morning or evening calisthenics, feel free to join the groups in the quad. Eve, I would appreciate if you kept your morning runs inside the fence, just running laps for now. The neighborhoods around here are lower middle class, for the most part, but I expect eyes and ears on the street. They can watch you from over there, but not hassle you personally without inviting more trouble than they ever dreamed possible."

The way he said that last left goosebumps on Gareth's arms. He had seen Baker angry a time or three, but Grodray was always the calm, intellectual type. Rather like Royston Loughty in that, although more of a hands-on type than the scientist back home.

Gareth angrily suppressed the flinch that wanted to shiver through his body. Pippa would be better off without him, if he could somehow convince them he was dead. She might not like it, but she would find a way to move on and have a life, rather than just hanging on forever.

"Dankworth?" Grodray asked.

Apparently, he had detected something.

Gareth shook his head and remained silent.

"Okay, then upstairs and pick out your rooms from the officer's area," Grodray said.

Gareth found all their clothing had apparently been packed and sent ahead, as there were footlockers with names on them in the waiting area at the top of the stairs. Quickly enough, everyone had rooms, with him third down, past Grodray and then Baker, followed by Talyarkinash and then the boys beyond a short gap.

They met up back in the upstairs area, which was filled on one side with empty triple bunks that were human sized, and the other was a lounge area where you could read or watch videos on a personal device. The majority of the population on *Zathus* was Warreth and Nari, with significant populations of Ramasayia and Enjev, so the human scale made sense, but at least his room was Vanir-sized.

"Okay," Grodray gathered them all together. "Dr. Liamssen, you, Xiomber, and Morty will be able to work here without much interruption, as we've brought over as much gear as you had there, and all your notes. Mostly, you'll continue what you were doing before, which was explore what's happening that Gareth's Star Dragon is suddenly bigger, while trying to identify what we might expect from Sarzynski. Baker, Dankworth, and I will be out on the streets."

"Any of my old friends still around?" Morty asked.

"Doubtful," Baker smiled. "We've either arrested everyone on your list, or chased them so deep under a new rock that they can't even find themselves."

"If that's the case, then you really only have two viable options," Xiomber interjected. "Either a second Star Dragon, which I doubt, or another rogue tube station, like we had here before Morty blew it up."

"Why do you doubt a dragon?" Grodray asked.

"Not his type, old Maximus," Xiomber grinned. "Hell, just convincing him to turn into a Vanir was a big enough pain in the tail. He only went along because *One*: he had to hide in plain sight, and *Two*: we made him the biggest, damned Vanir you could imagine. Those killer robots tell me he's not doing anything more to make himself a monster."

"We've cut off his friends here, for the most part," Morty chirped in. "Like I said earlier, I'm thinking you best look for him on Earth at this point."

"We've got all of the *Accord of Souls* to look in as well," Grodray said. "But I agree that he'll get tired of running. That's why we're here. We've got to find him, and stop him from getting to Earth, because if he uplifts their technology to what we have, then he can come back at the head of an army. The First Inspector has already made it clear to several of us that that is something we can never allow. If it gets to that point, they are prepared to take extreme measures."

"How extreme?" Gareth asked quietly.

Grodray nodded at him before speaking.

"As bad as you surmise, Gareth," Grodray said sternly. "They would be prepared to wipe out all humanity instead of allowing them to escape. You would be the last human."

"I'm not human anymore, Senior Constable," Gareth replied. "I am a Vanir now, even if I cannot join the *Accord of Souls* properly. At least, nobody has figured out how yet. And I am a Star Dragon. But I agree, I might have to be the last, if the alternative is a human crusade against the galaxy. As long as I can kill Sarzynski first."

"It may come to that, Gareth," Baker explained simply.

"I've known that for over several years, Eveth," Gareth replied. "Why do you think I've been trying so hard to prevent the rest now?"

THE CHASE

MARC HAD MISSED this part of the job. He was supposed to be in charge these days, and that meant that he sent others out to pull heists, but truly, there was nobody he knew round here with the skill or panache to do this.

Maiair was close. She had a cool head under that crest, as well as a willingness to shoot someone if pushed. Yooyar, on the other hand, would probably just shoot at the first sign of trouble.

Mishalska, the young Nari punk, was turning into a proper soldier these days, training himself harder than anyone else in the gang. It was almost like being back home on the football field. Watching that one kid who had no size or strength trying to compete with bigger, faster, stronger boys for playing time. That kid had had heart beyond anybody, finally getting to play a few meaningless downs at the end of his last game of his senior year, because Coach had never once seen him flag. Every down in every practice was approached like the winning play at the championship game.

Mishalska reminded Marc of that kid.

Zorge was home minding the store, so Marc had only those people with him.

Oh, and one of three remaining androids. Zorge had the other two, guarding the base against surprises, but Marc figured he could manage this possibly alone.

He needed the others because he still needed others. Gonquah had come perilously close to breaking Marc free of needing anyone in the *Accord of Souls*, before Gareth and that woman Constable, Baker, had taken him down.

Fine. You people want to play rough? Watch this.

Marc could have told these fools that the best way to move stolen and illegal parts around was to do it in the middle of the day. In the worst of the rush hour traffic. A time when the beat cop was too busy trying to direct traffic to step in and look closely at a tractor and trailer toodling along, running low on the axles because the equipment in back was too heavy to even move on repulsors.

Doing it in the dead of night, on abandoned back roads was just an invitation for someone to come along with guns and hijack it.

Marc smiled. Beside him, driving the small truck, Maiair smiled back, as if she could read his mind. Certainly, she had the best brain for it of all of them. She would make a good queen, a Grand Duchess of his new Empire.

In back, Mishalska and the android appeared to be competing with one another to be the most silent.

"One," Yooyar's voice came over the comm. "Countdown."

"Two," Marc picked up the device and keyed it. "Acknowledged."

There. Nothing incriminating, unless you were already paranoid and listening on all bands. Plus you would have to recognize the voices that quickly, and understand that the truck had just crossed the first intersection, coming off the highway, where his killer Warreth babe was sitting in another vehicle, a stolen car this time that nobody would notice until tomorrow.

Marc leaned forward just a little and looked down the long straightaway of the road. He had picked it because the road was old and narrow, almost an alley between a tall, brick wall outside an underworked factory on one side, and several new and used vehicle lots on the other.

If it had been Marc, he probably would have been able to break the ambush by jumping a curb and smashing his way through the parked cars, relying on weight and momentum to get him clear enough, fast enough. Noise and alarms here would bring police in a hurry, but they would have picked an innocent to drive.

Just another load that needed to be delivered tonight, officer. Don't know what was in it that made men and women with guns want it.

Or something like that.

There. Headlights as the vehicle rolled to a four-way stop, precisely looked all directions, and then made a right hand turn onto this narrow street.

I have you now.

"Pull forward and set your brake," Marc ordered, loud enough for the two in back to hear.

Maiair engaged the vehicle and drove it out of the little side alley they had chosen, pretty much blocking the lane and turning the road into a cul-de-sac.

"Everyone out now," Marc commanded, opening the door on his side and moving quickly around to the other side of the panel van. Wouldn't do be standing in front of an on-rushing vehicle, especially if anyone in the cab recognized him and decided to collect the bounty tonight.

The truck began to slow as he saw the roadblock. He wasn't going that fast to begin with, but he didn't immediately jam on his brakes and try to back out of the trap.

Pity. Should have.

Yooyar's stolen car rounded the corner and blocked him in. Rather than try to straddle the middle, she turned it diagonally and jumped out. Even from here Marc could see the glint of streetlights off the heavy disintegrator in her hand.

The driver of the big truck finally realized what was going on.

And panicked.

Marc couldn't see the whites of his eyes from here, but he could imagine them. The truck suddenly made a low roaring sound as the driver downshifted the gearbox for power and mashed the accelerator to the floor.

He was going to try to brush the van aside with his mass.

Inwardly, Marc had to give the man credit. He had been expecting an innocent who would roll over politely at this point. He had gotten a soldier apparently willing to push.

Marc drew his own heavy disintegrator and fired a shot past the hood of his van into the ground about midway between the vehicles. The asphalt steamed madly and exploded upward with rubble from the heat, but the driver didn't seem to flinch.

"Shoot the tires?" someone asked. It might have been Yooyar on the radio, he couldn't tell without taking his eyes off the impending avalanche of steel and chrome death.

"Everyone step back from the van," he roared over the sound of the truck closing.

He fired another shot, this time at a transformer box on a power pole. It exploded with a sound like a war, an echo that probably woke up half the town, only to discover that they had lost power.

Sparks flew everywhere, as well as a petite fireball ascending into the night sky.

Marc moved to a spot where he could dive to safety back in the alley where they had parked earlier. He raised his pistol and centered it on the driver's side of the windshield, falling into the classic stance of a Sky Patrol shooter: second hand cupped under the grip. Right foot pulled back behind him for stability. Hunched slightly. Eye, gunsight, and eternity about to pass to the horizon through the cab of the truck. Low, too, just about through the steering wheel, so you couldn't duck and hope.

You'd lose control of the vehicle if you did, at the very moment when it slowed way down from hitting a smaller van. Marc and his people would be able to swarm you, and they would be angry.

Marc doubted stories of human psychic ability. Nobody had ever been able to demonstrate such things in front of a scientific audience.

At the same time, his posture left no doubt as to his intent, and his willingness to kill at this point. The driver understood.

Inside the cab, the being jammed his brakes to the firewall and pressed the clutch down at the same time. Even that much mass can stop quickly, when you find the will to survive sure death.

The monster rig rolled to a stop less than a foot from the van.

Marc was up on the sideboard with the pistol pointed in quickly, but even as fast as he moved, the Nari driver already had his hands up and face turned to look at his ambushers.

Marc tried the door, found it locked.

"Open this," he snarled, centering the pistol on the man.

The driver reached over very carefully and clicked the lock.

Marc ripped the door open almost as fast as Maiair got the passenger side open.

"I surr-surr-surrender," the driver stammered.

"Out," Marc ordered him. "Mishalska, get in."

Wonder of wonders, the kid had known how to drive a rig like this, so Marc had not needed to recruit or kidnap someone to handle it.

Out on the street, Marc took the man's pocketcomm and smashed the face against a stone wall. That was good enough for now. Disintegrating it would have just been mean, as the man would have lost everything stored on it forever.

This could be fixed in a day.

"Start walking north," Marc ordered, gesturing the man back the way he came and away from his destination.

The Nari driver looked for the briefest moment like he wanted to argue, before he shrugged silently and started walking.

"Move it, people," Marc called to his team, but they were already moving.

Maiair quickly backed the van into the alley out of the way as her sister and the android climbed in, leaving the stolen car blocking the road behind them. Marc moved to the passenger side of the rig and watched his own Nari driver get it into motion.

Step one complete.

Now Marc just had to build himself a portal, so his new army could come over and show these people how it was really done.

HUNTER

THE SKY in this planet was still too purple, but at least the sun had set. Gareth had long since given up trying to identify constellations in the night sky, since much of the *Accord* was never closer than one thousand light years from *Earth*, but it did bring him some level of peace, just glancing up at the diamonds in the firmament of night.

He was dressed in his favorite cowboy outfit tonight. The place he was going wasn't a rough honky-tonk on the edge of town, where this outfit would go unnoticed, but a more upscale event, where he would draw whispers.

As intended.

He was bait. But even a stalking horse pinned for a tiger can kick, so he wasn't that concerned for his own safety. Besides, he might also be the tiger here. That thought brought a smile to his face as he approached the front gates of the facility, and the two Vanir that had been hired to check tickets.

Gareth had no clue how many such organizations his cover identity belonged to. With the Constabulary budget involved, he didn't pay any dues, just got tickets to a fund-raiser for some charitable organization from a messenger when he needed to go somewhere. And it was a good cause, so he didn't feel bad as a mole penetrating these echelons of social strata and perhaps spreading his middle-class American values all over the locals.

He was just sorry that Diệu Ahn was unable to join him. He made an even more effective secret agent when she was busy distracting everyone in the room with her competition to show off just a little more skin than was proper, at whatever event she chose to attend. Nobody usually even remembered she had a Plus One, afterwards.

But tonight was a different thing. The time for subtle was past, as the two Vanir men at the front gate inspected his ticket and very politely passed him into the interior. Prime tickets, apparently, at least according to Grodray. Requiring a middle-class manager's monthly salary just to purchase.

Serious money. Just none of it his.

Gareth's grin was irrepressible as he crossed the courtyard and climbed the eight, granite steps to the front door of the mansion. As back home, people with money had a tendency to want to show it off. Thus, a private fund-raiser in the home of some fabulously wealthy philanthropist.

Except this worthy had shown up in Gonquah's records. More than once. The secret records that weren't supposed to exist, suggesting that the man was perhaps not as clean and upright as his public persona appeared.

Elnon Ruaidhrí really did have a gorgeous home. Almost Georgian, in a place that had no idea who George was or what he might have meant to architecture. White marble exterior with three stories and pillars in front. Windows everywhere. Two long wings of the building reaching each direction from the massive foyer with twin staircases, each covered over with a lush, red carpet.

Perhaps half of the invited guests were already here, mostly in the process of moving from one place to another. Gareth felt a momentary twinge at being so underdressed, with everyone else gone to the nines and gems, but he was a reporter tonight, an outsider supposed to draw glares from the beautiful people.

And his smile could not be helped. He was back in the field, and playing a little game with himself tonight to guess how many of these people were also crooks in disguise.

A few faces he recognized from other parties, mostly with Diệu Ahn, but at this level the circles tended to be small enough. Interestingly, a significant chunk of the guests were Vanir, where he had been one of only a handful, other times.

Gareth passed through the foyer into a grand salon beyond where a side table was filled with finger foods. Wait staff with trays circulated, distributing tall flutes of wine and champagne, although he wasn't sure you could call it that, if it didn't originate in the French countryside. Still, lovely. And ticklish.

The crowd was a little thicker here, perhaps the gravitational center of the party, after all. The host was a Vanir, mostly holding court as Gareth meandered in.

One face jumped out at him as he moved to the fringes of a group studying a portrait of Ruaidhrí's parents over the mantle. Gareth nearly broke cover as his jaw dropped, because he had been expecting her here, just not like *that*.

Eveth Baker had rarely appeared around Gareth in anything more or less than the bodysuit of a Constable. It was a skin-tight outfit that covered her over in armored scales and authority, but she had left it at home tonight.

Instead, she wore a white, silk sheath that clung to every curve and plunged precariously in inviting places. Diệu Ahn would have gone out in such an outfit. Someone had done Baker's hair up, as well as her makeup, so Gareth assumed a professional, as Eveth never did neither herself.

Still: *Wow*.

She caught Gareth staring and grinned for just a moment. Grodray, on her arm, looked every inch the gentleman at leisure, in what Gareth would have classed as herringbone tweeds. Close enough.

"And how are we finding the occasion?" Gareth finally managed to ask, turning beside Baker so as to pretend to stare at the portrait over the mantle.

It was hideous. And he could say that with a professional opinion, given the amount of art he had been required to study and memorize recently. Ruaidhrí's parents looked almost demonic, as though the artist had intentionally overdone the reds and shadows in a way that left their skin almost sallow.

Grodray grunted with something approaching disgust.

"There is a rumor," Baker whispered to Gareth as they stood. "That Elnon took the original portrait and had it retouched later, to reflect his opinion of his sires."

"Do original pictures exist for comparison?" Gareth asked, dipping into his training.

"No one knows," she replied.

"Still, a useful tidbit," Gareth said. "Enjoy your evening."

He bowed to the two of them, as if they were strangers, and departed, seeking other clues and memorizing the layout of things, just in case he ever needed to break in at a later date.

Or just kick in the door with an arrest warrant in hand.

Gareth let the tides of the room draw him slowly around to where his host was standing with a group of people. They were the only two Vanir in this room at the moment, as shorter folks and staff came and went, so Gareth nodded to the man over the heads of a pair of Warreth with jewels in their head-crests.

"You look familiar," Elnon said, obviously trying to place a familiar-enough face.

"*Morthri*," Gareth supplied. "One of Gonquah's rolling parties, if I recall correctly."

He did. Perfectly. Tonight, however, was his role an art critic and reporter who just happened to recognize a face as well, as opposed to having read the man's hefty file, listing all the places where nobody had ever quite gathered enough evidence to put it to a grand jury. Until about a month ago, when Gonquah got arrested.

"Yes, of course," the man nodded. "On the yacht. How silly of me to forget. Enjoying things? Gareth, right?"

"That's right," he replied. "Rather enjoying the art and architecture. I was mildly surprised when the invite arrived and had your name affixed, as I had no idea you were such a collector. Had I known, I'd have probably been beating down your door long before this."

The two Warreth sensed the change in local environment and made polite excuses to abandon ship, leaving Gareth and Elnon alone for a moment.

"Would you like a grand tour?" Elnon asked. "My wife can handle the crowds for a bit, and this is really more of a meet and greet for the next few hours, at least until the silent auction begins to wind down. Or heat up."

Gareth had noted the collectibles put up for the silent auction tonight and presumed that several of them might bring in a nice annual salary individually, to say nothing of the entire group. This fundraiser would go long ways towards the charity's annual operating budget, all by itself, he gathered.

Pity the man behind it was so crooked.

"That would be lovely," Gareth exclaimed. "Although I might want to come back later with a camera and catch a few interiors and exteriors, just so my editor can put one over on some of the competition. I gather nobody has ever done a full architectural tour before?"

"That's right," Elnon almost preened as he took Gareth's arm in his and directed him to the south wing of the building.

"Truly a shame," Gareth noted as they made their way into a semi-formal library with paintings on the wall and a few sculptures in stone or metal on low pedestals.

Gareth stopped at one painting and cocked his head slightly.

"Early Eldritch Period?" he hazarded a guess quietly. "It's missing some of the later color and shading elements of the school, but I could see where they grow out of this piece."

"Amazing," Elnon said. "Yes, this was one of the very first transitional pieces when things first moved from the Skybourne School. It has been in the family for almost four centuries, so I'm not sure it has ever been seen in public. How did you know?"

"The Skybourne School always struck me as far too pretentious in their overemphasis on the blues and the use of that damnable, clay paint to add a third dimension to things." Gareth let his mouth sour, just a touch. He really hated that period of *Accord* art. "The Eldritch period reverted to two dimensions, and required the artist to master them well enough to force you to see the third, rather than cheating."

"Well said," Elnon agreed, turning them deeper. "I have a few other pieces in the private wing that should simply unravel you then."

"Lead on, then," Gareth smiled. "I find a sophisticated collector so rare a treat. Too many of them are *nouveau riche* pretenders who hire a buyer and never bother to actually learn about the art underlying."

"This collection has been slowly evolving for a little over five hundred years, my dear man," Elnon's voice got haughty, as expected. He really was old money on this planet. "I have taken it to heights previously undreamt of."

Gareth smiled and let the man lead him deeper into portions of the building no cop had ever seen.

STALKING HORSE

"SO WHAT DO WE KNOW?" Eveth asked as they assembled the next morning.

She was back in her armored bodysuit, feeling more like an professional and less like a bimbo. Undercover work required those sacrifices occasionally, but all she'd had to do last night was watch and study. Gareth, of all people, had managed to play to the target's vanity without them needing her as a pretty face to seduce the man.

But art nerds were a breed apart, and they had already established the Star Dragon with the perfect cover to penetrate that aspect of *Accord* society looking for bad people.

Eveth just wished that crime wasn't such a profitable venture for people. The *Accord* wasn't supposed to be so riddled with corruption. And she would happily take up a second career if they could somehow manage to put all the bad people in jail to the point that the Constabulary was no longer needed to keep the peace.

"Security system is possibly past State of the Art," Grodray replied.

It was just her, him, and Gareth this morning, in a small, private room reserved for a local officer in the unit.

"Past?" she turned and stared at him to clarify.

"I identified a few places where Elnon had installed things I couldn't even identify, let alone defeat," Grodray shrugged. "Not a problem if we just move in an arrest the man. However, trying it represents a problem."

"Correct," Eveth commiserated. "That might trigger Maximus to go underground again."

"Are we sure he's even here?" Gareth asked. "Would he risk staying put if the three of us are poking around?"

"That's what we need to find out," she said. "All the records we retrieved from Gonquah hinted at a connection between Elnon and Maximus, to the point that Elnon was the one that introduced them, but there has been nothing we could use to take him down. His legal team is too good and everything is far enough removed from his person as to make him invisible. Or invincible, as it might be."

"And nobody else had anything better?" Gareth asked.

"It all got burned," Grodray grunted. "Either metaphorically or literally, in a few instances. People panicked and scrammed computers hard enough to eliminate any possibility of recovering data from them. And if you pour water on warm ashes and stir vigorously, you'll get the same effect."

"Well, I agree with you that any paper records the man keeps will be detailed and meticulous," Gareth opined. "He just had to show off a few of the chains of acquisition around some of the more interesting pieces. Nothing illegal, although he was well beyond ethical behavior to accomplish some of it. But yes, everything is in a nested series of trusts and corporate entities so dense that they might stop a bullet."

"You saw paper records?" Eveth perked up.

"Yes," Gareth explained. "In art, you have to show a complete chain of ownership, all the way back to the original artist, to validate that you have something that is, in fact, not a forgery. That's where most forgers get caught. Copying a painting is relatively easy, but you have to spoof the ownership paperwork, and their professionalism frequently gets the better of them."

"Professionalism?" Grodray asked, eyebrows rising.

"They can't stomach a badly-formatted document, so everything is a little too perfect," Gareth said. "That sets people like me off. Can't tell you how many case files I read where the original, legitimate paperwork showed gaps that were filled in later with initials and dates on the sides, because something passed quickly a few times, and then sat in some dowager aunt's living room for fifty years unrecognized. You have to start a new chain, and then staple it to an incomplete one from the last company that insured a valuable piece."

"Huh," Grodray observed. "You all set to go into art fraud, after we catch Maximus?"

"It was that or a jail cell," Gareth grinned at the Senior Constable. "Needed to make myself valuable as a Constabulary agent somehow."

"But Art Fraud?"

"Jack, it was your idea," Eveth pointed out. "Use that eidetic memory of his for something useful."

"Well, yeah."

"So he's gotten us in the door a number of places," she concluded before turning to Gareth. "Can you get us inside to maybe crack his personal safe and find the key we need to turn him?"

She liked the way Gareth's face screwed up in concentration. He was a brilliant officer, much of the time, and was taking the time to think right now, rather than just blurting out an answer based on masculine ego.

"You two are too well known to accompany me inside on my next run," Gareth finally replied. "I would assume he'll remember both of you from the party, assuming he ever looked as high as your face, Eveth."

She started to say something tart, but blushed when she saw the smile on Grodray's face. Gareth was at least earnest.

"What will you need?" she asked, rather than sputter at the two men.

Again, serious pause as Gareth broke into the building in his mind, walking through the rooms to the office that apparently had no windows. His hands even pantomimed the process unconsciously.

"There was a dead space," Gareth finally said. "A spot that I can't account for, thinking back and counting steps."

"How big was it?" Grodray leaned forward almost as quickly as she did. They shared a knowing glance.

"Maybe six or eight feet deep," Gareth mused, eyes unfocused. "Depending on what the walls were made of. It ran between Elnon's bedroom and that office. The closet didn't seem that deep, when I glanced in, compared to the sumptuousness of the bathroom event."

"Event?" Eveth asked, unsure if she had heard the word correctly.

"Event," Gareth confirmed. "Bigger than my current cabin on *Irron* by about double. Makeup counter for his wife. Water closet that really was a closet. Double shower. Oversized, jetted tub that could hold six in a friendly orgy. Gold metal as tiles and plating everywhere, mixed with maroon and blue."

"Panic room?" Grodray asked.

"What's that?" Gareth turned to the older cop.

"If someone breaks in and the owner panics, he can retreat to a small, secured room, armored on all sides, with a separate water and HVAC system and hard-set communications to the outside world, to call for help. They are designed to be proof against anything hand-held, on the logic that you want someone alive."

"I didn't think the *Accord* was into that sort of thing?" Gareth asked, face all confused.

"Criminals almost always turn on each other eventually, Gareth," Eveth noted. "If you had enough money and bad friends, it might be a very useful thing to be able to be able to hide from them while calling the Constables to save you."

"Yeah, but that sounds too defensive," Gareth squinted at something she couldn't identify. "I'd want my bolt hole to have an escape hatch."

"Why?" it was Grodray's turn to get serious.

"You're in a small box, sure, but now I've trapped you there," Gareth said. "What's to stop me bringing something heavy enough to cut a wall away, if I don't mind smashing the rooms behind whatever beam I cut loose?"

"Tunnel?" Eveth asked.

"We were on the second floor of the North Wing," Gareth's eyes unfocused again and he started counting steps while she held her breath. "Crap."

"What?" she asked.

"There's another dead space on the first floor," Gareth said. "Not far from the Grand Salon. I put it down at the time as a simple pillar stabilizing things, but it's almost exactly under the blank space, maybe six feet across. Ladder down to first floor or maybe the basement?"

"North wing? Just beside the main rest room on the ground floor?" Grodray asked.

"Correct, where the bathroom looked like it had space for a second stall on the left, but the wall juts out at an odd angle."

"What's in the basement?" Eveth asked.

"Garage for his vehicle collection." Gareth started to say. "Crap. Of course. Pop out down below, jump in a car, run like hell."

"Yes, but that means we can get in that way as well," Eveth said. "When you tour the place again, get me pictures we can use for a floorplan diagram."

"Yes, ma'am," he smiled at her.

Eveth finally felt like they were getting somewhere. You didn't need a panic room, with as much other security as Elnon had, unless you were expecting trouble from people experienced at bypassing such systems, or willing to just blow them up in the process of the breaking part of breaking and entering.

One more note in the symphony. One more knot she had to undo, to make the galaxy safe again.

ART CRITIC

"SO GOOD TO SEE YOU AGAIN," Gareth heard as the auto-taxi dropped him in front of Elnon Ruaidhrí's mansion and flew off again.

Gareth waved and climbed those steps to greet the man at the door. As *Accord* bipeds went, Elnon was giant, but he was a Vanir, and they all were, for the most part. He probably outweighed Gareth by four stone, in spite of being several inches shorter, but Elnon looked like a pudgy, middle-aged businessman, not a field agent who needed to keep in top shape at all times.

They shook hands and Elnon escorted him to the back patio, where the early afternoon sun was just peeking over the building to keep things light but not yet hot. It had dawned an exceptionally gorgeous day, and promised to remain so clear up until sunset, when forecasters promised a fine mist to water everything.

Lunch was something Gareth called steak in his mind, served with something approximating fried mushrooms, at least by texture, and covered over with a rich demi-glace that was better than anything Gareth had ever had. The vegetables on the side were blue or yellow, crunchy, and pan-seared in butter.

It wasn't from a cow, but Gareth was past the point of comparing. They served the same purpose and even produced a similar-enough milk to make cheese and butter. Especially when you had a fantastically gifted chef on staff, apparently with instructions to impress a reporter wanting to let you show off your art collection to the universe.

Gareth belched appreciably and sipped a mug of coffee cut with chocolate and heavy cream in the Italian style.

"Wow," he said, letting that sum up lunch.

Elnon's smile turned up at both ends.

"So how else might I bribe you, old chap?" the art collector asked.

"I spoke with my editor," Gareth replied, referring to Eveth Baker even in his mind that way. "She would like me to get three or four good shots of places like the library and your bedroom, done in such a way that none of your security systems are obvious, so we don't advertise to the common criminal how to crack the place and make off with everything."

"The common criminal, Gareth?" he asked with a wicked tone to his voice.

"I presume that expert art thieves already know about your collection and have possibly tried their luck more than once, but either failed or were simply scared off."

"A little of both," Elnon laughed. "Not all the systems are obvious, and a few times, we have captured such criminals, but generally we don't advertise. But why the bedroom? There's nothing particularly noteworthy there. I prefer simple walls to art."

"There is nothing simple nor common about your bathroom, Ruaidhrí," Gareth laughed in turn. "Remember, in addition to art, we are selling a lifestyle. Your master bathroom is slightly larger than the biggest apartment I've ever had. Granted, I'm constantly traveling on assignment and single, so my needs tend towards the compact, but our readers like to be titillated with what the fabulously wealthy do with their money, while your competitors will suddenly demand that their interior decorator rip everything out and upgrade it, just to be better than yours."

That bolt struck home, as Gareth had known it would.

The rich all seemed to be alike in that way. Either they prefer to live simple, quiet lives where they alone knew they had money, or they actively competed with one another for ostentation. Take Gonquah and his yacht that was larger than Gareth's first independent command, the space-based Patrol Cutter *Bellerophon*, back on Earth. And the yacht never left the surface of that one planet.

"Oh, and perhaps a few shots of your vehicle collection would be useful as well," Gareth tossed that note in there nonchalantly. "Show everyone you are a well-rounded man of culture, and not just an art collector with some interesting paintings."

For a moment, Elnon's eyes grew dark and menacing, but then the gist of the phrase got through and he suddenly smiled.

"Yes, indeed," Elnon agreed. "This is so much more than merely art. It is, as you said, an entire lifestyle. Come, let us be off."

Gareth let go of the breath he had been holding and followed the man back into the building. As before, he counted steps carefully, building a three dimensional map in his head of the layout, but didn't bother pulling out his camera until they were upstairs and in that fantastic library.

Gareth fussed, asking questions and looking through the viewfinder as the sun lit the room with just the perfect amount of sunlight to add a line of whiteness to the air. He had wanted that early Eldritch Period piece, just because he couldn't find it any catalog, so it was either bought directly from the artist that many centuries ago, or had ended up here without any provenance at all.

"There," Gareth said, turning the camera around after he had gotten three or four good snaps for the folks back home to use in the future magazine article. "Do you think that captures the essence of the room? I'm thinking that might be the perfect image to lead with, setting you up as a most serious expert, reaching back centuries with the collection."

Elnon smiled proudly as he looked at the image on the screen.

"Yes," he said. "Elegant and subtle. What else would make the article pop?"

"I'd like to get one of you in your office, perhaps reviewing some meaningless paper of some sort at that desk," Gareth continued. "You, conveying forcefully that this is serious business that you must handle personally, instead of, as some others, merely hiring minions and giving them a budget to stock your domicile. Let's separate the serious collector from the poseur."

Again, the man preened, but Gareth understood how to play to Elnon's ego. Part of the journalist's job in something like this was to specifically make the subject look good. To make others jealous and competitive. To give the average wage-earner in their cubicle something to aspire to, or at least dream about.

Because the several magazines that carried Gareth's fictitious byline were all about the aspirational. The *Dream*. Even the Constabulary's help, secretly and quietly providing a significant amount of the funding for it, the folks running the magazine would go broke if they only sold to other elites, interested in outdoing one another. No, the money was in that dream.

In a way, Gareth had to crush the guilt he felt at peddling such a dream to folks that would never achieve it. At the same time, however, this was a much less destructive form of escapism, if he had to pick one, compared to say narcotics or alcohol. In that, he supposed that he was doing a public benefit. And that would make it all right.

The office had not changed. Four solid walls, lined with wood paneling rubbed a dark, rich mahogany that gleamed in the light of the desk lamp. There were no plants in here, but several bookshelves contained both knick-knacks and obviously-treasured tomes of some personal value.

"You sit there," Gareth directed. "Let me find the shot that makes you look the most heroic, and then I'll have you put on your serious face."

Elnon gladly sat, using a thumbprint to open a drawer in the massive desk and pull out a small stack of papers. Gareth didn't bother even glancing at them. Instead, he knelt down and looked at the walls behind his target. Framing the shot.

Looking at the space, there was an area just behind Elnon on his left where there were no bookcases, and only a small trash can designed to hold whatever Elnon needed disposed of, rather than having a flame-chute to immediately annihilate something with fire. Considering his bulk, the other gaps in corners and cases would be too tight a fit, if you wanted to open a concealed door and vanish from sight in a hurry.

Gareth lined up the shot in his mind, and the aimed the camera.

"Now, can you look down and frown seriously, sir?" he asked, snapping several quick images as the man complied.

To take advantage of the light, Gareth shifted to his side and snapped more. And then stood.

"I'm not sure the standing shots will work, but they might also capture your struggle against the entire galaxy, so I'd like a few, just in case," Gareth called.

Somewhere, probably from his mother, he had apparently gotten an eye for this sort of thing, because half a dozen images all looked like keepers to him. An art editor would make that decision, but at least they would have something to work with.

"Perfect," Gareth said, showing him the shots. "Even the overhead ones convey strength. I think my editor would be pleased. How about your bedroom and the bath, next?"

They moved on, and Gareth was pretty sure he could confirm the dead space. Eveth Baker had decided it was too risky to bring in any sort of portable scanner, camouflaged as something else, so Gareth had to just rely on intuition and whatever images he could get.

Nothing would be obvious, that much was clear. The man would have hidden any switches in such a way that even random chance would not reveal them. But at the same time, Gareth wouldn't need to break in this way, if they could access the space from below.

He could only hope.

And that damned bathroom had lost nothing on the second pass. He expected a number of folks would unhappily call their interior decorator after seeing these pictures and then make impossible demands about out-doing it. In that, his article on Elnon Ruaidhrí would be successful, if they ever ran it.

Wouldn't be of much value of course, if the man was in prison. Unless his wife was clean, and somehow managed to keep it in the face of Constabulary Auditors with green eyeshades and sharp pencils.

And Gareth managed a couple of good shots of the bedroom that just happened to catch the open closet door. Nothing much in there, except a confirmation of depth, side by side.

Downstairs, they went.

Gareth took a moment to use the main floor restroom as they did, partly because he'd had a lot of good coffee, and partly to measure that column of space against his memory. It only stood out because it made the room an awkward shape. All things considered, the man might have been better off moving a couple of other walls sideways, just so he could have a regular bathroom that didn't stand out in someone's memory like this.

As far as vehicles went when they got the underground garage, it was obvious that Elnon wasn't particularly interested in them. At least, not to the depth of some of the gearheads Gareth had known back home, or here in the *Accord*.

Xiomber, for example, would nerd out about private vehicles at the drop of a hat. They were rare in most cities, since auto-taxis could get you anywhere on short notice, including to orbit and across a wormhole tube, if you asked. But at the same time, not everyone wanted one, and they were not a requirement. Few people had or even needed their own car or flying sled to get around.

In that, Elnon showed money, but not much interest. He had a sleek, two-seater job in midnight blue that just screamed speed, especially from the way the landing gear would fold up into the bottom and give you smooth lines.

A larger vehicle was obviously intended to transport the man and his wife or business associates in luxury, facing each other across a small table where they could talk in comfort or negotiate in privacy. Beyond that, the *Accord* equivalent of a four-door sedan, presumably for the rarely-seen Mrs. Ruaidhrí to go places and do things.

Finally, a big box on wheels. Must be for hauling heavy loads around, except that the staff didn't look like the type. Perhaps, like an auto-taxi, you could dispatch it to pick something up, instead of relying on a delivery service to get around to you.

Still, for two people, an impressive garage. Gareth assumed that the nearly-invisible staff largely stayed in the other wing of the building from the master, and came and went via auto-taxi like normal people.

But it let him get significant pictures down in the underground space, including the ramp up and out the side, several sets of staircases, some of which were outdoors instead of into the building itself.

Pacing things off, Gareth also located a space that was surrounded by a small box of cyclone fencing, rather like where some office buildings would have people store bicycles out of the way in a parking garage. And it was in the right place for the rest of the column he was seeking, so Gareth walked all the way around to get the most shots.

"Why the vehicles, anyway?" Elnon asked as Gareth wrapped things up. "There's nothing particularly impressive here, as cars were never my thing."

"True, but consider how many people out there have never owned any private vehicles themselves, relying instead on auto-taxis and public transport their whole lives," Gareth nodded. "You have a stable, so you have wealth. At the same time, it's not that hollow ostentation that will turn some people off. As you said, you're not all about fast cars, too, so that will make you more personable, more impressive when they see the rest."

Gareth fixed him with a cold, calculating eye that was more journalist and art critic than cop. It felt weird, but it was also important.

"They want to pretend to be you, Ruaidhrí," he said firmly. "So you must be intimidating and fierce, but you must also be approachable, if they ever suddenly become fabulously wealthy themselves and run into you casually. That's the dream we sell. That's why people will buy the magazine. Does that make sense?"

Elnon paused for a moment, introspective.

"It does," he replied. "I just don't think I've ever run into someone with your level of passion for both the art and the journalism. If I get interviewed, they rarely know much, as this is just an assignment between doing a library opening and a wedding."

"More the fool them," Gareth let his own face turn to a scowl that wasn't pretend. "However, you have been most gracious, letting me take up your time this afternoon. I think I have what I need at this point, and my current schedule assumes that I'll have something written up for a quick review by your folks in about three weeks, if that works?"

"That would be lovely," he replied. "I'll be at a conference in a few days, and gone for about a week all told, so that timing lets me handle my other business first."

Gareth continued small talk as the man graciously ushered him out the front door, to a waiting auto-taxi.

As he rose into the sky, Gareth finally let himself smile. If the man was truly going to be gone, and Baker and Grodray would have the resources to confirm that, that would make his task so much easier.

And he might still write everything up. If the Constabulary seized everything, they would need to know how to value such a rare and probably priceless collection.

At least they had an expert on hand.

PORTALS

IT WAS A HACK JOB. Marc was aware of that, but it didn't really matter, as long as it worked.

Zorge and Maiair had brought in a couple of mechanics who worked under the table for the usual bribes, and they had assembled everything quickly enough, once the last bits of material were picked up from the middlemen.

And the suppliers had been willing to fall for the story about Marc needing to have a full set of spare parts up front. That, or perhaps they had understood that it would be easier to do this the first time given the political climate, rather than trying to order replacements later at a time when that was getting more and more difficult.

He had a full wormhole generator system now. Two of them, in fact. One packed up, back in crates after they had confirmed that everything worked, and the second pair assembled to make a full unit. Power would always be a problem, but an emergency system like this had two backup generators to power it, both topped off with enough fuel to last him a long time if he was careful enough to steal more later.

Marc laughed to himself that one of the tiny machines could probably output more power than the oversized, fusion reactors on either of Sky Patrol's primary LaGrange bases, despite being small enough to fit in a steamer trunk. But that would be necessary. Once he stepped through a portal and emerged on Earth, this system would destroy itself and nobody would be able to open it again. Or track where he'd gone.

If something went wrong, he'd be stuck on Earth for the rest of his life. Or at least until Constable Grodray found him. Or Gareth. His comrades would become freak-show performers, assuming the xenophobic peasants back home didn't just kill them out of fear or spite.

Sure, he could easily conquer Earth Force with his new technology, but who wanted to be king of an anthill just outside the walls of Versailles?

"What's so funny?" Maiair asked as the machine wound down from the latest calibrations tests.

The room wasn't all that crowded right now. He and the two Warreth females. The two Nari men. A Grace mechanic and his Vratha journeyman. Everyone else was at the far end of the garage space with the equipment, leaving him space.

"Playing out scenarios in my mind," Marc replied, letting some of the humor remain on his face for her to read. "I imagined all of us trapped on Earth when something went wrong, and having to settle for conquering that whole system for now."

"The Constables would still chase us, correct?" she asked. "Even there?"

"Even there," Marc assured her. "I'm sure they have agents in place somehow. Or at least watchers listening in on the radio signals, so they could report back quickly enough if something like us suddenly conquered Earth."

"You could always turn back into a human, Maximus," Maiair suggested. "That might let you hide. You'd be one grain of sand on a beach."

"I won't settle, Maiair," he growled back. "Everything, or nothing. And we won't be gone long. Just enough to set up a secret base in the Earth system, and I know many places we could do that. Then some recruiting and training, once we break my old comrades to the bit that there really are aliens out there."

"And then Empire?"

"Correct, First Wife," he smiled down at her. "Empire."

The sound was dropping to nothing in the rest of the space as the machines were finally wound down. The Grace mechanic approached, somehow conveying serious respect for Marc while maintaining the sort of attitude that showed he wasn't that impressed.

Marc nodded. A fine balance to strike.

"That's it for now," the man said simply. "We were able to target *Datha* with the scanners and pull something through. That's a representative shot over galactic distances, so everything should be ready. I'd run some more tests, if I were you, at least until so you're comfortable, before you put people through, but you don't need us for that."

He nodded back to his assistant.

"Zorge," Marc called. "You have everything you need?"

"We do," the Nari scientist replied.

Marc pulled an envelope from his inner pocket and handed it to the Grace with a smile.

"Thank you," he said. "We'll be in touch if something arises, but otherwise, I wish you the best of luck with your future."

And he meant it. Good technicians like this were rare. If Marc had just paid him the rough equivalent of two year's salary for this job, that just meant that the Grace would be able to enjoy better vacations or a better home. A better life, for not always having to play by the rules.

Quickly enough, Zorge got the two gone, leaving the inner gang alone.

"Understand this," Marc said. "Our next stop, once Zorge is ready, is a remote hiding place on *Earth*, in the Rocky Mountains not all that far removed from where I was born. Many of the back country places are accessible year around, but we should be timing this to arrive in the hardest part of winter, so the snows will be heavy and people will not be moving around."

"How do we know nobody will be there when we arrive?" Yooyar asked, coming up on her sister's other side.

"We don't," Marc assured her. "But the place I'm planning for has been used by underground gangs for a long time, so anyone we meet there will either be someone we can talk to, or someone we'll need to kill anyway. There will be no cops. And hopefully no sleeping bears."

"Sleeping bears?" Maiair asked, her crest ruffled. "How dangerous can they be?"

"They'll be a foot or two taller than me, covered over with thick fur, and weigh twice as much," Marc grimaced. "Grizzly bears hibernate by sleeping most of the winter, but they rouse occasionally, and can be angry and violent when they do. Shoot them without hesitation, if we encounter one. Understood?"

"This unit understands," the android said.

Everyone else had nodded, so it was a little jarring. Normally, the Ellis device was silent, but had apparently accepted those orders. Which was good. He could trust the killer robot to take down a grizzly.

"Okay, then," Marc concluded. "More tests on the wormhole machine, and then we'll need to figure out how soon we can depart. The next phase of our destiny awaits."

WALK IN THE PARK

ROYSTON HAD HOPED that by coming in to King's Cross station via Manchester and avoiding Westminster, they might be safe. After all, Camden Town had never lost its Bohemian nature, even as the rest of London itself had gentrified, renovated, faded, and reinvented itself over the centuries.

They had taken two rooms above a lovely, old Jazz café that still played live music every night, not all that far from St. Martin's Gardens. After breakfast, the three of them had taken a quick walk around Regent's Park on the Outer Circle, admiring the Zoo but not entering.

Royston had no idea how Terran animals might react to the smells of an alien Grace, and had no interest in finding out. Instead, they had continued the circle, arriving close to London's semi-ancient Central Mosque, where he and Fatima could murmur quietly back and forth. It wasn't her religion, or her heritage, but the woman she was impersonating was duly impressed and knowledgeable, which made it a pleasant experience.

At least until he turned and saw the figure almost stomping towards them on the sidewalk.

"And why, pray tell me, was I not informed you were in town, Loughty?" Sir West demanded as he got within yelling range.

Well, shit.

"Sir West, you remember my daughter, Philippa?" Royston asked as the man came to an angry halt in front of them. Royston pretended to ignore the rage seething off the man. "And may I present Ms. Fatima Darzi, niece of our old friend Firuz Alinejad?"

That deflected him, at least a little bit. Anger might be one thing, but good manners went bone deep with Sir West. Especially as both women were in Women's Auxiliary uniforms.

"Charmed," the old man said with a formal nod, vaguely mollified for the moment.

"Fatima, this is Dr. Sir Westfield van Duren-Abbott," Royston introduced her. "Professor Emeritus of Mathematics at King's College. Fellow of the Royal Society. Past Guardian of the Mathematical Union. Knight Grand Cross, Order of the British Empire. Knight Commander, Order of the Bath. My mentor and a dear friend of Firuz in the old days."

"A pleasure, Sir Westfield," Fatima replied, unsure what to say, obviously, since she could not know if the other Fatima had ever met Sir West in a previous life.

That had already tripped her up once with him. Royston stepped in to protect her.

Now was most assuredly not the time to expand their little conspiracy.

"And?" Sir West focused his ire on Royston again.

The man looked every one of his eighty-three years, with a wild ring of white hair surrounding a sea of liver spots on the bald top. Royston thought that Sir West's tweeds today might be older than Royston was. At least Pippa. The eyes were normally hazel, perhaps raging over into bronze today, and gave lie to the rest of the man's unkempt appearance as a fussy old duffer headed down to the pub for a pint.

"And we just arrived last night, Sir West," Royston tried to placate the man.

At least a little.

Royston wasn't going to let the man push too far. He was on vacation, after all. Even if it might take the form of saving the galaxy from hostile, alien invasion. Royston was still going to enjoy himself, damn it.

"What brings you north this morning, Sir West?" Pippa stepped forward and demurely injected her femininity into the conversation like a delicate perfume.

"Eh? Oh, consulting at Regent's University this month," Sir West took his anger down a notch. "Teaching a small group of advanced students in a special class on calculating the mathematical shape of space as gravity wells intersect."

"Fascinating," Pippa smiled at him. "We're secretly on vacation, but don't tell Alvin that. He thinks we've gone off to find more of Father's magical mathematical equations."

Royston nearly laughed out loud, but managed to contain it. Pippa could probably teach the class along with Sir West. She was certainly doing advanced, post-doctoral work, even if no serious college would ever admit her or Fatima into their graduate programs.

More the fools them.

Sir West focused his eyes on Royston, with silent Fatima nearly forgotten in the background, as intended.

"Alvin tells me that there's a flaw in your math?" the old man of science demanded.

"Perhaps, old friend," Royston allowed. "Remember, when I built the device we both concluded that significant portions of the equations had too large an error factor. Experimental evidence was necessary to see where we hadn't gone far enough."

"Blow up the Earth, Loughty?" Sir West's voice rose, just a bit louder.

"Oh, I don't think the probability gets much above about two percent right now, Sir West," Royston grinned. "Still, that's far too high, all things considered."

"And sneaking off to London?" he demanded. "Alvin said you were in Nevada, of all places."

"It made a useful cover story, Sir West," Royston replied. "What I'm really about right now is finding that young woman musician, and seeing if I can coax lightning to strike a second time."

"There is no space in proper mathematics for black magic, Loughty," Sir West growled, rather like a chipmunk threatening a terrier.

"Agreed, Sir West," Royston let his smile widen. "And yet, look where it has gotten us so far. We might be on the brink of another complete social and cultural revolution in human history, if it proves truly possible to lift a payload into orbit without a rocket. After that, it becomes a question of reach, but the math on the power necessary suggests something like an inverse square or perhaps an inverse cube of distance, so we'll be a considerable amount of time before we might be able to deposit a man on the Saturnine Gas Mining colony."

"You will keep me more regularly updated, young man," Sir West threatened. "And the day after tomorrow I was scheduled to have tea at

Buckingham. You will attend, and provide Her August Majesty with your latest findings. Am I understood?"

"You are, Sir West," Royston bowed, chagrined. "We will contact your office down in The City and get the details tomorrow. Today, however, I damned well intend to enjoy myself as a tourist. That means the Wellington Arch and Nelson's Column shortly, followed by the National Galleries. So be off with you to go torture your poor students."

Sir West bowed to the two women and departed, somewhat chagrined at Royston's own snappiness.

"Well, that went about as bad as I had feared," Pippa said as the man moved off, finishing an apparent morning constitutional, clock-wide around Regents.

"Indeed, daughter," Royston said. "The worst possible luck, but we will just have to make the best of it at the time when it can no longer be avoided."

"Is a visit to the Queen really that terrible, Royston?" Fatima finally broke her silence.

"No," Royston sighed, offering his elbows to the two women so they could walk some more. "It means that we'll be more under surveillance, however well-meaning it might be. We won't be able to just come and go as we please, at a time when I'd like to enjoy my old home town as something more of an innocent. At least one last time."

"I'm not sure I understand, Royston," Fatima's brow furrowed.

"If we fail, all of this will be gone, Fatima," he said. "Returned to a decaying wilderness as man disappears and the animals slowly reclaim it over the next few millennia. No more Mozart or Tchaikovsky, but also no more rock and roll."

That would probably be the worst part, stripping away the future from all these innocents around them, to die unknowing of his failure, but to die nonetheless.

Both women seemed to understand and leaned a little into him as they walked.

UNINVITED GUEST

GARETH WASN'T sure how to ascribe it, but he was willing to offer thanks for the blessing of Tyche, Roman Goddess of Luck. Both of the Ruaidhrí's had departed to attend the conference on *Churquark*, leaving the mansion largely empty.

According to surveillance teams and data collectors, about half the staff had gotten a long weekend, so there was almost nobody in the mansion. And, happily, no dogs. Gareth had a stunner, just in case, as well as a heavy disintegrator pistol, on the off-chance he encountered another Ellis device.

Not all of the killer androids had been accounted for, according to Gonquah's detailed construction records. And they still haunted his nightmares, from time to time.

The exterior of mansion was dark and the moons were both down. Plus there was the promise of rain later, so the sky was dark. Gareth had broken in to Gonquah's factory at Baker's side, and she had decided to repeat that process.

Instead of relying on lifterpacks, however, she was relying on Gareth.

They stood on a nearby block, in a darkened park that was closed at sunset. Both wore their blue-gray bodysuits with built-in scale armor, and dual holsters loaded for bear. Or at least dogs and androids. Grodray had a smaller team than last time, but just as heavily armed, plus more people on call in an emergency.

"Ready?" Gareth asked, glancing around, but he could see no witnesses.

Eveth smiled up and him and nodded.

Gareth took a step back and triggered the transformation into the Star Dragon. It was growing less painful each time, which was good. It was also bad, because he found himself looking forward to the other form. One of these days, he might not to come back to the alien form of a Vanir. What would he do then?

And yes, his eyes seemed a little higher this time, compared to his memory of Baker before. He really was still growing. What would he turn into at this rate?

Eveth turned her back to Gareth as they had practiced and relaxed as his paws came up and encircled her torso. He tried not to think about how he was holding her. And he was happy that a Star Dragon couldn't blush. At least visibly.

"Taking off," Gareth said. "Deep breath."

He could feel her draw the air in through is fingers and he tightened his hold, taking his own breath as he lifted her up and got a running start forward.

It was awkward, with her seventeen stone weight forward of his usual center of gravity, but he adjusted. Plus, it wasn't like he needed to set any speed records here. Just fly her two blocks over and land quietly near a side door, in a part of the mansion where they should be invisible. Still, bringing in lifterpacks would have been awkward, while walking, and would have signaled a problem if they left them outside the building.

Good thing he could fly.

Eveth Baker kept her muscles rigid as he flew, arms down and toes pointed so she didn't flail any.

Just like that, he was silently circling as he judged his landing. Even the quietest auto-taxi made more noise, but his wings flapped as though a large bird.

"Ready?" he repeated himself, quietly.

"Go," Baker replied.

Gareth relaxed and let the instincts Talyarkinash and the Yuudixtl brothers had programed take over. His tail came down as he fought to hover. He couldn't but it let him land like a javelin, rather than requiring a long, swooping pass. Baker's toes touched the turf almost as fast as he did, and then Gareth began to transform back.

At least the shift didn't involve him glowing. That would be weird. Okay, weirder.

How weird was it to turn into a dragon in the first place?

Gareth drew both pistols and backed up against the side of the building. They were below the level of the first floor windows, and thick hedges and trees blocked off any view of from the neighbors.

Baker seemed to be picking the lock with her eyes closed. Seriously. He checked.

She had explained the process to him once, the touch, but he hadn't practiced it. He saw his future either kicking in the door with an arrest warrant, or as a public, secret agent worming his way into the corrupt niches of wealth and breeding that had accumulated over the centuries.

Art Critic was as good as anything else he could have come up with.

The door clicked open, but all she did was turn the knob to confirm she had succeeded. Now she pulled out a small scanner and ran it over the entire frame. That was complicated, since the door was down in a small well, three steps below ground level, but she didn't seem to mind getting dirty.

The device in her hands beeped once and she grunted. Quickly, she pulled a small boring laser from one of her belt pouches and small camera. Gareth listened to all the night sounds, but wanted to watch her work, glancing up occasionally.

Eveth set the beam on a particular spot and quickly drilled a hole in the door frame, into which went the camera.

"Good," she muttered as she studied the tiny screen. "There."

Gareth heard a clicking sound so quiet he might have imagined it, but she pulled the camera back out of the hole and slid everything into pockets. She drew her stunner and glanced at him.

"Grodray. Step one," she said, letting the microphone built into her suit transmit the words.

Grodray wouldn't reply, but his team would know where they were.

Gareth grinned. She had drilled in, located a simple electrical circuit, and jumped it, so opening the door wouldn't break the existing circuit and sound an alarm. Nifty, but Gareth presumed that a cat burglar would do something similar. So the next step was probably where they tripped.

She pulled the door open and listened for bells or something to indicate an alarm. Grodray's team had someone on a Constabulary circuit, ready to interrupt the local police if they got an alarm and came to investigate.

Into the garage, pulling the door closed behind them. There was enough light down here to see, even at night. Gareth had noted the light levels earlier, so they didn't need complicated helmets to work right now.

Over to that cage.

Baker surprised him by simply sticking a key into the lock on the cyclone-fencing door and turning. It popped right open.

"Polymorphic master key," she grinned at his confusion. "I was able to identify the lock maker from your images, so I programmed something ahead of time."

Huh. This woman was even sneakier than he had thought.

Gareth turned himself sideways and watched the basement door where someone up in the kitchen would emerge. No word from Grodray meant no exterior alarms to this point, but someone might have gotten a silent ping upstairs and come down to see what was happening, even if the exterior didn't sound.

Maybe a rabbit had wandered in earlier and settled down, and was now frantically trying to escape the garage?

This was when things got interesting. He watched Eveth pull a larger scanner from her belt and begin to quarter the walls inside the storage unit.

"Bingo," she said quickly. "Helps knowing that he's Vanir."

She was pointing to a simple section of pipe that emerged from the wall at head level, and came down to a faucet with a twist-grip to open and close it. Water to wash off your hands, since there was a drain right below it.

Baker turned the knob and nothing came out. But behind her, the wall seemed to shift backwards. She put away the scanner and pushed on the wall.

"Grodray, that's two," she said, marking the next penetration step.

Still nothing on the airwaves, and nobody coming.

Baker nodded as an overhead light came on. Automatic, when this door was opened.

She went in first, and Gareth followed.

The space beyond was a narrow hallway, at least for a Vanir, that ended in a circular staircase going up.

"Close the door behind you," Baker ordered as she approached it, her scanner out again and pinging the space.

Gareth noted that this side of the heavy door had a simple handle, like any interior door, but it clicked firmly into place when he pushed. It was still built like a bank vault, to push it closed and feel the bolts set. And being inside a bicycle cage, nobody was likely to bump into it from the outside.

You had to know something was here. Or had strong suspicions and great need.

Hopefully, they were inside Elnon's security now. Since they weren't trying to steal any art from the walls, those sensors would be in rooms they did not need to visit.

"Grodray, confirm three," Baker said quietly.

They waited a moment, unsure now if their radios could penetrate the walls of the panic room.

"Confirm three," the Senior Constable said a moment later.

Gareth let go a soft sigh. Being out of contact wouldn't have scrubbed the mission, but it meant that he and Baker might get killed without anyone being able to rescue them, as had almost happened last time.

Paranoia in this business was not always bad.

From the look on Baker's face, she felt the same way.

"Climbing stairs," Baker said aloud, putting her scanner away, apparently satisfied, and aiming her stunner up and forward.

Gareth followed, making even less noise than the professional cat burglar in front of him.

Interestingly, there was a door on the ground floor, visible from this side. The whole front of the column would apparently hinge open, letting you escape from upstairs. Or perhaps just offering Elnon a quiet way to get to the ground floor. Old castles and manor houses on Earth had something similar, but that was generally for kings and folks to sneak between bedrooms at night.

Gareth wondered if Elnon had the need. Or just had hired an architect who believed in completeness. If you were in the Grand Salon, this was close enough to flee to, and you could lock the outer door, at least long enough to disappear from someone who didn't think about secret doors.

Up again they circled. The next floor was the panic room he had expected, but the stairwell continued up. Apparently, the master could exit into the attic, or perhaps he kept a pair of lifterpacks stored up there for a daring getaway.

A small bed in one corner. Only big enough for one person, which perhaps said something about Elnon that hadn't been obvious before. A small kitchenette, like you frequently found in nicer hotels, complete with a refrigerator block. A desk where Elnon could work.

A whole wall of fireproof filing cabinets, five drawers tall, since they were a standard size and Vanir scaled. Six of them, each three feet deep. Locked, but it was another simple lock. Mechanical as the others had been.

That made sense. If someone managed to kill the power to the building, you didn't want everything electronic to die with it. The alarms probably had some sort of uninterruptable power supply, good for days if you were serious. But the master would want to escape, and use his own muscles, especially if everything was off.

Baker tapped one of the cabinets, but returned to the stairwell, taking the first stride and nodding back at him.

Gareth followed her up. He had been right. The attic had been rearranged into a small flight bay. However, instead of lifterpacks, there was another small speeder up here. Not as impressive externally as the one downstairs, but Gareth suspected that this one was probably one of the fastest you could buy.

A man like Elnon, if pressed that close, would want to run hard and fast, and wouldn't skimp here. Not with as much money as he had spent downstairs to acquire his art.

"And none of this exists in any of the architectural drawing submitted to the city fire department," Baker murmured.

"Come again?" Grodray was on the line.

"Transmitting an image," she laughed, stepping back and pulling out a camera. "Slightly modified attic."

When Grodray whistled, they dropped back down a level. Gareth holstered his stun pistol and just settled for being able to kill androids and small vehicles. Baker could outdraw him if she needed to, and someone coming along now needed to be taken down quietly.

Or blown into smoldering, metallic wreckage.

THIEF IN THE NIGHT

EVETH STUDIED the panic room that Elnon Ruaidhrí had assembled. It was impressive, especially with all the other things she had known about the man. Stuff not even Gareth had been told, thus far. His whole life was probably locked up in these cabinets. Every piece of art. Every crime. Every bribe. And nobody had ever suspected anything until Gareth came along a year ago.

Some days, she wondered if he was blessed by the *Chaa*. Certainly, his advent into her life had altered everything. Maybe they had sent him as a quiet way to save everything, so they didn't have to come in and crack heads together.

Eveth had never been particularly religious, especially compared to many others, but some days, she questioned that.

They had been trying to nail Ruaidhrí for decades, and failing. In just a few weeks, Gareth had the man dead to rights.

"Where would you put the important papers, Gareth?" she turned to her new lucky charm and asked.

Gareth surprised her by holstering his disintegrator, his own lucky charm piece after Gonquah, and sitting at Elnon's desk. Both big hands went flat on the top for a moment, and then he rotated to his left, standing and taking one long stride to the cabinets at the farthest end of the room.

"This one," Gareth tapped that stack.

"Why?" she asked, intrigued.

"When he sat at his desk, this was the way he had to turn to open that door," Gareth pointed. "So I'm guessing it is a natural motion."

She nodded at the sound logic and slipped her picks into the keyhole at the top. She had read Gareth's report about a fingerprint pad in the office, but everything in here relied on mechanical rather than electronic solutions. Probably a key in the desk in here, which was also locked with a thumbprint, when she glanced back.

This lock took some effort. She was almost sweating when she finally got all the tumblers to surrender, although just cutting the damned thing out with her laser was still an option. An admission of surrender on her part, but an option.

She pulled the massive top drawer out and looked at the file folders contained. The front one caught her eye, and apparently her partner's as well.

"Damn it," Gareth murmured under his breath, reaching in and drawing it out.

Eveth followed the big Vanir agent back over to the desk and looked over his shoulder as he laid it flat and opened it.

"Grodray, stand by for action," she said simply.

"What's up?" he asked back.

"We are reviewing a file with Sarzynski's name on it," she said. "And he…crap. Oh, that's very bad."

"Talk to me, Eve," Grodray's voice got sharp.

"I need you to call it in and send a high level messenger off to *Churquark* faster than the news can get there. And then get here and quietly arrest all the staff," Eveth said. "From this file, Elnon sold Maximus all the parts that man needs to build himself two wormhole stations."

"Repeat that, Baker?" Grodray said.

"I think maybe Morty was right. Sarzynski's going to Earth for an army, Jack," Eveth felt the dread take over her entire body.

HOME

THE PERSONAL WORMHOLE tube was nothing like riding in the comfort of an auto-taxi on the short blip to orbit. Those took almost no time at all to complete. This trip was measured in the number of heartbeats Marc had to count as he passed feet first down what his mind kept interpreting as a gullet. As though he were in the process of being swallowed by a whale.

Marc kept those thoughts to himself. This was not the time to be thinking about burning bushes, either, or messengers from God, however it might look when he landed on the other side.

Hopefully, there would be nobody there and he could get organized quietly before reaching out to some old contacts to see how much of the network had survived, after his disappearance almost two years ago.

Marc saw the end of the tunnel appear, racing madly towards him. He already held a stun pistol in hand, against need, and took a deep breath against the oppressive atmosphere around him.

And then he landed. Just as he had before. One moment, tunnel to infinity. The next, he had popped into existence. Rebirth, as conquest.

The Bunker had been built by a crime boss more than a century ago, taking over an abandoned mine in northern Colorado and turning the place into an oversized complex almost like one of the ancient missile silos that still dotted the plains north and east of here.

Rough walls had been polished just enough that you wouldn't cut yourself on them. Concrete floors had been poured and leveled by professionals at different heights, creating large slabs like a multi-deck patio or mod living room.

In one hand, Marc held his stunner. In the other, a flashlight, but it was unneeded, as the lights were on in the large space where he landed.

"Cripes, what the hell is that?" someone yelled.

Marc spun and aimed at the four men that had been playing poker at an old-fashioned wooden table.

"Cops," another of the men yelled.

Before Marc could say anything, the men all exploded into action, reaching for pistols in belts or shoulder holsters.

There was no time to discuss this like rational beings, so Marc just opened fire, dropping the men like flies onto the table or floor. He paused as the they were down, looking around.

The space was large and open, almost vaulted like a church, with a number of doors along one side, opposite an area where a kitchen had been built. One of those doors began to open now.

"What's going on?" a man asked.

Marc shot him, too, and then raced to the door. Inside, a woman began to scream. The stunner silenced her.

Down each door, Marc thrust them open from the side, looked in, and moved on when each proved empty.

A pulse of power drew his attention back to the main room. Maiair stepped through, followed by Yooyar a moment later. Both were armed and prepared. Marc had deliberately had them hold back thirty seconds, just in case something bad happened and he needed a surprise. Or if the people here had reacted in a civilized manner, and not like criminals.

Of course, civilized people didn't even know this place existed, but Marc was playing with the cards he was dealt.

"Any more of them?" Maiair asked, covering a large door near the kitchen.

"Not on this side," he replied. "That's the garage. You check there and I'll clear the storage areas."

There was a small thorium reactor buried on one side of the next room under a protective shield. The other side held a massive cistern of pressurized water brought up from deep below. In between were a number of boxes and crates that held the sorts of sundries a man might need if he was going to hide out from the cops for a month or two, plus a pair of massive, walk-in units, one a freezer filled with meat and vegetables, and the other merely a refrigerator, also packed.

The men and women out there weren't going hungry. Nor would Marc's team, with the supplies that would be transported over.

He returned to the main room as the two Warreth women were locking the garage door from this side.

"What do we do with them?" Yooyar asked, gesturing to the four stunned gangsters.

"Tie them up for now," Marc said, as well the two back in the first bedroom. "How long until Zorge comes through?"

"Two minutes, as you ordered," Maiair replied.

Marc nodded. It was good to be dealing with professionals.

They gathered up the six and used plastic ties to hook the men and woman to chairs. The girl had the look of a bimbo the boss had brought along: extremely pretty and barely eighteen from the look of her, when the boss was in his fifties and badly out of shape. Had she been dressed when Marc arrived, he might have given her the benefit of the doubt and perhaps suggested daughter, but she was also of Caribbean descent, a darker, richer brown compared to the pastier white of the rest.

At least the gunmen weren't slobs. And had reacted quickly and efficiently with violence. That they had no chance against Marc wasn't going to count too much against them.

Zorge appeared next, off to one side with a pistol in hand. He looked around at the situation and nodded.

"Gear next?" he asked Marc.

"That's right," Marc replied.

The Nari scientist turned and vanished.

About the time the gangsters were stirring, crates began to appear over in one corner, as though materialized by an invisible genie. The first android came over in one load, leaving Zorge with the other two and Mishalska for now.

"What gives?" one of the men asked as he woke up and looked around. "Some sort of Halloween thing?"

Marc walked over and smiled. He had to remember that he wasn't human any more. That they wouldn't see him as one of them, even if any had been people that might recognize him from before.

"I needed your base," he announced in perfect English, which felt weird after all the time he had spent in the *Accord*, speaking their tongue. "It was unfortunate that you were here, but maybe we can work something out with your boss, because I only plan to stay here a little while before I go home.

"Which of the Nine Hells is home, you monster?" the man asked. Clearly, he was the leader, as the others just watched silently.

"A planet you wouldn't know, halfway across the galaxy," Marc smiled.

Behind him, a particularly large box came through the golden portal with a loud sound as it pushed several tons of other equipment forward a few inches.

"Jesus, what is all that?" the man's eyes were almost all whites now. "What are you?"

"You wouldn't believe me," Marc said. "So remain quiet for now and listen when I talk to your boss. If you boys are good, nothing bad will happen to you. In fact, really good things might happen instead. *Capiche?*"

"Uhm, sure, buddy," the man said. "Whatever you say."

The girl awoke first, and started screaming. Marc had to stun her to get her to shut up, and then tied a cloth around her mouth, making sure she could breathe, but not give him headaches.

The boss awoke last. Not surprising, since the effects of stun were best ameliorated by being healthy, and that fat little ball of anger was anything but.

He did remain more or less silent when he woke up, straining against this bonds even less effectively than the other four had.

"I'm going to boil the story down to the bits you need to know, understand?" Marc began, drawing all eyes in the room to him.

The two Warreth women didn't speak English, nor did the android, but they were mostly watching the prisoners for now. And ambushes that might occur.

"Two years ago, I was the boss known as Maximus," Marc's eyes bored in on the fat man. "Do you know that name?"

"Yeah," the little man replied. "But you ain't human."

"Correct," Marc said. "Something happened, and I got transformed into a race known as the Vanir. These two women are another race called Warreth."

All five sets of eyes turned to the women. Warreth might have feathers, bills, and head crests, but the Chaa had still made them mammalian bipeds on the same basic model as themselves. That Maiair and Yooyar were such exemplary examples just doubled the fascination of the men watching.

"The other is a combat-model android," Marc continued. "Fast enough to kill all of you before you even know what happened, so mind your manners. Am I understood clearly?"

All five nodded now. Cowed, perhaps.

"Good," Marc continued. "Two more men will join us shortly. They are Nari, and look like perhaps a Canadian Lynx, if you boys know what one of those are. As I said earlier, I needed your base. If you want to be cut in on my deal, I'm here to recruit a group of human killers, like I was, to help me go conquer the entire galaxy. The people out there are patsies. Pacifists, even, in some cases. But there are hundreds of planets of them, and I'm going to need gunmen like you to keep them in line."

"Aliens?" the fat boss asked quietly. "Like on the vid?"

Marc fought to keep the sigh and eyeroll contained. He was back in the bush leagues again, obviously. Surrounded by provincials and fools. One step at a time, trying to find enough straw to make bricks.

"Correct," Marc said. "I used to be human. They kidnapped me because they needed a killer. Now I'm in charge of the gang."

That got through to at least two of the mooks, the smart one at the far end of the poker table and one of the others. The sorts of men who understood what it meant to have an eye to the main chance. Those two moved up on his list to chat up individually.

"So why ain't you in charge over there?" the boss started like he was going to get smart.

"There are about a million cops in the *Accord*," Marc said. "Maybe ten million. It's a war, right now, and I'm one of the only killers. Even the two women here can't help me take on all that. Plus, those bastards went and got some help from Sky Patrol."

That got a good reaction from the four gunmen. All of them had probably seen the inside of a Sky Patrol jail at one time or another.

"Sky Patrol knows about all this?" the boss asked, incredulous.

"Parts of it do," Marc semi-lied to the men.

Gareth Dankworth was Sky Patrol, regardless of anything else. That was enough.

"So why are you here, Maximus?" the boss finally asked in a reasonable voice.

"I need an army of humans," Marc replied coldly. "Killers."

"An army?"

"Yes," Marc smiled. "You're going to help me conquer the galaxy."

IN HER MAJESTY'S SERVICE

ROYSTON APPROACHED this meeting like a duel in the old American West. High Noon Showdown, as it were. He had sent his best suit in for an emergency trip to the cleaners. Pippa and Fatima had broken out their best dress uniforms from storage.

Young Prince Henry of Wales greeted them at the door to the residential wing of the palace, once they had passed all the layers of security, armed or subtle, wrapped like layers of nacre around the place.

The young man had grown in the last year. He was probably nearly his father's height now, and would develop the man's breadth of shoulders soon. He looked down on Royston almost apologetically.

"Dr. Loughty," the young prince nodded to them. "Miss Loughty. Miss Darzi. Welcome."

He led them deeper into the palace, past more guards and functionaries than had been here before. They did not end up in the same, cozy chamber as before, but one closer to the Personal Quarters.

Royston wasn't sure if that made him feel better, or left him further on edge.

Through the door, he found Sir West seated to one side, and Prince Consort Daniel to the other. Her Majesty was seated at the center of a small arc, and the man next to her, opposite the Prince Consort, brought home to Royston just how dangerous the game had suddenly become.

Admiral Sir William Wellesley-Knox, *Commander, English Military*

Forces Earth and a former Sky Marshall of Sky Patrol itself. That is, Operations Commander of the entire force.

Royston had tangled with the man a few times over the years, but the Admiral had been Sky Patrol, and Royston's appointments and chain of command had only been Earth Force for the last fifteen years or so, so the arguments had been civil and bureaucratic, rather than risking breaking out into fisticuffs on the corridor outside an especially heated meeting.

It had come close more than once, though.

The admiral was a tall, lean, and bluff man who still managed to look rather like a shopkeeper from Manchester with his stern gaze.

Pippa and Fatima were introduced and seated on Royston's flanks, like wingmen he might need in a dogfight. The symbolism was not lost on Royston.

Prince Consort Daniel served tea, as before. Sandwiches and biscuits as only the Queen might rate. Small talk on various irrelevancies. More tea was delivered in silence by efficient servants.

Her Majesty, Elizabeth III, studied Royston over the edge of her mug as she sipped, remaining mostly silent. The Crown Prince explained some of his studies into the sciences, in response to general questions from his father and Sir West.

Even Fatima was interrogated mildly, both by Sir West and Prince Henry, but it was obvious after a moment that Sir West had never met the real Fatima Darzi, so he was at very little risk of tripping up the imposter seated with him now. And the questions were more curiosity about Persia than anything particularly personal.

"Rock and roll music, Dr. Loughty?" Her Majesty asked suddenly. "That might be the key to our future?"

"It does seem rather daft, on the surface of things, I will grant," Royston was at pains to keep everything bright and cheerful, both tone and body language. "However, my usual inspirations of syncopated jazz or the classical masters had failed me for the very first time. With Pippa's assistance, I sought inspiration in other venues. Other avenues of art, if you will."

"And now?" the Queen pressed.

"And now I have given much thought to the physics and mathematics I have uncovered, madam," he said simply. "As I noted previously, some of the basic theory was simply wrong, based on subsequent experimental data. Or perhaps incomplete would more accurately describe it. I needed a break from my labors, so I thought to locate that woman who had so inspired me the first time, in an effort, as I explained to Sir West, to see if lightning might be induced to strike a second time."

"And she is in London now?" Her Majesty asked.

"She will be, shortly," Royston said. "Thus, my heretofore secret venture. But for Sir West stumbling upon us, we would have attended the show tomorrow night and then been off on other jaunts immediately afterwards, with none the wiser."

A glance passed between Sir William and the Queen now. Royston steeled himself for whatever foolishness was about to issue forth from the man's mouth and fixed his gaze on the admiral, as though daring him.

The Admiral did not shrink.

"Should she be invited to the palace for a private performance?" Sir William asked.

"Certainly," Fatima, of all people spoke up suddenly, her voice tart with brilliant, sarcastic innuendo. Amazing, especially since she wasn't even human, but she had the intonation perfect. "If your desire is to ruin the entire impact of what we are attempting. Sir William."

"I beg your pardon," the Admiral's ruff came up.

"It would be as useful as demanding you regale us with all the verses of *God Save The Queen, a capella*, right now," Fatima stuck the burning embers under the man's fingernails, at least metaphorically. "The purpose was to recreate the original night in question, with that woman in complete and utter control of the entire auditorium, both psychologically and emotionally. Anything else is just a waste of everyone's time. I was not there, yet I have felt the power of it, merely from the stories Royston and Pippa have told me. So no, you should not ruin this woman's harmony by demanding she dance for her supper."

Royston bit his tongue rather than laugh. This woman was only impersonating Fatima Darzi, but he could actually remember the original woman unleashing that tone of anger, doubly rare in a land where the only way a woman had any power at all was to be born into it. In that, Admiral Sir William Wellesley-Knox might represent everything that both Fatima Darzi and a young Grace woman named Ilak Vorta might find wrong with present, human society.

The room had fallen to a shocked silence.

All the more so because a Persian woman might say such a thing to an English officer. Some memories went back centuries, to a less enlightened time, when the United Kingdom had not behaved with any great honor.

And Fatima had done her homework on the Nineteenth and Twentieth Centuries of Earth. And Anglo-Persian relations.

Royston had checked.

He sat quietly, waiting to be metaphorically thrown out of the palace for insulting Her Majesty's honor. Wars had begun over less.

Elizabeth Regina shocked him by grinning.

"Then perhaps Dr. Loughty might be induced to act *in loco parentis* instead," she said casually. "I expect that Prince Henry would find the performance enthralling, but, as you have noted, making a royal production of the event might despoil the very thing you sought."

As traps went, Royston found it masterful. The jaws were closed around his ankle before he even knew they were there. Prince Henry blushed. Prince Consort Daniel smiled. Sir William retained his gruff silence. They had all played their hands masterfully.

Royston couldn't remember the last time he had been ensnared so effectively. At least it had been Her Majesty that did it.

His honor could live with that.

"I would be delighted, Your Majesty," Royston surrendered gracefully. "The situation calls for subtlety, so the ladies with me were going to attend in mufti. If the Crown Prince's bodyguards were to maintain a discrete distance, none might even be aware that he had joined us. It will, of course, require utmost secrecy across the board. One hint to our supposed *Euterpe* of the gravity of the situation and all may be for naught, as she seemed to sense the power flowing in the air last time."

"So it shall be, Dr. Loughty," Her Majesty said with triumph in her voice.

Royston acquiesced, and hopes that nothing would go wrong, with an alien in their midst, magic poised to happen, and several dangerous men nearby with weapons.

He had simply run out of alternatives.

CONQUEST

GARETH HAD FOUND a new definition of professionalism that challenged every preconception he had ever had on the topic.

An entire Constabulary force had arrived at the front door, as well as every other entrance, and promptly and politely arrested everyone in the building, which came down to two maids, a groundskeeper, and the Ruaidhrí's personal chef. A maid, and butler, and a seneschal, for lack of a better description, had traveled with the Ruaidhrí's off-planet.

Security systems had been deactivated for now, but left intact, as the art in the building was still probably priceless and would need to be protected against theft. Plus, a small team of Gareth's new friends in the Art Fraud department had been called in and would remain on premises for the time being, cataloging and protecting the assembly.

There was one problem, however. The Chef simply refused to be arrested. Period.

She was a small Grace woman who somehow reminded Gareth of his maternal grandmother, both in their petite stockiness, and the fact that no stranger was allowed in the house without food in front of them.

So the entire team had moved down to the dining hall, minus only those people guarding the grounds or who had collected the rest of the staff and taken them away. Madam Streffa Vorkinnik was in the process of fixing what she called a quick snack for everyone.

If you were the kind of person who could just whip up a plate of chips covered with meat, cheese, and sauce, as a prelude to hot sandwiches, while cookies went into the stove. Two of the team had been detailed to oversee the Grace woman, lest she poison the team.

That had nearly gotten one of them slapped, when he made the mistake of saying it out loud.

Professionalism. Even in the face of being arrested under the possibility of being an accessory to treason.

And the cookies were delightful. Chocolate chip, more or less. Snickerdoodlish. And something closer to a sweet scone with dried fruit, that you dipped into a double cream.

And she had done it all from scratch, instructing her minders which jars to hand her and where to find the utensils. Without any recipe except experience.

Gareth burped as the first round of Italian-style sweet coffee arrived, flavored with chocolate and dulce de leche. He was just sorry he couldn't afford to hire this woman. Even for a day.

Grodray shared a commiserative smile as if he was thinking the same thoughts.

"What do we know?" Grodray asked.

All the eating was done at one end of the long table, with a towel stretched across the surface like a low curtain wall, to capture any spilled coffee that might threaten the stack of documentation at the other end.

Gareth had quickly sorted every folder into three, rough piles, pending their being scanned into evidence systems later when they forensics team arrived.

For now, he put his coffee down carefully and walked over to the smallest stack. The larger two were art documentation and histories of ownership, and Ruaidhri's personal records, mostly running the manor house, but also certain things about the many companies he either owned or sat on the boards of.

"Old money," Gareth said simply. "Well organized financial systems in place, dating back at least four hundred years to conserve his wealth generationally. We know they have two, grown children, one just finished with university and the other a few years behind. Trust funds have been established, so neither are at risk of ending up on the streets, if they are found to be innocent of their father's misdeeds."

"And what can we prove in the short term?" Eveth Baker asked, always one to go straight for the throat.

"Selling illegal and unlicensed wormhole technology to known criminals," Gareth said. "Namely, Marc Sarzynski. And recently enough, in the last month or so. That is enough to take him away and begin stripping away the rest of the layers. As with Gonquah, I expect we'll be years finding everything, but one man can only serve one lifetime in prison, regardless of the number of life sentences a judge might hand down."

"And Maximus has everything he needed?" Grodray asked sharply.

Gareth shrugged, looking at the documentation.

"He had everything he ordered from Ruaidhrí," Gareth offered. "I am the last person to ask about tube station engineering."

Grodray nodded at him.

"Correct," he said. "But I know just who can fill in the blanks here."

The Senior Constable rose from the table and walked to the far end of the room, talking quietly into his pocketcomm.

"Do we know where?" Eveth asked in hushed tones.

"In my wildest dreams, I cannot imagine that the equipment was set up where it was delivered," Gareth said. "Nobody is that dumb, when working that far outside of the law. Stupid people would have already been caught."

"So this is a dead end?" she pressed.

"The hardware is, most likely, yes," Gareth agreed. "We have more names to dig out and arrest. All the deliveries took place on this planet, so somebody has seen Sarzynski. We just haven't asked them hard enough yet."

Gareth returned to his excellent coffee before it got cold. Madam Vorkinnick delivered another tray of cookies, fresh from the stove and steaming slightly, smiling as she took the empty tray away.

"I've called in some favors," Grodray hung up and walked back over to grab a cookie and stuff it into his mouth all at once. Then he had to drink some coffee before he could speak again.

Eveth's face as she watched was a masterpiece of sarcastic tolerance that nearly made Gareth giggle.

"I've got a few friends being rousted to come here and take over this part of the investigation," Grodray finally managed to speak around the cookies. "Unfortunately, that means we'll have to settle for a pedestrian breakfast elsewhere, instead of whatever Madam Vorkinnick could achieve with a little time to plan. Hopefully it will also make up to the other team for getting up in the middle of the night."

"Where are we going, Jack?" Eveth asked.

"Gareth was right about this being something of a dead end, at least as far as our investigation goes," Grodray smiled at the two of them. "But I do know where we can lay our hands on a pair of experts on wormhole systems at this time of night. We'll grab them, and then head over to a lab and do some thinking."

"Why the hurry?" Eveth asked.

"He has the parts for building two stations, Eve," Grodray said as he grabbed another cookie and held it out like a weapon. "One gets him someplace where nobody could be expected to find him. The other one will bring him back when he's damned good and ready. We have to hunt him now."

"Where's he gone?" Gareth asked anyway, knowing in his soul what the answer was.

"*Earth*," Grodray replied. "Chaa help us when he decides to return."

EXPERT

IF IT HAD BEEN anybody but Xiomber waking him up, Morty might have gone ahead and bitten them. As it was, he still considered it.

"I don't care how good your dream was, you lazy bum," Xiomber grabbed the blankets and pulled them away before Morty could get a good grip and stop him. "Get your sorry ass up."

Morty grumbled a range of profanities at his egg brother and sat up in bed.

"What?" he demanded brusquely.

"Grodray just put in a call and they're headed over here to grab us," Xiomber said. "You got just enough time to shower and get dressed. They said they're taking us to breakfast."

Morty spun and put his socked feet on the floor beside the bed. He had learned to sleep in socks, since the floor tiles in here were always so damned cold, even on a hot day. He ran a hand down his snout, as if that would wipe away whatever silliness had gotten into his brother.

"Fine. I'm up," he groused, standing and stretching. Stripping off his pajamas, he grabbed a towel and headed towards the head.

There was a female Nari officer in the main room. Tonight's jailer, perhaps. She blinked in surprise at the naked Yuudixtl walking by her in socks, but remained silent.

Good for her. If they didn't want to see me naked, they should have let me sleep in.

Behind him, somebody wolf-whistled. Morty turned with a scowl and began to blush furiously at Talyarkinash's grin, as she stood next to the officer.

Women.

He sauntered into the bathroom, wiggling his stubby tail just a little extra as he did, listening to the quiet murmurs and giggles from the two Nari women until the door closed.

Clean, warm, and dressed, he and his brother met Talyarkinash downstairs as a small truck landed in the quad. The sun was about an hour from even starting to brighten the eastern sky, which didn't help his mood.

It was one thing to still be awake to watch the sunrise, after a night of partying and dancing. It was something entirely unnatural to get up and start your day this early.

"Let's move it, cute butt," Talyarkinash said as he stomped down the stairs.

Morty fixed her with a hard, deadly glare, but she seemed to be as utterly immune as most women.

Grumble.

Inside the vehicle, Morty allowed himself to be slightly mollified by freshly baked cookies. Trust those bastards to stop at a coffee shop before getting him, but Grodray had promised food.

Better be good, whatever the hell he thought was worth all this stupidity.

I'm doing my penance here, copper. You don't have to rub my face in it.

Grodray smiled and held out the tray, so Morty took a second cookie.

Okay, maybe.

"Last night, we raided someone you might have dealt with behind some middleman," Grodray said to the two of them. "The name Elnon Ruaidhrí mean anything to you?"

"Art collector?" Xiomber piped up.

"That's right," Grodray said. "He also sold Maximus two, complete wormhole stations worth of equipment, about a month ago."

"Two?" Xiomber asked. "What the hell does he need two for?"

Morty muttered something under his breath, but apparently not far enough under. Talyarkinash's ears and whiskers came forward and then flashed backwards in embarrassment.

"We were right, egg brother," Morty said. "Bastard's going to *Earth* for help."

"That's my theory as well," Grodray said. "From here, we're going to feed you two breakfast, and then head to a secret research facility the Constabulary keeps. Once there, we'll put you two to work."

"How long has he had the equipment?" Morty demanded in a quiet, fierce tone.

"Eleven days from the last shipment," Gareth spoke up.

"Okay, skip breakfast," Morty said. "We need to head to your lab right now. You can get some pizza delivered, or something, but that's enough time to build and tune one, and use it. That means he's probably already on *Earth*, looking for more killers like him."

"Or worse," Gareth spoke up.

"What could be worse than a hundred Sarzynski's in the *Accord*?" Grodray demanded.

"An entire planet of xenocidal humans finding out that aliens exist, Jack," Baker broke her silence.

Morty nodded to her.

"Finding someone like Maximus wasn't that hard the first time," Morty said. "There is a whole, damned star system filled with people we could have picked from. It was far harder finding Gareth, because there weren't that many heroes, when we went looking."

"Can you find Maximus again?" Baker demanded.

"We can try, Constable," Morty said. "Shouldn't be that hard, since they only have one tube station to look for."

"Then I have news," Grodray said suddenly to the three of them. "It cannot leave this vehicle, or you most likely will be put to death for leaking it. Is that understood?"

Morty watched Talyarkinash nod sharply. Then Xiomber. He was already looking at the walls around him for the rest of his life, so Grodray only had a partial threat. But the Senior Constable was also deadly serious in ways he hadn't even been when he walked into Morty's cell that first time.

"I'm in," Morty said.

"Probably as a result of your meddling, even with the good you have done, bad things have transpired on *Earth* since Gareth left," Grodray said. "Again, highest level security clearance there is, but you need to know going in, because it will change your equations."

"What the hell has happened?" Gareth demanded, blushing at the profanity that snuck out.

"A human scientist has managed to build his own wormhole generator," Grodray said. "Without our help, or Sarzynski's. It's tiny and short-range right now, but that's a just a matter of time. Especially if they come to realize that we aren't all that far away from them, as far as physics go."

"Crap," Xiomber murmured. "Humans breaking out?"

"Indeed," Grodray agreed. "We have to stop Maximus immediately, but we'll also have to figure out how to stop the humans from finding us. Or finding out about us."

Morty sighed heavily.

Had he really saved the *Accord of Souls* for only a couple of years, just to have Maximus return, at the head of a human army? Was there any, possible, worse outcome?

FIRST INSPECTOR

ANEN WARDSON REVIEWED the preliminary report filed by Prime Investigator Jackeith Grodray with something approximating existential terror. Just a quick note, but more than enough. She had to agree with him that the chances of a human invasion had suddenly gone from merely theoretical to horrifically realistic.

If Maximus had returned home to gather a plague of humans, then it was incumbent upon the First Inspector to protect the *Accord of Souls* at whatever personal or moral cost. She could turn into the worst murderer in history, if the outcome saved an untold future trillions from the sorts of savage death promised by the arrival of humans.

Anen put the document down and let everything inside her chest go for a moment, just because the tension was threatening to make her heart explode out of her chest. She had not gotten to this position by allowing her nerves to get the better of her, but nobody had ever faced a threat so terrible in the fifty thousand years since the Chaa departed, leaving the Vanir to protect the rest of civilization.

She picked up the handset nearby and dialed.

Commissioner Diazal answered quickly.

"How may I be of service, First Inspector?" he asked brightly.

Anen let the dread into her voice finally.

"I have a report from the field, Commissioner," she said. "I would highly recommend that the entire Commission be brought into emergency session, so that I might make a presentation and they can then decide the fate of the galaxy."

She heard the man's sharp intake of breath, but otherwise there was silence on the line for several seconds.

"That bad?" he finally whispered.

"Perhaps worse," she replied. "You and I are removed from the agents in the field, who are removed from the crime, but we may be facing the worst possible scenario my people have been able to think up. Possibly, though the reality maybe be even more terrible."

"We will need an hour to gather the Commissioners on planet," he said. "I will send messengers after the others, but we may have a quorum at hand. How long do we have?"

"I do not know, Commissioner," she said. "But we are facing the potential of an imminent, human invasion."

FISHERMAN

GARETH HAD NEVER ACTUALLY SEEN what a tube station looked like. He had only ever passed through the tubes themselves. And most stations were largely automated to the extent that an engineer pressed a button and perhaps slid a level to open and scale a tube, depending on traffic.

This thing in front of him wasn't quite home-brewed, but it had the appearance of something put together by a hobbyist, rather than purpose built.

"Where the hell did you confiscate this?" Morty asked as he followed Gareth into the room.

Xiomber was a step behind him, and the two Yuudixtl politely hip-checked the Vanir Constable who had been standing there out of their way. That their heads came up to the man's thigh didn't intimidate those two one bit.

Gareth stepped into a handy corner out of the way, with Talyarkinash standing close. Eveth and Jackeith followed Morty and Xiomber.

The machine looked like nothing so much as antique images Gareth had seen of a musical recording studio, where a sound engineer could individually control hundreds of settings with petite, vertical sliders, until he had the exact sound he wanted. Dozens of larger dials ran across the top, with needles next to them as you adjusted.

"You don't think we built the machine?" Grodray replied bluntly to the Yuudixtl as he got close.

"No," Xiomber said with a definite sneer. "You'd have ordered all the same parts ahead of time. This was whatever someone could find in every pawnshop and junkyard they knew."

Gareth had to agree with that. On closer examination, everything was slightly different as he went down the line. It was like someone had added the first slider, and then gone looking for the second, affixing it before they went for the third.

"Hey," the Constable scientist snapped as Morty began making adjustments, "You aren't supposed to touch that."

"Grodray, make him go away," Morty said flatly. "Xiomber and I can't work with mother hen here making noise."

"I beg your pardon?" the man started to get angry. At least until Grodray turned to him and sent him from the room with a head toss. The man departed, grumbling under his breath. Gareth assumed he was going as far as the next room, behind a mirror that looked two-way from the long angle Gareth had to watch.

"Also, cops wouldn't tune it like this," Xiomber turned his head and gestured at the row of dials and needle gauges. "This looks like a cat burglar rig."

"What's that?" Grodray asked.

Gareth couldn't tell if the question was honest or just humoring the two lizards.

"One man in, but the far tunnel entrance is soft," Morty said louder. "So the tube stays open, and someone can just chuck things into the tube from the far end and they'll come out here. Ya gotta be quick, since most security systems will scream bloody murder as soon as they detect the intrusion, but you still have maybe eighty seconds, depending on where a guard is."

"You've done this sort of thing before," Grodray accused him.

"We've been convicted of it, Grodray," Morty snapped. "Remember? Pages three, eleven, and fourteen of the grand indictment, in case you've forgotten."

Grodray fell silent as the two began running their hands over everything. Gareth noted that they didn't make any adjustments, at least not yet. More just familiarization, with sounds of happiness emerging from the two.

"Burritos or pizza?" Morty asked out of the blue.

"Burritos for breakfast," Xiomber decided. "We can get pizzas send over later."

Morty turned to Grodray and Baker.

"Four breakfast burritos, please," he even sounded remarkably polite. "Two extra spicy. Two with extra sour cream. Lots of meat and cheese."

Baker nodded and departed while the rest of them watched.

"Now what?" Gareth asked in a quiet tone as Grodray stepped close to them.

Grodray, at least, seemed satisfied with things for now.

"Now I play a hunch," the man replied. "Challenge their professional credentials to find the man and figure out if we need to send a team through or if we can just grab Maximus and his gang and drag them to justice."

"How long do we have?" Gareth asked. "I know you filed reports with your bosses. What will they do?"

"Right now, Gareth?" Grodray's voice fell so quiet that Gareth and Talyarkinash had to lean in to follow. "Right now, they may be deciding to destroy Earth if we can't stop Maximus before he does whatever it is he had planned."

Gareth felt the spike of cold adrenaline land at the pit of his stomach.

Pippa. Dr. Loughty. All of his friends in Sky Patrol. All of Earth Force.

All of Earth.

All of humanity might be doomed because of Marc Sarzynski's rage. And there was nothing he could do about it, except rely on a pair of semi-reformed, career criminals, and the very Constabulary that might decide to wipe out his entire species.

GENERAL

MARC WALKED BACK into the main chamber, holding the pocketcomm he had taken from the mob boss.

"Anything?" Zorge asked, looking up from a small piece of equipment he had been tinkering on, in the middle of the poker table.

"Maybe," Marc replied, reaching for the Vanir-sized table he had brought over and settling into it.

Maiair had been making tea. Yooyar had apparently been standing nearby her sister. Both drifted his way and took up the other two chairs. The three androids stood guard, and Mishalska had been left asleep on a cot in the garage for now.

Marc turned to check, but the three doors holding the six mobsters were closed. Locked from this side by some gadgets Zorge had brought.

"I was able to reach some of my old contacts," Marc continued. "Problem is, most of them got rolled up by Gareth Dankworth and Sky Patrol over the last two years when I disappeared. Several of the people I talked to suggested ever so vaguely that I had been caught by the cops, turned, and was now in the process of setting them up."

"Ouch," Zorge commiserated. "Where does that leave us?"

"I've got a couple of other places to look for help," Marc's smile gained wattage. "People like Cleveland Eddy and Two-Gun Kowalski are doing long stretches in federal penitentiaries right now. I just need to figure out which ones, and then we'll bust them out."

"Huh? Oh, right," Zorge snapped his fingers. "I'm not used to living in a place that doesn't have wormhole alarms everywhere. Will they even know what happened?"

"No," Marc turned serious. "The jailers will just discover them gone one morning, from a locked cell, with no indication how it happened. Better will be if they have life-monitors going, and both just go blank on the tape."

"Ya know, I could get to liking this place," Zorge said with a smile.

"What about the current prisoners?" Maiair asked, sipping her tea.

"Two of the grunts look like they'll play," Marc said. "O'Rourke might be a harder nut to crack, at least until Two-Gun walks in here and smiles at him."

"Why would that matter?" Yooyar asked, perking up.

"The man has a scar running from chin to hairline on the left side," Marc said. "Looks like an old, Prussian, dueling scar, but it was done by a razor blade when he was a teenager. Mob boss didn't like the kid smiling at the man's daughter, so he cut him."

"Really?" Maiair was shocked. "Did it scare him off?"

"Oh no," Marc laughed. "Two-Gun stalked the man and killed him later. Cut his body into pieces and left them in a pile on the man's front stoop. One of the two guns he got famous for later was taken from the guy. He's a real piece of work, but we go way back and he'll be grateful to be sprung."

"What about the rest?" Yooyar asked.

"I'll work on them some more, but we may just end up killing them afterwards to keep them quiet," Marc said. "Can't turn them loose right now, or they'll lead the cops right to us, most likely. And I need this place as a base for the station, at least until we can move it all somewhere else. And to do that, I need human agents who can take out a lease and things like that. Most of it can be done electronically these days, but I don't exist right now, and the machines responsible will balk if I tried."

"How hard are the machines to hack?" Zorge perked up. Nothing like a challenge to keep his head in the game.

"Child's play, compared to the *Accord*," Marc replied. "We've only had computers for about three centuries at this point, and Artificial Intelligence is still just a really complicated decision tree flipping coins."

"So get me access to a trunk and we can do something about that," Zorge nodded.

"Not quite as easy as walking into a café and connecting to their channel," Marc said. "Well, technically, that's not true. It is that easy. It's the getting out again afterwards that presents a problem. At least for a Nari or a Warreth or a Vanir."

"And thus, Cleveland Eddy and Two-Gun," Maiair completed the thought.

"Exactly," Marc agreed. "How soon to get everything set up and calibrated?"

Zorge shrugged, leaning back in his chair and letting his eyes focus on a distant horizon. He scratched the whiskers on the right side of his chin for a moment.

"Since we don't need to go off planet for the first jump, probably about a week or tenday," Zorge said. "I can refine things much tighter after that. How many people were you wanting to bring here?"

"Just those two, for now," Marc said. "Then maybe some members of my old gang that Gareth caught on that last day, if we can track them down. That gives us humans we can use as front men for the rest of things. Men who can't turn us in to the cops without going down themselves."

"Gotcha, boss," Zorge said. "Time to rouse the kid and get to work."

Rather than say anything more, he rose and headed towards the garage, where much of the equipment had been stored next to a late-model truck that had been converted to a limousine for O'Rourke and his gang.

Yooyar surprised Marc by joining the old Nari, leaving him alone with Maiair.

"We'll also need to set out to find you a wife," Maiair said quietly, placing one hand on his arm gently.

"That can wait," Marc replied. "We'll have years, if everything goes according to plan. I didn't really know any good candidates before, when I was a cop. Well, I did, but they're the kind that like cops."

"I know," she smiled. "We'll need to find you one like Liamssen. That will be my job, since she's going to have to measure up to my standards, if I expect her to keep you entertained."

Marc smiled back wanly. It was odd, falling into this sort of role, somewhere between Bonaparte and a Pasha from a fairy tale with a harem of beautiful women.

But she was right. Whoever they found would have to have a first-rate mind, on top of legendary beauty. That kid O'Rourke had brought had been attractive enough, until the moment she opened her screachy mouth.

She had at least gotten over her screaming fits, but Marc was pretty sure he'd had better and more rewarding conversations with house cats.

One step at a time. As she had said. Make Earth safe. Then recruit an army and take it over to conquer the *Accord of Souls*. Only then would he be able to come back and conquer his homeworld.

Humans were just too fractious a people. He knew that. But with *Accord* technology and an army composed of Vanir, Nari, and the rest that had broken to his will, he could keep his boot on humanity's throat.

At that point, the only problem would be the first three or four humans who tried to do the same thing to him, raising a human army on a crusade against evil and aliens.

Because only humans would fight other humans hard enough.

Still, Emperor Marc, Conqueror of the Universe.

Yes, that would do.

COMMISSION

ANEN STOOD before the body that represented the very *Accord of Souls* itself, wondering if she also faced the apocalypse.

Commissioner Diazal had managed to located eight of the others. That was more than a quorum. It was slightly over half of the worthies that sat on that body.

They had convened in strictest secrecy. Nobody else was allowed in the room, not even aides. although she had no doubts that it was being recorded and would eventually leak out. However, unlike most leaks, this one would potentially subject even an *Accord Commissioner* to life imprisonment. They would, at least, be careful.

For now, it was just important that the dangerous scope of things be abundantly clear.

Anen stood below the Commissioners on their raised, curved platform that allowed each to see one another and to surround whoever came before them.

Petim Diazal rose from his seat, next to the empty one where the Proctor would have sat, save for being on vacation this week, where a message was even now chasing after the man. In his stead, Diazal was discretely exercising executive authority. He would do that anyway, in another year or so, when the current Proctor finally retired after a lifetime of glorious service.

"Comrades," Diazal began in a serious voice, drawing all eyes to him magnetically. "I have been informed of a serious threat to the very *Accord of Souls* that we have all sworn to uphold and protect. As many of you are aware, I have been working with the First Inspector on an enquiry regarding the criminal known as Maximus. In the last fourteen hours, we have had a sudden escalation so critical that it became necessary to convene in Emergency Council, and perhaps make permanent, binding decisions. Our other Commissioners have had messengers sent to them, and will be joining us as soon as they can, but it may not be possible to wait even that long."

He paused there, hanging the room on pins and needles as he looked at each of the other faces, and the empty chairs. Finally, he turned his attention to her.

"First Inspector Wardson," he said simply. "Could you please bring the rest of the Commission up to date on the things you have previously told me?"

Anen studied all of those faces in turn. Most were friendly. A few dubious, but that was a personality trait on their part, and not hostility to her or the Constabulary. The crimes uncovered by Jack and Eve over the last year had been made abundantly clear to everyone.

The Commission was clean. Several members of the House of Worlds, on the other hand, had been arrested once all the evidence came out.

They would be a decade or more cleaning up this mess, but because of her people, and even a Star Dragon, they would have that time, rather than falling beneath the heel of a tyrant. She hoped.

"Commissioners of the *Accord of Souls*," Anen began. "We have been pursuing the criminal known as Maximus for over a year now. While he had managed to elude us on several occasions, his criminal brethren have not been so lucky, and the Constabulary has struck many telling blows against a criminal underworld whose scope had been previously unimaginable."

Many heads nodded. Everyone had been rather aghast at how badly corrupt other politicians had become.

"Recently, we have broken yet another criminal ring," Anen continued. "In the process, we have discovered that Maximus has in his control all the necessary components to build himself two, complete wormhole tube stations. He has escaped us again, but we have a scenario we are pursuing."

"At what point, madam, does this require emergency action on our part?" the Enjev Commissioner, Q'quivk'k spoke up. "As you have stated previously, you continue to hound him. Is it not just a matter of time until the criminal is in custody?"

Enjev were a bipedal species uplifted from something like an arachnid originally. Four major limbs, like a Vanir, plus two more, delicate arms mid-torso. Their mandibles gave little clue as to their thinking, unlike a Vanir's face, so you had to watch the four hands for unspoken cues. Q'quivk'k's body hair was blue-gray not that far removed from Anen's uniform, and beginning to age into the golden-yellow of his final stage.

"It is, Commissioner Q'quivk'k," Anen replied, keeping her tone under control. He wasn't an enemy. Just a sharp politician looking for an edge he could dangle over her. "However, it is the primary theory of my investigators in the field that Maximus has built one station and used it to flee someplace where he can hide from us for a very long time, while he puts in place a true threat to the *Accord*."

"Which would be?" the Commissioner nearly sneered at her.

"Recruiting a human army, with which he will return and attempt to conquer the entire *Accord of Souls*," she said flatly. Might as well brush the Commissioner's verbal games completely aside at the beginning, rather than fence with him all night.

That certainly got everyone's attention. It took Petim several minutes to get everything back under control from the various outbursts and howling.

"My apologies, First Inspector," Petim said as he finally got everyone to shut up. "Could you please give us a cursory background that brings us up to the current?"

"Why is that necessary?" Q'quivk'k's demanded. "Why not simply drop a force on Earth and arrest Maximus?"

"Because we don't know exactly where he is," Anen spoke before anyone else could. "We are searching, but there are ten billion humans in that system we must identify. It will take time we may not have."

"And what's your worst-case response, First Inspector?" Q'quivk'k's voice turned grim and dark now.

"I have spoken with Commissioner Diazal about the possibility of using a bio-weapon to end all human life, wherever it might be found in their entire home system," she replied, even more harshly. "We cannot wait until they break out, and only then attempt to inoculate our worlds, because something that virulent will no doubt begin to mutate with time, and might become a threat to the Vanir, or the Nari. Or the Enjev, Commissioner."

If the first outburst had been manic, this one was truly apocalyptic. Everyone was yelling, crying, demanding, pounding tables, threatening. Everyone except Q'quivk'k. Hs just sat and watched Anen. She returned a cold smile.

The Commissioner nodded once, and rose.

Q'quivk'k slammed his upper right hand into the table top like a gunshot. Everyone fell to silence in shock, as that Commissioner was normally a placid, quiet type.

Q'quivk'k turned to his right.

"Commissioner Diazal, my apologies for the outburst," he said in a polite tone before turning back to her. "First Inspector, what else do we need to know?"

Anen told them, watching faces grow pale as she did.

ROCKER

AS TRAPS WENT, Royston had been in worse and survived. Of course, those were just threats to his body. Tonight was about his soul. Or at least his intellectual reputation.

They had been waiting in a coffee shop not far from the British Library, he site of today's sightseeing. Pippa was dressed in green, and Fatima wore an abaya wrap the color of golden sand, with a blue hijab, both in silk, that she had bought at a local tailor who specialized in Muslim fashion.

It still made Royston's breath catch, watching her drink her tea and smile at him.

Two men walked in. Most of the customers in here barely noticed them walk up to the counter and order, but Royston had been a Sky Patrol agent when he was their age. Before science took over his life.

He recognized the way the men walked, if not the faces.

They got their coffee and retired to a table nearby, one watching the doors and the other the kitchen and the restrooms.

Royal Special Services.

"Our friend should arrive in approximately four minutes," Royston murmured to the two women.

Pippa looked perplexed, but Fatima fixed him with sharp eyes.

"The two men who just walked in?" she asked simply.

Royston nodded and sipped his coffee mildly.

Right on time, Prince Henry walked in, looked around, and smiled at them. Quickly, the young man ordered coffee and approached.

Royston found it terribly amusing that the young man had managed a Mod look tonight rather than the more-formal tweeds he had worn the previous two times Royston had met him.

For this evening blue dungarees, a little long and rolled up twice at the ankle, as was the style. Plain, white t-shirt under a black denim jacket. The boy's hair was not long enough to slick back into a large pompadour with a duck tail, but that was the only part that might make him stand out from the expected crowd.

Coffee in hand, Henry joined them. Royston found it amusing that Pippa had to fight the urge to stand in his presence, while he and Fatima sat companionably. Still, the boy was a natural as an actor. He fell into the fourth chair with a hearty grin and sipped his coffee, an innocent joining some older friends for a night of music.

"Good evening," he said. "Thank you for not putting up too much of a struggle with my mother. "

Royston nodded. The Queen could have done this so much less delicately, but that wasn't her style, either.

"We have about half an hour, Henry," Royston said. "The theater is a little over three blocks from here."

"Please, at least for tonight, call me Hank," the boy implored. "I don't often get to escape the confines of the Palace, where everything must be proper and precise."

"Hank," Pippa tried the name on a bit dubiously.

Two more men entered a few minutes after the prince, taking up the opposite corner from their compatriots and placing Royston and his party in a lovely, little box of safety. He had no doubts that several more men, perhaps a full rifle platoon, were someplace close against need.

Hopefully, nothing would ever come of it.

They made small talk for a time. Hank was interested in Persia, as an exotic location he might never visit, so Fatima was able to talk about her supposed home and show off the extensive research she had done.

Finally, they rose to depart. Considering the evening ahead, Royston had Fatima on his arm, while Pippa took charge of Hank. It helped that the man was so tall, and that his daughter had eyes for nobody but Gareth.

Fatima, in the interests of science, had chosen not to drug her sensory tentacles into quiescence tonight, but darkness on the streets and in the theater would hopefully shelter her from watchers. And nobody would be allowed to get close enough to them on the streets of London to present a threat to the Crown Prince.

Of that, Royston had no doubts whatsoever.

The theatre itself was an old, rundown sort of place. A neighborhood playhouse, when it was originally built, perhaps, with an excellent stage only three feet above the front row, and a well-designed bowl of seats, where everyone would have an unobstructed view of young Hamlet dying in the middle of the space.

The curtain was closed, as that night before. Red velvet as was classical. They had arrived a touch early tonight. Not quite first, but close enough for Royston to have his pick of seats, centered about two third of the way back. It would put him almost on eye level with the woman at the microphone, a necessity Royston didn't understand, but he wasn't willing to dispute his instincts.

Most of the early birds were down front anyway tonight, so Royston ended up with Hank on his right and Fatima on his left, with Pippa guarding the Prince's far side like a hawk. Fatima had kept her arm entwined with his for the whole walk over, and regained it now, once they were seated.

He gave her a questioning look, but she simply leaned her head against his shoulder with a smile, where he could feel her tentacles moving around under her hijab, even through the herringbone of his jacket.

Quickly enough, the room filled, every seat claimed and an extra row of people across the back, where a low wall marked off a small balcony for more folks to watch over their heads. At least four of them had followed the group from the coffee house.

The lights went down, plunging the room into near-ultimate darkness and a silence so complete Royston could hear the audience breathing.

The curtains peeled apart, revealing the same band as before in just enough light that the musicians could see each other and their instruments. The audience would be a black hole before them.

When he had attended other concerts of a similar ilk, at Henry or Pippa's age, the opening of the curtains was normally a cue for the audience to begin clapping and cheering, but tonight, everything remained utterly silent.

It was as though she had already cast her spell and captured them in her web.

The woman was dressed as before, in turquoise silk dress slashed to her hip and barely covering her to mid-thigh. Opera gloves in black. Black pumps. Her long, brunette hair was wild and loose, billowing lightly in the breeze of a fan at the front of the stage and centered up on her.

Before, she had only spoke at the very end, but tonight she seemed to feel the air of magic about her. She looked out over the darkness that hid the audience and seemed to find Royston with a smile and a tiny nod

"Good to see you again," she said, turning to the drummer with a harder nod, even as Royston's soul went cold with a dread he could not name.

Drums.

Syncopated jazz had a drummer to keep a soft, almost swishing beat, well in the background, against which the rest of the musicians counted.

This man, this *drummer*, was not interested in jazz.

The bass drum started first with a staggered, double beat. It was the heartbeat of the galaxy itself sounding.

Over it, the drummer began to play the rest of his instrument.

On a piano, a player can stab down the highest key on his right and then run the entire keyboard with the back of his hand, like an avalanche descending to the lowest notes. Doing the exact same thing with a drum set required this man to rotate gymnastically as he played more than twenty drums in sequence.

The effect was the same. The power was uncontrollable.

Bass player next. Upright and calling for the very dead to rise and take the world. Royston found his heart and his feet beating in tune.

The rest of the band joined in, the piano first and then two guitars, followed by a Siren calling all the foolish sailors to their deaths onto the rocks.

If Royston had imagined he had seen all of this woman's power and capabilities before, he was sadly mistaken. Or perhaps she had taken something from him as well, on that night when she gave him the higher physics, because tonight, she had ascended the very heavens and carried several hundred innocent music fans with her.

Royston leaned back to listen. And hopefully survive the onslaught of power embracing them.

As before, she spoke no more. Just a pause between song to tune instruments and drink water, before diving headlong into the next.

Somewhere in the middle, a torch song of love and loneliness. Royston was shocked at his behavior, but it felt perfectly natural to turn and kiss Fatima, and she seemed to feel the same way. They finally broke with a blush, but she did not withdraw. Just rested her head and tentacles on his shoulder again.

A quick glance over, but Hank was utterly enraptured and hadn't noticed. Nor had Pippa, hopefully. He was far too old to be fooling around with an alien secret agent.

The song was over all too soon anyway.

The woman on stage ended her tune with everyone breathless. Rather than close the curtains or take a drink, she looked up in surprise, the entire auditorium seemingly forgotten.

Royston felt it a moment later. Something drew his head to the heavens. And perhaps his soul.

"What is it?" Fatima whispered, but that was a question Royston could not answer.

And then the world ended.

RAIDERS

GARETH KNEW the moment had arrived by the way both Yuuixtl sat up straighter and stared at each other. He was the only other person in the room, the others having retired into the adjoining chamber to watch through the two-way mirror. Just in case, he rapped his knuckles smartly on the glass to get everyone's attention.

Morty and Xiomber had their heads together, murmuring quietly when the rest of the team burst into the room.

"What have you got?" Jackeith demanded.

"I think we've found him," Morty said. "Xiomber's certain, but I'm only rating it four deviations."

"That's a damned, high number," Baker said as she moved with Grodray towards the center of the room.

"Yeah, but multiply it by ten billion and you've still got a lot of other people it might be," Morty snarled back. "Even at this distance, it's a royal pain in the ass narrowing the field down."

"You did it once," Grodray accused. "Twice actually."

He nodded in Gareth's direction as the four of them, three Constabulary and one Nari scientist, hovered over the two Yuudixtl.

"And both times we were looking for an emotional signature," Xiomber snapped. "Cinra wanted a pure killer. Morty wanted a hero. Finding an archetype is a lot easier than finding a person. I can't just program in *Vanir* and have it look. We have to nail down a criminal psyche profile."

"Really?" Grodray seemed unconvinced.

"You got any idea how many criminals there are on Earth, copper?" Morty snarled.

"I do," Gareth spoke up to defuse them before emotions got out of control.

It was just the stress talking now. The risk that they were so far behind Marc that he would have time to raise an entire army of killers ready to come over and destroy the *Accord of Souls*.

Still, everyone paused, turning to Gareth.

"I was Sky Patrol," Gareth said. "Am Sky Patrol. My entire career has been dedicated to fighting crime. The few times I got to rescue maidens from something other than dragons I could probably count on one hand. If you think the Constabulary has had a hard time lately, multiply that by the centuries my kind have been trying to keep a lid on things here without the psionic resonance of the *Accord*."

He fixed Baker and Grodray with a hard look.

"There's one way to do this," he said. "Someone has to go through and determine."

"No," Grodray said. "If one person goes through, we have to send an entire team, otherwise one person might get killed before they can report back. At best, this tips Maximus off and he runs. At worse, it starts a war."

"And a whole assault force won't?" Gareth asked.

"If it does, it will be on our terms," Grodray replied. He turned to Morty. "Safe enough bet to scare the hell out of a group of innocents if we land on them?"

"Ain't nobody innocent where I'm going to drop you, Grodray," Morty said. "Maybe not Maximus when you get there, but it isn't the same thing as they don't have it coming. Personally, I'd take disintegrators instead of stunners, and just kill the lot of them, but I have a low opinion of someone that scores this high on the psychopath scale in the first place. Plus, he might have more of those android things that nearly kicked Gareth's ass last time."

Grodray was in command, so everyone waited for his decision.

"Talus, you listening?" Grodray asked out loud.

"I am," the Senior Constable in charge of the facility answered over the speakers.

"Alert One," Grodray said. "Get my team in motion and gear. Have local security teams ready to step in here, in case someone comes back through the tube other than us. I'll send a note to the First Inspector. Everyone has one hour to drop. Plan accordingly and meet here in full assault gear."

The room exploded into motion. Gareth followed Grodray and Baker to the suite where their rooms were in order to arm himself. Like the previous missions, stunner and heavy disintegrator pistols went into the holsters. They would do the same. The rest of the team would have both, but most likely keep the disintegrator holstered until necessary.

Gareth could shoot with both hands, as could Eve and Jack.

He didn't eat, knowing that the adrenaline would sour anything in his stomach, but Gareth did settle for a mug of honey-laden coffee to pep himself up without being so acidic that it curdled on him. He had to assume Marc would be waiting for them on the other side of the tube, probably firing as soon as he had a target.

Hopefully, they could flood the far end with enough guns and shooters to clear the room out, if it came to that.

Back at the staging area, he was surprised when Talyarkinash joined them, dressed for the field and with a bag slung over her shoulder.

"What do you think you are doing, Dr. Liamssen?" Grodray demanded in a low voice.

"You'll need a second medic with you," she said simply. "You only have one right now, and if something happens to him, you'll have none. I'm a fully licensed doctor, so I can join you as a field medic. Plus, I've been there since damned near the beginning, so I claim the right to be there at the end."

"You might get killed, Liamssen," Baker tried to dissuade her.

Gareth nearly laughed. Talyarkinash was at least as stubborn as the two Vanir.

At least.

"And Maximus might have killed me several times over, Baker," Talyarkinash snapped back at the woman. "He didn't stick a knife in your arm. Or offer to slice your throat. Keep that in mind."

Every eye turned to Grodray now. He studied the group closely. In the background, fifteen more troopers were filing in and lining up along the walls, but they remained silent in their field armor and firepower.

"On your head. Liamssen," Grodray finally decided. But he nodded.

"I would not have it any other way, Grodray," Talyarkinash replied.

Gareth turned to the two Yuudixtl scientists.

"Morty, will this tube hold a dragon?" he asked.

"Sure, kid," Morty said. "But this room's barely big enough just for you. And I got no idea of the space I'm dropping you, except that it's a room of some size. Wouldn't do it until you got there, just to be sure."

"Understood," Gareth said.

He could chance it. Transform into the Star Dragon in the middle of the transit and arrive at the other end in his great form.

But it was risky. He might come out in a place too small to maneuver. On the other hand, if he came out in his Vanir form, it would cost him several seconds to transform, possibly while a firefight was happening.

"Scout first, Gareth," Grodray ordered him. "You, Baker, then me into the tunnel. My team after that. Then Dr. Liamssen. If necessary, we'll hold them off long enough for you to change."

"Understood, sir," Gareth said.

He moved to a spot in front of the others, along the far part of the room where Morty and Xiomber would open a tunnel to *Earth*.

"Everybody set?" Xiomber called out across the rustling of bodies.

The noise fell to silence. Gareth drew both pistols and prepared to confront the man who had once been his closest friend in the world.

"Now," Grodray said simply.

Morty nodded and began shifting levers.

The generators behind the machine were in a separate part of the facility, so they weren't close enough to hear. At least not unless one of them exploded.

Still, the lights flickered under the enormous drain. They would be putting twenty bodies through a small generator station, rather than one of the big, industrial units for transporting vehicles. But those were permanently locked to a single tube and optimized.

Building this sort of apparatus required you to be able to target any point in the galaxy and lock onto it. And this unit had been home built from scratch by some criminal genius. It began to hum ominously as it drew power into itself. Not loud, but an unpleasant snarl of energy rather like a hive of angry wasps about to emerge.

"Grodray, we are go," Morty yelled over the noise.

"Open the tube," the Senior Constable, the Prime Investigator in disguise, ordered.

Gareth watched a Yuudixtl hand grab the big level on the end and push it all the way to the stops. In front of him, gold began to form in the very air.

He flashed back to leaving Earth the first time, under the control of those same two men. It felt right that they were the ones sending him back now, however temporary this mission would be.

At least he would be on *Earth* one last time in his life.

The portal opened. Gareth felt the softest breeze come over his shoulders and enter, like a whirlpool seeking to drown sailors.

"All weapons off safety and ready to engage," Grodray ordered the room.

They were going in hot. It was the only way to be sure.

"Gareth, into the tube," came the call.

Gareth stepped forward and felt the universe unravel around him as the tunnel took hold.

Last time, it had been frightening. Now, he felt nothing but anger.

He was going to kill Marc. Nothing short of that would ever make the galaxy safe. It saddened Gareth, but this was the moment when the greater needs of the trillions of being alive and yet to be born outweighed a handful of fools intent on upsetting the apple cart.

He took a deep breath, unsure how long it would take to arrive. He would need to land, scan the entire room, and probably open fire in an eyeblink. Or at least draw fire to him so that Baker and Grodray could get the drop on whoever was shooting. Hopefully, nothing but pistols shooting hot lead. His field armor would offer some protection.

A heavy disintegrator, like the one in his left hand, would just cut him in half.

Gareth felt his heartbeat surging, pounding in his chest and his ears.

The tunnel suddenly grew cold around him, rather than the normal warmth it conveyed.

Gareth felt a moment of panic as it felt like he was slowing down.

Was that even possible?

And then his entire universe lit up with white fire.

APOCALYPSE

IT HAD TAKEN TWO DAYS, but Marc figured that Two-Gun was finally starting to calm down. He didn't twitch every time he saw a Warreth female or a Nari male. The three androids had barely bothered him a bit.

"You ready to finally talk?" Marc asked.

The two of them were sitting at the poker table, sipping coffee. Zorge and Mishalska were in the garage, tuning the machine to make longer tubes. Maiair and Yooyar were over on the kitchenette side of the space, pointedly keeping a polite distance.

Two-Gun set his coffee down and stared up at Marc.

"It feels like some bizarre Halloween thing," he said in a surprisingly high tenor voice. He was a tall man, six two, but lanky and fast. The scar on his face made him look hideous, but the rest of him had once been pretty enough for the girls to swoon over.

"I understand," Marc said. "Over there, humans are unknown demons that mothers threaten their children with. I had to take on a Vanir form in order to hide."

"You planning to do that to me?" Two-Gun asked nervously.

"Not now," Marc said. "Maybe later, if you decide you want to. We might be able to erase the scar when we did, but I can't promise anything until I talk to a geneticist."

"It's all right for now," Two-Gun said. "Been this way for fifteen years.

Not sure I'd like looking at myself in the mirror without it. Or with the ears."

"Changing form takes some getting used to," Marc agreed. "At least for me it did."

"So you sprung me from prison," the shooter said. "What's the play?"

"I've got gold and some first-class forged paper bills and identity papers," Marc said. "You'll go into civilization in O'Roark's vehicle and set yourself up with a bank account and such. I think Seattle's a safer bet than the East Coast. They ignore outsiders up there, so you'll be able to work. Rent yourself a flat and find us a warehouse to move all our equipment to. Then rent a big truck and drive it back out here. We dismantle everything, pack it to wherever you landed, and set up again. From there, we build an army."

"Ya know, Portland's even smaller and more insular than Seattle," Two-Gun offered.

"True, but it's also a surprisingly racist town, even today," Marc countered. "After the way they treat non-WASPs, could you imagine the reaction to a Nari or a Warreth? At least a Vanir could be passed off as a human from a distance. No, Seattle doesn't really care what color or shape you are, as long as you have money."

"Gotcha, boss," Two-Gun said. "And you'll just trust me with money and a new identity? No chaperone? Nothing?"

"It's not like I can't find you if I wanted to," Marc threatened the man politely. "And you're back in the pen in a heartbeat if someone does recognize you, so you need someplace safe to hide as bad as I do. I can offer you the entire galaxy to vanish into. At least until we conquer Earth and you're no longer a fugitive."

That brought a rough smile.

"Sound good," he said. "When do I depart."

"Probably…"

Zorge came blasting through the door to the garage with a beam pistol in his hand and wild look in his eyes.

"Tube warning," he yelled as he found a spot with cover and dropped in. "Someone's coming through!"

Marc grabbed the table and carried it towards a side wall. It wouldn't stop much, but it would hide him for a second.

"Two-Gun, this way," he yelled, drawing the small human in his wake.

Around the room, Maiair and Yooyar also drew weapons, as did the three androids.

As armed laagers went, not much, but hopefully good enough. All he could offer right now was a rabid porcupine.

Marc felt the tube begin to take shape. The air tasted golden and warm over in one corner, where someone was about to drop Constables on him.

We'll just have to see about that.

And then the world ended.

THE COMMUNION

"HAVE ALL ARRIVED?" a voice asked the darkness.

"We are come, *Speaker for the Communion*," another voice answered.

Speaker for the Communion looked out and counted the sigils around him. Twelve, as in ancient times, when the last council of the Chaa voted to ascend to godhead. Even *Seeker for the Knee of God* was here, brought by no less than *First Immortal* herself, the two farthest wanderers having come home for the first time in a Chitra or more.

"I call *The Communion* to witness," he said to the other minds. "The vote to include the humans in the past was just and clear. The *Accord of Souls* was shaped without them, and has remained. But all of our expectations of human cultural development have proven inaccurate to a degree that requires a return to the original Plan. *Docent*, you would speak?"

"All such plans are estimates," the *Great Teacher* replied mildly. "Five Chitra is a long time in the life span of any species unmodified. Wrong conveys value. We cannot know God's plan without asking It."

"So noted," *Speaker for the Communion* said. "*Last Traveler*, how great is the danger?"

"When I first tasted the signs, the risk was measured in centuries," the most compassionate said. "However, look ye now and absorb the essence of change about to unfold around us."

Speaker for the Communion felt the sigils of two of his kin engulf this world of humans and draw forth the indications. One was *Glory in Sunrise*, named for the happiness in exploration for no greater reason than learning and seeing.

The other had been her brother, once upon a time incarnated. He had been called *Bowsprit* then, as the foremost point of the Ship of Heaven, but his sigil had grown inward, complicated over the Chitra. It might best be enunciated as *Astray in Darkness* today, indicating one that has gone deeper into the wilds and not yet found the way out.

Perhaps *The Communion* would need to assist.

"*Last Traveler* speaks truth," *Glory in Sunrise* spoke for her brother. "The risk is imminent, even on corporeal scales. We must act."

"I call *The Communion* to *Almar*," another voice broke in.

Speaker for the Communion joined the others in returning to the very soil from which they once departed, five Chitra ago.

"So," *Narrator of History* spoke now. "Our grandchildren have spoken for war on the humans of their own volition. They will wipe out the species in defensive terror. What says *The Communion*?"

"I will not allow it," *Merciless* spoke, breaking the silence of nearly a Chitra. "I must already stand one day before God for such a crime. No others should have to stand with me."

"Will you accept responsibility for a second expunging?" *Speaker for the Communion* asked, taking the taste of the minds about him.

"I will."

"Who else would speak?"

"We move in undue haste," *First Immortal* suddenly dominated them with her sigil. "It is true that we might have moments until such war breaks out, but it is acted upon in ignorance of *The Great Plan*. Of *The Communion*. Humans have no understanding that other species even exist as yet. We must judge them accordingly, but we must reveal ourselves to them first."

"And if they will not bow?" *The Mountain* asked.

"*The Communion* is already gathered," she replied. "We can summon the entire *Ascended Chaa* and place this vote before such a congress."

Speaker for the Communion noted the votes of his fellows and saw the way forward. Looking outward, he saw the terrified leaders of *Almar* preparing a crude biological weapon to unleash on the humans. He noted Constables of the *Accord of Souls* already in motion to kill or be killed, attempting to arrest the creature at the core of the troubles.

One such Constable stood out.

The creature wore the form of a Vanir, but was not of the *Accord*. He was human in a second guise. With a third contained within.

Most interesting. The human was capable of a higher form.

Perhaps they had chosen well, seven Chitra ago when they left the humans to develop. Such creatures might yet *Ascend*, if a Star Dragon was any clue.

But time was measured in seconds now.

The war was already begun. Only the Chaa could end it. Should end it.

Their own failures had brought the galaxy thus.

He reached out a hand and stopped time itself.

Humans acted in ignorance, it was true, but their crimes were no less savage for it. They would be placed on trial. The entire *Communion* would judge.

Speaker for the Communion caused his voice to emerge from every speaker device in the entire *Accord of Souls*, and every room on *Earth*, regardless of technology. He intercepted every wormhole traversing into or out of Earth and prevented the Commissioners on *Almar* from opening a new one to destroy the humans with their weapon.

Finally, he gathered up all of the souls responsible for the current state of affairs, including several humans who had no inkling of the coming role they would play.

"PEOPLE OF THE EARTH, YOU WILL HEAR ME."

TRIAL OF THE STAR DRAGON

AWAKENING

THE LIGHT WAS SO BRIGHT, so disorienting that it took him several seconds to remember something as trivial as his name.

Gareth St. John Dankworth.

Earth Force Sky Patrol.

Accord of Souls Constabulary.

For several moments he wondered if he was dead. Stories he had heard when he was young had suggested that such a perfect, white light that surrounded you when Heaven called you to your final resting place.

He wasn't ready to be dead. There was still at least one man he needed to make sure preceded him, after all. Marc Sarzynski. Maximus. The worst criminal mastermind in the entire, known galaxy.

The man who had been his best friend for nearly a decade when they were younger.

But then other voices intruded on Gareth's consciousness. Ones he recognized.

Hopefully, they hadn't died, too. He would rather be lonely in heaven, or hell, than to have all those others, those friends, join him.

But that was most certainly out of his hands now.

He looked up as a room seemed to come into being around him.

Around them.

White, but he was expecting that. Somehow larger than the sky, and yet it still felt tiny. Compact.

Overfull with emotions and beings.

And then Gareth understood who those beings were, the immense ones up on that platform, looking down at him and the other ghosts standing with him on the floor.

Was it a floor? There was something solid holding him up, but he could see stars through it and the walls, like they were all ghosts, too. And through the other ghosts in here with him. The air smelled like spring, right after that first good rain that makes all the plants wake up and look around. There was even a breeze that seemed to stir the air, so maybe he was onto something.

Jackeith Grodray. Eveth Baker. Those two were easy to recognize. Their intensity stood out against the others. Cops going to make perhaps the most important arrest of their already-storied careers.

Talyarkinash Liamssen. Doctor. Geneticist. Nari. Friend. The woman who would not allow the other two to leave her behind as he and the two of them walked into what might be their final battle.

Others were familiar, scattered through the space and indistinct, like they kept wanting to turn to smoke and never could quite make it.

Gareth opened his mouth and nothing came out.

Nothing? How was that possible?

No. Unacceptable.

"Who are you?" he managed to whisper.

The powerful being at the center of the dais above turned to face him, shock somehow registering on the face that appeared almost human. Almost Vanir.

Almost a god.

Gareth understood then, who they were.

All twelve of them had similar faces, similar features, that blend of Vanir and something else, but they looked almost like images projected on the side of a building, so huge they were compared to the folks down here on the ground with Gareth.

At the same time, they also appeared as tremendous clouds, white with energy and power.

Those were the Chaa themselves. The most powerful of the ancients. The ones who had shaped the *Accord of Souls* into a fixed form before transforming themselves into something else and setting out to find the Creator of the Universe, so they could sit at His knee and learn of His Plan.

"You would speak for the Humans?" the being communicated in a way that Gareth heard with his entire body, and not just his pointy, Vanir ears.

Speak for the Humans? Could he even do that? Gareth wasn't human anymore, at least as far as he knew.

Talyarkinash had transformed him physically into a Vanir, among other things, along with the help of the two Yuudixtl scientists/criminals: Morty and Xiomber.

Except he wasn't **OF** the *Accord of Souls*. Did not belong to that psionic collective that bound seventeen other species into the peace, the galaxy-spanning republic of worlds that excluded only the *Earth* from its halls.

"I am no longer Human," Gareth forced the words out with his mind, rather than his diaphragm. "But I would speak. For Justice, perhaps."

"It is noted, Gareth St. John Dankworth," the creature (Man? Being? Chaa?) said. "Who else would speak."

"If it is to be a judgment, then my words should be known," another voice spoke up.

Gareth did not hear it with his ears. Perhaps his soul?

But he knew that voice.

Royston Loughty, PhD, WMU, FRS, CBE, CStJ. Doctor of Physics. Warden of the Mathematical Union. Fellow of the Royal Society. Commander, British Empire. Commander, Order of St John.

More importantly, the Father of Philippa Loughty, the woman Gareth had been on his way to finally propose to when all this craziness began a year ago. *Pippa.*

How was Dr. Loughty here? Who else had joined him? Them?

"But for my arrogance, we would not be here," Dr. Loughty pronounced. "If a price must be paid, perhaps my soul will be of sufficient weight to offset the innocent."

"There are no innocents here," the Chaa in charge spoke. "Only shades of guilt beginning with troublesome and ending in xenocide. Who would speak for the *Accord of Souls*?"

A pause stretched, before another illuminated ghost stepped forward. He glowed white, like the rest, but Gareth got the impression of blueness from the man.

"In the absence of the Proctor, I suppose that such responsibility falls on my shoulders, Lord," the person said. "I would have led the *Accord* into making such a terrible decision, had you not intervened."

"The decision yet remains outstanding, Petim Diazal," the Chaa responded. "*The Communion* is gathered in Congress to judge."

Gareth heard most of the room now, erupting into whispers of awe and fear.

The Communion? The *Twelve* most powerful of the Chaa? The ones who had created everything? Here? Now?

Gathered In Judgment did not sound hopeful.

"How shall I address you, Lord?" the man known as Petim Diazal asked in a penitent voice.

"I am *Speaker For The Communion*," the Chaa pronounced. "The *Twelve* are gathered. All of the *Ascended Chaa* listen in on this deliberation, that they may make their wills known ere Judgment is rendered."

Gareth had studied some aspects of *Accord* history and law, in his quest to earn himself a proper place in the Constabulary, the police forces that protected the *Accord*.

A race of powerful mentalists known as The Chaa had found the way to free themselves from physical bodies. With immortality assured, they had set out to find the Creator, but before they left, fifty thousand years ago, they had taken most of the Chaa, those who did not wish to live forever, and transformed them into the Vanir.

Those Left Behind.

At the same time, they had chosen sixteen other species from across the galaxy and *Uplifted* them to sentience and civilization, where most had been barely animals at the time. Nari. Warreth. Yuudixtl. Grace. Quarrie. Elohynn. Borren. Moisa. Th'Tarni. Vratha. Enjev. Arawath. Ramasayia. Traakna. Drahvi. U'Chagi.

The *Accord of Souls*.

The *Twelve*, according to legend, had stood on the surface of their homeworld, *Almar*, the *Axle of Time*, and leapt into eternity. That hallowed soil today held the government buildings of the *Accord* itself, although Gareth had only ever seen pictures of it.

Gareth watched as one by one, the twelve beings before him lit up in turn and communicated their sigil to the assembly. It wasn't a name. Wasn't just a name. Instead, it somehow conveyed their entire being, their purpose.

First Immortal.

Docent, also known as the *Great Teacher*.

Seeker for the Knee of God.

Uplifter.

Glory in Sunrise.

Merciless, conveying implacable power as well as great sadness.

Speaker For The Communion.

Narrator of History.

Mountain.

Astray in Darkness.

Magistrate.

Last Traveler.

Of all of them, *Last Traveler* seemed to be the friendliest. Gareth caught a hint of true warmth as the being spoke.

"We are gathered in judgment," *Speaker For The Communion* pronounced. "Explanations will be heard. Guilt will be weighed. Worlds will be altered. The *Accord* must be protected."

Gareth felt his breath catch at that last bit.

"Why?" he demanded.

It sounded weak, even to his own ears, but he would not, could not remain silent.

"Who challenges?" *Speaker For The Communion*'s voice seemed to roar.

"Gareth Dankworth," he replied. "If you are truly gods, you Chaa, you could fix everything. Your failures of vision have brought us thus."

Inwardly, he gasped at his own audacity.

Certainly, Gareth expected that he should wash his own mouth out with soap for speaking to a god that way, but he could not stay his own rage at the situation. From the stirrings on the platform, Gareth expected someone to strike him down with lightning now.

Or at least snap him on the wrist with a ruler, like the sisters had once done when a pupil spoke out of turn.

Last Traveler brightened, drawing all eyes his(?) direction.

"The Human speaks truth," *Last Traveler* pronounced in a sharp, doom-calling tone. "We chose to exclude his type from the *Accord* during the organizing vote. That they did not subsequently chose to follow our Great Plan for their civilizing development is not necessarily a crime we should place at their feet. There are others much more culpable whom we should address first."

Gareth watched the creatures on the platform make their wishes known with light and sound. It would be easier if they had corporeal form, but each still seemed to manifest as a glowing cloud of gray/white light that was at times painful to even look at, rather than a body, and even the faces came and went as he watched.

But Gareth knew they had once shared a form similar to his own, even as he would have still looked somewhat like a human if he had a proper form.

Seven feet, four inches tall. Three hundred and forty pounds in his fighting trim. He could still pass a large human, such as the monsters of the interior, defensive line, even though he had played defensive end in school.

That much, Vanir were just large humans, externally. The ears were dramatically oversized and came to points, much like the elves that many fantasy artists liked to create. His eyes were larger, relative to the rest of his skull as well, almost like a cartoon character.

But he was also among the biggest, strongest of the Vanir he had met. Morty and Xiomber had done that on purpose, because they had transformed Marc Sarzynski the exact same way. The same build. Everything. Only the coloration was different, with Marc's normally darker skin and dark, curly hair preserved, even as Gareth's blond hair had.

They had at least started there. Before they moved on at Gareth's insistence and did something for which these gods in attendance might truly take offense. They had turned him into the Star Dragon so he could better resist the criminal known as Maximus.

Gareth turned in wonder at everything and spotted his old friend, his nemesis across the room surrounded by others that seemed possessed of the same, dark aura. Gareth tried to move, to attack the man, to finally kill him and make the galaxy a safer place, but he found himself held.

"No violence will be allowed, Gareth," *Speaker For The Communion* announced. "*The Communion* alone will *Judge*, and then punishment will be meted out."

Gareth felt terrible psychic fingers reach inside his soul and grope around. He had no other way to describe it. If his brains were a bowl of wet olives, someone was rifling through, looking for that perfect one, presumably to stick on the end of their finger, like everyone did when they had olives to munch. It didn't hurt, but the violation was something he would never forget, even if these people meant no personal animosity.

Still, it was wrong.

"But your intent is plainly known, Gareth," another voice said. "Your instincts will be judged by the outcomes you seek, and not merely the crime of being a human in the *Accord of Souls*."

Gareth turned and the one speaking seemed to be the Chaa known as *Astray in Darkness*. Gareth did not understand the implications of the sigil, but it did not seem as hostile as some of the others. *Mountain*, perhaps. Or *Merciless*.

Another name seemed to be resting behind *Astray in Darkness*. Gareth had the impression of a figurehead on a mighty sailing ship. Except *Astray in Darkness* was beyond even that.

Bowsprit. The closest bit of the ship to the horizon. That was the being's soul. He had gone astray in darkness seeking for something he did not understand. That none of them understood.

Gareth bowed, acknowledging the words and the intent. A human in the *Accord* was the single greatest crime possible. The only solution was dissolution.

Gareth could accept that, if it made the *Accord* safe again. If somehow, humans could be bottled up forever, or at least until they managed to grow up and become responsible, galactic citizens.

However long that might take. The Chaa had already waited fifty thousand years.

"There are two others whose crimes must be weighed first," *Uplifter* spoke next, the rage in his being palpable. "I did not give you art and civilization to have you cast it all away thus. You will face me."

Gareth recognized the forms of Morty and Xiomber. They even seemed to coalesce into their physical bodies as he watched, transforming from ghosts to bodies.

Both wore blue dungarees and T-shirts somehow not dripped on from lunch. They looked around with something approaching fear, but only for a moment before jaws clenched and eyes got all squinty.

"The *Accord of Souls* was designed to provide the greatest benefit for the greatest number of future being, Morty and Xiomber," *Uplifter* growled. "I see in your souls nothing but disdain for others and criminal behavior that leaves me appalled. What defense would you offer?"

Xiomber's snout opened, but no words came out. Morty, however, was having none of it.

"Hey, pal, we've pled guilty," the Yuudixtl scientist snapped. "We're already probably going to spent the rest of our lives in jail, okay? You wanna talk mitigating circumstances, maybe? It ain't all evil around here."

"What could you possibly offer that would offset the crime of bringing the human Marc Sarzynski into *Accord* Space?" *Uplifter* sneered savagely.

Gareth didn't even know gods were capable of that range of emotion, but then he had never met a god before.

"The Star Dragon, pal," Morty's jaw thrust out. "We went looking for a hero, when it became obvious just how badly we'd screwed up. I'd screwed up. How screwed the rest of you were going to be if we didn't do something. And don't give me that crap about us going to the authorities with what I knew, like good, little *Accord* citizens. Grodray and Baker here can tell you just how badly bent the cops were. Not just here, on most worlds. You people should have come back a thousand years ago, if you wanted to fix things quietly."

Gareth felt his blood pool in his stomach with sudden fear. This would be the point where Zeus would have blasted Morty off of Olympus, to fall to his death on the rocks below.

Instead, silence reigned. Awkward, extended silence.

Another voice suddenly broke the silence. *Narrator of History*, if Gareth had memorized them in the correct order.

"The Yuudixlt speaks truth, if rather bluntly and without charm," *Narrator of History* observed in a warm, alto voice that Gareth would have gladly spent all evening listening to. "We yet bear some responsibility, having fixed the structure the current generation of our descendants has inherited."

That voice reminded him of the woman who had been his kindergarten teacher, telling naptime stories before laying Gareth and his friends down to rest. Not that she would have even made something like this seem believable. Maybe a radio announcer instead, tucking all the little boys and girls into bed for the evening with a scientifiction tale, before moving on to play some soft, orchestral jazz as a way to get them to sleep without needing a glass of water in twenty minutes.

"The complexities are so noted," *Speaker For The Communion* announced in a voice that somehow seemed less angry, if no less powerful, to Gareth's weary ear. "All of the *Accord of Souls* can hear us. Every human alive will be made to understand their place, and their fate. This Court is in session. As *Speaker For The Communion*, I will preside, but *The Communion* itself will act as one. *Last Traveler*, you will present your findings that have brought us thus, for the first time in Five Chitra."

CHAA

HE HAD BEEN the last of *The Communion* to depart *Almar*, the *Axle of Time* itself. Not because of any great emotional attachment to the place itself, but so that others could race ahead and hopefully find the trail of the Creator. *First Immortal, Seeker for the Knee of God*, and *Glory in Sunrise* had left first, traversing several of the great wormholes in near space, listening for those echoes that said He had walked this way.

Last Traveler had remained behind nearly a third of a Chitra, watching over the newly-created thing that *Magistrate* and *Uplifter* had created. And perhaps to help the newly sentient species to find their places. The Grace would have eventually found themselves, but he had given them the suggestion to use art in an attempt to resolve their own sensory overload into something that others might understand.

Similarly, the Moisa were builders. Had always been builders. Perhaps *Last Traveler* had offered them architecture as a way of expressing their love of organization and strength.

As the *Last Traveler* to leave, he still looked upon his various descendants as grandchildren. The kind to be both spoiled and educated, as one did. To fire their dreams as well as their intellect.

It had brought him back to *Almar* time and again, just to bask in the glory of what his grandchildren had attained, and continued to explore. The new worlds brought into the *Accord*. The new art. Music. Even titanic, bronze statuary that was currently all the rage with the Grace.

To his many witnesses, *Last Traveler* communicated those visions, those dreams, those memories.

"And then the first seed of darkness bloomed," he said, turning his eye on the human Marc Sarzynski.

Maximus. A killer without hesitation, for whatever bits of remorse yet lived deep in his soul. There was light to be seen there, but even that was cast into service of evil.

He looked into the souls of several witnesses and brought the story forth.

In a galaxy that was not supposed to know crime, somehow the powerful beings of *The Communion* had missed the rise of a new creature called a crime boss.

Cinnra the Warreth had been such a creature. In a galaxy that was supposed to bind peace within the psionic resonance known as the *Accord of Souls*, some people had been born broken. Or somehow achieved it.

Last Traveler understood then that *The Communion* as an entity had failed. They had not foreseen that one could live only partially within *Accord* with one's neighbors. That poverty and want could exist in a galaxy where anything might be within the reach of your dreams. That the Uplifted could still prey upon one another.

He called forth the glyph of Cinnra the Warreth. Crime boss. Deviant. Dominator. But not a killer. Cinnra had determined that he needed a killer, in order to fortify his hold on a criminal underworld that was yet filled mostly with only-partially-broken souls.

He had tasked his best scientists with finding such a creature. They had located a human. Marc Sarzynski. And caused him to be brought to the worlds of the *Accord of Souls*.

Last Traveler was a compassionate being, filled with love and affection for *Those Left Behind*, including the ones he was not directly related to. The other sixteen clans.

He still felt a growl bubble up as a glyph that encompassed the two Yuudixtl criminals. The two had the courtesy to bow before his rage. Mitigation later they might have attempted, but the original sin was still theirs to own.

"These two bear that mark," *Last Traveler* said. "For their own arrogant motives, their own chance at a form of legend, of godhead, they brought Marc Sarzynski forth. This crime is not in dispute."

"No, pal, it is not," the angrier of the two, Morty, somehow managed to glyph back at him, although none but *The Communion* might hear it.

"Maximus, in due course, overthrew Cinnra the Warreth, killed him, and took over his gang, slaying many who would not bow to an alien, even one that would now pass as Vanir to the casual glance. One now may witness his crimes."

Last Traveler pulled forth many glyphs for evidence, as Maximus was a stain on all of civilization and everyone here needed to appreciate the depths of depravity to which a human might delve. Murder. Torture. Kidnapping. Extortion. Corruption of the Body Public and Politic.

All these things were shown to the assembled witnesses, *The Communion*, even those of the *Ascended Chaa* who chose to watch.

"And there are others," he spoke once the glyph had passed.

Zorge the Nari. Maiair the Warreth. Yooyar the Warreth. Mishalska the Nari. Other faces not present, but that was either because they had been captured and awaited their punishment, or had not accompanied Maximus to *Earth*.

Now *Last Traveler* showed a series of human faces that he extracted from the minds of the criminals. Demian O'Rourke, a human crime boss. Four other men who served the human, as well as a young woman of no great note, other than to want to belong.

"I could go on," *Last Traveler* said. "Without the Accord to bind them into peace, humans are just as dangerous, just as violent as we had expected them to be, seven Chitra ago when the vote was taken to exclude them from our construction."

"Members of *The Communion*, how do you vote?" *Speaker For The Communion* asked the assembled gods.

Each submitted a glyph, democracy being the only way to truly organize such a construct, where twelve powerful beings who might live forever did not wish to take permanent responsibility.

Quickly, the lopsided natures of things became clear.

"So it has been decided," *Speaker For The Communion* announced in a voice that even the ephemeral beings could hear. "The Earth and all of the humans are to be expunged. Thus will the *Accord of Souls* be protected, while not tasking any of the *Ascended Chaa* with having to watch over them and prevent their escape into the larger galaxy. *Merciless* has demanded responsibility for destroying humanity. If none would dispute that, he will now act."

"No," a voice rose out of the midst of the assembled watchers.

Last Traveler was shocked at the vehemence of the tone, especially coming from a young Grace woman. He could see one of the many humans wanting to rage, but this person surprised him.

"Speak, Ilak Vorta," *Last Traveler* commanded.

He had been granted the floor to present his case, and had done so, unaware that there might rise a defender. He would hear her testimony.

She turned to face him and pulled from her head a fine, silk cloth that had been obscuring her sensory tentacles. From the gasps around her, *Last Traveler* determined that only half of the humans were surprised that a Grace walked among them, disguised.

"If you act thus, you are no better than they are," she snarled in a tight, angry voice that almost caused *Last Traveler* to flounder back a step.

He looked within the woman briefly, and then within himself and saw the problem.

She was right.

GRACE

FATIMA KNEW that she appeared human to the men and women around her, including Royston, Pippa, and Hank. Even the ones that knew better.

The human musician Fatima somehow knew was named Ellen had understood that Fatima was something more. Fatima Darzi was only an identity she had assumed, in order to walk safely among the humans.

More safely. They were still the most violent, most dangerous species ever to achieve technology, according to the records, however ancient.

And yet, she had gone among them willingly. Met many humans, across the entire spectrum of behaviors and personalities. Had been accepted as one of them, with no more threat to her person than perhaps Sir West's towering indignation that Royston hadn't called the man and let him know they were in London.

Fatima picked Sir West out of the crowd from where he had been trying to slink to a corner, invisible as a mouse attempting to hide from the giants.

"So it has been decided," *Speaker For The Communion* commanded a death sentence on an entire species. "The Earth and all of the humans are to be expunged. Thus will the *Accord of Souls* be protected, while not tasking any of the *Ascended Chaa* with having to watch over them and prevent their escape into the larger galaxy. *Merciless* has demanded responsibility for destroying humanity. If none would dispute that, he will now act."

"No," the word exploded out of her lips before she could stop it.

One of the Great Ones turned to her now.

"Speak, Ilak Vorta," he commanded.

She was a spy, not an orator, but somehow, it was her rage that let her break through the fear that threatened to smother all these other beings that had been brought here to witness the Chaa known as *The Communion.*

"If you act thus, you are no better than they are," the phrase erupted from her like a volcano suddenly awakening.

"Why say you thus?" one of the others called down to her.

Fatima turned and glared back at the tremendous menace emanating from the one that she had heard called *Merciless.*

He glyphed her now, and she understood how he came to take this name, when he had been someone else before.

Fatima watched history unfold as the *Ascended Chaa* traveled the width and breadth of this galaxy in their quest to find evidence of He Who Created All. Watched them encounter another species like the humans, tucked in a distant corner of the spiral, almost across the Core from Earth.

Six worlds colonized from the seventh. Warlike. Violent. Xenophobic as they wiped out a planet where the natives were just beginning to understand stone tools.

They were perhaps the most dangerous element in the galaxy, while the *Ascended Chaa* were as yet only a collection of philosophers and seekers. Until *The Communion* spoke.

Fatima watched these same beings pronounce doom on the Tronafora. Watched the being who took the new glyph of *Merciless,* as he hunted down every ship, every creature, every bit of evidence that the Tronafora ever existed. Seven stars cast into sudden supernova stage by the violent expedient of dropping a black hole singularity into close proximity.

Seven star systems wiped clean of all life.

"Yes," Fatima agreed. "You have the power to destroy. And the will to commit xenocide. But you have not given the humans any chance to learn."

"They cannot learn better," one of the others sneered at her. "Look at Marc Sarzynski and tell me his is capable of civilized behavior."

"He is at the far end of human behavior," Fatima snapped back at the god. At all the gods "There are twelve billion others you could choose to study instead."

"And we would find the same capability for violence," that woman(?) called back. "The same murderous rages. The same disdain for helping their fellow creatures in need."

"You would find that walking the streets of *Orgoth Vortai*," Fatima sneered back in a similar tone. "You would also destroy all the amazing things that humans are capable of achieving."

Fatima tried to glyph back to them, as *Merciless* had done, but lacked the understanding of how such a thing was done. Perhaps she also lacked the power, but her rage would not be stilled.

"Allow me?" a new voice appeared in her head.

Astray in Darkness held out a hand, at least metaphorically. She took it and felt the Chaa reach into her mind and grasp at those things Fatima wanted these angry gods to see.

Art. Ancient architecture from her putative homeland of Persia. Music of the souq and the bandstand. Even American cooking, almost as bland and boring as English, but then she threw in Thai, Cameroonian, and Ecuadorian food, just to show them the range of humanity.

All of these images, these glyphs, *Astray in Darkness* lifted up and cast into the sky for her, like soap bubbles in a soft breeze.

"Thank you," Fatima bowed to the Chaa.

He surprised her by returning the bow.

Fatima turned the other way, scanning the crowd of beings until she found the one she wanted.

Ellen, the singer, had ended up not far from Royston, Pippa, and Crown Prince Henry, in disguise tonight as merely Hank, but still the man who would be King of England one day. Fatima tried to convey a smile to them, but she focused her attention on Ellen.

She had not known the woman's name until now, as the musical group went by a vague appellation that included no personal names. But she was Ellen. Her own glyph was nearly as bright as Royston's. Perhaps only Gareth's and Maximus' shown brighter, among the two score of humans who had been gathered up.

"I need your help," Fatima explained as she walked (floated?) over to the woman.

"Mine?" Ellen replied, stunned.

"Yours was the power that showed Royston how to achieve the higher physics and mathematics he needed, in order to understand how to step across space/time," Fatima said. "I need you to explain it to them."

Fatima gesture encompassed the twelve beings, but also included all the other species that made up the *Accord of Souls*, including herself.

"Explain?" Ellen asked.

"Your music," Fatima said. "I have never encountered anything with such power. It is a human thing that none but perhaps these gods have ever heard. And even they may be surprised."

"My band isn't here," Ellen said, turning this way and that to spy the crowd.

Fatima cursed under her breath. The Chaa had gathered together beings of power and importance, but not recognized the gestalt that this woman contained when she was up on that stage.

"Can you bring her band here?" Fatima turned to *Astray in Darkness* and asked.

It was a silly question. These creatures had stopped time and opened up and closed portals to a dozen worlds in order to gather this assembly. *Merciless* was prepared to pick up a black hole with one hand and drop it into the orbit of the human planet *Mercury*, in order to disrupt Earth's sun permanently.

"Why?" one of the angrier gods challenged.

"Because you do not understand," Royston suddenly appeared at her side.

Fatima could taste the rage boiling off the man as he took her hand and held it, almost as if it was the most natural thing in the world.

Like kissing him had been.

"Because I could not have achieved what I did without the power of this woman and her friends," Royston challenged them all loudly. "You need to feel that, experience it, and it is not enough to pick it up out of my memory and try to experience it second-hand."

Fatima felt rougher hands take hold of her mind, sifting it for what Royston knew. A moment later, they moved on, and she could tell that they moved on to the man by the way his breath caught.

Finally, Ellen felt the power, the intrusion of a dozen gods in her mind. Fatima reached out with her other hand and found Ellen's. Held it. Let the woman squeeze painfully while the gods ransacked her.

The Chaa withdrew after another moment.

"What says *The Communion*?" the most powerful voice asked.

"I would hear them," *Astray in Darkness* said quietly. "If their species is to end shortly, perhaps we owe them that much courtesy. Each of us will stand before *He Who Created All* at some future date. Each of us will have the stain of destroying the Tronafora on our souls, even if only one actually acted. *The Communion* still decided upon xenocide as a body. We all share that crime."

Fatima watched as the others were swayed by that logic, until all seemed to favor it. Even *Merciless* nodded.

Between one heartbeat and the next, a stage appeared. Five men in identical, black suits stood upon it, holding human instruments that Fatima still found esoteric and strange, but as with all things human, there was an edge of wildness that the *Accord of Souls* could not fathom.

Could not grasp.

"What the hell?" one of the guitarists murmured as he was suddenly transported from a darkened auditorium to the metaphorical hall of *The Communion.*

Ellen was still holding her hand, so the woman pulled Fatima enough to turn her back.

"I do not understand," Ellen said in a simple voice. "What do you need?"

"They do not believe," a new voice intruded.

Fatima turned to see Prince Hank suddenly close. Focused. Intent. Looking so much older than fifteen years in his poise and stance.

"It is like it was with my mother, Sir West, and Sir William," the young man said. "They had heard the stories, but discounted them. Sir William even went so far as to suggest that we summon you to the palace, in an effort to replicate it or prove Dr. Loughty wrong. That would have failed, for all the reasons that Ms. Darzi was right about and they were wrong. I was wrong. We need you, all of you. We need you to explain to these beings, these gods I suppose, what it means to be human."

"Who are you?" Ellen asked sharply.

Fatima smiled. Unlike the Americans she had met, Ellen was English, at least by her accent. Fatima only sounded Persian, because she needed to. She could speak English better than perhaps most of the people here. Or drift into any of the regional creoles necessary to hide among them.

"Henry Windsor," Hank introduced himself. "Crown Prince of England. Son of Queen Elizabeth III."

"Oh, shit," Ellen gasped. "Really?"

Fatima found it amusing that Ellen rounded on Royston at that.

"This is who you brought to hear me?" Ellen demanded angrily.

"No," Royston smiled in a way both serious and serene. "I brought Fatima to hear you. Hank was a necessary accompaniment because otherwise his mother might have insisted that you play the Palace. That was exactly the sort of situation I was hoping to avoid, but that is out of our hands now."

"Most of the people in here won't understand," Ellen tried to counter.

"Most of them won't matter, Ellen," Fatima said, gesturing. "Those twelve are the ones you need to reach."

"With music?" Ellen asked.

"With the power of rock and roll," Royston explained. "Like you did for me that first time, when you showed me the true music of the spheres, and how to unravel them."

"I'm not sure I can," Ellen faltered.

"I just witnessed you doing it," Fatima said. "I know what you are capable of."

ALIEN

GARETH FINALLY COULD MOVE, as long as he did not stray in the direction of Marc Sarzynski and his small band of criminal aliens. The ones Gareth had been coming to arrest, or destroy, leading Jackeith Grodray and Eveth Baker through a wormhole to *Earth*.

At the same time, he could not bring himself to place even a single foot in the direction he really wanted to go. Towards her.

This was what cowardice felt like. Gareth had never known it. Had never encountered a thing that caused him to retire and refrain. Even dating a volleyball player a foot taller than he was had been merely an adventure for an ambitious thirteen-year-old.

But he could not approach. Could not move.

Fortunately(?) she was not so inhibited.

Gareth watched Pippa detach herself from Royston and a Grace woman who had somehow become the speaker for the humans.

Pippa.

In his pocket, Gareth still had the ring he had been holding in his hands at the moment when destiny intruded. When Morty and Xiomber reached across the width of the galaxy, because they needed a hero if they were going to save the *Accord* from Marc.

But he could not move. Could not rush to her. Take her in his arms and feel he heart surely pounding as hard as his was.

She approached slowly. Almost timidly, like a forest creature who had never seen a man before and how no understanding of how dangerous they were.

But it was still Pippa. Still the woman he loved. Still the face that haunted him when he tried to sleep.

"Gareth?" she whispered as she got close.

He nodded, unable to even breathe lest this all be a soap bubble that would pop and evaporate before his eyes, like so many other dreams had been.

Gareth felt a hand on his back suddenly. It shoved, and he staggered forward a step before he could catch himself.

Gareth looked back and saw the tremendous grin form on Talyarkinash's face as her whiskers flared out and her ears seemed to scan the skies.

"Hi," he managed as he turned back to Pippa, unsure what to say or do.

And then she was in his arms, crying and hiccuping.

It felt so strange, holding her. He had been six foot two the last time he had seen her, then only a head taller than she. Now, she barely came up to the middle of his Vanir chest.

But he cried. And laughed. And held her tight, unsure if he would ever see her again.

"What are you now?" she finally asked, after they both managed to breathe.

"A Vanir," Gareth responded. "It was the closest form Morty and Xiomber could find for a renegade human, when they transformed Marc, so they did the same to me. At first."

"The little lizardman called you a Star Dragon, Gareth," she murmured.

Around them, the world went on, but he had eyes only for Pippa.

"That was the second part, Pippa," he whispered. "When I needed a tool that could stand against Marc. Could overawe his criminals. When I needed to be a symbol for all of the *Accord*."

"So you are truly a dragon?" she asked, shock resounding in her voice.

"I can become one, yes," Gareth said. "Talyarkinash helped with that part."

Gareth reached back and snagged the Nari woman by the arm before she could react.

"Pippa Loughty, it is my great pleasure to introduce you to one of my closest friends in the *Accord of Souls*, Dr. Talyarkinash Liamssen," he said. "Talyarkinash, the woman you've heard me talk so much about. *Pippa.*"

It was interesting, watching the two of them shake hands. Gareth had spent so much time around Nari, Grace, and Vanir that a human like Pippa appeared alien to his eyes.

"Gareth saved my life," Talyarkinash smiled. "I am so glad to be able to finally meet you. To thank you for making him such a wonderful person."

"Me?" Pippa was shocked.

"You," Talyarkinash said. "Let nobody lead you astray on this, but he has been pining for you, loyal to you, from the very first moment I met him. Everything he has done, after what was necessary to save the *Accord*, was with an eye towards somehow transforming himself back into a human so he could return home, if the authorities would allow it."

"Why would they not?" Pippa asked, her eyes going back and forth.

"Because I know too much," Gareth said. "I have had to study everything I could of the *Accord* in order to try and join the Constabulary, the police forces of the *Accord* that are just like Earth Force Sky Patrol. Humans are not supposed to know anything about the *Accord*, for reasons around us that are obvious."

"He even proposed kidnapping you, knowing that the two of you would never be able to return home afterwards, Pippa," Talyarkinash said. "Just so that you could be happy together."

"Would they have allowed that?" Pippa gasped.

"I don't know," Gareth felt his shoulders come up automatically. "We had to stop Maximus from conquering the galaxy first. That would have been later."

"Will we even survive?" Pippa asked. "Father knew there were aliens, that's how he unmasked Fatima as a Grace, but these being seem to be so much more powerful."

"They are the most powerful of the Chaa," Gareth nodded. "The ones who created the *Accord of Souls*. Who uplifted Talyarkinash's ancestors to intelligence and civilization. Marc and I represent the worst crimes imaginable, just by existing in the *Accord*."

"Father found out how you had vanished," Pippa smiled. "His experiments back-tracked what the two little lizardmen did. That's why Fatima came to us, to see what he knew, and if it could be derailed."

"I doubt that it could have," Gareth said. "Humans are too inquisitive."

"That's what Father said," Pippa nodded. "The best that could happen would be if he could least Sky Patrol astray for six months by claiming that something was wrong with the math. Then we went looking for the leaders of the *Accord of Souls* to ask them what could be done."

Gareth could not suppress the gasp that escaped him. How much had he missed, spending all his time trying to fight crime in this alien place?

"What happened?" Talyarkinash came to his rescue.

"We went out into the Arizona desert," Pippa explained. "Fatima stepped through a portal and went…somewhere. When she came back, it became our mission to find the woman Ellen and her band, so that Fatima could see what had happened."

"I don't understand," Gareth managed to squeeze out of the tension in his chest.

How close was the Chaa to just destroying everything? What could he do to somehow convince them to save all the innocents, even if they had to punish him for merely existing?

"Father thinks that it was only the combination of his brilliance and the woman's music that opened the pathways in his mind," Pippa said. "Perhaps without him and her, humanity would still require centuries before they developed the technology to find the aliens. We went out into the desert originally, in case the alien overlords decided that they needed to kill us, to stop things."

"Suicide?" Talyarkinash asked in a shocked, hollow voice.

"Sacrifice," Pippa corrected her. "Our lives, for the rest of humanity, if that was what was necessary. Nobody else knew, or perhaps even guessed that semi-benevolent aliens might be involved in Gareth's disappearance. That they might be watching us."

"And the musician?" Gareth asked. "Where does she fit in all this?"

"I took Father to see her and her band perform in London," Pippa said, still holding on to him with one hand. "Her music is simply impossible to describe, other than to call it the most powerful, most emotional thing I have ever heard. By listening to it, Father found the pathways to higher mathematics."

Gareth turned to Talyarkinash with a question on his face, but no words to express his need.

"It makes perfect sense to me, Gareth," she explained. "Humans have a powerful, latent, psionic ability. That's what you tap in order to transform, and to fly. Her father has similar capabilities for pure mental ability. This other human must express herself through her music."

Before Gareth could answer, a bright light filled the space where all the ghosts and gods were standing. One end of the auditorium was suddenly a raised platform, a stage, with five human men, dressed in skinny, black suits and holding instruments, standing around confused and concerned.

CRIMINAL

MARC STUDIED the room as his senses cleared. He had been holding a pistol in one hand, knelt behind a table that would provide some modicum of cover when the Constables came through their portal, but he had nothing now. Not a beam, not a knife. Nothing.

Maiair and Yooyar were the closest, standing on either side of him like bodyguards. Zorge was just ahead on his right. Glancing back, Mishalska and Two-gun Kowalski were behind him, watching his back, at least as much as they could.

O'Rourke and his people were in a second cluster. Not close, but not clear across the space, like the Chaa had picked everyone up and then put them down in a pattern.

Marc had heard about the Chaa. Some of his gang had been extremely superstitious when he took over, but Marc had thinned those ranks pretty quickly. Religion was nice, and a useful way to bilk suckers, but people concerned about going to hell for what they've done have a tendency to have second thoughts in the current world.

Eventually, enough of them would break under the stress and throw themselves on the mercies of the nearest priest. Which, in turn, usually meant a call to the cops, and a raid, possibly a shootout.

The rationalists had generally been the ones Marc kept.

Who in his right might expected to be called to the carpet by literal gods? And that was what Marc was looking at today.

There had been enough jokes in the gang. How bad could their activities be if the Chaa hadn't come back to stop them, after all?

Until they did. So maybe it had gotten bad enough. And maybe Marc was facing Hell finally, when he had expected it to be much farther off in his future.

He found he could not move in the direction of Gareth or those other two Vanir Constables: Grodray and Baker. Hopefully, they couldn't come over here. He had only a handful of his people, desperately outnumbered by the rest of the room, even before Dankworth turned into that damnable dragon.

And none of the androids were here. Marc assumed at this point that one of those twelve gods had understood what the machines were and simply annihilated them. It was what they should have done.

"What the hell is going on?" Two-Gun murmured from behind him.

"You know most of what I do, Two-Gun," Marc turned enough to answer. "Other than these are apparently the gods who originally created the *Accord of Souls* fifty thousand years ago."

"Gods?" the gangster asked with a growl. "Like Zeus and them?"

"Close enough for our purposes," Marc replied. "Ultimately powerful beings who aren't going to like us one bit for meddling in their sand box."

"I got no guns," Two-Gun muttered. "No knife. Nothing."

"Same here," Marc said. "They wanted us all in one room, it looks like, so they could judge us all."

"He said all of Earth was listening in," Two-Gun's voice took on a measure of broken awe now. "Is that even possible?"

"You tell me what limitations gods have and I'll tell you, Two-Gun," Marc snapped back.

"Crap, we're doomed."

"Probably," Mark said in a softer voice. "But we're going down fighting if we have to. I'd rather explain to Lucifer that it took a dozen gods to kill me, than to politely let those people line me up against the wall and stick a cigarette in my mouth."

Maiair's hand found his and squeezed. Marc drew some comfort from that. She wasn't his first choice for true love, but this woman probably understood him better than most. The one he would have chosen was over there, grinding salt into yet another wound, because that one had also chosen Gareth.

Marc was willing to grant that he had driven Talyarkinash into the man's arms. Stabbing a woman and threatening to cut her throat was not the way to any woman's heart.

But she had chosen to betray him when Morty and Xiomber came to her. She could have just as easily called Marc then and had his goons come over and rescue her.

He tried moving towards O'Rourke, to offer them some explanation and encouragement, but suddenly found his way blocked, almost as if his feet had been nailed to the floor.

One of the gods seemed to shine a light on him from their spot up on the dais.

"You will remain still, Marc Sarzynski," the being said. "We will get to you in good time."

COP

ANEN WARDSON FELT a surge of pride as she watched the agent known to the humans as Fatima Darzi step up and challenged the Chaa. Anen had sent the Grace woman to *Earth* to find a way to prevent this very tragedy, if possible. That Fatima had failed was not something that should weigh heavily on her conscience.

After all, they had all failed.

Very shortly, *The Communion* was likely to wipe out all the humans in existence, which would probably include Gareth Dankworth. Losing him would be a shame, because the man really had worked to redeem himself, but Anen did not expect gods like these to understand something so simple as that.

She turned and found Petim close. She found it interesting that, of all of the *Accord* Commissioners, only Petim had been brought here. She would have expected them to bring everyone when they brought her, but perhaps the one known as *Last Traveler* had understood already that Petim was the Commission, as far as that went. His will would carry the rest.

That they had also picked up the First Inspector of the Constabulary from that meeting meant that they still needed something from her.

Anen had no idea what she might contribute to such a decision. She had been trying to find a way to save the humans from themselves, right up until the moment when it became clear that Marc Sarzynski had made it to Earth. That had sealed his fate, and all of his kin, because there was no way except death to prevent an army of humans from coming through a wormhole one of these days and attacking *Accord* worlds. Whose death was just a matter of scale.

And nothing the *Accord* Constabulary could have done would have stopped them except to slaughter Sarzynski and his gang, and bring back the corpses for confirmation. Otherwise, it would have been a war.

Certainly, Vanir were physically more impressive figures, compared to the humans. But everyone would still be possessed of utter terror to confront a renegade human, especially an armed one. Prime Inspectors like Jack Grodray or Eveth Baker might not hesitate, but too many others would, and it would get them killed.

Even now, she had a hard time even contemplating taking a single step in the direction of the man who had brought them all to this point.

No, that wasn't fair.

Marc Sarzynski had brought them all here. Royston Loughty had merely been trying to solve a mystery, and accidentally uncovered a conspiracy instead. That he had found a way to open his own wormholes had only brought things to her attention, in time for the Constabulary to chase Sarzynski as far as Earth.

And to prepare to destroy all the humans.

Her methods wouldn't have been as comprehensive as the Chaa intended, but nobody knew a way to call on the gods and get them to listen.

Except that now they were here, and going to commit xenocide. While she watched.

There had to be a better solution. Anen had bet Fatima's life on finding it.

Perhaps she should have bet her own.

That thought broke her free from the stasis that had held her in place. She didn't want to think of it as cowardice, right as that might be. She needed to put her badge first now, and not her xenophobia.

She was a cop. Humans didn't know any better, for the most part. Gareth Dankworth did, and that knowledge just drove him to be as good a cop as he could manage, doing anything Jack or Baker had asked without questions.

That pushed her foot forward another step.

She quickly found herself standing next to Dr. Loughty and Fatima, even as something changed and the room was suddenly an auditorium, with a fresh crop of humans, all male, all dressed alike, all musicians, if she understood Darzi's reports correctly.

"Dr. Loughty, we have not met," she said as the man turned towards her, hoping that the Chaa had done something to let him understand her, even though they spoke different languages normally. "I am Anen Wardson, First Inspector of the Constabulary. Gareth Dankworth works for me now."

She got the impression that her much greater size did not intimidate the man in the slightest as he looked up at her. He was a human, so perhaps not.

A moment later, his face broke into a grin.

"First Inspector, thank you for sending Fatima," he said in a strange tone. "We have all tried to salvage the situation, but none have risked more than she. Please remember that when the rest of us are gone and blame and favor needs to be apportioned accordingly."

"You expect to die shortly?" Anen asked, shocked at the calm way the human seemed to accept his fate.

These monsters should have been fighting tooth and nail like crazed beasts, rather than philosophically accepting things.

"Madame, I have been living with that expectation since the moment that the Sector Marshal aboard The Arsenal told me that the niece of my old friend, Firuz Alinejad, wished to study physics with me," Loughty smiled calmly. "I had known Fatima Darzi when she was much younger. Given the circumstances, she could only be an imposter, but even then I had no idea how deep I might find turtles if I went seeking."

Anen wasn't sure she understood the reference, a cultural thing, but she got the gist of it. Royston Loughty was far more canny than anyone had given him credit for. And braver than she imagined, to simply continue on with what he was doing, trying to find a way to save things, even if it might cost him his life.

Should have cost him his life.

Was eventually going to.

Anen understood now more of what made Gareth Dankworth who he was. The unstoppable drive to make the galaxy a better place, even as he found himself trapped in a distant land and unable to return home.

Gareth had not even paused in his efforts, merely pivoted and turned himself into an Art Fraud specialist, working in a culture he had never imagined a year ago, because Jack Grodray had asked.

Yes, Gareth Dankworth was a cop. And Royston Loughty seemed to have something of that as well, even as he was closer in age to her than the youngsters in this room and was known to her as a scientist.

But they shared a glance and Anen knew. Yes. Royston Loughty had been an Earth Force Sky Patrol agent at some point. Something like Fatima, so deep undercover that nobody else in the room, except perhaps a dozen gods, knew the truth besides her.

Fatima and the other human turned to them now.

"Rock and roll?" the stranger asked one last time.

"It will be the greatest concert ever played," Loughty turned back to the woman and said calmly. "Not just the finest you ever play, but the most powerful thing ever recorded, because there are several thousand gods around us listening today."

The woman gasped.

"Thousands," she squeaked.

"Look around you," Loughty smiled. "You can see them, smiling back from the edges of the room. They are waiting for you, and you alone."

Anen could not see them when she glanced, but she also was part of the *Accord of Souls*, that psionic entity defined by the binding that brought seventeen species together into one.

It also excluded the humans, by design.

Perhaps, fifty thousand years ago, the Chaa had understood what these upstarts would be capable of turning into.

Or would become, had they survived.

ROCKER

ELLEN HAD NEVER WANTED MORE from life than to be able to stand up on that stage and sing, then go home and hide from the world when she was done. People didn't frighten her so much as exhaust her with trying to keep up with their unconscious communications.

She didn't understand it, most of the time. Doctors had called her a mid-functioning introvert. Any more so, and they might have prescribed drugs to *fix* her, had she let them, but Ellen knew she never would stoop to that level.

Fixing her involved taking away the one thing that gave her purpose.

Music.

She could impersonate normal enough of the time, but only in a world gone completely black and white, when she normally lived in such a rich sensorium that frequently it wanted to overwhelm her.

And then this strange woman held her hand.

Ellen had been consciously ignoring the fact that the stranger from the auditorium was a medusa, with tentacles instead of hair. Royston didn't seem to mind, so that must make it okay.

Right?

But Fatima held her hand, and suddenly Ellen felt her own power embrace the stranger.

Grace. That was what she was. Ellen smiled with understanding on so many levels.

Grace.

Every one of those tentacles was another set of eyes, nose, and ear, sifting the world around her constantly and feeding Fatima so much information that she must be mad. Except she wasn't.

She lived in a place where everyone else was black and white. Two dimensional.

Mundane.

"I'm not sure I can," Ellen tried to explain to all these people that the power wasn't hers to command.

"I just witnessed you doing it," Fatima replied with such surety of purpose that Ellen felt the ground grow solid beneath their feet.. "I know what you are capable of."

Yes, she probably did. Nobody else in this room would understand what it meant, to be subject to so many details constantly. To be unable to block them out, because anything she tried would drop a solid, glass wall three feet thick between Ellen and the rest of the universe.

But the Grace lived with that every day. Ellen could taste it as her powers touched Fatima's mind.

Ellen mastered her own soul and thrust herself into the ritual that carried her onto that stage each night. The deep breaths, counting by fives. The way she could push everything backwards four point seven three yards so they couldn't touch her.

In her mind, she turned the entire stage dark. Forced her audience to exist in shadows so they were nothing more than a suggestion of eyes reflecting at the edge of the fire.

Not people. Not watching her.

Not stealing her life energy, even as she was giving it away with as much effort as she could manage.

Ellen nodded to Fatima and let go of her hand.

The world turned a little more gray around her, but she could manage that.

She wasn't alone in the universe. She had the Grace to remember.

Even if the Gods were finally going to take their gift back and cast her forever into the hell of noise and madness.

Ellen blew out her breath and stepped up on the platform to stand before her band.

As always, she stopped seeing them as people. They became extensions of herself. There were no words to describe it, but she could tell what each of the men was thinking, as if it was printed on his tie.

Tommy, Lead Guitar, desperately worried about her, but putting on a brave face of the detached, rock guitarist, to provide her a platform she could grasp when the cold, dark waters she swam threatened to be too much.

Dave on Rhythm Guitar, set to hold the melody in place, regardless of what any of the rest of the universe thought they might do.

Mick on the upright bass, prepared to call forth all the hosts of Hell with his playing, an earthquake in his fingertips even now as he studied the very Gods around them and challenged them to meet his beat.

Rhys, surrounded by that tremendously-oversized drum set, from which he could give you almost anything if you let him know ahead of time the sound you needed.

Dalton, a ragtime, boogie-woogie pianist who could have played before kings and any classical conductor in the world, if he didn't want to rock.

They grounded her. Gave her peace. Forced her to breathe.

Ellen found the microphone just as she had left it five minutes ago.

Or a lifetime.

At her feet, a single piece of paper with a list of words. Dave always penciled in the set list after sitting perfectly still and watching her for ten minutes when they first got into the green room. Somehow, he could absorb her needs and flow, just right.

Every time.

This set had been perfect for London. For Royston, whom she had known would be there, and needing something special from them.

She would have to top it.

Ellen bent and picked up the paper, turning to Dave with a question on her face.

"I had two," he said quietly, almost apologetically as he handed her a replacement and took the old one. "Something told me that I needed a second list, as if we were suddenly going to play a whole other concert right after the first one. It made no sense to me three hours ago, but I did it anyway."

No, it wouldn't. How could any of them understand that they were a single, psionic entity when they played?

Until she had met a God, Ellen hadn't understood.

Until.

Quickly, she scanned Dave's alternate list.

Yes. This was almost identical to the one she had played for Royston the first time they touched across the darkness. When he had need, and she had power, and they had ascended the heavens together.

When they called out to the Gods for knowledge.

And somebody answered.

Ellen pushed her fears to the back of the stage and made them go away. The only thing they could do right now was infect her boys and make them play badly.

She would not allow it.

Ellen turned to Dave and placed his second list beside her microphone stand with a nod. Quickly, Dave pulled out a set of three by five cards and handed them out to the boys.

Royston needed her to go higher than she had ever touched before. Needed her to call down these ancient Godlike beings and demand that they sit quietly while she taught them what it meant to be human.

To be alive.

To be young.

SCIENTIST

ROYSTON WATCHED Fatima communicate with the young woman on a plane of existence he hadn't even understood existed, until he met the first of the beings who had *Ascended*.

Until he met a God.

Royston's soul was just small enough that he had to look around until he found Sir West, still trying to hide at the fringe of this strange mob. Trying to wrap science around everything that had happened.

There are more things in heaven and Earth, Horatio, than are dreamt of in your philosophy.

Human science was insufficient, just as Pippa had suggested to him before, when her pithy observation first drove him to consider rock and roll instead. *Accord* science, with all the magical wonder he had been able to somehow absorb from the corporeal beings around him, was not sufficient.

But now he was dealing with gods. *Ascended Chaa* who had somehow reached a stage of mental development that could not be explained, save to say that humans apparently held that same seed of potential greatness in their collective soul.

If he could find a way to keep these vengeful gods from ending everything tonight.

The room fell silent. Perhaps the entire universe, as *Speaker For The Communion* had said that every human in the Solar System would hear this *Judgment*. The *Accord of Souls* would likewise be poised on the edge of their seats, to have the Chaa themselves return in their lifetime.

Most would not appreciate that only the gravest risk possible would compel such an event, but they would understand the costs tomorrow, after they watched their Gods destroy an entire species.

The scientist in him would miss the chance to explore what would change in their culture from having been here today. Having witnesses the darkness that accompanied godhead.

"What is rock and roll?" the First Inspector, Anen, asked him in a quiet, nervous voice.

Royston took her hand in his and tried to press his understanding towards her with whatever psychic power he apparently possessed. It seemed impossible to describe, but that was because he lacked the vocabulary necessary, that of the gods themselves, to do any better.

"Power," Royston said simply, never relinquishing his hold on Fatima with his other hand.

Royston, the most scientific of minds, holding hands with two alien women and listening to rock and roll. Enjoying it, even.

Who would have imagined?

And then words were unnecessary. The man standing at the battered, wooden upright piano slid a hand down from the top of the scale to draw all mesmerized eyes to the keys.

Royston was prepared for the pulse of energy that seemed to emerge from the woman on the stage as the man began to play. Except that such a word did not do the act justice. As before, he attacked the keyboard as though mortal combat had begun.

Perhaps it had, and this would be the battlefield of choice.

Hard, rhythmic, almost *bombastic*. Here was a man who could challenge Rachmaninoff himself, bringing all that technique and experience to rock and roll instead.

The rhythm guitarist joined in, setting a basic melody in a way Royston hadn't understood, that first night. Such a simple progression of chords, yet it felt almost like a tiler laying a mosaic floor that would somehow vanish beneath your feet, until the moment you stopped when a child noticed it and pointed down with glee at the images.

A full measure later, the other man taught these assembled gods, perhaps the entire universe, the meaning of *Lead Guitar* with a power and emotion that Royston had only known the best violinists and saxophonists to achieve. At least until Pippa had suggested rock and roll might be the solution.

The pulse of energy was like a squall line had emerged from the stage and washed over the entire audience, a tide pushing them a little closer to shore, before the rip currents that would suck them back out to sea.

And then Ellen opened her mouth and sang.

That first night, he hadn't known what to expect. Jazz was famous for scat singers with technical excellence, or torch singers bringing their languid tales of woe to wring your heart.

Ellen was a rocker.

But more than that. She was power. Raw and unrestrained. Anger and love, sophistication and destruction.

It was like the ancient Hindu goddess Kali-ma stood before him on the stage, proclaiming the end of the world.

Considering the company, perhaps it was appropriate. She was facing the end of the world and challenging the gods themselves to stand before her and do their worst.

Royston hoped it would be enough.

SECTOR MARSHAL

IT WAS the worst feeling in the world, to be utterly powerless and to know it. Sector Marshal Alvin Siddall commanded the Earth Force Sky Patrol base known as The Arsenal, located in the L2 LaGrange Point.

The Far Side of the Moon.

Where experiments with dangerous energies or exotic weapons might not destroy the Earth. At least without destroying Luna first. And if they managed that, hadn't they already sealed their fate?

On the main screen, someone, somehow, had caused an image to appear. Alvin already knew that none of his men could control that screen, even as they still had basic control of the base itself.

It was like some alien being demanding that they witness what was happening, frightening as *THAT* concept was.

What was happening?

Alvin could see figures in a large auditorium, almost like a gymnasium in size. Perhaps a hundred lesser shapes, some of which he knew were friends, while the rest were those beings Royston had warned him about.

Aliens. At least a dozen different shapes and sizes, from a medusa to lizardman a stone giant. It was like the ancient Professor had brought his fanciful stories of elves and orcs to life in the modern age.

At the edges of the screen, the appearance of the dozen creatures that had assembled that congress to witness. Alvin had felt the glyph for *The*

Communion, as well as their individual names, even across whatever distance existed or didn't between the Arsenal and the Apocalypse.

"Anything on scanners?" Alvin called to the room.

"Negative, sir," one of the men yelled back, face down over an imaging projectors. "All space appears clear to a distance of four light seconds. *Arizona-Seven* is currently returning to Headquarters at L1 under emergency regulations."

"Who has control of the main projection screen?" Alvin asked the room.

"Working at it sir," another man called. "We have all other screens under our control, except…stand by. Sir, engineering reports that at least one screen in every chamber on the Arsenal is currently tuned to the same image we're seeing here. Same with audio. Nobody can break it. If they try cutting power to the screen, it still turns itself back on."

"How is that possible?" Alvin asked, finally setting the fear to one side for the pure wonder of whatever these Chaa had done, from wherever they were, to do this.

They could have easily blown the station up, if they had that fine of a control over his systems. Just overloaded the reactor and cut the humans out from the control circuits, until the only option left was to order everyone into the emergency escape pods and hope that help could arrive from one of the bases on the lunar surface fast enough to save everyone.

"Unknown, sir," the man answered what should have been obvious as a rhetorical question.

Alvin ignored him. Ignored all of them. Concentrated on the image on the screen.

Okay, mister alien god Chaa, you want us to watch? I'll watch.

Alvin reached down and found that he had the ability to manipulate the camera in three dimensions, zooming and turning. Quickly, he began recognizing faces in the mob.

At least he thought he did. Everyone there looked almost like phantasms rather than corporeal beings. Ghosts you could see through if you squinted just right.

But that was Royston, holding hands with…

What in Creation's name was Fatima Darzi? She had presented herself as a Persian Physicist, the niece of dear, old Firuz Alinejad, one of the great minds of his generation before that tragic accident.

Without that scarf on her head, she had tentacles. And he had touched the woman.

Alvin wondered if he needed something like a tetanus shot now.

But no, if she was an alien spy, she would have done everything in her power not to appear amiss. That would include her health.

It was the others who had suggested killing everyone on Earth with a bioweapon. That was high on the list of fears that Alvin had assembled with Royston before the man left. If the aliens could open a portal to pull a man like Gareth Dankworth into their universe, they could send a bomb this way.

Or the Black Death.

The other woman with Royston was an Amazon. Alvin was an inch or so taller than Royston, and he would still be looking up to that woman. Elf. Whatever she was.

Her uniform was identical to the one that Gareth was wearing, if that giant creature across the way was the missing man, and not just wearing a close approximation of his face. Except Philippa Loughty seemed to believe it was him.

There were two others as well, one another tall elf and the second a woman who probably out-weighed Alvin, as well as looking down on him.

Attractive too, if you liked Stone Giants.

Another time.

Alvin looked down at the device Royston had left him. The emergency scanner that would sound if it detected a wormhole opening within sixty yards, giving a vector that could be used to direct security teams. Alvin wasn't sure what they might do if it went off.

Still, he was supposed to be in charge. He needed to do something.

"Security, activate all your teams," Alvin said in a firm voice. "Put everyone in life suits for now, prepared to seal up at the slightest warning from their *NBC* scanners."

Nuclear, biological, chemical. All the ways that someone might kill you silently and effectively, without having to blow up your city. Or your base on the dark side of the moon.

"Weapons systems, sir?" the gunner asked, almost excitedly.

"Negative," Alvin replied. "What's coming won't be in a ship, Gunner."

"What will be coming, sir?" someone else asked.

"All of you men are familiar with how Gareth Dankworth disappeared?" Alvin looked around and got back nods and grunts. It was a painful, tragic failure for all of them that the man who might be their greatest agent had just vanished, whereabouts unknown. "Those aliens can open up a wormhole anywhere they want and pluck a man right out of space. Alternatively, they can send through a bomb to destroy us. Or something even worse. There is nothing we can do to stop them, except maintain our duty stations and act like the Earth Force Sky Patrol agents that we are."

On the screen, one of the greater beings suddenly seemed to turn and look right at Alvin. He felt the blood drain out of his soul, leaving everything hollow and cold.

"You are correct, Sector Marshal Alvin Siddall," somebody called *Last Traveler* said simply. "I should have brought you when I brought the others. My apologies, this will not hurt."

And then Alvin found himself standing in the middle of that terrible room. The device in his pocket beeped once and then fell silent. Like he had already traversed a wormhole and landed before either of them realized it.

He looked around in pure awe.

The screen had not done justice to the number of beings moving like will-o-the-wisps around the ceiling and far walls. Thousands of them, watching, studying, perhaps a few even smiling.

But he was the Sector Marshal of The Arsenal. The second most powerful and important base in Earth Force. He had a responsibility to his people.

Alvin turned in the direction that seemed to be where his invisible camera had last stood.

"Arsenal Forces, this is Sector Marshal Siddall," he said aloud. "I have been transported to wherever it was that the screen shows. Maintain your current duties and let the Commandant know he is now in command of The Arsenal. Otherwise, stand by."

Alvin just hoped that they would hear him. Would understand that there was nothing that they could do but watch. Would continue to act with the highest regard to duty and propriety.

If today was a good day to die, they needed to die well.

Everyone one of them had taken an Oath when they joined Sky Patrol, after all.

Last Traveler was suddenly there. Not confronting him, but well inside his personal space. He felt mental hands somehow rifling through his memory, his very being. It was not painful, but Alvin had the feeling that his entire life was being laid bare before this Chaa, that they could better judge him personally before they executed him.

So be it, he thought at the being. *We have all made mistakes, but there are very few that I regret in a career of service. Do your worst.*

"Oh we will, Alvin Siddall," the being smiled menacingly at him. "We will."

WITNESS

SOMEHOW, Gareth ended up with one arm around Pippa's shoulders, and the other around Talyarkinash as the music played.

He had never been one for the teenage rebellion of rock and roll, but he did understand the power that the band put forth. It was like Talyarkinash had said, the woman up there apparently had the same sorts of psionic potential that he did. That most humans had, perhaps in smaller amounts.

She could embrace an entire auditorium, or whatever this space was, and fill it with her emotions. Make everyone feel them. Live them.

But Gareth was still a human underneath. He hadn't been bound into the *Accord*. Couldn't be, unless one of the Chaa decided to perform the task. He had no doubts they had that sort of power, if they wished.

But with one arm around each woman, he could feel their hearts pounding through their skin. If Pippa's was ever so slighting faster, he could put that down to finally confronting the fact that he wasn't human anymore. That he couldn't marry her and start a family.

Not that it mattered much, if *The Communion* was about to destroy Earth and all the humans anyway.

But so much would be lost.

On the other hand, Gareth understood that the *Accord of Souls* was thousands of times larger than Earth. Trillions of souls would be saved by sacrificing humanity on the altar of the gods.

He just didn't have to like it.

So Gareth listened to the music with his soul, as well as his mind, and let Ellen's words and harmonies fill him with joy. It was like listening to a modern, pop interpretation of Friedrich Schiller's **Ode To Joy**, the anchor movement of Beethoven's Ninth Symphony. Or perhaps **Finlandia**, by Jean Sibelius, dedicated to revolution and resistance against the old Russian Empire.

Perhaps the latter was more appropriate, since rock and roll was always about rebellion.

Both women felt the power flow through them, so maybe human music could speak to an audience of aliens. Not that the *Accord* particularly mattered today, but at least everyone alive today would be able to remember what humanity had once striven for.

Once accomplished.

Gareth looked around and tried to study those beings known as the *Ascended Chaa* for clues. He was a cop. Part of his training had been to sit quietly in a restaurant, surreptitiously studying all the other patrons in the joint, so he could make a guess at their class, education, and how law-abiding they might be when nobody else was around.

Perhaps there had been a touch of magic, of this latent psionic ability, that he could tap. It was all a kind of magic, when you got right down to it.

The *Ascended Chaa* seemed politely inquisitive, at least those he could see, *The Communion* was a wall of blank, white clouds, giving nothing away at all during the performance. The humans and members of the *Accord* around him were as transfixed as he was, raptly absorbed by Ellen's loves, hates, fears, and triumphs.

Perhaps they had all traveled to Hamlin Town.

At one point, Gareth leaned down to kiss Pippa on the head, but she turned up and their lips met instead. It was good. At least they had that before they died.

Gareth had counted twelve songs, hopefully a good number, when the last notes tapered off and the whole world seemed to collapse, like a week-old helium balloon. He sagged with it as the emotions withdrew.

Pippa and Talyarkinash both snuggled closer to him as he held them. Around them, time seemed to start again, but that was just the rush of silence swelling over everything.

Gareth guided the two women over to where his partner and her boss were standing. They seemed to be recovering from the same emotions as everyone else, so hopefully they would have good memories after this as well.

"Pippa, this is Jackeith Grodray and Eveth Baker," Gareth introduced her. "They're with the Constabulary. It's like Earth Force Sky Patrol, but they protect the whole galaxy. I've been working for them. Inspectors Grodray and Baker, Philipa Loughty."

He didn't introduce her as his fiancé. It made no sense at this point, especially as he was only human enough now that he would be destroyed when those gods completed the task they had set out to do.

But the *Accord of Souls* would be safe. He had to keep reminding himself of that. Otherwise, Gareth knew he would fall into such a terrible funk that nothing could ever rescue him.

Not even death.

"Is there anything that can be done?" Pippa asked Eveth after they shook hands.

Baker glanced at him for the briefest moment before she spoke.

"Just before all this happened, Gareth was leading us on an assault that would have either captured or killed Marc Sarzynski," Baker said quietly. "With him gone, there probably would have been no need to do anything so gratuitous. At least one hopes."

"And that is where you are wrong, Inspector," a man's voice intruded.

Gareth spun and saw that Dr. Loughty had stepped close while he wasn't paying attention. Like Gareth, Loughty had two women with him, one a Grace dressed in the uniform of the Earth Force Sky Patrol Women's Auxiliary, which made absolutely no sense.

The other was dressed has he was, in the blue-gray bodysuit of the Constabulary. Unlike the neon-blue badge that Gareth wore, however, hers was brass. That meant that the woman was a Prime Inspector, like Jackeith and Eveth when they weren't undercover.

Looking at her face, Gareth goggled in shock.

This was Anen Wardson. First Inspector of the Constabulary.

Everyone's boss.

"How so?" Baker asked Dr. Loughty.

"The First Inspector and the *Accord* Commission were in the process of deciding that they should simply go ahead and destroy all of humanity with a bioweapon when *The Communion* intervened," Dr. Loughty said in a firm voice with traces of anger underneath.

"Jackeith Grodray and Eveth Baker, this is Royston Loughty," Gareth introduced the man now. "Pippa's father and one of the most brilliant men in the solar system. One of the greatest men it has ever been my pleasure to know."

They shook hands. Gareth got introduced to the young Grace operative who went by the name of Fatima Darzi. He also met his ultimate boss in the flesh for the first time.

Like Baker, Wardson was Vanir. Perhaps six foot three inches tall, but without the hard athleticism that Baker had, although Gareth could see traces of it in the way she moved.

"This is true?" Grodray asked their boss. "You were about to wipe out the humans?"

"It is," the First Inspector admitted. "Time had grown short, with Sarzynski known to be on Earth, with a working generator station he could use. Predictive modeling suggested that casualties from your assault on Sarzynski's stronghold would be at least seventy percent, so we could not take the chance that you would fail and the man would then be able to recruit an army that he could send back into *Accord* space."

"Then why even bother with the attack?" Baker asked in a voice filled with razor blades.

"You had the Star Dragon with you," the Boss said. "That might have been sufficient to win through. It would have taken my teams at least another hour to prepare the bioweapon, and then we would have begun the targeting process. Had you been successful in bringing me Sarzynski's body, and that of his gang, we could have called things off."

"Except that you would have already made the decision that you could justify wiping humanity out at a later time, correct?" Dr. Loughty asked the woman in a crisp tone.

Gareth felt a small thrill go through him when the First Inspector merely bowed, rather than trying to argue. Loughty was right. It would have been easy from there.

Perhaps the next time there was a hint of criminal activity involving humans. Or the time after that. Pop. Open a portal and throw a vial through it to shatter on the far side and infect anyone within range. Rinse. Repeat.

End of humanity. Perhaps the end of all life on Earth, depending on the nature of the weapon and its ability to quickly mutate across species, like influenza did. Bases like the Arsenal might hold out for a time, but what good would a few thousand men and women on a space station due, if they couldn't grow crops and it wasn't safe to land on any surface?

Another person joined them suddenly, stepping into the small circle of people, even as others stood back and watched in silence. Perhaps those others lived in fear, given the number of humans here and the fact that these people had never encountered such a dangerous creature in the flesh before.

"Excuse me," Petim Diazal said.

Quickly, the small Th'Tarni introduced himself to the folks who had never met him, including Gareth. Except he knew who the man was. Given another year, Petim Diazal would have probably been the one with the final decision on Gareth's fate, one way or the other.

He was nothing like the other Th'Tarni Gareth had met, especially not Gonquah, the fabulously wealthy arms merchant who had manufactured the killer androids for Marc. Gareth could feel the charisma coming off the man like the best cologne, but that was just a measure of what a successful politician would need to be like, at that level of play.

"I wanted to meet the person, the human, about whom so much fear and consternation had centered," Diazal said, bowing slightly to Dr. Loughty as two scholars met in an inn.

"You have the advantage on me, sir," Dr. Loughty replied. "But if I am to understand, you are the head of the *Accord* government?"

"That would be the Proctor, Khozo T'Yuugon," Diazal replied. "An U'Chagi. But circumstances had him on vacation fishing at the moment of our need, so we sent for him, even as we moved forward. I would have probably been the person who signed the declaration, though, yes. My soul would have born the stain when I went to stand before the Creator to explain myself."

Dr. Loughty bowed back and the two studied each other. The scientist was a little over six feet in height, while the politician was barely Pippa's height in her flats, but both men were mental titans that put the rest of the audience to shame.

"So where does that leave us?" Dr. Loughty asked the group in a simple voice. "We have heard the music of our illustrious songstress. We have gathered into a conclave that I hope will not devolve into a battlefield. All voices are hopefully present. What is next?"

"Now the Judgment will begin," *Speaker for the Communion* announced in a voice that echoed across a thousand worlds, and every place in the Solar System where humans existed to hear it.

DEFENDER

ROYSTON HAD the feeling that those twelve Gods, the beings of *The Communion*, had almost been waiting for someone to speak. To spark the inevitable. It had been his bad luck, perhaps, to draw that straw, but someone would have done it eventually.

He turned in the direction of the dais upon which the Chaa gods had assembled. Studied their glyphs again, since each seemed to be an identical cloud of light up there to the eyes.

First Immortal. Great Teacher. Seeker for the Knee of God. Uplifter. Glory in Sunrise. Merciless. Speaker For The Communion. Narrator of History. Mountain. Astray in Darkness. Magistrate. Last Traveler.

All of them represented so much power that Royston couldn't even begin to calculate it. Collectively, he had no idea if they had any limits, save their imaginations. With the lesser beings, the *Ascended Chaa*, present he wondered what it might be that they could not do.

Merciless had already made it known that he had once destroyed an entire species of star-traveling explorers. Brigands, granted, but probably no worse than humans might have been on a bad day. And that was merely one of them. He could call on the assistance of his peers, but that would be unnecessary.

Just dropping a singularity into *Earth*'s Solar System, close enough to disrupt the sun, would be sufficient to end humanity. It wasn't like they had ever sent generational colony ships to places like *Centauri* in order to expand humanity's footprint.

And until Royston Loughty had found the door, humans had been trapped in their home system forever.

"This Court is in session," *Speaker for the Communion* announced with a tone that implied a gavel striking the bench. "Much is already known, but there is much yet to understand. *Last Traveler*, you have called us thus, for reasons all too obvious, but the bulk of humanity cannot achieve glyphs, so their ignorance remains in place. Speak to this assembled body the basic facts. I would have humanity *understand* their crimes."

Royston watched the being move from his place at one end of the platform to stand down with the lesser beings, like a prosecuting attorney smiling grimly at the audience and the jury as he prepared his case. Royston almost expected him to put his thumbs into non-existent suspenders and grin as he turned to the rest of the room.

"Seven Chitra ago, the Chaa gathered together and planned that creation that would become the *Accord of Souls*," *Last Traveler* spoke with a florid, circular tone that seemed to emerge from all corners of the room simultaneously. "Roughly Seventy-two thousand human years, as such things are measured. Several worlds were known to have life upon them, but none other than *Almar* had advanced as far as even metals technology. Thus were the Chaa the first of the Creator's Children to be able to go seek Him."

Royston nodded, listening as the being glyphed his words as well as spoke them in what he heard as standard Queen's English. Gareth would probably hear a distinct, Indiana twang in his own head.

"The first Great Debate was whether or not humanity should be included in the roster of new species that would be uplifted to join the *Accord*," *Last Traveler* continued. "Unlike most of the other species, humans were already significantly advanced, with stone tools and cave art showing off a sophistication well in advance of any of the others we considered. The others were still yet perhaps highly intelligent animals by comparison, lacking language and tool use."

He turned and smiled at Royston, as if acknowledging the Defense Counsel who would become his principle opponent.

"At the same time, humans are an exceedingly violent species in their native form," the Chaa said in a darker tone. "They make war on one another for the thinnest of reasons and often no good excuse at all, save that *other* might be a different skin tone or speak the same language with a different accent."

Royston nodded back, all too aware of the history of his species when it came to violence. If anything, things had gotten so much worse, with the advent of ever-more-sophisticated technology, that humans should have probably never emerged from the Twentieth or Twenty-First Centuries, but rather destroyed themselves then.

When no guilt would fall on anybody but humans for the outcome.

"You would challenge my conclusions?" *Last Traveler* suddenly focused his attention on Royston, as if detecting a note of dismay.

"Not in whole," Royston countered him deftly. "But I would offer that humans do recognize such tendencies, and have, at least in modern times, worked to reduce such violence to manageable levels, as we try to become something better. Earth Force, and more particularly Sky Patrol, are dedicated arms of the World Government that exist to end wars, sir. Crime is a different matter, and there our efforts have not been as successful."

"Let it be noted," *Last Traveler* pulled a glyph directly out of Royston's mind as he watched, and then transmitted it to the others.

All the others: human, alien, and Chaa alike.

The founding of Earth Force in the late Twenty-First Century as a quasi-military arm of the World Governing Council and the Hall of Governments, before it simply became the government itself, while allowing all the nations to retain local control.

The advent of Sky Patrol, when it became understood that wars might have ended, but that humanity needed a single law enforcement agency tasked with protecting the entire Solar System, regardless of lesser jurisdiction.

Royston felt a smile as *Last Traveler* reached into the mind of Alvin Siddall and pulled forth some of that man's memories. Hopefully, the Chaa understood that some of the things in Royston's mind should be taken to his grave as secrets, rather than shared in open court.

Royston had been a Sky Patrol agent in his youth, although he never talked about it. Could never talk about it, without being brought up on charges for violating a number of Official Secrets Act sections. As he had said, war on an industrial scale might be gone, but there were still men and women born whose megalomania would not let them settle for anything less than domination of all things.

Some of those psychopaths turned to politics, where their faulty emotional wiring probably served them well.

But others…

Yes. Best not to discuss men like Gergely Cseh. Better still if everyone forgot the man ever existed, lest someone decide to emulate him and try to take over the entire world with blackmail and mad science.

He had been another one like Gareth or Ellen, possessed of an oversized psionic ability he could tap. And a heart as black a night.

Last Traveler had obviously seen those memories, and left them be. That was for everyone's benefit tonight.

Instead, they watched Alvin's memories play out. A much younger man, back when he was another one like Gareth, tall and muscular, and intent on making everything better. A successful career climbing the ladder, from 0-1 Deputy Agent all the way up to 0-7 and Sector Marshal, second only to the Sky Marshal himself, the Head of Sky Patrol.

Alvin's life had been much more public than Royston's, just another beat cop turned detective.

"I would pause now to prepare everyone." *Last Traveler* said quietly. "The memories I have shown until now have been Alvin Siddall, Sector Marshal of Sky Patrol and one of their top commanders; and Royston Loughty, PhD, WMU, FRS, CBE, CStJ. We have seen how Earth Force came about, and why it was necessary. We have witnessed the purpose and execution of Sky Patrol. All of these are simple things. Straight forward and public knowledge. Now we must turn to the present tense."

Royston watched the godlike being turn to face a corner of the room that everyone else had mostly ignored, partly out of necessity, partly out of spite. The spot where an invisible demarcation separated Marc Sarzynski and his gang from the rest, like an old-fashioned, three-strand electric fence holding in restive cattle, back home in Montana.

Royston got the impression of a hand waved across the room, much like the ancient wizards might have done on a vid for visual effect.

He watched Marc being bodily lifted into the air, hovering futilely as *Last Traveler* carried him to the center of the room, not all that far from where Royston and Gareth stood. At the same time, Royston felt a second force wrap psychic tentacles around his body, preventing him from simply grabbing Sarzynski by the neck and strangling that son of a bitch to death.

No doubt Gareth felt the same force. Glancing around, most of the people within close proximity were under the same compulsion. It was good to know that hatred of evil spanned cultures and species.

"Marc Sarzynski, also known publicly as the criminal Maximus, you are summoned," *Last Traveler* said unnecessarily, although people watching at home might not grasp the finer points of today's charade.

"We have seen the recent history of Earth Force and Sky Patrol," the Chaa prosecutor said in a harder voice than Royston had heard before. "It is my understanding that Marc Sarzynski once swore those same oaths as the Sky Patrol agents in this room."

Again, Royston caught what looked like a wicked gleam in the eye of *Last Traveler*, glancing his way and nodding at their shared secret. Not even Pippa knew, because Royston had retired from active duty and taken up science as a vocation when he married dear Elizabeth, God rest her soul.

"Now we will see how a dedicated, honored Sky Patrol agent turned to evil," *Last Traveler's* voice oozed a vicious ichor now.

Royston knew most of the story. Had witnessed it firsthand as the boys became men and the men moved from friendly rivals to deadly enemies. All over a woman. A very special woman, to be noted.

Pippa.

But then, the Trojan War had, at the end of the day, been driven by two men's love for the same woman.

Royston had read a number of translations of *The Iliad* over the decades. They all began with some variation of that most human, most powerful of emotions.

Sing for me, oh Muse, a song of the Rage of Achilles.

But everyone left out the other, greater battle: Menelaus and Paris. They spoke of the honorable warrior wronged and doomed to live and die such a short, powerful life, but left out two men's war over one woman, and the tremendous socio-political earthquake that resulted in the sacking of Troy, the wanderings of Odysseus, and the betrayal of Agamemnon.

Today was different, though. *Last Traveler* picked Marc's memories and turned them into emotional glyphs that others could absorb without words.

Two young men, as close to perfection as humanly possible perhaps, thrown together as freshmen roommates. Competitions in the classroom, on the track, and on the field. Friendly, for the most part.

Two men, never separated by more than a few hundredths of a point in academia, or as much as a tenth of a second in athletics.

Royston knew, from old records he had perused in his investigations of the man, that Elders of both Sky Patrol and Earth Force eventually expected that Marc Sarzynski had a significant chance to become Sky Marshal. To become the commander of the entire Sky Patrol.

That was the one place the two men differed temperamentally. Gareth would have had to have been blackmailed by his superiors to accept a promotion above Senior Special Agent, knowing that to become a Commandant, a base commander somewhere, would make the end of his days as a field agent.

But alas, it was not to be.

Instead, Royston watched as both men became Deputy Agents and first encountered him, and more importantly, Pippa.

If the rivalry at school had been nearly off the charts, the competition to catch his daughter's eye went an order of magnitude beyond that. Always friendly, but never-ending in the game.

And it had been so pointless, at the end. Marc Sarzynski had never lacked for available female companionship, as Royston knew. But Pippa had chosen Gareth, the simpler boy from Indiana over the one from New Metropolis.

Marc Sarzynski never got over losing that competition.

Royston understood better than the rest watching today, what had happened next. The subtle changes that came over the man, only evident in retrospect. The darkness that took root. The never-displayed rage that displaced the grief and depression Marc Sarzynski would never allow to take root.

The understanding that the Solar System really wasn't big enough for the two of them, like two old-time gunfighters facing off at high noon on a dirt street in front of a saloon. It had never happened that way, although the galaxy might be better off if it had.

Instead, Marc simply resigned his commission and walked away from Sky Patrol, in spite of all the conversations with superiors and attempted inducements to get him to stay.

Again, how might the world have turned out, the entire galaxy, had Marc been able to heal his broken heart and perhaps settle for the second greatest woman alive? Any number of them would have been happy to become Mrs. Sarzynski. Of that, Royston had no doubts whatsoever.

What would have happened to the *Accord of Souls* with another man? The crime lord known as Cinnra, a birdman creature known as Warreth, had asked his scientists to locate him a human killer, an assassin that he could use as a sharp instrument, in a galaxy that did not understand violence and could not apparently practice it upon one another.

The two Yuudixtl, Xiomber and Morty, had obliged the being, and found him the single most dangerous man alive in the Solar System. What would have happened had they just picked a common thug, like the one human who had been standing with Marc.

Royston didn't know who Two-Gun Kowalski was, but he read the man's glyph now, and saw a remorseless, merciless killer, but not one with the possibilities of Marc Sarzynski. No, that would have been satisfied with a galaxy of people he could kill, and not demanded more.

Not overthrown Cinnra and taken over his gang, as Marc apparently had. Did, as Royston watched *Last Traveler* pull those memories from Marc's mind and display his crimes to the whole galaxy.

Royston had a strong stomach. He had needed it in the old days, to do some of the things he had. He needed it now, watching Marc bring his brilliance and powerful drive to the task of purging Cinnra's gang of anyone who would not bow his head fast enough. The killings that cleared out any suspected of disloyalty. Rebuilding the gang with only the most ruthless men and women he could find and still trust.

Of surviving when he had been cast into an alien landscape where every hand was turned against him.

Royston watched the man's criminal genius blossom. He studied Maiair and Yooyar as Marc saw them: assistants, accomplices, and lovers. Like one of the ancient newsreels, the story unfolded, showing crimes and corruptions so brazen and expansive that Royston was amazed that anybody had been able to stop Marc, let alone topple him.

Last Traveler paused here, the waves of rage pulsing off the being even greater than that of the other eleven, if such a thin margin could be measured.

"That's only half the story, bub," a voice rang out, just as angry, if only smaller because the man projecting it wasn't a god. "Tell the other half before you completely poison the jury and I move for a mistrial."

Royston expected the Yuudixtl, Morty if he was correct in trying to tell them apart physically, would be snuffed from existence by one of The Communion for such effrontery, but instead the words drew a chuckle from one of the other Chaa.

"I doubt that you would be able to file a successful motion for a change of venue," *Narrator of History* seemed almost mirthful. "We have not located the Creator Who Bore Us yet and no others have advanced enough to be our peers, in any of the galaxies or planes of existence we have sought Him."

"Fine," Morty snapped grumpily. "It is my turn now?"

Royston found himself liking the little lizardman, as he read the complicated glyphs the Yuudixtl scientist projected, and saw how the others, the ones he thought of as the good guys, reacted to the man.

"Indeed," *Last Traveler* said. "Perhaps it is time to hear from the one most responsible for the greatest crime in the last five Chitra."

"And your salvation, princess," Morty snarked back hard. "Don't forget that part."

Rather than answer, *Last Traveler* picked up Morty in a field similar to Marc and held him aloft. A moment later, Morty's egg-brother Xiomber joined him.

Egg-brother? What an interesting concept. Royston looked forward to the little man's story.

He would need something useful, when he pled with the gods to do something less than simply wiping out all of humanity.

EGG BROTHER

SOMEHOW, Morty had always known it was going to end up like this. As he and Xiomber had always teased each other: how bad could it be if the Chaa didn't show up to stop us?

Until they did. You roll the dice enough times, and eventually the worst possible result will come up.

Statistical certainty.

"So, yeah, I own that," Morty said to the executioners up on their platform. "Cinnra wanted a killer, so I went and found him the best, meanest one I could. Not my fault that nobody would listen then I told them that they couldn't control a monster like that. Even Xiomber thought I was loony."

"Loonier than usual," his egg-brother replied, just before he squawked when the Chaa dude picked him up and added him to the shooting gallery. "What?"

"You hadda open yer mouth, egg-brother," Morty laughed. "Gonna get you in trouble, one of these days."

"You mean like facing a death sentence from a dozen angry gods with an axe to grind?" Xiomber snapped at him.

"Worse," Morty laughed. "I'll tell Mom on you."

You weren't supposed to laugh at gods. Stuff like that irritated the hell out of them, at least in the books. But that got a good chuckle from everyone, so Morty counted it as a win when nobody gacked him for it.

"Yes, I was the one that programmed the machine to locate Maximus," Morty said. "Already admitted to it in an *Accord* Court of Justice and just awaiting my final sentencing for treason, okay? But that's only the first half of the story."

He took a deep breath and wondered if he would land on his feet, if the Chaa dropped him from five meters in the air. He wasn't a Nari, or someone graceful like that. Probably faceplant pretty hard.

But how bad could it be if the Chaa didn't show up to stop you?

Indeed.

"Then one morning, I woke up in a cold sweat," Morty continued, feeling his voice dial itself down from sarcastic clown to serious scientist.

He hated when that happened, but really didn't have any control over it. Cost of doing business, when you worked for criminals who usually didn't have a sense of humor.

"It was a simple issue, really," Morty continued. "What the hell had I done?"

The room didn't laugh this time, but he hadn't expected them to. Shit had just gotten serious. Angry gods with itchy trigger fingers, and all that.

"I hadda ask myself a simple question: Could anything stop Maximus, once he decided he was going to just take over the entire *Accord of Souls* as Emperor Marc the First?" Morty asked the rest of them.

Interestingly, it was the cops that seemed to understand him and offer some level of support, from the looks on their faces. Even Liamssen smiled at him, and she had the most reason to hate him and his egg-brother, at least at first.

Gods alone knew what had changed after the raid that separated them. He and Xiomber had been too busy running for their lives.

"Like I told my egg-brother, if you've just burned your house down, you don't get to complain when you have to sleep in the backyard in the mud, while it rains," Morty's voice took on an even-more-sober tone now.

He could feel somebody rooting around in his head, but ignored it as much as he could. It almost felt like an itch under that one scale you can't reach, no matter how you twist. When you have to either find a good post to scratch against, or have an egg-brother who'll help.

Images ghosted the room as he watched, as he spoke, so Morty figured that he was just providing a running, color commentary as the Chaa broadcast all his secrets to the universe.

Of course, by now, every cop in the *Accord* had probably read his and Xiomber's initial statements, rather than the cut-down versions leaving out all the jay walking, parking tickets, and overdue library fines, so it wasn't like he had many things left to conceal.

"So now I had to do something about it," Morty explained matter-of-factly. "I had to undo the evil that I had caused to come into being. It was impossible at that point to just grab Maximus and send him home, because we had had to turn him from a human into a Vanir, at least physically, in order to hide in the *Accord*. Plus, any portal we tried to draw him through he would have avoided easy enough, and then come for us with guns blazing."

Morty had just enough freedom of movement to look over at his old boss and sneer at the man.

"Ya scare people too much, and they do stupid things, Maximus," Morty told the man, hopefully safe from the giant reaching over and crushing his skull with one of those giant paws.

But nothing happened, other than a flair of pure hatred in the man's eyes.

Betrayal, perhaps, but hey, you brought it on yourself, bucko.

Deep breath. You've already admitted it. Own it.

"So now I had to find something to stop the most dangerous monster in the *Accord of Souls*," Morty said, looking around until he found the one person he wanted to talk to now. "And I couldn't even tell my egg-brother, at least not until right at the end, for fear he'd decide he was more afraid of Maximus's reach than his rage. I went looking for a hero."

HERO

GARETH BLUSHED to hear the words from Morty.

He had never set out to be a hero. All he ever wanted was to do right and see good things happen in the world. So he supposed that maybe that made him a hero, at least when circumstances conspired to demand it of him.

How many other people took a step back, at that moment, instead of a step forward?

But he had taken an Oath. Earth Force Sky Patrol. Heroes, if you will. Stepping up to confront injustice and criminality, in whatever form it took.

"Since I had programmed the machine to find Maximus, from among all humans, it was easy enough to pretty much reverse everything when looking for someone to become his Nemesis," Morty continued, eyes locked with Gareth's now, as a strange river of energy seemed to connect them.

Fate?

"At the time, I had no idea just how exactly I had managed my settings," Morty said. "A human who was psychologically the exact opposite of Maximus in every way, but still his physical and mental equal. I would need that, in order to fight the ultimate crime boss and save the *Accord of Souls* from being conquered by that human."

Gareth nodded. He had watched the images drawn from Marc's

memory. From his very soul. Seen the man, who once might have been his best man, turn into his worst nightmare: a rogue cop.

Everything they had been taught, Marc perverted, because he understood both sides of the law better than anyone alive. And yet, it hadn't been enough, in the face of the might of Earth Force Sky Patrol. Gareth had come within eight minutes of capturing Marc at the same time as he caught the rest of the gang.

Although, in retrospect, Morty might have simply pulled him out of the back of a Black Maria van. Assuming, of course, that Marc Sarzynski was somehow taken alive.

What would those eight minutes have meant to humanity, had Marc died during that shootout?

Morty would have taken someone else, but whoever he had gone after in the absence of Marc Sarzynski would have been Junior Varsity by comparison. Maybe enough to do the job for Cinnra, but nothing that was a threat to the rest of the galaxy.

But then, would the *Accord of Souls* have simply collapsed, like the Roman Empire had, when people forgot to work every day at upholding their legacy? Maybe it would have taken another century, from what Gareth's studies had shown, but the structure was rotting and close to collapse when Marc arrived.

He had only hastened the final fall.

At least, until Morty had needed a hero.

"You roll the dice enough times, and bad things happen," Morty said. "But good things do, too. Xiomber decided to help me instead of shooting me, at the end. Him telling the rest of the gang wouldn't have stopped me, because I had my getaway planned and it worked. We were all gone to *Orgoth Vortai* with Gareth in tow before anybody could stop us. Scared the hell out that poor girl in the tea shop. Discovered that no woman can apparently resist the man's animal magnetism, species be damned. Fled again, until we found Talyarkinash and challenged her to outdo everything she had ever even dreamed of. I'm just sorry my and Xiomber weren't there at the end to see how it all worked, having run like hell when Baker and Grodray showed up."

Gareth felt the attention of the Chaa known as *Last Traveler* as it turned and located Talyarkinash, still snuggled up to his side opposite Pippa. It was like a searchlight seeking bombers overhead on a cold, dark night.

She stiffened and tried to grasp Gareth's side, but the Chaa pulled her away and into the air, just as he had the other three.

Gareth's motion to prevent the man never even made it to his nerves, so *Last Traveler* must have simply blocked him from moving, like he had stopped Gareth from killing Marc earlier.

Was there nothing he could do to protect his friends from these gods?

GENETICIST

TALYARKINASH WANTED TO SCREAM.

Would have, if the monster holding her aloft would have allowed it. It was almost rape, the way he simply overrode all of her motor control and turned her into a puppet, dangling in the air at his mercy and whim.

To take, without ever asking.

She wanted to rage. To tear his throat out with her teeth and hands, if she could just move. And if the creature had a physical body she could kill.

"Your hands are not clean," *Last Traveler* strobed his anger at her before relenting. "But neither are they entirely dirty. You will speak, or I will compel it."

Rape. That's what you're talking about, you son of a bitch. Do what I want and I won't hurt you.

If she could have only spoken those words aloud. But she saw something in his eyes (?) at that moment. Some understanding that he had let his gender do things to her that were not acceptable.

A tiny apology passed, and Talyarkinash found herself standing on the ground, instead of hanging in the air for a god's entertainment like the three men. Her feet would not take a step, but her hands were free.

The agony in Gareth's eyes turned to rage as she watched. Talyarkinash realized that his first instinct had been to step forward, to shield her from the anger of a Chaa. To even challenge the being and fight him. If that was even possible.

But this was Gareth. He would absolutely try.

Amazingly, Pippa and the Grace woman, Fatima, were both allowed to approach her. Perhaps they were also compelled, but it looked like a word of encouragement from *Last Traveler*, rather than taking possession of their bodies and forcing them to do his will.

Each stood close and simply took one her hands in both of theirs. Talyarkinash could feel the support, the love, flow from both women, to prop her up in those places where everything wanted to simply curl up in a ball and whimper.

Or leap at a god and rend him.

She still wasn't sure which emotion would win.

Talyarkinash took a breath and held it as long as she could, trying to find the center of her being.

Something from Pippa held her upright. But Talyarkinash knew Gareth as well. She would understand that man's instincts to protect. To fight, even against impossible odds.

To walk first into a wormhole, attacking Sarzynski's stronghold, knowing that there was a high likelihood he would be the first to die. Because that might open the way for Baker and Grodray to do something afterwards.

Yes, that was Gareth. And Pippa as well, as she studied the woman she had long since stopped thinking of as a rival. Philippa Loughty had no rivals for Gareth's love. That much had become evident quickly, and nothing Talyarkinash had seen had changed her opinion of the man.

Instead, she turned to the Chaa and let her anger show. There was nothing a Nari geneticist could do that would even get the attention of a god, and they both knew it, but the monster had the courtesy to look chagrined.

"Morty and Xiomber brought Gareth to me on *Hurquar*," Talyarkinash finally said when she felt like she could talk rationally. "I will never forget that day, because Gareth made such an unbelievable impression on me. I have not been able to isolate it to a pheromone or anything like that, but he had that effect on most of the women he had encountered, regardless of species."

She took another breath and let the storytelling wash some of the rage out of her soul. Thinking about Gareth calmed her. Explaining what

Morty's idea of *Hero* meant for the rest of the *Accord* was something that would keep her from wanting to kill a god for his arrogance.

"There is another Nari woman named Alicia, somewhere in *Hurquar*," Talyarkinash continued. "I heard the story from Xiomber later, about how she just happened to be behind them on the slidewalk and gave Gareth her scent card, with her contact information in vermillion ink."

She chuckled at the thought, mostly to herself, before looking back up and fixing her stare on *Last Traveler*.

"Had she known he was human, I doubt she would have behaved any differently," Talyarkinash growled at the god. "It is a measure of his charisma, his power. Something I later assumed was a factor of that same, immense psionic ability that allowed the Star Dragon. He has no comprehension about what he does to women, so his innocence is all the more endearing, but he walked into my lab and Morty and Xiomber needed a favor."

Deep breath to control her other emotions, before she showed everyone in the room, perhaps in the galaxy, how much she had been in love with the man from that moment. She could never tell him, he wouldn't have seen her. But he had been an even better friend than he ever would have been a lover. Had made her feel safe, even when they were on the run from Maximus. Had traded that criminal's freedom for her life, when he could have easily destroyed them both, that first night when the Star Dragon first appeared.

Flames, claws, or teeth, there was nothing Marc Sarzynski could have done to stop Gareth's rage. And Gareth had let him walk away, simply to protect her. Had risked the entire galaxy, to protect one Nari criminal.

Talyarkinash glanced at the man who had started it all. Another human like Gareth, but darker. Angrier. Another one she felt so deeply for that she sometimes didn't know herself.

But she could see the faint echoes of the man who had been Gareth's best friend a decade ago. Not all traces of that other man, another cop who had wanted to make the world better, were gone. Buried, perhaps, behind the rage and the will to power, but even then limiting things.

Punishing him with pain and regret, even as the criminal overlord found it necessary to torture another soul and kill him. It had brought him no joy. It brought him no solace now.

Just things that had to be done.

Talyarkinash had not understood that before. She had had to know

Gareth to understand that supremely human thing: to walk into the fire, at whatever personal cost, because that was the duty cast upon you.

"I was utterly opposed, until Morty and Xiomber explained to me what they were really about," she continued her narrative. "How Maximus was going to take over the entire galaxy if somebody didn't do something to stop him. How they had gone back to the well for another human, this one a cop who might be able to stop Maximus from destroying the very *Accord of Souls*."

She wanted to reach out and just touch Gareth on the arm now. Remind him of the good things that he had accomplished, because she could see the memories of that day taking center stage in his mind. The rage. The sadness. The commitment.

"There was one thing that the boys hadn't told Gareth," she said in a quieter voice, reliving it herself as she waited for a renegade human to go berserk and kill them all. "He was here to stop Maximus, but afterwards, it would never be possible for him to go home. No knowledge of the *Accord of Souls* was allowed on Earth, lest the humans realize that they really weren't alone and figured out how to escape and do something about it."

Gareth's eyes fell. She traced and realized that wistful sign was aimed at Pippa, standing close. As it should be.

"I watched Gareth commit to giving up everything in order to stop Marc Sarzynski's conquest," she turned back to the first god, and then the rest. "Everything. Earth Force Sky Patrol. His friends. *Pippa*. Because he would never be allowed to return. And that only caused him to pause for the briefest moment."

Talyarkinash reached deep into her memory and pushed that memory out to where the rest of the galaxy might understand.

Gareth, standing in her lab, having just learned the truth from her, without the careful, mental preparation that Morty and Xiomber had planned, to bring him along slowly.

Yes, the rage. The sadness. The commitment.

"Gareth's words: *He's here, and he must be stopped. Whatever the cost.*" Talyarkinash fixed her eyes on *Last Traveler*. "Do you understand what that means? What he sacrificed? Everything. And it was a price he was willing to pay. Can any of you say the same?"

She felt the being take a metaphorical step back, although none of them moved and Talyarkinash doubted that anyone else witnessed it. But she did. And that was enough.

"Tell me about the transformation," the Chaa ordered in a soft, polite tone. Finally asking instead of compelling.

"First, you need to understand Marc Sarzynski," she replied, casting her voice out to all the hosts of heaven and hell gathered around her. "He was human, like Gareth. Six feet, two inches tall. Roughly two hundred and forty-five pounds of Earth Force Sky Patrol Agent. Among the very best. Both of them."

Again, she glanced over at the dark man and read his soul, somehow exposed by the gods for everyone to do the same. So much like Gareth, and yet so different.

"They didn't tell me what Sarzynski was when they brought him to me, Morty and Xiomber." She picked up the thread and concentrated. "He was just a non-*Accord* alien they wanted turned into a Vanir. I am a geneticist. One of the very best in the business. My professional pride saw it as a challenge. I was able to turn him into the being you see now. Seven feet, four inches tall. Three hundred and forty pounds. Bigger, faster, and stronger than any of the Vanir I know. Morty and Xiomber tell me that after I was done they then turned Marc into a genius as well, functionally doubling his mental capacity to make him among the greatest warlords in history. Even human history."

Talyarkinash could not suppress the shudder that passed through her soul, thinking about what an Empire under Marc Sarzynski would have been like.

The non-gods around her gasped as well, whether it was because they saw what she saw, or merely understood the dreadful implications.

Talyarkinash wondered how close to immortality a human could get with the right geneticist challenging Time itself.

"So when they brought me a second human, and told me what he really was and why he was in my lab, I had an even greater challenge ahead of me," she smiled in spite of her emotional turmoil. "Especially when Gareth explained how he thought he could win."

STAR DRAGON

GARETH LISTENED to Talyarkinash's words and tried to keep himself composed. Centered.

Calm.

He represented all humans today, including all the billions who would never understand what was going on.

Last Traveler turned to him now. Faced Gareth from across the space. Gareth kept the growl inside when it really wanted to escape and paint itself all over a lesser god, however powerful the being might be.

"Star Dragon," the Chaa said.

Gareth couldn't tell if it was a question, a form of address, or something else. Gareth just nodded back at him.

"Star Dragon," he agreed.

"Why?" the creature asked.

Suddenly, all twelve of *The Communion* were focused on him. And thousands of their kin. And billions of humans.

And all of the *Accord of Souls*, however many trillions of people that was. And they were people, each and every one.

He didn't care what shape they took. What planet they were born. What gods they might worship.

They were his friends. His comrades.

The souls he had sworn to protect, first when he became a Deputy Agent of Earth Force Sky Patrol, even if he didn't know it at the time. Or later, when Grodray and Baker allowed him to take on the blue-gray body suit, and the neon-blue badge of the Constabulary.

To protect the innocent from harm.

"I have always been an even match for Marc Sarzynski," Gareth explained slowly, breathing the words in and out as he delved back into his memories. "In track and field, we swapped first and second place on a daily basis, even event by event. In academics, even a razor's edge was too thin to separate us. We are the same person, he and I."

And they were. The other gods, those watching over humans when the Chaa weren't around, could be credibly accused of playing a dark practical joke on humanity, to send two men to school together at the same time, and make them so alike in every way.

"Or were," Gareth continued. "Until we met Pippa and both fell madly in love with her."

He turned to look at the woman, ignoring the rest of eternity for a moment.

"She could only pick one, and for the longest time, neither of us knew which it would be," Gareth sighed, both with joy and sadness. "That was the greatest day of my life, when she chose me. None of us understood what that would mean, though."

He pushed his own memories up and out, letting one of the beings project it to the rest of the galaxy.

Nobody had understood what an inflection point had been passed, until much later. Marc didn't stop caring, but stopped caring as much. Found other things to focus on, but he had been infected with darkness.

Eventually, it took him fully, and the man walked away from his career as a crime-fighter, seeking another path. The darker one.

Destroyer, as it were.

The pursuit then, as Agents of Sky Patrol, often led by Gareth himself, chased the man through the underworld and darkness, never quite catching him.

Eventually, the UnderHives of Mars, where they had finally treed the fox and were circling for the capture when the man disappeared from sight. The rest of the gang had gone down with no understanding of how their boss had vanished.

Eventually, the best theory that remained, when the rest were discarded, suggested that Marc had somehow hypnotized his men to remember a flash of golden light and nothing else. One boss escaping and leaving his men alone for the cops.

Some rolled at that point, there being no honor among thieves, at least the angry kind. Marc's network was unraveled, dismantled. Eliminated.

And yet, nobody knew what happened to Marc Sarzynski.

Gone, without a trace.

Earth Force and Sky Patrol sought, but could find nothing that led them to how Marc had escaped, or where he might be hiding.

Gone, without any trace.

Gareth turned to study the man who was so much him that it was almost painful, some days.

Vanir, yes. Both of them, now, but he was still recognizable underneath, with the same jaw, the same hair, the same shoulders. Bigger eyes. Almost-ridiculous ears, at least to human sensibilities. Monsters compared to the humans around them that he had known and loved for so long.

"We are the same person," Gareth mused again. "When they made him better, they did the same to me, but that just meant we both started over with a clean slate, and a thousand times larger sandbox in which to pursue one another. And I would be just as much a hunted criminal as Marc, because I was a human, loose in the *Accord of Souls*, regardless of what Talyarkinash did to change me or what my mission was to save everyone else. I needed something more. An edge. A symbol, both of hope to the innocent, and fear to the criminal."

Gareth drew a deep breath and thought back to his youth. The comic books his parents let him collect, filled with stories both ancient and modern. *The Iliad* and the *Odyssey. Beowulf.* St. George and the Dragon. There and Back Again. Stories where a dragon was a monster to be feared and fought by the heroes.

But also King Arthur and his Knights. Arthur *Pendragon.* Heroes under a dragon's pennon. Protectors.

At first, he had been unsure if such a symbol would inspire as much awe and fear from the peoples of the *Accord* as it would humans, but then Morty had explained his psionic ability to Gareth in a way even a cop could understand. At least well enough.

He couldn't actually fly with those wings. His body would be too heavy, unless those wings were ten times as far across and he was built more like a Chinese dragon, a *Lung,* than the more European version he had in mind.

But it didn't involve physics, what he did. It was basically just *magic.*

There were other terms for it, but none of them were any more exact or illuminating than anything else.

Magic.

But if magic could make him over into a terrible, fire-breathing, flying lizard, what couldn't it do? Could it inspire the legendary dragonfear that had been at the heart of so many fables?

Only one way to find out.

Except that Marc had found them at the worst possible instant.

Kicked in the door while Gareth was woozy from the drugs and the transform viruses inside his system, *altering* him.

Marc walked in and stunned him unconscious. Helpless.

Failure.

Captured Talyarkinash, as well. Somehow Marc was able to ambush Grodray and Baker in the ensuing mess, taking everyone who might have been able to stop him.

Gareth felt the attention of *Last Traveler* waver at that moment. Like a light went out as the being turned his attention elsewhere.

To Gareth, his muscles sagged, and he suddenly realized how tense he had been, pushing back against the Chaa, even with his mind, if not his body.

"Prime Investigator Jackeith Grodray, I would have your story," the Chaa announced.

Grodray surprised Gareth by just smiling and the being and shaking his head.

"Not my story," Grodray said. "I was just a watcher. This is Eve's tale to tell."

Last Traveler turned to the other Constable. The other Prime Investigator.

Gareth could tell how much more careful the being had learned to be, when approaching a female with his powers and deciding to *compel* them to do something.

Gareth wasn't the only one in this room who had taken offense.

"Eveth Baker, I would have your story, then," the Chaa called out more politely than he had.

Baker scowled that magnificent way she did and stepped up. Gareth watched her take a breath and sneer at the assembled gods as she focused her attention.

Gareth smiled.

PRIME INVESTIGATOR

"WE HAD BEEN SEEKING rumors of a human loose in the *Accord*," Eveth growled at the man, the creature. The apparent Chaa of *The Communion* known as *Last Traveler*. Whatever that kind of a name really meant. "This was before Gareth, back when Cinnra first captured Sarzynski."

Had it really been less than two years ago when all this started? Eveth had a hard time framing everything into such a small window of time, such a small box.

And yet, that was the truth.

"As a young, hotshot Constable on *Orgoth Vortai*, I had been assigned to be the junior partner to a Senior Constable more or less brought in to watch me and see where my career was going," she continued, turning to Jack with a smile. "He might not have ever said that out loud, but I knew how to put disparate pieces together. They wanted to know if I was good enough to handle the job."

Eveth let her mind drift back. At the edges of her consciousness, she felt fingers tapping on the window pane of her soul, rather than just grabbing hold and squeezing her for information, like the being had done to Talyarkinash.

She had wondered if the Nari woman would jump the son of a bitch and rip his throat out over that. Eveth had almost done it for her, until *Last Traveler* recognized his mistake.

Power does not automatically make you right.

Eveth let the god have her memories to share.

"And then a rumor of a second human loose reached us," she continued. "We all had roles to play, and I played mine well. Bad cop, as it were, relying on intuition, while the cerebral Jack Grodray was the intellectual detective. We were chasing our second supposed rogue human."

She glanced at the *rogue human*. Laughed to herself at how far they had all come together in such a short period of time. That *rogue human* was possibly the best partner she had ever had, excepting only Jack.

"At the time, nobody understood just how deep so many planetary governments had fallen into corruption," Eveth snarled at the universe. "Petty things, but they add up, like water slowly carving a canyon through the mountains. *Orgoth Vortai* wasn't as bent as *Hurquar*, but we were on the trail and dared not tell anyone. At least until we had better evidence to take to Jack's superiors. This was when I still though he was just a Level-4, a mere Senior Constable forced to partner with a hothead to tone her down some."

That got a smile from Jack.

"Didn't work," he murmured just loud enough that several of the people nearby chuckled in response.

Including her and Gareth.

"So we pursued," she explained. "The investigation eventually took us to Talyarkinash's lab, where we got our first big break. But Gareth, Talyarkinash, Morty, and Xiomber made their getaway, although not without some luck and surprise."

Like Eveth running into a Quarrie and losing her pocketcomm. And then deciding to pursue Gareth alone, into an alley, where he and Talyarkinash ambushed her. And escaped without anyone being hurt. More than their pride, anyway.

Or walking into a bar and threatening the owner with all manner of physical implications if he immediately didn't give her everything she wanted to know, with the alternative involving jail, or a hospital.

Or both.

"Kicking over anthills, Constable Baker?" one of the other Chaa spoke up. *Astray In Darkness* seemed to be his name. Or something like that. Religion had never been her strong suit, and she wasn't impressed enough to start now.

"I was in a hurry," she replied, turning her attention to a more interested participant, from the tone of his voice. "Time was running out if we wanted to stop all this before it got out of hand. Oh, sure, Jack's friends would have been able to have a field day, unraveling things patiently over the course of months, once we knew where to shine the light, but Gareth would have gotten away from us, and Sarzynski probably would have disappeared."

"So using violence, or at least the threat of it is an acceptable form of policing in the modern age?" the man(?) asked.

Eveth shrugged.

"One can always choose to cooperate with a police investigation instead," she fired back. "There are criminals we're talking about. They have already broken Accord by their actions, so they need to be watched, possibly even arrested and put in a small cell until they come to see the error of their ways, or are no longer a threat to their compatriots."

She felt a surge of anger come up from somewhere unexpected, deep inside.

It had been a day. It had been a week of days, and now she was facing a plethora of angry gods intent on killing her partner and wiping out his entire species because they were too lazy to fix things.

Or too incompetent, but you didn't necessary say that to a god. At least not to his face.

Astray In Darkness apparently had really good psychic ears. She felt his back come up like an angry cat as he watched her, ever so slightly, but he refrained from rising to her snarling challenge, contained, for now, just between the two of them.

"But you failed," the being glyphed at her solemnly.

"We did," she agreed. "By the time we had a lead on Talyarkinash Liamssen and Gareth, Maximus had already gotten there and captured both of them. Worse, the geneticist had already done her magic to the human, so we had all that extra risk and danger thrown into the mix. And we got surprised and lost a firefight, Jack and I."

She actually felt the rage of a god touch her soul briefly as somebody extracted the next piece from her. They turned to their right, and suddenly two Warreth females and an older Nari man were hanging in the air, not far from Marc Sarzynski.

Unlike their polite handling of her and Talyarkinash, someone was playing rough. Eveth heard gurgles of pain and surprise from all three as they were manhandled into place.

Eveth snarled at the god.

That was still rape, as far as she was concerned.

"Maiair. Yooyar. Zorge," *Astray In Darkness* named them for the Court, and eternity. "You are broken failures. Poor examples of what the *Accord of Souls* was intended to become."

"Yeah?" Yooyar snapped at the Chaa. "And?"

Eveth nearly chuckled out loud at the Warreth woman's audacity, but then, what did they have to lose at this point? This wasn't going to be life in a prison cell. Not with these beings. There was going to be a house cleaning shortly.

Eveth suspected that it would be an ugly affair. At least for certain members of the audience.

Eveth got to watch as someone extracted glyphs from the two women a little more politely and displayed them for the others. The Nari male had apparently been sitting in the van, oblivious to the firefight behind him, even afterwards. She and Jack had gotten the drop on the two Warreth, but missed Maximus and let him sneak up on them.

The shot from the corner that got Jack. Her shot nearly nailing Maximus, but not enough to stop him. Both Warreth firing, the smaller one being the more deadly of the two.

Tossed bodily into the back of the van, along with Talyarkinash and Gareth. Transported to that secret warehouse where she and Jack were chained to a frame. Gareth more or less hung from another frame, because Maximus wanted to watch the man transform and see what Talyarkinash had done to him.

And Talyarkinash…

Eveth suppressed another growl. The Nari woman had regrown all the fur on her arm, but there was still a long, thin line of a scar visible underneath. Talyarkinash had kept the reminder, when she might have erased it with her science, because she wanted a souvenir of that night.

As if any of them actually needed something to remember what had happened.

The memories came also from Maximus now. Eveth could taste the extra layer of rage like frosting over them. That part warmed her soul, admittedly smaller than it should have been. The bad guys were also getting theirs tonight.

And they deserved it.

Eveth had been too groggy to remember much of the early part of the evening. Gareth had given everyone a good blow by blow account after that night, a result of Talyarkinash upgrading his excellent memory to be eidetic.

Gareth awakening first, dressed in white robes that seemed to bring with them some religious implications for the two men. Sarzynski on his throne, such as it was, but surrounded by his full Court of criminals.

At least those that had still believed in the man's power to that point.

Before…

Sarzynski waking Talyarkinash with a chemical smell, and then shaving a strip of fur off the Nari woman's arm. Before he stabbed her with his knife.

The rage that flowed back and forth between the two men like a river of lightning bolts between two magnetic poles as they screamed at each other. Two long-time friends, now at odds.

Worlds would fall before their battle was done.

Eveth glanced around the room at the truth of the words. Worlds were truly going to fall today. The *Accord of Souls* would be altered in ways that seemed impossible just yesterday.

A new future would be born tonight.

"Star Dragon," Eveth managed to say, loud enough that all eyes turned back to her.

The images displayed had been tinged with fear. Someone read her memories now and introduced them instead, since she had been awake enough at this point to witness the birth of a new life form.

A new symbol. Perhaps a new hope for the galaxy, in the face of Marc Sarzynski and his drive for *Empire*.

Gareth's scream of pure rage at that moment of transformation. The one that would have woken her anyway. Would have woken anyone in the building, since it was more than just audio waves.

The *Ascended Chaa* watched the man transform into something none of them had probably ever done before. Watched him break those chains. Take flight, pouring dragonfear into the souls of the assembled criminal underworld, where it would go on to infect planets like a virulent, new plague.

As intended.

And then Gareth started breathing fire.

Only now, watching with the added benefit of seeing the emotional impact that night had on the two Warreth women and the Nari male, did Eveth understand why Gareth hadn't just wiped them all out.

Would it have been better that night, for everyone involved if the human had chosen to destroy Sarzynski and Talyarkinash? Better for the entire galaxy?

She couldn't say. And that said a great deal. She hadn't realized how much she had come to respect the former career criminal, the Nari geneticist who had simply handed the Constabulary the keys to translate all her encoded records afterwards, so they could start the process of cleaning up *Hurquar*. Had even stood up to Jack, when the man wanted to throw her in a prison cell forever, because both Eveth and Jack knew that they would need Talyarkinash's help to understand Gareth.

When had that woman become such a friend?

"Star Dragon, why did you not destroy the human when you had the opportunity?" *Last Traveler* asked in a booming, angry voice.

"Because doing so would have killed my friend," Gareth said back in a tone so fundamentally calm that Eveth had to look over at the man. "Not Marc. Talyarkinash."

Eveth had had the same argument with the man five minutes later. And lost that one, too.

"One life lost, in balance for all of the rest," the being snapped.

"One friend given up, for no better reason than mere revenge?" Gareth countered. "I was raised better than that, *Chaa*."

As rebukes went, Eveth wasn't sure she had ever heard someone so solidly put into their place in so few words. But she felt the anger behind Gareth's tones. The Star Dragon wasn't far from the surface now.

She flashed back to the rage boiling off Gareth at that moment when they had proven beyond doubt that Gonquah had been building killer robots for Sarzynski. How hard he had worked to control it, in spite of wanting to unleash that impossible thing called *human anger*.

That thing that even the Chaa apparently feared.

"And I didn't let him go," Gareth continued in a snarl that almost made the air glow red. "The promise was one day's head start. That's all. His life that night, for that of the other three: Talyarkinash, Eveth, and Jackeith. One day. He got more, but only because it took longer than I expected to make my case to the Constabulary. However, his gang had been broken at that point. Dragonfear had served its purpose and was racing madly across the galaxy, taking criminals down or chasing them into their dens on world after world. And I never stopped chasing the man. *Will never stop.*"

Eveth felt a shiver. It seemed almost like a tide washing across the entire auditorium, touching every single being in the room, including the gods. Such was the power behind Gareth's words.

The rage.

The promise.

Something changed. She couldn't put her finger on it, but the room seemed to grow larger. And perhaps smaller at the same time.

Gareth was still Gareth, but it almost seemed like the Star Dragon had joined them in here, invisible, but present nonetheless.

Was that what it meant to be human? Among humans, Eveth had only ever met Gareth in person, and heard stories about Marc Sarzynski, but tonight she had met others. Pippa. Royston. Even the musician Ellen.

All of them had some manner of power about them that seemed lacking, compared to the rest of the chamber. At least the mortal parts.

"*Last Traveler*, is that why?" Eveth managed to cast her voice up into the maelstrom of the *Ascended Chaa* that were somehow above her, like witnesses up on a balcony, rather than down at ground floor. "Is that why you fear the humans?"

Everyone gasped.

ALL OF THE COMMUNION suddenly seemed close enough to touch, but they had never moved. Merely turned to look at a Prime Investigator named Eveth Baker.

But she understood now.

She and the others really weren't people to the Chaa. Those beings were already at least seventy thousand years old. Probably several times that amount, if she was reading them correctly with eyes that had been closed until now.

She and the others were merely facets of the *Accord of Souls*. Items on a checklist.

Not people with dreams.

Suddenly she was larger, but she had never moved. Someone had lifted her up to another place, somehow.

"Is that why humans were never admitted to the *Accord of Souls*?" she pressed, understanding what had triggered these gods into motion now.

Her voice contained no trepidation. That wasn't what Eveth Baker was about, but neither was the quaver mere curiosity.

"Because the humans had the potential to become you at some point?" Eveth let the inductive parts of her imagination fill in the gaps in the picture she had assembled in her mind. "So that they could join you in your quest, if they could somehow be kept isolated long enough to either mature, or wipe themselves out, as some others we have encountered have done?"

"You are correct, *Daughter of the Accord*," a new voice spoke up.

She turned to study the glyph of the one known simply as *Mountain*, even to its fellows.

Mountain. A thing of sturdy strength and beauty, but also a place from which you can fall if you are not careful. But if you do not, you can see sometimes forever, standing on those broad, strong shoulders.

Narrator of History spoke now, addressing herself to everyone who could hear her voice, which might be everyone alive.

"Twenty-nine Chitra ago, First Immortal **Awakened**," she said simply. "The Chaa were already a long-lived race at that point. Powerful with psionic ability, but the potential for more. She showed us the way."

They did not look all that different from the Vanir in the images, the glyphs presented to the galaxy. Perhaps they had merely stripped away most of the psionic potential, when they modified the ones who chose not to become gods?

Those Left Behind. The Vanir, because they were no longer Chaa. And the Chaa left them with sixteen other species, uplifted to provide companionship, but also in need of protection, which was why so many Vanir seemed to gravitate into law enforcement.

Protecting the innocent, as Gareth had understood.

"Within a Chitra, many others Ascended, including much of *The Communion*," Narrator of History continued. "We were the first. *Last Traveler* was not the last to Ascend, but rather the last of *The Communion* to depart from the *Accord of Souls*, waiting for a time so that his comrades could leap ahead on their quest for the *Creator Who Gave Us Dreams*. But we did not choose to include humans into our construction."

"Why was that?" Eveth asked *Mountain*, rather than *Narrator To History*.

He seemed like the one who wanted to say something, when everyone else would have trusted their storyteller to handle the task.

The room fell silent. So silent Eveth wondered if the heartbeat she was hearing belonged to a Chaa, or perhaps the galaxy itself, somehow awake and listening in.

"Humans, then or now, are a violent species," *Mountain*'s voice sounded like nothing so much as an avalanche beginning to find its way to the valley below. "But that is a facet of their emotional depth, which is greater than all other sentient beings we have met, save the Chaa ourselves."

Eveth could hear the truth of those words. Gareth was possessed of an inherent power she did not understand, but knew to be a human thing not shared within the *Accord of Souls*.

Looking around, she saw something similar in Pippa. In Dr. Loughty. Even in Marc Sarzynski.

Induction. The ability to make leaps of fancy that span bottomless chasms where logic is stopped.

Eveth was an inductive detective. That was why they had paired her with Jack, the master of logic. At least that was the story she had been told. And it had been enough of the truth that she wasn't going to bicker on the finer points of the rest today. She had made it to Prime Investigator, which was really that thing she wanted most out of life.

But even being confronted by gods wasn't going to turn that off.

"Those others, the ones you destroyed," she said. "They lacked that potential, and were thus an ultimate threat. But humans, if they could be contained long enough, might grow into something else. What is that?"

In the room, a few dozen corporeal beings. An even dozen gods. A few thousand *Ascended Chaa*.

Eveth somehow felt the stare of the entire galaxy, every man, woman, and child, focused on her alone.

A moment of uncertainty passed between the gods she faced. Eveth wasn't sure if that made her feel better or scared her entirely out of her wits, that she could back-foot beings such as this.

The next moment, eyes seemed to turn sideways, up on that platform, alighting on one of their number.

"To understand that, daughter, you must understand that which was destroyed," *Merciless* intoned gravely. "Perhaps it is time for their tale to be known."

MERCILESS

HE HAD NEVER TOLD the tale, even to his brother and sisters of *The Communion*. It was enough that the task was done. They did not need that stain on their own souls, when it came time to stand before *Eternity* and own the depth of this crime.

Modern Chitra called him *Merciless*, but in an earlier age they had teased him good-naturedly as *Restless*. Forever bouncing from place to place, seeking the clues that would lead them all to a higher understanding of the *Creator's Vision For All*.

Restless had found an advanced, alien species. Given the exacting nature of hindsight, he had wondered if the *First Cause* had intentionally put the Tronafora almost exactly opposite Humanity as the galaxy spun. One hundred and seventy-eight degrees, and only slightly closer to the galactic core.

Two more powerful, dangerous species that would stand in the path of the Chaa, and their goal of spanning the entire disk into a single, harmonious entity, populated by nearly forty intelligent species, eventually.

Thus might even the true gods have a sense of humor, black though it might be.

Merciless reached into the Pandora's Box he kept close to his soul, where the glyphs might be stored deep and never shared. He had only expected to share these memories with the Originator at the moment when he would be judged for his ultimate fate.

But he was *Merciless*. That title included ruthlessness. And Duty.

Merciless paused for one infinitesimal moment to nod to the Star Dragon. *Merciless* understood a duty that required you to give up all things for a greater good. The human Gareth nodded back, blood brothers separate from all the rest in this room.

He glyphed the first image of the Tronafora that any being had known six Chitra ago. Because the Vanir Constable Eveth Baker had been the one to ask, he Witnessed her reaction, as a measure of the rest.

They were a bipedal species, that still being the most efficient mechanism to move and still retain extra limbs that could be specialized into tool use. Baker found them spindly and a bit awkward, but that was her own estimate, having never seen them move.

A fast Vanir might outrun a Tronafora, in a race.

The species was lightly scaled, with three horns on their head in a manner that might span the space between Yuudixtl and Traakna, except that Tronafora were nearly Vanir height.

What separated them from all the other species that the Chaa had encountered, intelligent or not, was their culture, which had erased all religious overtones or references and embraced a purely mechanistic atheism almost as extreme as *Restless* found mathematically possible.

No greater afterlife existed in their worldview, where the *Creator Who Forgives* might judge them on the accomplishments of their lives and separate the worthy from those destined to whatever hell awaited. Each was merely a cog in a faceless machine, struggling constantly not with ethics and philosophy, but to attain, sustain, and expand one's personal power, generally at the cost to others from whom such power was of necessity stolen.

A ruthless pyramid of conquerors who found no value in any other species, and had discovered the same mathematics that had allowed them to escape the prison of their clockwork homeworld and begin slowly colonizing nearby systems.

Merciless showed the assembly image after image of the world known as *Bota Fori*. Gray skies thick with smoke and pollutants from the factories, hard at work putting out ever newer and more powerful machines designed to kill. Factories and barracks covering every bit of surface. Landdragons lumbering on four legs with beam cannon for eyes.

Skydragons to scout, with smaller beams, plasma breath, and adamantine claws to pounce and rake.

The Communion had met *In Congress Assembled* when *Restless* had returned with his news. The *Accord of Souls* had already been planned and was in the process of being born. The Tronafora had been missed, almost hidden in their distant corner of the circular galaxy, because the entire species gave off almost no psychic emanations whatsoever.

Humans, for comparison, as *Merciless* put the two side by side for all to see, contained almost enough psionic capacity for both species. And humans had yet to move past stone tools to anything so simple as metal, while the Tronafora had already fully hived the surface of their own world with metal and stone buildings and fortifications, and expanded to five others, one of which had not been empty when the invaders arrived.

Merciless let his anger color this glyph. To do otherwise would inflict harm on himself that was unnecessary. His kin would understand and think him no ill. The corporeal could not grasp, anyway.

Pr'Taxxu.

It had been a lovely, green and blue world. Once. By the time *Restless* discovered it, the planet's hiving was nearly complete, and he could only listen to the fading echo of the people who might have grown up to become the Taxxa.

Had there been any left alive at that point.

There were only Tronafora there now. *Restless* and the others had come too late to prevent a xenocide. At that point, even a geocide was imminent, as every native plant and animal was slowly being destroyed, replaced by things brought instead from *Bota Fori*.

"Most species are left alone," he spoke aloud for the first time. "Time will cause them to evolve into something more socially acceptable, or they will reach one of several biological or technological bottlenecks in their development and cease to exist as a viable species. We have witnessed this many times, and have the archaeological record of other species that might have reached our stage of development had they not."

"Were you the first?" a voice emerged from the crowd of corporeal beings below.

Merciless let himself ruminate on the topic for a long moment. *First Immortal* and *Great Docent* were the oldest of their kind, but *Bowsprit* and *Glory in Sunrise* had been the farthest roaming, along with the creature once known as *Restless*.

"We have found no evidence of other such *Ascended* in this galaxy," he finally said, carefully hedging his words.

"In this galaxy?" the creature asked, apparently reading the finer shading on the glyph better than *Merciless* had expected.

He turned to study the creature. One of the humans. A female. Daughter of another present, and emotionally mated to the Star Dragon.

Philippa Adeline Loughty. *Pippa*, to those who knew her. A woman thwarted by her culture, but unwilling to settle for failure. Her brilliance, while masked, approached that of her father in places. Her empathy for others outdid any of the human men present, and sat at a special, elevated level equaled only by the other human female, Ellen Denise Ames, leader of the musical gestalt.

"We have, by now, traversed roughly seventeen thousand other galaxies to some extent," *Merciless* told the woman. "In others, there has been some evidence that such beings as ourselves once existed. Some have galaxy-spanning civilizations, such as the *Accord of Souls* will eventually become, while others have left behind traces that such projects were attempted, but later failed."

"How does a galaxy-spanning civilization fail?" Pippa asked. "I could see on a single world, as resource depletion or warfare might do the trick. Even a single, unexpected meteor might unleash a cataclysmic, extinction-level event sufficient to undo higher civilization. How can that happen on this scale?"

Truly, the humans were more advanced than *Merciless* had expected. And he gathered, from the reactions of his kin, that others had discovered the same today.

It was good.

"On your own world, life exploded and then thrived for millions of years," *Merciless* brought up images from her own mind of great lizards that had once roamed. "But in your case, they have been gone for more than sixty thousand Chitra. We have only been **Awakened** for twenty-nine Chitra. Two hundred and ninety thousand human years. And even that is not as long as your species has existed. Who else might have evolved, *Ascended,* and departed even so recently as a thousand Chitra ago?"

He watched the woman nod her understanding, which surprised *Merciless* so much that he invaded her mind to see what it was that she saw. A moment later, both *Astray in Darkness* and *Last Traveler* silently rebuked him, and *Merciless* relaxed his hold on the creature's mind, allowing her to share, rather than forcing her to submit to his will.

How much have we forgotten, if we have lost even our manners? Merciless wondered at himself.

But she did understand. Such a primitive species, all things considered, and she understood that the galactic scale was just a matter of size over the planetary, and thus civilizations themselves could evolve so far that they eventually tired and died. *Merciless* thanked her for teaching him such understanding and returned to the Tronafora.

No others of his kin could tell this tale, as none had been close enough to actually witness it firsthand. *The Decision* had been made, to expunge an entire sentient species, as one might cut out a cancer to save the infested being. Or galaxy.

Six worlds. Hived over to provide a home for the Tronafora conquering machines. To stand as beacons for the various fleets seeking out new worlds to take. New species to eliminate.

New evil to be done in the name of whatever Tronafora culture venerated in their militant, mechanistic atheism.

Restless had found them. Had brought them to the notice of *The Communion*. He volunteered to end them, alone, so that none of the others might have such a crime to bear.

And it was a crime. An entire species wiped from existence and memory, merely to eliminate the risk to the fledgling *Accord of Souls* that was even then merely a dream of the two cousins, *Magistrate* and *Uplifter*.

Restless became *Merciless*. The assembled galaxy watched his transformational memories. *Bota Fori* destroyed first. *O'Pequiz. Xani. Ribble. Telea Mani.* Finally *Pr'Taxxu.*

Other worlds where the explorers had not yet begun to Hive with their militant civilization were left alone, once the infection of Tronafora was removed bodily from their solar systems. Fleets exploring were picked up and cast into nearby stars to purify them in fire. Tronafora were hunted down and eliminated.

Merciless.

An entire culture that evaporated in an afternoon, leaving only six dead stars behind as mute testimony. Monuments to…something. Even he wasn't sure what to call it.

But the task was done.

Around him, the *Ascended Chaa* fell silent, shocked to witness the thing, when most had been sufficient to know it had been done.

"So you failed," Pippa announced.

DAUGHTER

SHE COULD NOT CONTAIN herself any longer. Pippa had watched these powerful beings, proto-gods, perhaps, interacting with Gareth and Father. With the Constables and aliens all brought here for judgment.

Her words echoed off of whatever metaphysical ceiling might contain them, but she watched them sting the one known as *Merciless* the hardest.

"Failed?" he demanded in a soft tone that still contained all the rage he had internalized, that which allowed him to become *Merciless*.

"Failed," Pippa said. "Yes, you committed a most thorough xenocide, I'm sure. Eliminated every trace of the Tronafora from place or history. Wiped the slate utterly clean on six worlds. *What did you gain?*"

She couldn't help the anger that bubbled up. Her hands were still bound to the Nari woman Talyarkinash, and felt the woman's recoil of shock and dismay. Through her, Fatima as well, a linking of females across three separate species.

"We protected the *Accord of Souls*," one of the other Chaa spoke. *Uplifter*, she thought, but Pippa couldn't be sure.

"No, you destroyed a threat to it," she challenged his interpretation. "One of them, apparently. Why did you not go ahead and complete the task? Why were humans not eliminated then, before they rose to be a challenge?"

As audacity went, Pippa quailed inside, but she would not be stilled.

She could see it now, in ways that perhaps even these gods could not.

These creatures were reactive, not active. They displayed such a muddled thinking that she was offended by it. And let them know it.

"We did not see humans as a threat," *Narrator To History* spoke up. "Until today, that held true. Indeed, they needed to be kept isolated, but that was for their own good. Until your father, humans could not reach the *Accord of Souls* without assistance."

"He did not even seek you, until your kind, your grandchildren, meddled in our existence," Pippa sneered at the being. "And yet, the punishment will be ours to pay, and not theirs."

"It will not fall solely on your kind," *Uplifter* replied with a special anger it its voice.

"So humans are so great a threat to the *Accord* that they must be eliminated, because otherwise the people of the *Accord* will play with matches again?" Pippa asked the being a sharp tone. "Why do you not teach them not to play with matches in the first place?"

"Your kind have had five Chitra to develop and evolve, human," *Uplifter* snarled down at her. "We left you alone then, rather than incorporate you into the *Accord of Souls* because we believed that it would be possible. But we are gathered now to witness how badly that decision went wrong."

"No, you are here to gloat on the superiority of your culture and technology that you can do anything you want, to whomever you desire, and nothing but *God Himself* can probably stop you," Pippa let her anger lash at the man. "That does not make you better. It makes you infantile."

Suddenly, Pippa came to understand what it meant to have twelve, angry proto-gods focus themselves on you. Someone grabbed hold of her mind again, less politely than before. They squeezed, ever so slightly. Not enough to hurt, but sufficient that her thoughts and memories were exposed.

Hopefully, nobody but these gods could truly read her soul and all the secrets contained therein.

She felt herself sifted like flour, *Forty-niners* seeking every flake of gold that the riverbank might surrender to patience and will.

Finally, they let her go. Somehow, each of her own hands was now being held by the other two women, a triangle of support between Grace, Nari, and Human.

"Guilt is a human thing born of fear," *Speaker For The Communion* enunciated clearly as the being returned to their platform to scowl down at the ephemeral.

Pippa smiled at him. At all of them. She picked out the one she wanted and bored her mind in on him with her own ruthlessness.

"And yet," she crowed. "*Merciless* would not accept help in his xenocide, because of your overwhelming fear, all of you, that you will have to face *God The Creator* one of these days with such a stain on your souls. If that is not guilt, pray tell me what word I should use instead to describe your failure?"

Razor blades covered in honey still cut. She could see metaphorical blood dripping up there as they listened to her.

They had read her mind, these twelve. Seen her ideas, her suggestion, possibly her future, if she had such a thing.

"What you suggest as an alternative is so impractical as to be nearly impossible," *Glory In Sunrise* spoke now. Unlike many of the others, she glyphed from a primarily female point of view, although Pippa understood now that to be Chaa was to contain within one's self the ability to take on any form.

Even then, some had been born with male tendencies that colored their behavior and thought processes, just as *Glory In Sunrise* and *Narrator To History*, among others, had been born female.

If you could use such a verb to describe the arrival of one of these proto-gods, back in the distant history when they were merely nigh-immortal wizards of great power and vision.

"My idea is nearly impossible?" Pippa picked out the woman and smiled coldly at her. "From a species that can pick up a black hole and drop it anywhere they want, as a way to punish upstart species?"

Pippa had a moment of sadness overtake her, as she considered her mother and how Elizabeth might have handled these beings. Mother would have been even less flexible than Father, and in that Pippa strove to emulate the woman she had not kissed goodnight in nearly two decades.

Elizabeth wouldn't have taken a gram of shit off these people. Pippa wasn't about to start.

Around her, gasps, from mouths human as well as other. One did not sass gods, apparently. At least in their worldview.

Pippa had never allowed a man to dictate things to her, including Father. If these proto-gods were going to kill her, to kill every single one of her friends, she would meet them on her feet, not her knees.

Suddenly, the triangle of power was broken as Talyarkinash and Fatima let go of the hands they had been holding together, even as they somehow retained their grip on her. Pippa thought they were moving away from her, but they were each turning to stand at her side, joining her in facing off with these beings, these angry children who expected to bully people out of their way.

Tough.

"What would it gain?" *Mountain* spoke in a voice like an earthquake reaching up for the surface of the planet.

"Time," Pippa fixed her terrible gaze on the Chaa and glyphed at him. "You had all expected humanity to reach a special place in another Chita. To be able to join you in your grand quest, your mad adventure, even as you guaranteed that no other species in this galaxy would ever even come close. This would give you time to find out if that is possible."

"And the cost?" *Mountain* asked.

"A few worlds, a few millennia," she replied. "You, who have already spent nine Chitra exploring seventeen thousand galaxies cannot be that greedy, can you?"

Dead silence. Even the grave might make more noise.

Pippa found the light in here different, as though the room had changed, or the galaxy. One could never be too sure, with dreamers like these involved.

"The *Ascended Chaa* will retire to consider this proposal from the human, Philippa Adeline Loughty," *Speaker For The Communion* announced in a voice that seemed to echo across eternity.

And just like that, they were gone. All of them.

Pippa looked up and all those faces that had been on the platform had vanished. All the lesser beings that had been floating like ghosts went with them.

Only the ephemeral remained behind.

"What have you done, Daughter?" Father was there.

He looked like he wanted to hug her, but held back, no doubt a little awed by the circumstances, but also by the two menacing shield maidens holding her flanks. Pippa stepped forward and hugged him instead.

"Maybe I have found a way to save us," she whispered.

BROTHERS

GARETH FELT THE CHAA LEAVE, in ways he didn't think he could explain to the others. But he also wasn't just one person, anymore. Around him, he could feel the Star Dragon flying, almost as if they were separating into two beings, at least for today.

He would miss that thing, if he were indeed to lose it, but if it would make things better, then he would be happy for the loss.

Still, the hands holding him in place were gone now, as well. He could move without anyone stopping him.

Gareth felt his head turn to the left. One Vanir form, surrounded by several others, not all that far away from him.

Marc.

He took a step. Watched Marc suddenly freed from whatever cage had held him up in the air, so that they stood eye to eye watching.

Gareth reached a hand out tentatively as he approached the barrier separating Marc and his gang from the rest of the room. Probably a wise choice, especially if the Chaa were truly as gone as they seemed.

Still he walked close. Watched Marc do the same, even as his associates, the Warreth sisters Maiair and Yooyar, and the Nari Zorge, stepped back, away from him.

But for the thing between them, they might talk alone for the first time in nearly four years.

Behind him, Gareth felt the rest of the room also seem to recede, as if everyone understood that this conversation needed to be private.

"Hello, Marc," Gareth said simply.

"Gareth," the man answered in a tone more weary than wary. "I'm sorry that it had to come to this."

"And I as well," Gareth replied. "But I don't suppose that there really were any other options, were there?"

"No," Marc said. "It had grown too big to be contained in just the Solar System. Or even the *Accord of Souls*. Eventually, either you would have found a way to stop me, or I would have conquered the galaxy and created a human-dominated Empire."

"Why?" Gareth asked simply, that one syllable containing all those years, all the arguments never had.

All the possibilities gone.

"I couldn't handle being second best, Gareth," Marc said. "I used to think you knew that, but I've learned more in the last hour than I had in the previous twenty-nine years. Until now, I never truly understood that it was never a competition to you. Or rather, the only person you were competing with was Gareth."

"Yes," Gareth said. "I wanted to be the best me I could. I'm sorry it took all this for you to understand. What could we have accomplished, if you had?"

Marc laughed lightly, suddenly sounding more like the man Gareth remembered from their youth rather than the criminal warlord intent on conquering the universe.

"Eventually, I would have probably become the Sky Marshal of Sky Patrol," Marc said. "That was one of the enticements they dangled in front of me when it became clear that I was leaving. You never would have wanted the job, so it wouldn't have been a competition."

"No," Gareth nodded. "I would have fought tooth and nail if they ever wanted to promote me past Senior Special Agent, because that would have meant a desk job. Not my style."

"And it really wasn't you, in the end, Gareth," Marc said.

Gareth watched the man's eyes wander back over his shoulder, but he didn't need to glance to know that Marc was looking at Pippa, wandering mentally back to a moment where she had chosen him instead.

Again, how much better might the world have been? Gareth would have been heart-broken and crestfallen, but he also knew that he would have gotten over it eventually. Somehow.

Marc never had. And it no longer mattered.

Their eyes locked again after a moment. Gareth could see all the pain of his memories in there, but there was also a new resolve.

"If we hadn't gotten ourselves into this mess, I might have even found myself a new Empress from among the humans on *Earth*," Marc said. "I had found a template, the perfect woman, but she wasn't human, so she couldn't help with my long-term plans. And then she went and betrayed me."

It was Gareth's turn to let his eyes find a horizon and contemplate. He knew who Marc was talking about. And he agreed.

"Talyarkinash would have been perfect for you," Gareth said. "The old Talyarkinash, that is. From before."

"What did they do to her?" Marc's concern was genuine, with a tiny flare of real anger underneath.

"She had to reinvent herself into someone else when I came along," Gareth said with as much sincere honesty as he could press into the words. "When she was captured by the Constables and given the choice to cooperate with them or rot in a prison cell for the rest of her life. But she would have made a great mate for you. She has been an exceptional friend when I needed one."

Marc nodded.

Gareth knew he should feel something more. Some rage or jealousy, but they had moved past it all, it seemed, the two of them. They could just stand here and talk, like two old friends in a bar who haven't seen each other in several years, catching up before returning to their separate lives.

Except nobody would ever return to their old lives. Most of their friends wouldn't have life shortly. At least he hoped he had made a good enough impression on people like Grodray and Baker. And on Talyarkinash.

They would be the only memory of him tomorrow.

"So why were you on *Earth*, Marc?" Gareth asked.

"It was the last place I expected anyone to look for me," the man chuckled. "And I had enough contacts there that they could hide us for a while, and enough wealth to get what I needed. But it never would have been enough for me. I would have eventually recruited an army of gunmen and tried to conquer the *Accord of Souls*. That's just the way I'm wired these days."

Gareth nodded this time. He could recognize such a stark truth. Even *Earth* wouldn't have been enough for Marc.

How are you going to keep them on the farm, after they've been to gay Paris?

"And I did need to find myself an Empress," Marc continued. "Someone like Pippa, but more ruthless. Or like Talyarkinash, but human so that I could start a Royal House. I had planned to live forever, once I found the right geneticist. At least several millennia, rather than decades. I would have reshaped everything in my image, like Machiavelli always demanded."

"What would you have done when the Chaa came back and objected?" Gareth asked with a smile.

"Yesterday, they were just a myth, old friend," Marc smiled back. "Fables told to children to keep them in line, like the bogeyman. I would have spit in their faces, and they would have probably snuffed me out, and then spent a century undoing everything I had been trying to build. But what the hell do us pitiful humans know?"

They shared a chuckle at that. Yes, it would have played out about like that.

How do you plan for angry gods to return? You don't. Not rationally. And it wasn't like there was anything he or Marc could have done to stop beings of such enormous power.

But time was growing short. The Chaa would return soon, from wherever they had gone to talk without the children listening in.

"Marc, I'm sorry it turned out like this," Gareth said earnestly. "I wish we could have found a way to make it work, back then, or somehow since."

"And I as well," Marc said, his eyes growing sad and somber. "The follies of youth we can never undo. The choices we can never go back and make right. But these Ghosts of Christmas Past, Present, and Future will not lead us to the sort of happily-ever-after that you find in the vids."

"I am still honored that you were my friend, even if we lost that later," Gareth said.

He held up a hand and placed it on the shield that separated them. There was no greater symbol for all of this that he could find.

"And I you, Gareth," Marc replied, placing his own hand opposite Gareth's, separated by nearly a foot of invisible barrier. "Perhaps in our next incarnations we will get it right. Or at least closer."

"Next incarnations, Marc?" Gareth chided him. "You don't think we aren't both immediately going to hell for this?"

"Were I still of your faith, I would expect that, Gareth," Marc replied. "You would not, for reasons I don't think you have the emotional capacity to understand, but that's fine. I went elsewhere, looking for something to fill in that hollow spot in my soul. I found a militant form of Buddhism that spoke to me well enough."

"Did it bring you joy?" Gareth asked.

He watched Marc look inward for a moment before the man nodded. "It did."

"Then I'm happy for you," Gareth said. And he meant it. "All I ever wanted was for my friends to find joy. Even you, afterwards. I never stopped hoping that you would find your way out of that darkness."

"All it took was the intervention of a cadre close enough to gods that nobody could tell the difference," Marc laughed. "And the destruction of everything either of us had ever known, ever loved. So when you're in heaven, and I'm being reborn, maybe we can both work to make the universe a better place."

"I hope so, my friend," Gareth said. "I do not ever intend to stop trying."

Marc nodded and stepped back, letting his hand fall to his side. Gareth did the same.

They would be destroyed by the Chaa shortly enough, and none of it would matter, but he had at least had a chance to talk to his old friend again.

It was enough.

Around him, Gareth felt the arrival of the Chaa, all of them, like an invisible squall line passing overhead, bringing with it a change in temperature and pressure, as the impending storm prepared to take you.

"People Of The Earth, you will hear me," *Speaker For The Communion* called to all corners of the galaxy again, just as he had before. "The time has come."

DEFENDER

ROYSTON FELT THE CHAA APPROACH. Like the others, he had been standing back, watching Gareth and Marc perhaps finally come to peace, even as they were separated by a barrier none could crack.

The two men could finally talk as equals. Hopefully expressing those things that had been buried for so long.

But the moment passed.

"People Of The Earth, you will hear me," *Speaker For The Communion* commanded. "The time has come."

Royston slid away from the others, as interesting as such alien people were and as pleasant as their earlier conversations had been. All eyes had been watching Marc and Gareth, breaths held so tight that no noise would interrupt.

The Gods were returning.

Royston approached the two men. They had found peace, it was obvious. Either would have been acceptable as a son-in-law five years ago, when such a thing was possible and Royston had called in every favor he was owed to know the background of the two.

Just like that, it was as if the intervening years had passed.

Thus do we all grow up, he mused.

The barrier separating them was present for Marc and Gareth, but Royston stepped right up to that point and apparently through it, as if even it understood that the time for violence was over and the shield no longer necessary.

"Gareth, Marc, come," he ordered the two, surprising both men by taking one of their hands and pulling them back to the center of things.

"How…?" Marc started to say, but Royston just smiled at him.

"It is time to deal with this as adults, young men," he said back sternly.

He could do that. Royston Loughty was old enough to be their father, and had been a Special Agent of the Earth Force Sky Patrol, back in his highly-classified younger days, before Elizabeth.

Neither man resisted as Royston pulled them along, much like the triangle of power that Pippa had formed with Fatima and the Nari woman Talyarkinash earlier, when his amazing daughter had challenged the gods themselves to behave.

Glancing back, the group of criminals that had attended Marc followed, sucked into Royston's wake but still protected from harm. If you were about to watch someone be executed, why bother stepping in?

The group did not split into facets, as he had expected, but merged seamlessly. Everyone understood that the time for violence was done.

The completion of all things was upon them.

Pippa stood front and center, glancing back at him in surprise and awe as her triangle of power matched his: Talyarkinash and Fatima standing at her wings, just as Gareth and Marc did his.

Chevrons aimed at the gods like arrows ready to be loosed.

"The *Ascended Chaa* have undertaken to discuss your proposal, Pippa Loughty," *Speaker For The Communion* announced. "The vote was the barest majority opposed, but even *The Communion* recognizes that pure democracy is not the method by which such a grave situation should be resolved. We would hear your dreams in your own words, that the vote may be swayed to a more secure and permanent majority."

Royston wanted to speak, but it was not his place. He had brought the two most dangerous poles of power into alignment, and perhaps that was enough. With the musician Ellen, the four of them might represent the most psionically powerful humans in existence right now.

"You destroyed the Tronafora, rather than let them continue expanding," Pippa observed in a slow, teaching voice. "Their militant atheism ran counter to everything you believed as a culture, so I feel that such anger colored your emotions too much."

Royston wondered if she had picked up the same shades as he from the glyphs *Merciless* had communicated. Perhaps she was a fifth part of their whole, and he had never truly appreciated that his daughter was his equal in so many ways.

It would be necessary to correct his behavior if they managed to survive this. Pippa truly was his peer. She should become his intellectual partner in all things, and not a mere assistant, even on paper.

Earth Force could get stuffed.

"They would have eventually sought to conquer the entire galaxy and subsume it beneath their Hives," *Merciless* replied grimly.

"That is entirely possible," Pippa agreed. "But with all your power, I have yet to see any hint of true precognition among you. You can estimate and theorize, but none of you can pierce the veil and actually see the future."

Royston felt a ripple of mild surprise roll across the *Ascended Chaa* as if such a thing had never even been considered. Perhaps there were limits to their godhead.

What would today have been like, had the Oracle at Delphi been able to advise these Olympians?

"So, yes, they would have tried," Pippa continued. "Or perhaps not. Perhaps an encounter with truly sentient aliens, rather than the verging-on-intelligent Taxxu, might have caused their society to recoil and evolve. *We cannot know.*"

"We cannot know," several of *The Communion* echoed, as if a call and response of the Kirk.

Royston could see fault lines emerge up there. Destroyers and Protectors, wavering back and forth on the decision to eradicate Humanity. It had been a razor-thin thing, he could tell.

"You cannot know what might have happened to them or to Humanity, irredeemably confronted with the greater galaxy and true gods," Pippa said, turning from left to right to take them all in as Royston watched with pride. His daughter, standing in for all humans. And Earth Force barely recognized that women might have something useful to contribute to science, to say nothing of politics. Fools.

"But you also have it in your power to refrain today, that you might find out," Pippa continued.

"We have heard your proposal, Pippa Loughty," *Speaker For The Communion* replied. "The Communion is split evenly on the idea, not because we do not see the merit of it, but because of the scope of potential power that it represents, and the cost to us. Explain yourself."

"I already know that you have the power to interrupt wormholes," Pippa said. "Gareth, Eveth, and Jackeith were in such a structure at the moment you blocked it, extracted them, and returned the rest of their team to their starting point. Such was the glyph you shared when announcing this Court."

"That is an active act," *Speaker For The Communion* said. "It requires a watcher to intercept such a thing."

"True," Pippa nodded. "But why can you not set up such a structure in space and power it with your will, or perhaps some psionic device you cause to be constructed. This was a technological advancement of yours before it was a mental one."

"Humans will not accept a cage," *Astray In Darkness* spoke up now. "Such a thing will cause them to redouble their effort to escape and return to being a threat, trebled now with the understanding that there are ranges out there denied to them. And people that could be conquered. Worlds looted. Technological advancements beyond their wildest dreams."

"Thus are humans engineers," *Glory in Sunrise*'s mirth seemed to infect everyone, both gods and the ephemeral below her. "Tell them a thing is impossible and watch them prove you wrong."

Royston could not debunk her theory. Look at what he had done when challenged by Pippa that his understanding of physics was insufficient.

"But if the cage is large enough, it might give the humans time to expand into the galaxy and find themselves," Pippa's voice took on a softer tone now. Not pleading, but invoking perhaps. "If there is an entire sandbox into which they might play, perhaps it will be enough to contain them. You yourselves expected it to take another Chitra before humans were evolved enough to approach. We have not even possessed metal-working technology for a full Chitra. What could we do with as much as another Chitra to explore one small corner of the galaxy, secure that we have it to ourselves. What art could we create?"

"And later, the humans would still be entirely contained, if it became necessary to eliminate them," *Merciless* offered in the most practical voice Royston thought he had ever heard.

"Why do you propose fifty light-years, Pippa Loughty?" *Speaker For The Communion* inquired in his magisterial voice.

"If I remember my studies correctly, a sphere fifty light-years across, centered on my Solar System, contains roughly fourteen hundred star systems, and approximately two thousand stars, when you factor in how common binary systems are," Pippa said. "And there are nearly one hundred and fifty stars similar enough to our own that they should have inhabitable planets around them."

"You are correct, but two of them already possess advanced lifeforms that may yet evolve into beings that could join the *Accord of Souls* at a later date," *Narrator Of History* noted.

"So you would not form a perfect sphere," Pippa nodded. "You should still be able to erect and maintain a barrier that keeps humans in. Or out, as it were. The *Accord of Souls* would be protected, including future worlds you wished to admit. The human xenocide is at worst delayed. But at best, humans will evolve into someone that could eventually become a partner to the Chaa in their quest. Any you will go to meet God without an unnecessary stain on your souls."

"It will not work," *Mountain* announced. "As *Astray in Darkness* notes, humans will spend all their time trying to break out. One of us would have to maintain a constant, eternal vigil to prevent that."

"Not necessarily," Royston spoke up now.

He couldn't tell if the ideas were his own, or somehow flowed from one of the men with him. He wasn't even sure they were three separate beings now, rather than one composite gestalt that had formed under the pressure of the situation.

Like a second diamond, after the one Pippa had formed.

What would advanced humans be capable of, once the species got there? Royston didn't know, but he had half a dozen examples from which he might theorize.

"Speak, Father of Pippa," *Mountain* challenged.

Royston understood that the being was seeking a technical solution, and not just a sociological one, so he reached deep to tap the power suddenly at his command, unsure if it was Marc or Gareth offering hints. Probably both of them.

"Yes, I agree," Royston nodded in general to the Chaa. "A simple barrier a millimeter thick will fail quickly in its intended purpose. As a human, I would build a platform capable of sailing through the wall until I could set myself up on the other side and start my mischief again."

They had all seen the failure of such a solution immediately, but nobody here was apparently as sneaky as Marc, and Gareth, truth be told, to circumvent.

"Make the suppressor a light-year thick," Royston offered as a solution. "Humans do not have the capability, with our modern, chemical rockets, to traverse that distance in anything less than generations anyway."

"Even for us, the power requirements would be astronomical," *Mountain's* voice almost contained a sneer, the first emotion Royston could remember coming from the being.

"Not necessarily," *Merciless*, of all people, spoke, echoing Royston's earlier words. "True, to relocate the number of black holes necessary to power such a shielding would greatly disrupt the gravitational tides of galactic plane, but we could also rely on a network of red and white dwarf stars. The result would not be uniformly spherical, but would also be more easily maintained for perhaps as long as a Chitra, before enough stars drifted to open gaps in the shielding effect."

"Is this your logic or your guilt speaking?" *First Immortal* asked, joining the conversation for the first time. "Are we hearing hope or shame?"

Royston had heard *First Immortal* referred to earlier as one of the female-born Chaa, but this powerful being sounded almost like the Goddess/Mother that all primitive cultures on *Earth* had worshipped in the beginning. There was nothing soft or compliant in those tones or glyphs. This was the Crone of ancient religions.

In that, she almost sounded like Pippa.

"Both, I would expect," *Merciless* answered honestly. "One cannot be separated from the other at this point in history. Is not one crime sufficient to take to our *Final Judgment?*"

And that, right there, was why it was perhaps necessary and acceptable for the Chaa to have destroyed the Tronafora. Royston had read the being's glyphs and understood that primitive species to have suppressed all religious belief. Doing so, like the various *Industrialisms* of the Twentieth Century always left man empty and hollow, for what was he without ethics?

What was any creature without an ethical structure upon which he could frame his actions? Scientists had long failed to provide an adequate demarcation between man and the higher animals. Many so-called lesser creatures had language. Had beliefs.

Only a few had ever been shown to have ethics. To look up at the scientist and say "*This is I will not do, because it is* wrong."

Thankfully, proposals by *Earth* scientists to uplift such creatures to a level that might rival humans had been turned down again and again as *Unethical.*

Let them evolve their own way, into the thing that they should be rather than forcing them to meet our standards.

But then, wasn't that what the Chaa had attempted, so long ago? Uplift sixteen. Modify the seventeenth. Ignore most of the rest.

Hope that Humanity would find its own way.

Interestingly, Royston felt one of the Chaa extract from his gestalt and then from Pippa's a map of the near systems to Earth. At least as he understood them. One of the professional astronomers working at the Arsenal, with Luna providing a shadow against various radiation pollution from Earth itself, could have given them a more precise mapping, but if this was decided upon, the Chaa would handle it themselves anyway.

They wanted to know that it could be done. And done with efficiency and cost-effectiveness tossed in, so that one of them wasn't on duty to maintain it constantly.

Royston watched an image take shape above them, like a massive hologram, except this was entirely in his mind, as he understood it.

Just as it was in the mind of every human in existence, down to the smallest infant that might grow up to someday be an astronomer, a ship's captain, or an explorer.

It was not a perfect sphere. Once such an elegant solution was no longer necessary, it took on a more mechanical appearance.

No, better to describe it as a series of giant, transparent snowballs surrounding the *Earth* at a distance and enclosing it in a bumpy box. There was enough overlap in all places that the structure would appear to hold water.

And humans.

"Is this a task worth doing?" *Seeker For The Knee Of God* broke zir silence.

Unlike the others, this Chaa's voice contained no clues that might suggest a gender. Not that it was machine-like, but rather, so androgynous that it might be both genders at once.

When you controlled your form, anything was possible, limited only by your imagination and your need.

Look at the Star Dragon, for example.

Nobody answered the question posed, at least not where he could hear it.

Royston had a feeling that the *Ascended Chaa* were voting, in some secondary cloak room hidden from the ephemeral creatures. Voting again, perhaps.

Shifting like tides in response to the case made by Pippa to save her species, if that could be possible.

Like Gareth, Royston could live with having to be executed today, if not everything else was lost.

"The vote is amended," *Speaker For The Communion* announced as the *Ascended Chaa* returned. "*Merciless* and *Astray In Darkness* will cause the barrier to come into being, and power it sufficient for half a Chitra, at which time *The Communion* will reconvene."

Everyone understood the dark overtones of his voice, a rip current threatening to overwhelm you and drag you to a watery death at sea. Humans, you have five thousand years to get their act together and form a more perfect union.

Or perish.

It would not be his problem, dead for so long by then that those humans might have forgotten his name.

Looking back, the progress over the last five thousand years did give Royston hope. It had only been thirty-six centuries since Homer's Ilium had fallen. Fifty centuries of time more or less encompassed written, human history, dating from the first writing systems attributed to the ancient Sumerians.

Where would another fifty centuries find us?

It was good. He and his friends had just saved billions of humans, potentially trillions, from extinction.

"Now we will address the criminals among us, and their punishments," *Speaker For The Communion* continued in a voice that filled this room with dread.

FIREMAN

MORTY FELT the gaze of that old bastard on the stage center on him.

Sure, start with me, you sanctimonious shit. I started it all, didn't I?

"Morty the Yuudixtl, your crimes, as you note, are the most significant, because without your efforts and genius, none of the rest of this situation could have occurred," *Speaker For The Communion* began.

Many of the other Chaa growled at him as well. He couldn't really blame them. Nobody likes to have to come into work on their day off just because somebody else screwed something up so badly that only a monumental effort will salvage things before the shit comes completely unraveled.

Not even gods.

Morty took a step forward and lifted his jaw at them. He wasn't daring them to do their worst, because they could, but he hadn't once backed down in his life. He wasn't about to start today.

Xiomber joined him a moment later, standing at his side through thick and thin, like his egg-brother always had. They were a team, going back decades. Maybe Mom had never understood why they could never get real jobs, but she had loved them both anyway.

And nobody else had been good enough to do what Morty and his brother had accomplished. Y'all keep that in mind, too, suckers.

"Your soul has been read," *Speaker For The Communion* continued in a voice just as serious as Morty's was sarcastic. "Each glyph has been noted and filed."

Morty hadn't really grasped what true power was until he realized that those people could create a perfect copy of him tomorrow if they wanted to, just from the amount of information they had stored, like organic computers with a nearly-infinite drive array.

Morty refused to show fear. They knew it was there, but they knew everything.

"Your punishment should be the greatest," Speaker For The Communion said. "But others have spoken in your defense."

Morty felt a presence walk up behind him, like someone had just put up a skyscraper and suddenly he was standing in its shadow.

Gareth put a hand on his shoulder in companionship. Xiomber, too.

"Kid, we've known this was coming from day one," Morty turned to look up at the Star Dragon who had shaped so much of their lives.

"I don't care," Gareth stated flatly. "Evil never recognizes itself as doing wrong, so it never reconsiders its actions. It certainly never tries to step back and fix things. Sure, both of you have decades of other things to account for, but I've already heard that list, including all the parking tickets, jaywalking, and library fines. You still decided that you had to save the *Accord of Souls* and sacrificed almost as much as I did in the process."

Morty wasn't going to cry. Not even Gareth could make him, but it was a close thing. Xiomber and several others all seemed to have colds coming on, though.

So maybe a human could qualify as an egg-brother, too.

Grodray surprised the absolute hell out of Morty by stepping up on the other side and adding a hand on the other shoulder.

"You tried, Morty," that big, dumb cop said in a soft voice.

Damn it, I was doing fine holding it all together, Grodray. Why can't you just let me be killed in peace? It's unseemly to be crying while the gods snuff you out.

"As I said, others have spoken for you and your egg-brother," *Speaker For The Communion* announced in a softer tone. "Half of your actions warrant your execution as a warning to all future generations. But the other half cast you into a new light, one that we will hope foreshadows your ability to be properly rehabilitated by the Constabulary. Prime Investigator Jackeith Grodray already intends to ask the Court for a sentence of ten years to life, contingent on good behavior. We find that sufficient for you and your egg-brother. Perhaps you will meditate further on the nature of sin and redemption, and be able to make something useful of your future existence."

Morty thought he might collapse. But for the hands of the two Vanir cops on his shoulders, somehow giving him strength, he might have. He couldn't stop crying, but that was okay. Vanir cops had spoken up for him. It didn't get any weirder than that.

But if you burn the house down, you got no call to bitch about having to sleep in the mud. He and Xiomber had managed to call the fire department in time to save the *Accord of Souls*. Ten years in a small box would be just enough time to read everything in the prison library, and then get bored enough to start writing his autobiography. Somebody needed to tell these people *WHAT REALLY HAPPENED!*

Might as well be the truth.

FRIEND

TALYARKINASH CONTAINED as many of the tears as she could, which wasn't that many, all things considered. Morty and his brother had utterly upended her life twice. First by bringing her Marc Sarzynski to upgrade, and everything else that might have gone with it, perhaps.

Second, Gareth.

How could one word contain everything? Even the glyphs of The Communion were barely sufficient in their data-density to sum up what had happened since a human cop had walked into her lab and proposed to save the *Accord of Souls* with her help.

"Talyarkinash Liamssen," *Speaker For The Communion* turned the spotlight of his attention on her next.

She stepped forward, surprised when Pippa and Fatima came with her, adjusting wordlessly so that she was suddenly at the apex of their triangle. Two women she had met less than an hour ago, and they stood with her like Gareth and Grodray had done with Morty and Xiomber.

She squeezed their hands in thanks.

"Your crimes rank perhaps one step less than the two Yuudixtl," the Chaa continued. "But you worked in ignorance when modifying Marc Sarzynski, and with intent when presented with Gareth Dankworth. Like Morty and Xiomber, your actions show a growth and maturation that we find mitigates your sentence."

Talyarkinash nodded. That about summed it up: a decade of pure greed and subtle evil, and then everything since that moment dedicated to saving the *Accord of Souls* from her own actions.

"As with the Yuudixtl, the Constabulary will see to your punishment," the being announced. "We find in you the opportunity for true rehabilitation, and not just the punishment of social isolation. We also note your intent to continue working with the others to improve the galaxy, rather than simply working with a Damoclean Sword overhead. The Constabulary could free you tomorrow and your essential beliefs would no longer bend towards evil."

It was a good thing that Nari didn't blush like the furless species did. Gareth probably knew her well enough to see the whiskers twitch, and the ears rotate, but hopefully the rest would be ignorant.

This was what growing up felt like. Taking responsibility for helping others, and not just yourself.

For building a longer table, rather than a higher fence.

Pippa and Fatima both stepped close and engulfed her in a hug that said more than anything words might possibly contain. A moment later, she felt Gareth wrap his arms around the entire group and then his love for them all flowed, even Fatima, who had been a complete stranger.

But that was Gareth.

It was Eveth Baker grasping her after the others stepped back that broke something inside her, and she could no longer contain the tears. But the tall woman just held her close, like her mother had once done.

Around them, she felt even the *Ascended Chaa* smile down at her, once she finally could stand on her own, although Baker kept an arm around her shoulders like a sister. And Pippa stayed on the other side, with Fatima close enough to catch her if she fell backwards.

"Now we must confront true evil," *Speaker For The Communion* announced in an angrier voice.

Talyarkinash felt a polite force brush her to one side, clearing a pathway into which Marc's various sidekicks and hangers on were thrust.

Two Warreth women: Maiair and Yooyar. Both young, perhaps just barely adults as the *Accord* might measure things, but already hardened criminals and killers.

Two Nari men: Zorge and Mishalska. One old and one barely older than the Warreth sisters.

Seven humans. Two-Gun Kowalski. The crimeboss O'Rourke and his gang: a young woman whose purpose was obvious and four other gunmen who almost looked like the two-dimensional caricatures of humans everyone seemed to have in their heads.

Talyarkinash wondered if she was too used to the five powerful beings around her as representatives of the species, and the others would truly be what humans were like, when viewed on this plane of existence. She would have to ask Royston, if she had the chance, or perhaps one of the survivors.

"The human associates of Bigby O'Rourke are mere criminals, caught up unknowingly in the greater tides of history," *Speaker For The Communion* intoned. "Human law can deal with all of you, but we will add one geas to your punishment. Upon incarceration, each of you will be compelled to detail all of your crimes for the authorities, that you will serve sufficient time in prison to have the opportunity to learn regret and be rehabilitated. The examples of Talyarkinash, Xiomber, and most importantly Morty should serve you as examples."

In the blink of an eye, six of the humans were gone. Somehow, Talyarkinash was certain that they had all just been dropped into a prison cell, somewhere on Earth, with the glyph of a Chaa welling up inside them for enough notebooks to contain their multitude of sins.

Minor players, serving only as examples of what the Chaa might do, even on a day that they had found the capacity for mercy. Especially the one known as *Merciless*.

"Two-Gun Kowalski, your glyph is known," *Speaker For The Communion*'s voice suddenly was filled with an anger she had not detected earlier. "You are a flawed example, even for the psychotic and homicidal humans. You lack the possibility of empathy that might someday lead to remorse. Time spent in prison would be dedicated to pretending to be rehabilitated that you might fool a warden into releasing you."

Talyarkinash watched the weak glyph of Two-Gun Kowalski snap his fingers at the gods around him.

"We find no redeeming qualities about you, human," *Merciless* spoke up. "Even as others of your kind have impressed this conclave with their wit, intelligence, and empathy. You are a waste of resources and will be dealt with as such."

This time, a flash of light seemed to descend on the human and engulf him. Rather than blinking out of existence, as the others had, he seemed to dissolve over the space of a second, like sugar dropped into hot water and stirred.

Probably a better death than he deserved, all things considered. She had seen what kind of person Kowalski was. Even at his worst, Marc Sarzynski still retained a core of humanity, of empathy, that she had been able to detect today. Two-Gun Kowalski had been a broken man, a rabid dog to be put down because there was nothing else one could do with him.

At least it was silent, both physically and emotionally.

"And now, broken children of the *Accord*, we come to you," *Speaker For The Communion* addressed the four remaining criminals. "We created this place for all species to live and grow in harmony by creating an accord that linked all into one being. You represent our failures, broken children."

The acid that he dripped on those words was heart-rending, as Talyarkinash listened. They saw themselves as parents who had failed to raise good children.

Worse, they would punish those children for it.

"Wait," Talyarkinash managed to bubble up a glyph from the depths of her own soul, interrupting the others.

As before, all eyes turned to her, most of them hostile now, as the Chaa worked themselves up to the sorts of anger necessary to punish their own children.

"Can you not fix them?" she asked.

"Fix them?" *Last Traveler* asked, after being silent for so long. "Why would we fix them?"

"Because they were born without accord," Talyarkinash felt the pleading in her tone but couldn't help it. "They lack the link to others that is the psionic resonance known as the *Accord of Souls*. Others do as well. After five Chitra, the bonds have grown weak."

Talyarkinash stepped closer to the four and breathed in the scent of their glyphs. Yes, criminals guilty of terrible things, but utterly bereft.

At least she had maintained some empathy, so she perhaps wasn't as broken as these others, but she had found her way back. They were to be destroyed without any opportunity to experience the love and friendship that most of the *Accord* took for granted.

But then, wasn't that true of most criminals?

"Only partly," another voice intruded on her thought processes.

Talyarkinash turned as she recognized the glyph from Pippa. Fatima joined her a moment later, sharing a memory of a conversation the two women had had previously.

"Most war and crime is a result of want," Pippa had said then and

Fatima glyphed it now, speaking of the human capacity for development, but unknowingly describing the underlying failures evident in the *Accord of Souls* as well. "Of poverty, both physical and emotional. As Roosevelt once said, freedom from want will lead up to freedom from fear. If we could move past poverty at a global and systemic scale, humans can be fantastically warm and giving people."

"The same can be said of the *Accord*," Fatima added, turning to encompass all of *The Communion* with her fierce gaze. "Crime today is a factor of want as much as it is of broken individuals choosing crime. Without need, they would have no reason to turn to the uglier side of life. The *Accord of Souls* is broken because too many people are not sufficiently engaged in productive lives, in the sorts of personal art that improve the species. All species and not just mine."

Talyarkinash turned and discovered that she had formed the gestalt again, three souls almost one, despite being Human, Nari, and Grace.

Or perhaps because of it.

Criminal (however reformed), outsider, cop.

"Yes," Pippa glyphed powerfully, drawing elements and knowledge from all three. "The Constabulary has been fighting a losing war for centuries to prevent crime. To contain it."

"Is this true?" *Narrator For History* suddenly reached out an angry hand and two other beings joined the trio at the center of the room.

Accord Commissioner Petim Diazal, representing the government. First Inspector Anen Wardson, of the Constabulary.

A tiny male, standing shoulder to shoulder with a giant woman. Confronting the very gods themselves, returned angry.

The gestalt stepped up and stood beside them. Another one joined on the other side a moment later.

"It is," Wardson said simply. "The Vanir, as *Those Left Behind* have the greatest investment in the *Accord*, but that very commitment has alienated many others. Civilization has been breaking down for a long time, one bad choice at a time, in spite of everything my officers could do to hold it together. Thus the fear of humanity as too great of a stress for the system to survive."

"And all our efforts to bring more people into a greater understanding and support of the system have not been enough," Diazal added. "We have lost too many souls to alienation and lethargy. To crime and despair."

"So we are to take this foursome as an example of what has gone wrong with the *Accord of Souls?*" a new voice chimed in as the part of the entity known as Talyarkinash watched and listened. "And our own culpabilities?"

Uplifter, who had given the seventeen species form and capability. The other *Creator*, if you wanted to envision an entire pantheon of gods, all searching for the most powerful, but gods nonetheless.

"Five Chitra have passed," Talyarkinash spoke. Or perhaps Pippa. Or even Fatima. It was hard separating them into constituent parts at present. "None of you could see the future, so you could only establish a path, but not guarantee it. As with all, it is now necessary to correct the course against the drift of more than six hundred lifetimes lived."

"Fix all of the *Accord?*" Uplifter probed.

"Reinforce accord itself," they answered in harmony. "Strengthen the ties that bind. Let the lost children come in from the cold."

"Some will resist," Uplifter challenged.

"Resist a god?" the gestalt mocked the being. "Epicurus would laugh in your faces, were he able. *If a god is unable to prevent evil, then ze is not all-powerful. If ze is not willing to prevent evil, then ze is not good. If ze is both willing and able to prevent evil, then why does evil exist?*"

Talyarkinash had never heard of the Hellenic philosopher Epicurus before now, but was stunned at the jar of power that rocked the Chaa assembled here to *Judge*.

Rocked them to their very cores.

They recovered quickly, but the entire conclave had seen them learn doubt. Experience it firsthand for the first time in perhaps Chitra.

Perhaps they learned shame as well, if she read the glyphs correctly. That was the other side of a coin marked arrogance.

"You would need less Constabulary," someone up there challenged the First Inspector.

Nobody was prepared for the laugh that emerged from Wardson's mouth.

"I can think of no greater success than to spend more time rescuing people from emergencies and less time arresting them," she called back. "I would retire tomorrow and take up watercolor painting, if I thought that we would be needed less and less."

The *Ascended Chaa* vanished again.

Talyarkinash had no doubt that this vote would be just as contentious as the one to save humanity had been, but they had made a collective case to the Chaa.

As the running joke in the underworld had always gone: *How bad could it be if the Chaa didn't come back to stop you?*

Except they had. That was how bad it had gotten.

Talyarkinash could see new religious movements springing up, merely from the joy of having lived through such a thing as to watch all the gods return.

Abruptly, the gods returned.

Not there, and then present.

"Your jails will be overfull, when we act," *Narrator Of History* announced to the group. "Many more than you expect will return to the fold."

"So be it," the Arawath Commissioner replied. "We can always sentence them to the community service of helping their fellows rehabilitate. And I am sure that there are many murals to be painted, and parks that could be cleaned, by way of serving penitence. The *Accord of Souls* has never been about punishment. The goal was always to make the galaxy a better place to live, for as many beings as we could. It was only in falling short of that dream that we have failed. That you have failed, but only in your ability to envision far enough into the future to understand today's needs."

"It was never our goal to return again and again," *Narrator To History* replied. "We seek the *First Cause*."

"And yet, you are our elders," the small man said. "Our role models. If it is to be that we will face the *Creator* before you do, it is your duty to help prepare us, just as it is our duty to honor and reflect your values when you finally join us."

Talyarkinash found that last bit a trifle thick and gooey, but she had never had any patience for the sort of glad-handing that was necessary if one wished to pursue political power as a vocation. Perhaps that was simply the nature of the game.

"So *The Communion* agrees, speaking for the *Ascended Chaa In Conclave*," *Speaker For The Communion* pronounced. "The *Accord of Souls* will be altered. All beings will feel our touch. Few will feel our wrath, but there are those that cannot be saved, even by such as us, and they will join the human in dissolution."

For a moment, the entire universe seemed to ring, like church bells calling the faithful. Talyarkinash felt something touch her deep inside, and then pass, like the kiss of a flower petal on a spring breeze.

"Now we will deal with the three humans who have caused us to return."

FALLEN

HE HAD KNOWN the moment was coming, but there was nothing Marc could do to prevent it. He had never gotten up one morning and decided to embrace evil. Never even thought of himself that way until recently.

Ambition was a relentless taskmaster.

At least there had been the chance to talk to Gareth. To acknowledge everything that had gone wrong, and assume the blame for it, as much as a younger version of Marc Sarzynski had deflected everything onto the other man before.

He was going to die, but he could do that with a clear conscience. He had done evil things in his anger. Later, because nothing less would keep the other gangs at bay, when this same man had been pursuing him across two different galaxies, first for Earth Force Sky Patrol, and later for the Constabulary.

Gareth wouldn't have stopped short of death, and based on the things Marc had learned today, he wasn't even truly sure now that death would be all that much of a barrier to Gareth's unstoppable rage. They had transcended into another place.

Marc felt the hands of one of the Chaa draw him front and center again, even as the remaining members of his gang vanished. But they were returning home, chastened by the power of these beings such that they would never again be criminals. The *Accord of Souls* would become so much stronger. Another would-be conqueror would utterly fail where Marc might have succeeded.

One tiny part of his soul held onto that tidbit, even as he had let the rest go. He could have succeeded, were Gareth not there to stop him.

But Marc Sarzynski had grown appalled at where his ambition would have taken him, once he had the chance to stop and truly consider that future, rather than spending every waking moment trying to stay one step ahead of the Constables.

Ahead of a Star Dragon.

Emperor Marc the First, if he had lived long enough to hand power down to one of his children. And the Chaa hadn't noticed him first and decided to undo things.

Yesterday, they had been merely the sorts of founding legends primitives told in order to justify themselves, and let their kings claim descent from gods.

Except there really were gods out there. And in here.

Marc drew a breath and let one true regret linger. He had chased Pippa, and that other Marc might have turned out acceptable, had she not broken his heart in ways he just never got over.

But there was another. She had broken his heart as well, although she would never know it. Her betrayal had been all the worse, for what it had engendered, but she was still perhaps the very model he would have used, when he went to Earth to select an Empress for himself.

As if she could hear his thoughts, Talyarkinash turned now and met his eyes.

Marc sighed at what might have been and turned to face his defeat.

"Marc Sarzynski, your list of crimes is so long that *The Communion* itself will adjudicate your punishment," *Speaker For The Communion* said simply.

Marc bowed his head and let go the breath he had been holding. Two-Gun Kowalski was most certainly in hell by now, and he would be joining the man shortly.

Drawing images from Gareth's mind, shared during the gestalt, the galaxy would truly be a better place without Marc Sarzynski in it. He shrugged. Not much more you can say about a man at that point.

"And that's where you're wrong, Marc," Gareth suddenly said aloud.

Marc's eyes flew open to find his oldest friend and deadliest enemy standing close.

"I know he had done evil, terrible things," Gareth said to the assembled vengeance above them. "But I also see the kernel of truth, or goodness at the core of the man. There is repentance for his deeds, little good though that he expects it will do him. I've just watched you alter an entire congress of species. Why can you not fix what ails Marc Sarzynski?"

Marc felt his jaw drop open. Gareth Dankworth had been *Nemesis* for so long that it was sometimes hard to remember what came before. Both of them remembered the rage, that night when a Star Dragon was born.

And yet, they had transcended everything else.

Standing in the hall of the gods for final judgment did that.

"Why?" Marc turned to Gareth, almost forgetting those above in his shock. "I'm evil. You know that. Nothing would change what I've done. Nobody can bring those lives back."

"I know that, Marc," Gareth said. "But I also remember the man that many thought would one day lead Sky Patrol. Who would embody that thing we all strove for. Repentance means you regret what you've done. Rehabilitation means that you could still do good in the world. I believe you still have that good in you."

"Truly, Star Dragon?" *Mountain* called down. "You believe that he could be made a productive member of society without falling back on the old ways, the old evil?"

"I do," Gareth turned and challenged the very gods with his solidity.

"Would you be willing to trade your life for his, on that belief?" *Mountain* asked.

"Yes."

Marc nearly cried, much like the two Yuudixtl had. He had forgotten what it was like to have true friends. Perhaps he hadn't known one in the years since he and Gareth had parted ways.

"Marc Sarzynski?"

"No," Marc yelled back with all his might. "I will not allow it. You will not find a higher example of all the best of humanity that Gareth Dankworth. You should be holding him up for everyone to emulate, even knowing that in falling short they will elevate all things."

"Marc, all I ever wanted was for you to find peace," Gareth said. "To be happy. I've done the thing that would save everyone. You should have a chance."

"Don't you see, Gareth?" Marc implored him. "I can never undo those crimes. I can never make it right."

"That is where you are wrong, Marc Sarzynski," a new voice broke in.

Astray In Darkness. The darkest, bleakest of the gods.

"Wrong?" Marc almost demanded.

"We have both walked in shadows," the man said. "We have both gone *traik*. But it is possible to find one's way home. I am no longer *Astray In Darkness*, for I have found my path now. You should do the same. I will take the name *Polaris*, for the star by which Human navigators in the northern hemisphere of your world could sail their primitive ships and find their way home."

"The Star Dragon would speak for Marc Sarzynski," *Speaker For The Communion* called. "As would *Polaris*. Who would gainsay them?"

Silence, on a practical as well as psionic level, and Marc found he could sense those things now.

He felt a touch, almost a kiss on his cheek from a proud father. Everything seemed to settle in his soul and his eyes cleared from the tears.

He found Gareth standing shoulder to shoulder with him, like in the old days.

"If he is to return home healed, I would ask the *Ascended Chaa* a favor," Talyarkinash was suddenly standing close enough that he was able to reach out and take her hand.

The Communion paused.

"That can never be undone, Talyarkinash Liamssen," *Narrator For History* spoke. "The barrier will prevent it, and we will not be present to hear your regrets."

Marc felt something stir as she turned to study him. He had not forgotten her cobalt-blue eyes, or the Imperial Russian blues to her gray fur. Until her betrayal, he had considered other dreams.

Her eyes held a pleading question in them, one that took Marc's breath away.

"Are you sure?" he whispered to her.

She smiled at him, with eyes, whiskers, and ears.

"I am."

Marc hadn't realized that he could become more emotional than escaping a sure death, but he suddenly was. The gravity of her decision weighed on him like somehow walking on the surface of a neutron star.

"And I, as well," Marc offered weakly.

"Would any offer challenge?" *Speaker For The Communion* asked the room.

Marc waited on pins and needles, but nobody spoke.

"It is good," *Speaker For The Communion* announced. "*Uplifter*, I think it would be most appropriate in your hands."

Marc watched a blue light rise, like a whirlwind of cerulean sand, and Talyarkinash disappeared inside it.

A moment later, it evaporated, leaving behind a vision Marc found as compelling as *Venus Rising*.

It was still her, still Talyarkinash Liamssen, but she had been transformed. She was human now, rather than Nari, with those same eyes, but no whiskers, and human ears. The hair on her head was still the Imperial Russian blue it had been before, with gray and black stripes in it where it tumbled down to her shoulders.

Marc realized that she was nearly as tall as he was, but when he turned to his right, he realized that he was staring Gareth in the center of the man's chin.

His mouth fell open in awe.

"Correct, Marc Sarzynski," *Uplifter* smiled down at him. "Many chose to speak for you, so we will parole you to live out a human life on a human world."

He found Talyarkinash's hand, human now, and pulled her close to him. He even kissed her when her arms went around him and she insisted.

This woman would be giving up everything, choosing eternal exile on an alien world, and losing all her friends and family, but Marc also realized that she didn't really have friends or family, save for Gareth.

And she had chosen him.

Maybe he could be happy.

"That is settled," *Speaker For The Communion* glyphed. "Royston Loughty, we must consider your crimes next."

SEEKER

ROYSTON CONSIDERED the beings around him. The many things he had learned today, forming a new entity in the gestalt with Marc and Gareth. Discovering the other gestalt with Pippa, Talyarkinash, and Fatima.

He would never think of her as other than Fatima, in spite of it merely being a role that a Grace woman named Ilak Vorta was playing. He had never met that stranger, only the one purporting to be the niece of his old friend Firuz.

But Humanity was protected. As was the *Accord of Souls*, in some esoteric way that would see it almost reborn into a newer, stronger entity. And many criminals had gotten their just desserts.

"The wars of Maximus and the Star Dragon created a desperate situation, Royston Loughty," *Speaker For The Communion* intoned severely, his entire being seeming focused on Royston. "However, it was your effort to open the portal that represented the greatest threat to the galaxy in seven Chitra, as humanity would have found the path to reach nearby stars in perhaps as little as a century. Less, had their fears played upon them, to know that aliens truly existed out there."

Royston nodded. Truly, he had done the most, having taking the starting point of Gareth's kidnapping and relentlessly pursuing his investigations, until they led him to a bunker in the Arizona desert, and a special, lucky catseye that he had traded two silverfish and a bloodstone to Tommy Wilson for.

And a hole in the universe itself.

There were many steps on that path, but he had taken them.

"We have undertaken to understand a new humanity today," *Speaker For The Communion* continued. "Seven Chitra removed from your primitive forebears. Five of its most powerful representatives stand before us."

Royston considered his compatriots. Gareth and Marc collectively represented the very best that Earth Force Sky Patrol had ever striven for. He himself was the foremost expert on solar radiations in the entire Solar System, and a close competitor to Sir West, still hiding somewhere around here watching, when it came to raw physics.

Pippa was perhaps the most intelligent, most capable woman he knew, across a lifetime of powerful females. She even outscaled the members of the *Accord* that he found surrounding him now.

And Ellen Ames. How does one describe the Goddess of Music herself, descended to Earth and incarnated in such an avatar? Nothing Royston had attempted would have succeeded without the gestalt he had somehow been able to form with that woman and her band.

What were future humans going to be capable of, if this group represented the promise of that destiny?

"That is the question that has bedeviled *The Communion* time and again, Royston," *Docent*, the *Great Teacher* spoke up now, drawing their conversation into the personal, as if everyone else in the room were mere witnesses.

He studied the being, reading the glyphs of the man he had once been, one of the oldest and truest friends with *First Immortal*. This was the one who had showed the others of the *Ascended Chaa* how to translate themselves out of corporeal existence once she had done it, that they might grasp enough immortality to find the *Path of God Herself Written In The Stars*.

"Some have advocated for removing you and Ellen entirely from the context of Earth," he continued in a deep, broad voice that seemed to echo of the stars themselves. "They are driven by a fear that you might yet surpass us in depth and breadth of your power."

Royston tasted the magnitude necessary to achieve that sort of outcome, and felt it take his breath away.

How many Chitra would that take, even at the astounding pace that humans had developed since conquering fire?

"That, my friend, is why *The Conclave* will return in only half a Chitra," *Docent* smiled at him privately. "That will be sufficient time for Humanity to choose a direction, either towards power or evil, or perhaps they will have destroyed themselves before we return."

Yes, he supposed so. These gods might yet fear what humans could do, having seen the five beings of power of the current generation. It left Royston a little in awe, but he also understood why they had been able to achieve so much.

"How likely is such a concentration of power to occur again?" he asked the *Great Teacher*.

Amazingly, the Chaa shrugged back.

"We have studied the pattern of human genetics that each of you carry within," he replied. "Within the grand depths of ten billion humans, statistical analysis suggests it is low, but we also know that the five you will not be subsumed into the greater whole to disappear. Your various descendants will contain that spark, at the very minimum."

"You do not foresee a regression to the mean?" Royston asked.

Again, a simple shrug, as if the Chaa truly were incapable of such an extrapolation.

That might be where and how humanity could pass them, if we contained the seeds of the Oracle of Delphi.

"I have been alive for twenty-nine Chitra, Royston," *Docent* said, containing in his glyph a measure of what three hundred thousand human years might reveal. And what it might conceal. "All things are eventually possible."

All things are eventually possible?

Royston sighed and smiled, regretting, finally, that he would not be around to see them. He understood now what it meant that this group had chosen to live forever, rather than allow death to shortcut them to the *Creator Of All.* What might they miss here, if they passed on to another place and could never return?

That brought a feeling of brotherhood with this ancient being, this god descended to speak with a mere human. The Chaa who had become *Docent* had wanted to live long enough to see the everything that was possible.

Royston mourned that he would die first, but that was the nature of what it meant to be Human, and in that, he differed from the Chaa.

"Now, you see," *Great Teacher* nodded.

Suddenly, the rest of the room returned, as if that conversation had been truly private.

"I do," Royston nodded back.

They would leave him on *Earth*, where whatever mischief he might undertake would be small potatoes.

Even the first interstellar colony would not be a threat, because the clock had started, the walls were secure, and in five thousand years, this Judgment would continue.

"Royston Loughty, we note that your time is expected to be shorter than that of the others, as you have perhaps a few decades at most until death claims you," *Uplifter* spoke, drawing Royston's eyes away from *Great Teacher*.

"That is correct," Royston said quietly.

He turned far enough to finally spot Sir West, noting that the man had finally found his way into the center of the group, once there were no other places to hide.

"Members of *The Communion*, I would like to present my own mentor, Sir Westfield van Duren-Abbott," Royston said. "He is perhaps as elderly as a human scientist can be expected to be, and retain that spark of life and intellect that makes him such a challenging foe."

And it was rather rude fun to watch a man like Sir West blush. But he deserved it, both the good and the bad.

"It is a pleasure to make your acquaintance, Sir West," *Uplifter* replied politely. Others did the same with their glyphs.

"Royston, we have received a request."

Royston felt his chin come up. Not quite defiance, but he was no less adamantine in his outlook than either Gareth or Marc had been.

He was not prepared for Fatima to step close and study him from less than two feet away. Close enough to kiss her again, were either of them of a mind. And had the galaxy allowed it.

But the galaxy did. And the future would be upon them all too soon.

So he kissed her, reveling in the feel of all those tentacles tasting his hair and flesh as he did so. In doing so, he was able to read her soul, perhaps an after-effect of the gestalt he had contained.

Her vision nearly knocked him for a loop, so much so that he recoiled enough to look her in the eyes.

"You are audacity itself, my dear," Royston whispered.

She smiled demurely, looking very much the young Persian woman she was impersonating.

"My options as a deep cover agent seem to have evaporated, Royston," she said. "I have been *blown*, to use your term for it. Burned."

"And this would bring you joy?" he asked, contemplating how he might explain such a thing to his friends and family.

Except that Pippa stepped close and put an arm around each of them. So he knew what her vote was. Gareth joined a second later. Others did as well, reaching out to simply touch him on a shoulder or arm.

He had never experienced such a vote of confidence. But these were his friends and family. Even Alvin Siddall smiled at him and shook both their hands.

"Such will your destinies become intertwined with ours," Royston finally found *Uplifter* and smiled a knowing secret at the being.

"That is our hope, as well, Royston," *Uplifter* said. "Prepare yourself."

How does one prepare?

He took Fatima's hand in his and let his normally-tightly-held emotions flow into and over the woman, even as she did the same.

The blue flame descended, but it brought no pain.

When it cleared, he had to look at his hands, noting that the liver spots he had come to live with were gone. The color was better, as was the muscle tone.

So they had done it. He was thirty years old again, and Pippa could pass herself off as a younger sister, rather than a daughter.

And Fatima…

Her hair was black and long, lustrously flowing past her shoulders. The subtle, unconscious clues that might have suggested this woman was an alien were gone, noticed only because she was fully human now, and not merely pretending to be one.

She kissed him again, with promise. Decades of promise. Perhaps a second family, once he managed to explain everything to the bureaucrats who would not take the word of a mere god as evidence necessary to fill out new forms.

But that was tomorrow's problem. He had a honeymoon to consider first.

"Star Dragon, yours is the final decision."

STAR DRAGON

AND JUST LIKE THAT, they had come to the point that Gareth had been dreading all day. And perhaps for months.

What would become of him?

Ever since that moment when he had been standing in Talyarkinash's lab and she told him he would never be allowed to return to *Earth*. That no human could be allowed to know about the *Accord of Souls*.

They all knew now. He suspected it would haunt Humanity almost as badly as the thought of Humans had terrorized the *Accord* for so long.

Still, it was his time. He would not quail before it. Pastor Jacob had taught him to understand his place in the grand scheme of things, and nothing these Chaa had said or done would cause him to question that today.

Gareth stepped up and found *Speaker For The Communion* at the center of the line of Chaa.

"What would you have?" he asked simply, knowing that it no longer mattered.

Nothing really mattered at this point.

Gareth St. John Dankworth had accomplished everything he had set out to when Morty and Xiomber had asked him to save the universe. Even the totality that could be contained in the oath a new Deputy Agent of Earth Force Sky Patrol took when they earned their badge.

"You have no fear," the being observed.

It didn't feel like a question, so Gareth just shrugged his shoulders. He already knew that. Or rather, what fear all creatures knew would never be allowed to interfere with Gareth doing his duty. Doing what was right.

"The *Conclave of the Ascended Chaa* has spent the longest time in their debate on the merits of the Star Dragon," the being in charge said to the entire galaxy. "Until the decision was made to alter the very *Accord* itself, many were of the opinion that the galaxy needed such a protector."

Gareth nodded. He had come to the same assessment. The Star Dragon was a powerful symbol, inspiring fear among the criminals, as he had always intended, while also offering inspiration to the common folk that they didn't have to live with the criminality that had preyed on them for so long.

Already, Grace art had begun to incorporate his icon as a symbol for the Constabulary itself. Where he wasn't seen as a Herald of The Chaa themselves, like tomorrow might bring.

Gareth was uncomfortable with some of the religious movements that seemed to have sprung up, venerating him as some sort of archangel. It wasn't right. He was just a man, a cop trying to do his best.

"Similarly, arguments were offered for altering Humanity in a manner similar to how the *Accord* will change," *Speaker For The Communion* continued. "Thus would a Star Dragon perhaps become unnecessary."

"It is unnecessary now," Gareth countered them all before they got up too much a head of steam to derail. "The purpose of the Star Dragon was to provide a tool that could stop Marc Sarzynski and his intended conquest of the galaxy. That is done."

"The purpose, perhaps," the Chaa replied. "But the powerful symbolism remains."

Indeed. How much of Human history contained such a powerful image?

Pendragon. St. George. Bilbo. Beowulf.

Gareth St. John Dankworth?

Frightening to even consider.

"All I want to do now is go home," Gareth glyphed at the beings, trying to compress all the rage, the sorrow, and the anguish that had been his since that day. "To see my family again. To get on with my life."

"To make the world a better place," *Speaker For The Communion* finished the thought for him.

"As long as I breathe," Gareth whispered the promise.

"Without the Star Dragon?" *Speaker For The Communion* asked.

"Happily," Gareth replied, feeling his chin come up just the slightest amount.

It was a tool he had undertaken, and nothing more. His identify, much as others might not believe, was not wrapped up in a twenty-nine-meters-long bronze dragon, flying overhead and breathing fire.

"It is part of your genetic makeup now," the Chaa continued.

"So is being a Vanir, if I am given to understand the amazing genius of Talyarkinash Liamssen," Gareth nearly growled the words back. "Such was it with Marc, and you undid that. Undo the dragon from my soul and let me go back to being me."

"And thus, the crux of the argument, which grew quite heated by our standards," *Speaker For The Communion* said. "*Polaris*, who was once known as *Astray In Darkness*, and before that *Bowsprit*, you led the discussion. Let the people of the galaxy know your mind."

Gareth turned to face the newest of the Chaa, if you measured them by their souls.

He had been *Astray In Darkness*. Now he had found a polestar against which he could finally navigate, and it had turned out to be Humanity, of all things.

Thus, in questing, perhaps we all find the thing we seek.

"Indeed, Gareth," *Polaris* nodded to him. "We do find the thing we seek, even though we often cannot articulate what it is until it lands in our grasp."

Gareth had stopped being surprised that they could read his mind. In this strange place that he had been summoned, all things seemed possible. Arguing with gods was the least weird part about it.

Polaris laughed heartily.

"Many were of the same opinion, Gareth," Polaris said. "That the purpose of the Star Dragon had been fulfilled. That he was an unnecessary complication in the future planning of where Humanity might evolve, at a moment when the Chaa were shown to be deficit in such vision."

Gareth nodded. Exactly.

"But others felt that Humanity needed such a symbol, as long as they remained *unreconstructed* by the Chaa," the man continued. "That perhaps the very concept of the Star Dragon transcended even Gareth Dankworth and became a Human need. Your own historical studies reflect the continuing inspiration of dragons."

Pendragon. St. George. Bilbo. Beowulf.

"We would return you to *Earth*," Polaris said. "To Earth Force Sky

Patrol, in their quest to bring Humanity to the very paradoxical place of no longer needing them."

Gareth felt a spike of fierceness overtake him. The First Inspector had said it best. If you don't need us, then we have succeeded beyond our wildest dreams.

"Humanity might not get there in the time remaining," *Polaris* cautioned him, marking that day, fifty centuries thus, when this conversation would be renewed with whichever of his descendants might have it. However they had gotten there.

"And?" Gareth prompted the being, when he realized that even a Chaa might know doubt.

"We would send you home," Polaris said. "And send the Star Dragon with you. If you are willing to hear my logic."

Gareth nodded. These were the most powerful beings in the galaxy. Maybe in the universe, ancient and hopefully commensurately wise.

"Humanity will need a Star Dragon, even after your time," *Polaris* said. "But we would make such a thing recessive within the core soul of Humanity itself, rather than linking it to your line. The next Star Dragon after you might and might not be any son or daughter of Dankworth."

"Pendragon," Gareth understood.

"Pendragon," *Polaris* agreed. "Already, you contain the myths of such a man, rising at need to fight injustice again. So shall Humanity have a Star Dragon today, and thus, perhaps, more Star Dragons later, if the need becomes acute."

"But not my children?" Gareth asked, finally anxious.

For so long, ever returning to Pippa's arms had been too much to hope for. Now, it was within his grasp, but what would it be like for his descendants, to be Dankworths, scions of such a famous man?

But if any could reach for the power, then they wouldn't necessarily need him.

He had been a hero, when the situation needed one.

Now he could just be a man.

Polaris nodded to him, and a blue fire erupted.

SKY MARSHAL

IT HELPED that every man he might have to deal with already knew the story. And the judgment of a panel of what might be gods.

Alvin Siddall was going to have one whale of an argument on his hands when he got home. And he didn't care. He was the Sector Marshal in charge of *The Arsenal*. Royston and Gareth, and even Pippa, fell under his jurisdiction. Marc Sarzynski would as well.

He remembered what the man had been like. Before.

The light in Sarzynski's eyes had returned. There was no other way to describe it. The same was in Gareth's eyes, now human again.

He turned to Royston and managed not to goggle at the man, suddenly three decades younger, or the woman that Fatima Darzi had turned into, holding his hand.

"Are you satisfied, Royston?" Alvin asked, with as much professionalism as he could manage.

"I am, my friend," the great physicist replied with a nod.

Alvin turned slowly in place, counting noses to make sure he had everyone.

Gareth and Pippa.

Marc and the now-human Talyarkinash.

Royston and Fatima.

Ellen Ames and her band: Tommy, Dave, Mick, Rhys, and Dalton.

Sir Westfield van Duren-Abbott, representing England, one of the Founders of Earth Force.

Across the way, a group of alien beings that would recede into legend shortly.

Yuudixtl.

Nari.

Grace.

Warreth.

Arawath.

Vanir.

Chaa.

Alvin bowed formally to the woman he recognized as his true peer: First Inspector Anen Wardson of the *Accord of Souls* Constabulary. She would actually be the equivalent of the Sky Marshal himself, Alvin's boss, but the rest of these folks were cops, like Gareth, or politicians.

Plus the hosts of Heaven and Hell, arrayed around him.

"I will speak for the *Accord of Souls*, when we must face the Sky Marshal and the governing bodies of Earth," Alvin nodded to the Chaa as well.

"And you will do us proud, Alvin Siddall," *Speaker For The Communion* replied with a bright tone to his voice.

One of the Yuudixtl separated from the rest of the crowd and stepped close now, drawing himself up proudly before Gareth before turning to smile at the rest of the humans.

"You did it, kid," Morty said to his partner in crime.

"We did it," the now-human Gareth agreed. "I couldn't have done it without you."

Both appeared to be in tears as they embraced, Gareth dropping to one knee and squeezing the tiny lizardman tight against his chest.

Alvin nodded, only tangentially embarrassed at such a display of emotion between two men, but it felt right.

Earth Force and Sky Patrol had taken a wrong turn. It was obvious now. Looking around at the many strong, capable women of the *Accord*, Alvin understood that things would need to change, going forward.

He could dedicate his remaining years to doing something about that. He had no doubt that the three women returning home with him would be powerful totems on his side.

Finally, the two separated. Gareth rose, and Marc Sarzynski stepped up and hugged Gareth as well.

Alvin heard Marc whisper something into Gareth's ear, but he was too far away to understand it.

He didn't need to. Those two had come home.

Now it was time for the rest.

Alvin looked up at the being who had apparently transformed itself during the course of this single day, taking a Human name to remember Human things.

He nodded to *Polaris*, glancing once to make sure that the two groups had separated, but he trusted these beings to be able to handle something so simple.

Polaris nodded back, smiling at him with pride. At all of them.

Light.

READ MORE!

Be sure to read all of the Star Dragon books!

Birth of the Star Dragon
Flight of the Star Dragon
Call of the Star Dragon
Shadow of the Star Dragon
Trial of the Star Dragon

ABOUT THE AUTHOR

Blaze Ward writes science fiction in the Alexandria Station universe (Jessica Keller, The Science Officer, The Story Road, etc.) as well as several other science fiction universes, such as Star Dragon, the Collective, and more. He also writes odd bits of high fantasy with swords and orcs. In addition, he is the Editor and Publisher of *Boundary Shock Quarterly Magazine*. You can find out more at his website www.blazeward.com, as well as Facebook, Goodreads, and other places.

Blaze's works are available as ebooks, paper, and audio, and can be found at a variety of online vendors. His newsletter comes out monthly, and you can also follow his blog on his website. He really enjoys interacting with fans, and looks forward to any and all questions—even ones about his books!

Never miss a release!
If you'd like to be notified of new releases, sign up for my newsletter.

I will never spam you or use your email for nefarious purposes. You can also unsubscribe at any time.

http://www.blazeward.com/newsletter/

Connect with Blaze!

Web: www.blazeward.com
Boundary Shock Quarterly (BSQ):
https://www.boundaryshockquarterly.com/

ABOUT KNOTTED ROAD PRESS

Knotted Road Press fiction specializes in dynamic writing set in mysterious, exotic locations.

Knotted Road Press non-fiction publishes autobiographies, business books, cookbooks, and how-to books with unique voices.

Knotted Road Press creates DRM-free ebooks as well as high-quality print books for readers around the world.

With authors in a variety of genres including literary, poetry, mystery, fantasy, and science fiction, Knotted Road Press has something for everyone.

Knotted Road Press
www.KnottedRoadPress.com

ABOUT THE AUTHOR

Blaze Ward writes science fiction in the Alexandria Station universe (Jessica Keller, The Science Officer, The Story Road, etc.) as well as several other science fiction universes, such as Star Dragon, the Collective, and more. He also writes odd bits of high fantasy with swords and orcs. In addition, he is the Editor and Publisher of *Boundary Shock Quarterly Magazine*. You can find out more at his website www.blazeward.com, as well as Facebook, Goodreads, and other places.

Blaze's works are available as ebooks, paper, and audio, and can be found at a variety of online vendors. His newsletter comes out regularly, and you can also follow his blog on his website. He really enjoys interacting with fans, and looks forward to any and all questions—even ones about his books!

Never miss a release!
If you'd like to be notified of new releases, sign up for my newsletter.

I will never spam you or use your email for nefarious purposes. You can also unsubscribe at any time.

http://www.blazeward.com/newsletter/

Connect with Blaze!

Web: www.blazeward.com
Boundary Shock Quarterly (BSQ):
https://www.boundaryshockquarterly.com/

ABOUT KNOTTED ROAD PRESS

Knotted Road Press fiction specializes in dynamic writing set in mysterious, exotic locations.

Knotted Road Press non-fiction publishes autobiographies, business books, cookbooks, and how-to books with unique voices.

Knotted Road Press creates DRM-free ebooks as well as high-quality print books for readers around the world.

With authors in a variety of genres including literary, poetry, mystery, fantasy, and science fiction, Knotted Road Press has something for everyone.

Knotted Road Press
www.KnottedRoadPress.com